I0583362

Dedicated to

All my amazing fans who crave my particular brand of emotional torment.

We all probably need therapy, but you are my people, and I love you for it.

Jennifer Saviano, my bestie and author soul sister. You always inspire me to do better and lay my heart on the page.

Danny Nagel and **Kayla Bowers**, my test bunnies, I owe you so much. Without your incredible feedback, ideas, and support, I'd be lost. Thank you so much!

And **Eric Deardorff**, the love of my life, my continuous well of romantic and humorous inspiration. But shh…Don't tell anyone. It will ruin his reputation.

Lilith Adams Series

Blood Lily
Rose of Jericho
The Lotus Tree
Ghost Orchid
Wormwood
Hellebore

Novellas in the same world

Draga & the Savage: Dragobete
Draga & the Savage: Dracul
Draga & the Savage: Corvinus
Draga & the Savage: Ţepeş
Draga & the Savage: Snagov

For more information about permission to reproduce selections from this book, write to Permissions, Jenny Allen Books & Original Art, 872 Stoverstown Rd., York, PA, 17408

Manufacturing by Ingram Spark.
Book Design by Jenny Allen
Editing by Horrorsmith Editing
Cover Art by Blonde Design and © held by Jenny Allen.

ISBN: 979-8-9928592-2-5

Jenny Allen Books & Original Art, 872 Stoverstown Rd., York, PA 17408
JennyAllenBooks@gmail.com
www.JennyAllenBooks.com

Your mental health matters. Some may find this as a checklist of endorsements, but for those who have triggers, please read this list carefully.

Trigger Warnings include but are not limited to:

Strong violence & murder
Suicidal ideation & actions
Realistic depictions in an ICU setting
Brief Mentions of child abuse & neglect
Mentions of substance abuse, overdose, and recovery
Implied mentions of child SA
Viral pandemic
Intrusive thoughts
PTSD & trauma response
Graphic night terrors/nightmares
Survivor's guilt
Mentions of domestic violence & abuse
Severe mental & emotional manipulation
Strong sexual content with dubious consent, breath play, knife play, biting and blood play.
Forced suicide

The **988 LifeLine** provides 24/7 free and confidential support to people in crisis via phone call, text, or chat.
988lifeline.org

SAMHSA (Substance Abuse and Mental Health Services Administration) offers 24/7 free and confidential treatment referral and services
1-800-662-HELP

The National Domestic Violence Hotline provides 24/7 free and confidential help. You can chat at thehotline.org, text "START" to 88788, or call
1-800-799-SAFE

Official Wormwood Soundtrack

True Love Waits – Radiohead – Ch 3, page 18 at the chapter break

Careless Whisper – State of Mine – Ch 8, page 57, paragraph 8

Something Beautiful – Needtobreathe – Ch 10, page 70, 5th paragraph after the chapter break

Oceans – Seafret – Ch 14, page 98, paragraph 9

Lose Control – Teddy Swims – Ch 19, page 142, 2nd paragraph

Where Is My Mind? – Pixies – Ch 22, page 167, 1st paragraph

The Outsider – A Perfect Circle – Ch 25, page 191, 1st paragraph

Mouth – Bush – Ch 26, page 206, 5th paragraph

Love is a Bitch – Two Feet – Ch 32, page 257, 4th paragraph from the bottom

How Villains Are Made – Madalen Duke – Ch 36, page 284, 8th paragraph

Change (In the House of Flies) – Deftones – Ch 38, page 304, 3rd paragraph from the bottom

I Dare You – Amber Run – Ch 53, page 435, 1st paragraph

Slip Away – UNSECRET (feat. Ruelle) – Ch 59, page 480, 4th paragraph

Compelled – Jack Trammell – Ch 62, page 511, 3rd paragraph

Heal – Tom Odell – Ch 64, page 524, 5th paragraph

Hurricane - Fleurie – Ch 65, page 532, 4th paragraph

Special Note

The *Draga & the Savage* Novella Series chronicles the history of Luminita Dragomir and Aaron Bogdan's tumultuous relationship, beginning in 1241 Romania. It is a tragic tale of heartache, horror, trauma, and passion which continues here in *Wormwood*.

Events from the novellas are mentioned within this book. Although it is done in a way that does not take away from the story and should not cause confusion, the emotional impact of certain situations within this book and the next will hit much harder if you read the novellas first, especially the first two: *Dragobete* and *Dracul.*

Wormwood

by Jenny Allen

Jenny Allen Books
York, PA 17408

Chapter 1

Darkness…cold, unshakeable darkness permeated Lilith's skin, and the world narrowed to two black eyes swirling with malice. The basement stretched out between them. The silence felt oppressive, as if the entire world collectively held their breath in anticipation of this moment.

The scars littering Ashcroft's face pulled and pinched his features into a horrid mask of pure, unrelenting evil. Blood dripped from his taloned fingers, and they twitched, eager to rend more flesh.

This is the monster. The one who slaughtered Gregor's family, who killed my mother, who murdered my partner, who caused my father's execution, and now…

Lilith's eyes drifted to the floor. Anguish squeezed her lungs. At Ashcroft's bloody feet lay Chance, bleeding out from the lacerations across his chest, shoulder, thigh…and beside him, Andrew with four gaping holes in his torso.

She couldn't save them. The beast had already claimed them both, and now his eyes were on her. There was no one left. Only her.

The final moments washed over her again.

Chance was fighting Ashcroft. Lilith had tried to reach him, but Andrew trapped her in his arms. He spoke to her, but Chance was losing.

Her heart had cracked wide open at that sight.

Andrew's thumb had brushed her cheek, and she finally gazed up at him through her tears. His eyes were shining orbs of molten sunlight. They captivated her, but then he said those words…the ones she couldn't ignore or unhear.

"I love you, Lilith Adams."

Those words hadn't truly sunken in until later…until it was *too* late…until he was already gone.

When Andrew kissed her after his tear-filled declaration, she had felt every single emotion ricocheting through him, as if she'd drowned in Durand blood. The overwhelming depth had left her speechless, even if she didn't love him in return.

It hadn't mattered to Andrew. He loved her…enough to die for her, enough to tell her to live and be happy without him. How could she not mourn the death of someone who cared about her that much? How could she not be gutted by his sacrifice?

Lilith's gaze returned to his pale corpse at Ashcroft's feet and the cavity where Andrew's heart had once beat for her. *It's my fault. It's all my fault.*

She shifted her attention back to Chance, the man she loved with every stitch of her soul. His chest didn't move, his skin had taken on a deathly pallor, and blood stopped trickling from his wounds. The absolute agony she felt in that moment was worse than anything Ashcroft could do to her.

Lilith sank to her knees on the cold concrete, and sobs wracked her body. "I can't do this anymore."

She hadn't realized she'd said the words out loud until Ashcroft replied.

"Then stop fighting. Come to me. I'll end your suffering." The monster practically purred the words, but they were false. Ashcroft desired her pain more than anything else in the world, and he would savor every drop, prolonging the moment, until nothing remained.

"Is this not enough for you?" she cried.

When he only smirked, she slid her dagger from its sheath and sliced across both her wrists. "Is this what you want? Pain *and* blood. Take it." Her fractured heart cracked more with every drop splashing against the floor. "I have nothing else to give you. You've taken everything!"

Ashcroft moved closer, like a shark in blood-scented waters, eyeing his prey, but Lilith didn't care. She *couldn't* care. That part of her was already dead. It had died with the two men at Ashcroft's feet.

A small voice inside screamed for her to not waste their sacrifices, but she didn't deserve them. If it hadn't been for her, they would both be alive. She wasn't some hero or the key to a rebellion. Lilith was nobody, unimportant, and they had both died trying to protect a person as insignificant as her when their lives had been worth so much more.

Ashcroft's talons dug into her arms, piercing her flesh, but she barely felt them. He dragged her to her feet, but her eyes remained locked on

Chance's face. Teeth punctured her skin, tearing into her neck, but all she felt was relief.

"Marie?"

A hand touched Lilith's shoulder. She startled from the traumatic dream, nearly falling out of her chair.

"Oh goodness, honey. I'm so sorry. I didn't mean to scare ya."

Lilith panted for breath, trying to shake off the horror still gripping her chest and the acrid taste of unworthiness.

"I truly am sorry."

Lilith pulled on the only smile she could manage and blinked up at the ICU nurse—Kayla, according to her name badge. "I…uh…was having a bad dream."

While Lilith's heart still hammered away, the nurse opened the box in her hands. "Well, Dr. Preston brought in donuts, and I thought you might like one. You've barely eaten these past few days."

Lilith opened her mouth to refuse, but when her eyes fell on the open box of rich confections, her stomach growled in answer.

"Thanks," she said softly, grabbing a pinwheel-esque French cruller— her favorite.

"Big day today." Kayla beamed a smile which slightly dimpled her cheeks. Apparently, the nurse had decided overcompensating with cheeriness would brighten Lilith's mood, but her words summoned conflicting emotions.

A mixture of nervousness and excitement churned in Lilith's gut, but it did help shake the nightmare's torment. Her gaze drifted up the ICU bed to Chance's sleeping face. *Ashcroft didn't kill him three days ago, but I came so close to losing him.*

Scenes from the van flashed through her mind—Chance coughing up blood, the deep lacerations across his chest bubbling with each breath, the slashes to his shoulder and thigh bleeding steadily, her frantic attempts to cover the wounds and staunch the flow, Chance trying to talk to her…to apologize to her…to say goodbye.

Lilith pushed the heart-wrenching memories away before the tears fell. She couldn't focus on that. *Chance is alive*, she reminded herself for the millionth time.

"Are ya excited?" Kayla asked. She slid the box onto the bedside table. It seemed the nurse felt Lilith required more than one donut and a few snacks from the vending machine after three days.

Lilith took another bite of her cruller and nodded. Today was the critical test. Physically, Chance had been healing at an impressive rate, by human standards anyway. Blood transfusions had helped, but the Durand ability of rapid healing seemed dormant. Perhaps that was because they had kept him sedated to protect the breathing tube. It did seem to be a skill which required conscious effort.

This afternoon, Dr. Preston intended to remove the chest tube and perform a *sedation vacation,* where they turned off the sedative drip. If Chance woke up—*once he wakes up,* Lilith corrected herself—they would be able to tell if he had suffered any brain damage from the blood loss.

Keeping the despair at bay was a true challenge. The possibility he might never recover from that night, that he might not be *her* Chance, clawed at Lilith's insides like a wild animal hell-bent on destruction.

"I think Allen is gonna do great," Kayla continued happily while cracking open the blinds.

Even the few rays of weak morning sunshine made Lilith's persistent headache worse. She had barely slept since that night, and when she did, her subconscious tormented her.

For the sake of anonymity, Chance was Allen Jones, and she was his wife, Marie. Too many people were hunting them, but it still caught her off guard when someone called Chance by his middle name.

"I think so too." Part of her was terrified to hope, especially after that tragic night. Lilith had almost lost Chance, and she *had* lost Cohen. Despite her best attempt to block it, the memory of Ashcroft's talons embedded in Andrew's chest flashed through her mind again.

Live and be happy. That was the last thing he had told her.

Andrew hadn't been in her life long, but she struggled to picture a world without him in it. Things between them had been…well, complicated seemed like a horrifically inaccurate word, but she genuinely cared about him, and he…

I love you, Lilith Adams. He had been crystal clear about his feelings at the end. *You saved my soul,* he had said. God, how wrong he'd been. Cohen died because of her…*for her.* Loving her was what got him killed. How could anyone confuse that with salvation?

Lilith grabbed the remote and turned on the TV, hoping it might distract her while Kayla moved about the room, checking the IV lines, jotting down vital signs, and marking a line on the chest tube drainage system.

"Welcome to the Channel 8 news break."

Wormwood

The sound barely registered past the rhythmic *beep, whirr, shh* of the machines in the room. Lilith tried to steady her breathing and clear her mind.

"Our top story today comes from Madisonville…"

Lilith's head snapped toward the TV. Madisonville was a very small town. It couldn't have been a coincidence.

A picture of a smoldering house on a familiar plot of land appeared beside the news anchor. Lilith quickly turned up the volume.

"Tragedy struck in the sleepy farm community of Madisonville three nights ago, when a fire destroyed a home, resulting in the deaths of seven people."

Seven? Orchid must have lost quite a few men. Then an awful thought occurred to her. *What if Ashcroft escaped? What if all this was for nothing? What if Cohen and Chance died for nothing?*

No. Stop. Chance is alive. He's right here…living and breathing.

Lilith bit down on the rising panic and tried to focus on the broadcast.

"Investigators suspect possible arson but are not releasing details at this time. In other news, the steady rise of Parvo B-20 cases in the states of Alabama, Tennessee, North Carolina, and Kentucky are forcing the CDC to consider lockdowns in those states."

Shit. The virus was spreading at an alarming rate. In a week, it had appeared in three other states. Of course, they had no idea how long the blood supply at Goditha had been contaminated and how many vampires had been infected. Enough to reach the Durand, at least. The two species didn't commonly mingle.

Regardless, there was no way they could keep the source hidden forever. The CDC was all over it. Eventually, they would find Goditha…

Which Luminita violently took over. Alexis said the Romanian intended to slaughter everyone at the facility. Fuck. This is going from bad to worse.

"Parvo B-20 displays the same symptoms as other strains of the virus—fever, headache, cough, sore throat, rashes, and joint pain. Unlike its more common variant, B-19, this new strain has also caused life-threatening anemia, liver failure, and encephalopathy in otherwise healthy adults.

"The CDC advises citizens to self-quarantine for two weeks if showing any symptoms listed and to call 911 for emergencies only. They also recommend the use of masks and gloves when in public."

Masks and gloves? Lilith frowned at the screen. The cult's virus only seemed to spread through blood and sexual transmission, not contact or droplet. *Is it different for humans? Has it mutated already?*

"Some scary stuff, huh?"

Lilith nearly jumped at the sound of Kayla's voice. She had been so focused on the news stories that she forgot the nurse was still there.

"Uh, yeah. It sounds pretty serious."

"We've had a few cases here, but they're keeping them in a specialized unit. I expect they're gonna make masks mandatory any day now. Anyway, is there anything else I can get you? Water? Ginger ale?" The woman made no move to reclaim the donut box.

Lilith flashed a slight smile. "No. I'm good. Thanks, Kayla."

The woman nodded with another cheery expression and strolled through the door to her computer on wheels.

When Lilith turned back to the television, the morning show was revealing must-buys for the last days of summer, as if the world wasn't starting to come apart. After lowering the volume to mild background noise, Lilith curled up in her chair, rested her hand on Chance's arm, and watched his chest rise and fall with every puff from the ventilator.

The dark emotions from that dream still haunted her, but she pushed them as far away as she could.

"Please be okay. I *need* you to be okay." Tears misted her eyes when her gaze moved up to Chance's slack face. She would give anything in the world to see his mischievous grin…to witness that adoration shining in his eyes…to feel his hands cupping her face…to hear him say her name.

The fractured thing in her chest cracked a little more while Lilith watched him sleep. Her hope lived on borrowed time. The moment they tried to wake him up would either destroy her completely or answer her prayers. The powers that be had not listened before, and she was scared to believe they would start now.

Chapter 2

Nicci leaned against the doorway to the ICU room, watching her partner whisper to Chance. She tried to hold her own tears at bay. Everything had gone so wrong. Somehow, Luminita's men had found them and managed to delay Nicci, Tim, and the others. They hadn't gotten there in time. Now Chance was fighting for his life, and Cohen…

Her thoughts halted on that name with violent confliction. She had never liked him, had always questioned his motives, but he had sacrificed himself to get Lilith and Chance away from Ashcroft. The asshole had given his life and proven Nicci wrong.

God, she wanted to hate him for that, but Cohen was the only reason Chance was still breathing.

"Hey, shorty," Tim said, exhausted.

Nicci smiled up at him with all the pep she could muster. "Hey, big fella. You know, you really should get some sleep. You were here standing guard all night."

A wide yawn escaped, and Tim rubbed the back of his neck before leaning against the wall. "Yeah, well…Eileen said Dr. Preston is done waiting. He wants answers from Lilith, and I can't leave Chance alone. I'll be okay until she's done talking to the doc."

"This is so fucked up." Nicci sighed, and her gaze drifted back to Lilith curled up in the chair, her hand on Chance's arm.

"I know."

Nicci's head swiveled toward him. "How did they even find us?"

"I don't know. Cohen said Orchid was an expert tracker, and we were in a hurry. Maybe we missed something. I mean, we never did figure out how she found us at Cohen's cabin in the first place."

Nicci frowned, running through every possibility again. "Eileen changed clothes. You searched her bag and shook any possible tail."

Tim nodded with a tired frown. "I've gone over it again and again, Nicci. I missed something. I *must* have missed something. I mean…"

The guilt in the man's voice made Nicci's heart heavy.

"Maybe if I hadn't been distracted like a hormonal teenager…" His eyes flicked to Chance in the hospital bed, and his face crumpled.

"This is *not* your fault," Nicci stated adamantly. "No more than it's mine or Lilith's or Eileen's, or…" Nicci swallowed her instinctual dislike and continued. "…or even Cohen's. This whole thing falls on Luminita. She's the one that brought that fucking monster back."

Tim nodded. One corner of his mouth lifted, but his eyes remained sullen. "Why don't you take Lilith to Dr. Preston's office? I'll stay here with Chance."

"Tim." Nicci waited until he actually looked at her. "This is *not* your fault. You did everything you could. We all did."

A heavy sigh rushed past his lips. "Yeah, but it wasn't enough, was it?"

"He's not dead, Tim."

The man merely nodded, his attention shifting back to Chance and Lilith.

Nicci patted his arm when she passed and moved into the room.

"Hey, partner." She managed to infuse a little more brightness into her voice.

Lilith turned in her chair.

God, she looks awful.

"Have you slept at all?"

"Not much," Lilith admitted. "Every time I close my eyes…I see things I only want to forget."

"I'm so sorry, Lil." Nicci closed the distance and wrapped her arms around Lilith, who clung to her in return. "I'm sorry about all of it. I'm sorry we didn't get there sooner."

"Chance is alive. That's all that matters." Lilith spoke the words as if trying to convince herself more than Nicci.

"Yeah. He is, and he *will* wake up."

Nicci squeezed Lilith tighter, dreading the next part. The last thing she wanted to do was take her away from Chance to dance around a litany of questions.

"I hate to do this, Lil, but Dr. Preston isn't willing to wait any longer. He wants to talk."

Lilith pulled back, sniffling and wiping at her eyes. "I know. It needs to be done."

"I'm going with you. Tim is gonna stay with Chance, okay?"

Lilith nodded before standing. She ran her fingers down Chance's arm to his hand and gave it a squeeze. "I love you, *beau*." After releasing a weary sigh, Lilith turned away from the hospital bed.

"I'll keep an eye on him," Tim stated softly. He strode across the room to wrap his arms around Lilith. "He's gonna be okay," he whispered against her shoulder.

Lilith smiled up at him, but it didn't reach the woman's eyes, and it made Nicci's heart ache. Hopefully, everything would go well this afternoon and give her a little more hope.

"Nicci," Tim started when they turned to leave. "Make sure she eats something. Real food, not snacks and donuts."

"I'm right here, Tim." Lilith peered over her shoulder with a distinct Lilith-like frown.

"And if I gave you that order, would you listen?"

Lilith paused before flashing a genuine smirk. "Probably not."

"Exactly why I told Nicci and not you." Tim smiled while settling into the seat beside the bed. "It wouldn't kill you to get an hour or two of sleep too."

The smile slowly slid from Lilith's face, and her eyes drifted back to Chance. "I can't. Sleeping is worse than being awake right now."

That sobered Tim quickly, and he nodded in understanding.

Nicci led Lilith out of the room and through the ICU doors. "So, what's your plan here?"

Lilith remained silent for a long moment but finally responded once they were alone in the hall. "I plan to tell him as much truth as possible. Did you see the news? The virus is spreading too fast. We have to get ahead of it."

"The Elders are gonna be pissed."

"Well, I'm not planning on taking things public today." Lilith frowned down at her partner. "If we can get our hands on a viable vaccine, that will be the best way to go public—with a solution. The Elders will have to recognize that."

"Well, I'll follow your lead."

Lilith rubbed her hands roughly over her face. "I need coffee and perhaps something real to eat. Tim is right. I've been living on vending machine garbage for three days."

"Let's hit up the cafeteria first. Dr. Preston will understand."

Lilith and Nicci loaded up to-go boxes with eggs, bacon, and hashbrowns and snagged two large coffees before heading back to Dr. Preston's office. Warning bells were blaring in Lilith's head. Confessing their secrets to humans went against everything she'd learned, but she had already broken that seal when she told Gorman, Hersch, and the others everything about a week ago.

Still, this felt different. Perhaps it was because the man was a doctor. Of course, confessing to the FBI should have been scarier, but it was Gorman and Hersch. In a very short time, she'd learned to trust them. All she knew about Dr. Preston was that he had saved Chance's life, had kept their secrets the past three days, and had slipped Lilith and Nicci a few units of blood from his research lab without question. Plus, Eileen trusted him. That should have been enough, but was it?

I guess we'll find out.

When they turned the final corner, Lilith spotted Agent Hersch waiting outside the door. The woman was staring at the sparkling floor, arms crossed over her chest, a deep frown pulling at her delicate features.

Guilt.

Lilith recognized it in all their faces—Nicci, Tim, and now Eileen's—but the blame didn't belong to them.

This was all *her* fault. It had been *her* plan that failed, *her* father's demon who killed Cohen and almost Chance, *her* complex relationships which caused two men to risk their lives to save *her*. She wished she could steal away their guilt like a Durand. They didn't deserve to bear the blame weighing them down.

"Good morning, Eileen." Lilith pulled on a smile, hoping it might ease the agent's mind.

"Lilith." All the negative emotions leaked from Eileen's face when she turned toward them. "You look…better," Eileen offered with a small chuckle.

"Coffee and real food." Lilith held up the heavy to-go boxes. "Brought enough to share." Now that she was out of that ICU room and concerned about people beyond just Chance, she was able to pull on a more cheerful persona.

Maybe one day I'll really feel it, but for now, I can at least fake it.

"Great! I'm starving." Nervousness slid into Eileen's expression before she spoke again. "So, are you ready for this?"

Lilith noticed the doubt in Eileen's eyes, but she didn't have much choice. "It needs to be done, and Dr. Preston isn't willing to wait any longer."

Eileen nodded with a slight frown and patted Lilith's shoulder. "I'll help however I can."

"Thank you, Eileen…for everything. Really. I can't thank you enough." Tears threatened to spill again at the thought of what would have happened if Eileen hadn't brought them here. Lilith would have been planning a funeral for her fiancé, not praying he would wake up.

Eileen's smile seemed forced, and Lilith understood. The agent didn't feel like she had done enough.

"It was the very least I could do."

"Okay, girls. Let's tackle this shit before our food and coffee get cold," Nicci interrupted with a tight smile, clearly wanting to escape the emotionally deep waters of their mutual guilt.

An hour later, Lilith stared across the desk at Dr. Preston while he ran his hands through his pitch-black hair. Everyone remained silent. Lilith, Nicci, and Eileen nervously held their breath, waiting to see how the doctor handled the explanation of vampires and—to a minimal extent—the Durand.

Lilith hadn't delved into Ashcroft, the Council, or anything not medically relevant. She also hadn't mentioned their involvement in the current viral outbreak. One problem at a time.

"So, let me get this straight." Dr. Preston rose from his chair to pace the small area behind his desk. "Vampires are real…"

He glanced at Lilith, who nodded.

"…and there's a separate race that draws on emotional energy to heal…"

Again, he glanced at Lilith, who nodded.

"…but you can't go into detail on the second one because it's too risky."

"Yes, but all you need to know is that Chance is both. If he wakes up, he may be able to heal completely with the other ability."

The man rubbed his chin and continued to pace. "The science makes sense, as far as vampires go. Half-bloods presenting as severe cases of thalassemia, the deficient hemoglobin levels causing hypoxia if not replenished…" He stopped and peered at Lilith with a healthy dose of skepticism. "But you ingest blood. You don't take it intravenously." His eyes darted to the two blood packs on the table he had brought for Lilith and Nicci.

"That's correct."

"And you obviously eat and drink normally." He waved at the half-empty boxes and paper coffee cups.

"Yes."

"How does the hemoglobin survive the stomach acids to be absorbed? Any normal digestive system would denature the proteins and break down the blood."

"I'm afraid I'm not an expert on the subject. I'm just a CSI, but my uncle Duncan used to say the body adapts. He mentioned something once about a special ability to absorb what we needed before the blood reaches the stomach. I'm sorry I can't be more specific."

Dr. Preston seemed to consider her words for a while, still rubbing at his stubbly chin. "And your reason for such secrecy?"

"There are many." Lilith sighed. "As for vampires, full-bloods—like myself—can live very long lives. That is something humans have always coveted, and throughout history, they have not been known for their acceptance of anything new or different.

"In regard to our current situation, the Elders among my kind are divided on a number of issues and are actively looking for us, but so is this other species, who are even more radical about securing their secrets. We need to keep our anonymity until Chance is back on his feet."

"This other race…" His hand flourished in the air. "…whatever you want to call them, sounds like mystical pseudoscience."

"I can only vouch for their existence and their ability. I don't know how any of it really works."

"Why are you telling me all this?"

Lilith frowned in clear confusion. "You said you wanted answers."

"Yes, but you could have lied. Are you? Lying?"

"No, Dr. Preston, I am not. I've told you what I can. Anything more would severely endanger your life."

"Okay. What is it you want?"

Lilith had known this question was coming but hadn't expected it so soon. Hersch had been right about this guy being open-minded.

"I want you to keep this between us for now. Certain situations will most likely force us to come forward soon, and we could use a respected human on our side. Assuming you *are* on our side."

Dr. Preston stopped, planted his hands on his desk, and leaned closer. "If I promise to keep all this secret for now, will you allow me to take a blood sample from you?"

The man's keen eyes studied her while Lilith thought over the request.

"It stays off any records? For your eyes only?"

"Yes."

"And you'll keep everything quiet until I ask otherwise?"

"Yes."

An almost manic spark lit his eyes, like Lilith had seen with Dr. Nichols when he explained Ashcroft's blood sample. Perhaps it was a common trait for research doctors. Of course, Dr. Nichols had turned out to be an enemy hell-bent on ridding the world of vampires. He was the mastermind behind the virus currently plaguing the Southeast.

"You can have your blood sample," Lilith said reluctantly.

"Mine too," Nicci added. "I'm a pureblood from an old Italian line."

The doctor's eyes narrowed and then shifted to Eileen, as if expecting her to reveal an unexpected heritage too.

"Sorry. I'm Grade A human." Eileen flashed a smile, which made the doctor's lips curve into something similar.

"All right. Well…" The man settled back into his seat and folded his hands on the desk. "I suppose we should discuss this afternoon."

Wow. Straight on to other business. Anxiety gripped Lilith's chest again. Part of her couldn't wait, and the other dreaded the moment of no return. Once there was certainty, she couldn't pretend anymore.

"I'm going to remove the chest tube while he's still sedated. It's rather painful. The nurse will dress the site, and we'll get a chest X-ray to ensure there's no air trapped in the pleural space. Kayla will redress his wounds, and then we'll taper back the sedative until he wakes up. We still want him drowsy, or he might fight the breathing tube, but he'll be conscious. Once I perform a few neuro tests, we'll have a better idea of what we're looking at."

Lilith kept her tears and sorrow at bay, focusing on facts and science instead. "When will he come off the ventilator?"

"Assuming he passes the neuro tests, we can perform an SBT while he's awake." When Lilith merely frowned, Dr. Preston elaborated. "Sorry, medical jargon…a Spontaneous Breathing Trial. If he does well enough, we might extubate…Sorry. Take the breathing tube out today."

For the first time in three days, Lilith felt a true flicker of hope in her chest, but she was terrified to believe it. Once again, she prayed to whatever higher powers would listen.

Please, let him be okay.

Chapter 3

Chance turned away from the black SUV's window and jogged through the woods toward the cabin. He needed to get back before people started growing suspicious.

It had to be done. There was no other option. No other way to save her. Still, guilt weighed heavy on his heart. *She'll never forgive me for this, but at least she'll be alive.*

Tim and Eileen paced outside the van while Lilith peered through the driver's window. *Lilith.* A smile eased across his lips. The new blond hair made the woman glow.

I'd do anything for her. Anything to protect her.

Guilt slid across his shoulders again. Chance couldn't seem to maintain eye contact as he continued toward them.

There's no other way.

When his boots hit pavement, he came to an abrupt stop. Nothing at the cabin was paved. There was only a dirt road and a gravel drive.

For a moment, Chance stared at the smooth concrete, and fear tightened his chest. Slowly, his eyes rose to Duncan's basement. The light bulbs flickered, revealing irregular flashes of light down the long space. Enough to know he was alone.

No. She should be here. Panic started to take over. Chance whirled around, searching every inch, opening every door, but there was no one else, not even outside. *None of this makes sense. Where is Lily? Where is Cohen?*

"Lily!" His voice echoed through the empty basement—the only sound breaking the oppressive silence besides his panicked breaths.

Not even the frogs and crickets were singing outside. Everything was unearthly still, like a crouching lion waiting to strike.

Pain seared across his leg, and he dropped to one knee.

Angry gashes transected his thigh, blood quickly seeping into his jeans and running down his leg. His eyes searched the space wildly but saw nothing, no one. The same stifling silence made his ears ring. Once again, the world waited, hunched, ready to pounce.

His body twisted when another strike sliced through his shoulder, like red-hot knives carving into his skin. Chance growled in pain, squeezing his eyes closed, and clutched his injured arm. *Can Ashcroft really move that fast? Be that silent? Like a goddamn ghost?* Unfortunately, he knew that answer. He'd seen the footage from the PMIC lobby.

"Chance." A strangled whisper reached his ears, and he snapped his head up.

Ashcroft stood nearby, but he wasn't the one who had spoken.

With an unbearable pain in his heart, Chance diverted his eyes to Lilith, who knelt on the concrete before the monster, a knife in her hand.

"No!" he screamed when the blade slid across one wrist. Chance attempted to move…to stop her, but he was rooted to the spot. His muscles refused to obey, as if they were controlled by someone else. "Lily, stop! Please! Don't do this!"

Either the words didn't reach her or she ignored them. The knife sliced across her other wrist.

"Is this what you want? Pain *and* blood? Take it," she cried out in a voice so strained with tears and anguish that it cleaved his heart in two. "I have nothing else to give you. You've taken everything!"

The heart-wrenching words twisted Chance's insides even more than watching Ashcroft's talons dig into her arms. Lilith didn't struggle, didn't fight him.

She's giving up? How could she just give up? After all we went through, everything we sacrificed, the things I did to keep her safe…

When Ashcroft lifted Lilith to her feet, Chance caught a glimpse of two bodies on the floor—Cohen, with his heart ripped out, and…

The world came to a screeching halt and narrowed in on one thing—Chance's lifeless body.

This is a dream. It has *to be a dream.*

The image of Ashcroft jend Lilith disintegrated into smoke, slowly disappearing until only the corpses remained.

No. I'm not dead. This is a fucking dream.

"Are you sure?" The voice whispering over Chance's shoulder dripped with venom. "Death might be preferable to what awaits you."

Wormwood

Talons raked across his chest, cutting deep until each gargled breath was a fight. He couldn't seem to get enough air, no matter how hard he tried. Panic made everything worse, clawing at the shredded remains of his lungs, making them burn.

Then Chance was on the ground, coughing and gasping. The world went dark around the edges. *Lilith. I need Lilith. I need to see her. I need to apologize. Fuck I can't die like this. I have to live or...*

Lilith hovered over him, tears streaming down her face, and God, she was beautiful. The panic eased, and Chance reached out to wipe her cheeks. He hated seeing her cry. It always felt like a personal failure on his part.

When his fingers brushed her wet skin, her eyes snapped to his, and the look in them nearly stopped his heart right then and there.

"How could you?" she cried through angry tears. The betrayal was blatant and bare in her haunting olive eyes.

Chance struggled for some wisp of air, some breath which would let him apologize, explain, but he only coughed harder. Blood splattered across his already shredded chest.

"I'll never forgive you...not for this."

Chance reached for her again, desperate to make her understand somehow, but she pulled away from him, as if his touch were poisonous. An old familiar feeling coiled around him: rejection, something he never thought she would make him feel, but there it was. Her eyes cut through him with such heartbreak and fury, like a dagger to his chest.

"I trusted you."

Those horrified words were the final blow. Chance squeezed his eyes shut, sending tears rolling. One last strangled breath rushed out of his blood-filled lungs, and he couldn't draw in another. He had no desire to live without her. If he had truly lost her, he just wanted to dissolve into the darkness, to disappear.

The crack of a twig caught his attention, and his eyes flashed open. A familiar black SUV sat on the dirt road leading to the cabin. Chance frantically patted his body, expecting blood and ruined flesh, but he wasn't injured. The window of the SUV rolled up. He was back where he had started.

It's a dream. Just a fucking nightmare, he told himself. But it didn't erase the image of Lilith's anger and heartbreak or the pain he had felt at her words. They were seared into his brain.

Chance started through the woods toward the cabin, convinced this nightmare intended to torment him with this hellish loop for as long as possible.

"Okay, Kayla. Let's start titrating down the drip."

Lilith's pulse pounded in her ears when Dr. Preston gave the order.

Removing the chest tube had gone smoothly, and according to the doctor, the chest X-ray looked fantastic. Kayla had redressed all Chance's wounds, which were nowhere near as deep as they had been when Lilith tried to stop the bleeding that night. So far, everything was going according to plan, but this…waking him up…was the real test.

The nurse punched buttons on the IV pump before entering numbers into her little handheld device. "Decreasing the propofol by 0.4 micrograms."

It sounded like gibberish to Lilith, but she studied Chance's face and waited. Seconds ticked by, then minutes until her lungs began to burn.

Tim squeezed Lilith's hand, drawing her attention. "Breathe."

She couldn't tell if he was reminding her or himself.

After five minutes passed with no change, the slowly mounting panic threatened to snuff out the spark of hope in her chest.

"Decreasing by another 0.4 micrograms," Kayla reported, pressing buttons on the IV machine again.

The seconds stretched out painfully slow.

Chance's eyes moved frantically behind his lids. The tiny flicker in Lilith's chest began to grow, beating back her fear and panic.

She waited, but his eyes didn't open. Tim squeezed her hand again, but she barely felt it. All her focus was on Chance.

"Decreasing another 0.4 micrograms," the nurse repeated.

Time slowed to a crawl again, the anticipation stealing Lilith's breath.

Chance's eyelids flickered and slowly opened. The relief flooding Lilith's body nearly sent her to her knees, and Tim wrapped a firm arm around her shoulders to keep her steady.

Dr. Preston moved closer to the bedside and pulled out a penlight. "Chance. I'm Dr. Preston. Blink twice if you can hear me?"

Lilith darted her eyes to Kayla, who frowned in confusion. "It's his nickname. I told the doctor he might respond better to it."

As soon as the tension left the nurse's face, Lilith refocused on Chance.

"Good. The ventilator is helping you breathe. It's important that you remain calm and let it help you. Now, I need you to stare at my nose. I'm going to check your pupils."

The doc flashed the light across Chance's eyes several times before standing up and taking both of his hands.

"Okay. Can you squeeze my hands? Good."

Then the man walked to the end of the bed and pulled the blanket back, exposing Chance's feet.

"Can you wiggle your toes for me? Both sides at the same time, if you can? Excellent."

After replacing the blanket, Dr. Preston turned to Lilith and Tim.

"He seems to be neurologically intact as far as following commands, but we won't know for certain until he's off the ventilator and I can run more tests."

Relief and hope surged through Lilith's body until she could barely breathe.

"Brittney, let's start the SBT." The doctor nodded to a woman in sky-blue scrubs standing near the ventilator.

She pushed a few buttons before staring at the numbers on the screen. "Respiratory rate is steady. Normal volumes, no increase in pulse."

"Marie, you should come talk to him. Keep him calm." Dr. Preston gave Lilith the warmest smile she'd seen the man wear.

Tim squeezed her shoulders again with a happy grin and kissed the top of her head. "Go on, sis."

Lilith took a deep breath, steadying her nerves, before stepping up to Chance's bed. His hazel eyes, flecked with green, tracked the movement until they met hers. Tears filled them while they searched her face for something. It was the oddest thing…

He looked…afraid…

Afraid of *her* for some reason.

"I'm right here, Chance." Lilith's fingers drifted down until they slid between his.

"Slight increase in pulse and respiratory rate," Brittney reported.

"That's normal," Dr. Preston added.

"Hey, you're okay. You're going to be okay." Happy tears flooded Lilith's eyes, blurring Chance's face when she bent down to kiss his cheek. "I love you, *beau*," she whispered softly, her voice threatening to break. "Do whatever you need to finish healing…if you can."

She squeezed his hand to emphasize her point.

"Everything is within normal limits and holding steady."

Brittney's report brought a smile to Lilith's lips she'd thought she would never genuinely display again. Then she felt it—the small little pull, the tug—and a fraction of the fear which had controlled her ebbed away, leaving relief and happiness in its wake.

When Lilith pulled back, those same emotions were in Chance's eyes and so much more. She brushed the stray locks from his face and ran her fingers lightly through his chestnut hair.

I almost lost him, but he's alive and he's okay. I know it.

Just as she became certain, his eyes drifted closed. A dart of panic flashed through her chest until Chance squeezed her hand again.

"Okay. Ten successful minutes, X-ray looked perfect, and he's a healthy young adult. Marie and Tim, you should get something to eat. We'll extubate and see how he does, but I don't want you two underfoot if we have to re-insert the breathing tube, okay?"

Lilith nodded before leaning to kiss Chance once more. "I love you so fucking much." Her lips brushed over his cheek, and she closed her eyes, sending happy tears streaking down her face.

"Come on, Lil. Let's join Eileen and Nicci in the cafeteria and give them the good news." Tim rubbed her shoulder. "I knew you wouldn't give up, brother. Welcome back to the land of the living."

Tim started to guide her away, but Chance had a death-grip on Lilith's hand.

"It's okay. We're safe. I'll be back as soon as they let me. I love you."

After she squeezed his hand, he finally let go but kept his eyes on her while they turned for the door.

Walking away from him in that moment was one of the hardest things Lilith had ever done.

Chapter 4

"That's fantastic!" Eileen beamed at Lilith and Tim while they settled into chairs at their table. Relief washed over her, as it probably had for all of them.

Chance is awake.

Her gaze drifted to the man beside her, who barely seemed able to keep his eyes open. Worry knitted her brow. "Tim, you really should get some sleep. I'll keep an eye on Lilith and Chance."

A slight smile tugged at his lips, and he slid his hand onto her thigh, which summoned all sorts of inappropriate thoughts that Eileen quickly shut down. Now was *not* the time for her hormones to roar to the surface.

"I know. I should, but—"

"No!" Nicci stabbed her salad with a little too much zeal. "You *all* need sleep. I know Lilith won't listen to me, so I'm not gonna waste my breath, but the two of you"—she pointed her fork, swinging it between Tim and Eileen—"are going back to the hotel and getting some damn sleep."

When they opened their mouths to protest, Nicci narrowed her eyes.

"Don't even *try* to argue with me. Eileen, you don't have to babysit Dr. Preston and run interference anymore. Tim, you don't have to stand guard outside Chance's room. I'm more than capable of taking over that responsibility. So, eat and then get back to the hotel. You can tell Gibson and Keller the good news and finally fucking sleep. I mean it."

Tim shut his mouth and nodded obediently. Eileen chose to do the same. After all, the woman was right. They had been burning the candle at both ends for three days straight, and if they didn't rest soon, they'd collapse.

"Good." Nicci shook her head and stabbed her salad again.

Eileen slid her hand over Tim's, squeezing it lightly before taking another bite of her buffalo chicken wrap. *Honest to God sleep*...Now that it was a possibility, she felt incredibly tired.

"Well, since Nicci is dishing out orders, I'm gonna take my burger and head back to the hotel." Tim darted his warm brown eyes toward Eileen. "What about you?"

"Yeah, we can eat at the hotel." Eileen tried to ignore the fluttering in her stomach when he looked at her. Instead, she closed the lid on her box before rising from the table. "Quite honestly, I'm exhausted. I'll probably pass out on the way."

"Hopefully, the driver wakes us up when we get to the hotel." Tim chuckled while he stood.

"Thank you, Tim...for being there with me." Lilith pushed out of her chair and threw her arms around him, hugging him tight.

"I'm just glad he seems okay," Tim said while kissing the crown of her head. "If he wasn't..." Words seemed to fail him.

"I know, but he is," Lilith reassured Tim. "Please, get some rest... both of you."

"Exactly, big fella," Nicci emphasized between bites.

"I hear you loud and clear, shorty." Tim winked and put his arm around Eileen's shoulders.

The movement seemed so natural, like muscle memory, even though they'd only had one quick but incredibly hot moment at the cabin mere days ago. Being around Tim felt...comfortable. He was so easy to talk to: open, honest, fiercely protective, and funny.

A grin curved Eileen's lips while they strolled toward the hospital's front entrance, his arm still resting across her shoulders.

"Cab should be here in about five to ten minutes." Tim tucked the burner phone back in his pocket.

"I can't wait to take a long shower and sleep." Eileen sighed longingly. She hadn't had a nice hot shower since the cabin.

A light chuckle rumbled from his chest. "Hey, when we get back to the hotel...before we pass out..." His words trailed off, as if he had a question he wasn't sure he wanted to ask.

"What is it?" Eileen peered up at him while they stepped outside and moved to a bench beside an elaborate fountain.

A crease formed between his brows, and he sat down before looking back at her. "Can I go through your bag again? I've gone over every detail, trying to figure out how Orchid tracked us down, and I must have missed something. That's the only thing that makes sense."

"Sure. I don't mind at all." Eileen flashed a bright smile, hoping he didn't notice the nervousness behind it.

It wasn't a matter of trust. The bag contained one thing she didn't want to look at ever again—the file from John's murder. Eileen hadn't been able to stomach the photos that first night in the cabin, and she wasn't sure she could do it now. Seeing her partner, the man who had saved her life so many times, sitting in a bathtub of blood, lifeless…

The brief memory of finding his body was enough to twist her insides, and she didn't need crime scene photos to bring it all back.

Tim tightened his arm around her. "Hey, you okay?"

Shit. I guess I don't have much of a poker face.

Eileen snuggled against him, resting her cheek on his chest, and chose a half-truth. "I'm exhausted." She sighed and left it at that.

His strong hand rubbed circles over her back, almost lulling her to sleep by the time their cab arrived.

After finishing their food, Eileen decided to hop in the shower, but Tim sat on the bed, combing through the contents of her bag. He understood why she didn't want to be present while he rifled through her things, why she had been hesitant to agree. It had nothing to do with privacy and everything to do with the FBI file resting on the bed. That was the main reason he had been reluctant to ask.

After taking apart her hairbrush, rummaging through every little item, and thoroughly inspecting the bag, he still hadn't found anything.

Fuck. Tim rubbed his hand over his neck. The exhaustion pulled him toward sleep, but his mind refused to let things go. If he had missed something which led to all this, to Cohen dying and Chance almost following suit, he *had* to know.

A week ago, Tim might not have cared about Detective Andrew Cohen meeting an untimely end, but he did now. The man had made amazing strides to put things right. He had opened up and actually let them in, allowed them to help him. Cohen deserved better.

Tim grabbed the police file on Special Agent John Gorman, Eileen's partner, and flipped it open again. He rifled through every single page and photograph, laying them out on the bed, but still came up empty.

The shower turned off with a squeak. Tim hastily grabbed all the photos and tossed them face down in the folder before Eileen opened the bathroom door.

"I almost feel human," she said with a sigh, then stopped abruptly, her cheeks turning pink. "Sorry. Was that rude?"

Tim snorted a laugh and quickly averted his eyes when he realized she was only wearing a towel. "Not at all. I almost feel human all the time." He glanced back, unable to stop himself.

"Is that so?" A bright smile curved her lips until her gaze moved to the papers spread across the bed. "John's file?"

"Yeah, sorry. I was trying to get it cleaned up before you were done."

Eileen tightened her towel and gave him a nervous smile. It somehow made the woman even more attractive. His body was entirely too tired to indulge in anything right now, but his brain—or perhaps another part of his anatomy—didn't seem to care. Eileen was positively ravishing, with the pinkish flush from the hot water still lingering on her skin.

"It's okay." Eileen wandered closer, her focus still on the folder and scattered papers.

Tim tried to rein in his desire to explore everything underneath that damn towel. *This is not the fucking time*, he reminded himself again.

Eileen came closer, wrinkling her brow. "Huh."

Tim glanced back at the chaotic mess. While he had managed to shove the photos in face down, the file lay open, with scattered reports and statements surrounding it.

"What is it?"

Eileen bent over the bed beside him—which did *not* help his self-control—and brushed her fingers over a round FBI seal on the inside cover. It had been hidden by the autopsy and toxicology reports.

"I've never seen a sticker here before…Doesn't make much sense. No one would ever see it."

Tim cleared his throat and released a slow breath, desperately trying to concentrate. "Eileen, could you do me a favor?"

She turned her head and peered at him in confusion. Her blue eyes sparkled. Tiny drops of water clung to her long lashes. "Of course."

"Can you put some clothes on while I check out the sticker?"

A soft frown started to form. She glanced down at the towel, and hurt flashed in her eyes.

Does she actually think I don't like the view? That couldn't be further from the truth.

"Eileen, I am far too tired to do the things I really want to do right now, so if you could take it easy on me and put some clothes on, that would help."

The woman's surprised expression turned into a grin that was downright impish. "Are you sure? I mean, I'm absolutely spent, but—"

"Yes, I'm sure." Tim chuckled. "You've already had one subpar performance from me."

Eileen stood up straight, with an endearing smile on her lips he definitely wanted to kiss. "I disagree with that assessment, but you're right. We're both worn-out." She reached past him to grab her clothes and placed a light kiss on his cheek.

It took all Tim's self-control not to just grab Eileen and pull her onto his lap. No woman had ever affected him this way. He had gone more than twenty years without a woman and had been perfectly content on his own, but something about Eileen just felt…right.

As soon as she was out of arm's reach, he grabbed the folder and started picking at the FBI seal. It seemed raised, like a security sticker on high-end items at Target. It took several attempts, but Tim finally started peeling it away. Sure enough, a delicate overlay of gold filament coated the back.

Son of a bitch.

"Was it the sticker?" Eileen asked from the bathroom door. She was now dressed in a T-shirt and sleep shorts, which did little to suppress the desire roiling inside him.

Tim nodded, averting his gaze to the GPS-tracking sticker in his hands—a Bluetooth model which had limited range. Orchid had tailed them, and he'd missed it.

Guilt settled over his shoulders like a two-hundred-pound weight.

Eileen sank down on the bed next to him. "I am so sorry. This is my fault."

"No, it's mine. Orchid knew that if she made your partner's murder look like a suicide, you'd grab his file before you left. I should have seen that, and I should have spotted her tailing us, but I didn't. It was my responsibility to keep you and the others safe."

"But you didn't *have* to help me, Tim."

"Yes, I did…for multiple reasons." His gaze lingered on her, memorizing the woman's concerned yet glowing expression. Then he stared down at the carpet with a heavy sigh. "But my carelessness cost Andrew his life and almost got Chance killed."

Fingers gripped his chin, turning his face toward hers.

"You couldn't have found the tracker. I'm the only one who would know the ins and outs of an FBI file, and I couldn't bring myself to look at any of it. Cohen said Orchid was like a ghost. She can change hair color, facial features, eye color…No one would have noticed her following us when she can alter her appearance."

"Yeah, but still—"

"No," Eileen interrupted firmly. "Everyone is quick to take the blame, but what we need to focus on is the future, not dwelling on the past. Punishing yourself won't change things, and Chance is going to be okay."

"But Cohen—"

"Made his choice. He chose to give us time to get out by distracting Ashcroft. He knew the risks. Burying ourselves in guilt won't bring him back."

Tim stared down at the round sticker in his hands. "So, what do we do with this?"

"Doesn't really matter. We've been here for three days. If it's still active and she's close by, she already knows where we are. Just throw it in the trash."

He started to stand, but Eileen put a hand on his arm and waited for him to meet her eyes.

"Tim, you can't control everything. You didn't fail anyone, especially not me." She slid her fingertips up his cheek and into his hair before pulling him closer. Eileen rested her forehead against his and released a soft sigh, warming his lips. "Don't overthink things. Let's tackle one problem at a time and not get hung up on the things that went wrong, okay?"

How does this woman know me so well? We met a week ago, and she already knows my tells and how my brain works. Once upon a time, that would have scared the hell out of him—and in some ways, it still did—but it was also oddly comforting to be *seen…understood.*

"Okay," Tim whispered, his lips nudging hers in a light kiss. He didn't trust himself to stop if he deepened that contact, and after being up the past thirty-two hours on roughly three hours of sleep, a kiss was all he could handle. "Let me toss this in the can out by the vending machine. I don't want housekeeping in here until we leave. Then we can finally sleep."

"Deal."

Tim dragged himself off the bed and headed for the motel door.

Chapter 5

When Lilith and Nicci returned to Chance's room, it was empty. Lilith's heart nearly stopped dead in her chest.

What happened? Everything was going so well? Where the fuck is he?

"Marie!" Kayla interrupted her spiraling thoughts.

Lilith glanced over her shoulder to see the nurse jogging over with a smile on her face.

That has to be a good sign, right? Lilith tried to quell the panic searing through her brain.

"Sorry. We didn't have a phone number for ya. Dr. Preston moved Allen to a med-surg room closer to his research lab. He's doing fantastic. Here, I can take you up there if you want."

Once again, a surge of relief ran through Lilith's body, leaving her exhausted. "Thank you, Kayla. That would be great."

The nurse led them back toward the elevators. "It's really amazing how well he did off the ventilator."

"Was he awake? Talking?" That little tendril of fear still slithered around in her head. *What if he isn't the same? What if the Durand side can't heal the possible brain damage?*

"The doc performed his neural tests in private, but he said Allen did great. He answered every question correctly, with no sign of impairment."

The weight on Lilith's shoulders lifted when they stepped into the elevator. Kayla pressed the fourth-floor button and smiled over at them.

"Whatever you all did before he got here made a difference."

Lilith shoved away the horrific memories from that night before they fully formed. "Thank you."

"Oh, I will tell ya…It's normal for him to have a sore throat and a raspy voice for a few days."

Lilith nodded, and the elevator dinged. The nurse quietly led them down the hall to a small nursing unit with perhaps ten rooms.

"He's over there in 407. Dr. Preston's lab is the set of double doors just past it. He typically spends more time in there than his office, if you need anything."

"Thank you, Kayla." Lilith flashed a grateful smile before the woman hurried back to the elevator.

"I'll keep watch out here and give you some privacy." Nicci wrapped her arms around Lilith in a huge hug, making her take a step backward. "He's really okay." Nicci sighed happily, still squeezing her partner.

"Nicci. I need to breathe." Lilith chuckled but was half serious. The petite detective was stronger than she looked.

"Stop being a wuss." Nicci backed up and swatted her arm. "Give Chance my love. Ya know…the platonic kind."

Lilith rolled her eyes playfully, but the bright glow of happiness in her chest was nearly overwhelming.

Live and be happy.

Andrew's last words repeated in her head, and the sudden guilt dulled her glow. *He sacrificed himself so that I could have this exact moment. He loved me that much.* It felt wrong. If the roles had been reversed, would she have sacrificed her life for Andrew's happiness? A wave of guilt accompanied the answer—no, she wouldn't…she hadn't.

"Lil, are you all right?"

"Yeah," Lilith lied. "I'm just really tired."

"Well, I'm not surprised. You've barely slept at all the past few days. I should take you back to the hotel after you see him."

"No. Thank you, though. I'd rather be here." After flashing a smile, Lilith hurried over to room 407.

Only the steady beep of the heart monitor filled the room. There was no collection of machines, no breathing tube, just Chance asleep in the hospital bed. He looked peaceful. Lilith leaned against the doorway, watched the steady rise and fall of his chest, and smiled.

He's okay. He's really okay. If she said it enough, maybe she would finally believe it.

Movement on the opposite side of the room caught her attention, and Lilith instinctually moved for the gun she didn't have. The only way the hospital would allow her to carry was if she used her credentials, which would defeat the purpose of using false names.

"I'm not a threat." A feminine voice emerged from the shadowy corner.

When the light fell across the woman's face, Lilith didn't recognize her, but the hazel eyes flecked with green seemed impossibly familiar.

"Who are you?" Lilith took a step back, noticing Nicci's approach in her peripheral.

"Can we talk in private? Please. I am not here to cause anyone harm."

Lilith had zero reason to trust this stranger, but a nagging familiarity made her hold a hand out to Nicci, stopping her partner short. "Who are you? Tell me that and maybe we can talk."

"You most likely know me by my code name, Orchid."

Lilith had suspected, but the confirmation made her blood run cold. *Luminita found us. But Orchid said she wasn't here to hurt anyone. Of course, that doesn't exclude kidnapping.* "Why the hell should I trust you?"

"Because my real name is Helena Vieux."

Lilith blinked, shock flaring through her body. Certainly, she had misheard the woman. *Impossible. Helena Vieux died over twenty years ago.*

"That's not possible."

"I assure you, it is. May we talk now?"

Helena fucking Vieux…Chance's mother. It could be a lie, a way to make me drop my guard. But…something about her eyes…They looked just like Chance's. *Idiot. She can change her eye color. It's part of her ability. There is no reason to trust her.*

"Please, Lilith." The woman seemed sincere. "I'm only here to talk. That's it. I promise."

After locking eyes for several moments and weighing her options, Lilith darted her gaze toward Nicci. "It's okay."

Once her partner roamed back to the nurse's station, Lilith stepped inside and softly closed the door. If Orchid wanted to kill them, she would have done it already. It had only taken her seconds to snap Xander's neck at the cabin.

"Thank you. I know you don't have much reason to trust me, even after knowing my real name." The woman's gaze drifted to Chance, still asleep in the bed, and tears misted her eyes. "All these years…I thought he was dead."

"He thought the same about you." Lilith had no idea what else to do or say. Chance's mother was alive. Lilith's brain just couldn't seem to make sense of it.

"I suppose in a way I did." Helena continued to stare at Chance, as if he might disappear at any moment. "I was supposed to take him with me, you know. That was the deal I made with Luminita—me *and* Chance. When I woke up at the hospital…" The woman paused, drawing in a shaky breath, as if the event had happened recently and not twenty years ago. "She told me he died in the crash." A tear escaped her hazel eyes and streaked down her cheek.

"*Luminita* told you that?"

Orchid's visceral reaction seemed genuine. Lilith wanted to believe her, but she had learned the hard way that the Durand were capable of anything. She'd trusted Luminita once, and Andrew had hid more than a few things before the cabin. Even if this was Chance's mother, it didn't mean her story was real.

Helena nodded, allowing a few more tears to escape.

"Cohen said you used to work for Farren?"

The woman raked a hand through her short brown hair, just like Chance did when he was nervous or frustrated. "Yeah. A long time ago."

Obviously, a subject she didn't want to discuss.

"And now you work for Luminita?"

"*Worked* for," Helena corrected. "I have a new mission now, which is why I wanted to speak with you."

Lilith frowned in confusion. "I'm supposed to believe you're just switching sides after you snapped Xander's neck and nearly killed Chance in the woods?" Defensive anger leaked into her voice, mostly to remind herself that this woman was an enemy.

Helena turned to fully face Lilith, rage evident in every feature. "I didn't know who Chance was that night. And after I learned about Luminita's lies…that she kept him from me and stalked him for her own personal fucking projects…after he endured God knows what? Yes! You *are* supposed to believe that I want to destroy everything Luminita has and see her beg for her fucking life."

Okay, pissing off a deadly assassin is probably not the best idea. "I understand. You want revenge. There's a lot of that going around."

"Not revenge…*retribution*." The wrath drained from Helena's face when she turned back toward Chance. "I wasn't always a good mother, but I thought I'd have an opportunity to change that if we got away from

Bastien. That man always brought out the worst in me, kept me high and under his control. I failed my son in so many ways for so long."

Lilith couldn't deny the heartbreak on the woman's face. It seemed too raw to be an act, even for a Durand. Still, if Helena was who she claimed, she hadn't been a good mother. Chance had shared his experience of being locked in a closet for days, and that was probably one of the milder stories.

"Yes, you did," Lilith stated adamantly, her protective urges taking control. "He won't talk much about that time in his life, but the few glimpses he's given me…were not flattering."

Lilith expected defensiveness, but Helena's shoulders slumped forward, and her face fell.

"I know." The words escaped on an agonized sigh, tearing at Lilith's heart.

Fuck. The last thing Lilith wanted to do was feel sorry for her, but with that reaction, how could she not? "He does have good memories of you, though."

Helena didn't meet her eyes, as if terrified to believe her.

"Chance had to escort me to a gala, and I didn't know how to dance." A happy smirk crossed Lilith's lips when the memory played out in her head—Chance taking her hand and wrapping his arm around her waist in her kitchen…the smell of musk and the gleam of sunlight surrounding him…the teasing smile he had worn. "While he taught me the waltz, he told me about days watching old musicals and dancing with his mom. He said those were the happiest days of his childhood."

Helena's hand flew up to her mouth, blocking a strangled sound from her throat.

"Those movies definitely left him with a hopelessly romantic side. I suppose I have you to thank for that."

Helena seemed to smile behind her hand, but her shoulders shook with muffled sobs.

"Is that why you're here…to see him?" Lilith asked tentatively. The woman might be Chance's mother and be pissed at Luminita, but that didn't necessarily mean they were all safe.

"No." Helena's voice almost broke. She wiped her cheeks and let out several slow breaths, steadying herself. "That is not the *only* reason. I need you to tell me everything you know about Luminita."

"Well, that's a tall order. You work for the woman. Surely, you know more than I do."

"This is my first assignment in twenty years. I'm only aware of recent events, not their motivations."

Lilith considered Helena but couldn't see the danger in sharing a few details. "Basically, Luminita wants to make the Durand more powerful to stave off extinction. At least, that's what she claims. Ashcroft was an abomination, a Durand-turned-Vampire with unfathomable abilities. Luminita tried to replicate the results with Cohen but was interrupted. She wants Ashcroft, the Voynich Manuscript, Chance, and me. I'm the last descendent of the vampire who turned Ashcroft. As far as I know, that is her end game."

"She won't be able to resurrect the monster this time," Helena said with a satisfied smile.

"Why's that?"

"After I let you escape—"

"How *did* you find us?" Lilith interrupted quickly.

Helena frowned at her for a moment. "The same way I found you the first time—a tracking device. Luminita gave me orders to find you, incapacitate Ashcroft, retrieve the book, and take the brunette male traveling with you. She refused to give me his name, of course. As if I wouldn't recognize my own son."

Disdain dripped from Helena's words, but Lilith's thoughts halted on her list of priorities.

"Chance? But not me or Cohen?"

"Chance was a primary target, Cohen was secondary, but I was under explicit orders to ensure you lived and allow you to escape."

"That doesn't make any sense." Lilith shook her head. Even if Luminita had decided against the ritual, Lilith couldn't picture the woman purposely letting her go.

"She did not explain her orders. She never does," Helena stated with more than a little resentment. "Anyway, back to your original question. Once you were gone, I slaughtered the rest of my team, killed Ashcroft, and took precautions—as instructed—to ensure she doesn't bring him back."

The monster was finally dead, but how? "As instructed?"

"I asked Andrew Cohen what to do."

"Andrew? But I saw him—" Lilith stumbled through the words, too shocked to think clearly.

"Die? No. I mean, he was dying when I spoke with him. I had to give him a few drops, just so he could speak."

Tears prickled Lilith's eyes, and she swallowed hard before asking the one question she was scared to hear the answer to. "Is he…alive?"

"I don't know. I had two men take him to Goditha, but he was in rough shape. He asked about you, though."

Lilith wiped at her eyes and tried to stuff everything back down. "What do you mean?"

"He asked if you made it out. When I said yes, the man was beyond relieved, as if that was the only thing that mattered. I've never seen something like that from another Durand."

Those words cracked the dam she'd so carefully built, and Lilith sank into the chair to cover her face and cry. *Why me? Why am I so fucking important?* First, her partner, Alvarez, and then Cohen. Both had sacrificed themselves to keep her alive, but why? She wasn't worthy of devotion on that level.

After clearing her throat a few times and rubbing her face, Lilith managed to reinforce the dam holding her emotions and questionable self-worth at bay. She had to rein things in. Lilith couldn't afford to lose it now.

*Andrew might be alive. There's a chance…*But she was scared to believe those words. *Come on. Focus.*

"Perhaps…" Lilith's voice broke, so she took a few more breaths and tried again. "Perhaps you should tell me what you want from me."

"Look, Lilith. I'm not here as Luminita's agent. I'm here as your ally. Ashcroft is dead, I have the book, and I know where you are, which will remain secret. However, if I want to keep up appearances with the she-devil and find out more, I need to give her something. So, can I give her the book? Will that be enough to buy us a few more days? Is it too dangerous to hand over? I…have people I need to keep safe."

People? People she cares about, judging by her expression. "Who?"

The woman darted her eyes away and brushed her fingertips over her brow—Shame. "That doesn't matter."

She has a family. That's the only thing that makes sense, but the woman obviously wants to avoid that subject. "The book will probably satisfy her for a few days, but once she knows Ashcroft is thoroughly dead, she'll come after me. She thinks I'm some magical fucking key to making more like him. And she'll come after Chance. I'm guessing a half-breed between a vampire and Durand is uncommon?"

Helena dipped her chin and sighed. "Between two weak half-bloods, it's not uncommon, but both Bastien and I were purebloods. Fertility is rare among my kind. It's nature's way of balancing the scales, and I assume the same is true of your kind?"

"It is, especially between two purebloods…But are you sure Bastien *was* a pureblood? Everything I've read claimed he wasn't, and Chance has always presented as a weaker half-blood. At most, he only needed replenishments every four to six weeks."

Helena eased into a chair across the room, deep in thought. "Because of his top secret work, he kept his identity and heritage hidden to most. At least, that's what he told me. He said his boss wanted to keep him off the radar."

"Top secret work? Chance never mentioned what his father did for a living." An apprehensive chill raced down Lilith's spine. What kind of project could Bastien have been working on in Louisiana? They didn't have any major facilities in that state.

"Chance never knew. His father forcibly retired before Chance was born. I never asked for specifics…It's a long story."

"Do you remember who his boss was?"

Helena swung her deep hazel eyes up to meet Lilith's. "I remember." A warning hid in her expression which Lilith didn't understand. "Aaron Bogdan."

Lilith couldn't hide the shock on her face. Her mouth fell open. *Aaron had some top secret lab in Louisiana over twenty years ago? And no one knew?*

"Farren wanted the lab disabled and sent me. The mission fell apart, and I was pretty badly injured when Bastien found me." A soft huff escaped the woman's lips, and she stared off into the distance. "I actually thought that asshole was my savior when he got me out and took me home."

Helena shook her head, her shoulders sagging once again.

"In part, that's what made it hard to leave. I felt I owed him. I should have left sooner…if not for my sake"—she peered over at Chance sleeping peacefully—"for his, but the drugs made it so much harder. It started with pain pills after my injury. When I couldn't get those anymore, I turned to illegal drugs and eventually heroin."

"But you're a pureblood Durand." Lilith frowned, unable to follow the logic. "Why would you have lingering pain issues?"

Helena rubbed the skin above her eyebrow and kept her gaze on the floor. "I didn't. I was okay after a few days, but…the damage was done. The heroin was harder to give up than Bastien, but when Luminita told me Chance died…" Her voice broke again. "…I went from the hospital to rehab. It took over a year, but I've been clean about nineteen years now. I just wish I'd been strong enough to do that for him sooner."

The woman rose from the chair and took a step closer to the bed but froze when Chance's eyes moved quickly behind his lids. Something like fear flickered across her face, and she moved back toward the door.

"So, I can give Luminita the book?"

Lilith shrugged. "It's just an encrypted journal. It doesn't have any power. Luminita thinks it does, but she's delusional."

Helena nodded and came to a stop beside Lilith. "Please. Don't tell him who I am yet. I'd like to do that in person, once I get my people to safety."

Lilith immediately felt conflicted. As much as she didn't want to break yet another family secret to him, keeping this from Chance seemed inherently wrong. Helena should be responsible for telling him. This wasn't Lilith's secret to share, but how could she lie to the man she loved, even by omission?

"Please," Helena begged.

With a heavy heart, Lilith nodded. "Okay, but I'm only giving you three days. If you don't tell him by then, I will. We made a promise to each other. We don't keep secrets."

The woman placed a hand on Lilith's shoulder but didn't quite meet her eyes. "He's a good man, then? Despite my failures?" Hazel eyes with flecks of green rose to Lilith's, still brimming with tears.

Lilith swallowed hard and pulled on a soft smile. "He is the best man I know despite the things he's endured."

A few of Helena's tears fell, rolling down her cheeks. "Thank you for speaking with me. I will be in touch."

"Three days," Lilith warned.

Helena nodded. "That should be all the time I need."

Chapter 6

Late evening sun was filtering through the blinds when Chance opened his eyes. His lids were impossibly heavy, as if he'd slept for weeks. His gaze roamed around the unfamiliar room in confusion at first. Then he remembered: a doctor asking him questions, Lilith crying while kissing his cheek, the death grip he'd had on her hand. Chance had been so terrified she'd disappear.

The same doctor had returned to ask even more bizarre questions after they brought him to this room. Lilith hadn't been there.

Lilith.

A dart of panic shot through him, and he lifted his head, peering around the room. *If something happened to her…if Luminita found them…*

Chance finally spotted her curled up in a chair near the head of his bed, sleeping. Anxiety leaked from his system while he watched the steady rise and fall of her chest.

She's okay.

Lilith rarely looked peaceful when she slept. Relentless nightmares had tormented her pretty much every night since Miriah's apartment, but for the moment, she didn't seem to be dreaming. At least, he hoped she wasn't, not after Duncan's basement.

As if he had summoned them, the memories of that night flashed through his mind. Even weakened by the virus, Ashcroft had been stronger, faster, and Chance had lost. That final blow, talons raking through his chest, splitting his skin with searing agony…Chance shouldn't have survived that.

In the van, Lilith had been so desperate, scrambling to patch him up and stop the bleeding, forcing him to feed. But he kept trying to apologize, to tell her how sorry he was…that he loved her.

Tears flooded his eyes while those memories whirled around him. She wouldn't listen. Lilith had refused to let him say goodbye. She never gave up on him. *Never*, even if he had.

A sudden scratch in his throat made him cough, and pain flared across his chest. He lifted the gown enough to reveal bandages stretching from his left collarbone to below his ribs on the right. More surrounded his right shoulder.

"Chance?" Lilith's shaky voice caught his attention, and he turned toward her again with a soft smile.

"*Cher...Cherie.*" The voice that emerged was raspy and almost unrecognizable.

Lilith's smile went from tentative to absolutely radiant, and her olive eyes misted. She shot out of the chair, rushed over, and cradled his face, searching his eyes frantically.

"Please, tell me you're okay." Her chest heaved with each labored breath, and tears rolled down her cheeks. Even now, she was the most beautiful thing he had ever seen, and it made his heart ache.

"I'm...okay." His throat felt raw and itchy, like he'd tried to swallow fiberglass. "Can I have...some water, *amour...de ma...vie?*"

A beaming smile stretched her mouth before her teeth sank into her bottom lip. She nodded, then jogged over to the door and called for Nicci.

Chance carefully pushed himself into a sitting position. The wounds across his chest screamed in protest. When Lilith turned back to face him, she stopped and stared, as if she had seen a ghost. Considering the shape he'd been in, it wasn't far off the mark.

"You okay, Lily?" He knew the answer was no. How could she be, after all they had been through?

Lilith covered her mouth with her hand, trying to keep her tears at bay, and made her way back to his bed. "It's just"—she swallowed several times before she could continue—"seeing you sitting there, awake..." The words trailed off, and she covered her mouth again, trying to hold back the sobs threatening to take over.

With a few careful movements, Chance scooted to one side and patted the empty space. "Come here."

"I...I don't think I'm supposed to," she said quietly, but there were small tremors in her hands, nervous energy trying to rattle her apart.

"I don't...care." Chance cleared his throat with a wince and patted the bed again.

"I don't want to hurt you. You're still injured." Tears fell when she lowered her eyes to the floor, and it broke his damn heart.

"Lily, I…need you to come here, please."

She didn't argue after that, but only perched on the edge of the mattress, facing away from him. Lilith took slow, deep breaths, but her tumultuous emotions still rioted over his skin.

"*Cherie*…" Talking became a little easier each time. "Please."

An irrational fear took root the longer she refused. *Does she know? Did she find out somehow? She may be happy I'm alive, but that doesn't mean she's not angry at me. Although…I don't sense anger.*

Then her shoulders shook, and she slid into the bed, curling toward him gingerly while continuing to weep, as if some mental dam had burst. Chance wrapped his arms around her and pulled her against his chest despite the sharp stab from the movement. Pain didn't matter. It was temporary. *She* was all that mattered, and he needed to touch her, hold her, surround himself with her.

"Shh, *cherie*. I'm okay," he whispered against her hair. He moved his hand up and down her back in soft strokes. The warm weight of her in his arms felt like the missing piece to a puzzle. Lilith completed him, gave his life meaning…purpose. He rested his chin on her head, his eyes drifting closed while he inhaled the light lavender scent of her hair.

She's here. She's okay, he reminded himself.

"I…God, I really thought I'd lost you." Her voice dissolved into more tears, and Chance tightened his arms around her.

Grief, sadness, guilt, elation, and love poured through his skin like a tidal wave, but he held onto her, refusing to let go. The emotions mingled with his own, ebbing and flowing until it reached an equilibrium.

Movement at the door caught his eye.

Nicci snuck into the room. She flashed a sheepish smile, placed a cup on his bedside table, and tiptoed out.

Reluctantly, Chance let go of Lilith long enough to take a few sips of cold, refreshing water and then nestled into the bed with her. Lilith's tears began to slow while his fingers drifted through her blond curls. He soaked in every sensation, down to the rapid beat of her heart.

Once he told her what he had done, she would be furious, they would fight, and Chance might not be able to hold her like this for a while…if ever.

They'd made a plan. The whole group had agreed on it, and he'd changed it without anyone's knowledge. Part of him wanted to regret his decision, but he didn't. At the time, Chance had believed it was the only way to keep her safe, and he'd been right, even if things didn't go as planned. The fact he was here with her proved that much.

"I love you, *cherie*...more than anything in this world," he whispered with complete conviction. His life meant nothing without her, which made *her* life more valuable. If he hadn't made it...if he had died in that van, she would have survived. The others would have seen to that. Had the roles been reversed, he couldn't say the same.

"I love you," she whispered against his chest, her voice still thick with tears. "But don't you dare try to die on me again. Twice is enough."

An amused grin curved his lips, and he held her tighter, ignoring the flaring pain.

"Seriously." Lilith leaned her head back enough to lock eyes with him. "Never again." All the humor drained from her face with those words, leaving behind only fierce determination.

"You say that like I had a choice in the matter, *mi amour.*"

"Didn't you?" Those two words coupled with her stern stare made his chest tighten.

Shit. She knows. Panic flared, and Chance fumbled for some sort of answer, but she didn't wait for one.

"You told Cohen to get me out...You knew you were losing to Ashcroft." Her olive eyes searched his again, riding the line between sadness and anger.

If she knew the full truth, there'd be no doubt. She'd be furious.

"I didn't think there was time, and..." A heavy sigh rushed past his lips. "All I could think about was getting you out of there, away from him."

The crease between Lilith's brows deepened the longer she stared at him. "What aren't you telling me?"

Fuck. Even without Durand blood, she can read it all over my face.

"Lily, *mi amour*, please. Can we just lay here for a bit and appreciate the fact that we all made it out?"

For some reason, Lilith's face crumpled with fresh tears.

"Lily?"

Grief and sadness tinged with shame roared against his skin, and his eyes widened.

"What happened?" Chance barely got the question out past the panic squeezing his throat. Someone else had been hurt, perhaps worse.

"We didn't *all* make it," she whispered shakily. After a few steadying breaths, she finally continued. "Andrew…He…" An inexplicable blush tinged her cheeks. "He distracted Ashcroft so Tim and Gibson could get you out of there."

"What?" Chance's brain couldn't comprehend what she had just said.

"Cohen. He told me to 'live and be happy' and yelled for the guys to get you out of there. Then he passed me off to Nicci and charged Ashcroft. I saw that monster stab his claws into his fucking chest."

"He's dead? He died for me…us?" Chance was still struggling to understand. Sure, Cohen had made real strides at the cabin, but self-sacrifice?

"We don't know for sure, but Orchid said—"

"Wait, *what?* You've talked to Orchid?" Fear and panic returned with a vengeance.

"Um…yes…Maybe we should wait to discuss this. You just woke up, and you need to finish healing." Lilith's gaze fell to the bandages peeking out of his hospital gown, and she lay back down.

Chance sensed a rising level of anxiety before she started reeling in her emotions, burying them again, and he hated that she felt she had to.

"*Cherie*, talk to me." His fingertips ghosted down her cheek and over her bottom lip in a lingering caress.

Lilith's eyes didn't rise to meet his. They remained locked on the bandages while she held that emotional dam in place. "She wants to help us take down Luminita."

Confusion knit Chance's brow. "Why?"

A flicker of panic rippled over her skin. "Luminita betrayed her, and she wants…retribution. Orchid told me she killed Ashcroft and ensured they couldn't resurrect him this time. The monster is dead. It's finally over." A relieved sigh escaped her lips. Its warmth spread across his neck.

"What else did she tell you?" Chance tried to keep the nervousness out of his voice.

Lilith carefully snuggled closer and rested her head against his uninjured shoulder. "Can we just lay here for a while? Please?"

Chance slid his hand into her blond curls, cradling her neck and drawing her closer. She obviously wanted to delay this particular conversation, but he had to know.

"Lily…" He breathed against her ear. "Please, tell me what she said to you."

After an audible swallow, she inhaled and released it slowly. "She has the Voynich Manuscript, and she's going to hand it over to Luminita to buy more time but wanted to ensure it was a safe move. But she told me something else I don't understand…Luminita's orders. They just don't make sense."

She doesn't know. That thought brought equal measures of relief and anxiety. He had to tell her. If Chance kept it from Lilith, it would only make things worse. She deserved the truth. He'd made a promise. No more secrets.

"What were her orders?" Once again, he tried to keep his voice from shaking, but she didn't seem to notice.

"To retrieve Ashcroft, the book, and you. If possible, she was to deliver Andrew too, but she was ordered to ensure I made it out and to let me go. I don't understand it. Luminita needs me. Or at least she's convinced she does. I'm Gregor's last descendent."

Chance's pulse became erratic. The pivotal moment had arrived. He either told her the truth now or lied, hoping it never came to light. But things always found their way out of the dark eventually.

"Chance?" Lilith pulled back enough to search his face. "What's wrong? Your heart is *racing*."

For a moment, he stared at her olive eyes, the curve of her cheek, her full lips, and the light reflecting off her blond tresses.

God, she's beautiful. I can't keep this from her. I have to tell her, but…

The scene which had repeated in his nightmare surged to the surface—the angry tears, the look of utter betrayal.

If I lose her…

"Chance?" she prompted again, worry etched in every line.

"Lily, *amour de ma vie*…I have to tell you something, but please…just listen, okay?"

Her worry deepened to outright fear, and it almost changed his mind.

Chance took several deep breaths. The pain in his chest lessened with each one, but his arms tightened around her to stop his hands from shaking.

"I didn't disable our tail at the cabin that night."

Lilith peered up at him in shocked confusion but didn't say anything.

"I had them call Luminita, and I…" Words failed him when her features hardened. Chance squeezed his eyes closed and tried to memorize the warm weight of her in his arms. "I made a deal with her."

Lilith stiffened, and Chance's pulse throbbed in his throat.

"What deal?" she asked with carefully neutral tones.

"If she tracked our location and provided backup to take down Ashcroft..." *This is it. Once I say this out loud, I can't take it back.* "I agreed to surrender to her men...to give myself up *if* she let you go."

Lilith's emotional dam burst in an overwhelming rush of fear, anger, and betrayal. He had expected it...known it was coming, but it was still a devastating stab to his heart.

"You did *what?*" Her voice shook with those same emotions. "We had a plan!" She scooted back, taking her warmth with her, and every inch of him mourned that loss.

Slowly, reluctantly, Chance opened his eyes. Lilith sat up, her fierce stare pinning him in place.

"We had a bad plan," he said, "and you know I'm right. We all would have died in that basement. I..."

"You *lied* to us." She pushed the words through gritted teeth. "You promised me no more lies, yet you went behind our backs to play the fucking martyr?"

"Lily, you wanted to do the same thing. You were on the fucking verge of handing yourself over to Luminita."

"I didn't *lie* about it." Each word came out clipped.

"I had no choice," Chance whispered, knowing she wouldn't understand.

"There is always a choice. Why the hell would you offer to turn yourself over? Why would you just give up on everything...on *us?*"

Angry tears flooded her eyes just as they had in his nightmare.

His heart cracked.

"We couldn't win, Lily." He reached out to touch her cheek, but she jerked away from him.

"You don't know that." Uncertainty lingered in her voice.

"*I do,* and so do you." He released a heavy sigh. "I love you, *cherie*, and if something happened to you...if *you* died...I wouldn't survive that. I had the power to give you every possible chance, and I used it."

"And you think your life means less? You thought I'd just...what? Move the fuck on?"

Tears constricted Chance's throat, making each swallow an effort. "My life...means nothing without you."

Lilith's face contorted with fiery indignation, and the sight slid between his ribs like a knife.

"And you think mine does without you? God, you are fucking selfish." Lilith pushed off the bed to pace the room. Her hands shook with a rage that flooded the entire space.

"Selfish?" Of all the things Chance had expected her to say, that wasn't one of them.

Lilith came to a halt at the foot of his bed and stared him down. "Yes! You'd rather force me to live without you than face the possibility of living without me. You couldn't survive my death, so you'd rather make me try to survive yours. *Selfish.*"

Chance blinked. His brain scrambled to make sense of her argument. He had never looked at the situation that way.

"And did you ever stop to think about what would happen if your plan succeeded? You don't think I'd fight tooth and fucking nail to rescue your ass? That I might die trying to *save* you?"

"No," Chance admitted quietly.

A scathing laugh escaped her lips, and she started pacing again. "You just expected me to walk away and be grateful? To give up the man I love with every stitch of my soul and cherish the fact that *you* gave up?"

Shame settled across his shoulders. "Lily, I was only trying to keep you safe. You would have done the same."

Lilith stopped, and her body went rigid. "But I didn't! Do you want to know why?"

When he frowned in confusion, she continued.

"Because it wasn't just *my* life to give…not anymore. If I handed myself over to Luminita, I knew I'd be signing *your* death warrant because we are fucking tied together. My life *is* your life."

"*Cherie…*" Tears filled his eyes. The hollow ache in his chest became nearly overwhelming.

"No! Do you realize what your actions say?" Lilith eased onto the bed but stayed out of reach. "You don't believe that I love you as much as you love me. That's what this says." Her lip trembled, and her throat bobbed several times. "You think I'd be just fine without you."

"No, that's not—"

"*Your actions say otherwise!* Ask Nicci or Tim or Eileen about the past three days. Ask them about how I'd rather starve than leave your side. Hell, you can ask me about my fucking nightmares…Slashing open my veins to Ashcroft because he'd taken everything from me….because I had *nothing* left without you."

Recognition shot right to Chance's core, and his eyes widened. He had seen that in his nightmare loop, but how was that possible?

"Are you ever going to believe me?"

His shock-addled brain couldn't make sense of her question. "What?"

"Are you ever going to believe how much I love you, or are we destined to keep having this same fight?" Her olive eyes searched his for an answer, desperate for some sign she apparently didn't find.

Lilith squeezed her eyes closed, sending tears streaming down her face. Her heartache thrummed across Chance's skin like the prick of a thousand needles.

"Lily, I—"

"Good evening, Allen," a voice said cheerfully from the doorway. Dr. Preston strolled into the room, clicking away on his cell, oblivious to what he'd walked into. When the doctor finally glanced up from his phone, the man frowned. "I'm sorry. Is this a bad time?"

Chance wanted to scream "yes," but he needed a few minutes to compose his thoughts. Everything Lilith had said was true. Why couldn't he see that? Why couldn't he believe how much he meant to her?

Chance blinked back the tears and cleared his throat while Lilith quietly wiped her cheeks. "No. It's okay."

"Oh, good." Dr. Preston gave a relieved sigh. "I'll keep this short. All the labs, imaging, and tests look good. I want to keep you overnight, but I anticipate releasing you sometime tomorrow, as long as everything continues to go well."

"Thank you," Chance replied.

The doctor glanced between him and Lilith. "Try to get some rest tonight."

With that, Dr. Preston stepped out of the room, leaving them alone with the emotional turmoil separating them. It felt like a goddamn ocean.

"He's right. You should rest, and I should too." Lilith said stiffly, rising from the bed.

God, she sounds so…hollow, so heartbroken. It gutted him. "Lily." His voice broke on that one word.

"I'll have Nicci come sit with you."

She wouldn't even look at him. Lilith merely strolled toward the door, lost in thought…despondent.

"I love you, *cherie*," he called out, his heart fracturing into pieces.

She paused at the doorway and peered over her shoulder with tear-filled eyes. "Maybe one day, you'll believe I love you too."

The sadness in her voice cut through him more than Ashcroft's talons had, but before Chance could respond, Lilith slipped out of the room.

Chapter 7

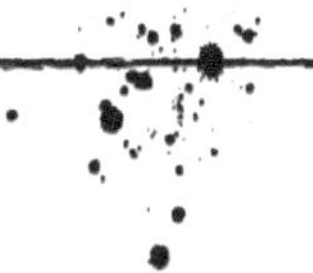

"**B**reathe…Just breathe. You're almost there," Lilith whispered to herself, frantically swiping her card at the motel lock. She whipped her head both ways, praying no one opened their doors. Lilith couldn't face anyone else, much less talk to them. Running out on Nicci without an explanation had been hard enough.

She had to get inside before the wall around her emotions completely shattered. Lilith needed to be alone with the pain tightening her chest, threatening to tear her apart. The idea of anyone witnessing her completely lose it mortified her, and it was about to happen. The inevitable collapse hovered so close. Tears already blurred her vision.

The box on the door finally flashed a green light, and Lilith barreled inside, closed the door behind her as quickly and quietly as possible, and locked it.

Alone. I'm finally alone. Lilith sagged against the door while every internal stone tumbled from the dam. The overwhelming weight and agony of everything she'd held at bay through the ride back to the motel crashed over her, and she sank to the floor in tears.

So many thoughts raced through her head, and Lilith didn't know where to start. Her throat constricted, her lungs burned, and her stomach twisted. While she covered her face with her hands and sobbed, her mind settled on the thing that hurt the most.

Chance had lied. He went behind her back and made a deal with their enemy. Once again, he hadn't trusted her…hadn't trusted in them as a couple or everyone as a team.

Instead, Chance had made a deal—his life in exchange for hers. But it wasn't noble. Chance would rather force her to live without him than risk having to live without her. If his plan had worked, she would have drowned in that unsurmountable guilt. How could he not see that?

Besides, Luminita would have never honored the deal…not forever. Eventually, she would come for Lilith.

But what cut the deepest was Chance's lack of faith in how she felt about him. What else did she have to do to prove it to him? Would he ever see it? Truly believe it?

Fuck! Lilith screamed internally while rubbing her face.

Then the shame settled in. She had kept secrets from him tonight too. Lilith could have told him the full truth about Andrew—what he had said to her, the kiss that still summoned a host of confusing emotions—but she didn't. She could have told him the truth about Orchid, but she didn't.

Perhaps he's right not to fully trust me, she thought with utter despair. She scrunched her face against another bout of soul-rending tears.

Sure, Lilith had given Orchid three days to get her things in order, but she had withheld the full story with Andrew because…She paused, searching for the truth.

Because she thought Andrew was dead and it shouldn't matter? Because she was scared of how Chance would react? Because she was terrified he might sense something she didn't want to discuss? Because she still didn't know what in the hell to say about it, especially now that he might be alive?

Lilith raked her hands through her hair and squeezed her eyes shut. *I'm too tired to do this. I can barely think straight. I've had, what? Five hours of sleep in the past three or four days seems like a generous estimate.*

The sight of Chance's grief-stricken face when she walked out of the hospital room flashed through Lilith's mind again, bringing fresh sobs and a crushing wave of guilt. *I walked out on him. He came back from the very brink of death, and I fucking walked away.*

No matter what he had done, she couldn't justify that. Her guts twined into knots, making her nauseous, but it cleared her mind enough to focus.

Shower. I need a shower. Lilith finally forced herself away from the door and stumbled toward the bathroom, which summoned memories of their night in New Haven.

Even after she'd gone off on him about the candles, Chance had meticulously removed every article of her clothing and carried her into the shower. Everything he had done that night was a slow, purposeful devotion. He'd been determined to make her feel better and had more than succeeded.

Lilith gripped the bathroom counter to stay upright. *Have I ever done anything like that for him?* She stared hard at the sleep-deprived woman in the mirror. The answer was obvious, and it made crimson blossom over her cheeks.

Accepting what Chance gave was different than expressing her own feelings. Words only went so far. Had she ever truly shown him how much she loved him back? Perhaps there was a reason he thought she didn't feel as deeply, that she would survive losing him. It wasn't true, but did he know that?

Maybe, after Boston, she wasn't capable of fully revealing her heart. The constant rejection had been just as painful as the physical abuse, and she rarely initiated intimate encounters. Perhaps Boston had drilled that fear of rejection so deep that, even with Chance, she didn't feel comfortable starting things.

What if that asshole ruined me? What if I just can't be that open again?

Lilith shoved away from the counter, stormed over to the shower, and turned on the water. The idea that David Boston's abuse would forever haunt her, forever change how she acted, how she responded, made rage burn through every cell.

No. Stop giving that asshole any of your time and energy. He's taken enough.

A large part of Lilith wanted to race right back to the hospital, but she couldn't face Chance like this: irrational, unable to think, sleep-deprived to the point of insanity. They needed to talk, and she wasn't capable of that currently.

A shower and then sleep, Lilith told herself.

The steamy water did little to quiet her rambling brain, which jumped from one problem to another as if incapable of a coherent series of thoughts.

Emotions and flashbacks only spun faster when she curled up in the bed. Her mind inevitably settled on that night in the van, and tears flooded her eyes. There had been so much blood. Chance kept trying to talk to her, to say he was sorry. At the time, she'd thought he was giving up, apologizing for leaving her, but what if he wasn't? What if he had been seeking forgiveness, trying to tell her about the deal with Luminita?

Lilith hugged the pillow tighter. It didn't fill her with warmth the way Chance did, but she still sobbed into it, like she had against his chest. There was so much, too many things, and she couldn't pick out anything from the chaotic storm in her head anymore. It surrounded Lilith like overwhelming white noise, threatening to obliterate her.

For one purely selfish moment, she wished it would.

Lilith stared down the familiar earthen tunnel. Dread blossomed in her chest. She couldn't count how many times she had stood in this exact spot, staring at the faint pinpoint of light at its end.

"I can't do this," she said, too tired and emotionally burnt-out to endure the tortures in store for her.

Lilith closed her eyes, took steady breaths, and tried to change the dream. She'd heard of certain people eventually controlling lucid nightmares like these.

When the panic finally eased, she found herself crawling through the infernal tunnel. Mud squished between her fingers, and rocks bit at her knees, like they always did.

So much for control.

The tunnel narrowed, forcing Lilith to her belly. She continued to claw forward. The walls closed in until she couldn't move. Her lungs seized with panicked breaths while she squirmed but made no progress. The mud and stone pushed against her naked body, suffocating her. Pure chaos swirled through her mind. Lilith couldn't suck in any more air.

This is a dream, she reminded herself. Once again, she squeezed her eyes closed and tried to focus through the roaring noise in her head.

"One…two…three…breathe," she repeated until the panic receded.

Lilith dragged in another slow breath and released it through pursed lips. Then she wiggled forward, reaching the tunnel's end.

When her feet landed on the smooth concrete floor, she frowned. This wasn't the rock-strewn ground she was accustomed to. It wasn't a cavern full of stalagmites and stalactites which greeted her. There were no pools of blood or flickering light from old lanterns.

An impossibly long room stretched out before her, with two interior doors to the right, a boarded-up door to the left, and an exterior door with blinds at the other end.

Duncan's basement.

The absolute silence made her ears ring, and Lilith stood frozen, waiting for the first horror to appear. There were plenty of things her mind could use to inflict damage here—Ashcroft's attack that first night,

Cohen's confession, that inexplicable kiss, Chance being struck down, Ashcroft's talons stabbing into Cohen's chest…

She waited, but no one appeared. The basement seemed as vacant as a tomb.

"No!" A muffled scream cut through the silence, most likely emanating from behind one of the interior doors.

Against her will, Lilith's feet moved toward the first room. A growing sense of apprehension accompanied each step and made her hands shake when she reached for the handle.

"Stop, please! It's enough!" The shrieking voice from inside the room was clearer now and…familiar.

Lilith paused when Andrew's blood-curdling screams came from inside. Her throat bobbed, and his last words to her echoed through her head—*Live and be happy.*

After swallowing hard, she twisted the knob and shoved the door open. It wasn't the bedroom she remembered. This seemed more like a prison cell, with a toilet, sink, and barred window.

When she stepped into the small room, she noticed someone curled up on a cot against the wall. Lilith recognized the man's features and sandy blond hair immediately.

Andrew seemed to be sleeping, but not peacefully. His eyes moved rapidly behind his lids, and his face contorted in pain before he screamed out Luminita's name. When his body thrashed, blood blossomed on the thick bandages around his chest.

Lilith rushed inside and sank to her knees beside the cot. This was a dream, it wasn't real, but she felt compelled to help him anyway. After all he had done for her, the least she could do was comfort him in a nightmare.

"Andrew," she whispered near his ear. "Wake up."

His golden eyes snapped open with shock and recognition, and his face turned toward her. "Lilith?" The word held such desperate hope.

When she reached out for his hand, Cohen's form dissolved to smoke, and her fingers passed right through. Confusion and fear strangled her heart while his image melded into the darkness and vanished.

Gone. Cohen is gone. The same grief she had felt that night washed over her.

Before she had time to move, the entire room tilted, and her hands swung out to grab the cot's frame. The thing shifted and slid toward the door along the rapidly increasing angle of the floor. When the bed collided with the wall, the jolt cost Lilith her grip, and she slid.

Then she was falling.

Her stomach lurched into her throat until she landed hard on a rocky surface. The impact to her shoulder and hip sent pain flaring through her body. Her head cracked against the stone, and everything went black.

When her eyes finally opened again, she stared up at the mass of stalactites hanging from the ceiling, like wicked teeth dripping with blood. Flickering light made shadows dance along the ceiling, and her eyes followed them to the massive stalagmite dominating the room.

Back to our regularly scheduled program, I guess. Lilith sighed heavily, too worn-out to summon her usual sense of urgency in these nightmares. *How many ways can my brain torture me? Eventually, it'll run out of ideas, right?*

"*Criiiiin!*" Luminita dragged out the word, her melodic tones filled with malice.

It reminded Lilith of the siren.

Crin—Romanian for Lily, Luminita's nickname for me.

Odd. Typically, Ashcroft and his victims dominated this space.

Lilith tried to climb to her feet, but a violent wave of nausea sent her right back to the ground. The unrelenting pounding in her head felt real, and every call from Luminita made it worse.

Lilith curled onto her side, cradling her head in her hands, and fought to breathe through the nausea making her mouth water.

This is just a dream, she reminded herself again. *This is a fucking nightmare.*

After a few minutes of steady breathing, her head began to clear, and her nausea receded.

Good. Now wake the fuck up!

Apparently, that exceeded the limits of her power. Luminita was still calling for her.

When Lilith rolled onto her back, a hand clamped over her mouth. She froze, eyes widening. Her heart pounded against her ribs in a violent assault.

"Shh," a voice to her right whispered.

Slowly, Lilith turned her head.

Xander, another in a long list of names weighing on her conscience.

His face was a mask of concentration while he stared ahead, but what caught her attention was his neck. Bones protruded through bruised skin at impossible angles. The injury was exaggerated but still disturbed her.

"*Crin!*" Luminita called out again.

Xander shook his head. The bones in his neck crunched hideously with each movement.

"I'm losing patience, *Crin*." An icy malevolence slithered into Luminita's voice, making Lilith's heart race even faster.

The tone reminded her who Luminita truly was. The Romanian had been there when Ashcroft tortured Lilith's cousin Miriah for days. She had happily watched while Duncan devolved into a self-mutilating thing incapable of cognizant thought. Luminita had lied to Chance and Orchid, keeping them apart. She'd strapped Cohen down, a man she supposedly loved like a son, and cut into his flesh for the mere possibility of power.

She is just as much of a monster as Ashcroft.

No…

Worse.

Ashcroft tormented the body in horrific ways, but Luminita shredded a person's sanity, weaponized their emotions, irrevocably broke people like she had with Andrew, Duncan, Orchid…Chance. The woman needed to die…even if it was only in a dream.

"I'm sorry," Lilith whispered, pulling Xander's hand away from her mouth.

Sorrow pinched the man's face, and he nodded. Xander touched her shoulder, stood, and walked across the rocky floor. He didn't flinch when sharp stones sliced his feet, leaving bloody footprints behind. The man kept moving, as if on autopilot, stepped right into the rancid pool of blood beside the stalagmite, and sank below the surface.

Come on. Just get through this. Lilith slowly stood and slid her foot forward, navigating the spaces between jagged rocks.

Once she reached the massive stalagmite, Lilith flattened her back against it. Rough stone bit into her bare skin while she tiptoed along the edge, but Lilith kept her eyes on the putrid blood. The surface remained placid.

There were no ripples, no bodies rising to the surface, and little Emily—Ashcroft's victim who had plagued Lilith's nightmares recently —didn't make an appearance.

Either my brain recognizes Ashcroft is dead and has decided not to torment me with his victims or even my nightmares are exhausted.

"Crin!" The word echoed with a sharp snap.

Lilith continued to edge around the stalagmite until the lantern revealed what lay in store. It felt as if her heart had stopped dead in her chest.

Luminita lorded over a metal table, twirling a scalpel in her hand, but it wasn't Andrew laid out before her. Blood welled from several deep cuts across Chance's chest while he struggled against the leather straps.

"Ah! Finally!" Luminita's aquamarine eyes glinted in the lamplight, and a maniacal grin split her lips.

"Put the scalpel down." Lilith demanded, walking into the open space.

Luminita raised one elegant eyebrow, as if Lilith had said something amusing. "But aren't you curious?"

Lilith took careful steps forward, and Chance's eyes finally locked onto her. He tried to scream, but the rough cloth shoved in his mouth muffled the sound. She swallowed hard, refusing to give Luminita the satisfaction of her tears.

"Curious about what?" Lilith asked, closing in.

"Stop!" With one clipped word, Luminita swung the blade to rest at Chance's neck.

Lilith froze, her body going rigid. *This is just a dream*, she repeated, but this time, the mantra didn't help.

"Good girl." Luminita's hideous grin returned, and the scalpel trailed to hover over Chance's heart. "Now…don't you wonder what makes him different? What makes him special? You're a woman of science. Surely, you want to know." When Lilith didn't answer, Luminita's stare hardened. "I know I do."

The blade pushed into his skin just below his sternum, and even with the rag in Chance's mouth, his shrieks echoed through the cavern.

"No! Stop!" Lilith screamed, as if the woman was cutting her open as well. Perhaps, in a way, she was.

Luminita paused, with the scalpel still embedded in Chance's abdomen. "Why should I? He's mine, after all."

Those words struck Lilith like a physical blow.

"A life for a life. That was the deal. I can do what I want." The Romanian's lips curved into a haunting smile. "I. Own. Him." She slowly spoke each word to emphasize her point.

White-hot rage burned through Lilith, and she curled her hands into fists. "No!" Anger drove her forward without even thinking.

Luminita dug the scalpel deeper and pulled up, dragging the blade against the bottom of Chance's sternum, which produced a sickening sound.

Lilith came to an abrupt halt. The world seemed to shatter around her. *No, no, no. This is just a dream. It isn't real!*

No matter how many times she repeated them, the words didn't stop the wild beating of her heart or quell the panic tightening her lungs. Despite her earlier resolution, tears gathered along her lashes.

Chance's blood pooled and then trickled to the floor in a steady drip. *Blood. There's so much blood.* Lilith stared at the lacerations across Chance's chest while the van shot out of the driveway. She called out directions to the others and applied as much pressure as possible. Blood welled up between her fingers. Chance coughed and gagged, trying to breathe.

Lilith blinked and the flashback ended.

Luminita now stood at Chance's side, blocking Lilith's view, but his screams echoed through her head with heartbreaking brutality. He thrashed against the restraints while Luminita continued to work.

No, no, no!

Lilith lunged forward, but some invisible force kept her from reaching them. "Chance!" Tears blurred her vision, and she raged against the barrier, slamming her fists against it until the skin split.

His body went still, his legs no longer kicked, and it broke something in her...*everything* in her.

Luminita spun, inspecting something clutched in her bloody hand. Lilith couldn't make sense of it at first, no doubt protecting her from the horrific sight.

"Hmm," the woman mused.

She raised her gaze to meet Lilith's, and Luminita stepped closer. Her dark grin sent tremors coursing through Lilith's body.

"I think this...belongs to you."

When the woman held out the object, recognition hit Lilith like a bolt of lightning. The world spun. Her gaze narrowed on the ragged lump of muscle.

Every inch of her soul shattered into agonized shards while Lilith stared at her name carved into Chance's heart.

Chapter 8

"Andrew," a feminine voice whispered. "Wake up."

Cohen jolted awake from his latest Luminita nightmare, his heart hammering against his ribs and his breathing labored. He scrambled to a sitting position and wildly scanned the small room.

It hadn't changed. Only the toilet, sink, and bed kept him company. There was no one in the room.

Did I imagine the voice? I must have. It sounded like...No. Impossible.

When the adrenaline began to leave his system, the pain set in. He winced with a grunt and peered down at the bandages across his chest. Crimson blossomed from the center.

"Great. I'm bleeding again." A heavy sigh rushed past his lips, and he pulled his knees up, resting his forearms on them.

The small, barred window in his cell was dark. It was night. *That makes...three days? Four?* Cohen couldn't be certain since he had been in and out of consciousness, especially in the beginning.

Luminita had to be the one holding him captive. The assassin had sent Cohen to Goditha before he passed out that night, despite his desperate pleas to let him die.

Assuming I'm right, my delayed healing is probably punishment. Someone obviously had given him enough Durand blood to keep him from dying, but not enough to fully heal him. Being isolated also eliminated any chance of leaching off others to heal the damage Ashcroft had inflicted.

He drew in a slow breath, and his mind inevitably returned to that fateful night. The events played out in his mind vividly, as if they were happening all over again.

Chance had put up a hell of a fight with Ashcroft, but the monster eventually got the upper hand, slashing at Chance's thigh and shoulder.

Instead of calling for help, Chance had screamed for Cohen to get Lilith out.

He'd tried, but Lilith…*God, she is a force of nature. The most stubborn woman I've ever met,* he thought with the ghost of a smile.

As soon as Cohen grabbed her, she'd elbowed him in his already broken ribs to get away. He couldn't breathe, especially not with the damn Kevlar vest. Cohen had ripped it off and sucked in a painful breath, just in time to watch Lilith bury a knife in Ashcroft's side. The monster had turned on her…stalking her like a ravenous lion.

The fear had been crippling. Thankfully, Chance intercepted Ashcroft, giving Cohen a second opportunity to get Lilith out of the infernal basement. Again, he had tried.

Stop! I'll never forgive you if you don't let me go right fucking now! Lilith's words had utterly destroyed him. He'd tried to reason with her, but the devastation in her eyes told him everything he needed to know. She was right. If he had forced her to leave the basement without Chance, she would always hate him for it, and he couldn't survive that. Without her in his life in some way, his held no meaning.

Every cell in his body had screamed for him to ease her pain, to do *something* right for once.

Even then, I failed. His stomach soured at the thought.

Tears stung Cohen's eyes when he recalled that pivotal moment. He could have shoved her toward the door and rushed in to save Chance, but no. Instead, he had selfishly confessed his love for her, caressed her cheek, kissed her…all while her fiancé was losing his fight with Ashcroft.

Fucking selfish. It didn't matter that he had ultimately done the right thing. He didn't do it when it counted. Cohen had seen Tim and Gibson dragging Chance out, observed the vicious wounds across Chance's chest…known his odds of survival were slim to none.

If I'd acted sooner…

The thought of Lilith out there, grieving yet another tremendous loss he could have prevented, tormented Cohen's soul, assuming he had one. He had failed to save her partner, Alvarez, in Phipps Bend. Cohen had failed to protect her father, Gregor, in Farren's courtroom. And now, he had failed to save the love of her life.

As if the point needed to be emphasized, his mind returned to the kiss—his ultimate betrayal of them both. It had been a taste of heaven and would forever haunt him.

Live and be happy. Those had been his last words to her while her fiancé bled out. *Fucking cruel.*

Andrew angrily wiped the tears from his eyes and smoothed his blond hair tight to his scalp.

If this is hell, I deserve it. Fuck. I deserve worse.

As soon as the self-deprecating thought left his mind, it was replaced by the memory of Lilith in his arms, his lips caressing hers in absolute devotion. All he remembered sensing from her during that kiss was shock, but for him, nothing would ever be its equal, and he had *stolen* it.

The fact that he still dreamed about it, wanted it, craved it, made his stomach twist in knots.

He had prayed on the porch that night to let her friendship be enough. The hug she'd given him then had been pure and real. He hadn't taken it by force. But when his actions counted the most, he had failed her.

Is it really love if I didn't put her first when it truly counted?

Cohen slammed his fists against the mattress, but the action was far from satisfying. He surged off the cot, ignoring the blaring pain in his chest, and punched the wall with every ounce of strength. The concrete held steady, and bones fractured, but he didn't care. It didn't matter.

He reared back again, driving his fist into the wall. It left blood behind this time. The sharp stab up his arm quieted the chaotic noise in his head, if only for a moment.

When Cohen readied for a third strike, the clunk of a lock made him freeze. He whipped his head toward the door.

It was definitely a lock, not the slide of the opening where they pass me food once or twice a day.

The metallic squeal of a handle turning followed. Andrew dropped his arm to his side and turned with anticipation. His rage would finally have a target other than himself.

Each second stretched out, making his chest heave with quick breaths. He locked his eyes on the door, as if the hatred they contained could burn holes through the metal.

The door swung open and clanged against the wall. Two men marched inside with stun rods slightly smaller than cattle prods.

"On the bed!" one man barked, but Andrew stared him down and straightened.

There would be consequences, and Andrew welcomed them. Anything to drown out the emotional torment in his skull. If he was lucky, they would knock him out and he would have a temporary reprieve from it all.

Without a flicker of emotion, the guard jabbed the baton into Andrew's side, hitting him with 50,000 volts. Every muscle seized. Every joint locked in place. Cohen gritted his teeth against the burning current. When the shock finally ended, adrenaline flooded his system, keeping him upright.

"On. The. Bed!" the guard repeated, emphasizing each word.

When Andrew still refused to comply, the second man stepped forward and slammed the rod's handle into Cohen's jaw. The teeth-rattling blow sent his head whipping back sharply. The room spun, then plunged into darkness for several seconds. Cohen's knees hit the concrete.

Every part of his body hurt, but the sudden stabbing pain in his chest doubled him over. Cohen clutched the saturated bandage and fought to drag oxygen into his lungs. Agony threatened to tear his heart apart. Sweat beaded on his skin, and darkness bled into the edges of his vision.

Something hard pressed into his throat, cutting off his meager air supply. The object jerked his head backward. Then it clicked. The guard was behind him, pressing his stun baton against Andrew's throat and forcing him to face the door.

Either this guard is new or Luminita arranged this.

All mercs employed by the Durand were issued a unique cocktail of mood stabilizers and psych meds to suppress emotion so no one could draw on them from a distance. Touch, however, allowed Cohen to siphon off energy regardless.

Andrew struggled long enough to grab the baton, positioning his hand against the guard's, and drew miniscule amounts of what he needed. The blinding pain in his chest eased, as did the pressure against his throat, but the baton stayed in place, a continued threat.

The sharp click of stilettos echoed before a familiar silhouette appeared at the open door. Equal measures of fear, panic, and rage blocked out everything else.

"That is enough," Luminita said in a surprisingly soft tone.

Her heels continued to sound against the polished concrete floor. She paused before him and crouched to meet his eye level.

"My dear, Andrew." Luminita lifted his chin, but when he averted his gaze, her touch quickly retreated. "I do not like seeing you this way."

Concern flooded her every word, but Cohen knew better.

"Then let me go. Problem solved," he growled through clenched teeth.

Luminita clucked her tongue with a wry smile. "I do not think so, *fiul meu.*"

Cohen froze. She hadn't called him that in years, and he despised the fact that it still had such an effect on him.

No. I will not let her fucking win. Andrew summoned his memories from the medical center—every cut, every slice, every desperate plea, every blood-curdling scream, every promise of power, and every bullshit speech about the *greater fucking good.*

"*My son?* You don't get to call me that after what you've done!"

Luminita leaned back on her heels and considered him for a long moment. "How did you finally heal the scars?"

Cohen balked at the unexpected question before the moment with Lilith on the porch filled his head again, cooling his anger. The warm weight of her arms around him, her face pressed against his chest, her soft breaths tickling over his arm, the sweet lavender scent of her hair… The pure moment belonged to him, and he refused to let Luminita sully it.

"That doesn't concern you," Cohen snapped.

The woman's startled expression quickly transformed into one of malice. "Oh, but it does, *fiul meu.* I gave them to you for a reason." Her nail tapped his chin, and she dipped her head, peering at him through thick lashes. "It will be a pity if I have to recreate them."

A snarl contorted Andrew's face, and anger flushed his skin. "Fuck you!" He lunged forward, but the stun rod at his throat reined him in, crushing against his windpipe.

Cohen coughed and gagged while Luminita stood.

"You had such promise once," she said with a wistful sigh. "Perhaps, in time, you will again." Luminita lifted her gaze to the guards. "That's enough for now." After one last lingering look, she turned to the door.

"I will *never* trust you, and I will *never* forgive you," Andrew called after her, each word biting with venom.

Luminita stiffened but didn't turn around. "We shall see."

Chapter 9

Luminita stormed down the hallway, silently cursing herself. She had lost control and snapped at Cohen viciously, which would only make her mission to sway him back to her side more difficult. However, when she'd asked him about the scars and how they had healed…

The *ocean* of emotions which filled him before he refused to answer had struck her like a physical blow, and she'd retaliated by threatening him. It was a foolish and reckless move she would have expected from a youngling like Alexis, not an ancient such as herself.

The unfortunate truth was, Luminita truly loved Cohen like her son. That hadn't been a lie. She had tried to cut him out of her life after their meeting in the cabin. Luminita had said as much to Alexis, with good reason. Still, when it came time to give Orchid her orders, she had included Andrew because she could not let him go.

Her thoughts returned to the swell of emotions from Cohen. The overwhelming longing, peace, and devotion made Luminita curl her hands into fists again. Even at their best, Cohen had never cared about her so deeply.

She had practically raised him after Farren slaughtered his parents. Luminita taught him how to feed, how to skirt Farren's notice, how to survive amongst the cut-throat Durand…how to be a man.

He is my son. What makes this vampire so special? I know it must concern Lilith. She does not deserve his love, when she doesn't even return it.

Luminita yanked open the central lab door and stormed inside. Anger and jealousy still twisted her stomach.

"Ms. Dragomir," a guard said from across the room. "You have a visitor."

After straightening and smoothing her scarlet jacket, Luminita walled off every single emotion with precise expertise and pulled on a smile. "I'll receive my guest in my quarters." Without waiting for a reply, she stalked toward the door on the right which led to the staff's living spaces.

Once she was alone in the hall, she released a heavy sigh of disappointment. She had chastised Alexis for letting her emotions get the better of her, for allowing her turbulent history with Andrew to get in the way of her mission, and here Luminita was, doing the exact same thing.

Pathetic.

After rolling her shoulders, she exhaled slowly and released the gnarled lump of ugly feelings. Such things were beneath her and her cause. After all, Lilith didn't matter, only her blood did. He would see that eventually or...

Wheels turned in Luminita's mind, devising a path which just might suit her better than her original plan. A smile graced her lips, and she strolled toward her small apartment at the end of the hall with renewed confidence.

"Come in," Luminita called from her chair after a series of rapid knocks sounded on her door. She checked the gold watch on her wrist. "You're late. We were scheduled to meet two hours ago."

Orchid dipped her head and hurried inside but kept a reasonable distance. "My apologies. I was tracking a few leads."

"And how are your searches progressing? It has been four days now." Luminita narrowed her eyes, stretching her senses for any emotion the agent might reveal.

"I still don't have any leads on Ashcroft. If he's feeding, the bodies have not been found. The tracker I had on the FBI agent went dark, but I do have something for you."

Hmm...she seems truthful. "What do you have?" Luminita raised one delicate eyebrow and studied Orchid's every movement.

The woman slung her backpack around and extracted something wrapped in cloth. "I found it outside Duncan's home. Thankfully, the fire missed it."

Orchid unwrapped the mysterious item while she approached, and when the thing lay exposed, a weight lifted from Luminita's shoulders. Although...its condition left much to be desired.

"Very well done." She delicately extracted the fragile book from Orchid's hands. Two bullets marred its blood-stained cover, but a careful peek inside revealed the necessary pages and cipher were still usable. "The Voynich Manuscript is critical to my research."

Orchid was wearing a prideful smile when Luminita glanced back up at her.

"Thank you. I want you to double your efforts to find Lilith Adams and her male companion. Whatever you require to accomplish that mission is yours."

"But…" Confusion radiated from the woman. "You expressly ordered me to let her go."

Luminita gently laid the book on her end table, turned in her chair to fully face the assassin, and glared up at her. "And now I am changing your orders."

The woman blinked, as if suddenly remembering who was in charge. "Yes, of course."

However, Orchid didn't leave. Instead, the woman's curiosity perfumed the air.

"Is there something you wish to ask, agent?" Luminita kept her voice neutral this time. Orchid was a deadly enemy, and keeping her loyal was worth a few concessions.

"Three things…if I may."

Luminita waved her hand, inviting the woman to continue.

"The asset I sent you, Andrew Cohen, is he…alive?"

She hadn't expected that question. "Why do you ask?"

Again, Luminita watched Orchid carefully, studying the brief flickers in her expression as she raised her chin.

"I take pride in my work, and he was in bad shape. I wasn't sure he'd make it to Goditha."

After considering the assassin for a moment, weighing the consequences of answering, Luminita responded. "He is alive, although still recovering. What are your other questions?"

"Why the change in objectives, and who is her *male companion?* Refusing to give me a name does not inspire my trust."

The last part made Luminita pause. This went beyond a mere concession into truly dangerous territory.

"Sit, please." Luminita gestured to the chair across from her while gathering her thoughts. Orchid discovering Chance's identity seemed inevitable now, and withholding the truth from her would only hurt the mission. Luminita needed to keep the agent on her side, to make her understand.

Orchid slowly sank into the chair as directed, keeping her eyes locked on her host.

For a moment, Luminita remained silent, considering the best tactic to use. Intimidation might secure her loyalty but could easily backfire. Telling the truth…

"I lied to you twenty years ago."

"What?" the woman whispered in blatant surprise.

"Chance did not die in that car crash. *He* is one of your targets, Lilith's brunette companion."

As expected, rage flooded the room, and Orchid shot to her feet. "He's alive? You lied to me, and *this* is how you tell me?"

Every ounce of the woman's anger felt genuine, and Luminita internally sighed in relief.

"I understand why you would be upset—"

"Upset?" Orchid shouted. "You *stole* my child!"

"No," Luminita stated plainly. "I saved him…from you."

The woman's mouth snapped shut.

"Do you honestly think he'd have been better off *with* you? You told me the stories…what happened in that house." Luminita rose from her chair with regal grace. "What would you have done with him during the year or more it took for you to get clean? Would you have locked him in another closet? Would you have left him in the care of an abusive man like Bastien?"

Orchid swallowed hard, and shame shimmered over her skin. She collapsed onto the chair, eyes distant and glassy.

"And what if you relapsed a third time? How desperate would you have to be to use your son as payment?" Luminita stared down at the woman. "I needed an operative, and he needed safety. *That* is why I lied."

Shame still burned Orchid's cheeks when her head bowed. "But…all these years…" Her voice cracked with tears.

"After your first two relapses, I couldn't trust your recovery, and once I did…" Luminita stepped forward and crouched before Orchid, just as she had with Andrew. "Do you think your husband would understand? Does he even know your history?"

After swallowing hard, Orchid shook her head. "Only that I'm a recovering addict. I never told him about Chance and Bastien."

"I thought not." Luminita patted Orchid's knee and pulled on a sympathetic smile. "I did you both a favor. Besides, I kept an eye on him until the vampire Elder took him under his wing. Gregor gave him a good life."

Orchid lowered her gaze. Nothing but sorrow and guilt emanated from her.

"Now, to answer your first question. Your son made a deal with me. He agreed to come here, as my guest, if I let Lilith go. But as you know, he didn't honor his end."

Orchid snapped her head up, furrowing her brows. "He was half-dead when they pulled him from the basement. He might not even be alive. I was fighting off Ashcroft and couldn't intercede. It is *my* fault."

An amused chuckle escaped Luminita, and she rose from her crouched position. "Fault is not my concern. Now that I have the book, I require them both. Are you still capable of your mission, or should I enlist the services of someone else?"

After hastily wiping her cheeks, Orchid stood up, straightened, and lifted her chin once more. "I am more than capable."

"Are you quite sure? If tracking down your son and his fiancé is something you cannot handle—"

"No," Orchid interrupted. "If you don't intend them harm, I see no problem with the assignment."

"Quite the contrary." Luminita smiled softly. "Although they may not believe it at first, I mean them no harm. I merely need blood samples and to study their interactions, test their abilities. Nothing invasive."

"Then consider it done." Orchid turned on her heel, marched to the door, and exited without another word.

Luminita sank back into her chair. Her fingertips grazed the book's surface in a loving touch. "Guilt and shame are such effective tools." She sighed happily. Some dark corner of her mind protested with memories of old wounds, but she ignored it.

Even if Orchid had somehow managed to find out the truth before today, Luminita's words would haunt her as much as her past.

However, giving Orchid what she needed was crucial to success. The woman had failed her son in so many ways. Allowing her an opportunity to protect him for once and safely deliver him here...

That will be her motivation, to do what she couldn't when he was young. But if she fails—or she turns on me—I'll remind her what it's like to lose a child.

As soon as Orchid was alone in her car, she pressed the call button for Noah's cell, her finger shaky.

Come on, come on. Pick up!

When Noah's cheery voice announced he was sorry he had missed the call and invited her to leave a message, Orchid's gut turned sour. She hadn't been able to reach him since the night she dispatched Ashcroft.

Luminita has to have them. Orchid turned her gaze back to the sprawling building.

She could storm in there and search for them, but the layout was constructed for easy defense, and the men Luminita kept in residence were highly skilled, more so than the team she had sent after Ashcroft.

The odds of Orchid pulling off a successful rescue solo were horribly slim, but if she recruited allies with a common goal…

Orchid quickly looked up the Econo Lodge North in Knoxville and dialed the number. "Room 107, please…Yes, Mrs. Jones."

Chapter 10

A loud metallic ring, like an old alarm clock, woke Lilith from a restless sleep. She threw a hand out, fumbling over the items on the nightstand and knocking several things to the floor before her hand landed on the clunky phone. With a groan, she snatched the receiver and held it to her ear.

"Hello?" She tried to focus on the clock. *10:00 a.m.? I've been asleep over twelve hours? God, it only felt like four.*

"Lilith, it's Helena."

A jolt raced up Lilith's spine, burning away her drowsy stupor in an instant. "How did you get this number?"

A huff crackled through the line. "I found you at the hospital. Did you really think I didn't know where you were staying?"

Lilith worked her way into a sitting position. Every muscle ached from days of sitting in those hospital chairs. "Fair point. Is everything okay?"

The woman sounded...different, agitated, and that probably wasn't a good thing.

"No. I need to meet with you and your team. I'm about six hours away."

The nervous tremble in Orchid's voice raised every hair on Lilith's body.

What if Luminita got to her? What if it's a trap?

"Are you still there?" Orchid asked impatiently.

"Yes, but—"

"You don't trust me," the woman finished for her. "I understand, but I *need* your help. I do not want to hurt any of you. Please...for the sake of both my children."

Both? Lilith's mind ground to a halt.

"Chance and my daughter. She's only seven."

The desperation in Orchid's voice was undeniable. Maybe it made Lilith an idiot, but she believed her. Plus, the woman already knew where to find them.

"We'll be here at the motel. The hospital is discharging Chance sometime today." Lilith didn't feel the need to point out the obvious implications, and thankfully, Helena picked up on the message.

"I understand and will honor my deal." The line went silent for a moment. "Thank you."

"Don't thank me yet." Lilith hung up before Helena had an opportunity to respond.

Fuck. This is not going to go well.

Frustrated exhaustion rippled through Lilith's body, and she rubbed her face. How much more could they all take before they inevitably broke?

Hell, maybe we already have.

T im groaned at the muffled ring of an old telephone. *Fucking motels and their paper-thin walls.*

He rolled on his side and stretched out his arm for Eileen, but his hand hit the empty sheets. Tim frowned and peered around the dimly lit motel.

When he didn't immediately spot her, panic darted through his chest. He sat up, scanning the area more thoroughly. The bathroom door hung open, and the room was empty. No one else was there.

Tim hopped out of bed, grabbed his jeans, and hastily pulled them on, his mind running through the possibilities. *Technically, she's rooming with Nicci, but all her stuff is still here. She could have gone over to talk to Lilith...or maybe she went back to the hospital.*

The door swung open while Tim was yanking on an olive-green T-shirt, and he whirled around. Eileen stood in the sunny doorway with eyebrows raised and two cups of coffee in her hands.

"Are you going somewhere?"

A cross between a sigh and a chuckle escaped while Tim sank onto the bed's corner. Once the relief wore off, the embarrassment set in, and his gaze fell to the carpet. "No...I just..." *God, stop being an idiot and just spit it out.*

When he looked up, she was still standing in the same spot. The sunlight at her back highlighted her brown pixie-cut like a warm halo.

"Are you okay?"

"Yeah." A smile curved his lips while he soaked in every beautiful detail, from her curvy yet athletic figure to her sparkling blue eyes. "I just woke up and you weren't here, so…I was worried."

"Oh." A delicate blush graced her cheeks, which only made her more irresistible. "I went to grab us some coffee. Two sugars, right?" Eileen slid the cups onto the table and closed the door.

"Yeah, thanks." Coffee was exactly what he needed right now, or he'd fall into another fourteen-hour coma. He felt every one of the sleepless hours standing guard as he crossed the room.

"Yours is the one on the right," she said over her shoulder while she opened the curtains to let in a little light.

Tim hesitantly sipped, expecting it to be piping hot. To his surprise, it was the perfect temperature, and he took a deep swig. "How long were you out getting coffee?" The question left his mouth before he could think it through. *I sound like a damn stalker. Real smooth, Bardow.*

When Eileen peered over her shoulder with a raised brow, he quickly amended his words.

"It's just the coffee isn't scalding hot."

"Oh, that." Eileen chuckled. "I hope it's okay. It's habit. I always pop in a few ice cubes so I can drink it faster."

"Huh." Tim took another swig, already feeling more energized. "I like it."

While he drained the last of his cup, Eileen closed the distance, rested her hands on his hips, and stared up at him. "I'm sorry if I scared you."

After placing his empty cup on the table, Tim grinned and slid his fingers through her short hair. "No apology needed. I'm just on edge, but if you're feeling generous, I wouldn't turn down a—"

Before he even said the word, she gripped his face and pulled him closer. Her lips crashed against his like she'd been waiting for an excuse to kiss him…*as if she needed one.* The intoxicating sweep of her tongue over his sent a heady rush straight down to his stomach and lower. The heat was instantaneous and exhilarating.

Tim instinctively drew her against him before backing her up to the bed. A need he had never really known pulsated through his center. It was inexplicable yet undeniable. He *needed* this woman…now… tomorrow…the day after…

Before his brain could finish that thought, Eileen's legs hit the bed. They tumbled onto the sheets, and a giggle of excitement interrupted their kiss. It was the most beautiful sound he had ever heard.

Tim rolled, propping himself up on one arm, and gazed down at the dazzling smile Eileen wore. He brushed his fingertips over her lips, her cheek, and then sank them into her silky hair. A deep well of emotions hovered on the tip of his tongue, but he couldn't seem to find the words.

Slowly, her smile transformed into an expression of hunger and longing which affected him on an entirely different level. The compulsion drew them together like magnets.

Suddenly, he understood why Chance had acted so irrationally at the thought of losing Lilith. It had seemed insane to him at the time, but now…

"Where'd you go?" Eileen caressed his cheek, her eyes searching his. The way this woman just…knew him, still caught him by surprise.

"Nowhere. I'm right here," he whispered, softly capturing her bottom lip.

Eileen deepened the kiss with a zeal that stole his breath. Tim didn't fight it when she rolled him onto his back and slid on top, straddling his waist. She planted a palm in the center of his chest and sat up, staring down at him as if trying to understand something.

"I've never been like this…" Her eyes widened a touch, like she had surprised herself by saying the words out loud.

Tim rubbed his hands up her thighs to her hips and grinned. "Like what? An intoxicating hellcat who knows what she wants and takes it?"

Eileen tilted her head with a shocked expression. "Is that what I am?"

"It is with me," Tim stated simply. "And that is most definitely *not* a complaint."

A smirk lifted one corner of her mouth, and a vibrant blush made her skin glow. "You're right. *You* bring that out in me. It's like…" She frowned in thought, and Tim held his breath, waiting for her to finish.

When she didn't, he placed a hand over hers, still resting on his chest. "Eileen." Once her eyes met his, he continued. "You can talk to me. It's okay. Whatever you need to say, you can tell me."

Those stunning blue eyes glistened while she stared down at him. "It's like you've made me comfortable enough to be the person I've always wanted to be."

The confession made tears sting his eyes and Eileen's blush deepen.

Her gaze drifted to his hand on hers. "You…make me feel beautiful and irresistible…You irradicate the rejection and unworthiness I've been forced to feel my whole life. It hasn't even been a week and I…" She paused, swallowing hard, and found his eyes again. "I don't know how to explain it."

Tim's heart swelled, and he pulled her down against him. "I know the feeling," he whispered into her hair. "I can't explain it either. When I was young, I dated but never let myself get attached. Being…*different* comes with certain rules, and when I got shipped overseas, I just…stopped trying. I didn't see the point, especially after the shit with Jill's husband."

While he spoke, Eileen traced her fingertips up and down his arm. Every stroke stirred something inside him deeper than lust, urging him to keep going. Romantic heart-to-heart conversations were not his specialty. Hell, he'd never actually had one before that he could recall, but with Eileen he felt safe to share his thoughts.

"I've never been drawn to someone. And with you…it's more than that, more than attraction."

She tilted her head up with a hopeful smile, and Tim drank in every line and detail of her face.

"You are fierce and brave yet vulnerable and delicate. I shared the darkest parts of myself, deeds most people would condemn me for, but…here you are, and I…I've absolutely fallen for you."

As soon as the words left his mouth, the fear set in. Tim couldn't unsay it. He couldn't take it back. Eileen made him feel safe to talk freely, but what if he had overshared.

What if she isn't at the falling stage yet? What if it's too soon and I just wrecked everything by opening my dumbass mouth? What if it's all too much…if I'm too much? It's not like I have a basis for comparison.

Eileen's lip trembled slightly before her mouth found his in a kiss that wasn't insistent or carnal, as they usually were. This one was tender, slow, accepting, and completely devastating in the very best way. It held all the answers she couldn't seem to voice, and Tim's fear of rejection withered away with each press of her lips.

He sank his hands into her hair, and her tongue caressed his in leisurely strokes. The heat between them was like burning coals instead of the raging bonfire it had been moments ago, and it tasted sweeter, deeper, more meaningful.

I could get lost in a moment like this…linger there forever. Well, perhaps not forever, but—

A loud knock came from the door.

Of fucking course, Tim internally groaned.

Eileen broke the kiss to peer over her shoulder. The sheer curtains were still drawn. She would only see an outline, if that.

After the second knock, Eileen peered down at Tim with a slight frown. "I *should* answer that, right?"

A low chuckle rumbled from his throat. It seemed he wasn't the only one reluctant to let the moment slip away. "It's probably important, so…"

After a heavy sigh, she patted his chest. "To be continued, but…" Eileen paused, a brilliant smile slowly unfurling. "I've fallen for you too, Timothy Bardow." She snuck a quick kiss while he lay there in stunned silence.

Once Eileen slid off him to cross the room, Tim sat up and quickly adjusted himself so it wouldn't be immediately apparent what they had been up to. The woman had a definite effect on him in more ways than one.

I've fallen for you too. How could he not grin like an idiot at that?

"Hey, Lilith," Eileen stated clearly from the doorway. "Come on in."

When Lilith stepped into the room, her gaze shifted from Eileen to Tim and back again. "Sorry to bother you, but can we grab breakfast and talk? The three of us?"

"Is something wrong?" Tim asked.

Everything about Lilith's demeanor, from her fidgeting hands to her shifting posture, screamed that there was.

"I need to fill you in on a few things."

Okay. Vague. "Give me five minutes to finish getting dressed, and we'll head out, okay?"

Lilith nodded with a forced smile. "I'll be in my room." She left without another word.

Tim stared at the door after Eileen closed it.

Something is not right…Maybe a lot of somethings.

"At least it looks like she actually slept," Eileen said, as if trying to find a bright side.

"Yeah. I'm still worried about her, though. She doesn't seem…right." Tim sighed and grabbed his duffle from the dresser.

"She's been through a lot. More than most people experience in a lifetime."

"True." Tim pulled on his socks before grabbing his boots. Knowing that didn't ease his concern, though. He had seen that despondent look before, that expression of feeling utterly lost. "I just hope we can end things before she breaks."

"We will."

He peered up at Eileen's soft yet confident smile and desperately wanted to believe her.

Chapter 11

The quick walk across the street and down a block to Waffle House passed in silence. Lilith led the way, with Tim and Eileen right behind her. Somehow, that only increased her anxiety.

A few times, she thought about slowing down to walk beside them, but perhaps being alone with her thoughts would allow her to organize them into a cohesive narrative.

Probably not.

Lilith wished Nicci could have joined them, but her partner was still at the hospital, keeping an eye on Chance.

Chance.

Her thoughts halted on that subject with equal measures of panic and heartbreak. The way they had left things…Correction—the way *she* had left things…

No. Business. You can dwell on how to fix things later, assuming they can be fixed after I tell him everything. Now is not the time to dwell.

Lilith stuffed those thoughts back into a neat little box and trudged across the diner's parking lot to the front door. Once she opened it, Tim reached out, holding the door for Lilith and Eileen.

Ever the gentleman.

The place was packed with truckers and travelers from I-75 seeking either breakfast or lunch, plus a few who seemed local. Although the cacophony of noise would cover their own conversation, it also made Lilith's head ache. All the boisterous voices, the sizzle of the grill, the metal spatula's sharp clang, kids screaming, clanking glasses…It all seemed overwhelming until they found a vacant booth in the back corner.

Lilith slid into the near side, giving Tim and Eileen the seats against the wall. Over the past few months, she had adapted to Chance's need to watch the exits and assumed Tim would be the same. It made sense, with their background in security.

"Mornin', folks. Coffee?" The waitress swooped in with a steaming pot and plastic menus before they had fully settled in.

All three of them covered their cups.

"Ice water will be fine," Lilith replied with a strained smile. Even social pleasantries required too much effort this morning.

Once the frazzled waitress nodded and trotted off to the next table, Tim cut right to the chase. "Okay, Lil. What's going on?"

After checking the server's location to ensure she wasn't about to surprise attack them again, Lilith answered, keeping her voice low enough to avoid casual eavesdroppers. "Orchid came to the hospital."

Both Tim and Eileen's eyes widened.

"And you're just telling me now? When did this happen?"

Lilith understood the edge to Tim's voice, but it didn't make it any less abrasive.

"Last night. And I'm telling you now," Lilith snapped. *Yeah, twelve hours of sleep wasn't enough.*

Although a frown wrinkled Tim's brow, he remained silent this time.

"She wants to work with us to take down Luminita."

"What?" Eileen blurted in surprise.

Meanwhile, Tim's eyes tightened in clear suspicion. "Why would she do that? Why turn on her boss?"

For a minute, Lilith carefully considered her answer. She had promised Orchid three days, but that only applied to Chance. However, if she told Tim and Eileen now, they would have to carry that secret too.

"I can't tell you…not yet." Lilith sighed and dropped her gaze to the menu.

"*You can't tell us?*" Tim huffed while rubbing the back of his neck. "What *can* you tell us?"

The anger made sense. They had become close, shared secrets, and now, she was holding back. Lilith had expected Tim to be upset, but asking him to keep something this big from his best friend until Orchid talked to Chance…that would be selfish and cruel. She needed to carry the burden alone for now.

"Look, Tim. I'll tell you everything soon. I promise. But for now, please trust me. She has a very compelling reason to hate Luminita *and* help us."

After a few seconds, Tim nodded. "Fine. You might wanna know that Eileen figured out how Orchid tracked us down."

"A GPS location sticker inside the FBI file on John," Eileen added. "We tossed it."

"That explains a lot." That's how the woman had found the cabin, how she located Duncan's, and how she knew which motel to call. But it didn't explain everything. "Before I discuss my conversation with Orchid, there's something else you need to know."

Lilith swallowed down the betrayal and pain the subject elicited before continuing.

"Chance made a deal with Luminita."

"What?" Tim's voice rose to a concerning volume. "What the—"

"Here ya go." The waitress placed three ice waters on the table before grabbing her pad and pen. "Are y'all ready to order?"

Tim continued to stare at Lilith, which made her skin crawl for some reason. Maybe it was the internalized guilt his glare seemed to reinforce.

Everyone quickly gave their orders, but the tension only increased around the table. As soon as the waitress gathered the menus and headed for the kitchen, Tim broke the silence, keeping his voice lower this time.

"What do you mean, *he made a deal?* What fucking deal?"

Lilith focused on the table and fought back the tears threatening to rise. "He didn't disable our tail. He had them call Luminita, and he…" God, she didn't want to say it out loud. "He offered his life for my freedom. He agreed to go with Orchid and her men if they let me go."

Her shoulders slumped forward under the weight of a dozen mixed emotions, from anger to shame.

"That's why they let us go and didn't follow," Eileen said while Tim glared through the window, his jaw flexing. "I wondered why. She had enough men, and when they intercepted us on the way to Duncan's, they only blocked our way for a few minutes and drove off. It was…weird."

"Orchid told you this?" Tim managed to ask, though his jaw remained tight.

"No. Chance did." Despite her best efforts, tears welled in her eyes.

"And I'm guessing that's a big part of why you look miserable right now?" A gentleness infused his words that Lilith hadn't expected, especially after his gruff question.

After swallowing a few times, she met Tim's gaze. "He lied to me, to us, and…he still doesn't understand my point of view. Still doesn't understand why it bothers me so much."

Tim slid his hand across the table to grab hers. "I'm sorry, Lil. I didn't know."

Lilith gave his hand a squeeze and flashed a tight smile. "I know you didn't. No one knew. He didn't want anyone to talk him out of it."

"I would have kicked his ass if I had. Hell, it's still not off the table," he grumbled.

"But," Lilith began, trying to get the conversation back on track, "the important thing is that he *had* a deal with Luminita, and we don't know how that will change things or what her response will be. Obviously, he was unable to hold up his end."

She refused to think about what would have happened if he had.

"Okay, something to keep in mind. Now, what did Orchid tell you?"

"She wants to meet with us. She…needs our help."

Tim raised his eyebrows. "And we just trust her?"

"I think Luminita has her daughter. At least, that's what she inferred."

"I don't see how that would make you trust her more. *If* it's true, that only gives her more incentive to turn us over to her boss."

"I understand what you're saying, Tim, but…" *Fuck. How the hell do I explain this without giving away Orchid's secret and putting Tim in an awkward situation?*

"Why can't you tell us what makes you trust her?" Eileen asked simply, as if trying to tackle the problem from a different angle.

"Because it's not my secret to share, and if I tell you, you'd have to keep that secret too…for now, at least."

Eileen nodded, but Tim narrowed his eyes again.

"Does it concern an orchid tattoo?"

"What?" Tim's unexpected question caught Lilith completely off guard. "What tattoo?"

"He didn't tell you that either?" An aggravated sigh rushed past his lips.

"Who? Chance?" The idea of another secret between them made her stomach twist.

"Yeah. The night Orchid attacked—"

"Here we go!" The server slung plates of steaming food in front of them, oblivious to the tense atmosphere. "Anythin' else I can get ya?"

"We're good, thanks," Lilith replied hastily. She couldn't even summon a polite smile this time.

Once the waitress retreated with a slight huff, Tim continued. "Chance told me the woman put up a hell of a fight, but he had the upper hand until he spotted an orchid tattoo on the woman's forearm. *Apparently, his mother had one just like it.*"

The emphasis he placed on the last sentence made his train of thought quite clear.

"Why wouldn't he tell me that?" Lilith sighed and covered her mouth, as if that could stop the frustrated sob trying to break free.

"I know why, even if I don't agree with his decision." Tim rubbed the back of his neck again. "He was embarrassed. He froze, and he almost paid for that mistake with his life. Plus, he thought he might have just imagined the whole thing. Because it's not possible, right? Helena Vieux died in a car crash twenty years ago."

Omission was one thing, but lying…Lilith refused to do that. Of course, she didn't need to *say* anything. The expression on her face and the pained sigh she released gave Tim everything he needed.

"Dear fucking god. Are you serious?"

All Lilith could do was nod. She had no idea what to say anymore.

"Orchid is Chance's mother?" Apparently, Agent Hersch needed the clarification.

"Yes," Lilith replied quietly.

The woman's mouth opened and then closed when something occurred to her. "She didn't know about him, did she? That's why she wants to take down her boss?"

"After the crash, Luminita told her Chance died. She didn't know."

"That doesn't exactly make the woman a fucking saint." Tim clenched his hands into fists on the table. "The shit he's told me about his childhood paints a dark fucking picture."

"I am not arguing that fact, but if you'd seen her in the hospital, watching Chance sleep…I *believe* she wants to kill Luminita for what she did. Orchid told me the plan was for her to escape Bastien *with* Chance. She wanted an opportunity to get clean and be a good mom for him. Luminita stole that from her…from both of them."

"That's easy to say twenty years after the fact," Tim snapped.

"I know, but she's our best weapon against Luminita, and she told me something else. Did Gregor ever tell you about a research facility down in New Orleans?"

"New Orleans? No. As far as I know, there's never been one in Louisiana. I mean, there's blood banks in Lafayette and Shreveport, but that's it."

"Orchid told me her last mission for Farren was industrial espionage at a research facility in New Orleans…owned by Aaron Bogdan. I was hoping she was wrong, but—"

"Wait, her last mission for Farren? When was that?"

"Before Chance was born. It's how she met Bastien. He was a scientist at the facility."

Tim's brows shot up. "Bastien Deveraux was a scientist? The same druggie piece of shit that beat Chance and stole cars to pay for his habit?"

"She said they forced him into retirement before Chance was born. And apparently, Aaron hid his lineage too. Bastien was a pureblood. She's sure of it."

"But didn't you tell us Chance was in Nichols's database and it showed he was a half-blood and something else?"

"Yes, but according to Orchid, the fertility rate between two purebloods like her and Bastien is basically non-existent. That's why Luminita and Aaron have such an interest in Chance. The combination must have skewed Nichols's results."

"Unless…" Eileen added. "What if your uncle knew about the database and changed it to keep anyone from knowing about Chance?"

The agent made a very valid point. They already suspected Aaron. If they could prove he had access—or better yet, had changed something in the database—perhaps the Elders would finally back them.

"It's possible. I'll run it by Nicci when I get a chance. Until then, I told Orchid to meet us at the hotel. She should be here in about five hours or so."

Tim sucked in a deep breath, still rubbing his neck, and closed his eyes. "Fine. We'll meet her, but it has to be *all* of us."

"I know, Tim. She wanted me to keep her identity secret until she can tell Chance face-to-face. I gave her three days, or I'd do it for her."

Tim smirked in approval before digging into his omelet and hashbrowns.

Lilith took a few bites of her cheesy eggs, then asked for a box. The entire conversation had left her stomach uneasy. Maybe she would have an appetite later.

Probably wishful thinking, but what else do I have?

Chapter 12

Nicci stood outside of Chance's room, watching him through the door. He was still sitting on the side of his bed, fully dressed. The man looked absolutely miserable.

The way his shoulders slumped and his head hung low broke her heart. He hadn't moved since the nurse told him the doctor would be in soon with discharge instructions, and that had been forty-five minutes ago.

She had no idea what Lilith and Chance had talked about last night, but it obviously upset them both. Lilith basically ran out in tears, without a word, and Chance…He had tossed and turned all night, and after he woke up, he'd been like this: despondent, defeated, and devastated.

It's none of my business, Nicci reminded herself for the thousandth time.

But when Chance rubbed his face with a pained sigh, like it ripped from his very soul, she couldn't just standby anymore.

"Hey," Nicci said softly, stepping into the room.

Chance glanced at her with red-rimmed eyes before returning his attention to the floor.

"Do you want to talk about it?" Nicci asked tentatively. She sank onto the chair across from him and waited.

"There's not much to say. I fucked up." The man's voice strained under the weight of those words.

"We all fuck up. I'm not Tim, but I'm here if you want to talk."

Again, Chance glanced up at Nicci. "I appreciate it, but…" His face pinched, as if trying to hold back tears, and he raked a hand through his hair. "It's bad. I'm not sure she'll forgive me this time."

Nicci arched a brow. Her protective instinct had kicked in, but she tried to keep it light, for his sake. "Come on. What did you do? Kiss your nurse?"

When Chance's glare pierced right through her, she got the message. *Now isn't the time for jokes. Noted.*

"This is serious, Nicci. Lilith is…beyond pissed. I *hurt* her."

The last three words summoned her fierce loyalty. No more kid gloves. "Tell me what happened." The statement was firm this time, and Chance seemed to understand it was no longer a request.

"I couldn't let her die, Nicci," Chance pleaded. His red-rimmed eyes overflowed with tears. "We needed a better plan, more resources, but I knew everyone would veto it."

Apprehension blossomed in Nicci's chest as the gravity of the situation sank in. "What did you do?"

Chance rested his elbows on his knees and stared at the floor as if it held the answers. After a rattled breath, he finally spoke again. "I made a deal with Luminita. I'd go willingly with her men if they made sure Lilith lived and let her escape."

"What the actual fuck, Deveraux?" Nicci huffed and launched out of the chair to pace the room. Anger, betrayal, and frustration fluctuated through her body with every step. "No wonder she was so upset last night."

"I know," Chance replied with a weary sigh.

"What?" Nicci rounded on him. her hands curling into fists. "You didn't think she was carrying enough fucking guilt?"

Chance blinked, somehow surprised by her reaction or maybe her words. "I didn't…I didn't think of it like that. I just *had* to keep her safe, no matter the cost."

"What about the cost to *her*?" Nicci took another step closer, barely containing her rage. "Did you honestly think sacrificing yourself wouldn't break her anyway?"

Chance exhaled slowly. He returned his gaze to the floor, and his shoulders slumped further. "Like I said. I fucked up. I couldn't face losing her, and I acted out of fear."

Somehow, that cooled the anger surging through her. Nicci slid back onto the chair and took his hand. "If your plan had worked, you would have lost her anyway. Worse, you'd have to live lifetimes without her."

Slowly, Chance raised his eyes to meet hers. "But she'd be alive."

"For how long? Days? Weeks? She'd run headfirst into a damn suicide mission to save you. You need to get it through that thick skull of yours that Lilith is *not* interested in a life without *you*."

Chance searched Nicci's eyes desperately, and a few tears trickled down his cheeks. "Do you think that's still true…after last night?"

Chance barely managed to get the words out, and it was one of the saddest things Nicci had ever heard. After giving his hand a squeeze, she asked, "What did she say before she left?"

"*Maybe one day you'll believe I love you too.*" His throat bobbed several times, and his face pinched in pain.

"She didn't say *loved*…as in the past tense?"

"No," he whispered, like he was afraid of the hope she offered.

"See? You two are gonna be okay. Come on, Chance. You and Lilith are like fated mates in a cheesy paranormal romance. Personally, I find it disgustingly, nauseatingly, infuriatingly adorable."

One corner of Chance's mouth curved upward, and Nicci took that as a win. *Maybe a change of topic is in order.*

"Hey, did she happen to say anything about your visitor yesterday?" Lilith had run out so fast last night, Nicci hadn't gotten an opportunity to ask.

"Visitor?" Chance frowned. "Who?"

Nicci shrugged. "I don't know…Some woman. Lilith gestured for me to stay at the nurse's station. They talked for about half an hour, and then the woman left. I didn't recognize her."

"No, she didn't mention it. Although…I didn't give her much opportunity to talk." He raked his hands roughly through his tousled hair.

"Did she tell you about Cohen, at least?"

"That he stepped in to distract Ashcroft so we could all get out? Yeah."

A half-smile emerged when Nicci sat back, shaking her head. "It's kinda difficult to fathom, isn't it? Cohen…taking one for the team."

A muscle ticked in Chance's clenched jaw. "He didn't do it for the team."

"I know, but still…He could have let you die."

Chance's stare hardened. "He nearly did. I only survived because Lilith and the rest of you got me here just in time. The doc said I coded in surgery three times. I think the only reason Cohen stepped in was because he knew she'd never forgive him if he didn't."

"Well, if you're right, his plan sucked. I mean, does it matter if Lilith is pissed at him if he's dead?"

"That's a matter of perspective." Chance huffed. "I tried to be understanding, even supportive, but the man kept pushing his limits. He crossed a damn line when he said *she* was his purpose."

Nicci patted his arm, hoping to de-escalate the conversation. "Well, I'm glad you're the one who's still here. I mean, Andrew did seem to make some progress, but you're right. Besides, you're my third favorite person." Nicci flashed a brilliant grin, which earned a genuine smile from Chance. "There ya go! An actual smile."

"I'm guessing Lily is number one and Tim is number two?"

"Naturally. You better get your shit together, though, or Eileen is gonna knock you down to fourth place."

"Wait. What about Alicia? Or is your girlfriend on a scale of her own?"

Nicci sensed all the bright humor draining from her face, and her hand slipped away from Chance. "I…uh…broke up with her while I was in New York."

The entire fight flickered through her mind again—Alicia's teary pleas for honesty, how she had begged for Nicci to just let her in…But she couldn't.

"What happened?"

Nicci shrugged with a heavy heart. "I love her, but…she's human. It had to happen eventually."

"But does it? Tim doesn't seem to think so."

"Tim is thinking with his dick." Nicci frowned.

"Come on, Nic. You know better than that. Things are changing."

Nicci hopped up from the chair and out of the conversation. "I'll see what's taking the doc so long."

Alicia was a can of worms Nicci wasn't prepared to open just yet. The fact that Alicia was human and Nicci was a pureblood capable of living for centuries wasn't the only problem. Nicci's job had become a danger to everyone close to her, especially her girlfriend.

If Alicia had been at Nicci's apartment when Aaron's men tossed the place, she would have been dead, just like Tim's friend Ray, who had been guarding the place. Putting an innocent civilian in that position was selfish and reckless.

"Thank you, Nicci," Chance called after her.

"No problem, big guy." Nicci flashed a smile and jogged toward Dr. Preston's lab.

"Miss DeL...Smith."

Nicci turned around when a deep voice almost used her last name. Dr. Preston stood by the printer behind the nurse's desk.

"I'm just about to give Mr. Jones his discharge papers and go over a few things, but perhaps I could speak with you first...in private?"

Once she nodded, he grabbed the papers from the printer and led Nicci toward his lab, stopping in the doorway.

"I placed a biohazard cooler packed with ice in his room during shift change. Take it with you. It's only four units, but that's all I could spare without drawing attention."

"Thank you, Doc. We appreciate it." That would at least get her and Lilith through the next few days—maybe a week if they rationed.

"Just don't forget our deal. You and...*Mrs. Jones* promised me blood samples." A rather clear threat lingered in the man's eyes.

"That won't be a problem. We'll both come in tomorrow. You have my word."

Doctor Preston nodded, apparently satisfied with her answer. "Let me talk things over with Mr. Jones, and you two can get out of here. I'm actually quite surprised Marie isn't here."

Chance had insisted on not telling Lilith when he was discharging. After their conversation, Nicci wondered if he was scared Lilith wouldn't have shown up.

"She's probably still sleeping. The woman had to crash eventually."

"I suppose so. She showed a lot of dedication, sleeping in those god-awful chairs."

Chance stared out the cab window while they headed to the motel. Thankfully, Nicci seemed to be done talking.

On second thought, maybe that was a bad thing. Being alone with his thoughts only twisted the knot of panic tighter in his chest.

He had to apologize. Chance needed to convince Lilith he realized how bad he had fucked up and would never do it again. He *had* to fix things between them. The mere possibility of her rejecting him now, after all they had been through, made bile rise in his throat. He couldn't lose her...not now, not ever.

Rain pattered against the glass, and Chance watched the drops streak across the window. He loved the summer rain, especially when it broke a heat wave like this. The drops were the perfect temperature. Still, his heart weighed too much to enjoy it.

An ocean stretched out between him and Lilith, and he wasn't certain how to navigate those waters to find his way back to her, if he even could. He wished he shared Nicci's confidence about their future.

When they reached the motel, Nicci slipped him a keycard. "That's your room *with* Lilith—107. If things don't go well, I got a spare bed in my room right next door—108." Before he said anything, she lunged in for a hug. "I really think things are gonna be okay, though. Lilith *loves* you."

"Thanks, Nicci." He bent down to give her shoulders a squeeze. "I appreciate everything."

"You're welcome." Nicci flashed an encouraging smile and headed off toward her room.

Chance faced down the door to 107 with fear and uncertainty. He frowned at the keycard in his hand.

Given the situation, maybe I should knock?

His gaze traveled to the T-shirt and sweatpants the hospital had provided, and he felt utterly ridiculous for being self-conscious. *This is my fiancé, not a first date.* But some part of him wondered if that was still true. He didn't know what to expect after the way they had left things.

Chance closed his eyes and stretched his senses for the first time since Duncan's basement. *Nothing.* Either she wasn't inside or…

He pushed farther and recognized Nicci's signature next door but no one else's. *Okay. The rest of them aren't here.* At least, he hoped and prayed that was the reason.

Chance slid the card across the box and opened the door to an empty room. The relief of not finding a body didn't last. Reflexive panic quickly overpowered it, and Chance struggled to suppress his emotions.

Tim is an excellent bodyguard, and Eileen is very capable. Wherever Lilith is, Tim and Eileen are probably with her. Breathe.

Chance sank onto the edge of the bed, trying to quell all the thoughts racing through his head. He rubbed his face, his temples, his neck, but nothing eased the knots in his chest and stomach.

Nothing would help until he made things right…assuming he could.

Chapter 13

Shifting hues of red, purple, and orange filtered through the small window, illuminating the steel door keeping him captive. Cohen sat on his cot, with his bare back against the cool concrete, legs drawn up, and arms resting on the knees of his black pants. He watched the sunset's subtle color changes with conflicted thoughts.

Fiul meu—Romanian for *my son*. Luminita hadn't called him that since he had left for the police academy, one of their last private moments together.

After the lies, the betrayal, the torture, the endless fucking mind games, that word shouldn't have had an effect, but it did, and that disgusted him.

A heavy sigh full of anguish rushed past his lips, and he counted the door's rivets once again.

What did she say the last time she called you that?

Cohen's entire body stiffened when the disembodied voice broke the silence. *No. I will not respond. I will not give the demon power.*

That cruel inner voice had disappeared after his confession to Lilith about Alexis and all the other women he had slept with, pretending they were *her*. Apparently, it was back to haunt him again. After days of isolation, sparse nutrition, and virtually no energy to feed on, he shouldn't have been surprised.

Tell me, the voice hissed.

Andrew turned a laser-like focus on the concrete blocks, searching for hidden images. He shut everything else out—or tried to.

You'd tell Lilith…

Her name broke his control, just as the demon had known it would, and the memory bubbled to the surface.

Jenny Allen

It had been a sunny day in early July when they had met in Greensboro—a week before he was due to report to APOSTC Police Academy in Tuscaloosa. Luminita had chosen an old hotel in a neutral city to avoid Farren's attention and keep their meeting secret. It had become routine by that point, after thirteen years of concealing Luminita's role as his mentor and friend.

"Dis is a mistake," she had said in her thick Romanian accent, the fake one she had used around him until the medical center last year.

"I'm twenty-three. The Council can no longer stop me. It gets me away from my grandfather's control, and it puts me in a position to truly assist the Durand."

"And vhen you do not age?"

"I'll transfer to a new city. We need more of a presence in the police departments, especially in the lower ranks. If we can quell problems before they become political issues, it will only help our cause."

The pride that had shone in her smile that day was forever burned into his soul. Perhaps his mother would have looked at him like that if she had lived long enough. Maybe she had and he couldn't remember.

Cohen wasn't sure which thought hurt more.

He had only been seven when Farren executed both of his parents. His grandfather had wanted him to witness the price of weakness.

Perhaps that was the reason the memories of his parents were so fragmented and fragile. The more he reached for them, the farther away they slipped. Maybe his mind was simply protecting him.

He had been there. Cohen had watched the bodies fall to the floor of Farren's courtroom, just like Lilith's father's had. But he couldn't remember the blood…couldn't remember their faces…

"Fiul meu."

His mind returned to that July day and Luminita's words.

"You have come so far, my dear sweet Andrew," she had said before wrapping her arms around him in a rare show of physical affection.

Luminita had cradled his face in her palms and studied his eyes. They had been gold that day—his true eye color—for the first time since he developed the ability, and he instantly knew what that meant.

Luminita had seen him for who he was.

Sadly, he had thought that meant she truly loved him like a son.

"Careful, informed decisions vit multiple advantages…De Council vill see you as an asset, but not so important dat dey pay close attention. Farren vill be disappointed."

Cohen still recalled the anger and rage he had felt at her last sentence, how his jaw had clenched until the muscle twitched.

"No!" Luminita had snapped sternly. "Dat monster does not deserve your emotions, not even your anger. *No vone does.* Dey are for you and you alone. *Ve are Durand!* Ve do *not* give away vhat ve need to survive. *No vone* deserves your essence…your heart. Do you hear me, Andrew?"

And now you wish you'd listened, don't you? the demonic voice interrupted. *You confessed your love to the vampire…gave her your heart…and for what? So you could die a better person? Or just a selfish one?*

Cohen's stomach soured, and he pulled his knees closer to his bandaged chest. Pain accompanied the motion. The continual isolation forced him to heal at a human rate, which was no doubt part of Luminita's plan.

"Just more fucking mind games."

What was it like? the disembodied voice whispered through his head, like an alluring siren's call growing stronger each time. The silence, the fucking ravenous need for some form of stimulation, clawed at his brain and wound tight around his aching chest.

What harm could it really do? It's just talking to myself. Plenty of people—No! he mentally screamed, returning to his search for patterns in the wall's texture. Giving in meant allowing that part of him power—the part that sought nothing but destruction.

How did she taste? As sweet as you imagined?

Cohen swallowed hard but managed to prevent the memory from rising…barely.

Fuck. I need a better distraction.

"What does Luminita want from me?" He spoke the words to block out the voice and keep his mind active. "Why save *my* life? Why keep me alive?"

Because she cares about you.

Cohen ignored the ludicrous statement and shoved off his cot. He paced the small room barefoot, working the problem just as Luminita had taught him.

Because she cares about you.

He curled his right hand into a fist, cracking the scabs and sending jolts of pain up his arms from the fractures. He used them to drown out the demon's voice.

"Without the Voynich Manuscript, I have no value…Even with it, she has to know she's lost my loyalty. Alexis said as much when she came back to the cabin."

But has she?

Cohen refused to acknowledge the question and continued his train of thought. "What does she want? Lilith, for certain…Chance, if he managed to survive…Ashcroft…"

He furrowed his brow and stopped. "Either she believes she can sway me back to her side…or…"

Cohen forced a breath in past his constricting throat. *Or she thinks I can deliver Lilith to her.* He couldn't even say the words out loud.

The only thing that made him unique from any other Durand, besides his history with Luminita, was his connection, kinship, friendship— whatever it was—with Lilith.

"I won't do that," Cohen stated clearly. He scanned the room again. Luminita had to be listening or watching, most likely both. "Do you hear me, Nita? You can't fucking have *her*! Do what you want to me, but I will *not* give you Lilith!" The words tore from his throat in a feral cry.

Why? Because you love her? Because she made you feel something? She held your heart in her palms and rejected you! Why do you owe her loyalty? Why sacrifice yourself—your body, your heart, your soul—for someone who doesn't even want you?

Despite his firm resolution not to interact with the demon in his head, tears flooded Cohen's eyes in response, and his body went rigid.

She doesn't want you, even after your declaration…after that kiss…the one she didn't return…Even after your sacrifice. She only wants him.

Every word twisted the metaphorical dagger further into his chest. It was all true, every last word, and yet…

Luminita actually loves you. She wants to make you better!

The demon's words sent rage burning through Cohen's veins, like molten lava.

"Luminita loves no one and nothing! She lied to me! Played me for a fucking fool. I don't even know who she really is, and she had no problem carving into me, even when I begged, fucking pleaded, for her to stop!"

Andrew sensed the demon's triumphant grin. It had finally gotten what it wanted—a true response.

Luminita tried to make you stronger—a pinnacle of your species, the ultimate apex predator who feared no one. Can you say the same for Lilith? What has the vampire ever given you?

Tears rolled down Cohen's cheeks, and he padded to his cot. His shoulders slumped under the weight of too many things.

"Everything that mattered," he whispered, sinking onto the thin mattress.

Sentimental bullshit. Have you regressed that much? Are you that pathetic? How has any of it made you stronger?

"Sometimes, it's not about strength. The most powerful moments have been learning to be vulnerable…"

A collage of moments cascaded through his head.

The first time he had seen Lilith in Miriah's apartment, an unexpected beauty filled with light.

Her candor and passion in the interrogation room while she spoke about her father and Chance.

The moment Cohen had pulled her fragile and beaten body from the farmer's truck after Spencer's attack.

The first time he had given her his blood to keep her from dying.

His desperation to save her in Phipps Bend.

The disgust and awfulness which had consumed him when Ashcroft forced Andrew to cut her.

The way she had absolutely shattered when Farren killed her father.

Lilith lying across his lap after the car crash in New Haven, hands trembling around the gun, terrified but determined.

The way tears had filled her eyes when Andrew begged Farren to spare her life.

The harrowing escape from Haverty's apartment on a repel line, when she trusted him not to let her go.

Lilith's sobs when Luminita tortured him, her words coaching him through the worst cuts.

Lilith arguing with Chance, refusing to leave Andrew behind.

How beautiful and raw she had been the night of Gregor's funeral.

Her willingness to hear him out when he had shown up in New York City, unannounced.

Her patience with him when he lashed out.

The absolutely stunning vision Lilith had been in that lavender lace gown at the gala.

Every time she had reached for him.

Every time she had seen though his facades.

Every time she had forgiven him, even when he didn't deserve it…

Especially when he didn't deserve it…

Every time she had believed in him, trusted him.

Every time she had *wanted* to see him.

Every time she had offered her friendship.

The hug she had freely given him on Duncan's porch…

Cohen had meant those words in Duncan's basement…all of them. It was okay she didn't think of him in a romantic sense. On some level, Lilith loved him—genuinely loved him—and had proven it many times. *That is enough.*

Is it? You still haven't answered my question. How has the vampire made you stronger?

There were many points Cohen could have argued, such as his scars finally healing or finding a sense of purpose, but none of it mattered, not anymore.

"What makes you think I deserve any of it? I don't deserve strength or power, and all I've ever done is fail Lilith at every turn." Certainty settled in his stomach like a block of ice, the chill seeping into his bones.

And that is your purpose? To finally do one thing right…for her? The one who will never warm your bed? The one who will never see you as anything more?

"She's seen *me*…She *wanted* to see *me*…She *fought* to see *me*…And that is enough. It's more than I deserve. I will protect her with everything I am. That is my *only* purpose."

Chapter 14

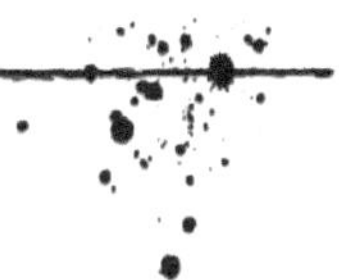

The electronic chime of the keycard lock sent a jolt down Chance's spine. His heart raced so fast it threatened to beat right out of his chest. The door swung open, and the world narrowed to that space, that moment, and then there she was.

Lilith stopped abruptly in the doorway when she spotted him. The summer rain dampened her blond hair, marked her clothes, and sprinkled her skin. Wherever she had gone, she had walked. Just the sight of her like that stirred something in him.

Her eyes widened, and her breaths came quicker, but she stood still. Lilith didn't run to him, didn't slam the door. She just stood there, emanating an indecipherable hurricane of emotions.

"*Cherie*, I…" He slowly rose to his feet, trying to find the right words.

Lilith's throat bobbed. She tossed her to-go box on the table but remained in the doorway.

"I can't tell you enough how sorry I am…" His voice trailed off while she stepped inside, swung the door closed, and stormed toward him. He still couldn't make sense of her signature. Anger, fear, love, hatred, betrayal, regret—none of them seemed right, yet all of them were there.

Fear coiled tighter until he could barely draw in a breath, but when she reached him, there were tears in her eyes. Before the realization fully registered, Lilith flung her arms around Chance and pulled him closer, capturing his mouth in a kiss that moved through him like a nuclear blast, irradicating everything in its path.

His arms tightened around her, pressing her body firmly against his. Chance had thought he would never have this again after last night… have *her*. The absolute relief flooding his body brought tears to his eyes.

Lilith broke the kiss with a breathless gasp, and Chance leaned his forehead against hers. There would be fights, but he hadn't lost her.

She's right here in my arms, where I desperately wanted her to be…need her to be.

"I am so sorry…" she started, but her voice broke.

The words took him by complete surprise. "What? No. *Cherie*, you don't have anything to be—"

"Yes, I do," she said adamantly, leaning back to meet his eyes. "I *never* should have walked out of that room. You almost died—no, you *actually* died, multiple times—and I…I walked away." The sorrow and shame in her expression was too much for him to take.

"*Amour de ma vie.*" Chance cradled her face and searched her deep olive eyes. "You were exhausted and angry. You needed rest. You didn't walk away from me."

"Yes, I did."

The words struck him like a physical blow, but he forced himself to remain calm. *She's here now*, he reminded himself.

"You lied to me. I'm mad about that, but I was *furious* with you last night because you *still* don't get how much you mean to me." She lowered her gaze to his chest, and guilt greeted his touch. "Then…I realized it's my fault you don't know."

Chance crooked a finger under her chin and tilted her face back up toward him. "What are you talking about?"

Lilith drew in a breath and avoided looking into his eyes. "Do you remember the night in New Haven? The candles…the shower?"

Despite the serious conversation, the memory summoned things which brought a grin to his face. "As if I could forget, *cherie*, but I don't understand what that has to do with this…why you're blaming yourself."

After a few deep breaths, she met his eyes again. "You took care of me that night, gave me *everything*, even the things I didn't know I needed. You were patient and devoted. It was the most beautiful thing anyone has *ever* done for me." Tears spilled down her cheeks, and the sight tore at him. "I've *never* done anything like that for you."

His heart cracked, and he pulled her against his chest, resting his chin on her head and running his fingers through her damp hair. "No, no, *cherie*. You've given me more than you'll ever know." Emotion constricted his throat, but Chance pushed past it. "I'm sorry for being too blind…too scared to truly believe it. That is on me, not you. I fucked up, and I'm sorry."

A tendril of fear caught his attention, and he pulled back enough to see her face.

"Lily, what's wrong?"

The fear only increased when her eyes rose to meet his. "There's things I need to tell you…things I didn't get a chance to say last night."

"Okay, but—"

"No. I need to tell you. I don't want secrets between us, and if I don't tell you now, that's what they'll be."

Lilith slowly slipped away, and he let her, only because she needed him to. All he wanted was to hold her and forget about the world for a while, but that would have made him selfish, and he wouldn't make that mistake again.

Chance lowered himself back onto the bed and waited for her to start.

Lilith rang her hands and sank into the chair, like she didn't have the energy to stand.

"That night in the basement, you told Andrew to get me out of there. I got away once, but the second time…" Color spread across her cheeks, but Chance still didn't understand her nervous fear. "I told Cohen I'd never forgive him if he made me leave you."

There it was—the guilt.

"Lily, his death is not your fault."

Lilith flinched. "Of course, it is, but that's not what I'm…" She drew in a deep breath, blew it out heavily, and straightened. "Before he raced over to Ashcroft, he told me…Fuck." Another deep breath. "He told me he loved me and that I saved his soul…"

Anger flared through every cell. "He did *what?*" No wonder Lilith blamed herself. *That fucker told her he loved her.*

"Then…" The shakiness in her voice caught Chance's attention more than her refusal to answer. Lilith rubbed her face with trembling hands and avoided his gaze. Fear rippled off her in waves and each one crashed against him with the force of a hurricane. "He kissed me, told me to live and be happy, and threw me toward Nicci when she burst through the door."

Lilith rushed the words, like ripping off a Band-Aid, but Chance's mind halted on the first part. His heart plummeted.

He kissed her. He fucking kissed her.

"Chance?" Lilith's voice shook between labored breaths.

Nausea twisted his stomach when the image formed in his head, but he forced himself to meet her eyes. Only one question truly mattered.

"Did you…" Just saying the words seemed impossible, but he *had* to know. "Did you kiss him back?"

Lilith's face immediately crumpled. "What? No!" She quickly crossed the room while Chance tried to tame his racing pulse. Lilith crouched in front of him, resting her hands on his knees. "Of course not, Chance. *Never.*"

The raging storm in his head eased, and a relieved sigh rushed past his lips.

"You actually thought I would?" The wounded question made him feel like shit for even asking.

"No, *cherie*. But I had to know for certain. I'm sorry." He slid his hand over hers, but the anger still raged through his body. "It's too bad Ashcroft killed him before I could."

A sudden thought occurred to him.

"Ashcroft is dead, right? Or did Luminita get her way?"

"Yes, he's dead, but there's something else I *need* to tell you."

Chance pressed a finger against her lips. "Does it concern me and you…our relationship?"

Lilith shook her head.

Relief flooded his body again. "Then save it for later."

"But—"

"I can't handle any more revelations. There's only one thing I need right now."

"What?" Lilith asked tentatively, as if afraid of his answer.

Chance guided her up off the floor and tugged her onto his lap. "You, *cherie*. Just you."

A vibrant blush raced up her neck and colored her cheeks in the intoxicating way it always did. However, eliciting that familiar response wasn't enough to satiate the anger in his head or obliterate the mental image of Cohen kissing her.

"I need to know you're mine, Lilith. All of you."

Sadness filled her eyes, and she cupped his face, studying him. "I *am* yours, Chance. *Only* yours. Don't you know that?"

"Logically, yes, but…Cohen kissed you." He swallowed the bile those words summoned. "I need to burn that thought from my mind. You wanted a moment to take care of me? To give me what I need? This is it. I just need *you*."

Chance closed his eyes and leaned his forehead against hers again.

The seconds stretched into an eternity, the old fear of rejection humming in the background.

"You are mine, and I am yours." Her voice was thick with tears, and it broke him.

Deep-seated need roared to the surface, surpassing everything else. He snaked his fingers through her hair, gripped the back of her neck, and drew her to him. When her lips crashed against his, the world felt right again, like he could finally take a full breath, but Chance needed more.

The timid flick of her tongue ignited every territorial instinct. *Mine. She kisses* me *back because she's mine, not his. Never his.*

One hand tightened in her blond tresses while the other grabbed her hip, tugging her closer. A delicate moan vibrated through the kiss. He needed more of those sounds…louder.

With a frantic compulsion to feel her skin, he grabbed her shirt and slipped it over her head, only breaking their kiss for an instant. Her tongue didn't move in timid strokes anymore. It danced and swirled with his in a rhythm that made other parts insanely jealous.

When Lilith sat back, panting, the animalistic drive in him started to scream. *No, I need this. I need her.*

"Take this off." She tugged at his stiff T-shirt. Desire darkened her eyes, and a breathless grin curved her sensual lips. The sight was exquisitely beautiful, even before she started unhooking her bra.

Chance grabbed the back of his shirt with one hand, yanked it off, and tossed it on the floor. He didn't give her time to focus on the long, thin bandages crossing his chest.

In one smooth move, he secured an arm around her and rolled, putting her back to the mattress. Chance hovered over her, studying every gorgeous line of her face while his hips rolled against hers. The slight hitch of her breath just before her teeth raked over her bottom lip was a particular favorite of his.

When he slid off the bed, she peered up at him with a frown. "What are you doing?"

He flashed a grin and reached to unbutton her shorts. "I did say *all* of you."

That delicious blush colored her skin again, a maddening blend of bashfulness and desire. Chance gripped her panties and shorts, wiggling them down her hips. He let them fall to the floor with everything else.

Chance stood there for a moment, gazing down at every perfect curve—even the ones she hated. Every part of her was sacred to him and deserved to be worshipped. He wanted to spend his whole life doing just that.

In that moment, he knew.

Chance never could have kept his deal with Luminita. How could he have even entertained the possibility when it meant walking away from *her...willingly* walking away?

Never again because she's mine and I'm hers.

After shedding the rest of his clothes, he bent to lightly kiss her knee. An amused sound, like a suppressed giggle, brought his gaze to hers, and he sensed heat racing down her spine. His eyes never left hers while his lips skimmed up her thigh, over her hip, up her ribs, to hover over her already pebbled nipple, which rose and fell with each heavy breath.

Anticipation and desire swept over her skin, deep enough for him to drown in, and it broke his control. Chance kept his eyes on hers and claimed the delicate flesh with his mouth. A surge of pleasure tickled over his skin, urging his tongue to dance in swirling circles.

A mewling moan left her throat, but when his hand glided between her thighs, it transformed into something more primal. Chance knew every spot to stroke, what made her arch against him, squirm, and writhe, what drove her to madness...*Because she's mine.*

His teeth raked lightly over her nipple, and she inhaled sharply, her thighs clenching. A wide grin curved his lips before he trailed teasing kisses up her chest, collarbone, neck, until he found her lips again.

This time, Lilith kissed him like a woman possessed, hauling him closer with a desperation that seared into him.

Chance abandoned all pretense of control. His hands dove into her blond curls, clenching into fists, and Lilith wrapped her legs around his. The intoxicating taste and feel of her filled his very soul.

This is where I belong, with her, nowhere else.

Suddenly, Chance found himself on his back, with Lilith straddling him. A devilish grin graced her lips when she pulled away.

"I don't think you need to claim every part of me to know I'm yours." Her grin widened. "I mean...you are always welcome to, but—"

Chance grabbed her hips jend rolled his beneath her in answer.

Lilith's teeth sunk into her bottom lip, and her eyes almost fluttered closed. "Let me finish."

"Oh, believe me, *cherie*. That's exactly what I'm trying to do." He couldn't help himself when she made it that easy.

Lilith suppressed a laugh, snatched his wrists, and pinned them to the mattress above his head. That definitely stoked the already raging inferno. "I think what you really need is to know that *I* claim *you* as mine…that *I* need you…that I want *only* you."

Chance stared up at her wild eyes, drinking in the desire and certainty seeping into his skin. She stared right into him, past every layer, straight to his very core. In his entire life, Lilith was the only one who truly chose him…kept choosing him.

She's right. That's what I really need. "God, I love you, Lily. I'm sorry for ever thinking I could walk away from you for any price. I *never* could have done it."

Lilith leaned closer. Her lips hovered just out of reach. "That's the correct answer. If you want to marry me, we are in all of this together, no matter the outcome. I won't accept anything less because I am yours and you are *mine*."

The way she growled the last word was his undoing. Chance captured her mouth in a fevered kiss steeped in something more carnal than even their first time, in the alley. He couldn't wait, couldn't fucking breathe until he was inside her.

When his hand slid beneath her, she tensed, and it made him pause.

"Are you sure it's okay?" Her fingers drifted over the dressings on his chest.

"It's a little late to ask that question." Chance chuckled darkly.

When she didn't move, his hand glided up her shoulder, into her hair, and cradled the back of her neck. "*Amor de ma vie*, I'm okay. And this will only help me, not hurt me."

The tension left her body, and she claimed his mouth with that same animalistic fire, bringing his all-consuming need right back. Chance put an impatient hand between them again, positioning himself. Before he moved his hips, Lilith shifted hers, taking him in deep.

The sudden rush left him stunned…overwhelmed.

Lilith gasped against his lips, but when Chance withdrew almost completely and thrust in again, she lifted her head with a deep moan, making him drive harder. His hands curled around her hips, holding on tight. Each plunge brought them both closer to the edge, and nothing in the world felt better.

This…This is my heaven.

Lilith's moans turned louder, feral, more feverish, and as much as he loved them, they were in a motel with paper-thin walls, and people who knew them were right next door.

Chance pulled her back down to him, stifling her heady cries with a possessive kiss. Her breath hitched a split second before her body quivered and clenched, and he lost it. He tensed, arms banding around her. He tried to stifle his own groan and buried himself deeper while their combined pleasure rocked through him.

They stayed that way—panting, a sheen of sweat coating their skin, hearts racing. Everything was euphoric, fucking magic, even as the orgasmic waves began to ebb. He *never* wanted to let go.

Finally, Lilith lifted her head to smile down at him. The woman glowed, and Chance stared up at her in awe. For thirteen years, he had loved her from afar, but this…if he'd known, *truly* known this was what awaited him, he never would have wasted a single second without her. He reached out, brushing the damp strands of hair from her face with a reverent touch.

When her smile widened, a burning question rose to the surface. "Can I ask you something, *cherie?*"

Her head tilted in the way it usually did when someone said something ridiculous. "Of course."

"If I'd told you how I felt before you left for UCLA, would you have stayed?"

Lilith blinked before folding her arms over his chest and resting her chin on them. "Told me or made me believe it?" Her chuckle rumbled over his skin.

"So, you wouldn't have just taken me at my word?"

Lilith cocked an eyebrow and grinned. "You had quite the reputation until our trip to Tennessee." Her expression dimmed once the words left her mouth.

"Meaningless distractions because I couldn't have the one person I wanted," Chance said, trying to reassure her. He would have done anything to bring that glowing happiness back to her face.

"I know." Lilith flashed a smile, but it wasn't as bright. "Seriously, though. Talking with you…exchanging banter…was always the highlight of my week, and you *are* pretty easy on the eyes. So…if you made me believe it…yes. I would have stayed."

Wormwood

Chance cradled her cheek, moved but conflicted by her answer. So much could have been prevented if he'd had the balls to tell her back then—Boston Sr. and his impending manhunt, for example.

"I'm sorry I waited so long."

Lilith placed a kiss in the center of his palm, and when she smiled back at him, that euphoric glow returned. "We're here now. That's what matters."

Chapter 15

Luminita had decided to review the footage from Andrew's cell in her apartment for a reason. She had already watched it five times, and a heaviness weighed on her heart which required privacy. Luminita had to understand every second, no matter how painful, to choose the right path.

Still, witnessing the man pace his cell, argue with a voice she couldn't hear—his confessions and heartache, his utter brokenness—it affected her in a way Luminita hadn't expected and summoned old memories which still haunted the fringes of her mind. There was a time when she had been broken, a time when everything had seemed hopeless.

Yes, inflicting harm on Andrew, slicing him to the bone, ignoring his screams and tearful pleas for mercy, had been difficult, but they were all for a cause greater than them both—the survival of their race. As horrific as that night had been, she never fully regretted her actions. Perhaps until now, when she was forced to observe the fallout.

Luminita stiffened in her chair, pausing the footage. "No. Emotions are weakness. This…what is happening to Andrew, is precisely *why* they are so dangerous…why you should never let anyone in. I learned that lesson myself at Vlad's hands." Those emotions hadn't belonged to Vlad, but he certainly had taken advantage of them.

For the past five hundred years, she had avoided that pitfall. With the death of Vlad Dracul, her abusive and vindictive husband, Luminita had sealed her emotions in a tight tomb.

Since then, she had watched empires rise and fall, the Victorian age of enlightenment, the industrial revolution, world wars, the birth of technology and its meteoric rise. Nothing and no one had touched her in all that time…or so she had thought.

Of course, deep in that emotional pit, there was one other who would always affect her, but she refused to acknowledge it. *That* man had abandoned her long ago, chosen a different life.

With a tired sigh, Luminita rubbed her face and tried to see reason, but the boy she had raised, the one she considered a son, had lost himself. Cohen was drowning in a sea of despair, reaching for a lifeline that could never save him, and she…*felt*…

Luminita knitted her brow while sorting through the unfamiliar feelings. *I've failed him. I taught him better than this…or perhaps I only thought I did.*

"He thinks Lilith has somehow saved his soul"—she brushed her fingers over the screen in an affectionate caress—"but I am the only one who can truly save him. Lilith can never be what he wants…what he needs. He'll see that eventually."

A crackle preceded the voice which echoed through the intercom on her desk. "Ms. Dragomir, there's a call holding for you on the secure line."

Luminita narrowed her eyes and ran through every possibility before landing on the most likely one. With a delicate finger, she pressed the button.

"Patch it through." Before she released the talk button, her eyes caught on the screen and Andrew's screaming face. "Give Cohen an hour and send the girl in." She didn't need to specify. That part of her plan had already been mapped out, and the guards knew her wishes.

"Yes, ma'am."

Luminita needed as much information as possible to plan future moves. If that meant pushing Andrew's boundaries, so be it. The days of isolation, cut off from a feeding source, would make it easier for him.

He can only fight for so long.

A tiny flicker of guilt pulsed against the obsidian walls Luminita had assembled to contain the few emotions she possessed, but it sputtered out and died before fully registering.

"I *will* bring him back to me. I *will* find a way."

Luminita spoke with certainty, but haunted memories lingered in the dark recesses of her mind. She refused to let them reach the light, to acknowledge how similar her actions were to Vlad's. Intent was everything. Vlad had only sought her pain and suffering, a way to punish her for not loving him. Luminita had a purpose, a goal worthy of devotion. The two were not the same.

Luminita closed the laptop before picking up the ringing phone.
"Aaron. How nice of you to call."

The second of stunned silence made her smile.

"You are a very difficult woman to reach." The clear anger and annoyance in his voice killed her amusement, but it was the bitter subtext which riled her.

"Quite a hypocritical statement coming from you, considering I had to show up on your doorstep because you refused to answer my calls."

"What the hell is happening in Tennessee? The arson and homicide at Duncan's house is all over the news. Sloppy work. And now I can't reach anyone at Goditha."

"You weren't interested, remember? Too busy hiding out in your apartment, playing the dutiful Elder." Saccharine sweetness infused every single word.

"And now you have my rapt attention. Explain."

Part of her wanted to stonewall him simply for the condescending tone, but matters needed to be addressed. "We originally thought Goditha was Ashcroft's destination, so I sent in a team to neutralize and prepare the site."

"You attacked a research lab?" The question sounded hollow, as if Aaron expected it all to be a joke.

"You'd rather I leave human and vampire witnesses to Ashcroft's abilities? It had to be done."

"You said *originally*..." Aaron reminded her, once again utilizing a judgmental tone which grated her spine.

"Yes. He had a different location in mind. Lilith figured it out, but I wasn't made aware until after the Goditha takeover."

An aggravated sigh rattled the handset. "Please tell me you at least have Ashcroft."

Luminita rubbed the bridge of her nose, already tired of the conversation. Aaron had his moods, most of them unpleasant these days, especially when forced into good behavior. The watchful eyes of the Elders put him in a foul disposition, but knowing that didn't make dealing with it any easier.

"No. My agent is tracking him, but if you are so concerned, perhaps you'd like to contribute instead of criticizing me at every turn."

Silence loomed between them for a few moments. Luminita waited patiently. She refused to be the first to break the tension.

Let Aaron sweat.

"Michael discovered who Mannix met with—David Boston, Sr. That's the father of the missing FBI agent, correct?" Aggravation still lingered in his words.

"Do you have any information I *don't* already know?" The irritated bite stemmed from a deep desire to be proven wrong on that front. The confirmation would force her to accelerate the timetable. Things had to move faster.

"There are rumblings from my contacts about the FBI's plan to drop both the investigation and the search for Agent Boston." Aaron's snarl was almost detectable over the phone, but Luminita ignored it.

"Sounds like Mannix made his deal. Our assets are in danger."

Another heavy sigh rumbled through the speaker, and it broke her tenuous patience.

"I am more than aware of your disapproval," Luminita snapped. "You don't see the value in Chance or Lilith, but they are vital to my research."

"Luminita, Ashcroft is—"

"Aaron. You are either with me or against me. Remember, *you* are the one who came to *me*. *You* are the one who wanted *my* help to secure your place in the world."

"I know," he growled. "But things are falling apart. There was a breach at Solasta a few nights ago. The Elders are scrambling to assess the damage, and once they discover the slaughter at our most prolific blood research facility, they'll assume we are under attack."

"Do they suspect you?" Luminita kept her voice neutral, as if the question were routine.

"What? For Solasta?"

"Yes."

"No. Not that I'm aware of…" His words trailed off, and he went silent again.

Luminita hoped her partner would connect the dots and prove he had been a worthy choice, that the pain of enduring his presence in her life had been worth it.

"Nita…" A clear warning buzzed through the line, and it brought a broad smile to her lips.

She found Aaron most attractive when vicious and truly threatening, like he had been when she'd first met him. Too often lately, he had been annoyed, almost whiney—neither of which she cared for.

"Did *you* have something to do with it?"

"Why would you ask me that?" Her question didn't feign innocence. It was a challenge, a test.

"The others won't tell me much, but research was targeted. You took out Goditha—the lab Lilith believed to be contaminated by a virus—and then the research team studying the same virus was targeted."

A brilliant grin lit her face. The man did excel at connecting dots, if given enough time.

"Did you make a move on Solasta?" The fine tremor of fear in his words made the grin slide right off her face.

"You have two choices, Aaron. You can either join me here as a full partner to further the cause, or you can continue to play the dutiful Elder and try to convince your leadership that you are not the villain. Just know, if you choose the later, *we are done*. Your cover is blown, and I refuse to let the mission die with you."

"You are giving me an ultimatum?"

"It's time to choose a side."

"And my son? Must he chose as well?"

"Michael's loyalty is on your head. Bring him or don't. It is up to you."

The man heaved a sigh. "Be honest with me, Nita. Did you truly attack Solasta?"

"You already know the answer. You have forty-eight hours to make your decision."

After hanging up the phone, Luminita took a deep breath, opened her laptop, and pulled up the live feed for Andrew's cell. The anxious need to be distracted by anything else was all-consuming. There was a chance Aaron would walk away, that she would lose that connection, that source of kinship and amusement…

No, it ran deeper than that, even if she wasn't prepared to admit it. Aaron meant far more than she would ever allow him to know. He was the source of her greatest pleasure and greatest pain. In that regard, he would always be unique.

"Such sentiment is nothing but weakness," she reminded herself and concentrated on the screen.

Andrew was pacing again, fists flexing at his side. Every so often, he would stop, as if listening to someone. Then his shoulders would slump, and he'd resume his back-and-forth pattern.

Luminita wondered about the voices. Had they started before his isolation here? Had he heard them at the cabin? Perhaps that was why he had been so unhinged during her visit. What did they say to him?

Judging by his sporadic verbal responses, they seemed to revolve around the vampire...

Could I use that? Perhaps Luminita could sway him to her side with promises of safety for the woman he had almost died protecting. Given the right circumstances, Andrew might even help bring her in, despite his earlier declarations.

Lilith. The depths of Cohen's feelings for the vampire still burned in Luminita's gut. No matter how much she reinforced the obsidian walls keeping her detached, jealousy still reared its ugly head.

The devotion is meant to be mine. I protected him. I trained him. I cared for him. I loved him, but she *gets his loyalty.*

On some level, she knew her jealousy didn't end with Lilith. Luminita envied Cohen's emotional abandon, how freely he embraced his devotion to the person he loved. It was weak, but a sliver of herself had wanted that same freedom once...centuries ago, when she'd had someone's love.

Luminita pulled up the footage from earlier. Andrew screamed while spinning around the cell, clearly searching for a camera.

"I won't do that!" he had said. "Do you hear me, Nita? You can't fucking have *her!* Do what you want to me, but I *will not* give you Lilith!"

Fiery anger quickly overpowered her mental shields and flooded every nerve. "Why *her?*" Luminita scowled at the screen before slamming the laptop shut.

The one person she most wanted to end was the one person she *had* to keep alive at all costs.

"What a cruel turn of fate."

After swallowing the rising bile, she picked up the phone and dialed. With Boston, Sr. on the hunt, reassurances and contingencies were required.

A deep male voice answered on the third ring. "Drăgaica."

Luminita found the codename grating. The memories attached to the name—to that time in her life when someone had called her *Draga,* Romanian for Beloved—those were things she no longer wanted to recall, but Azrael insisted on using it.

"I require a favor. A contract is expected, if it hasn't already been issued. Chance Deveraux and Lilith Adams. Others may be listed as well. I need you to spread the word. I will double the bounty for anyone who takes out an assassin targeting them and triple the amount if they find the targets and bring them to me *alive and unharmed.* They were last seen in

Madisonville, Tennessee, four nights ago. That should provide a sufficient head start on the other contract."

"Received," was his only response.

Luminita hung up the phone, eased into her chair, and rubbed her temples. This manhunt was going to cost a fortune, but Lilith and Chance were irreplaceable.

Things would have been so much simpler if Orchid had found them. Of course, after certain revelations, her loyalty was uncertain, which was precisely why Luminita had an insurance policy.

Sending Orchid to Duncan's that fateful night dramatically increased the odds of her assassin recognizing Chance. Telling Orchid the truth had been a calculated risk, but if the guilt and shame hadn't been enough to quell her rebellion, the lives of her husband and daughter should do the job.

The woman was incredibly skilled, but breaking into *this* place required more than an assassin and a handful of vampires. The lab was built like a siege fortress for a reason.

Mannix, however…He was the true threat. If the FBI dropped the case, leaving him free to move and utilize his resources, he could become a real complication. Luminita still had supporters on the Council, but not enough.

"He needs to work faster." Luminita pushed out of her chair and stalked to the door. The guards outside nodded in deference, but she remained focused on her destination.

More men stood guard outside the central hub. They dipped their heads when she passed. The lab itself sat quiet and waited for a purpose, which only spurned her on. The clicks from her heels increased with her pace.

She continued straight across the lab to another door. After passing more armed guards, she marched down the hall and came to a stop at the vault-like door sitting at its end.

What appeared to be a large peephole in the door lit up, scanning her retina. The ring turned green, and a hidden panel slid from between the cinderblocks. When Luminita pressed her hand against the screen, she recited the verbal password, "Wormwood."

A series of metal thunks echoed within the wall, and the thick steel door cracked open. Luminita wasted no time slipping inside and shoved the heavy door closed. The thunks within the wall sounded again—locks clicking into place.

Only then did Luminita scan the artificially bright lab. Her gaze settled on a heavy-weight man with a shock of bright red hair bent over a microscope.

"I need it ready within forty-eight hours," she stated firmly.

The man moved away from the microscope but only to scribble a few notes.

Luminita folded her arms over her chest and stalked closer. Each step was accentuated by a sharp click on the tile. "At least tell me the cure is ready?"

"Aye, the Wormwood file was quite thorough," the man said on an irritated sigh. "I'm working as fast as I can with what I have."

"If you require something, tell me. It's yours. But we are running out of time."

The man swiveled on his chair. His boyish face pinched in a scowl, and he extended a list pressed between his thumb and forefinger.

Luminita held his stare while she snatched the paper from his grasp. She scanned the list. Most items were easily obtainable, with a few noteworthy exceptions.

"You need *everything* on this list?"

The man pressed his mouth into a firm line before finally answering. "For what you're asking? Absolutely."

A tired sigh escaped Luminita. She would have to rearrange things, move assets to make the most difficult ask on that paper happen.

"I'll see to it."

"Once my work is complete, I'll be free to leave, as promised?"

"Of course." Luminita pulled on a genuinely warm smile. "I assure you, this is necessary work that will benefit both our species."

The last part wasn't a lie. The first, however...

Luminita had never cared for loose ends.

Chapter 16

Red blazed across the skyline of New York City in a bloody swath of sunset, reflecting off the sparkling towers of glass and steel. Far below, the city buzzed with chaos, but the primal parts of Aaron yearned for the days of true lawlessness within the Carpathian Mountains. For a time when he had been free.

While the Mongol's Golden Horde marched across the Romanian territories, conquering everything in their path, flooding the country in a haze of war, Aaron had roamed, drank his fill, reveled in the blood of his victims without consequence…at least, until he met her.

Luminita Dragomir, Drăgaica, the Eater of Souls.

The woman summoned an uneasy host of warring emotions. They shared a rather complicated and tumultuous past. In the first seven thousand years of his life, no one had affected him, not until her. Since their first meeting in 1241, no one else had accomplished the task either.

Luminita was a devastatingly beautiful woman, with her wild raven-black hair and sinful body. But it was the woman's devious intellect that had intrigued him. She was always plotting ten steps ahead, which he found equally intoxicating and infuriating.

She referred to them as partners. The truth, however, was that her strategic mind surpassed his, though he would *never* admit that. Aaron had no doubt she knew, though.

There had been a time where they could have been more. They had been so close…But those memories hardened over the years. He had formed a callous to protect what little remained of his tattered soul—the one thing she had gifted him.

Aaron's hand drifted into his pocket, fingers drawn to the tiny item hidden in its lining.

Fate had brought them together. There was no arguing that. She had found him trussed up by villagers who had caught him off guard. Luminita drained all but three of them—including women. She had freed him, tossed a sword at his feet, and issued a challenge.

Prove your worth, Sălbatic.

In the beginning, she had merely seen him as a strong tool for her ritual, but over those first three days, they had grown close, formed a connection which had brought something to life in him. The way the torchlight danced in her sea-blue eyes during her Dragobete ritual, the fascination and arousal in her expression while he drank that village maiden dry… Luminita hadn't looked at him that way in quite some time.

When they met again two hundred years later in Beszterce, Luminita's husband, Vlad Dracul III, stood in his way. The abusive monster had almost been the death of her. Aaron had tried to save Luminita, to fix the damage Vlad had inflicted. But something had irrevocably broken in her during that time.

The last night in Oarzina, before he left to recruit the Ottoman Empire for his war against Vlad, was the last night Luminita had truly shown Aaron love. At least, he thought it was love. After five hundred years, perhaps his recollection was inaccurate. Maybe he merely remembered what he desperately wanted and not what had happened.

As painful as the years which followed had been, Aaron still didn't regret meeting her. She had taught him valuable lessons, most of them painful, but necessary.

Luminita made her stance on their business relationship very clear. It started and stopped with the mission. The past was just that. Still, it didn't stop his daily devotion of touching the item in his pocket. The act was an undeniable compulsion after so much time, nothing more. At least, that was the lie he chose to tell himself.

The mission. To rise above the constraints of humans. To become powerful enough not to cower to their laws, not to fear their numbers.

The blood packs and hemoglobin capsules had been a very recent development. For many millennia, most of their kind relied on devoted humans or lone travelers, taking a small amount, just enough to survive.

Aaron had strongly disagreed with his brothers on that point.

Gregor and Duncan wanted to coexist, intermingle, lessen themselves until they blended into the ocean of mundane humans.

They succeeded, Aaron thought with a sneer. If humans turned on them now, there would be no fight. It would be an extinction…genocide.

That's why he had gone to Luminita after leaving her in Ahnenerbe back in 1945. Aaron despised her methods, but they shared the same vision—to not only fight a war, but ensure its victory—and Ashcroft was the key.

Aaron found it deeply ironic that his peace-loving brother had snapped in Scotland. While Aaron was fighting a righteous war against Vlad Dracul III, Gregor was drowning in the blood of an entire family line, slaughtering men, women, and children alike. Then he unwittingly created the abomination which would eventually be their salvation.

Aaron wondered if Luminita was right, if there had been some special element to Gregor's blood that forced the transformation. It made a certain sense. The sun had never affected Aaron like it had his brothers. It would stand to reason they might have had some special trait as well. If this ability to turn others existed, Aaron didn't share it. They had tried. So how could Luminita be so certain it had passed on to Lilith?

The very thought of his niece brought another sneer to his face. He had always disliked the girl and the way Gregor doted on her. Duncan's children as well. They were all useless.

No. Lilith was *worse* than useless. She was meddlesome and smart enough to be a threat. Lilith had already sabotaged their plans several times and caused this mess with the Elders. She just couldn't let things go. Personally, Aaron would rather bury her in the ground than risk another setback, especially now.

Goditha and Solasta, two of their biggest labs, hit within days of each other. Luminita was taking risks. making bold moves, and Aaron was already in the hot seat, thanks to his bothersome niece.

The apartment door opened and shut, but Aaron continued to stare through the floor-to-ceiling window at the dying sunrise and its delicious crimson hues.

"You wanted to see me, father?"

As always, the title bothered Aaron. "Yes, Michael. I'm going on a trip," he said simply, eyes hardening on the horizon.

"Sir? I thought, after Philadelphia, we agreed to stay in town until the Elders reach a decision."

"Plans change." His voice remained flat, but he finally turned to face his only son. "Luminita has complicated the situation and issued an ultimatum."

Michael's dark eyes widened, and his stiff posture softened. "So, we are abandoning ship?"

"Not exactly." Aaron focused on the floor, wrists clasped behind his back, and strode toward Michael with measured steps. "Lilith and her people are talking to one of the Elders…probably Antonio. He was closest to Gregor after Duncan."

Michael wrinkled his broad forehead. "We already knew that."

"Yes, but as long as I'm safely tucked away in this tower, I'm not only a target, but also a suspect." Aaron paced around his son slowly, his gaze focused on the tile. "But…if I were to disappear under suspicious circumstances…"

"Suspicious? I don't follow."

Aaron laid a hand on Michael's shoulder and came to a stop at his side. "You've served me well, my son."

Michael swiveled his head toward him, clear confusion etched on his face. Aaron didn't often give Michael praise, much less address him as his progeny. The shock was expected. Aaron had counted on it.

With a quick movement, Aaron released the blade from his sleeve. The handle hit his palm, and his fingers instinctively curled around it. Before Michael even opened his mouth, Aaron shoved the blade deep between his ribs.

The shock and confusion deepened, and pain contorted Michael's features. Blood bubbled past his lips with each gurgled breath.

Aaron clutched him close. His hand remained steady on the blade. "It will be quick, Michael."

Some part of him mourned the loss of a valuable tool, but if his life depended on Michael's complete dedication to the cause, it was a price he refused to pay.

As Luminita had told him many times, attachment and sentimentality were nothing but weaknesses. Ones Aaron could no longer afford.

It didn't take long for the light to die in Michael's eyes, and Aaron lowered him carefully to the floor, ensuring the proper placement. Then he began setting the stage.

Forced entry, signs of a struggle, Aaron's only son lying dead on the ground…The Elders' emotional weakness would put Aaron above reproach, turn him into a victim. After all, what sane man would murder his own son?

But Aaron wasn't a man. He was a *true* vampire—a fact none of them seemed to recall.

Wormwood

With everything perfectly set, the Elders would assume Aaron had been attacked and taken, especially if he left everything behind…or at least seemed to.

With careful precision, Aaron stepped over the growing pool of blood, tapped a panel in the bottom corner cabinet, and retrieved one of two bugout bags hidden there.

I'll have to stick to public transport…to the train station, he thought, swinging the bag over his shoulder.

Aaron side-stepped the blood without giving the body a second glance and pulled out his burner cell. He pressed call for the only number saved on it.

As soon as someone answered, he spoke in angry, clipped tones. "Tell the Lady Dragomir I'm on my way."

It was time to shed his façade, to escape his temporary role as Nefîrtat, the mimic from the Romanian creation myth. Aaron would finally emerge from the darkness of self-deception, embrace his nature, once again become Fîrtat, the shining one, and choose truth.

Chapter 17

Soft breaths tickled across Chance's chest in a rhythmic pattern. A brilliant smile curved his lips. For a moment, he simply enjoyed the feel of Lilith curled up against him. After slowly opening his eyes, Chance peered down at her peaceful face resting over his heart.

Peaceful. No nightmares. That alone seemed like a miracle.

He slowly tightened his arm around her bare waist. Chance didn't want to wake her but felt compelled to make sure she was really there, that he hadn't imagined the past few hours, that she wasn't a figment of his imagination. The warm weight of her body eased the pressure in his chest, but it wasn't enough.

As if drawn by a magnet, his free hand reached for her, unable to resist. The petal softness of her skin was too inviting. When his thumb coasted lightly over her bottom lip, she made a small sound which brought a smile to his face.

Her eyes started to flutter but didn't open while his fingers trailed in a feather-light caress over her cheek and into her hair.

Chance knew he should let her sleep. Lilith had more than earned a few restful hours, but he *had* to touch her, couldn't *stop* touching her. The number of times he had almost lost her…the number of times they had almost lost each other…

He focused on the naked ring finger of her left hand—something he needed to rectify soon. If they hadn't been hiding out in the woods and on the run, he would have already seen to that. Chance never wanted Lilith to second-guess his sincerity. He wanted to marry her. He'd never wanted anything more in his life.

Lilith's burner rang on the nightstand, and he snatched it up, answering before it woke her.

"I'll be there in forty-five minutes." Chance didn't recognize the strange woman's voice.

"I'm sorry. Who is this?" he asked as quietly as possible.

The line buzzed with road noise but no answer.

"Who is this?" He used a little more volume in case the woman hadn't heard him.

Lilith wrinkled her brow in her sleep, eyes darting behind her lids.

"Can you hear me?" Chance asked impatiently.

"Yes." The word was barely audible over the roar of a passing semi.

"Who are you talking to?" Lilith asked groggily.

"I wish I knew. Someone you're expecting to arrive soon, who doesn't want to give their name."

Lilith's eyes snapped open. In an absolute panic, she reached out, climbing over him to grab the phone. "I'm sorry. I'm here…Yeah, I'll have everyone ready. Room 107, yes."

Lilith hung up the phone and stared at it in her palm for a long moment. Chance could feel every hammer of her heart against her ribs.

"Care to explain, *cherie?*"

Very slowly, almost hesitantly, she turned to face him. Fear, anxiety, sorrow, pity—it all swirled around her. Lilith darted her tongue out to wet her lips. "It's Orchid. She's meeting us."

Chance raised his eyebrow and studied every line of her face. "Luminita's assassin?"

She immediately lowered her gaze to his chest. "Not anymore," she whispered, as if reminding herself more than telling him.

"Lily."

Her eyes met his again.

"What do you mean?"

Lilith drew in a deep breath and pushed away from him. She sat up, pulling the sheets nervously around her bare figure like a shield.

"She's helping us."

When her gaze locked on him, it made his heart race, not because she was an irresistible vision with the blush creeping over her cheeks—she was—but because of the intensity in her eyes.

"I made a promise not to tell you the reasons why, but…" Lilith drew in another deep breath and slowly released it. "I told you before, I don't want secrets between us. Either you can wait until Orchid gets here or I'll explain everything right now, but it *has to be your choice.*"

"About why Orchid changed sides?"

Lilith bit at the inside of her cheek and nodded. The conflict was clear in her eyes—she wanted him to know but desperately didn't want to be the one to tell him.

"It involves me?" An inexplicable fear darted through his chest.

Lilith nodded, her eyes already glassy.

Chance shifted to sit up against the headboard. One image popped into his head—the Orchid tattoo.

No. It's not possible. She died.

Then he recalled his conversation with Tim and how he'd asked if Chance was sure she had died in the car crash. The twenty-year-old memory was a garbled mass of tears, shrieks, blood, and flashing lights.

No. Gregor told me. No one came for me. It's not possible…but what if he didn't know? What if she lived and decided a new life was a better option? What if…

Chance tried several times before he finally swallowed past the lump in his throat. Lilith watched him with a heartbroken expression that said everything, but he had to hear the words.

"You know Orchid's real name?" he asked as gently as he could.

Lilith nodded again, biting at her bottom lip. Tears clung to her lashes.

"Tell me."

"Chance, there are things you need to know—"

"Stop," he interrupted.

She mashed her lips together with a wounded expression, making his heart hurt more than it already did.

"Come here."

Lilith hesitated but eventually wiggled a little closer.

Chance grabbed her hand as soon as she was in reach. "I said here, not closer." Then he tugged her onto his lap and cradled her face between his palms. "All I want is a name. If it's the one I think it is, *she* needs to explain the rest. That's not on you."

The flood of relief was almost palpable, and her stiff muscles relaxed a touch.

"Lily, *cherie*…What is Orchid's name?" Chance searched her eyes and saw the answer before she released a breath and spoke it.

"Helena Vieux."

The words left her lips in a hushed tone, and although he had expected them, they hit like a nuclear bomb, throwing everything inside Chance into chaos.

"I'm so sorry. She showed up at the hospital and—"

"Lily, stop," he pleaded.

She snapped her mouth closed.

The white noise, the roaring anarchy in his head, was too much. Chance couldn't handle anything more. Even the flickers of sentiment rolling off her skin felt painful. With measured movements, he moved Lilith off his lap and slid from the bed.

A hundred questions and an entire cavalcade of volcanic emotions erupted, as if they had been waiting just below the surface for the perfect moment. Nothing made sense. He couldn't breathe. The world was simultaneously upside and spinning, suffocating him.

"Chance?" Lilith's timid voice acted like a lifeline in dark seas, pulling him back.

No. There's still one thing that makes sense…the only thing that will always make sense.

"What can I do?" The heartbreaking plea almost undid him.

Her fingers brushed his shoulder, leaving shivers in their wake. Lilith stood there with the sheet gathered around her, her tousled blond hair spilling over her shoulder. Tears shined in her hypnotic olive eyes.

How could I possibly love this woman any more?

With a shaking breath, Chance slid his arms around her waist and buried his face in her shoulder, desperately drinking in the solace and peace her touch brought.

"I love you," she whispered against his hair.

Chance drew her closer, his fingers digging into the sheet. "I…" he started but had to clear his throat. "I love you, *cherie.*"

After a moment, Chance leaned back enough to see Lilith's face.

"Thank you for telling me and not letting her blindside me."

A frown crinkled her brow, and she reached up to cradle his cheeks with heart-searing tenderness. "No secrets, remember?"

Those words reminded him of one thing he hadn't told her—the event which had allowed him to make the leap in logic. Chance gathered his strength, forcing himself to confess the mistake that had almost cost them everything.

"*Cherie*, the night Orchid attacked…I had her…and then…" His throat bobbed when the moment came back to him. *Why are the words so difficult?*

"The tattoo?" she asked.

He peered down at her in surprise. "How do you know?"

A half-smile lifted one corner of her mouth. "Tim told me."

A subtle current of pain greeted his touch, and it made his heart race with a need to erase it.

"*Cherie,* I'm sorry. It's just that things happened so fast, and…"

No excuses.

He allowed his gaze to drift from hers. It was easier that way. "I was embarrassed for being so sloppy…for almost dying because I got distracted." His heart thrashed against his ribs like a caged animal, and he clung to her, trying to fight through the panic those memories summoned.

"Chance." Lilith didn't speak again until his eyes met hers. "It's okay. Tim explained it to me."

Just as his heart rate started to slow to a normal rhythm, her smile faded, and a frown wrinkled her brow.

"Lily, what's wrong?"

"I…" she started in an almost breathless voice. "…don't know."

When she sagged against him, a panic far more potent than what he had felt moments ago ripped him to the very core.

"Lily!"

Her legs buckled, and he hauled her into his arms.

"What's…happening?" she asked faintly.

"Tell me what's wrong, Lily. Talk to me!" Chance carefully moved her to the bed.

"I'm just…dizzy and don't feel right." Her eyes drifted closed.

It felt like a steel vise clamped around his ribs, coiling tighter with each breath.

"Lilith!" His hands surged up and cradled her face between his palms. "Look at me."

Her eyes fluttered open on command, but only for a moment. "Just give me a second. I'm…tired."

Her signature was weaker than it had been earlier.

Chance immediately withdrew his hands from her face and scrambled to his feet in pure horror. The incessant screaming in his head stretched time from seconds to minutes to an eternity. He watched her chest rise and fall, but he couldn't form a single coherent thought until her eyes opened fifteen minutes later.

Lilith winced, rubbed her temple, and let out a little groan. "What happened?"

Her voice was stronger this time, and the relief it brought made Chance sink to the floor.

The motion drew her attention, and she rolled onto her side to look at him. "Chance? Why are you on the floor?"

All the words caught in his constricted throat, and he lowered his tear-streaked gaze to his hands.

"Chance?"

"I didn't mean to," was all he managed to get out.

"Didn't mean to do what?"

Her voice sounded closer, but he couldn't look away from his traitorous palms.

"Chance. Talk to me. What just happened?"

She reached for him, but he pulled away and met her eyes. "Don't. I…I drew from you. I didn't mean to, I swear. I'm so sorry."

"It's okay. I'm okay. I just got a little dizzy and—"

"No. It's not okay. I was careless. I didn't even know I was doing it, and I…I hurt you." Just saying those words out loud turned his stomach.

To his complete surprise, a chuckle escaped her lips.

"What could possibly be funny about this?"

Lilith cocked an eyebrow and tilted her head, as if he should know. When he merely continued to glare at her in disbelief, she finally explained.

"You don't remember that night in Gregor's hotel, when I kept running from you because I thought I'd hurt you the same way? I seem to remember you pinning me to the door to prove your point, in more ways than one."

"But I *actually* hurt you," he insisted. "It's not the same."

She inched a bit closer but didn't try to touch him. "Isn't it? When we showed up at the hotel fire and I was spinning out…you grabbed my hand and, seconds later, had a bad dizzy spell. Do you remember that?"

"Not really," he admitted. Truth was, Chance didn't remember much before the alley, except Lilith slugging Cohen in the jaw.

As if summoned, the memory surged to the forefront—Lilith against the brick wall, her legs wrapped around him, her nails digging into his shoulders, her moans echoing through the dark, the impulsive rapture of their first time.

"Chance? Where did you go?"

His cheeks flushed, and he lowered his head but peered up at her. "The alley," he confessed, with a curving grin he couldn't contain.

That delicate blush he loved so much colored her cheeks, and her teeth sank into her bottom lip for a second.

Then she found her words again. "It was a momentary slip in the midst of an extreme situation, and I'm fine, just like you were that night."

When Lilith reached out this time, Chance didn't pull away, but his heart still hammered against his ribs.

"See?" Lilith guided his hand to her bare chest over her heart. "I'm fine."

Chance watched his hand rise and fall for a full minute before meeting her eyes again.

"I'm fine," she stated clearly.

When he still sat frozen from the memory of her losing strength in his arms, she moved closer. Lilith crawled into his lap, wrapping her legs around his hips and her arms around his neck.

"I'm okay," she repeated, leaning her forehead against his. "You're not going to hurt me."

"But I did—"

"You won't now." Her warm breath rushed over his lips. "Touch me. I trust you."

Everything came to vivid life, as if he let down the wall keeping her out. The warm press of her skin against his…the heat of her breath…the lavender scent of her hair…the racing beat of her heart—it all surrounded him. The woman was pure magic and impossible to resist.

He slid his fingertips gingerly over her hips in a feather-light touch.

"See? Everything's fine," Lilith whispered. Her voice was thick with desire.

His palms surged up her back, pressing her body against his.

"But"—she giggled when Chance's lips touched the sensitive part of her neck that always made her thighs clench—"we only have…" Lilith paused, most likely glancing at the clock, but he didn't care. "…half an hour to shower, dress, and inform the others before Orchid arrives."

"Sounds like plenty of time," he growled against her skin.

"Chance…" Lilith leaned back as much as his arms would allow, which wasn't much. "You don't have to prove anything to me. We should shower, change, and spend the rest of our time mentally preparing."

"*You* are the one who crawled naked into my lap and told me to touch you." Despite everything, the woman still coaxed a roguish grin from him. *Fucking magic.*

"To prove a point to *you*." The dazzling smile faded. "This…I can't even imagine how hard this is going to be for you…" Delicate fingers brushed the hair from his face. "I didn't want you going into that afraid to touch me."

The deep well of gratitude in his chest cracked, and Chance captured her mouth in a kiss full of the things he couldn't seem to say in that moment.

When Chance leaned his forehead to hers, he whispered against her lips, "Thank you, *amour de ma vie*."

Chapter 18

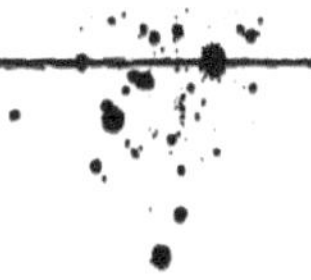

Chance sat silently on the bed. A thousand questions weighed on his shoulders while Lilith explained things to Nicci...or tried to.

"Orchid? The *assassin* who tracked us down, snapped Xander's neck, and almost killed Chance?"

"Yes." Lilith sighed heavily. "I invited her here."

"Why?" Nicci firmly folded her arms over her chest and glared at Lilith with open disapproval.

"One, she already knows where we are. She found us at the hospital last night."

Nicci opened her mouth to say something, but Lilith barreled ahead.

"And two, she has a compelling reason to turn on Luminita." Lilith's gaze slid to Chance but didn't linger.

His brain still couldn't accept it as fact. The concept was surreal, impossible, but worst of all, devastating. If Helena was alive, it meant she *chose* to leave him behind, *chose* to let him suffer.

"And the reason is..." Nicci prompted with an edge of impatience.

"Nicci, I'm asking as your partner. For now, please just trust me on this."

Chance had never seen the petite detective's jaw clench so tightly. It was a tall ask.

"She told Lilith that her real name is Helena Vieux." Chance broke the tense silence. Just saying the words out loud was like plunging a dagger into his own scarred heart, but they would all find out soon enough. Chance refused to let it cause a rift between Lilith and Nicci.

A frown pinched Nicci's face. "I know that name..." Once her mind worked out the details, her brown eyes widened, and she looked to Chance. "But that's..."

"Impossible?" Chance offered. "So I've been told my entire life."

Nicci raised her hand to quickly cover her gasp. "Oh God, she almost…"

"Killed me? I'm aware." The words emerged more clipped than intended. It probably had to do with the constant white noise filling his head and burning his synapses.

"Yes. It's an all-around fucked-up situation," Lilith said, pulling Nicci's attention away from him.

Chance was grateful for the brief distraction. The detective's constant stare of horror made his skin itch. Forming coherent thoughts beyond the barrage of questions circling his brain was difficult enough without the added pressure of social niceties.

A hard knock on the door made his heart slam against his ribs with equal force. However, when Tim and Eileen strolled inside, his wild pulse tamed—at least, at first.

Fuck! Chance shoved off the bed and paced the room in a useless attempt to work off the surge of adrenaline. *I can't fucking do this. I can't see her. I can't know she chose to leave me. I can't fucking handle that. God, I feel like I'm ten years old again. I just want to hide in the fucking closet. How could she just leave me?*

"Chance?"

He came to an abrupt halt when Lilith stepped into his path. *Lilith.* He drank in every bit of her, from the shimmering strands of copper in her blond hair to the deep sea of love and understanding floating in her olive eyes. The spiraling thoughts fell away, one by one, until there was only *her*.

"Chance, *beau*, you don't have to do this. You can wait next door. I would never force you—"

"I know," he said quickly. "And I love you for that." He drifted his palm over her cheek, summoning a smile that warmed his heart.

Helena might not have chosen him, but Lilith had, many times over, even when he fucked up so bad he thought she would never forgive him. She had chosen him, and *that* was what truly mattered. The *only* thing that mattered.

"I'm okay," he whispered and actually meant it.

Before Chance said anything else, Tim spun him around and captured him in a bear hug. "Damn! It's good to see you up and around, brother." After clapping Chance's back, Tim released him with a relieved sigh. "How are you feeling?"

"Physically? Fine. Better than fine." Chance let everything else hang in the air between them.

Tim nodded somberly. "This is fucked up, but we're all here for you."

"Anything you need," Eileen added, scooting closer to Tim.

The happy hum between them brought a genuine smile to Chance's face. At least *something* good had come from all the insanity. It had been over twenty years since Tim had even gone on a date, and the man had never looked at *anyone* the way he looked at Eileen. Their radiant smiles reminded Chance of his own whenever Lilith was nearby.

As if Lilith had read his thoughts, fingertips brushed over his back in a soothing stroke, and she appeared next to him.

A series of rapid knocks resonated from the door and echoed through Chance's skull like warning sirens. The breath froze in his chest, and his pulse sky-rocketed.

Time slowed to a crawl while Tim moved toward the door. Lilith slid her fingers down Chance's tense arm to grab his hand. It was his anchor in the storm, something to cling to, and the panic eased enough for him to take a few shallow breaths.

Lilith leaned close and whispered against the shell of his ear. "Remember, nothing she says will change who you are, especially to me."

Those words sank into his very soul, becoming permanently etched there, and he squeezed her hand. But Chance couldn't pry his stare from the opening door.

A woman in all black stood on the threshold—the same woman from the woods. Evening sunlight framed her instead of diffuse moonlight, but it was her. He had no doubt.

A broad hood covered most of her downturned face, and the few strands of hair which escaped were an unfamiliar straw color.

For a moment, disappointment and relief wrestled for control. Chance had the same chestnut hair as his mother. Maybe they were all wrong. Maybe his mother had died in that crash two decades ago, and this was nothing but an imposter.

The woman swiveled her head right to left in a long movement, most likely surveying the room before stepping inside. Once she did, delicate gloved fingers reached for the hood, and Chance tightened his grip on Lilith's hand.

Everything else fell away. Chance fixated on the woman's shadowy face. His heart hammered violently with every beat while she slowly slid the hood back.

At first, Chance frowned. He didn't recognize the woman, but after a moment, her features rippled. The blond hair darkened, and the blue eyes bled into hazel. Even her nose shrank slightly, and her cheekbones rose.

In a matter of seconds, Chance stared at the face he had both loved and feared since childhood. Every emotion swirling inside him like a tornado stopped as if frozen in shock too. Everything went still, and he couldn't tear his gaze away from the glassy eyes of his mother.

The woman cleared her throat, which tensed several times before she spoke. "*Petit renard.*"

Little fox. The nickname struck him like lightning, and he couldn't move, couldn't speak, couldn't even breathe, but his eyes misted.

"May I…have a few minutes alone with…my son?" the woman managed to ask.

My son. His brain tried to make sense of the words, tried to absorb them, while everyone turned to look at him. Chance was dimly aware of dipping his chin in a nod.

Nicci, Tim, and Eileen filed outside, but when Lilith moved, Chance reflexively tightened his grip on her hand.

"Are you sure?" Lilith asked gently.

He still couldn't rip his gaze from the ghost before him. "I…" Chance swallowed hard, closed his eyes, and finally met Lilith's compassionate stare. "I can't do this without you."

Her bottom lip trembled, and she pinched her brows together with a flood of love and devotion, soothing the ache in his chest a bit.

"Then, let's sit," she suggested, guiding him toward the bed.

When he looked back at the door, Orchid watched them, her eyes never leaving his. She seemed just as mystified, just as overwhelmed, just as haunted as he was.

"Why?" was the only word Chance managed to get past the lump in his tightening throat.

Helena's eyes misted, and she lowered herself into a nearby chair. "I didn't know. All this time, I didn't know…" Each word strained to break free, drenched in unshed tears.

Chance averted his gaze jend tugged Lilith's hand closer. Once again, he thought, *She is my anchor, my compass, my future. The only thing that matters.*

"*Petit renard,* Chance. I don't know how much you remember."

"Don't call me that." Sudden rage burned up his spine, seeping into every cell, and he snapped his eyes up to meet hers.

"I remember plenty. I remember the closet, the hunger, the beatings, finding you both passed out, with needles in your arms. The time you convulsed from a bad batch and nearly died, the way you both treated me like an annoyance when I got in the way, the broken bones, the bruises…But most of all…" Chance's entire body quivered, along with his voice, until he thought he might rattle apart at the seams. "I remember the all-consuming feeling of *not being wanted*. You come here now…over twenty years later…calling me *son*? Your *little fox*?"

Helena lowered her head with a sob, and her shoulders slumped. "You're right…to be angry." She barely got the words out, her shame surging through the room like a tidal wave.

His rage dulled enough for him to breathe but still burned beneath his flushed skin. "Do you even know what happened to me after the crash? What fresh horrors I went through at the hands of *charitable* people?" Chance allowed all his misery to seep into his voice.

Memories of things he had never told a soul—not even Lilith or Tim—rose from the dark recesses of his mind, where he had buried them long ago. The beatings from foster parents had been nothing new, but the creak of footsteps on the stairs at night still haunted him.

"No," she admitted on a shaky breath. "Luminita…She told me you died in that crash, and—"

"You just believed her?" he asked with an incredulous huff.

Hazel eyes overflowing with tears rose to meet his. "No. Of course not. She showed me police reports, pictures of"—Helena's voice broke—"pictures of a mangled little corpse. The deal I made with Luminita was for us *both. I wanted you*, Chance."

The muscles in his jaw clenched and twitched while he held onto his anger with a death grip. Pretty words were easy.

"She lied. Luminita lied to me. She stole you from me."

"Why?" Once again, it seemed like the only word Chance could force out.

"Because she wanted you on your own…wanted to see what you were capable of without my influence."

Cold disbelief hardened around his heart. "It had nothing to do with the drugs?"

Helena went still, and her back stiffened. "Recovery was difficult, but I've been sober for nearly nineteen years."

"Better late than never, I suppose," he responded bitterly. A new life she could get clean for, but not for him. Her son hadn't been reason enough to try. He wasn't worth salvation, not even then.

A heavy sigh escaped, and she rubbed at her brow. "Life with your father was…toxic."

"I remember," Chance hissed.

"But you were too young to truly understand."

Chance pulled his hand away from Lilith's and surged to his feet. Lava burned through every vein, threatening to consume him in a violent eruption.

"Too young to understand? Was I *too young* to know when you were both strung out…too busy fucking on the couch to feed your kid? Was I *too young* to comprehend the vicious fights, when dad would beat and threaten you, but you'd still leave anyway? You'd leave for weeks, and do you know who he'd blame for it? *Me.* I took his wrath every time you ran away and left me with him. And you *always* came back, not for me…for *him* and the fucking drugs."

Tears cascaded down the woman's crimson cheeks, but Chance didn't care. Crying now wouldn't make up for the things he'd endured.

"The pity from neighbors and free school lunches were the only reasons I didn't starve to death. That all happened *before* Luminita!"

"I know," she said quietly. "I failed you so many times, and nothing I can say or do will make up for that."

Lilith grasped his hand, pulling his attention away from Helena. Sadness and heartache filled her olive eyes and infused her touch. "Remember."

He barely heard her whispered word over the blood thundering in his ears, but the rage cooled.

What she had said earlier flashed through his mind, and Chance sat back down on the bed, wrapping an arm around her shoulders. Listing all his mother's sins in a screaming tirade wouldn't change anything, and he didn't need it to. Everything that had happened, every torment he had endured, had led him here, led him to Lilith, and he couldn't regret that.

"Chance," Helena said in a tentative voice. "I am sorry. I do wish I could change things. You deserved so much better. When Luminita offered me a way to escape Bastien and Farren—"

"Farren? Cohen was right? You worked for him?"

Helena nodded with a sigh. "I was a spy and assassin for Farren. When I *ran away*…the times I left and Bastien took it out on you…it was because I had no choice. When Farren called with a mission, I *had* to accept."

There was a reason. She didn't just run away and leave me to pay the price.

Logically knowing that and letting it truly sink in were two very different things. Before he could even fully process this latest revelation, Helena continued.

"But…the drugs made me sloppy, careless. Farren's patience was wearing thin. When Luminita offered a way out for me *and* you, I took it. Anything had to be better than how we were living. I wanted to get us both away from Bastien. I wanted to get clean *for you*. It was *all for you*." Tears poured from her hazel eyes, and all he sensed from her was an endless ocean of shame and regret.

Everything told Chance to believe her, but life had taught him not to trust. He simply stared at her, conflicted and raw, with misty eyes. Maybe he was too terrified to believe her. Releasing his pain to embrace a new narrative seemed impossible. It would change everything, and who would he be if he let it happen.

"Remember," Lilith whispered against his shoulder, as if she could read his thoughts.

Even if it were true, even knowing the full story, it didn't change his experience, the things he had been through. They were all part of him—scars on his soul. They made him who he was, the man Lilith loved.

"Bastien discovered my plan somehow. He got my phone, called Farren, and made a deal of his own. He'd hand Farren his missing agent in exchange for money and a promise of safety."

Helena curled her hands into fists and narrowed her watery eyes at the carpet.

"The stupid bastard had no idea what he'd done. As soon as Farren realized what you were…" Her eyes found his again. "Farren would have killed us all. He'd have seen you as nothing but an abomination and would ensure we couldn't make another. That's why I *had* to cause the wreck."

Chance stiffened at the last sentence. Shock and confusion creased his brow. "But I caused it…" The words began with certainty but drifted off. "I kept asking if you were okay. Dad reached back to slap me, and we drifted into oncoming traffic."

Helena clamped a hand over her mouth to stifle a whimper and shook her head. "God, no, baby. It wasn't your fault. When Bastien reached over the seat, *I* turned the wheel. I knew we were safely strapped in, and

Bastien hated seatbelts. I refused to let him touch you ever again. You didn't do anything wrong, Chance. You *never* did."

Chance frowned down at the floor with a lifetime of guilt weighing on his shoulders. For over two decades, he had blamed himself for his parents' deaths, even if they hadn't been perfect. The whole world was spinning out of control, shifting to morph around this new truth, changing him on a cellular level.

"I woke up at the hospital, and Luminita…convinced me you were dead. I didn't know. I swear."

Silence invaded the room, hovering in the air like a poisonous cloud until everything went numb.

"May I ask a question?" Lilith's voice was a welcome distraction.

Chance tightened his arm around her shoulders, drinking in her warmth while being careful not to pull from her like he had earlier.

"Yes."

"How did you figure it out? Chance was ten when you last saw him, and the woods were dark that night."

"I didn't figure it out until Goditha. Luminita wanted a full lockdown. Part of that procedure includes going through guest logs for the past year to anticipate any unwanted surprises. I saw both your names and immediately pulled up the surveillance footage from your first visit in October. As soon as I saw his grin…the way he looked at you…I knew. He always had the most radiant smile when he was happy."

That broke him.

Chance pulled his arm away from Lilith, buried his face in his hands, and wept. Every stroke of Lilith's hand over his back brought him comfort, safety, something to hold on to so he didn't drown in the onslaught of emotions.

"Chance?" The voice of his mother. From those rare moments when they would watch movies, dance to musicals, and laugh…That voice came closer.

Fingers touched his arm, and they didn't belong to Lilith. Fear, shame, guilt, and agonized grief accompanied her contact, and he froze, seizing like an engine with no oil.

"I will *not* let Luminita have you…either of you. I *will* destroy her, if it's the last thing I do. She's taken too much from both of us and now she has…"

Helena halted with a quick burst of fear.

Chance lifted his head to meet her wide eyes. "She has what?"

Wormwood

Helena rose from her crouched position and returned to her chair, probably buying time. "My husband and"—the column of her throat shifted with an audible swallow—"my daughter. She's only seven."

All the logic in the world couldn't stifle the irrational jealousy erupting in his chest. It wasn't the girl's fault she had gotten the version of Helena Chance had deserved, that he had barely survived while she probably thrived in a drug-free existence. He couldn't blame an innocent seven-year-old girl, but envy still burned in his veins.

"That's why you're here? You want *my* help to save your new family?" Chance huffed angrily.

"No! It's not the only reason." The plea seemed sincere, but the acrid sting of abandonment felt more familiar than the hope her words offered. "I mourned you for twenty years. I've walked around with a hole in my heart all this—"

Her voice broke, and she dissolved into a heart-wrenching sob. It cracked the ice around his heart but didn't melt it.

"Chance. I failed you before…many times. Let me help you now. I won't fail you again."

Every cell waged war until Chance thought it might tear him apart. What if it did? What if this moment irrevocably broke him? What if he couldn't come back from this? What if—

"*Beau*," Lilith whispered. Her breath heated the shell of his ear, and the panicked thoughts began to fade. "Breathe, *amour de ma vie*."

Chance closed his eyes, sending a few tears streaking down his cheeks, and concentrated on her voice.

"I'm right here. You're okay. We are okay. This is your choice, and I will stand by whatever you choose. I love you."

The rest of the world disappeared, lost in the void, burned away until Lilith was all that remained. Chance wrapped his arms around her and buried his face in her shoulder. The sweet scent of lavender engulfed him, and the gentle hum of her compassion suffocated the hateful jealousy in his heart.

This is what I need…the only thing I need. Nothing can change the past, especially not pretty words, but this…this gives that suffering meaning. Lilith is my future.

She pulled back and cradled his face in her palms while searching his eyes. "I'm here…with you. No matter what." Lilith spoke each word with firm conviction, as if trying to sear them into his brain.

Chance stroked her blond tresses, wonder filling every touch. This woman loved him so fiercely it made his heart nearly burst. "I'm so sorry about the deal. I was such a fucking idiot," he whispered in a spontaneous confession.

A broad smile crept across her lips. "We finally agree on something."

The sassy wink which followed did him in.

Despite everything, a chuckle rumbled into the air between them. The fact that now, in *this* moment, she could make him laugh…*Fucking magic.*

"May I ask something?" Orchid's timid voice broke the bubble surrounding them, pulling him back to reality.

When they both turned to face the woman, Chance nodded.

"Why would Luminita be interested in blood?"

Apparently, Orchid felt broaching a tactical question might make things easier, though Chance wasn't sure if it was for her benefit or his. Either way, she wasn't wrong.

"Blood?" Lilith asked before he could. "What do you mean?"

"At Goditha. The team had a secondary objective I wasn't privy to, but I noticed they wiped out the blood bank. They took everything."

Chance swung his gaze to Lilith, mirroring her dawning expression of dread.

"Oh, God," Lilith whispered. Her breaths came quicker. "Aaron must have told her my theory about Goditha's blood supply."

Chance peered at Orchid's confused frown. "Do you know where her lab is?"

"Yes, but—"

"We'll get the others in here and start brainstorming."

A hopeful smile cracked through her expression, and the woman slowly exhaled.

"We will help each other as temporary allies, Orchid." When Chance used her code name, the smile dimmed. "Everything else…" He rubbed a hand over his face. "It's a lot to fucking process."

The woman nodded silently, but tears flooded her hazel eyes again.

"What do you want from me?" The question tumbled past Chance's lips before he'd thought it through.

"An opportunity to earn your trust and, perhaps, eventually, your forgiveness."

Chance saw a flash of the same mother who had cuddled with him on the couch, shared popcorn, and sang along with Gene Kelly to *An American in Paris.*

"I can't guarantee any of that," Chance responded stiffly. As wonderful as those moments had been, they had also been rare and couldn't eclipse the pain he'd suffered.

"I know. I would never ask for a guarantee. Just let me help."

He considered her for a long time, weighing all the options, before angling his head toward Lilith. "Can you grab the others? And tell Tim to get Gibson and Keller."

"Are you sure you want them here?" Lilith gestured toward Orchid.

"If I can sit here and be reasonable, so can they. Luminita is more important than our personal issues. If they want to walk, let them."

Lilith flashed a tight smile, pressed a kiss to his cheek, and rose from the bed.

"Oh, I almost forgot. One other thing." Orchid's words made Lilith pause. "Your friend, Detective Cohen. He's alive. Luminita has him."

As if drawn by a magnet, Chance flicked his gaze to Lilith, who stood rigid in the center of the room. A conflicted mess of emotions radiated off her skin, but the relief and happiness buried among them brought a new surge of anger to Chance's core.

She considered Cohen a friend. Naturally, she would be happy he was alive. But the image of Cohen kissing Lilith dominated Chance's thoughts despite her reassurances and the many ways they had claimed each other. That had been when they both thought he was dead, and this news resurrected his fear.

"Of course he is," Chance growled, rubbing his temples. *What else can go wrong today?*

If the past year had taught him anything, it was that he should have known better than to even think that question.

Chapter 19

*T*wo *hundred and twenty-five…the number of cinderblocks comprising my cell.* Andrew had no illusions that it was anything else. The reinforced bars on the window and the locked steel door were a clear indication. *Luminita plans to keep me here as long as she sees fit.*

One…two…three…Cohen started the count over again, like he'd done at least fifty times. The number never changed, of course, but it helped keep his mind active.

Just give Luminita what she wants, the demon hissed.

"Four…five…six…" He counted out loud to drown out the intrusive voice, but it didn't work.

What do you really owe the vampire?

"Seven…eight…nine…" Cohen's voice rose until it echoed through the small room.

The demon's taunts were getting old and predictable. That should have made them less painful, but it didn't. Every word cut at him like lemon-soaked paper.

Do you think she knows you're alive?

The count faltered. *God, I hope she doesn't.*

Liar.

Cohen went rigid and fixed his eyes on the ninth block. Lilith had rallied the troops to rescue him at PMIC. If she knew he was alive and came for him here, she would play right into Luminita's hands.

What if that was the plan? What if Luminita didn't need his cooperation at all? What if he was nothing more than bait?

No, he thought. The raid on PMIC had been focused on the cult and their virus. Rescuing him had been a secondary objective. Lilith wouldn't risk her life and those of others solely to save him.

Would she?

His conversation with Lilith in the stairwell of Haverty's building rose to the forefront. Lilith had made it crystal clear she would sacrifice Cohen if it meant keeping her and Chance alive.

But…that was *before* the medical center, before they had grown close, before she had seen past his masks, before she had seen his true eye color, before—

Before she knew you were fucking look-alikes and pretending they were her, before Alexis showed up, before you confessed your undying love like a psycho stalker and kissed her while her fiancé was dying. She'll never come to your rescue again.

"Good." Fresh pain lanced Cohen's already wounded heart. "If her happiness means me dying in this miserable pit, so be it."

A maniacal cackle that didn't belong to Cohen filled his head. *You aren't that selfless. You won't let yourself rot away in here, and you still want her.*

"I'll always want her…" Cohen frowned. The realization sank in with a sting. "I'll always love her, but that's on me. She owes me nothing. I'd never ask her for a fucking thing."

Idealistic, delusional nonsense. It's easy to spout altruistic promises when you have no choice. If you were free…if she was standing in front of you now…would you say the same? Would you walk away, content to leave her in the arms of another? Would you deny yourself, curl into a ball, and wither away?

Cohen's throat constricted, and nothing escaped but a strangled cry. Would he be strong enough to let her go if he could physically touch her?

He wanted to scream "yes," but the demon was right. It was easy to believe in himself, to have conviction, when he didn't have a choice.

You couldn't resist anyone, much less her, in your current state. The demon chuckled darkly.

Once again, he wasn't wrong. Need itched beneath Cohen's skin like a thousand fire ants crawling and biting. Not only was he still injured, with fractured hands and the deep punctures from Ashcroft's talons, but he also hadn't truly fed since the night of the gala over a week ago.

That was the last time he had given in to his obsession, pretending the redhead was Lilith, imagining *her* scent of sweet lavender, picturing *her* face flushed, moaning *her* name, creating a whirlwind of sexual energy to drink, plunging into *her* heat…

"Fuck!" Cohen threw all his frustration into the scream and slammed his fractured hands onto the mattress. The accompanying pain searing up his arms was a soothing balm in comparison, masking the emotional agony tearing him apart, if only for a few minutes.

When the wave of mind-numbing pain began to ebb, the thunk of the lock stole his attention. His eyes darted toward the door, and his heart rate doubled until the pounding blood in his ears drowned out everything else.

Whatever came next wouldn't be good, but anticipation still laced his fear. His desperation for stimulus, his compulsion to block out the voice, his burning need to feed—it consumed him. Even torture would be preferrable to languishing in the cell, weak and alone in the inner demon's unrelenting grip.

The steel door swung open, and a woman screamed.

"No!"

A figure stumbled into the room and collapsed in a heap on the floor. The heavy door slammed shut, followed by the resounding thunk of the lock.

Cohen fixated on the shivering woman and the dark red curls falling around her face in a frazzled mess. He didn't move. Each muscle locked. Wild desire pulled at his center, beckoning him to take what he needed…what he craved.

A few shades too dark. His gaze moved from the garnet hair to the hands covering her sobbing face. *Too tan.* The cherry-red nails were too flashy for Lilith, but…

Recognition hit him like a blow to the gut. "Alexis?"

The woman's shoulders stopped shaking, and her hands fell, revealing watery emerald eyes surrounded by black smears of makeup. A line formed between her brows before relief flashed across her face.

"Andrew? Oh, thank God." Then worry tinged her expression as she truly took him in. "You're injured."

Take what you need, the demon roared in his head. *You know she'll let you.*

"What are you doing here?" Cohen demanded, still refusing to move.

"Luminita…She…" Sorrow pinched Alexis's face, and she swallowed hard before trying again. "There were men waiting with my brother when I returned. They took us both. She never intended to let us go. She lied…"

The woman's agony perfumed the air, and he wanted it, needed it, but if he drew it in now, he would never stop. His control was nothing more than tissue paper facing a hurricane. Despite all the woman's mistakes, he didn't want to kill her.

Cohen drew his knees up to his aching chest to keep from launching off the bed. "She doesn't like loose ends. I tried to warn you."

"I know. I'm sorry." Alexis wiped at her mascara-streaked cheeks and started to stand.

"Stop!" Andrew screeched in panic. "Stay where you are."

The woman's eyes widened, and she froze mid-motion. "Why?" Alexis searched his face, her own crumpling. "I'm sorry about everything, especially…" She lowered her gaze to the concrete but still rose to her feet. "My jealousy got the better of me. I had no right to hurt you."

The demon roared in his head, demanding him to devour, and it took all Cohen's control to stay on the mattress. "None of it matters. Stay there. I don't want to hurt you."

You don't have to hurt her, the voice whispered seductively. *There are other more fulfilling ways. Indulge your fantasy and heal yourself at the same time. She looks enough like Lilith. You've done it before.*

Andrew's stomach flipped, and his throat went dry. He had sworn to himself after confessing to Lilith that he would never do it again, never imagine *her* when he—

"Andrew." Alexis's tentative voice stopped his spiraling thoughts. "You don't have to hurt me." Her echoing the demon's taunt thickened the tension between them, and Andrew curled his battered fingers in the sheet. "We could…help each other."

Alexis straightened, smoothing her hands down her wrinkled shirt. Andrew tracked every motion with a predatory stare. When she took a step closer, his heart thrashed against his ribs, as if trying to break through the bone and cartilage.

"Stop! Please!" Andrew wrapped himself into a ball, buried his head, and squeezed his eyes shut. Every inch screamed for Andrew to pin her to the wall and devour every ounce of sexual energy she offered, regardless of the consequences.

I promised. I fucking promised her, and Alexis resembles Lilith too much for me to see anything else.

Then the answer is simple. Dread accompanied the demon's words. *If you want to keep your promise, take what you need and drain her.*

"Andrew." The voice sounded closer this time, which sent a shiver of anticipation down his spine despite the bile burning his throat. "I know you're mad, but this doesn't have to mean anything. You're hurt. You need me."

He threw every ounce of strength into ignoring the breathy proposal and focused on the pounding beats of his heart.

Kill her or fuck her…Either way, you need it.

No! That's not who I am anymore!

It's what *you are. A predator. Denying yourself for the sake of a woman who doesn't want you won't change that. There are no prizes for playing the fucking martyr. Do you honestly think some vow of celibacy and suffering will save your soul? Do you even have one? You are a* Durand. *You take what you need to survive.*

"Talk to me."

Fingers touched his forearm, accompanied by flickers of fear, sadness, and longing. The delicious caress of energy, power, ruptured his thin skin of control, drawing the ravenous monster to the surface.

Andrew shot his head up, his wide eyes slowly narrowing on Alexis's face. She looked so much like Lilith that it made every inch of him ache with a consuming desire.

Alexis parted her full lips in a shaky breath and pulled her hand away, but not fast enough. Andrew snatched her wrist, caught somewhere between insatiable lust and starvation. Alexis gasped while arousal and fear warred in her emerald eyes.

She tried to pull away, though didn't put her full effort into the motion. Her compulsion to taste the frenzy inside him overpowered everything else.

Andrew unfolded his legs, slid off the mattress, and rose to his full height, towering over her. Her pulse violently thrummed in a hypnotic rhythm against his fingers.

"You should have listened." The almost unrecognizable voice which passed his lips held no warmth, no anger. Nothing. "I warned you to stay away."

"I…" Alexis swallowed, and her blown pupils studied his face. "I don't want to stay away." She expelled her truth on a heated sigh drenched in wanton desire, but fear still swirled within her.

The intoxicating combination flooded his senses, and he drew it in, welcomed it.

Just like that, the demon had won.

The rush after being denied for so long forced a shuddering sigh from Cohen's throat, and his eyes fluttered closed in surrender.

"That's it. Let me help you." Alexis caressed his cheek, leaving a trail of shivers behind.

They rippled through him, but a nagging voice in the back of his head told him it wasn't right…It wasn't *her.*

In one swift motion, he snatched her free wrist and pulled it away from his face. When he opened his eyes, she was peering up at him with a confused frown.

"You want me. I can feel it. You're practically vibrating with desire. I know you want me."

Cohen stepped forward, forcing her backward, and continued until her body hit the cinderblock wall. The woman moaned while he raised his hands, pinning her wrists above her head.

Alexis stared up at him, wide-eyed, her chest heaving, plump lips parted, skin flushed a heated pink. Carnal desire flooded the air between them.

It would be so easy. She wanted him to lean in, to pin her to the wall with his hips, to give into his desire, but she didn't understand, could *never* understand.

He moved closer until his lips hovered above hers, almost touching, but not quite. Cohen whispered while her hot breath washed over his skin.

"You aren't the one I want."

Alexis's chest stopped heaving for an instant. When Cohen retreated, crimson blazed up her throat and across her cheeks. Her rising anger and embarrassment were even more delectable than her erotic heat.

"What?"

"You heard me. You're nothing but a cheap imitation, Alexis." Although his body screamed and yearned to tear off every shred of her clothing and sexually punish her for not being the woman he loved, his promise, his oath, refused to be ignored. It burned beneath his skin like a holy sigil on his battered soul.

The room shifted, darkened, until he stared at Lilith's tear-streaked face from the basement that fateful night. That moment had meant *everything*. *She* meant *everything*. He wouldn't sully that in a perverse moment of weakness with a substitution, and Alexis would never be anything more than that.

"Please, don't do this," the woman before him whispered on a terrified whimper, but the words came from Lilith's mouth—the one he would sell his soul to kiss again.

Andrew dropped her wrist and brushed his thumb over her cheek, wiping away a tear. "I *love* you, Lilith Adams."

"Andrew!"

The angry shriek tore away the mirage, and Lilith vanished, revealing Alexis's enraged face. The sudden loss felt like a dagger twisting between his ribs.

"*I* am the one here! *I* am the one who can help you! *I* am the one who *wants* you."

The paper-thin veneer of restraint ruptured, and the intrusive demon roared to the surface, taking complete control. While Alexis's emerald eyes widened, Cohen drifted his hand from her cheek to encircle her throat with slow, purposeful movements.

"Then help me," the demon whispered with a vicious grin.

Alexis choked when his hand tightened. He began ripping away energy, layer by layer.

"Andrew…Stop…Please!"

The raspy plea didn't sway the monster in control, but it tore at Andrew while he watched, trapped, unable to pull away, unable to stop.

The light in her misty emerald eyes began to fade, and strength infused every single cell of Andrew's body. He hummed with power.

The woman weakened beneath his grasp. Bright red nails dug into his forearms, but the demon ignored the stinging pain. The half-moon cuts healed as soon as they had formed.

Eventually, her biting grip loosened, her hands fell away, and her lips parted in one last desperate gasp.

A tsunami of energy tore through him until the demon receded, happy and sated, leaving Andrew to deal with the fallout.

He released her throat as if the woman were a poisonous snake. Alexis's body crumpled to the floor, and Andrew staggered backward, horror echoing through his brain in one endless scream.

He peered at the unmarred flesh of his chest, then flexed his hands at his sides—no longer a source of pain. His eyes locked on Alexis again.

She didn't move. Garnet curls haphazardly covered her pale face.

God. His shoulders shook, and tears finally flooded his eyes. *What have I done?* He sank onto the mattress.

Alexis's lifeless eyes seemed to follow him.

Fuck, fuck, fuck.

You survived. You took what you needed.

Andrew buried his face in his palms, trying to block out the image of the body before him.

You are the one who insisted on keeping your promise to the vampire. Was it worth it? Do you feel more righteous? Do you feel clean? Was Alexis's life worth your virtue?

A tortured whimper escaped, and Cohen curled into a ball on the bed, facing the wall.

Maybe the demon was right. Maybe he had no soul to save. Maybe he was no better than Ashcroft.

Maybe he deserved this place.

Chapter 20

Andrew Cohen is alive. The thought kept echoing through Lilith's mind while everyone gathered in the hotel room.

Each time her conflicting emotions rose to the surface in a stifling swell, she glanced at Chance. He sensed everything, but she couldn't stamp out the recollection of that night. Andrew's confession had been burned into her memory, along with his reverent kiss, which had been filled with promises but asked for nothing.

Lilith hadn't lied. Chance *was* her future, the man she loved, the man she claimed, the only one she wanted, but the thought of Andrew in Luminita's clutches haunted her. Even if she didn't feel the same, Andrew *loved her.* He had tried to sacrifice himself to save her, and now he was the one who needed saving. She couldn't abandon him.

Fingers threaded through hers, and she expelled a relieved sigh. She tightened her grip on Chance's hand and pulled on a smile before facing him again, hoping it would give him some measure of solace.

"I'm sorry," she whispered, low enough for only him to hear.

For a split-second, guilt pulled at his handsome features in the classic signs—eyes cast down and away, cheeks raised, the corners of his mouth depressed.

"Stop apologizing, *cherie.* He's your friend. You have every right to be worried."

The words sounded hollow, as if they were nothing more than a conditioned response, and that tightened her throat. Chance wanted to believe the words—that much she could tell—but he just…didn't, and after her confession about that night, she couldn't truly blame him. He had worried about her closeness with Andrew Cohen ever since the Medical Center, and now…

Lilith swallowed hard around the lump in her throat. She wanted to talk to him, convince him nothing was different, that nothing had changed, but now wasn't the time. They had things to deal with, plans to make, and everything else would have to wait.

"I love you," she whispered while the others were finding places to sit or stand.

Chance strengthened his grip on her hand. "I love you too, *amour de ma vie.*"

At least those words he spoke with conviction, and it eased the tension in her chest a bit.

Lilith forced her eyes away from Chance and peered around the room. Orchid still sat in her chair, while Eileen claimed the other. Tim moved to stand behind the FBI agent, and Nicci leaned against the wall near their bed.

However, Gibson and Keller had chosen a position close to the door, still maintaining as much distance as possible. They fixated their heavy stares on Orchid with an intense hatred Lilith understood.

The woman had killed Chris Xander, their brother-in-arms, after all. She had snapped his neck like a twig during her attack on the cabin.

Orchid twisted, looking at the two men with a mask that was neutral but somehow respectful. "Before we begin, I wish to apologize for my role in your team member's death. I was given a mission to complete but did not know pertinent facts. I am sorry."

"Your role? You fucking killed him." Gibson took a step forward, curling his hand into a fist, but Keller threw an arm across his chest, stopping him short.

"Don't do it, brother. It won't bring Xander back."

A muscle twitched in Gibson's jaw, but he retreated to the wall and leaned stiffly against it.

"Your apology won't bring our man back either. Skip to what we need to know." The low growl in Tim's voice drew everyone's attention.

"Of course," Orchid replied, with a business-like nod.

"Start with what you told us about Goditha," Lilith prompted.

"Once we secured Goditha, I spotted Luminita's men on the surveillance cameras, packing up items in one of the labs. I asked about it but was given no information. Apparently, I wasn't granted clearance to know their alternative mission. On my security sweep, I narrowed down the lab they targeted. It was the blood supply. They took *everything.*"

"Why would…" Nicci started, but her voice trailed off when the realization finally struck her. "Holy shit." She swung her eyes to Lilith, who sighed with resignation.

"Aaron must have told her my theory on the virus's origin."

"A virus?"

Luminita must have kept Orchid in the dark about more than Chance's identity.

"Yes," Lilith answered before anyone else could speak. "I believe the blood supply there was contaminated with the same virus that has infected both vampires and the Durand and is currently spreading through the surrounding human population."

"Why would she want that?" Orchid asked with a frown. "If it's capable of infecting the Durand, it's extremely dangerous."

"I'm not sure. Perhaps she wants to contain it as much as possible."

But Lilith didn't have much faith in that theory. Luminita was a calculating person and never did anything without a clear reason which would benefit her cause. Simple precaution didn't fit her personality profile. Everything the woman did had an offensive purpose.

"Or weaponize it," Chance added.

Lilith turned toward him while trying to work through his words.

"According to *Cohen…*" He cleared his throat after saying the detective's name, as if the act itself were painful. "Luminita still has enemies among the Durand. With the exposure of her experiments, she might have more now."

"Yeah, but the virus is a blunt instrument. It would infect more than her targets. She could kill off the entire species and ours too. That directly opposes her mission to empower the Durand."

"If she had a scientist who could manipulate the virus and modify it…"

As Nicci thought out loud, an eerie feeling crept down Lilith's spine.

"She'd want an antidote first," Lilith blurted out when the thought came to her. "Luminita would only take the risk of having it close if she *knew* she couldn't be infected."

And there was only one person who was currently working on a cure—the same person who hadn't returned her text messages, which wasn't like him.

Lilith shot off the bed, grabbed the burner phone, and dialed a familiar number. The line rang for what seemed like an eternity before someone finally picked up.

"Solasta labs, research department. How can I direct your call?"

Lilith didn't recognize the unenthusiastic female voice at first but finally placed it. Claudia, Gerard's phone-obsessed intern with the thick bangs.

"Dr. Gerard Scott, please."

The heavy silence filling the line brought a growing sense of dread which squeezed Lilith's chest in a death grip.

"Um, I'm afraid that's not possible." The woman's tentative tone only made that grip tighten until Lilith could barely suck in a breath.

"Why is that?"

"I'm not supposed to discuss that."

"I'm calling on urgent business concerning the virus he's been working on. It is critical that I talk to him as soon as possible." Lilith let the stress and desperation soak every word to drive her point home.

The longer the silence stretched, the more Lilith's panic built until it rattled through her very bones.

"Is this CSI Adams?"

The woman whispered the question, and Lilith hesitated.

If she said yes, it could easily get back to Aaron, but she was calling from her burner and could switch the SIM cards. If answering truthfully persuaded the woman, she would take the risk.

"Yes."

"Mr. Bogdan left very clear orders not to talk to you, but…you worked with Dr. Scott. He always spoke so highly of you."

Lilith picked up on Claudia's use of the past tense, and her heart plummeted. "What happened?"

A soft sigh crackled through the cheap phone's speaker. "There was an attack several nights ago. Dr. Scott was taken, along with all his research on the virus."

Shock ricocheted through every cell, and Lilith sank onto the bed like a boneless heap. She wasn't surprised someone had taken him. Lilith had expected it, from Claudia's cagey behavior, but an outright attack on Solasta was something she had never considered.

"The night guards were all killed, the lab was ransacked, as well as his office, and Solasta isn't sharing any information. Mr. Bogdan had all the evidence shipped out to a private lab. He claims there may be some inside connection."

Fucking Aaron. Of course, there was an inside connection. He either handed everything over to Luminita or was covering her tracks. That was the only thing that made sense. Perhaps Luminita's research facility was the one he had sent everything to. "Do you know this lab's location?"

"No. There's no record of the shipping address."

"Can you answer one other question for me?"

"If I can," the woman said confidently.

"You said his office was ransacked. Is his map of Scotland still hanging on the wall?"

"The map?" Obvious confusion filled the question. "Yes. That thing is adhered to the wall. I think the whole building could collapse and it wouldn't move. Why?"

"Curiosity. He always loved that thing. Thank you for your help."

Lilith hung up before the woman said anything else and stared at the phone. With the skills of Dr. Scott, Luminita would not only have a cure, but also a deadly weapon in time.

"What happened?" Chance asked softly, sliding his hand over hers.

"I think you're right." Lilith couldn't pry her eyes from the phone resting in her palm. "I think Luminita has Dr. Scott. There was an attack at Solasta."

"When?" Orchid fired off the question with urgency.

Lilith finally lifted her gaze to meet the woman's eyes. "She didn't specify. A few nights ago."

"And this scientist had a cure?"

"He was working on one, but I haven't spoken to him since he received the cult's computers. There's a possibility they already had a cure formulated. It would make sense, to ensure they didn't fall victim to their own virus."

"Why did you ask about his map?"

Chance's question pulled Lilith's attention away from Orchid, and she glanced up at his green-flecked eyes.

"Dr. Scott is severely paranoid. He has a ghost drive embedded in the wall behind that map. It backs up everything automatically. He showed it to me once when I worked with him after college. Gerard trusted me with a lot because of his relationship with my father, and he always worried that something might happen to him one day. He wanted someone to know where to find his secrets."

Heaviness weighed in her chest. The men who had taken Dr. Scott didn't know about the drive, but Lilith couldn't reach it. Solasta would be locked down even tighter after a blatant attack, and she had no doubt

Aaron had them all blacklisted. They wouldn't be able to get anywhere near Solasta without an Elder to override her uncle's orders.

"We need to call Antonio," Chance stated, as if reading her thoughts. He gently pried the phone from Lilith's grip and rose from the bed. "I'll call while everyone else catches up."

Judging by the tension around his eyes when they briefly flicked in Orchid's direction, Chance wanted privacy for several reasons. Once again, Lilith couldn't blame him.

Facing down the ghost of his mother had dredged up a host of painful memories, some of which he would probably never share, but she had felt them somehow. Not like she had with the Durand blood, but like a specter hovering on the edge of her own memories, just out of sight. Maybe she had become skilled at reading him, or perhaps it was their closeness.

"Okay, partner." Nicci interrupted Lilith's swirling thoughts when the door clicked closed behind Chance. "Does *she* still need to be here?" The petite detective nodded in Orchid's direction.

Lilith cleared her throat and refocused. "Yes, Nicci. She does." Lilith opened her mouth to explain, but Orchid stepped in.

"We have a common enemy. Luminita deserves destruction. The demon stole my son, and now she has my husband and daughter. I won't rest until I've stripped everything away from her."

"And she has Cohen," Lilith added.

"What? Cohen? No." Nicci pushed away from the wall and crossed her arms over her chest. "Cohen's dead. I saw Ashcroft kill him."

Although Nicci's gaze was firmly locked on Lilith, Orchid was the first to respond.

"I gave him a bit of my blood. I needed to know how to permanently end Ashcroft. Then I sent him to Goditha with two of my men. I figured supplying Luminita with a secondary target would appease her for a day or two, at least. I asked when I met with Luminita this morning. She confirmed that Andrew Cohen is alive and in her care."

Care. What a bastardization of that word. Lilith's stomach twisted when the image flashed through her mind—Cohen strapped to a metal gurney, body convulsing against the restraints, shrieks of agony echoing off the tile walls, Luminita's scalpel carving into his skin and nicking the bone.

"No fucking way." Nicci paced the small area, trying to work through everything. "Ashcroft is dead?" Nicci turned her narrowed gaze on Orchid.

"Yes. I decapitated him, threw his head in the river, and burned his body. Luminita will *not* revive him a second time."

A heavy huff escaped while Nicci continued to pace. "How are we supposed to believe you?"

Orchid turned away from the detective to face Lilith. "I've read your profile. You are skilled at reading micro-expressions. Am I lying when I say Ashcroft is dead and Luminita is my enemy?"

Lilith studied every line and movement of her face while Orchid spoke. "No," she stated simply. "But…you are a Durand, and in my experience, they are exceptionally gifted liars. Luminita and Cohen both had me fooled."

Something in Orchid's expression appeared impressed by her truthful admission.

The ding of a phone broke the tense silence in the room, and Orchid pulled a cell from her pocket. Her hazel eyes roamed the screen, and something cold leaked into her expression.

Great. More good news, Lilith thought with a healthy dose of sarcasm. *When it rains, it's an apocalyptic flood.*

"Well, this complicates things," Orchid muttered before tucking her phone away. "We need to move fast. Pack everything as quickly as you can. We won't have much time."

"Why? What happened?" Agent Hersch asked.

White noise buzzed in the back of Lilith's head, growing louder with every passing second. A vague impression of anger and heartache threatened to consume her, but she wasn't sure where it came from or why. It didn't seem to belong to her…or anyone in the room, for that matter.

"David Boston, Sr. has officially offered a contract for Chance Deveraux, Lilith Adams, Detective Andrew Cohen, Detective Nicci DeLuca, Timothy Bardow, Special Agent Eileen Hersch, Special Agent John Gorman, Derek Gibson, Christopher Xander, and Brian Keller. He wants Chance alive. The rest are optional."

Lilith had known it was coming, but hearing the reality didn't compare. Despair seeped into her very marrow and twisted around her bones like a thorny vine. The madman wanted Chance alive so *he* could punish him for killing his son, but everyone else present that day would die for their complicit role in his murder.

"But they couldn't know our location," Nicci objected.

Orchid arched one brow. "I found you rather easily, detective. Besides, Boston isn't the only one issuing a contract."

Lilith frowned and locked her gaze on Orchid.

"Luminita is offering double to kill anyone who tries to harm you and triple for delivering you all *alive* to her instead. She also threw in your last known location—Madisonville. Every agent for hire will see these contracts. If they're loyal to Boston, they won't care about the money, and if they are not, they'll be instigating a bloodbath around you, which will draw far too much attention. We need to move."

The hotel door swung open again, and Chance rushed inside. He looked pale as a damn ghost.

"What now?" Lilith groaned before rubbing her hands over her face.

"Michael is dead. They found him in Aaron's apartment. The entire place was trashed, and no one has seen or heard from Aaron since. Between the Solasta attack and this, the Elders are panicking."

"Michael?" Lilith frowned deeply, stunned by his response. "Did they give you any details about the body?"

"Stabbed through the ribs." Chance shrugged and pulled out the SIM card.

"Was anything else missing besides Aaron?"

"Not that they mentioned." Chance snapped the thin plastic and reached in his pocket for a replacement.

Lilith stared at the carpet while she ran through every possible scenario. *Who would want Aaron? One of the other Elders? Maybe he had a falling out with Luminita. Perhaps he wasn't onboard with her attack on Solasta. Or...*

She halted for a moment. Her mind was unwilling to accept the possibility at first, but...

What if Aaron wanted to disappear?

"I need you to call Antonio back. I *need* to know if Michael had any defensive wounds."

Chance tilted his head and peered at Lilith, but he eventually nodded and stepped outside again.

"Everyone else, pack what you can. Orchid is right. We need to move."

"I hate to point out the obvious here, but we don't have a vehicle and renting one would defeat the purpose at this point. They have all our names." Tim looked to Eileen for a split-second. Guilt tightened his mouth.

"You're right, and moving as a group might be a mistake." Lilith released a weary sigh.

"No. We are *not* splitting up again." Tim's steely tone left no room for debate, but authority figures commonly brought out Lilith's rebellious side.

"Chance and I are who Boston wants—"

Orchid cut her off quickly. "Correction. *Chance* is the *only one* both sides want alive. Splitting up puts people in *more* danger, not less. A killer will hesitate if Chance is present, to ensure they capture him alive as ordered. If he's *not* present, there will be no hesitation. Precious seconds mean the difference between life and death."

"I have to agree," Tim muttered. "But all eight of us aren't gonna fit in your tiny-ass SUV."

"I've been thinking about that," Eileen said with a spreading smile. "There's an old storage lot on John Sevier Highway east of the city. They store RVs and other vehicles there, and I can tell you from personal experience, their *state-of-the-art security* consists of two exterior cameras and a chain link fence."

"Wouldn't a stolen RV stand out like a sore thumb?"

Eileen leaned in her chair to meet Keller's questioning gaze. "Only if it's reported as stolen. If we pick the lock and avoid looking at the cameras, no one will think twice about someone picking up their RV in the height of summer vacation season."

"Until someone comes looking for their RV and it isn't there," Tim added.

Eileen merely shrugged. "No plan is foolproof, but it's less likely to be missed than a work or personal vehicle."

"Fine. Chance and I will go." Tim appeared resolute, but Eileen's cheery laughter stopped him short.

"No offense, but you two would definitely stand out. Nicci, Gibson, and I have much more…*generic* body types. We'll be hardier to identify."

"Absolutely not." Tim huffed. "I'm not sending you out there with a goddamn assassin to steal an RV."

Eileen twisted in her chair. She shot Tim a piercing stare that gave Lilith chills. "You aren't *sending me*. I'm *choosing* to go. I know the facility, where the cameras are. I can pick the lock, and I'm an FBI agent, not some wilting damsel who needs protection."

Tim's throat bobbed, and pink tinged his cheeks when he took a step back. It was the first time Lilith ever recalled seeing the man rattled.

"I'm grateful for your concern, Tim…" Eileen softened her voice, and the panic in the man's brown eyes waned. "…but it's not warranted. I can handle myself."

"And she won't be alone," Nicci added, patting his shoulder. "I'll watch your girl's back."

The blush returned to Tim's cheeks and deepened, but he nodded stiffly.

"Then it's settled." Orchid rose from her chair and dug the key fob out of her pocket. "Everyone else should pack and be ready to go when we return."

"Wait." Lilith scooted off the bed and ventured deeper into the room to retrieve her forensic kit. After putting it on the bed, she popped the case open and pulled out two things. "This will help."

Lilith handed Eileen her lockpick gun, which was far easier than manually picking the lock.

"Thanks." Eileen smiled in appreciation.

"Who knows how to hotwire a vehicle?" Lilith glanced around the room.

Gibson and Nicci both raised their hands. Lilith tossed the wire strippers to her partner, who caught them with a nod.

"I'd give you all gloves, but it would look suspicious on camera."

"Agreed." Eileen flashed a conspiratorial smile and stood.

At least someone appeared to be enjoying themselves.

Chapter 21

"**B**efore you go…" Tim tried to swallow past the nervous constriction of his throat. "Can I speak with you…in private?"

A hesitant smile reached Eileen's lips, and her gaze bounced around the room. Tim could sense everyone's impatient stare, but this was important to him. He needed her to understand.

"Just a minute. It won't take long. Please."

Eileen's roving gaze stopped on him. Her electric blue eyes locked on his, and her smile brightened. The pressure in his chest started to ease.

"I need to grab something from my room anyway." Then Eileen pivoted toward Orchid. "I'll be right back."

With an expectant side-glance at Tim, she headed for the door, and he wasted no time following.

"Where are you two going?" Chance asked from the sidewalk when Eileen barreled past him to unlock the hotel door.

"The others will explain." Tim clapped him on the shoulder. He jogged to catch the door as it started to swing shut.

After rushing inside and closing the door, he turned toward Eileen, who was rummaging through his luggage.

"Uh. What are you doing?"

"I need your hat…the one from the Tennessee Aquarium."

"Sure. It's in there somewhere."

Not even a second later, Eileen yanked the hat from his duffle with a triumphant grin and slid it on her head. "Perfect!"

Tim couldn't help but smirk at how damn adorable she was, with her big blue eyes shaded by the brim and whisps of her pixie cut curling around the hat. The reason he'd wanted to speak to her resurfaced, dimming his smile.

"I, uh…I just wanted to apologize. I didn't mean to…" *Fuck!* He wasn't even sure how to say it.

"Hey." Eileen's soothing voice tempered his racing pulse, but not as much as her palms sliding up, cradling his face. "It's okay. You aren't the first man to mistakenly think I need his protection."

Tim grasped the hat and tossed it on the bed. It hid the fierce blue in Eileen's eyes he desperately wanted to see. He brushed a few short locks from her forehead and released a soft sigh.

"I don't doubt your abilities, Eileen. I know how capable…how deadly, you are. I've just…" He furrowed his brow, sorting through the chaos in his head.

"Just what?" she prompted gently.

Tim expelled a heavy breath and spoke the truth. She deserved it, no matter how much it frightened him.

"I've never felt this way about anyone, and the thought of you in danger… It's not about you needing my protection; it's about me needing to *see* you're safe, needing to *know* what's happening. It's the panicked uncertainty when you're not with me."

Eileen's wide-eyed stare made Tim groan and step away. He raked an aggravated hand through his curls.

"I sound like a fucking idiot. I'm sorry. I just wanted you to know that I *don't* see you as some damsel in distress. You're more like a pixie warrior goddess, especially in tactical gear."

The memory of their first kiss brought a smile to his lips. The night of Orchid's attack, he had been so rattled by the thought of losing her, like he had lost Xander, that it forced him to confess his feelings. The way the light from the kitchen window had made her blue eyes blaze… She had looked like a divine sprite dressed for battle. And then…she had kissed him with that same ferocity.

Eileen tugged on the back of his shirt, pulling him from the memory. "Tim."

He sighed again, bracing himself for a fight or worse—rejection—and turned around.

As soon as he faced her, Eileen gripped the back of his neck and pulled him down until her lips crashed against his, catching him completely off guard.

Once the initial shock wore off, Tim gripped her waist and hauled her up, lost in the ethereal beauty of the devastating kiss. Every nudge of her lips, every deliberate stroke of her tongue, every breathy sigh, felt like a touch of divinity, and damn, he wanted to worship every bit of her.

Her legs wrapped around his hips in a possessive grip, making his head swim. *All I want to do is lock that fucking door and spend the entire night giving her reasons not to leave. Hell, if I do a good enough job, she won't even have the energy to stand.*

Eileen's fingers delved into his hair, sending delicious tingles over his scalp, and her tongue darted past his lips in an intoxicating dance. His pulse raced from the overwhelming effect she had on him. Eileen was like the purest drug swimming through his veins—a high he never wanted to come down from.

A sharp knock on the door broke the spell, and Eileen pulled back. Heat flushed the delicate column of her neck, all the way up to her cheeks. Her chest heaved with each heavy breath. Tim couldn't take his eyes off her. She was an absolute vision.

Another swift knock elicited a growl from Tim's throat. There was never enough time. Of course, while he gazed at her, he realized eternity probably wouldn't be enough time either.

Well, that's a sobering and terrifying thought after a few days. Definitely do not say that shit out loud.

"Thank you," she whispered against his lips. "For seeing my strength *and* for worrying about me."

Tim crushed her against him and buried his face in the curve of her shoulder, breathing in the heady mixture of earthy florals from her shampoo. "Just…come back to me."

"Of course I will." The promise tickled through his hair.

Three more knocks.

Tim lowered Eileen to her feet, grabbed the hat from the bed, and placed it on her head while she beamed up at him.

"You be careful too."

Tim nodded in agreement. The knocks became an endless barrage, which could only mean Gibson was on the other side. Tim clenched his jaw and stalked to the door before yanking it open.

"Yes, Gibson! What is it?" The biting words dripped with anger and frustration, but his friend ignored it.

"The assassin is getting restless. Is Agent Hersch ready to go?"

"I'm right here. All set." Eileen sauntered by him, her hand grazing his arm when she passed.

"Orchid's already in the car." Gibson nodded toward the white Toyota 4Runner, and Tim's gaze followed Eileen while she walked up to the passenger's side and climbed in. "Keller is packing up all our gear. Don't worry, boss. Nicci and I will keep an eye on her."

"Absolutely, big fella," Nicci added, strolling up to Tim. "Trust me."

Tim smiled and pulled Nicci into a hug. "Thanks, shorty."

The petite detective shoved at his midsection with a playful scowl. "Stop calling me that."

Tim arched a brow and chuckled. "I will when you stop calling me 'big fella.'"

Nicci snorted a laugh and winked up at him. "Never gonna happen, *big fella*."

Once Nicci and Gibson hopped into the backseat, the SUV backed up and sped away. With a heavy sigh and uneasiness twisting his guts, Tim reluctantly headed back into his room to pack.

After Chance watched Tim and Eileen disappear into their room, he entered his own to deliver the news but stopped short inside the door. Fear, anger, and confusion swirled through the air in every direction, but he kept his eyes on Lilith and the sadness in her expression.

"What did I miss?"

"Boston's dad put out a contract on all of us," Nicci stated, heading toward the door, but Chance didn't even glance in her direction.

Nervous energy encompassed the space between him and Lilith, crackling with a thousand unspoken things.

"He wants *you* alive and the rest of us dead." Lilith's reluctant confession tightened every muscle in his body until the tendons and ligaments ached.

Chance didn't regret playing the executioner, punishing David Boston for his crimes. The man had deserved far worse than two bullets to the head. Not only had Boston physically and emotionally abused Lilith in college, scarring her very soul, but he had almost killed her at PMIC.

Boston had held her at gunpoint. The powerlessness Chance had felt in that moment, staring into Lilith's tear-filled eyes while the barrel pressed against her temple…It had been absolutely crippling. Boston had had every intention of pulling the trigger. He *wanted* to kill her, *would have* killed her if Eileen hadn't distracted him.

Chance had refused to let Boston have another opportunity. He'd ended the threat with calm, purposeful precision and, in the process, might have signed all their death warrants, even Lilith's.

"Luminita has countered his offer," Orchid added, pulling Chance from his thoughts. "Double to take out anyone who attacks you, triple to deliver all of you to her alive. Chaos is about to descend upon us."

Still, Chance's eyes never left Lilith's, even while he clenched his hands at his sides. All he wanted to do was hold her. He sensed every ounce of her barely restrained tears, the caress of her marrow-deep fear, and the confusion threatening to tear her apart. It called to him like a taut string tugging at his center.

"I am taking Eileen, Nicci, and Gibson to secure a vehicle," Orchid continued. She rose to her feet in his periphery and started toward the door. "Pack and be ready."

Chance only somewhat noticed everyone filing out of the room, but the moment the door clicked closed, he became acutely aware he was alone with his fiancé.

Lilith practically vibrated with nervous tension. "Chance..."

Before she said anything else, he strode forward, quickly eating up the distance between them. Her olive eyes widened in a swirling vortex of emotions, and the confusion in them stung, but Chance grabbed her wrist and tugged her against him.

His arms enveloped her, and the feel of her body made his throat constrict. Between the conflicted feelings she had for Cohen and the looming threat of Boston's wrath, the deepest part of him screamed in panic. He couldn't lose her—he wouldn't survive it.

"I'm so sorry, *cherie*...for all of this." The tears straining his voice summoned a surge of compassionate sorrow from her which stole his breath.

Lilith leaned her forehead against his for a moment before gripping his face and leaning back to meet his eyes. "Stop. This is *not* all on you."

"I killed him...and I'd do it again. But I'm the reason we're all in danger."

"David Boston and his abusive, obsessive psychosis are the reason, not you...not even me. The asshole lured me in...knew I was heartbroken after my mom's death, homesick, vulnerable, young, living away from home for the first time...*He* is the only one to blame."

Pride surged through every cell, not because she had defended him, but because she had defended herself. For once, Lilith was finally assigning the blame to someone else—the one who truly deserved it.

"We'll figure this out. We always do, remember?"

Hearing their familiar mantra brought a smile to Chance's lips.

"I love you, *beau*, more than anything or anyone."

A deep-rooted tension in his sinew finally relaxed, and he dropped his forehead to hers, inhaling her delicate lavender scent.

"You are everything, the only purpose that matters, the only thing holding me together." While he spoke, he caressed her neck. Her pulse thrummed violently against his skin in time to his own racing heart.

"You're the only thing holding me together too."

For some reason, a panicked dart of doubt seeped into his bones, and before he could stop himself, the question tumbled from his mouth. "What about Cohen?"

The second the words escaped, he wanted to claw the air and take them back.

The stab of betrayal she felt ricocheted through him like a frenzied bullet, and she pulled away, taking all her warmth with her.

"What are you talking about? Why would you even say that?" Lilith narrowed her olive eyes, and he looked away, unable to withstand her withering stare.

Truth. I promised her truth. Always. Still, opening this particular can of worms meant facing possibilities he would do anything to avoid. "I know you're worried…and confused." *Not eloquent or particularly insightful, but it's a start.*

"I'm *worried* about my *friend* and what's happening to him," she snapped. "I'm confused about how *he* feels about *me*, not the other way around."

"Lily…" Chance sighed, still unable to meet her heated gaze. "You can tell me—"

"I am!" Her angry shout nearly stopped his heart. "I am *not* confused about us. *We* are not the source of my confusion! Interpreting my emotions without context is a dangerous thing, Chance. Stop and fucking listen."

Conviction and frustration infused every word, and he finally met her gaze with more hope than fear.

"I am yours and you are mine," Lilith stated clearly, with an absolute certainty that rang through his very bones. "Cohen being alive does *not* change that fact!"

Chance merely watched while Lilith paced and expelled an exasperated huff. No sound could escape the shame and guilt constricting his throat. Then she stopped in front of him, her gaze colliding into his with the power of a freight train.

"If you question my feelings about you again…especially after this morning, I swear to God…I will kick your fucking ass."

The combination of her unexpected threat and fierce stare teased a roguish grin to Chance's lips. "You'd try."

Apparently, Lilith didn't see the humor in his playful response. She leveled him with a glare that made his grin falter. "I am not kidding. *You* are *mine*. I don't want *anyone* else." Her olive eyes blazed with a possessive threat, stealing the air from his lungs.

Chance reached for her, overcome by an aching need to touch her, but she evaded him and took a few steps backward.

"First, tell me what Antonio said." Lilith crossed her arms over her chest in an irrefutable demand.

Chance shifted gears with difficulty and forced his thoughts back to the phone conversation. "Um, right." He raked a hand through his hair and averted his gaze to concentrate. "No defensive wounds on Michael. Why did you need to know?" He had an idea but wanted to hear her say it.

"I think…" She hesitated, and he dared a brief glance at her biting her bottom lip, which conjured delicious images from this morning. "I think Aaron killed Michael and staged the apartment."

"Walk me through your thought process." Chance struggled to focus on anything but her mouth. It wasn't that he didn't believe her—quite the opposite—but she obviously needed to talk things out.

Lilith paced the small room, probably picturing the crime scene. "Signs of a struggle but no defensive wounds. A staged scene is the most likely answer. Michael took out Ray with no trouble, who as we both know was professionally trained and highly skilled…"

Chance continued to track her movements back and forth.

"The only way someone could get close enough to Michael without a fight was if he trusted them…and Michael only trusted *one person*—his father."

A smile curved Chance's lips when Lilith came to a stop, her eyes finding his.

"It's the only logical answer. Aaron staged everything to disappear."

Chance nodded. "That was my assumption too."

Relief flooded her expression. "What about the Elders?"

"Antonio came to the same conclusion. There are more votes to his side, but there are still a few holdouts. For now, Antonio is acting leader of North America."

"At least it's progress," she said with a weary sigh.

"He's also lifted the manhunt on us. One less thing to worry about."

"That's helpful." Her eyes lit up. "Wait. What about Solasta? Does this mean we can get in?"

Chance couldn't contain his broad smile when excitement danced in her eyes. "Yes. Antonio ensured you and I are on the list, and he'll add Tim and Nicci when he has time. They didn't know about the attack on Goditha, and Antonio is wading through a ton of records. Aaron kept a lot from them."

"Okay. We need to make that a priority. Dr. Scott's ghost drive is crucial."

"What do we do with it when we get it?"

Lilith paused, her eyes shifting rapidly while she worked the problem. Then her gaze snapped up to him again. "I need to go back to the hospital."

Chance furrowed his brow. "You made friends with a virologist while I was comatose?"

Apparently, it was too soon to crack jokes about his brush with death. The light leaked from Lilith's face, and she swallowed hard.

"No."

"I'm sorry, *cherie*. I didn't mean to make light—"

Tears filled her eyes, clumping in her dark lashes. "I sat in your room for three days. I cracked and fractured, Chance. I was *not* traipsing around the hospital, making *friends*."

Chance's cheeks flushed. Every word cut him to the core, carving themselves into his bones. He rushed forward when her tears began to fall and folded his arms around her.

"I'm sorry, *amour*. It was a stupid thing to say." He crushed her against him while her shoulders shook. "Shh, *cherie*. I'm here. Right here."

Lilith slid her hands up his back and clutched him close, as if he would disappear at any second. Tears soaked his T-shirt, summoning a visceral ache, and he buried his face in her shoulder. The intoxicating scent of lavender surrounded him like a warm, familiar caress in the storm of pain radiating from her.

After a moment, the sobs stopped, and she pulled away, wiping angrily at her cheeks. "Never joke about it again," she demanded, looking away.

"I swear." Chance placed a finger under her chin and lifted her face until she met his eyes. "I am sorry, *amour de ma vie*. For all of it."

When her lips captured his, he tasted the salt of her tears, along with the utter devastation she had experienced. The heady mixture brought with it a calm resolve to never doubt the depth of her feelings, to never question Cohen's place in her life, to never let her fracture like she had in the van, when she had been desperate to save him.

She is mine, and I am hers.

Chapter 22

Andrew kept his eyes locked on the cinderblock wall behind his bed. Hours had passed, with Alexis's lifeless stare boring holes into his back… into his soul.

Sixty minutes ago, the door had opened, but Andrew hadn't moved. He'd remained curled up on his bed, facing away. Shuffling footsteps had preceded the sound of something heavy dragging across the concrete— Alexis's body, most likely.

Even after the door swung closed and the lock clicked, Andrew hadn't braved a look. If he was wrong and she still lay there, drained and pale …He couldn't handle that.

Do I even have a soul anymore? Did I ever have one? Do you require a soul to love someone? He'd told Lilith she had saved his soul, but what if he didn't have one to save? What if he merely deluded himself into believing he had one?

Love and obsession are not the same thing, the demon whispered.

"I'm not sure I know the difference," Cohen admitted. Agony twisted his heart.

Love means caring for another, wanting what's best for them. It's selfless.

"I tried." Cohen's voice broke, and his raw eyes flooded with tears.

Obsession is possessive, the demon continued. *It's compulsive, selfish. Before you tried, you admitted your selfishness and even begged forgiveness. You don't love Lilith…You want to possess her…claim her as yours. You didn't kill Alexis for Lilith's sake. You killed her because the idea of letting your obsession go was more abhorrent than the alternative.*

Cohen's throat bobbed while he curled tighter into himself, as if that would protect him from the demon's harsh truths.

"No," he finally whispered. "I know I'd be no good for her...I'd just destroy the things I love about her."

And yet...you kissed her.

"I was about to die..."

And felt you deserved a reward? You took without even asking. One kiss to take to hell with you. A selfish obsession, not love.

"You're wrong," Cohen protested, but his voice strained, becoming weak.

Dark laughter in his head was the demon's only reply.

The heavy lock clicked, the steel door creaked open, and stilettos tapped against the floor. Despair and dread raged through every cell, but he still didn't move.

When the heels came closer, the muscles along Andrew's spine stiffened to the point of pain, but he welcomed the agony, used it to distract from the fear strangling his heart.

"Andrew, my sweet boy. I know you're awake." Luminita's voice held an unexpected compassion which slithered past his defenses. "I'm sorry, *fiul.*"

The mattress dipped behind him, and her sorrow perfumed the air, tickling over his skin in a familiar caress. He recalled all the times he had lost someone, all the times Luminita had comforted him. She had meant everything to him once.

Tears escaped his lashes, soaking the mattress, and Luminita's delicate hand touched his shoulder. Part of him wanted to pull away and scream at her. Alexis had only been there because Luminita had wanted it.

However, the shattered pieces of him were desperate for the solace offered by the one person he'd depended on through every dark time in his life...until last year. He was a man dying in the desert, starved for any drop of comfort, whether real or only a mirage.

When he didn't resist her touch, Luminita ran her palm in soothing strokes up and down his arm. "Shh, *fiul.* This is my fault. I should not have waited so long. I didn't expect...but perhaps I should have. You tried to tell me, and I did not listen."

Luminita ran fingers through his hair, and Andrew let her. Each pass eased some of the ache, and for the first time in hours, his eyes drifted closed.

"That's it, my sweet." The softness in her words reminded him of his mother after he woke from a nightmare. Of course, he didn't know if the memory was real or imagined.

"Deep breaths."

Andrew drew air in through his nose, filling his lungs, and expelled the breath through his mouth. The act summoned a memory which unfolded in his mind.

He stared across the room, eyes fixed on Lilith's olive-green ones. "Breathe…one…two…three," she coached him.

He studied every line of her face, the misery and compassion in her expression, the way her tears gathered in the corner of her eye before rolling over the bridge of her nose.

Silver flashed in his periphery, and Lilith's eyes widened. "Stay with me, Andrew."

Her words didn't make sense. He would never leave her. Then the pain came. Luminita's vicious blade cut into his chest, and a scream ripped from his throat.

Luminita's hand stilled in his hair, sensing every emotion accompanying the recollection. "I never wanted to hurt you." The woman's voice sounded strained with tears, but that was impossible. Luminita *never* cried.

Cohen finally tore his gaze away from the wall and rolled onto his back. Luminita stared down at him, her Caribbean-blue eyes glassy— such a rare and mystifying sight.

Andrew found himself entranced, frozen.

"I wanted what was best for you…to protect you from the world, but…" She hesitated. The silence felt heavy, like the air before a storm. "I broke your trust, and for that…I am sorry, Andrew."

The moment she caressed his cheek, some desperate part of him broke. His eyes closed, and he leaned into her touch, ravenous for some measure of genuine affection.

When his eyes opened, the truth struck him like a physical blow. He had been so preoccupied with finding comfort from his demon he'd missed something crucial. Compassion filled her touch and even sadness, but a critical component was missing—regret.

"But you'd still do it again…carve me up for your ritual."

Luminita withdrew her hand and swallowed hard, but her steady gaze never left his. "If I'd taken the time to properly explain first…if I'd persuaded you to see the beauty and power in what I was doing *before* beginning the ritual…"

The hope in Andrew's heart shriveled into ash under the heat of his anger. "Nothing you could say would persuade me to lie down as your sacrificial lamb."

"Okay." The word rushed past her lips. "I'm no longer asking you to. I just…miss you."

Cohen pushed up, sitting with his back against the cool wall, and eyed her with wary caution.

"The ritual requires a Durand, but it doesn't have to be you. I will no longer force you."

"But you'll hold me prisoner." Cohen couldn't bring himself to trust the woman, no matter how pretty and comforting her lies were or how desperately he wanted to believe them.

"For your benefit and safety."

A sardonic laugh rumbled from his throat. "Keeping me safe from what exactly?"

"Boston, Sr. has a contract out for everyone involved at PMIC… including you."

"I had nothing to do with Agent Boston's death. I wasn't even there when it happened."

Although, if he had been, the federal agent would have suffered far worse than Chance's bullet. The man had hurt Lilith many times— Andrew knew that much. Letting the bastard live had not been an option, an opinion Chance and Cohen shared.

"It doesn't matter to him. You left the building with them." Luminita peered at one of her pale-pink nails. The emotional mask from earlier was carefully tucked away.

"What color are my eyes?" Cohen asked coolly.

A line creased between her brows. She met his icy stare but didn't answer. Luminita didn't need to.

"I think your act needs more work. I'm not here for my protection. I'm here because you don't like someone else messing with your toys."

Luminita stiffened, her ocean-blue eyes narrowing. "I don't know what you mean."

"Oh, I think you do." Cohen pushed to his knees on the mattress, forcing Luminita to quickly stand. "I think it crawls under your skin…the fact that I've sworn my loyalty to someone else…that I love someone else…someone who sees me at my very core and cares about me anyway."

Luminita's frown deepened with every word until her nostrils flared and she curled her hands into fists. Rage flooded the air between them with crackling energy.

The hungry demon inside drank in every drop.

Andrew stepped off the bed with the same cool confidence the demon had given him earlier with Alexis, but this time, it was all him.

Lilith had seen him, the real him behind the masks. She had grabbed his hand and pulled him *closer*. If he was really a soulless monster crippled by obsession, as his demon wanted him to believe, Lilith would have pushed him away. She wouldn't have fought to befriend a pure predator.

Yes. He desired Lilith. Andrew wanted everything with her, but it would never happen, and that…was okay because she loved him on *some* level. He had felt that, even when he didn't want to believe it. Her acceptance and forgiveness outweighed the primal urges.

That's why he'd killed Alexis. Because her life meant nothing compared to protecting Lilith from more pain. *He* meant nothing in comparison. That was love, not obsession.

"Andrew." Luminita backed up when he took a step forward, hovering over her petite form, but the rush of fear didn't come.

"What do you want?" Cohen growled.

Luminita stopped with a hand against his chest. The woman fearlessly met his eyes, and her stare bored into him.

"I want Chance to study. He is a rare specimen, after all. I want Ashcroft as well. I want you by my side, where you belong. I want Lilith here, where we can treat her and keep her safe."

Cohen's bravado faltered. "What do you mean *treat her*?"

Luminita tilted her head, as if surprised he didn't know. "She's infected with the Wormwood virus. Surely, you knew that?"

Cohen took a step back, shaking his head. "No. You're wrong. She's not infected. She can't be."

Luminita raised her eyebrows. "My poor sweet, Andrew. Of course, she is. *You* infected her. I can only hope it hasn't altered the properties of her blood."

Andrew sank onto the cot. Panic flared through his chest like a lightning strike. "That's…not…possible."

"Oh, but it is. Haven't you noticed the voice, the fevers, the lack of impulse control, delusions? You're infected."

Cohen's mind tore through every moment to disprove her words. The voice had started after the medical center, but everything began spiraling out of control *after* the cult kidnapped him. He had assumed it was merely compounded trauma and the tight quarters at the cabin ramping up his PTSD, but he admittedly didn't remember the entire ordeal with the cult. What if they *had* infected him?

"No. You're lying." Cohen gritted his teeth but couldn't even make himself fully believe those words.

"The cult did more than torture you," Luminita said, echoing his thoughts. "And then…you kissed her."

Andrew's heart contorted into a twisted thing before plummeting to the ground. He couldn't speak, couldn't move, could barely breathe.

It couldn't be that simple, could it? Surely, it took more than that to infect a vampire.

"As it stands," Luminita continued with confidence, "I happen to be the only one with a cure—since procuring Lilith's scientist from Solasta. I am her only hope…and yours."

The triumphant smile unfolding before him made every hair rise on end. If it was true, Luminita would have a price, and it wouldn't be a pleasant one.

"What do you want?" Cohen asked again. Panic and guilt clawed at his insides with razor-sharp talons.

"I already told you." Luminita turned her back on him and sauntered toward the door, her heels clicking sharply. "If you would like to help"— she paused to peer over her shoulder, sending her raven curls spilling down her slender back—"you could think of some way to persuade Lilith to come here, peacefully, for her own good, before Boston's men find her. They have no interest in keeping her alive, and many mercenaries like to play with their targets first, especially when they look like her."

Andrew's blood ran as cold as arctic waters sludging through his veins. "Then give me the cure. Let me out. Let me help her," he pleaded, but Luminita turned back toward the door.

"Not until I trust you, *fiul*."

Chapter 23

Hostile silence filled the vehicle like poisonous gas, but Eileen did her best to sit still and ignore it—an impossible task. Of course, *all* of it seemed impossible to her. Two vampires staring holes into an emotion-feeding assassin who had supposedly died twenty years ago? The whole thing sounded ludicrous, like an absurd plot on some teenage paranormal drama.

Eileen stole a glance over her shoulder. The blistering glares from Nicci and Gibson weren't even directed at her, but she felt them in her marrow. If looks could kill, Orchid would be a shriveled corpse.

"How far?" Orchid asked in a surprisingly calm voice, as if the two people behind her weren't fantasizing about her death.

Maybe the Durand were adept at blocking people out and ignoring their emotions. They must have developed the ability, or sensing everyone all the time would drive them mad. Then again, most of the one's she had met weren't sterling examples of sanity. Even Chance seemed to have his moments.

Eileen wondered if it was different for him—being a half-blood. Was his ability to read people weakened? Did he heal slower? Is that why he'd been in the ICU for three days? Would a full-blooded Durand have recovered faster?

"Agent Hersch." Orchid broke Eileen's spiraling train of thought. "How far?"

"Sorry. Um…" Eileen glanced at their surroundings, getting her bearings. "About ten minutes or so, on the left. You'll see the big chain link fence.

Orchid nodded in confirmation, and the uneasy silence settled over them again.

This time, Eileen's thoughts wandered to Tim, and a private smile begged to be released. She still couldn't seem to wrap her mind around the vampire concept. He seemed so…human.

A pixie warrior goddess. The description made her heart sing. For Eileen's entire life, everyone had treated her like something fragile, even her ex-husband, Karl. Granted, he liked to break fragile things, but still…No one had ever viewed her as strong or fierce. Even her late partner had done everything he could to protect her, shelter her. Then there was Tim.

She had come so close to just blurting out those three dangerous words tonight, and part of her regretted not doing it. Eileen didn't want to hold back with him. Tim made her feel safe, valued, respected for everything she had to offer, and he brought out sides of her she hadn't known existed.

Shit. I've completely fallen, and there's no turning back. Not that she actually wanted to, but the future was uncertain. Tomorrow wasn't guaranteed, and eventually, her bereavement leave would end. That alone would force a serious decision: Stay with the FBI or follow a new path?

"So…" Detective DeLuca's scathing tone made Eileen tense in her seat. "When you said Luminita stole your son, you were talking about Chance?"

Eileen uncomfortably glanced sideways, noticing Orchid stiffen.

"Yes," the assassin replied in a flat tone, clearly indicating she did not wish to discuss the subject.

Eileen might not have known Nicci long, but even she realized the woman wasn't easily deterred from a truth she wanted. Usually, it was a quality Eileen admired, but this seemed like dangerous territory.

This is not going to end well.

"And how did she do that? Steal your son after you faked your death?"

Eileen blinked at the blunt questions and tried not to squirm in her seat amidst the building tension.

"I don't see how that is any of your business," the woman replied in clipped tones.

"Chance is engaged to my partner. That makes him family, which makes it my business."

Orchid's hand flexed around the steering wheel. "I wasn't aware they were engaged."

Nicci ignored Orchid's statement. "I'm guessing Luminita told you Chance died in the crash? I mean, that's the only thing that makes sense. Still…you never looked for him? Not even once?"

Everything sounded more like vicious accusations than actual questions. Nicci wanted to drive home a point, not find answers.

A muscle ticked in Orchid's clenched jaw, but she said nothing, refusing to rise to the detective's bait. Unfortunately, Nicci wasn't done.

"I'm just saying, if it was *my* child, I wouldn't take anyone's word. Chance's name never changed through all the foster homes, through his stay in the children's hospital, even through college in New York City. *I* know because *I* checked."

Orchid glared through the windshield, her hands tightening around the wheel until her knuckles blanched white.

"You know what I think?" Nicci continued to push. "I think deep down you didn't *want* to find him. I think Luminita offered you a blameless way to leave him behind, with your old life. I think you took it and never looked back."

The tension in the air became absolutely suffocating. Eileen sat perfectly still, studying Orchid in her periphery, waiting for her to snap.

"No answer?" Nicci taunted fearlessly.

"Detective, perhaps this isn't the time or place—" Eileen began in a desperate attempt to diffuse the situation, but Orchid cut her off.

"No. She wants an answer." The woman's words didn't hold the venom Eileen had expected. She just sounded sad.

Orchid swallowed hard and flexed her hands again.

"Luminita showed me horrific images of his mangled little corpse. They still fucking haunt me, even now that I know he's alive. I never *looked* for him because I couldn't bear to see those images again…or see his modest little grave. That would make his death absolute, irrefutable. It was my way of keeping his spirit alive…with me. *You* aren't a mother."

Although Orchid's confession tugged at Eileen's heart, Nicci was a tougher critic.

"From what I've heard, you weren't much of one either," Nicci snapped with venom.

Eileen sank deeper into her seat, wishing she had listened to Tim and stayed behind.

"None of us are perfect, detective. Despite my mistakes, the loss of Chance…it crushed my soul, threatened to snuff me out. His memory was all I had to hold onto, the only thing that kept me going for a very long time."

The woman's voice broke, and she sucked in a deep breath, collecting herself before speaking again.

"I don't expect your sympathy. I don't *want* your friendship. I merely want to help my son, save my family, and make Luminita suffer."

At that, Eileen threw a pointed glare over her shoulder at Nicci. She understood the detective's desire to protect her friend, but there were some lines which should not be crossed, especially when Orchid was the one driving. Thankfully, Nicci held up her hands and nodded, conceding to Eileen's silent demand.

"As long as we have common goals," Nicci stated, her voice unenthusiastic.

When Eileen turned back around, she spotted the fenced enclosure up ahead. "That's the place."

She dropped her gaze to the vehicle's clock: *7:05*. The staff never stayed past six at the latest, which only left the cameras and gate. *Perfect.*

"Okay. The first camera is to the left, pointing at the call box. Just ensure you face away from it when you pull in. I'll hop out and get the lock."

Orchid drew her hood down in answer before turning into the RV lot. Once the vehicle came to a stop, Eileen slid out and pulled the lockpick gun from her pocket.

The second camera sat on the building's top right corner and looked over the entire area, but the resolution was shit. No one would be able to see her clearly at the gate.

Eileen scanned her surroundings for any movement in the dwindling evening light. She spotted a dry-docked party boat, two mid-sized fishing boats, a defunct tour bus, the same old RV she had seen a hundred times, and two newer RVs, but no people.

After one last scan, Eileen tugged down the brim of her hat and grabbed the chain. The lockpick gun made quick work of the generic padlock. In seconds, Eileen pulled the chain through the gate and began swinging it open.

Orchid edged the SUV forward, but Eileen jogged up to her window and knocked. The woman stared at her for a moment, as if trying to figure her out, and then rolled down the window.

"I forgot to tell you. Pull it straight in. It'll make the license plate pretty much impossible to read. Also, you should probably stay in the car, in case we need to leave in a hurry."

Eileen peered into the backseat at Nicci and Gibson.

"You two are with me. Face away from the right corner of the building."

Once everyone nodded, Eileen stepped away, and Orchid pulled the SUV straight forward as directed.

Eileen scanned the area again. Something felt off, but everything appeared the same as it always had. Nothing stood out. Maybe it was just the uncomfortable conversation from the drive unsettling her nerves or the fact she was once again breaking the law.

She'd cared about that at some point, but when shit dissolved with Karl, when the system failed her so miserably, she had started to lose faith in it, and now…The law didn't seem relevant anymore, as if it were some juvenile concept for people who didn't peer behind life's socially acceptable curtain.

"So, which one's our target?" Gibson strolled up beside her, rubbing his dark goatee.

It was odd to see the man in jeans and a T-shirt, without an AR-15 in his hands. He had practically lived in tac gear the entire time they'd been at the cabin.

"The brown and tan monstrosity on the end. It's been here every time I've come by. I don't think the owners use it much…if ever."

"You come here often?" Nicci inquired. Apparently, she'd left all her animosity behind with Orchid.

"The owners have storage units in the building and, as you can see, are pretty lax on security. They've found signs of human trafficking, murder vics from out of state, large amounts of narcotics, you name it. It's an FBI dream. I'm called out here no less than once a month."

"Won't they recognize you on tape, then? I mean, if you're here that much…" Gibson frowned over at her with a look that almost seemed like disappointment.

"Hence the hat. Plus, I'm not in a suit or tactical gear, which is the only ways they've ever seen me. People never look the same out of uniform, and trust me, they aren't *that* observant. Tonight, I'm just your average RV owner itching for a vacation."

The last part wasn't far from the truth. Eileen desperately needed downtime on a beach somewhere, perhaps with a certain ex-Army Green Beret with impossibly broad shoulders.

"Hmm. Smart." Nicci flashed an appreciative smile.

"Speaking of smart…" Eileen peered over at Nicci. "Pissing off the assassin driving us around may not have been the best move."

To Eileen's surprise, Nicci shrugged, without a glimmer of regret or apology. "I wanted to know her intentions. Sometimes, the only way to get to the truth is to push a few buttons."

"So, you're done pushing buttons?"

Nicci chuckled warmly. "For now. So…shifty storage units, huh? You definitely make it sound exciting."

"It's usually more disgusting than exciting," Eileen admitted, grateful for the subject change. "John always hates coming here." The grin on her face faltered when reality hit home. John, her partner, was dead. "I mean, he always hated it," she amended. Eileen would never work a case in this dump with him again…or anywhere. That part of her life had died in a blood-filled bathtub.

"You sure you want this one?" Gibson called out, dragging her back to the present. "The tires might be dry rotted."

"I think it'll be the least likely to be missed. Let me check it out."

Gibson and Nicci flanked Eileen, guarding her while she picked the door's lock. It took longer than the gate, but not by much.

As soon as Eileen opened the creaky door, that sense of unease in her chest grew. But judging by the stale air, thick with a myriad of odors, and the coating of dust, no one had been inside the thing in years.

"Damn!" Nicci covered her nose with the back of her hand. "Did something crawl in there and die? Maybe multiple somethings?"

Eileen cautiously climbed up the RV's steps. The stench only grew worse. She coughed and gagged before hauling her shirt over her nose.

Of all the luck. She recognized the pungent odor of decay when she smelled it. Nicci was right. Death shrouded the RV's interior, and she'd bet money it wasn't animal corpses hidden inside. *Fuck.*

Eileen raced down the steps. "Yeah, that's not gonna work for several reasons."

"What clued you in?" Nicci asked with a laugh. "It's probably your next official crime scene."

Eileen cracked a grin. "Honestly, I'd call it in, but we don't need the added attention of an FBI task force. On to option two."

After wiping away any trace of her presence, Eileen locked up the RV of death, and they moved on.

The second one was newer and had been used more recently, but most importantly, it didn't smell like the house of a thousand corpses.

Nicci slid under the dash with her wire strippers while Eileen scoped out the interior. A three-person couch sat opposite a dining table, followed by a galley kitchen and two bunk beds. The back of the vehicle sported a bathroom with a small shower and a bedroom with a king-sized bed.

The thing was bigger than Eileen's first apartment. Not only could it transport all of them, but they could skip the hotels. Most RV parks preferred cash and didn't insist on IDs. It was perfect on several levels.

The engine roared to life, and Nicci hopped to her feet with a proud grin. "We have liftoff."

"Why don't you and Gibson drive the RV back? I'll ride with Orchid and lock up behind you."

"I don't think that's a good idea." A deep frown furrowed Nicci's brow.

"Look, you and Gibson clearly have a lot of reasons to hate her. I don't mind riding back with her by myself."

"*I* mind. Tim is my best friend—besides Lilith, of course—and I don't trust Orchid."

"I'm a federal agent." This particular argument was getting a little old. Eileen found it rather insulting coming from Nicci, who had surely faced the same adversity as Eileen since they were similar in size.

"And she's an assassin who kicked the shit out of Chance…the best hand-to-hand fighter I have ever met."

The argument died in Eileen's throat. Orchid had done a number on Chance. Hell, she would have killed him if Tim hadn't gotten there in time.

"You still don't trust her motives?" Eileen asked.

Nicci arched a brow. "You do? Come on, Agent Hersch. You're too smart to trust a perp."

The accusation in her statement made Eileen bristle. "I trusted Chance after he shot and killed a fellow agent in cold blood."

Nicci's expression fell. "That was—"

"Different?" Eileen interrupted. "Not to me. I didn't know Chance at the time any more than I know Orchid now. *You* don't know her either."

Nicci held up her hands. "Okay, you make a valid point. We don't know her. We should be cautious. I don't think any of us should be alone with her. Luminita has her family, and I'm not sure her desire for revenge will take precedence over that when pushed. She could hand us over at any time in exchange for their safety. Plus…" The woman hesitated, which seemed unlike her.

"What?"

"I didn't want to point out the obvious here, but…Orchid murdered your partner, staged his death as a suicide, all simply to find us. Why would you trust her?"

Eileen blinked. *Why didn't I make that connection? At the cabin, Cohen clearly stated John's murder was Orchid's handiwork. So, why am I not trying to kill the woman myself? Why didn't it sink in?* It was like she had somehow suppressed the fact, as if she was unable to truly deal with it.

"I'm sorry, Eileen. I didn't want to bring it up, but…" Nicci's words trailed off.

"No, you're right. I guess I just wasn't letting myself think about it." Now that the seal had been broken, the aching pain and righteous anger seemed overwhelming.

While Eileen stood there, despondent and lost in thought, Nicci leaned closer to the door and called out for Gibson.

"Do you have a class C driver's license?"

"Yes, detective."

Nicci turned back to Eileen and flashed a smile. "Problem solved."

Gibson jogged up the stairs. When he reached the top, his gaze bounced between them. "Everything okay?"

"Yep. You're gonna drive this beast to the Waffle House near the hotel. I'll ride back with Orchid and Agent Hersch. We'll all meet you there."

"You got it." Gibson slid into the driver's seat with a genuine smile this time.

"Come on, Eileen. Let's go." Nicci started down the steps but stopped when Eileen hesitated. "I won't start a fight if you don't. Promise."

The woman flashed a grin which seemed more impish than sincere, but Eileen followed her anyway. "And if you do…I'll help you finish it." Nicci winked before bounding down the steps.

Chapter 24

Tim drew in a deep breath, leaned forward to rest his elbows on his knees, and glanced at the clock *again*. Even slow, purposeful movements didn't help the riot of emotions in his head.

Ten minutes after seven. Every second ticking by made the tension in his chest tighten until he thought his ribs might crack under the pressure. They all had a price on their heads. It wouldn't take long for the vultures to descend, and Eileen was out there, without him. It felt unnatural, like a missing piece of himself.

Less than two weeks and he couldn't remember how to breathe properly in her absence. *How is that even fucking possible?* he wondered. *Why can't I seem to remember what functioning without her looked like? Maybe because I don't want to...*

With a tremendous effort, Tim pried his intense gaze away from the torturous clock. "So..." He peeked up at Lilith and Chance, who were both packing the last of their things. "Aaron finally chose a side, huh?"

Perhaps he could distract himself from the tumultuous thoughts about Eileen.

"It seems so," Lilith said. "I don't see any other explanation for the evidence."

"Damn...Killing his own son. I know we all questioned the man's motives and loyalties, but hell..." Tim shook his head, still trying to comprehend what could have driven a man to that extreme. "Those two have been inseparable for decades."

"It was one-sided."

Tim frowned up at Lilith. "How so?"

"Michael always worshipped his father. He'd *regale* us with stories at our family reunions about his father in the *old country*. None of us could stand it."

Lilith dropped her forensic kit near the window next to the door.

"Aaron, however, always treated Michael more like a loyal lapdog or a valuable employee than a son. At least, that's the impression I formed during our limited interactions."

Still, Tim thought. *The man got close, looked him in the eye, and stabbed him.* He had only met Aaron a handful of times, and although he never liked the guy, Tim never pegged him as a vicious killer. Of course, plenty of people had liked Ted Bundy before the truth came out.

"How many units do you have in the cooler?" Chance's question drew Tim's focus away from his dismal thoughts.

"Four," Lilith quickly answered, heading toward the door with her suitcase. She kept her eyes trained on the thin carpet.

"Wait."

Lilith froze and peered over her shoulder at Tim with a pleading look, which he ignored.

"I thought the doc only gave you four when Chance discharged."

A delicate blush blossomed over Lilith's cheeks. "Yeah, he did. I had a unit yesterday. I'll be fine until morning."

"Warm one up now," Chance said, his tone almost gentle.

"I'll be fine," Lilith insisted with an irritated huff.

"*Cherie,* we don't know what will happen between now and the morning. I need you at your best…your strongest."

Lilith whirled on her heel to face him. "And what if we need it? What if someone else gets hurt and I can't save them because we don't have enough?"

Regret flashed through Chance's eyes, but Tim didn't understand it.

"Lil, he's right. I mean, I get what you're saying, but what happens to you if we lose the blood or you get separated? Or *you* get injured? You're already pushing your limits."

The piercing glare Lilith flung at Tim pinned him to the spot but quickly softened, as if she realized he wasn't the true target of her anger.

"*Cherie.* Please. You'll feel better…less irritable."

Sincere concern filled Chance's words, but when Lilith glanced back at him, her enraged expression confused Tim again. She opened her mouth to say something but stopped.

"Point made," she muttered before strolling to the door and opening the cooler with a flourish. A saccharine smile stretched her lips while she snatched a unit and showed it off.

Tim shifted his gaze to Chance, who appeared less than amused and more than a little guilty.

"I'll go warm this up in the bathroom sink." Her eyes lingered on Chance with an odd expression when she passed him.

Once the door closed, Chance's shoulders slumped. It took a few moments for the man to tear his attention away from the bathroom door and notice Tim's expectant glare.

"What?"

Tim arched a brow before nodding toward the bathroom. "What did you do now?"

A deep crease formed between Chance's brows, and he opened his mouth but stopped. The defensive anger melted into guilt, and he paced over to sit on the bed, facing Tim.

"I let stupid shit get to me and made an asinine comment." Chance rubbed a hand over his mouth and shook his head.

"What stupid shit?" Tim asked in a flat tone. The last thing they needed was Chance spinning out again.

A dark chuckle escaped before he answered. "Cohen, of course. What else?"

"I thought you two already settled that issue at the cabin?"

"Yeah, well…" Chance swiped his hand over his mouth again with an aggravated huff. "That was *before* he kissed her."

Tim sat bolt upright. "What?"

"In Duncan's basement, before you guys arrived…while I was fighting Ashcroft…He told her he loved her, that she saved his soul, and then he fucking kissed her before *running to my rescue*."

"Wow." Tim sat back in the chair. His brain struggled to accept the new information.

"Yeah," Chance uttered with a sigh. "I asked her…well, basically accused her of being confused about us now that she knows he's alive, and that…didn't go over well."

"No shit. What did she say?"

A soft smile fought against the misery in Chance's expression. "That I'm hers and she's mine and Cohen being alive doesn't change that." Chance lifted his gaze to Tim's. "I believe her, I do. I just…I'm fucking furious with Cohen. She wants to save her friend from Luminita, but all I want to do is *tear him apart.*"

"I get it, man, but *you* have the girl. You don't have anything to prove."

The skin tightened around Chance's eyes, and for the first time since Agent Boston, Tim recognized real malice in their depths.

"It's not about claiming my damn territory or eliminating a romantic rival. I gave him the benefit of the doubt. I *helped* him, talked him through things, even when it was the *last fucking* thing I wanted to do. And he…took advantage. The bastard told her he loved her and kissed her…despite *everything!*"

"So…" Tim rubbed his jaw, debating what to say. "You're angry Cohen betrayed *you?*" He kept his voice tentative, hoping to make his friend less defensive.

Chance pressed his lips into a firm line, obviously biting back a few choice comments. "He betrayed us all…everyone who tried to help him, not just me."

"Maybe it was what he needed to say goodbye. Do you really think he expected to live?"

"That's irrelevant," Lilith answered from the bathroom doorway, then wandered into the room. "It was selfish. He even admitted as much and asked for my forgiveness."

While Tim digested the new nugget of info, Lilith's narrowed gaze landed on Chance with a scorching heat. "Do I need to uphold my threat?"

Although Tim stared in utter confusion at the stern tone, Chance cracked a lopsided grin. "No, *mon petite cherie.* I was just explaining things to Tim."

The hard edges of her expression softened but didn't disappear. Her eyes stayed locked on his.

"I swear, *amour de ma vie.*"

Lilith continued to study him for a moment before a smile finally tugged at her lips. "Fine. I'm gonna go next door and grab Nicci's stuff."

Chance caught her hand and pulled her closer. With a smirk, Lilith bent to give him a quick kiss.

"Don't take long," Chance warned before letting her go.

"*Aye, aye, mon capitaine,*" Lilith replied with a thin layer of sarcasm, then slipped out the door.

Chance's smile broadened, but Tim still saw traces of sadness, as if there was a weight attached to his happiness, dragging it down.

"What else?" Tim groaned.

Chance dragged his eyes back to meet Tim's, and his smile dimmed. "I made a stupid joke that upset her."

"About?"

The man dipped his head and peered up from beneath his furrowed brow—the human male equivalent to a dog tucking his tail between his legs.

Shit.

"A stupid ass joke about Lilith making friends with virologists while I was in a coma."

White-hot rage flared through Tim's body, and he clenched the chair's arms to keep from slugging his best friend. "You said what?" He ground the words out between clenched teeth.

Chance blew out a heavy sigh. "I know, I know."

But he didn't *know,* and that only enraged Tim more. "No. You don't," he growled. "If you did...you *never* would have made a joke about it."

"I know *now,*" Chance amended quickly.

"Do you?" Tim narrowed his eyes to mere slits. "You didn't stare into her shell-shocked eyes, begging her not to give up hope, while we waited to hear if you survived surgery. You didn't see her fall to fucking pieces in your ICU room and weep until she had nothing left. You didn't watch her waste away at your bedside, clutching your hand. You didn't have to force her to eat and drink. You didn't hear her wake up, screaming for you, after nightmares tormented the few hours of sleep her body forced her to take!"

With each statement, Chance grew paler. Tears filled his eyes, and his throat bobbed.

Good. He needs to hear this!

"You know who she *didn't* wake up calling out to? *Cohen.* Do *not ever* make the worst days of Lilith's life a fucking joke again, or I swear to all that's holy, I will knock you the fuck out!"

After several hard swallows, Chance nodded solemnly. "I'm sorry."

"You fucking should be," Tim snapped. "It didn't just affect Lilith, ya know." The memories of those days and nights, pacing outside of Chance's room, weighed heavy. The guilt, though...That's what Tim struggled with the most. If he'd gotten past Luminita's men fast enough, perhaps he would have made it there in time.

"Tim." Chance's voice pulled him from the vortex, and Tim angrily wiped at his eyes. "I am sorry, *mon frère*. Like I said, it was stupid and asinine."

Tim cleared his throat and pushed out of the chair. "Don't let it happen again. I'm fucking serious."

"It won't. I promise."

The door swung open again, and Lilith tossed Nicci's stuff into the growing pile. "You guys done sharing?" she asked, with only a slight edge to her voice.

"You mean, am I done threatening him with violence for being an unfunny, insensitive asshole?" Tim threw a pointed glare at Chance, demanding reassurance.

"Yes. I promised and I meant it." Chance raked a hand through his hair and sighed heavily. "I'm sorry."

"Good. I'm gonna get some air. Maybe help Keller gather up the equipment." Tim headed for the door but turned his attention to Lilith. "I'm happy to set his ass straight any time."

Amusement quirked her lips, and a soft chuckle escaped. "Thanks."

"I take care of my sisters." He captured her in a tight hug. "Blood related or not."

"Thank you, Tim," she whispered, with tears in her voice. "For everything."

After one last squeeze, he released her, threw a warning look at Chance, and opened the door.

Humid evening air and the faint scent of gardenia greeted him, but no sign of Orchid or the others. The anxiousness returned with a vengeance, clawing and scraping at his bones.

It shouldn't be much longer if everything went right. Maybe they had to stop for gas.

When Tim turned to close the door behind him, a sudden pressure in his left thigh made him stop—a *familiar* pressure. *Fuck.*

"Get down!" he screamed.

Tim ducked milliseconds before the wood above him splintered with an unmistakable thud. He threw himself inside before the next shot barreled through the flimsy door. Lilith kicked it closed.

"They must be using a rifle, mid-range, with a suppresser. I didn't hear the shots."

Contrary to most movies and TV shows, silencers did *not* make guns silent. It was false advertising at best. They merely muffled and diffused the loud sound, but combined with enough distance, it could make them difficult to hear over the ambient noise.

"Shit, Tim. You're hit!" Lilith scrambled closer, crossing in front of the door.

Tim held out his hand and crawled toward the wall.

"Stay away from that piece-of-shit door. It won't stop a bullet if they decide to shoot blind. Get your gun and take cover on the other side of the bed."

After a quick but conflicted nod, Lilith stayed low and did as directed.

"Just keep watch. I'm fine," Tim ordered when Chance moved toward him. It wasn't his first bullet wound and sure as hell wouldn't be his last.

Once he positioned himself against the concrete wall, he finally set eyes on the hole through his jeans, which oozed blood down his leg. That's when the searing pain finally registered.

Thankfully, the blood wasn't flowing in rhythmic spurts, meaning the shot had not hit a major artery. Unfortunately, it wasn't a through-and-through. The bullet was still in there somewhere.

"Lil, do you have gauze and tape for a pressure dressing?"

"Yes. In the bottom center of my forensic kit, next to you."

While Tim dragged the aluminum case closer and popped it open, he peeked up at Chance. "Any movement outside?"

"I've counted three so far, but they're staying low, taking cover behind the cars a few rows out. They're waiting."

"Call Keller on the walkie. He always keeps it on."

"I got it," Lilith said, carefully crawling forward to snag Chance's duffle.

"Tell him to scope out the rear of the hotel. They're probably waiting for others to get in position and flank us," Chance added, without taking his eyes off the window.

While Lilith relayed everything to Keller, Tim found the pack of gauze and immediately covered the wound with his left hand, then applied pressure. The burning flared sharp, and he grimaced, searching for the tape.

"Is there an exit wound?" Lilith asked after finishing with the walkie.

"No." Tim grunted through gritted teeth, tearing the tape and securing the dressing as tight as possible. The pressure and sizzling pain racing down his left leg reached a fevered pitch. Tim leaned his head back against the wall, drawing in deep breaths until the worst of it passed. "Fuck! I hate bullet wounds."

"We'll have to get the bullet out."

The glare he leveled at Lilith wasn't entirely intentional. "I know, but that's a *later* problem."

When Lilith opened her mouth to say something, the walkie crackled.

"Only one target out back," Keller reported with a slight air of disappointment. *"Cheap vest and an even cheaper piece-of-shit semi-auto rifle. Over."*

"Toss me the walkie, *cherie*." Chance held out his hand, and Lilith sat up before tossing it over the bed.

A quick whistle, cracking glass, and a *thunk* sent Tim's pulse racing. He snapped his gaze to Lilith, who quickly ducked behind the bed, revealing a hole in the wall.

No blood.

"Are you okay?" Frantic panic lined Chance's words. "Lily?"

"Fine," Lilith called out.

"Then stay the fuck down," Tim added with an irritated grunt. The microburst of adrenaline passed quickly, making the damn hole in his thigh throb in time to his slowing pulse.

"Keller, can you take out the perp behind the hotel? Over."

"Yes, sir. Over and out."

Chance crept over to the pile, snagged Lilith's vest, and tossed it over to her. "Put it on."

Thankfully, the iron-clad order didn't raise an argument from Lilith. She complied without hesitation.

"I'm gonna sneak out the bathroom window and meet up with Keller," Chance said. "I'll borrow your vest."

Tim tried not to think about how Chance had lost his vest during the fight with Ashcroft. Now wasn't the time for more guilt-fueled trips down memory lane.

"You stay here with Lilith," Chance continued.

Once Tim nodded, Chance made his way past the bed. Whispered words were exchanged with Lilith, but Tim focused on crawling to the far side of the window, taking Chance's previous position.

Each movement sent a new surge of pain down his leg, but he powered through and eventually sat up against the wall, where he could scan the lot.

The men outside were shifting position. Three…no, four attackers, civilian-style protective vests, a mix of defunct camo patterns probably from an Army surplus, movements organized but not smooth—

definitely not military or police formations. They were probably privately trained mercs, either freelance or militia.

"Chance," Tim hollered, not taking his eyes off the enemy.

"Yeah?"

"Four perps out front. Be careful. Radio when you and Keller are in position. I'll lay down some cover fire to distract them until you get closer."

"That'll start the clock," Chance warned, though it wasn't an outright "no."

Tim released a heavy sigh. The second they shot back, whether pistol or rifle, someone would call the cops. Breaking the window's glass alone would draw attention much less the gunfire. Hell, it was possible someone had already called them.

"Unavoidable at this point. And I don't want you taking chances. Cover fire is the safest play. As long as they think you're still in here, it's unlikely they'll light the place up. You'll have to neutralize the threat fast so we can haul ass before the cops show up. No fucking games out there. Fast and efficient."

"Will do."

The bathroom door opened and closed, then silence descended. Tim sharpened his focus on the men outside, trying to ignore the burning pain in his thigh and the anxiety squeezing his chest. Eileen and the others could return at any time, walking right into this shitstorm.

"How's your leg?"

Tim stole a quick peek at Lilith, who now sat against the wall on the other side of the window. "I won't be running any marathons the next few days, but I'm fine."

Lilith nodded in his periphery but continued to stare at the bloody dressing.

"It's not your fault," Tim stated, tracking two men talking between the cars. "I know that look. Stop feeling guilty and get angry. Those assholes out there are trying to kill us for money…money from the corrupt father of your abusive ex. Keep the blame where it belongs."

"Oh, I am…I should have told Gregor about David. My father would have flayed the flesh from his bones and anyone who cared he existed."

The lethal tone in Lilith's voice brought a grin to Tim's face.

"I have *no* doubt about that. I understand why you didn't, though. Your first time alone in the world, something you fought tooth and nail for…You didn't want to admit Gregor was right."

"No—"

"Right about the world being a dangerous place, no matter your species. Not that you need constant coddling," Tim corrected quickly.

A thoughtful hum came from her direction. "You aren't wrong. I didn't stray far from home after coming back from LA until Gregor sent me to find Duncan, with my very own bodyguard."

"Speaking of which…" Tim briefly glanced at her, chewing the inside of his cheek. "Go easy on him with the Cohen stuff."

"Tim—"

"Just hear me out, please." When she remained silent, he continued. "It's not that he doesn't trust you or believe in your relationship, Lil. For a very long time, you were this impossible dream he'd never be able to touch, and now…he has everything he has *ever* wanted—you. It's been less than a year, and someone is already trying to steal his happiness. And that's *after* he shoved down all his insecurities and genuinely tried to help the guy. He's angry and feels Cohen betrayed *his* trust, so please…be patient with him."

Tim snuck another peek at Lilith, who stared off into the distance with a melancholy expression.

"I will," she replied softly.

As if summoned, a crackle preceded Chance's voice on the walkie. *"In position. Keller? Over."*

"In position. Over and out."

Tim sat up tall and aimed his pistol, wishing like hell his AR-15 wasn't in Keller's room. The likelihood of hitting targets over twenty feet away, in partial to full cover, with a 9mm Beretta weren't optimal, but a distraction would pull focus from Chance and Keller, allowing them to maneuver for a fast takedown.

Movement on his left drew Tim's attention from the men outside. Lilith mirrored his stance, aiming her pistol, just like he had taught her.

When in doubt, mimic your partner.

Tim gave her a nod of approval, which she returned with a small smile.

The first shot shattered the window, and the rest rang violently through the night.

Chapter 25

Chance crept along the side of the hotel with careful, silent footfalls, his AR-15 aimed and ready. Focusing on the threat helped push all the riotous emotions into the background.

Tim was injured, Lilith was scared and angry, and a sense of helplessness had been shredding his insides since he woke up in the hospital, but *this*...This gave him calm purpose. This was something he could control, and it was the only time he didn't need emotions. Eliminating a threat was the *one* thing Chance knew how to do without question.

Until the fight with Orchid.

The onslaught of memories from that night halted his steps. Chance wanted to blame the loss on the damn tattoo, but in truth, he had barely gotten the upper hand on her...

Orchid...Helena...his mother. *Fuck*. The whole thing made his head hurt.

Granted, the woman was a highly skilled assassin for a powerful shadow organization, but that didn't lessen the sting of defeat.

Chance expelled a slow breath and flexed his fingers around the gun, letting the weight of it in his hands shove the thoughts back into the abyss, where they belonged. The men out front weren't formally trained, much less high-powered merchants of death.

After rolling his shoulders, he put his back to the wall and crept the last few feet, stopping at the corner to listen. The ambient sounds of traffic filled the evening air, but nothing else.

The stillness wasn't a peaceful one. It was the held breath before a pounce, the tensed muscles before the chase, and it brought a subtle grin to Chance's lips.

These were the moments where all civilized things fell away. Complex emotions were muted, morals became obsolete, and reality narrowed to his target. Everything else ceased to exist, including the demons from his past which haunted him. It was pure freedom of self, a surrender to something simple and primal—the hunt.

Chance pressed the button on his mic. "In position. Keller? Over."

"In position. Over and out," Keller answered a second later.

The pause after seemed to quiet the background noise, but the tension gathered to a breaking point.

Chance exhaled one slow breath before shattering glass and shots ruptured the burgeoning silence. He took off, staying low, keeping his gun braced against his shoulder, sweeping his vision over the lot.

Chance didn't stop until he reached the row of cars the perps were using for cover. He didn't spare a glance back at the hotel. Lilith was the one thing that would break the focus he needed to maintain.

Several bullets *thunked* against vehicles. The softer shots indicated the mercs were blindly returning fire. *The fucking assholes.* Chance bit back his rising anger and shoved away the thought of one of those bullets finding Lilith.

She's wearing her vest, and Tim is with her. She's fine, he told himself.

Another deep breath and a tighter grip on his rifle brought the calm back, and Chance crept along the cars, closing in.

The loud gunshots from inside the hotel stopped.

"Two and Three, move forward! Remember the primary objective and check your targets!"

Chance peeked over a trunk at the tall man barking orders with authority. That's the one he wanted—the Alpha.

After crouching back down, Chance pressed the mic and whispered. "Keller, take the two heading for the door once you hear my shot. Over."

"Copy. Over and out," came the quiet reply.

Chance deftly maneuvered around a few cars for a better view, then propped his arm against the trunk of a black sedan. The metal burned at his skin, still hot from the baking sun, but he ignored it and lined up his shot.

The Alpha, dressed in mismatched camo, leaned on an SUV, intently watching his men race across the lot to the hotel. He didn't even have his gun at the ready to protect their backs. The shorter man beside him had his rifle aimed, but not to cover the advancing mercs. Instead, he scanned the surroundings.

Eventually, the sentry's gaze met Chance's scope, and a split-second of recognition made the man's eyes flare. A grin lifted the corner of Chance's mouth, and he squeezed the trigger, hitting the man square between the eyes. Two quick shots cracked through the air, followed by heavy thuds, but Chance didn't shift his focus.

He moved his scope smoothly to the Alpha, who hopped back, frantically looking around while clutching his rifle like a damn security blanket. The man didn't even aim it.

Fucking amateur.

Chance kept him in his sight, tracking the merc's erratic motion. Part of him wanted to throw down the gun and fight him hand-to-hand, make him suffer, but the police would be here soon.

Fast and efficient, like Tim said.

After another deep breath to curb his disappointment, Chance exhaled slowly and squeezed the trigger. The man's head whipped back, and he went down surrounded by a spray of red mist.

Before Chance lowered the rifle, headlights cut across the lot. His heart nearly stopped dead in his chest. No way the response time to *this* part of town was *that* fast.

The white SUV pulled up to Room 109, and relief chased the brief shot of adrenaline. Chance jogged over, joining Keller while Orchid jumped out of the driver's seat.

"What happened?" she shouted, taking in the shattered hotel window and the two bodies lying a few feet away.

"Low-level mercs. Amateurs. We handled them, but we gotta move fast," Chance reported when he reached the vehicle.

Orchid scanned him but didn't bother with Keller. "Any injuries?"

"Tim—" Chance started, but Eileen's trembling voice cut him off.

"What?" The sprite-like woman clambered out of the backseat. "Where is he?"

"Inside with Lilith…"

The woman took off like a shot.

"He's okay," Chance called after her with an amused smile.

"How bad?" Nicci now stood at his side.

"Shot to the thigh. Didn't hit anything major, but we'll have to get the bullet out soon. No luck at the RV park?"

The detective chuckled darkly. "Well, Eileen's first pick turned out to be a crime scene. The absolute *worst*. But we found a suitable substitute.

Once we cross the state line, we'll see about switching plates. Anyway, Gibson is waiting at the Waffle House down the street with it."

"Good." Chance nodded thoughtfully, organizing the next series of events in his head. "We'll help Keller load all the gear into the SUV. Lilith and Eileen can help Tim into the backseat, and the rest of us can walk, but we gotta hustle. The cops will be all over this soon."

"You got it, boss."

"Everything except Keller and Gibson's stuff is in 107," Chance relayed before following her toward 109.

T he door to 107 had three bullet holes: one down low, with blood misted around it, and two at about six feet high, which were clean. As soon as it swung open, Eileen locked her gaze on the blood coating Lilith's hands. Somehow, she managed to swallow past her racing heart, which seemed to be lodged in her throat.

Lilith followed her line of sight and flashed a sympathetic smile. "This looks worse than it is. I just finished changing the dressing."

The words barely registered past the noise roaring in Eileen's head. She just kept replaying the utter chaos in the van the night Chance had almost died. There had been so much blood, and it had coated Lilith's hands, just as it did now.

"He's okay." Lilith stepped aside to let her in.

Eileen moved past her, trying to shove the horrific memories of the van ride out of her head.

After clearing her throat and blinking back the tears threatening to spill, Eileen made her way to the bedside. But as soon as her gaze collided with Tim's, she lost the fight. Tears slid down her cheeks, and she furiously wiped them away.

I am a goddamn FBI agent! She had witnessed plenty of people hurt in the line of duty, and Tim wasn't dying. *This shouldn't be a huge deal.* But she understood why her heart thrashed against her ribs like a wild animal.

The very thought of being separated from Tim after having just lost her partner, John, terrified her. In a shockingly short time, Tim had become important—no, *crucial*, if she was being honest—and Eileen couldn't handle the idea of losing him.

It all came back to those three little words she had almost said earlier, and the strength of the emotions scared her almost as much as the bullet lodged in Tim's thigh.

"Eileen…"

She heard him but didn't respond, too lost trying to remember what her life had looked like before she met Tim at Chance's place in New York City. The authority he'd commanded while laying out the plan of attack for PMIC was almost as attractive as the man himself in head-to-toe black tactical gear. The draw had been instantaneous, but the natural ebb and flow of them moving together through PMIC…That had been something special.

Shit. It's been what…two weeks, if that? Why does it feel like a lifetime ago?

"Pixie."

The corners of her mouth lifted. That one word dragged Eileen from her thoughts, and her gaze focused on his rich brown eyes.

"There you are." Tim flashed a sly grin which melted her damn insides. "Can you and Lilith help me to the SUV? We can't stay here."

Eileen blew out a breath and shoved her chaotic emotions aside. "Of course. Lilith? Gimme a hand?"

Seconds later, Lilith appeared on Tim's injured side. At five foot nine, she would be able to support his six-foot frame easier than Eileen could at five three.

After a few groans and winces, they got Tim on his feet. He was able to put weight on the leg—a good sign—but he leaned against Lilith with each step. The arm he draped over Eileen's shoulders seemed to be for moral support, or perhaps he merely wanted her to feel useful. Either way, the distraction helped.

Once they got Tim situated in the SUV's backseat, Eileen climbed in with him.

"What happened?" she finally asked.

Tim peered over at her with a half-smile. "Lucky shot when I left Lilith and Chance's room to help Keller. The bullet didn't hit anything major."

Eileen expelled a breath but couldn't shake the anxiety roiling through her body despite the reassuring words.

He's okay. See? Breathing and smiling right in front of you…Okay, now he's frowning, but still…He's okay, weirdo.

"Hey, I'm all right, really. Not my first rodeo…definitely not my worst either."

The words were meant to make Eileen feel better, but it just made the ache in her chest worse for some reason.

Tim leaned forward and brushed his fingers through her short hair, sending a comforting shiver down her spine. "Are *you* okay?" he asked with genuine concern.

Eileen frowned at first, confused why he would even ask. She wasn't the one with a bullet in her leg, but she forced a quick smile and nodded.

"Yeah, of course." An absolute lie. She allowed her gaze to drift to the dressing, which was already half saturated. Moving him probably hadn't helped matters, not that they'd had a choice.

The rear hatch slammed closed, and then the front passenger and driver's side doors opened. Lilith twisted in her seat after fastening her seatbelt.

"We're gonna drop off the luggage and equipment at the RV. Then we're heading to the hospital. Can you call Dr. Preston and ask him to meet us?"

"I don't need a doctor. I can sew this up myself," Tim argued while the SUV pulled out of the lot.

When Lilith's fierce stare narrowed in on him, the man went still.

"Someone has to dig the bullet out of your leg before it heals, and I don't feel like doing it. Besides, I need to talk to him anyway."

Eileen already had her phone out. She pressed the call icon on Dr. Preston's contact before Tim even opened his mouth.

"Agent Hersch. To what do I owe the pleasure?"

At least Dr. Preston seemed to be in a good mood, which was rare.

"Is there any chance you can meet us at the hospital?"

"I'm already here. I stayed late to type up some notes. Why?" He didn't bother to veil his suspicion.

"Lilith wants to discuss something with you and…" Eileen paused, not because she hated asking for help—though that was part of it—but because she suddenly couldn't say the words.

Come on, Eileen. Get your shit together. FBI agent, remember? You are not civilian seeing blood for the first time.

"And?" Dr. Preston prompted with slight irritation.

"One of our group is injured—"

"Jesus Christ, Eileen. I can't be your on-call surgeon."

"It's not bad. Not like last time. We just need a bullet dug out without a police report."

Tense silence hummed through the line, and Eileen held her breath, hoping and praying. Dr. Preston had every right to tell her "no." This wasn't his fight.

"Fine." The man huffed begrudgingly. "But I want my blood sample. What's your ETA?"

"Twenty minutes…Thirty tops."

"I'll meet you outside the ED."

"Thank you, Dr. Preston. I owe you one."

"Evan. I think we're beyond formalities at this point."

"Thank you, Evan." Eileen ended the call. "He'll meet us at the ED," she relayed, tucking her phone away. "Lilith, he wants his blood sample."

"That's fine."

Orchid turned into the Waffle House parking lot and pulled alongside their new vehicle. Sirens screamed through the night, drawing closer. It only took a few minutes for Gibson, Keller, Nicci, and Chance to catch up and unload everything from the back.

The plan they settled on was for the RV team to buy takeout from the restaurant to legitimize them being there. Then they would make their way to the hospital afterward so Orchid could ditch her SUV, which had been seen at the hotel.

Once everything was settled, they took off, passing by the growing sea of flashing lights without incident.

Eileen sank into the backseat, finally able to draw in a full breath. But as soon as her gaze landed on Tim's injured leg, the anxious fear in her belly began tearing at her again.

"Hey, pixie warrior."

A smirk curved her lips at the moniker, and she raised her eyes to meet his.

"Come here." Tim held up his arm, and she happily accepted the invitation, curling up against his side and letting his arm drape around her. "Are you okay?" he whispered into her hair. His soothing voice quelled more of her internal panic.

"No," she admitted on a soft breath. "But I will be once you're all fixed up." Eileen sensed the burning flush travel up her throat to her cheeks, but she pretended no one else could see it.

A surprised little sound rumbled in his chest, and his arm tightened around her shoulders. The world felt right again.

Eileen still couldn't understand how she had gotten to this point so soon. Actually, she had never been in this position at all. She had never found the feeling of *home* in another person, and she had never felt this sure about anyone. It should terrify her, like it had in the hotel room, but right now, in his arms, it didn't.

Tim rested his chin on her head. He swallowed before drawing in a deep breath. Eileen closed her eyes, allowing the rhythmic rise and fall of his chest to eradicate the tension left in her body.

When the vehicle came to a stop outside the hospital, the bubble burst too soon, and reality crashed back in. Tim's first groaning wince when he moved his leg to climb out of the vehicle brought the anxious tension right back, though not as all-consuming as it had been earlier. Eileen hopped out and hurried around the SUV to help him.

Although Tim wore an amused grin, he took Eileen's hand and let her help…a little bit.

"Well, at least this one's still conscious." Dr. Preston strode toward them, his white lab coat smoothly pressed, along with his slacks. But his black hair seemed tousled, as if he had been running his fingers through it continuously.

"I don't need all that." Tim waved at the tech with the gurney trailing after the doctor.

A tight smile pressed the doc's mouth into a thin line. "We don't hand out medals for masochistic bravado. On the gurney."

Tim bristled but reluctantly complied without further comment, with Lilith's help.

"Take him to my exam room on the fourth floor."

The tech nodded and wheeled Tim off, but Dr. Preston turned toward Lilith instead of following. "I get my blood sample *before* you leave."

It wasn't a question.

"Of course. Like Eileen said, I need to talk to you anyway."

"All right." His gaze traveled over Eileen and landed on Orchid standing by the SUV. "A new addition?"

"Of sorts, yes," Eileen answered before Lilith said too much or nothing at all.

The doctor shrugged. They weren't his secrets to hide.

"Orchid and I will park the car and meet you both upstairs." Lilith flashed a smile and jogged toward the SUV.

When Eileen turned back, Dr. Preston was already striding toward the ED doors.

"Thank you again, Evan," Eileen said, catching up to him.

The man threw her a side glance while they walked. "Are you in danger, Eileen?"

The unexpected question made her miss a step, but she swiftly recovered, at least physically. After debating her options, she settled on the truth. "Yes."

"Because of them?" he asked without judgment.

"*In addition* to them," she corrected.

"And you trust these people?" His navy-blue eyes found hers while they strolled through the sliding doors.

Eileen didn't hesitate. "With my life."

Evan nodded at the transport gurney waiting on the elevator. "And our patient? Who is he?"

"Confidentially?"

"Of course."

"Timothy Bardow. He's ex-Army, Green Beret, highly decorated. He works security now. Why?"

"No. Who is he to you?"

Eileen's confused expression deepened. "Why do you want to know that?"

His sardonic laugh surprised her. "Because I want to know if I'd be out of line asking you to dinner when you aren't dodging life-threatening situations."

Eileen blinked up at him. "You're kidding."

She had worked with Dr. Preston on several cases over the past four or maybe five years, and not once had she gotten the impression he had *any* romantic interest in her.

"Actually…no. I'm not."

"I'm with Tim." The hurried words flew out of her mouth without a second thought. "It's serious," she added as the truth sank into her bones.

"Ah." Evan's smile tightened a bit, and he pressed the button for the visitor elevator. "Well, thank you for the honesty."

"Sorry." The flush heating her cheeks felt like a damn inferno, and she was about to step into a suddenly tiny-seeming elevator with the man.

"No apology needed." The smile was genuine and warm this time when he waved her ahead. "I'll get him patched up for you."

"Thank you."

The embarrassment died down, but Eileen still stood as far from him on the elevator as possible, uncomfortably aware of his presence while the floors ticked by.

Chapter 26

"You're sure?" Luminita clutched the phone, certain she had misheard him, but each note held a clear warning in case she hadn't.

"Yes," Dr. Scott snapped. "There is no trace of the virus in the blood sample you gave me."

Luminita's mind whirled when faced with the startling truth. Andrew Cohen's descent into madness was genuine. She'd been certain the virus had caused his intrusive voices and delusions.

As for Lilith...

Through Dr. Scott, Luminita knew with certainty that Cohen—even if infected—couldn't have passed the virus on to Lilith. That was a blatant manipulation on her part.

A pureblood vampire would require *repeated* exposures—*many* of them—to slowly wear down their superior immune system. One simple kiss couldn't have caused Lilith any harm, but Cohen clearly wasn't aware of that fact.

It had been a risky move. If he had known the truth of the virus, it would have weakened her position with him. But she had made a calculated decision in the moment based on his reactions, and it had paid off.

"And the cure? Is it ready?"

"The first batch will be ready by morning. I'll need test subjects to ensure its viability."

"I have a mix of purebloods, half-bloods, and Durand, all infected and ready for you. Once you've proven its efficacy, I want everyone in the facility inoculated. In the meantime, I want to administer the cure to Andrew."

"You did hear the part where I told you he is *not* infected, correct?"

"Yes, doctor," she responded with seething derision. "But *he* is not aware of that. Do as you're told."

Luminita hung up before the infuriating vampire said anything else to worsen her mood. After a moment's consideration, she picked up the phone again and dialed the extension for the prisoner's wing.

"Yes, ma'am?"

"Cell 17. I want you to slowly increase the temperature to one hundred degrees over the next twelve hours."

"Of course, ma'am," the man responded without question or hesitation.

If only everyone could be that cooperative. It would make life so much easier, but then…I'd miss the challenge.

Arranging pieces like a coordinated offense on a chess board stoked her instinctual desire for control. Forcing someone to accomplish a task with violent threats was one thing, but convincing them to willfully complete it as if it were the missing step to achieving their life's mission? That was an art form which made her pitch-black soul sing an operatic tragedy worthy of immortality.

Luminita set the phone's receiver down in the cradle and cracked open her laptop. One click brought up the live feed from Cohen's cell.

Andrew had changed into the white cotton T-shirt and sage-green scrub pants she had left for him, but he paced the small space like a rabid animal. He smoothed his blond hair against his scalp repeatedly while whispering indecipherable things to the empty air.

Every few rounds, his voice rose to yell, "Selfish piece of shit!" He would stop, the tension gathering in his limbs. Then he would haul back and punch the cinderblock wall with a sickening thud.

After the second time, blood dripped from the split skin over his knuckles and trailed along the floor, but the pattern kept repeating, as if he were stuck in a loop of self-punishment.

A brief pang of guilt slithered past her ribs. The emotional scars were as clear as the physical ones she had carved into his skin at the medical center, although those were gone now. There was a chance Andrew might not survive this, that he would irrevocably break, that she might lose him forever. It had been a very long time since she had mourned a loss.

Permanency lost its context after witnessing a thousand years of history. Everything and everyone was temporary. Well, with one notable exception in her long life—one vampire who seemed tethered to her.

The odd fear of losing Andrew soured her stomach until she recalled his biting words. He had chosen his side and pledged his loyalty to Lilith. Andrew refused to see the world the way Luminita did. He didn't comprehend the point of no return approaching and the necessity of a plan to weather the public hailstorm. Humans en masse were dangerous creatures.

Manipulation was Luminita's only recourse now. Andrew had brought this all on himself. He had chosen the difficult path strewn with pitfalls. The man couldn't even blame the virus for his deteriorating mental state. Andrew Cohen had *willingly* chosen madness. He chose *Lilith*.

That fact still made her blood transform into lava, scorching through her veins on a destructive path. Luminita let the sensation sweep over her, consuming everything until it burned out the irrationality. Once the anger died to embers, she could safely return to her normal state. Too much hinged on her plans to allow petty emotions to influence her actions. She needed to maintain control.

If Andrew refused to forgive her and listen to reason, she would guide his actions through other means. He claimed Lilith was his sole purpose, so Luminita would use that carrot to influence him while upholding the illusion of freedom—in choice, at least.

Orchid, however, was a genuine problem. There hadn't been a single police report fitting Ashcroft's M.O. since Duncan's basement. At the rate he had been feeding, one day was too long between meals, much less four.

The most logical answer was that Orchid had lied. The woman had never taken more than forty-eight hours to locate a target—at least, not while sober—and she had nothing to report on Ashcroft, Chance, or Lilith after *four* days.

Two possibilities existed: Either Ashcroft was finally dead or someone else had captured him. The likelihood of Orchid being involved or, at least, being aware of the players was almost a certainty. Fortunately, Luminita held two irresistible bargaining chips. With the correct amount of pressure...

The desk phone rang with a shrill pitch which burrowed under her skin and short-circuited her thoughts. After expelling an aggravated breath, Luminita snatched up the receiver.

"Yes?" The curt tone earned a hesitant pause. "What is it?"

"Ms. Dragomir, Mr. Bogdan has just arrived on the premises and is demanding to see you."

Luminita stilled in her chair. An unexpected thrill had accompanied the man's words. "Let him in," she directed, a grin creeping over her lips.

Aaron had finally chosen a side, and he was *here*. That should not have affected her the way it did, not after so much time snuffing out those emotions, but excitement zipped through every nerve.

After rising from her chair, she strolled to the door and unlocked it. The moment Aaron entered the hall, she knew and slowly backed away. His ancient hunger, tinged with fury, flooded the air like a roiling storm cloud, crackling with energy and threatening devastation. It was primal, feral, and *gods*, she had missed it.

A slight tremble began in her hands while she smoothed over her crimson silk blouse and black pencil skirt. Luminita drew in a deep breath, savoring the riotous storm drawing closer, and leaned against her desk with a hungry grin.

This was Aaron unleashed. This was Aaron as her Dionysus. He had *finally* shed his civilized façade of indifference and derision to reveal the blood-thirsty barbarian she had met in war-torn Romania centuries ago.

Three powerful knocks echoed through the room, and her elation cooled. The savage she desired, the one she knew he could be, wasn't dissuaded by any obstacle.

Then the door burst open, slamming against the wall like a clap of thunder, and her devious grin returned. Aaron stood on the threshold, his white buttoned-up shirt spattered with dried blood, his broad chest heaving with each sawed breath, his hands clenched into fists. But his silvery grey eyes…they glowed with unbridled anger.

"Aaron." She emphasized her Romanian accent, letting his name leisurely roll off her tongue as if the sight of him in this state had no effect on her.

He narrowed his venomous stare and stormed into the room, flinging the door shut behind him. Aaron moved toward her with a confident purpose she hadn't seen from him in centuries. Luminita's eyes widened with wicked delight when he didn't stop at a safe distance.

She kept perfectly still, even when he marched up to her and banded his hand around her throat. As deviant as it might have been, she missed the searing touch which had haunted her skin for decades. Luminita wouldn't allow him the pleasure of seeing that, however. She merely locked eyes with him, wearing a knowing grin.

"I should end you for what you've cost me!" he snarled, but his hand didn't tighten.

"And what have I cost you?" she asked in obvious amusement.

The man's lip twitched, and he stepped closer until he towered over her, forcing Luminita to look up at him. "Everything I've worked for, Nita. My power among the Elders, our resources…it's all gone. And that is only what you've taken *recently*." He squeezed her delicate neck, but not nearly hard enough. Aaron was still holding back, controlling himself, and she had no interest in his restraint.

"Whose blood are you wearing?"

Aaron drew his brows together as if he had forgotten, but rage surged through his touch again, dark and delectable. He pressed forward until he had her pinned against the desk. That hand tightened a little more, bringing a delicious burn to each shallow breath.

"Michael's," he growled between gritted teeth.

Luminita's grin faltered. She hadn't predicted that move, which was a rarity. "You killed Michael?" The question was barely audible past his crushing grip on her throat.

Aaron leaned down. Those piercing gray eyes pinned her in place. "You left me little choice, Nita."

She struggled to drag in air around his constricting hand, and warning bells blared in her head to put an end to this, to stop playing with fire, but…she wanted the burn, craved it.

Just like Vlad said you would, a sinister voice in the back of her mind whispered. Luminita ignored it.

"How?" she asked gruffly, with the little air she could force out.

Something shifted in his eyes, and his strong features softened for a moment. But once he understood, she felt it—the animalistic roar of control snapping, a surge of heat swirling into his fury. Long ago, Luminita had feared his control, his dominance, but right now, she craved it beyond reason. She didn't bother to stop and consider why.

His face loomed closer until his breath warmed the shell of her ear. "I slid a blade between his ribs. Is that what you want to hear?"

Venom coated each syllable like thick honey, and her grin broadened.

When Aaron pulled back enough to crowd her vision, he shifted his eyes between hers, as if searching for something. Luminita had no idea if he found it, but his grip loosened enough for her to drag in a breath. Oxygen flooded her air-starved lungs with a heady rush.

"Why?" Luminita studied his stormy gaze with ravenous delight.

The heat banked to embers, and he clenched his strong jaw painfully tight, but his hand relaxed a little more.

"Tell me the truth, Sălbatic." Luminita hadn't called him by *that* name since he had adopted his civilized mask hundreds of years ago, but she knew it would trigger an entire host of memories.

Aaron's eyes flared with primal lust, betrayal, and vicious fury, as if that one word had summoned his true base nature.

Perhaps she should have called him that sooner.

Would it have eradicated his Elder persona? Did it truly have that much power?

"He served his purpose. I had no further use for him, and his death divided the Elders long enough for me to make a clean escape. The mission is what matters."

Uninhibited practicality accompanied his cold confession. But his heated gaze was far more passionate. It raked over her intently, like a physical touch searing through her skin.

Luminita had missed that too.

"You feel no remorse." It wasn't a question. Not a drop of guilt, regret, or sadness lingered in his exquisite signature of wrathful carnality.

A hauntingly brutal smile snuck across his lips. "Progeny only serves a purpose if you do not intend to live forever. I have no compulsion to rest my legacy on the shoulders of others."

His hand was merely a weight against her throat, hovering over her throbbing pulse. The fingers no longer squeezed. She craved the violence. Perhaps some distant part of her felt she deserved it, after all these centuries.

Luminita stared at his forearm exposed beneath his rolled-up sleeve. She trailed her nails lightly against the blood-speckled skin at first, but then she pressed harder until Aaron drew in a hissing breath.

"All this petulant anger is for me?" Her gaze collided with Aaron's, and the embers sparked into licking flames. "If you're mad at me for spoiling your games, why don't you show me what *true* fury is…*if* you remember."

The steely glare galvanized, and Aaron leaned in again. "You're the one who enjoys games." The growling words vibrated over her skin. He tightened his hand to the point of pain once more. "What? No Datura Seeds to satisfy your appetite, or do you simply miss Vlad?"

Those words struck a definite chord. Despite the crushing pressure cutting off her air supply, Luminita leveled him with an indignant stare and dug her nails into his arm. When he still didn't ease up, she dragged them down to his wrist, leaving bloody furrows.

Aaron released her with a violent shove which nearly laid her out on the desk. She drew in gulping breaths, slowly soothing her burning lungs, while Aaron inspected the oozing wounds she had inflicted.

"Do not mention *him* to me," she hissed with a snarl. "And I do not *play games*, Sălbatic. I orchestrate events, create change, make bold moves, but *none* of them are mere games!"

"And what do you call this? Is there some grandiose scheme in your duplicitous head which requires pushing my buttons? Reopening old wounds? Teasing me?"

Once again, he towered over her, his grey eyes gleaming a deadly silver. Energy hummed and crackled between them, swimming through her veins like a siren's song, and her breaths quickened. She hadn't felt their connection this strongly in so very long.

"It isn't a game." Luminita gripped his strong chin with her thumb and finger, drawing him closer. "I want to free you from this apathetic mask you've grown accustomed to. I want to remind you of who you once were. I want your fury, your passion, your savagery…or are you no longer capable of those things?"

The clear challenge burned in her eyes, earning her a scathing scowl.

The monster lurked inside him, behind the thin veneer of civility he still clung to. She wanted to tear that mask away and burn it to ash for suppressing the chaotic frenzy she had seen in him the first fateful night in the old country.

Aaron had resembled a mad god of blood, Ares himself, with an endless hunger which would never be sated. Even during the wars against the Ottoman Empire and Vlad, he had indulged himself on the battlefield. But over the centuries which followed, Luminita had watched his spirit wither and burrow deep inside. Perhaps severing his last ties to vampire politics had finally allowed his divinity to reemerge, for him to reclaim himself.

In one swift move, Aaron traded his hold on her throat to sink his fingers into her raven-black hair. His hand twisted in the strands, and he kept her close enough to whisper over her lips.

"*You* want *my* savagery or just my body's?"

The swell of excitement proved impossible to hide. The chaos, the tenuous restraint, the salaciousness smoldering in his eyes and under his skin—this was her wine of choice, a vicious bouquet capable of pulling her free from the meticulous control she constantly had to maintain.

Perhaps she was the one who needed to be reminded of who she had once been. This wasn't just about Aaron's freedom, but hers as well, at least for a brief time.

"*Yours*. If you still have it in you," she whispered in defiance, tracing her nails up the blood-splattered shirt. The modern garment annoyed her. Another piece of his civilized mask.

Luminita's grin turned feral. She curled her fists into the fabric and tore. Buttons pinged across the tile in delicate tones, but Luminita focused on Aaron's quickened pulse.

The fingers in her hair tightened, and she sucked in a breath at the pain prickling her scalp. Still, the man hesitated. All that energy, rage, and erotic heat trapped beneath a paper-thin skin, straining to be released, desperate for it.

"Stop holding back!" Luminita demanded. She slapped his cheek with such force, his head turned away from her. "Prove your worth, Sălbatic."

Those had been the first words she had ever spoken to him—a direct challenge.

As if in slow motion, Aaron turned back to face her with blown pupils, leaving only silver rings of cold flame. Sawed breaths flowed between clenched teeth, and his entire body hummed. It was mesmerizing.

The hand in her hair twisted with a sharp sting, and she absorbed the delicious violence roaring to the surface, scorching her skin everywhere their bodies touched.

"You'll regret that." The gravelly threat made her breath hitch.

"Prove it!" When she lashed out, her nails drew blood along his chest. He hissed before his brittle control *finally* snapped.

Aaron's mouth collided with hers in a violent demand. There wasn't a shred of softness in the bruising kiss, and it sent her pulse racing, but it wasn't enough.

Luminita captured his bottom lip between her teeth and bit until the coppery tang of blood reached her tongue. Aaron whipped back, retreating a few steps. He touched his swollen lip while he stared at her, wild ferocity drenched in a voracious hunger that made her thighs clench.

Aaron glanced down at the crimson drops on his fingers. He lifted his zealous eyes back to her while he tore off his bloody shirt.

Before her ravenous grin fully formed, he hauled her ass onto the desk, gripped her neck, and pinned her down, knocking the wind from her lungs.

"You're a fucking demon," he snarled, but his rage wouldn't win this war, and she knew it. Aaron had wanted this too badly for too long.

On the night of Dragobete, they had shared a true Dionysian union, but because of the Datura Seeds, Aaron's conscious presence hadn't been there. He had no memory of it.

Over the years, they had shared certain sexual aspects, but the haunted memories of Vlad's abuse and the imprints which lingered on her skin had prevented her from allowing Aaron inside her. Then…he had abandoned her in Hungary.

"Perhaps…" The "R" rolled seductively with her natural accent. "…but so are you, Sălbatic, and you're starving for the frenzy. So, what's stopping you?"

Something shifted in his eyes.

"Maybe you"—Aaron tore off the top button of her blouse—"are the one"—he snapped off a second and a third—"who is"—he snatched the delicate silk and tore it roughly away, leaning over her—"desperate for the frenzy…to surrender control."

Luminita stared at her nail marks in his skin, still wet with blood. He was right. She wanted the blissful oblivion where nothing existed but pleasure and pain. It would never replace that fateful night, but she still wanted it. Despite that, she resented his deliberate choice of words.

When Luminita pushed against him, he clinched his grip on her throat tightly and pinned her to the desk with his weight.

"Oh, no, Nita. You demanded *my* savagery, remember?"

When the pencil skirt halted the progression of his knee moving between hers, he reached down with his free hand and tore the skirt from the bottom hem to her hip.

As much as she had craved all this, especially his unbridled devastation, the fact he *knew* it affected her made her defensive. She reflexively wanted to take back the control and distance she had maintained since their bitter reunion in Los Angeles. The only way to escape the instinct's grip was to push Aaron further, to force him to take without mercy.

Luminita used her enhanced strength and knocked his hand away from her throat with a condescending glare. The surprise granted her enough room to stand.

"Pathetic. Leave the insights to the intellectuals, Sălbatic." The crimson silk of her ruined blouse fluttered to the floor and pooled at her feet.

Aaron grabbed her jaw. "Always pushing," he snapped.

Her grin only widened.

"Then. Push. Back." Luminita emphasized each word with a snarl of her own.

Without a second's hesitation, Aaron spun her around and pulled her back against him. He pinned her hips to his with one hand while the other surged firmly up her stomach and shredded the delicate lace of her bra.

She tried to move against him, to find a way to escape, although she didn't really want to. The feel of his already hard length pressing against her was far too inviting, and the struggle made it twitch. Aaron quickly leaned forward, trapping her between his solid body and the desk.

The searing touch of his hand slid roughly over her breast, the palm raking over her already pebbled nipple, and a traitorous moan escaped her throat. Aaron's hands on her skin felt far too good, too familiar, too addictive.

Hot breath rushed over her ear, sending shivers down her spine. "Your body gives you away, Nita. You want me as much as I have *always* wanted you."

The confession intruded on her hunger with the weight of so many pivotal moments. The Dragobete ritual, their time together in Poiana Negrii, the fateful night he left for Turkey because she was too broken…the night in Hungary she woke up alone. They were old wounds she wasn't eager to explore.

"I don't want *you*. I want *your rage and frenzy* unbound."

Those very emotions washed over her, burning white-hot everywhere they touched, and it felt fucking glorious. She had missed its caress.

"I believe the second part, but not the first."

He clutched her hair again and forced her down. Her cheek collided with the wooden desk. Harsh tugs and the sound of shredding fabric preceded the remnants of her skirt falling away. The cool air was frigid against her feverish skin, except where Aaron's unrelenting weight kept her warm. His control over her body drove her pulse to thrum violently in her ears.

The breath halted in her lungs when he slid his fingers between her slickened thighs and pressed firmly against the soaked satin.

"You are an infuriating creature, and I've waited long enough."

The husky groan vibrated through her bones and tightened her very core. It was the last gentle thing Aaron did.

The satin panties were torn without much difficulty, but when he touched her most sensitive places, he was rough, unyielding, feral, and she drank in every intoxicating drop. His other hand stayed firmly in her hair, keeping her face pressed to the desk.

Luminita breathed through the hollow ache in her center—one he quickly remedied.

The sound of his slacks and belt falling to the floor made her breath hitch, and thrilling anticipation swirled through her.

"You wanted Sălbatic, *mica ispita*." The rumbling tone was nearly as delicious as the feel of him nudging at her entrance.

There was only a moment of hesitation.

His first merciless thrust tore a screaming moan from her throat. The second and third were just as thoroughly brutal, but then he stopped. Her fury was instantaneous.

Before she spoke a single word, Aaron yanked her upright by her thick tresses and crushed her against his chest again. He banded one hand across her body, clutching her breast and pinching the nipple painfully tight between his fingers.

Aaron dove the other between her thighs, working in slow but firm circles, commanding she come undone. It wasn't enough for him to simply be inside her after all these centuries. He wanted, *demanded*, every part of her.

His hands were not what dragged her closer to the edge, however. It was Aaron's hot breath rushing over the curve of her shoulder. Teeth raked the delicate skin in a teasing touch which stole her breath, but he didn't bite. He had given her an oath all those years ago in Poiana Negrii, one she no longer wanted.

"Drink."

Aaron stilled his hips, with him still buried inside her. "What?"

Not only confusion saturated the word, but a mixture of desire and confliction.

Luminita twisted her head enough to catch his eyes. "I did not tell you to stop. Drink, Sălbatic, and take what you've always wanted." To emphasize her point, she tensed her body, squeezing his hard length. "Unless you no longer want me."

Rage and lust roared against her skin in a boundless tidal wave, making her walls quiver and clench. While his brutal thrusts resumed, two sharp points broke the surface, and her breaths became ragged and desperate.

Still, nothing compared to the ecstasy which wracked her body when those delicate fangs sank viciously into her skin, followed by the harsh bite of his teeth. Pain seared and ebbed, breaking her free, letting her surpass her plans, the drudgery, the confusion, even the past, until she only existed in this moment.

Aaron continued to violently play her body like an instrument, with brutal thrusts and swirling fingers. His teeth remained clamped on her shoulder. The coil tightened with each agonizing moment until she shattered.

The freedom in her absolute bliss made the room spin, and Aaron was the only reason she didn't collapse from the relief. It was a feeling she hadn't known, not ever. In fact, it was the fear of this, craving the loss of control, which had made her push him away when they first met.

Luminita was only dimly aware of Aaron following soon after, with primal groans vibrating against her back.

He didn't linger, thank the gods. Aaron pulled away from her with a conflicted storm of emotions, but Luminita couldn't decipher them, not in her pleasure-addled state. She watched in her periphery while he scooped up his ruined shirt, wiped off his cock, and tossed the stained fabric in her trash can.

The calm began to settle into her center, her pulse regulated, and her breathing slowed. The euphoria leaked away too fast. Something trickled down her chest, and she traced the deep bite mark between her neck and shoulder.

Every touch brought a delicious shock of pain and pulled that euphoria back. Her eyes drifted closed, and she allowed the sensation to swim through her veins.

It should have frightened her, should have reminded her of Vlad's violent abuse, but it didn't. Perhaps it was the passage of so much time, or maybe it was the knowledge that Aaron still sought permission first, unlike Vlad.

Or maybe Vlad's dark promise to her had been true. He said she would crave the violence one day and seek it out in others.

The confusing thoughts burned away the bliss and left her irritated.

"You should settle into your room." Luminita kept her typical tone of indifference and sauntered toward a changing screen, where a satin robe hung from its side.

She felt Aaron's eyes raking over her nude form, felt his hunger already returning. His appetite for her had always been voracious, at least until he had abandoned her.

After sliding on the robe, Luminita pivoted on her heel and raised one eyebrow. "In other words, Aaron, you can leave."

A frown pinched his strong features while he zipped up his slacks. Aaron crossed the room with purposeful strides. His silvery grey eyes searched hers, but she avoided his gaze with a bored expression. She knew what he was looking for, but she wouldn't give it to him.

Aaron gripped her jaw with crushing strength and forced her to meet his eyes. "Nita."

The feral growl of her name almost weakened her resolve.

Almost.

Her defiant stare made his blood heat. It scorched through his enticingly painful touch.

"Get. Out." Luminita spoke each word with venomous fervor.

Aaron's top lip twitched, and his heavy stare bored into her, but she didn't falter.

"And if I'd rather lay you out on that desk and feast on you until you beg me to stop?" The corner of his mouth lifted in a salacious grin, more threat than promise. But beneath it, she felt the soul-deep sting from her callous dismissal. It made something old and far too familiar ache in her chest, something she wanted to forget.

Luminita rose on tiptoe, and his vise-like grip left her jaw. She stopped just before reaching his lips. His pulse thrummed beneath his skin, still drunk in an erotic haze.

In slow seductive tones, Luminita whispered against his slightly parted lips. "I no longer have an interest in men who ask *permission*. Leave my room, or I will have you escorted out."

Once again, she prodded that old wound.

The tidal wave of fury, embarrassment, and primal lust left her lightheaded.

His emotions had been buried for a long time, and they ran *so* deep. *Gods*, she had forgotten.

Part of her prayed he would defy her and take what he clearly wanted with the same addictive intensity. Her body still ached and throbbed from every rough touch and brutal demand. The bite at the sensitive junction of her shoulder and neck burned exquisitely, and she wanted more, but she refused to simply hand him that power.

Luminita took a step back, and to her disappointment, he let her. The resolve hardened into steel, and she took another step away from Aaron, who merely glared at her with open contempt.

For some reason, the expression on his face made her feel… uncomfortable, perhaps even remorseful.

"Always playing fucking games." Aaron clenched his jaw and scanned her body with a scathing disapproval, which crawled under her skin. "I suppose you'll summon me the next time you have an itch you can't scratch. I'll give you fair warning, Nita. Next time…I won't be so fucking nice."

Luminita pulled the robe around herself a little tighter and watched Aaron's muscled back when he stormed through the door, slamming it closed behind him.

The threat echoed through her head, and she couldn't tell if it excited her more than it scared her. In fact, everything which had taken place since he had walked through that door had done both.

Chapter 27

While Orchid navigated the SUV to the hospital's farthest parking lot, she stole a quick side-glance at Lilith. Then her eyes fell to the vampire's naked ring finger. Orchid should have kept her mouth closed, minded her business, but it nagged at her. Chance was all grown-up. She had missed everything, and this little sliver of insight into his life proved too tempting.

"So…" Orchid cleared her throat when words failed her. "I heard that you and Chance are engaged?"

Lilith swung her gaze slowly to Orchid with an incredulous expression, as if the woman had just asked if unicorns existed. "Um… yes."

"But you don't wear a ring." Orchid pulled into a spot and put the vehicle in park.

Lilith continued to stare a hole through the side of her face. "No…obviously not," she replied in a hesitant cadence.

"May I ask why?" Orchid swallowed her nerves and turned to face Lilith with a smile she hoped read as polite curiosity.

A line formed between Lilith's brows, and she narrowed her eyes. "Are you…" She paused, as if deciding whether to continue. "Are you questioning my intentions?"

If Lilith's face hadn't clearly stated the concept was offensively ludicrous, her clipped tone relayed the message loud and clear.

"No. I merely wondered why you don't wear a ring."

Lilith considered her for a long moment before opening the door and climbing out of the SUV. Orchid followed suit and fell in step beside her, keeping her mouth shut this time. The silence felt sharp and uncomfortable, but she trudged on without another word.

"It's new," Lilith stated after a few minutes. "Chance proposed the night we left for PMIC. He didn't have time to get one, and we've been on the run since." Lilith finally glanced over at her. "I don't see how any of this is important information to you."

The words stung, but they weren't unwarranted. "I was merely curious about your relationship with my son."

Lilith came to an abrupt halt, and Orchid paused beside her. A mix of anger and confusion perfumed the air. When Lilith turned to face her, she wore a conflicted frown.

"I get your curiosity, but please understand...I don't know you, and neither does Chance. I believe you are who you say you are. I believe you're sincere in your desire to help. But I think *Chance* should be the one to decide what to share with you. You owe him that much, at the very least."

"Yes." Orchid's throat constricted around the word. Lilith was right. It should be his choice. Trying to glean bits of information about him from others wasn't fair. "I just want you to realize that I lost him that day too. I didn't get to see him grow up. Perhaps Detective DeLuca was right. I should have looked for him, even after Luminita convinced me he was dead, but I was...scared to see things I couldn't forget if he'd really died."

Lilith's expression softened slightly. "I understand, but..." She expelled a weighted breath. "This is a conversation you need to have with him...when *he's* ready to listen. He endured more than I think either of us knows, and it should be his decision."

Orchid nodded, unable to speak. If she said anything else, the dam would break, and her barely restrained tears would flow.

They started to walk again. This time, the silence didn't prickle her skin. They had nearly made it to the door when her work phone rang.

Orchid stopped, still as stone. Lilith peered at her suspiciously.

"Luminita. I should answer. I'll meet you inside."

Lilith scanned over her one more time before continuing toward the hospital.

After a slow exhale, Orchid pressed the answer button.

"Be faithful, even to the point of death." Luminita's voice sounded different, less smooth and composed somehow.

"And I will give you life as your victor's crown," Orchid replied automatically.

"I need you to come back to the facility. I have another job for you."

"But I'm still tracking Ashcroft and the others."

A significant pause stretched out between them, and the hairs on the assassin's nape rose.

"Orchid. I am giving an order. I assume by now you know the consequences of disobedience?"

The implied threat struck home. Luminita had her family, and ignoring orders would get them killed.

"Yes," Orchid managed to squeak out.

"Good. I expect you here in six hours. If you are late, I will have a choice to make. What is the old saying? Age before beauty?"

Orchid swallowed around the painful lump in her throat. It felt like she had ingested a handful of razorblades. "I'll be there."

"Six hours," Luminita reminded her before hanging up.

After pulling the phone away from her ear, Orchid stared down at the screen. Tears flooded her eyes. It was obviously a baited trap—one Luminita knew would work. Orchid had no choice. If she didn't go, the Romanian would execute her husband and then her daughter.

She lifted her eyes to the hospital doors a few dozen feet in front of her. If she left, she couldn't protect Lilith and Chance. Even if she stayed, she couldn't guarantee their survival. But they weren't helpless. Chance had proven that tonight.

However, Noah and Desiree were innocent *and* helpless. And they were only in this danger because of her. Even if Orchid obeyed, Luminita would most likely kill them anyway, but not trying to save them was a shame she couldn't endure. She would rather die with them than leave them to suffer in her place.

Orchid pulled up the phone number Lilith had given her and dialed.

"Hello?" Lilith asked hesitantly.

"It's Orchid. I'm sorry, but I have to go."

"What?"

"Luminita wants me to report back, and I have no choice. She's threatening my family. I realize it's basically suicide, but I have to try. Please, tell Chance..." Once again words failed her. What could she possibly say? "...that I'm sorry and I will do everything I can to help your cause."

She hung up before Lilith could yell or worse, change her mind.

Lilith glared at the phone in her hand. Not only was Orchid running off to Luminita and abandoning Chance *again*, but she couldn't even stay long enough to tell him herself. Once more, Lilith had to be the bearer of bad news, a role she was *really* tired of playing.

"May I continue?" Dr. Preston asked impatiently.

Lilith closed her eyes for a moment, reining in the surging tide of livid frustration. She released a calming breath before turning back toward him.

"Yes, please."

"While my resident is stitching up your friend, I'd like to get some blood samples."

"Of course." Lilith flashed a tight smile and followed Dr. Preston's gesture to a chair beside a table littered with supplies. "I will tell you that I just fed. It will most likely skew the results."

The doctor pressed his mouth into a firm line. "How so?"

"I'm not an expert, but it makes a difference with luminol. Blood from a vampire that has freshly fed will glow because of the human hemoglobin. A sample from one who hasn't will not glow because the hemoglobin levels are too low to create an effect."

"Interesting, but I should be able to decipher your blood from the donor's, correct? Or does your system dismantle the human red blood cells? To merely harvest what it needs and implement it into your own cells?"

The questions exceeded her base knowledge. "Uh, I'm not sure. My uncle Duncan would know that answer, but unfortunately, speaking to him isn't possible."

"Because of your secrecy?"

"Because he's dead," Lilith replied in a flat tone. "He had tons of research notebooks that I haven't had the time to delve into. Perhaps…if things go well, I could pass them on to you."

A brilliant light sparked in the man's navy eyes. "That would be incredible."

"I do have a favor to ask in return, though."

The glimmer dimmed a little, and the skin around his eyes tightened. "And that would be?"

"Do you know a good virologist that you trust? Someone who will keep things confidential, for now?"

Dr. Preston eyed her with suspicion and fastened the tourniquet painfully tight around her arm. "Why do you need a virologist?"

The blatant question made Lilith hesitate. She had already entrusted this human doctor with a tremendous amount of dangerous information, but it was nothing which truly affected the human population. The virus, however...

"I plan to retrieve research material on a virus which may include a cure or vaccine. I need someone who understands the data and can utilize it properly and quickly."

"What virus?" The man pinned her in place with a piercing stare Lilith found rather uncomfortable.

Once again, she paused. Revealing secrets, especially to a human, just felt wrong, but without his help, the entire world might suffer—vampire, Durand, and human alike.

"Do you know someone?"

Dr. Preston tapped the antecubital space of her elbow, helping the vein swell and surface. He rubbed the entire area with an alcohol pad.

"I do. What virus?"

Lilith bit her lip and hoped she wasn't making an enormous mistake. "Parvo B-20."

The man's eyes widened. He sat back on his stool, staring at her.

"It's an ancient virus from Greece. A cult released it, but I believe they may have developed a failsafe first to ensure they didn't contract it. An associate of mine was working on the data recovered from the cult's stronghold, but he's gone missing. I know where he keeps a backup. I just need someone experienced with viruses and vaccines to put the information to use."

Dr. Preston's eyes lost their focus. They peered through Lilith like she didn't exist while he worked through everything she had said. "An ancient virus...That makes sense. The samples I've studied didn't seem like an evolution of B-19...More like a predecessor, but one we haven't seen."

The man blinked, and his gaze rested on her again.

"Have you considered approaching an expert on ancient viruses? There's one in Pennsylvania—"

"Dr. Rachel Thomas?" Lilith interrupted with a barked laugh.

"Yes..." His brows lowered and pinched together, then he grabbed the needle.

"Dr. Thomas and her brother, Dr. Wolfe, are the ones responsible for the virus. They found it during his dig at Apollo's temple."

"And they released it on the public?"

His horrified tone made Lilith like him a bit more.

"In a way. I don't think they expected it to cross into the human population, though."

A tiny hiss of pain escaped her lips when he slid the needle into her vein. Once the little flash of red appeared, he started filling various tubes.

"So…this virus targeted vampires?" After asking, Dr. Preston huffed a laugh, as if he couldn't believe those words had left his mouth.

"Not just us, but yes. An attempt at genocide."

The last sentence sobered him. "I see." He switched tubes before speaking again. "I had an assistant last year. She's a virology major about to complete her doctorate. Absolutely brilliant. I wanted her to come back this year, but she missed the deadline to apply due to a family emergency, and the college wouldn't allow me to make exceptions."

"A student?"

Dr. Preston placed a cotton pad over the puncture site, applied pressure, and withdrew the needle. "An *exceptional* student who has already completed most of her education. She would do literally anything for time in the lab, including keeping her mouth shut."

"But if the college won't let you make exceptions…" Lilith prodded.

A grunt of displeasure escaped him while he wrapped the coban dressing tightly around her arm. "I can hire her as an assistant. It just won't count toward her practical hour requirements. For an opportunity like this, I don't think she'd mind."

"What is your actual field of study?"

Lilith realized she didn't have the faintest clue. Dr. Preston was a general surgeon—she had learned that much—but his lab didn't seem geared toward operating.

"I started as a surgeon out of college. I keep my credentials up-to-date and perform minor surgeries for the hospital as needed, but my research grant is on DNA anomalies and their resulting attributes. That's why Agent Hersch comes to me with her weird cases she can't explain."

Lilith had no idea what she had expected, but DNA anomalies *wasn't* it. "Like *X Files*?"

For the first time, Dr. Preston laughed with a genuinely broad smile. "Something like that. I've consulted on everything from complex genetic samples from a new species, like the Capitojoppa amazonica wasp, to severe abnormalities from inbreeding and rare genetic disorders. I can't say I've dealt with alien DNA."

"Well, I suppose you can add vampire to your list." Lilith chuckled.

"And whatever other species you insist on keeping private. Mr. Deveraux's sample is quite…interesting so far."

"Keep that private, for your safety and for that of anyone you've considered telling. Vampires might be secretive, but…this *other species* will kill anyone they suspect knows about them without hesitation or fact checking."

Thankfully, the doctor seemed to consider her warning. "I will focus my energy on your sample, then."

Lilith released a breath of relief. "That would be best for everyone involved, especially you."

The doctor nodded thoughtfully while cleaning up his supplies. "May I ask a social question that I'm curious about?"

For a minute, Lilith merely stared at him in confusion. "A social question?"

"Yes." Dr. Preston leaned against the counter and crossed his arms over his chest. "A question about your social structure."

"Okay…" Lilith couldn't tell if she was more nervous or curious about what he wanted to ask.

"You said before that you and the detective are purebloods, but Chance, Timothy, and Gibson are half-bloods."

"Yes." Although Lilith wasn't quite certain where this was going, a defensive itch began to form.

"Is there a rift between the two within your culture?"

"You mean, do purebloods look at half-bloods as lesser citizens?" The idea seemed ludicrous until her thoughts landed on her father.

"Precisely."

Lilith had to swallow hard before she could get the words out. "A few of the older ones harbor some prejudice. Not because they see them as weak, though. It's more…practical than that. Half-bloods don't live nearly as long. A pureblood might live centuries or more. Most half-bloods only live an extra twenty years or so, depending on their heritage."

"So, longevity is the social standard."

Her first reaction was revulsion, but when Lilith truly considered it, he was right. The Elders ran their society—the oldest members of their race.

"I suppose it is."

"And yet you—a pureblood—are engaged to Mr. Deveraux—a half-blood."

This entire conversation was delving into uncomfortable territory, and Lilith rubbed at her arms. "Uh. It's more complicated than that in our specific case, but…even if it wasn't, I'd still chose him." She bit at her lip, praying this little interview would end soon.

"Fascinating." Dr. Preston pushed away from the counter. "Thank you for answering my questions. Should we check on your friend?"

When he gestured toward the door, Lilith couldn't have been more relieved.

"Yes. Thank you." She crossed the room in quick strides, desperate to be anywhere else.

Dr. Preston remained silent while he led her past the patient rooms. When they rounded the corner, Lilith spotted Eileen pacing in front of a closed door.

"Everything okay?" Lilith asked when she got closer. The panic in Eileen's fidgeting hands had Lilith's mind spinning.

"I don't know," Eileen confessed in a rush. "Tim kicked me out."

Lilith tilted her head in confusion. "What? Why?"

"He said he couldn't handle seeing me upset."

Lilith tried to suppress a smile and failed, which only made Eileen's frown deepen.

"I'll check on our patient," Dr. Preston offered stiffly. He moved past them and slid through the door.

Eileen watched him the entire time, shifting her posture more than once.

After the door clicked closed, Lilith leaned close to whisper. "Is there a problem with Dr. Preston?"

"What? No," Eileen stammered.

"Your reaction says differently."

A heavy breath rushed out, and Eileen put her hands on her hips. "He just…" The woman's bright blue eyes rolled, and she resumed pacing. "He tried to ask me out. It was weird."

An amused smirk lifted the corner of Lilith's mouth. "Okay. Not what I expected. And from the looks of it…you didn't either?"

"No," Eileen replied adamantly. "I've worked with the man for…five years, I think?"

"What did you say?"

When Eileen leveled her with an almost lethal stare, Lilith held up her hands.

"Hey, no judgment. I'm just curious."

"I told him the truth." The woman continued to pace, avoiding Lilith's gaze completely. "That I'm with Tim, and…" She stopped and stared at the tile floor.

"Eileen. Seriously, if you need someone to talk to…confidentially, you can trust me. I won't say anything."

The petite agent chewed at her bottom lip but finally met Lilith's stare. "It's ridiculous. I've known him less than two weeks."

"You know…I've known Chance since I was thirteen, but…I never really *knew* him as a person. He was just this handsome guy who worked for my father. We traded jokes once in a while, but that's it. Then my dad sent him with me to Tennessee to find Duncan. It took me all of three or four days to admit I loved him. Granted, I did think he was dying at the time, but still…it was the truth. The heart knows long before we choose to consciously admit it."

Eileen studied her for several silent seconds. "I've never experienced that…at least not before Tim. Karl, my ex-husband…he just kinda wore me down. I remember thinking that he must *really* love me to work that hard. I didn't realize then that he was grooming me for a life of accepting hollow apologies and empty romantic gestures to make up for the bad things he'd do."

The pain in Eileen's voice mirrored Lilith's own scars from surviving David Boston. She knew those manipulations, that delicate balance he had practiced to keep her from leaving for so long.

"Tim is the furthest thing from that," Lilith reassured her.

"Oh, I know that. Believe me. It's all just…new. I didn't freak out when John took a bullet to the leg, but seeing Tim on that bed…injured…" A few tears jostled free of her lashes.

"It's different." Lilith nodded with a knowing smile.

Eileen's face fell in a horrified expression. "Oh my god, I am so sorry. I'm standing here, blabbering about a leg wound, after what you…and Chance…I'm sorry."

"It's not a competition." Lilith chuckled. "Of course, if it was, I'd win. That's the second time Chance has almost died on me."

After a hesitant moment, Eileen joined in Lilith's laughter. "How have you not had a heart attack?"

"Well…to be fair, I've almost died on him at least twice as much."

"Since Tennessee? Eight months ago?" Eileen blinked at her in shock.

"Yeah. Cohen's blood was the only thing that saved me at least three of those times."

The amusement slid right off Eileen's face. "So, he actually has a purpose?"

The words summoned that night in the cabin after Luminita had left, the night Andrew confessed *she* was his only purpose. He had been there, involved in some manner with saving her life each time. In a weird way, perhaps he had been right.

"I suppose so."

"Sorry." Eileen huffed. "I know you two are friends. I just don't see why."

Lilith considered that statement for several minutes while Eileen tried to wear a path in the tile.

Why *did* Lilith want to be Andrew's friend? It wasn't simply because he was a lost soul, a broken person. It wasn't just because *he* cared about *her*. She had wanted to see the real person behind the masks since he had revealed what he was. Lilith had tried to believe he didn't matter…until the night Luminita's scalpel had dug into him.

The psychotic woman had stripped everything away, exposing Cohen at his core. She had drawn every single emotion out of him until she had almost killed him, and he had survived. Cohen had lived through decades of Farren's horrific abuse. He had survived the loss of every single person around him. Sure, he was broken but still breathing, and Lilith admired that.

Over the past year, she had nearly lost every recognizable thing in her life. She knew the struggle, and unlike her, Cohen hadn't had anyone to support him. His coping mechanisms were disturbing, to say the least, but they gave him a reason to face the world every day.

"Hey, you okay?"

Lilith snapped her gaze up to Eileen. "Uh, yeah."

"I'm sorry if I brought up a painful subject. It was a dumb thing to say."

"It's fine." Lilith forced a smile, but thankfully, the door swung open, stealing Eileen's attention.

"I believe it's safe to enter now," Dr. Preston said with an amused smile.

Eileen hurried past him without a second's hesitation. Lilith started to follow, but her phone rang again. She held up a finger to Dr. Preston and answered the call.

"Lily. I just wanted you to know we're here." Chance's Cajun-flecked voice always soothed her frazzled nerves—well, almost always. "How's Tim?"

"I'm pretty sure he's fine. Eileen just went in to see him."

"And you're okay?"

A gentle smile graced her lips. "Yeah, I'm okay. We should be heading down in a few minutes."

The few beats of silence seemed to stretch taut, pulling the words out of her.

"I truly love you, *beau.*"

"Are you sure you're okay?"

A soft chuckle escaped. "I'm sure. I was just talking to Eileen about things, and…I needed tell you."

"I love you too, *mon cherie.*"

Lilith desperately wanted to rip off the Band-aid and tell him about Orchid, but breaking that kind of news over the phone was cowardly. He deserved better.

If only Orchid had understood that.

Chapter 28

As soon as Lilith and the others exited the hospital, a weight left Chance's shoulders. After what had happened at the hotel, letting Lilith out of his sight transcended pain, and her tone on the call had sent his pulse rioting. She had sounded so sad but insisted she was okay.

Chance jogged down the RV's stairs and out to meet them. He told himself it was to see if Tim needed help, but that was a complete lie. The man was limping a little, but nothing crazy. Eileen kept a close eye on Tim, though. Her gaze darted to his leg every now and then with a worried pout.

Once Chance locked eyes with Lilith, a warmth filled her face which soothed his soul. He stopped a few feet away and forced himself to smile over at Tim.

"Glad to see you on your feet, *mon freur.*"

"Tis but a flesh wound," Tim stated, in the most godawful British accent Chance had *ever* heard.

"They gave him a little something for the pain," Eileen said with an amused grin.

"Pff. I didn't need nothing." Tim waved a dismissive hand, his glassy eyes tracking the movement.

Chance chuckled and watched them pass by, heading for the RV.

Then Lilith touched his shoulder, and everything else drifted away. He turned and wrapped her in his arms, squeezing her against him before she said anything. Chance needed a moment to hold her, to feel that she was safe. Everything had happened so fast, and he had barely seen her after the shooting.

"Hey…" Lilith's soothing voice warmed the shell of his ear. She slid her fingers into his hair, and he soaked in that touch like a starving man. "We're okay."

Chance swallowed hard and tried to absorb those words into his damn marrow. Tim was the one who had taken a bullet this time, but what about the next? With multiple contracts out on all their heads, tonight's attack wouldn't be the last.

"Chance." Lilith pulled back enough to search his eyes. "What's wrong?"

He lowered his gaze. "I…don't know. I just…Everything happened so fast." Chance drew in a deep breath and blew it out. "I just needed to know you were really okay, especially after that phone call."

Relief trickled over her skin, and she flashed a bright smile. "I'm fine, *beau*. We should get moving."

"But you sounded so sad on the phone. It felt like you were saying goodbye." Chance let the fear roll right off his tongue this time.

"Oh, no, handsome." Lilith caressed his cheek with an almost heartbroken expression. "I was talking with Eileen right before you called. I…told her about how we met when I was thirteen but I didn't *really* know you until that trip to Tennessee…and…" A vibrant blush colored her cheeks, making his pulse quicken. "And how I completely fell for you in…four days?"

"Three days."

Her smile broadened at his correction. "Might have been less. Anyway, after the way we left things, I just wanted you to know that I still love you."

Chance leaned in to lightly whisper, "You are the love of my life, Lily. You're stuck with me."

A little giggle tickled against his lips, and she gave him a quick kiss. "Happily so." She winked, then pulled away.

A bright grin lit his face, and he turned to follow her toward the RV. After just a few steps, he stopped. Something had occurred to him.

"Wait. Where's Orchid?"

Every muscle in Lilith's body tensed, and a whirlwind of emotions brushed against his skin.

"Lilith? Where is she?" A familiar dread trickled down his spine.

Finally, she turned around to face him with an expression of pure determination. "She left."

"Left? I don't understand. Left *where*?"

Lilith pressed her lips together and slid her hand into his. "Luminita called and Orchid left. She's not…coming back, Chance."

Some distant part of himself he had thought incapable of being hurt again cracked. She had *chosen* to leave him behind, to abandon him for a second time. As hard as he had tried not to let the woman in, he had done it anyway and allowed her to wound him once more.

"Why?" It was the only word he could get out.

Lilith squeezed his hand tightly. He clung to it like an anchor, preventing him from drifting out to sea.

"She said Luminita threatened to kill her family if she didn't return."

Anger roiled in his guts. *That* family she'd risk her life for, but not him. Logically, Chance realized they needed more help than he did, but that didn't matter to the fissure in his chest. Yet again, *he* was not enough.

"She asked me to tell you—"

"Stop," he interrupted quickly. "I don't care what she said. If she'd meant any of it, she would have told me to my face."

Lilith's eyes filled to the brim with tears. "I am so sorry."

The breathtaking sight of her sadness cooled his anger to smoldering embers. He slid his hands up to her face, cradling it between his palms.

"*You* have nothing to apologize for, *mon amour*. You're the only thing keeping me sane." He brushed a thumb over her bottom lip when it curved into a smile. "Thank you for never giving up on me."

With an uneven sigh, Chance pressed his forehead to hers.

"I *never* will," Lilith whispered. "Not even when you piss me off so much I have to kick your ass."

Chance couldn't help but laugh and pull her tight against him.

"You two coming or what?" Nicci called out from the RV. "There's a damn bedroom. You can make out later. Let's go!"

They both laughed, and Lilith stepped back, wiping her cheeks.

The shit with Orchid hurt more than he had expected, but Lilith was still here. She kept choosing him every time. Lilith had stayed by his side the entire time at the hospital, holding on to hope. She had fought for him. *She* was all that mattered.

"Nicci's right. We need to go." Lilith held out her hand with a stunning smile.

He slid his fingers between hers and fell into an easy stride beside her, where he belonged, where he had *always* belonged.

"Where's our ghostly assassin?" Nicci asked when they reached the RV.

Lilith hesitated, but Chance didn't. "She chose a side, and it wasn't ours."

Nicci merely stared at him while they climbed the steps into the RV.

"Gibson, are you good to take the first shift? I could use some sleep."

"Sleep. Right. Like anyone believes you two are gonna sleep." Tim snorted a laugh, which clearly reinforced the power of pain pills.

Chance glared over at the bottom bunk, and Tim held up his hands in surrender.

"Yes, sir." Gibson replied from the driver's seat. "Where are we heading?" Gibson asked.

"New York City."

"Uh, are we waiting for Orchid?" The man's tone indicated he'd be more than happy to leave the woman behind.

Lilith studied Chance's reaction, but honestly, he didn't know how to feel. If Luminita was threatening the woman's family, she had probably realized Orchid wasn't on her side anymore. Luminita would either kill her or force her compliance.

Abandoning him was one thing, but would she betray him? Would she hand them all over to the enemy to save her new family—the one she *actually* cared about? And if she didn't…if Luminita killed her…

"No." Chance sighed heavily, shoving the thoughts away. "Solasta is our immediate concern."

"Got it, sir. Keller and I will take turns. We both have our CDL."

Eileen cleared her throat and made a suggestion. "We should stop at an RV campground once we cross over into Kentucky or Virginia and swap plates with someone…just to be safe."

"Eileen makes a good point. First campground you come to after we cross the state line." Chance nodded his appreciation at the petite FBI agent curled up against Tim.

"Yes, sir."

With that settled, Chance turned his attention to Lilith. "We should both get some sleep, *cherie*. It's been an exhausting day."

Now that they were on the road, everything weighed heavy on his bones, especially his battered and bruised heart.

Chapter 29

Cohen opened his eyes to a lightless void, a black so deep it pressed against his skin like the waters of a bottomless ocean. He struggled to draw oxygen into his lungs. Panic seared every nerve ending until he thought he might implode from the pressure.

A pinprick of light appeared in the inky black. He moved toward it somehow, though he wasn't sure if he was running or swimming, maybe neither. His sole focus remained on that light—a guiding star in the seemingly endless void. If he could just reach it, escape, he knew with certainty he would be saved.

The darkness tightened around him, slowing his progression as if it refused to let him go. It became thick like molasses coating his body, pulling at him, but he kept his eyes on the light and continued to fight.

It was so close. Cohen reached for it, fingers dancing in the sun's rays. Hope surged through him on a cellular level. The void coiled around him like a snake, squeezing until he couldn't even draw a breath.

Tears filled his eyes while he struggled, but the dark slowly dragged him away from salvation. Nothing he did made a difference. It was all over. Cohen had lost.

The darkness engulfed him once again, blotting out everything else, and Andrew stilled. He closed his eyes, sending tears down his cheeks, released a breath, and surrendered.

When he opened them again, the scene had shifted. He stood in Duncan's basement, surrounded by oppressive silence. Blood covered the floor and walls in arcs, splashes, and pools, but there were no bodies. He turned slowly, absorbing every detail while he waited for whatever horror was in store for him.

Nothing changed.

Curiosity consumed him, and Cohen wandered toward the bathroom.

At first, everything seemed in order, but then his gaze snagged on the mirror. The scrawling letters written in blood hit him like a hot poker, straight to the heart.

Let it be enough.

But it hadn't been. Healing his scars, offering her friendship—it hadn't been enough, and now…

Andrew's throat bobbed. He turned away, shame overwhelming him. Cohen slowly stalked into the main room but stopped dead in his tracks when he took in his surroundings.

Lilith stood in the middle of the basement, looking exactly as she had that night. Her dark tank top and shorts made her pale skin glow around the splotches of blood. Her blond curls were damp with sweat, but her eyes…Her gorgeous olive eyes were fixed on him.

Cohen couldn't sense anything from her, not even a whiff of emotion. She just stood there, watching him, with an expression he couldn't decipher.

Guilt made his skin flush, and he lowered his gaze to the floor, but Cohen moved toward her regardless. She was that light in the void, his North Star, and he would *always* be drawn to her. That certainty might as well have been tattooed on his damn bones.

"Andrew," she whispered in the softest voice.

He closed his eyes, savoring every single note.

She took his hand, raising it, and released a heartbreaking sigh. "Why are you doing this?"

He opened his eyes when her fingers grazed the split skin of his fractured and swollen knuckles. "I deserve to be punished," he admitted.

"Stop."

Andrew's gaze collided with hers, and he couldn't breathe again. The tears lining her lashes glistened in the light, and she stared up at him with a melancholy smile which tore him to pieces.

Cohen couldn't help himself. He had to touch her. It was an irresistible compulsion, and he was so fucking tired. His thumb skimmed her cheek, tucking her blood-streaked hair behind her ear.

Just that simple touch resonated through his body, and she didn't pull away. She stayed there, watching him.

It's a dream. Only a fucking dream. This isn't real! The words screamed through his head, but he didn't care. It *felt* real. When he touched her, it drew him closer, made him feel something other than the abject misery he had been wallowing in for days.

Andrew sank his fingers slowly into her hair and studied her expression. She didn't stop him, didn't walk away. Lilith just stared up at him with that same heartbroken look. His tentative touch reached her nape, the fingers barely brushing against her skin, and she shivered.

It was his undoing.

Andrew cradled the back of her neck and drew her closer. He brushed his lips over hers in the faintest touch. It was all he could do to not kiss her with all the passion and desire swelling in his heart.

"Why are you doing this?" Lilith whispered against his lips.

Andrew froze. Heat flooded his cheeks, and he pulled away. Lilith still stared at him with that same melancholy.

"I'm sorry." He lowered his gaze and removed his hand from her hair.

"Why?" she insisted.

Cohen peered up at her from beneath his furrowed brow. "I already told you. I *love* you."

Lilith took a shaky step backward, her face suddenly flushed. "I…don't feel right."

With a sudden dart of panic, Andrew caught her in his arms. "What's wrong?" He smoothed the hair from her face while frantically searching her eyes. "God, you're burning up."

"Why?" she asked again, moaning in pain and clutching her abdomen.

Absolute hysteria erupted in Cohen's mind, and he sank to the floor with Lilith held tight against him. A deathly pallor had crept into her complexion, and the skin beneath her eyes appeared bruised. He raised his wrist to his mouth, intending to rend through the flesh with his own teeth if it meant saving her, but Lilith halted the movement by grasping his hand.

"It won't help," she whispered.

The truth struck him then. *The virus.* This is what it would do to her because of his moment of selfishness. He had condemned her to this fate.

Andrew crushed her against him, his arms squeezing around her thinning form. "I am so sorry." Tears strained his voice until it broke.

The fullness of her beautiful face slowly disappeared, leaving sunken hollows. Still she stared at him with that *same* expression. Her eyes never left his, even when they yellowed, along with her skin.

He couldn't watch anymore. Andrew squeezed his eyes shut and just held her until all he felt in his embrace were dry bones. Sobs wracked his body when even those disintegrated into dust beneath his touch.

His selfish desires had done this. *He* did this.

"Andrew?" Lilith's confused voice sounded from the stairs.

He whipped around in shock.

Lilith stood a few feet away, healthy as ever, dressed in her lavender nightgown.

Cohen stared down at the ash coating him and frowned. While he tried to make the connection that it was all a dream, the soft sound of bare feet on concrete moved closer.

"Andrew?" she repeated, moving her hand over his shaking shoulder.

After swallowing hard, he turned his tear-streaked face toward her. Confusion and concern filled her eyes while she crouched beside him.

"Are you okay?"

Cohen peered back down, but the ash was gone. A hundred emotions and thoughts all swirled into a cacophony of static. He couldn't tear his eyes away from the spotless scrub pants.

Her fingers softly traced his jaw before guiding his chin, pulling his focus back to her.

"Andrew." Her confused expression deepened. "Are you okay?"

The breath caught in his lungs, and he shook his head, unable to speak. Lilith was so close. God, he could even smell her lavender scent.

It's just a dream, a nightmare, he reminded himself.

Sadness surged against his skin in an unexpected barrage, leaving him dizzy. However, when Lilith bit her bottom lip and ran a palm over his cheek, he nearly fell to pieces.

"How do I help you?" She searched his watery eyes with a determination that somehow felt real, as if it were *really* her staring at him, not some figment of his own demented mind.

"I'm not worth helping." Andrew covered her hand with his, holding it against his cheek and closing his eyes. "I'm sorry, Lily. I should have been better…should have tried harder, but I was selfish. Fuck, I'm *still* selfish." He tried to will his hand to fall away, to let her go, but he just couldn't. The warmth of her touch was too addictive. He craved it like a suffocating man yearned for oxygen.

"Andrew, stop punishing yourself like this. Please."

The desperate plea made him open his eyes. The way she gazed at him, with a mixture of compassion, fear, and devastation, cut him straight to the core.

"I deserve much worse for what I've done." He studied every gorgeous line of her face, memorizing it.

Lilith would suffer, she would wither away, and she would die… because of him.

"What have you done?" she asked with disbelief, as if he couldn't possibly have committed an act bad enough to warrant this punishment.

She grazed his raw and bloody knuckles with her fingers—a delicate touch filled with aching sympathy. The sensation brought fresh tears. He didn't deserve this, any of it, not even in a dream.

"Andrew…none of it matters. We can start over. Be friends. I just need you to hang on until we find you. Please."

Cohen raised his gaze to hers. "There is no way to start over. The damage has already been done. I'm sorry. So fucking sorry." As he had done before, Cohen skimmed her cheek with his thumb and tucked a few blond strands behind her ear.

Lilith's face pinched, and tears escaped her eyes. "I don't want to lose anyone else. Please. *You* matter. *Your life* matters."

"It doesn't," he replied simply.

"It does to *me*," she insisted, with absolute certainty.

The air froze in his lungs, and he stared at her in disbelief. Some small part of himself glowed with hope, but he quickly snuffed it out.

She only feels that way because she doesn't know. She doesn't know what I've done…what I've sentenced her to.

Cohen opened his mouth to tell her, to confess the truth, even if it meant losing her forever, but she disappeared in a blink. His eyes roamed the basement, but it remained as silent and empty as a tomb.

A loud clang of metal woke Cohen from his fitful sleep.

An aluminum serving tray slid through the slot, but when he tried to sit up, a swirling dizziness sent him right back to the mattress. He felt weak, drained somehow, and hot.

A quick glance down his body confirmed his shirt was soaked with sweat. The room felt like a damn sauna. It had to be the virus finally manifesting physical symptoms. The cult *must* have injected him at some point during his torture.

It was all real. Luminita was right, and Lilith would die if he didn't do something. He had to save her.

She was his purpose, his North Star.

The RV came to a stop, startling Lilith awake. She exhaled in ragged gasps, and her head spun when she finally managed to sit up. The nightmare had started as it usually did—in that infernal tunnel—but the end…

Pain flared between her brows, and she rubbed at her temples, trying to make sense of it. Andrew had appeared in her dream again, and he had seemed so broken, so lost, so *real*.

It had to be some manifestation of her guilt over leaving him behind. She had failed him, and now he was at Luminita's mercy.

Mercy. A dark chuckle escaped her lips. Lilith doubted the woman had a single drop of it in her body.

Still, his misery and sadness had seemed so damn real. She had sensed him hovering on that dangerous line, tipping toward oblivion, but why? Kissing her had been a mistake, but no one would end their life over something so insignificant, right? What if there was more? What if there was something else?

Fuck. It was just a dream. Another in a long line of nightmares. Get a fucking grip.

A warm hand caressed her back, and it brought a faint smile to her lips.

"Another nightmare, *cherie?*"

Lilith wiped the tears from her eyes. "Yeah. Another nightmare."

"Me too. Come here." Chance opened his arms, and she curled up against him, resting her cheek on his chest, while he hugged her close. After placing a tender kiss to her forehead, he sighed into her hair. "I wish I could take them away for you."

Lilith traced the lines of his chest. "No one can do that, but you're here when they're over, and that means just as much."

Lilith closed her eyes and let the rhythmic beat of Chance's heart chase everything else away.

Chapter 30

Orchid stared through the windshield at the sprawling concrete building shrouded in darkness. The hulking thing sat there, waiting to devour her, like a dragon crouched among the tall trees. Or perhaps the lab closer resembled the sadistic ship from *Event Horizon*, possessed by hell itself, preparing to torment her with her past.

That metaphor seemed more fitting.

Walking inside meant surrendering, admitting defeat. The odds of her leaving this hellscape were beyond dismal, but what choice did she truly have?

Even if she fought her way in and miraculously defeated Luminita's considerable forces, it would take too long. Noah and Desiree would be dead before she reached them.

But if she could figure out a way to cooperate without endangering Chance, maybe her family could still walk away. Orchid *had* to believe that. She *had* to cling to that desperate hope.

Orchid peered down at the phone in her hand and hesitated. After her internal debate, she sent a quick text to Lilith's phone.

"I want to leave a voicemail. Please, don't answer my call."

Three dots bounced in the left corner and anticipation sent her pulse racing.

"Okay."

A simple reply, but that was best. Orchid took several deep breaths and cleared her throat before pressing the call icon. Blood pounded in her ears with each ring. She was terrified either Lilith or Chance would answer despite her request.

When the generic voicemail greeting started, she exhaled heavily and tried to calm her nerves.

"Chance. I've thought about what to say the entire drive. Nothing will ever be enough. I'm sorry I couldn't tell you this in person. Even if there'd been time, I'm not sure I could have gotten through it. I love you. I have *always* loved you. I'm so sorry I was never the mom you deserved, but…"

Her voice broke with tears, and she forced a few rapid breaths.

"I'm proud of the man you became in spite of everything. I wish I had the time to get to know you, learn about your life, try and make things right between us, but…I *have* to do this. *Please*…don't think I chose them over you or that you're not enough. You were my *everything*. I died that day…when I thought I lost you.

"You are strong…capable. You have people who love you and fight by your side. I'm all Noah and my daughter have, and I can't leave them to suffer for *my* sins. I…" She forced another breath through her constricting throat, determined to finish. "I hope you have a beautiful life that helps you forget the horrible things you've gone through. I wish I could be there to see it. I love you, *petit renard.*"

Orchid jabbed the end-call icon and surrendered to the sobbing tears. Her heart had cracked in two. Discovering her son was alive had summoned starkly contrasting emotions—joy warred with horror, love with guilt—but only having a few hours to see who Chance had become…That *tore her to pieces*, and now…she would never truly know him.

The demonic building waited for her, ready to consume her soul and spit out her bones. Orchid wiped away the tears, but more followed. It took her a moment to make out the clock through her watery vision, but when she did, dread riddled each nerve.

Time was almost up.

Orchid looked down at her phone, a tear splashing on the screen. She couldn't allow Luminita to get her hands on it, but Orchid couldn't bring herself to wipe it either. *If* she managed to get out of this situation, it was the only way she could find Chance and Lilith again.

After a moment's thought, she wedged the phone beneath the driver's seat, ensuring it wouldn't be seen without serious work.

Then she furiously wiped her face, inhaled several deep breaths, steeled her nerves, and opened the SUV's door. The humid night air clung to her skin with the scent of pine, and the waning moon cast everything in a deep blue hue. The gentle whir of machines disrupted the songs of crickets and frogs, like an intrusive predator.

Orchid forced her body to march forward. Each muscle screamed in protest. They instinctually wanted to run in the opposite direction, but her mind refused to give in. The door loomed closer, and her heart thrashed violently against her ribs. When she reached for the handle, tremors ran through her hand, and her throat closed.

Once she opened this door, she could never go back. This was a one-way ticket, and they were expecting her.

Orchid expelled a shuddering breath, rolled her shoulders, and swung the door open to two assault rifles trained on her face.

"Agent Orchid. We need you to disarm. Place all your weapons on the table."

Orchid complied without a word, removing each dagger—nine in total—and her pistol. Once they were all splayed out, one of the mercs spun her around and shoved her face-first against the wall.

A hand between her shoulders kept her pinned while the man patted her down. Several rough kicks to her instep forced her feet apart, and the man moved his hands slower up and down her thighs, which was unnecessary. The black leggings she wore made it impossible to hide anything.

Once satisfied, the merc snatched her wrists and yanked them behind her back. The zip tie he used bit into her skin, but thankfully, it wasn't tight enough to cut off circulation.

Any hope that Luminita might still trust her withered and died. This was Orchid's worst-case scenario.

"Luminita wants to see you in the central lab," the man said gruffly, pulling her away from the wall and shoving her forward.

When she didn't move, the man jabbed the muzzle of a gun into her back, and she stumbled.

"Move!"

Orchid clenched her jaw, biting back her instincts. If it wasn't for the threat to her family, she would sever their spines in a heartbeat. It wouldn't be difficult. A few quick moves and she would have at least one of her daggers.

The muzzle urged her forward again, and she obeyed.

Meeting Luminita in the lab didn't bode well. The tile floor and central drain made cleanup much easier than the woman's apartment. Orchid tried to push the thought from her mind, but the little sliver of hope she had clung to fell away.

They marched her past the closed doors, like the condemned walking Death Row. None of the rooms had plaques or numbers, no identifiers to divulge their secrets. This obviously wasn't where they kept prisoners. With the exception of the security offices, the rest of these rooms were probably staff quarters or general supplies. But Noah and Desiree were in this building somewhere, confused, terrified.

A guard swiped an access key over the sensor, and the lab doors opened. An elbow crashed into her spine this time, sending her shuffling forward awkwardly. When the doors shut behind them, the sound summoned a sinister sense of finality.

"Helena." Luminita's voice dripped with condescension.

Orchid's glare snapped up to the Romanian. Her focus remained there while the mercs shoved her into a chair and zip-tied her legs.

"I'm very disappointed."

Luminita stepped closer, with a vaguely familiar man by her side. Orchid couldn't quite place him. Perhaps she had met him when he was younger, or maybe he just resembled someone she knew. She studied the man's tall form, his silvered hair, and the faint wrinkles lining his angular features. However, it was his light grey eyes, burning with violence, and the regal posture beneath his polished suit which gave her pause.

"Do you recall Aaron Bogdan?" Luminita waved a hand at the man, but as soon as his name left her lips, blood pounded like thunder in Helena's ears. "It was his facility you destroyed when you bungled the job in New Orleans for Farren."

Helena tried to swallow past her tightening throat. She may not have had many interactions with the man, but she'd done her research. Before his life as a seemingly ill-mannered Elder, he had been a warrior, The Great Barbarian of Hungary, feared by the Ottoman and Romanian armies alike. The human histories had been altered, but the Durand kept thorough records.

One corner of Aaron's mouth twitched. "That was...*costly* in many ways." The barely restrained malice in his voice chilled Helena to the bone.

"But..." Luminita interjected. "That is not why I called you." She cast Aaron a sharp glare, which he merely returned. After a tense moment, Luminita dragged her stare back to Helena. "You've been lying to me, little Orchid."

It wasn't a question.

"About what?" Amazingly, Helena managed to keep her voice even.

A vicious smile swept across Luminita's face. "Let's start with Ashcroft."

"Where is my family?" Helena countered, sitting up a bit straighter.

The women locked eyes, a clear challenge waging between them. Luminita's ocean-blue ones were soulless, frigid, and calculating.

"Aaron." Luminita addressed him but kept her piercing scowl on Helena. "Have the guards bring our guests, please."

Despite the staring contest, Helena shifted her attention to Aaron, who bristled at the order. He didn't seem particularly happy with Luminita, or perhaps he didn't like being told what to do. Both seemed equally possible.

Still, the man turned and nodded toward the door behind him.

"Where is Ashcroft?"

Helena refocused on Luminita. "I don't know." *Technically, not a lie.* After throwing his decapitated head in the river, it could have landed anywhere. Maybe it was still out there, bobbing in the water, with fish and creatures nibbling at it.

Luminita's grin widened, and her high heels clicked sharply against the tile, moving closer. "Ah, but you know something, my little tracker. What happened that night? The two men who brought Andrew gave me a full report. Ashcroft and the other targets were injured, and you had six men with you."

"Ashcroft was dangerous, even injured. The men fought him and died." *Again, not a lie.* All six men had battled the monster, and all six men had fallen, although four of them did so by her hands.

"Clever wording." An amused huff escaped Luminita's lips, but before she continued, the door behind her opened.

Helena swung her gaze to Noah, who carried their daughter, Desiree. Guards prodded him forward while he looked around the room. Then, his wild eyes landed on Helena.

"Lena?" he gasped.

"Noah, I'm sorry." It was all she managed to get out.

"Mommy!" Desiree screamed in blissful excitement, but her enthusiasm dimmed when Helena didn't run to her.

"Hi, baby." Orchid's strained voice cracked, and tears flooded her vision. Noah and Desiree became nothing but blurry bits of color.

"Why are you sad?" Her daughter's cherub-like face pinched into a sympathetic pout, and she wiggled out of Noah's arms.

"No, Des! Stop!" he called out, reaching for her, but the girl shot past Luminita and barreled into Helena.

Desiree's little arms wrapped around Orchid's middle, and a memory of Chance doing the same thing as a child plunged Helena into abject misery. She had failed Chance, and now she would fail Desiree too.

"Don't cry, Mom. I missed you too."

"Desi, baby...Look at me." Tears glistened on her daughter's cheeks when she looked up at Helena. "I need you to stay with your dad and be brave, okay? I love you, sweetie."

Although a frown wrinkled the girl's forehead, she wandered back to Noah, peeking over her shoulder the entire time.

"As you can see, they are unharmed." Luminita gestured behind her with an edge of impatience. "Whether they remain that way rests on you."

The click of a gun cocking rang through the lab, and Helena forgot how to breathe. Aaron stood beside Noah, his gun pressed to her husband's head, while Desiree cowered by his feet, crying.

"No! Stop!" Helena shouted in sheer desperation.

Luminita stormed over to Aaron, whispering something in vehement tones. The man narrowed his haunting silver eyes, but he let his arm fall to his side.

"Fine. Have your fucking games," Aaron grumbled.

Luminita smoothed her emerald blouse and dark grey pencil skirt, then met Helena's panicked gaze. "You have until morning to consider your options."

She signaled the guards behind her.

"Take them back to their cell and put Orchid in with them."

Relief flooded Helena's body, and for the first time since she had arrived, her muscles relaxed. The tiny sliver of hope she had abandoned reappeared. Perhaps there was still a way out of all this.

The mercs cut her loose and escorted her over to Noah and Desiree. Her daughter immediately hugged her waist, but her husband kept his distance, staring at her like he would a stranger. It wasn't far from the truth.

He knew next to nothing about her life before him—not the jobs, the assassinations, the Durand, Bastien, or Chance. Noah didn't even know the true extent of her previous heroin addiction, just that she attended weekly NA meetings.

Wormwood

Helena opened her mouth to say something to him…anything…

But nothing came.

She merely stared at Noah, heartbroken and shattered. Even if they all made it out of there alive, she had lost him.

The guards nudged them roughly through the door and into the prisoner's wing.

Chapter 31

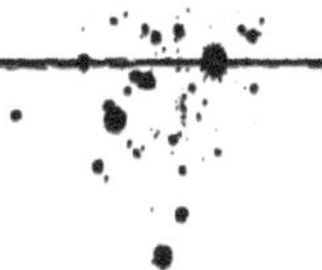

A soft breeze rustled the leaves, making the humid night a little more tolerable. For a second, Nicci stood on the RV steps, eyes closed, breathing in the scent of pine and gardenia.

She missed camping. Alicia had *not* been an "outdoorsy" kind of gal, and Nicci hadn't taken a solo trip in years.

For an RV park, this place was nice. Strings of warm white lights illuminated the campground's center, lending it an ethereal quality. Picnic benches ringed an unlit firepit and several grills. It made for a beautiful communal meeting place, where campers could get to know each other. Of course, at three in the morning, the other visitors were fast asleep.

Nicci glanced down at her reheated box of eggs and hashbrowns and her ice-cold Mountain Dew. *Breakfast of champions.* Despite her rather active and athletic lifestyle, she had the diet habits of a college frat boy.

Nicci grinned at Tim and Eileen, who sat quietly in the softly lit hangout, and headed for their bench. Lilith and Chance were still struggling to wake up, and Gibson and Keller were attending to their license plate exchange. That left Tim and Eileen for company.

Third wheel it is. Nicci didn't mind, not really. Tim was far too entertaining to poke fun at, and she doubted they would mind her crashing their party.

"Hey there, big fella. How's the leg?" Nicci plopped down across from them with a smile.

"Sore, but I'll live," Tim grumbled between bites.

"Aww. The drugs wore off, huh?" Nicci flashed a smirk at Eileen, who grinned conspiratorially.

"Yeah, about an hour ago," the agent supplied before Tim could answer.

"Such a shame." Nicci sighed for dramatic effect. "He was funny on pain meds."

Nicci took a bite of eggs and peeked up at Tim's deep blush.

"I'll have you know, I'm always funny."

"Not *that* funny." Nicci snorted, rolling her eyes.

Eileen unsuccessfully tried to stifle a laugh.

Tim swung his attention to her with a playful glare. "You're supposed to be on my side."

The pixie woman bit down on her lip but still grinned. "I am!" she squeaked, laughing once more.

Tim refocused on Nicci, jabbing his fork in her direction. "Do you see what you've done? My girlfriend is laughing at me."

As soon as the words left his mouth, Tim seemed to register that he had never really called her that before, bringing the blush right back to his cheeks. Eileen's eyes went wide, but her smile turned positively radiant.

"So, it's all official, then?" Nicci glanced between the two of them with a hopeful gleam.

Tim opened his mouth to say something, but Eileen spoke up before he could. "Yes. All official."

Tim peeked over at her. They shared a look, then he grinned back at Nicci.

"Are you sure? I mean, Tim doesn't have a track record. Like…at all."

Tim's grin turned to a glower, but Eileen's laughter softened it some.

"You." He jabbed his fork again. "You are always causing problems."

"And yet you love me anyway." Nicci beamed a sugar-sweet smile. "Hey, Eileen. Do you know how I met this gentle giant?"

"Nicci." The growled warning didn't seem playful this time.

"Oh, come on! It's funny!"

"It's really not," Tim replied flatly.

After giving him a brilliant smile which clearly said "trust me," Nicci turned toward Agent Hersch. "So, I get this call from Lilith, asking for my help. Officially, we were partners, but Lil was out on bereavement. We hadn't met in person."

"Seriously, Nic. Please," Tim pleaded, dropping his fork.

"Anyway, Lilith shows up at my apartment, with this big guy and Cohen in tow. Needless to say, Andrew immediately pissed me off."

"Makes sense." Eileen giggled.

"But this one"—Nicci poked her fork in Tim's direction—"he was so polite…asking me how long I'd lived in New York City and if I liked it."

A glance at Tim told her she was treading on dangerously thin ice.

"Anyway, I straight-up accused him of hitting on me and told him he had the wrong equipment for my tastes. The blush on his face was positively radioactive!"

Eileen covered her mouth and chuckled, which eased the tension in Tim's face a touch.

"I was completely wrong, by the way," Nicci continued, which brought a surprised expression to Tim's face. "After centuries dealing with misogynistic vamps and being a female detective in the NYPD, I'm a little hypersensitive to male attention. Turns out, Tim is just a great person."

Nicci grinned warmly at her friend, and the corner of his mouth tilted in a lopsided smile.

"And now, the big lug is my best friend *and* the best sparring partner I could ask for."

"I thought Lilith had the top spot."

"Okay, so you're tied for first. That's still pretty special."

"Well, thank you, pipsqueak. You're tied for first on my list too. Although, Chance really needs to get his head out of his ass, or he's gonna drop a rank. Hopefully, a little sleep did him some good. There's a few things we need to discuss as a group."

"Such as?" Nicci shoveled another bite into her mouth. Electing for onions, mushrooms, cheese, and country gravy had definitely been the right move.

"We have to take some precautions because of the contracts out on us. We aren't the only ones in danger."

When a deep frown creased Tim's brow, Eileen rubbed his arm with a sympathetic expression. Whatever he was referring to, they had obviously already talked about it.

"What's wrong?" Chance asked, rounding the table with Lilith close behind.

"Something we need to do while we're in the city," Tim replied.

Chance nodded, as if he already understood. "We need to create a list…anyone publicly linked to us."

Nicci frowned and turned to Tim. Maybe it was the sleep deprivation, but she needed more clarification.

"Jill. As long as there are professionals hunting us, she's in danger."

For some reason, that had never occurred to Nicci. Possibly because Jill was human, or maybe because Nicci didn't want to think about who else could be a potential pressure point. A chill crept into her gut.

"I mean…in Jill's case, it might take some time to connect us. She…still uses her married name"—a fact which obviously disturbed Tim—"but I visit her at least once a week. Everyone at the group home knows me as Jill's brother, Tim."

Nicci was listening, or rather, she was *trying* to, but the growing awareness and dread clawing at her skull drowned out some of the words.

"Gloria and the girls. I spend a lot of time there, and a quick search will show Alvarez as my late partner. It wouldn't be a stretch to assume I'm still close to his family."

About half of Lilith's words registered, but barely. Nicci couldn't seem to focus past what all this meant, what she would have to do.

"Anyone else?" Chance peered around the table.

Nicci's shoulders slumped. She had no choice. "Alicia," she muttered.

Everyone at the table seemed confused by her reluctant tone, except Lilith and Chance. They were the only ones who knew what had happened.

"I…uh…broke up with Alicia before I left New York to join you guys at the cabin."

"What?" Tim blurted. "Why?"

The weight of everyone's stares made Nicci's skin want to crawl right off. She scratched at her arm reflexively and shot a glare at Tim, but she quickly lowered her gaze to her half-eaten food.

"Precisely because of shit like this! If the woman was *ever* on time, she would have been in my apartment when it was ransacked. Alicia would have died *because of me*. It's not fair, especially when I can't be honest about why."

Tim reached across the table to grasp her hand. Nicci peeked up at his compassionate frown and nearly cried.

"I'm sorry, Nic."

One side of her mouth lifted in a weak smile. "That's the life we lead. Being a cop is dangerous enough, but secrets are part of the deal." She allowed her eyes to drift to Eileen. "At least, they usually are."

Pink blossomed over the agent's cheeks.

"Nothing against you, Eileen," Nicci swiftly added. "I'm glad the big fella found you. The man needs someone to keep him in check, and you're an exception to pretty much all the rules."

"Thanks," Eileen replied quietly.

Nicci rubbed her face and groaned. "Can we *please* change the subject already?"

"What about Gibson and Keller? Do they have anyone we need to consider?" Eileen swooped in, rescuing her.

Nicci couldn't have been more grateful.

Tim shook his head. "No family, no significant others. I'll double-check with them when they get back, though."

"Okay." Eileen took a bite of her egg-white omelet while she thought. "We have three adults and…how many kids?"

"Three," Lilith stated.

"I can call in a few favors. The suits in the New York office owe John and I for taking the Cappalletty case. I should be able to arrange a safe house and a few men to stand guard."

"Are you sure?" A wary look creased Tim's face. "This could be construed as an inappropriate use of resources."

"My name…and John's are on a hit list for professional killers. If the FBI doesn't already know, they will soon. I can use that to ask for manpower and resources legitimately."

"What about your dad and sister?" Tim asked.

"I'll call Kim, but they live in Tucson. I doubt she'll take anything I say seriously." The anger and resentment in Eileen's voice indicated they had a less-than-stellar relationship. "As for dad…we don't speak."

"What if Boston has spies in the bureau? I mean, he kept David from losing his badge."

Lilith had poised an excellent question, but Nicci was confident she already knew the agent's answer.

Eileen shrugged. "I can ask them to keep it off the books, and I know someone in New York I can trust. Still…I can't promise it's foolproof. I'm all ears if anyone has a better idea."

Of course, no one did.

Solasta had already been breached once, and at least an FBI safe house would provide some anonymity, even if only temporarily. Nicci couldn't really see a safer option.

"Okay. Eileen, make your calls. We'll get everyone settled into the safe house before heading to Solasta." Chance laid out everything calmly, as if Nicci wasn't about to upend Alicia's life *after* breaking her heart.

"What's the plan once we have the ghost drive?"

Nicci, so grateful for the subject change, could have kissed Tim. However, when she peered over at her partner, Lilith wore a tight smile that wasn't the least bit comforting.

"First…" Lilith shifted her focus to Nicci. "We'll need to decrypt it."

"I can handle that. No problem." Hacking was simple. It was all ones and zeros—pure and simple logic, unlike relationships.

Lilith nodded and idly pushed her food around with her fork.

Fuck. Whatever she has planned, we are not *gonna like it.*

"Then…we need a virologist."

Nicci froze, a forkful of hashbrowns halfway to her mouth. She knew damn well where this train of thought was going.

"What about Solasta?" Tim offered.

But it wasn't that simple if Lilith was acting this cagey.

"They all have different specialties, but Dr. Scott was the only virologist. They had one at Goditha, but—"

"Luminita slaughtered everyone," Chance added.

"Right. I…" Lilith sucked in a deep breath. Her eyes danced around the group.

Here we go, Nicci thought.

"I asked Dr. Preston, and he has someone he trusts."

Nicci just stared at her partner, as did everyone else. *A human? She wants to entrust this to a human?*

Chance recovered first. "You want to hand the cult virus and *all* their research to a human?"

Lilith pushed out a heavy sigh. "Dr. Preston already knows about us."

"What?" Chance dropped his fork.

Apparently, Lilith hadn't gotten around to filling him in on that part.

"I had no choice, Chance. He performed surgery on you, helped keep our identities hidden, supplied Nicci and I with units of blood…Hell, I gave him six vials of my blood tonight."

Chance peered around at everyone, still shocked. "You all knew about this?"

"Yeah," Nicci answered first. "She's right. We didn't have a choice. Dr. Preston has been trustworthy so far."

"That doesn't mean—" Chance began, but Lilith cut him off.

"The virus has already crossed into the human population. It's only a few stages away from a full-blown pandemic. Time is critical, and they'll have incentive to complete the work. This isn't just about us…not anymore."

Chance leaned his elbows on the table and dragged a hand through his hair. "This really should be Antonio's call. We need to fill him in."

"Okay. I know, but—"

Chance turned a glare on Lilith, making her pause, but Nicci jumped right in.

"Lil, this is not Aaron. Antonio is *not* the enemy!"

"I get that, and I'm not disagreeing. I just want to wait until we *actually have* the ghost drive. There's no sense kicking a hornet's nest if the drive isn't there…if I'm wrong."

Nicci tossed her fork down and locked eyes with Lilith. They needed *very* clear terms.

"*If* the ghost drive is there, *if* we retrieve it successfully, and *if* I can decrypt it, we call Antonio *immediately*. *If* any of those steps fail, we *still* tell Antonio about everything we know. No more conversations with Dr. Preston until we speak to Antonio. *Period.*"

"Agreed," Lilith responded hastily.

Thank fucking God. Nicci had expected a fight or, at least, resistance. Maybe Lilith was finally starting to understand the hierarchy's importance.

One can hope.

Chapter 32

Aaron glared at the dark liquid, tightening his hand around the glass of bourbon. His third drink hadn't even taken off the edge. Everything itched ferociously beneath his skin, *especially* Luminita Dragomir, for multiple reasons.

She wanted him feral and bloodthirsty but, apparently, only with her. When he had moved to dispense some long-overdue punishment, Luminita had tugged on his damn leash, pulling him up short, as if he were merely her dog. The thought summoned an old memory of the inn at Deva, but Aaron shoved it aside before it could fully form. That was a very long time ago…a different life entirely…before she had corrupted everything.

Orchid's fiasco at his lab thirty-four years ago had set back their joint venture by decades, cost him one of his best scientists—Bastien Deveraux—and spawned the man who was currently a thorn in his side. Orchid *deserved* to suffer.

He'd wanted to dole out justice much sooner, but instead he'd waited while Luminita orchestrated her games. She'd let Orchid play house, allowing the agent to believe she had a future, freedom. It was an illusion, but as the years dragged by, Aaron's impatience had festered, like so many other things.

Now that the agent had failed spectacularly, it was *finally* time for retribution, or so he had thought.

No. Of course, Luminita has more damn games planned. The woman always *has plans.*

To his irritation, she rarely decided to share them, much less include him, at least since his departure from Oarzina. There had been a brief time when they had been equals, when they had plotted together, shared a life. It seemed like some impossible fever dream now.

Luminita was absolutely infuriating, but that had always been part of her appeal, always drawing Aaron to her like a magnet. She challenged him like no one else ever had, which made her frustratingly irresistible. Of course, ever since Vlad's capture, she had been more interested in keeping Aaron at a distance—detached control.

A slow grin formed, and his thoughts wandered to earlier this evening when Luminita had finally pushed him enough to take the power from her.

For that one exhilarating moment, she had been putty in his hands, and the feel of her shattering around him had been worth the pain, worth her sharp words, even worth her callous dismissal. In his impossibly long life, he had never desired anything more than to bury himself inside her heat and feel her come undone.

Aaron craved her like blood from the first time she'd put him on his knees nearly eight hundred years ago. And it had been everything he thought it would be, but…some crucial component was still missing. Perhaps her lack of acknowledgement soured the moment.

Luminita could pretend all she wanted that he hadn't touched something true in her, but Aaron knew better now. If only she had allowed it to happen centuries ago on Dragobete instead of corrupting the moment. He couldn't help but wonder what their life would have looked like.

Would they have avoided Vlad Dracul and all the pain he'd brought them both? Would they have had all those centuries together? Did it matter now?

They had allowed an ocean of misery to separate them, to turn them into something dark and twisted. He couldn't change that fact.

His thoughts returned to one specific moment. She had *asked* him to bite her.

There had been a time when even his lips on her throat had thrown her into absolute panic. It was something she had feared so completely, she had made Aaron vow never to taste her blood. Now, he truly knew why.

He had felt it when she shattered, not the physical reaction, but the fracture of her mental armor and what lay beneath.

A knock drew him from his thoughts, and he narrowed his eyes on the door.

Another knock—louder this time.

Aaron drained his glass and lounged back in his chair. Only one person would bang on his door at this late hour, and he was more than happy to make her wait.

The anger he sensed roiling on the other side of the door was another delicious clue.

It was odd, *feeling* her emotions. Since they'd met, Luminita had only allowed him to see what she wanted and had used that to manipulate him. Even those raw moments between them, in the small villages around Beszterce, were suspect. Aaron could never be sure what was real. But now, he knew with certainty.

The doorknob turned but not far since he had locked it. A series of rapid knocks made him grin. Her mounting frustration built like a gathering storm, and he was waiting for the lightning to strike.

"Aaron!" Luminita yelled sharply, banging on the door in a staccato rhythm.

With a devilish smirk, Aaron finally rose from his chair. He took his time, enjoying each pound of her fist on the wood and every biting word which passed her lips. By the time he flipped the lock and cracked the door open, she was positively fuming, vibrating with an intoxicating rage.

"Nita," he stated calmly. His gaze raked over her flushed skin and piercing blue eyes. "Did you want something?"

Her glare sharpened to a point, and she shoved past him. "I suppose you think your little plan to rile me up is clever."

Aaron closed the door with slow, careful movements. Something about witnessing Luminita in this furious state brought a sense of calm, easing the incessant itch beneath his skin. Perhaps because it was something honest from her instead of more lies.

He strolled over to where she stood, purposefully avoiding eye contact until he towered over her. "Ah, that's right. You don't like being ignored."

Anger flared, and she shot her hand out to slap him, but he intercepted her wrist. "Not tonight, Nita." In a smooth movement, he wrenched her arm behind her back and used it to press her lithe body firmly against his.

"Let me go," Luminita demanded in a lethal tone, only increasing his arousal…and hers, he noted.

Aaron leaned down, brushing his lips along the shell of her ear when he whispered. "I know that's not what you really want." He captured her lobe in his teeth, biting only hard enough to make her tremble, before releasing her and backing away.

Luminita glared at him with malice and smoothed her emerald blouse. "You know notingk of vhat I vant, Sălbatic."

He didn't need her ability to sense emotion in that moment. The way her accent thickened betrayed her true feelings. The slip only occurred these days when she was truly furious.

"If you say so." Aaron scoffed. "Why *are* you here?"

"To explain why I couldn't let you kill Orchid's husband and why we can't just slaughter them."

"And why is that?" Aaron poured himself another bourbon to stave off his own anger. It was bad enough the woman never filled him in on the full breadth of her schemes, but the condescending tone made his bones ache.

"I have plans."

"You said that already," Aaron growled. "It's not an explanation. Of course, you've never excelled at those, have you?"

Luminita rolled her eyes, as if *he* was the one being dramatic. "I have one last job for her, and I can't ensure her cooperation if you kill both the hostages."

"A job?" Aaron downed his drink, slammed the glass on the table, and moved to loom over her again. "Drawing her into this plot *at all* was idiotic."

"She served a purpose."

Luminita's defiant glare made his blood heat. He wanted to pin her to the wall and fuck the look right off her face, replacing it with pain and ecstasy, but he tempered his desire for now.

"Did she?" Aaron took a step closer until their bodies nearly touched, forcing her to tilt her head up to hold eye contact.

"She found Cohen's cabin."

"And cost us a priceless asset," Aaron snarled. "You can't trust her. She wants to destroy you…us, and you want to let her walk out of here?"

"On this job, I *can* trust her. The target is one she will *not* refuse, and we will have her daughter for leverage."

Aaron studied her, taking in every line of her face and flicker of emotion beneath it. "And after this job?"

Luminita's hooded gaze bored into him. "I don't leave loose ends."

"What about the husband? What is your *plan* for him?"

The cunning glint in her eyes, the wicked curve of her lips, the predatory sense of her delight, all seduced him, had *always* seduced him.

Follow me, Sălbatic, and I'll whisper my secrets while we tear a bloody path through the world. She had said that to him once, when they'd first met.

"You'll see in the morning," she teased.

Of course, she had never fulfilled her first part of the promise, never whispered her secrets. Like always, Luminita had kept them to herself.

Aaron skimmed his fingers over the thin fabric of her blouse, the delicate column of her throat, and sank them into her raven curls, gripping tight. "Or you could tell me now."

Arousal pulsated over her skin, but her lips pressed into a firm line. She was fighting her desire in favor of control, but it still existed, burning like smoldering coals. Perhaps it always had.

A twist of his hand pulled her hair tight. Her lips parted, and she sucked in a sharp breath, which ended on a faint moan.

Ah…there it is.

Aaron leaned in closer, wearing a devilish grin. "What's that, Nita? I didn't hear you."

Hatred seethed in her eyes, but lust still vibrated beneath his fingertips. "This is a pathetic display, even for you!"

The woman's biting words sounded venomous, and if he hadn't drunk Luminita's blood, he might have believed them. He wondered just how long she had been hiding behind that façade. Before Dragobete? After? Did it truly matter anymore?

Regardless, he wanted to rip away her carefully crafted veneer, now that he saw it for what it was. Lies, nothing but lies.

"Is it now?" After releasing her hair, he stalked around her, soaking in every delectable inch tensed with pure need. He now knew what affected her and how. The advantage he held made him positively ravenous, but Luminita needed to be taught a lesson.

The woman straightened, pretending his assessing eyes didn't bother her, and started toward the door.

Aaron swiftly cut off her retreat.

"You are *not* leaving," he stated firmly.

"Yes. I. Am." She emphasized each word, and her luminous blue eyes narrowed with honest anger.

Aaron took a step forward, and Luminita backed up, maintaining her distance.

"No." He took another, and so did she. "You. Are. *Not.*"

The dance continued until Luminita's back hit the wall. Her eyes widened slightly, and he placed his hands on either side of her, caging her in.

Apprehensive desire quickened her breaths, making her chest rise and fall rapidly. The dark of her eyes expanded until only a rim of blue remained.

Gods…The energy pulling taut between them, like it had all those centuries ago, was exhilarating. It was the first breath after drowning in an ocean of meaningless motions, cowering to mediocrity in order to stay hidden. This…Luminita…reminded him of who he was.

"I should thank you for my gift." When a crease formed between her brows, Aaron clarified. "Your blood."

The realization struck her like a bolt of lightning, and her eyes locked on his with fear—a *bone-deep* fear. That intoxicating sensation scorched through Aaron, blistering his arteries. She must have been truly distracted if it took her this long to make the connection. Vlad had told him what drinking her blood would do, but…the reality paled in comparison to his malicious comments.

"You can't hide behind your games and venom anymore, little Nita. I sense your emotions…I know what you crave." Aaron hovered closer, to whisper against her ear and drink in her scent. "You want the frenzy. You want the consuming chaos to snatch control from your grip. Perhaps you always have."

He dragged his lips over the rioting pulse beneath her skin.

"But you don't want to surrender. You want it savagely forced from you…at least in appearance. You don't crave abuse. You crave dominance…*my* dominance."

"Stop!" Luminita shoved at his chest with an angry snarl, but only because he was right. Her wanton need flooded the air until it was all he could sense.

Aaron met her gaze with deadly conviction. "No. I warned you, Nita. I told you next time I wouldn't be so fucking nice, and *you* are the one who didn't want me to ask permission, remember?"

"I'm not interested in fluffing your ego, Aaron." Her ocean-blue eyes turned icy, but her body flushed with more heat than a damn inferno. The woman was practically melting in front of him.

"Take off your skirt." He snapped the order with commanding authority.

Luminita stood still as stone, but he sensed the confliction in her.

Aaron snatched her throat, squeezing the delicate thing while she swallowed. "I am *not* asking."

When she still refused to move, his grip tightened until he sensed her pain and panic start to boil over.

"Now!" he growled against her ear.

A choking gasp escaped her lips, but her hands stiffly moved to her waist, unzipping the infuriatingly tight skirt.

Aaron eased his hold enough to let her drag in a few breaths. "That's a good girl." Those words elicited a hypnotic rage from the petite Romanian.

As desperate as she was for oblivion, to lose the control she held onto so tightly, she resented that weakness and despised him for seeing her vulnerability. But obviously not enough to stop him. She could, easily. At any time, she could drain him, weaken him, put him on his knees. Instead, Luminita fisted his shirt and tore it open.

Of course, Aaron had no interest in her regaining any ground.

Before her nails could scratch his chest, he released her throat, snatched both her wrists, and pinned them to the wall above her head. "No claws tonight, kitten." He forced her wrists higher, lengthening her body to its limit while still allowing her high heels to touch the ground.

The blend of sexual heat, fear, and fury made every inch of him rock hard until his cock strained against his slacks.

"Let go," Luminita demanded slowly, but it held no substance.

Aaron maneuvered to pin her wrists with one hand, testing her. He knew Luminita's strength. His grip would only hold if she wanted it.

She continued to stare at him, her breaths labored, but she didn't fight. *Pity.*

With his free hand, Aaron roughly shoved her skirt down until it pooled around her candy-apple red stilettos. Her muscles flinched and quivered, but Luminita still didn't push against him, didn't struggle to get free.

"See…you tell me to let you go, you snarl insults, and yet…" He raked his nails up her thigh with enough pressure to redden the skin without breaking it.

A hissing breath washed over his cheek, and her muscles trembled beneath his touch. When his fingers reached the apex, a feral grin split his lips.

"And yet, you…" He leaned back enough to capture her fierce gaze. "You, my Goddess of Blood and Chaos, are absolutely soaked."

An audible swallow preceded an erotic moan, which rushed against his lips. Her hips moved, desperate for more friction from his fingertips, and Aaron drank it all in with a triumphant grin. Then he pulled his hand away.

The surge of fury was almost as enjoyable as her carnal need. Aaron took a minute to savor it before pushing off the wall and stalking toward his bourbon.

"What are you doing?" Luminita's sharp tone held an edge of desperation.

Hmm…Pushing her seemed to weaken that callous façade of hers. If only he had tried that sooner.

Aaron peered over his shoulder. The woman still stood against the wall, skirtless and breathless.

"Having a drink. I'm done. You can leave." Aaron turned his attention back to his glass and poured a generous serving. Every cell in his body screamed to pin her against the wall and thrust inside her with violent abandon, but a message had to be sent.

A malevolent laugh rang through the room. "*You're* done? *I* can leave?"

Aaron took a slow swig, ignoring her.

A rustle of fabric sounded, followed by the whir of a zipper, and she approached with a tidal wave of outrage.

"Either tell me what you have in store for Orchid's husband or get out. Your choice."

The furious footsteps halted.

Aaron took another long sip, waiting. He silently prayed she would just give in. If Luminita responded with a true answer, he could surrender to his lust and ravage the woman in every way he had always wanted to.

Her heels clicked toward the door and a bittersweet smile curved his lips. *Luminita Dragomir does not simply give in. She never has.*

Aaron's hand gravitated to his pocket, like it frequently did when memories resurfaced. His fingertips grazed the outline of the object hidden there, both a familiar comfort and an old wound.

Chapter 33

Helena ran her fingers through the dark silken hair of her daughter, who was asleep on her lap. The poor little thing was exhausted, and it hadn't taken long for her to drift off after the night's excitement. A soft smile played across Helena's lips before she looked toward Noah.

Since the guards shoved them in the cell, he hadn't moved from his position by the door, leaning against the wall with his back to her. He hadn't spoken a single word.

Of course, neither his stance nor his silence shielded Helena from the constant ebb of anger and betrayal pulsating through his body, but he wouldn't have known that. Noah had no clue who or what she was. He was only aware of the persona she had worn for the past few years.

"Who are you…really?" Noah's sharp tone cut through the quiet, threatening to cleave her in two.

"I never wanted to lie to you, Noah. I swear."

Her husband stood away from the wall and turned an unforgiving stare on her. The once happy and loving face, with soft green eyes, thick stubble, and a dimpled chin, contorted into something unrecognizable.

"Answer the question," he demanded with steely resolve.

This is not the man I married. I did this. I caused this callous change, made a wreck of his life, lied to him.

Helena swallowed the sudden swell of guilt. "My real name is Helena Vieux."

"The woman called you Orchid. Why?" His stare raked over her like a burning touch until it landed on her tattoo—an orchid with a purple background gracing her forearm. "A nickname?"

"No," she replied. Helena was done lying. The likelihood of them surviving was remote. The least she could do was come clean before they died. "A code name."

Noah raised his eyebrows in surprise before the scowl returned. "Code name? Like, a spy?"

"Of sorts." Helena knew he would assume the government, but one problem at a time.

"And you work for these…people?"

"I *did.*"

"But not now?"

"No," she admitted with a pained sigh. "I…disobeyed orders."

"And that's why we're here? Me and Desi? Because you fucked up a job?"

The accusation cut through her heart like razor wire, mostly because it was true. Helena averted her gaze to take in the gentle curves of Desi's face. Her eyes misted.

"Yes."

"Why?"

"Why what?"

"Why did you go against orders if you knew *this* was a possibility? Is that why you asked us to go to Frankie and Jen's?"

Guilt clogged her throat like condensed bile. "Yes. What happened to Frankie and Jen?" Helena hadn't even thought about that until now. If they had found her family there…

"Nothing. A neighbor called me. She said the basement was flooding and I needed to get back right away. When Desi and I got there…Well, someone knocked me out, and I woke up here."

A sigh of relief escaped before Helena considered the neighbor's fate. Luminita didn't leave loose ends. At least one innocent person had already died because she had kept Noah in the dark.

"Why did you disobey orders?" he repeated in clipped tones.

"Luminita—the woman you met—is dangerous. She needed to be stopped." But that wasn't the true reason. She had always known the Romanian was a formidable and deadly woman. Helena hadn't made it her mission to destroy Luminita until Goditha, until she had uncovered the demon's despicable lie.

A huff from Noah brought her back to the present.

"All for the greater good, huh? Are our lives worth it, Lena…Helena, whatever the hell your name is?"

Helena focused on the floor, unable to answer those questions.

"How long?"

When she didn't answer, Noah tried again.

"How long have you been a fucking spy?"

The seconds it took for Helena to meet his indignant stare felt like hours. The man deserved the truth. The *entire* truth.

"Forty-five years, although I've been retired for the past twenty."

Noah balked, wrinkling his forehead. "Forty-five years," he repeated in a whisper. "But...you're only thirty-six."

"I'm not," Helena replied, slumping her shoulders. "I'm seventy-eight."

The hesitant step back seemed instinctual, and his eyes opened impossibly wide.

"What?" Noah shook his head, refusing to accept her answer. "No. That's *not* possible. I mean, Desi..." The words trailed off when his eyes landed on his daughter.

"It is possible." Helena returned her stare to the concrete, avoiding the horror in his eyes. "My people siphon off emotional energy. It keeps us young, heals wounds, prevents disease, and grants us some unique abilities."

"This isn't funny, Lena. Seriously? What the hell are you talking about? None of that can be true." The frantic, disjointed rebuttal barely registered over the man's panic.

A heaving sigh pushed past her lips. "It's all true, Noah. Watch."

Helena slid the tie from her blond hair, letting the tresses spill over her shoulders. She closed her eyes and focused on Helena Vieux, the woman Chance knew as his mother.

"What the hell?" Fear surged from Noah's direction. "Your hair...your face..."

Helena opened her eyes but still couldn't meet his.

"Even your irises are a different color." Sawing breaths followed his words, and Noah's panic flooded the room.

"This is Helena Vieux, the woman I was before I met you, the woman who died twenty years ago."

"What do you mean?" Not a single prickle of compassion lingered in his voice. The question was a demand for information, and her heart fractured a bit more.

"Noah...you *have* to understand."

"No! I don't." The snapped response was another sharp jab to her chest.

"Please, just let me finish." When he remained silent, Helena continued. "I was trapped in a horrible hell twenty years ago. I was living with an abusive monster who kept me high to control me. I…I tried to escape with my son, but—"

"Son? You have other kids?"

Something in Noah's tone drew her attention, and she met his gaze. It actually seemed a little softer.

"One, although…I was told he died in the car crash that almost killed me. Some days, I wished it would have. The person I was…she died the moment Luminita convinced me I no longer had a son."

For the first time, a flicker of regret flashed in his green eyes. Silence filled the space between them while Noah studied her. "You said 'convinced you'…She lied?"

Helena nodded, not trusting her voice.

"He's alive?" Noah leaned against the wall, arms crossing his chest.

She nodded again.

"And that's why you disobeyed orders? Because you were mad at her?" His tone hardened, making the implication clear.

"I thought I could keep you and Desi safe. I never wanted to put your lives in danger."

A muscle ticked in Noah's jaw, and her heart sank even further. She hadn't thought that was possible.

"Yet here we are. They could kill us because of what you've done, and we don't even truly know you."

Tears flooded her eyes. "You knew the best parts of me. Desi is proof of that. I was the person I wanted to be with you, Noah. That should count for something."

Noah's eyes glistened, but he lowered his gaze. "Playing house is not a relationship. None of it was real, was it?"

The fissure in her chest cracked open, like the Mariana Trench, and tears spilled down her cheeks. "Of course, it was! I love you. You and Desi gave me a reason to keep living…" Her voice broke with the threat of heaving sobs.

Noah rubbed his watery eyes but didn't move from his spot by the door.

"I left everything behind when I met you. I didn't want any part in this life. I just wanted you and Desi."

This time, Noah covered his face and crouched against the wall. His shoulders shook.

Helena wanted to go to him, hold him, and kiss apologies into his skin until he forgave her. But the weight of Desiree in her lap pinned her to the spot.

"How am I supposed to trust anything you say?" Sobs strained his voice, making it ragged.

"There were things about my past I *couldn't* tell you. My kind are very secretive, and telling you would put you in danger. There were also things…I didn't *want* to tell you because it's not who I am anymore."

Noah surged to his feet and knelt in front of her, but the anger in his eyes seared right through her. "That is *obviously* not true, or we wouldn't be here right now."

"I didn't have a choice! If I had…I would have chosen you."

Noah's stare softened again but still pinned her in place. "What was the job?"

A frown creased Helena's brow. "Why do you want to know that?"

"Because I want to know who the hell I married."

Helena studied his clenched jaw, the tight skin around his eyes, the determined line of his mouth…

"Luminita needed me to track down a group of assets…people. That was my mission."

Suspicion clouded his gaze. "What *exactly* did that entail?"

The nervous swallow immediately gave her away. She couldn't sugarcoat things, not if she wanted a chance at forgiveness.

After glancing down at Desi to make sure she was still asleep, Helena locked eyes with her husband.

"In order to flush them out, I had to kill an FBI agent, plant a tracker on his partner, and follow them to Alabama."

The color drained from Noah's face. "You…killed someone?"

"It wasn't my first time or my last." Helena flashed a sad smile full of defeat.

"How many people have you killed?"

Helena diverted her attention to the cinderblock wall across the room. She felt every flicker of disgust and horror cracking her marriage apart. "More than I care to remember."

"How many?" he insisted.

"Noah, you don't understand. As soon as my gifts developed…as soon as my people knew I could shift my appearance, I was thrown into a life of violence. I trained for fifteen years because I had *no choice*. I was either useful or I was dead."

"How many, Lena?" Sadness infused each word, but she didn't dare hope Noah would truly understand.

Helena released a heartbroken sigh. "One hundred and thirty-three."

Noah shot to his feet and stumbled backward. For a few moments, he simply gawked at her and tried to breathe. After a flickering glance at Desi, still curled up in Helena's lap, he found his voice again.

"How many since we've been together?"

"None until Luminita forced this mission on me. I swear it."

"And since then?"

"Six…including the FBI agent. But three of those were Luminita's men, and one was a *true* monster. That's why she's so angry. Luminita wanted the demented thing alive, and I couldn't let an insatiable killer live, much less hand him over to her."

"So…that's the real reason we're here? Because *you* passed judgment on another murderer?" Noah hurried forward, pulled Desi into his arms, and sank to the floor on the other side of the room.

"Noah," Helena pleaded, immediately missing the warm weight of her daughter. "You don't understand."

"Make me understand, Lena. What did you do?"

"I killed Luminita's monster and saved my son."

"And our lives were worth accomplishing that? Was it a fair trade? Us for them?"

Helena drew her legs up, resting her cheek on her knee. "I thought I could keep you safe. I'm sorry, Noah. I'm sorry for all of it."

"I don't think that matters now." The anger left his voice. He just sounded tired.

"I'll do whatever I can to save you both. If…" She drew in a breath, trying to let herself hope. "If I can get you out of here, my phone is under the driver's seat of my SUV. Call the last number. Tell them who you are. They'll help you. I know they will." Helena hugged her legs tighter and stared at him through watery eyes. "I wish I'd met you first."

A wounded expression crossed his face, and tears filled his hypnotic green eyes. "I wish you had too."

Chapter 34

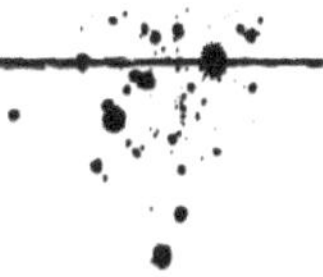

Andrew expelled a sigh of pure relief after splashing cold water over his head and neck. It only lasted a few seconds. The heat seemed impossible to escape. The air blistered his lungs while rivulets of sweat ran down his spine. Were all fevers like this? Stifling heat?

Fuck. Andrew gripped the sink when another dizzy spell threatened to send him to his knees. Once the room stopped spinning, he peered up, but there was no mirror. Luminita was probably right not to trust him with sharp objects. He would do almost anything to escape this torment.

After rolling his neck, Andrew hauled his sweat-soaked shirt over his head and let it sit under the running water. He worked the fabric, wringing it out several times until it was chilled. Then he settled the saturated cotton across his neck and shoulders with a shuddering sigh of contentment.

Shivers set in and goosebumps rose over this flesh. The shirt wasn't the only culprit. The air suddenly felt chilly against his feverish skin, making every muscle tighten and tremble. It was such an odd sensation, but then he had never been sick, never had a fever. One of the few benefits of being a Durand.

The heavy clunk of the lock made Cohen whip his head to the side. He watched the door in his periphery, although he was fairly certain who stood on the other side.

The door swung open.

Just as expected—the devil.

Luminita stalked into his cell, and Andrew twisted to face her with raised brows. In the nearly thirty years he had known the woman, Cohen had only seen Luminita in a pair of slacks a handful of times. She *heavily* favored skirts.

"Good morning. How are you feeling, *fiul?*" She started toward him, but he held up a hand, internally flinching at the empty endearment.

Cohen truly was not in the mood for her theatrics today. Just inhaling required too much of his strength.

"I've been better, obviously. What do you want?"

"I brought you something. A peace offering."

When he peeked at her again, a bright smile lit her face. It stirred memories of better times, when he had trusted her with blind adoration. *I was such a fool.*

The woman turned and waved a hand. Movement drew Andrew's attention back to the doorway. A mousy man in a white lab coat shuffled inside, carrying a small stainless steel tray.

"What is it?" Cohen eyed the syringe lying next to a few alcohol pads.

"Dr. Scott completed the cure."

Cohen refocused on Luminita, studying every nuance carefully. "Why should I believe you?"

Sadness tinged the air around her, but Cohen knew better than to trust it.

"You are sick, and I want to help. I'm the only one with the cure, *fiul.*"

"Stop calling me that!" he snapped.

"Andrew," she amended. "Let me help you."

Nothing stood out as a transparent deception, but Luminita was a next-level manipulator. She had fooled him for nearly three decades. Still, something about her felt off, different.

Typically, Luminita allowed very little emotion to slip past her mental walls, which was what made her difficult to read. But today, a steady stream of anxiousness emanated from her, with peeks of other, stronger feelings.

"You're fighting a fever. Please, let me help you before things worsen."

Cohen's studious gaze lingered on her. Maybe this change in Luminita was all in his head. Perhaps he was hallucinating it, desperate for some sort of hope to cling to. Did it matter?

Either Luminita was offering the cure or she wasn't and he would die anyway. Truth made the most sense. If she had wanted him dead, Luminita would have let him die from his wounds.

She wanted him alive. Not because she cared about his survival. He had no illusions about that anymore. No, she still needed something from him. In the end, the reason didn't matter. Only one thing did—Lilith—and he couldn't save her if he was dead.

"Fine." Cohen expelled the word on a weary sigh as another bought of chills racked his body.

The awkward man in the lab coat ripped open the alcohol pads the second Cohen agreed, as if he was anxious to get the hell out of the room. He approached Cohen's left side, hands trembling slightly. Somehow, Cohen doubted he simply had a dislike of needles.

As soon as the cool pad rubbed over his upper arm, Cohen averted his gaze and settled it on Luminita. "It's been a very long time since I've seen you wear pants."

A strange tingle of anger and embarrassment glimmered beneath her indifference. "It's not common. True," she admitted with reluctance. "But it is necessary today."

Although her tone remained the very picture of calm, there was a cryptic weight to her words.

"Is there something—" A sharp jab interrupted his train of thought. Cohen sucked in a hissing breath. "Is there something special about today?"

While the quiet man gathered his supplies, a dark grin spread across Luminita's red lips. Coupled with the excitement dancing in her eyes, it wasn't a good sign.

"All done, ma'am." The man snatched up the tray and hurried through the door before she said anything else.

"Nita."

She winced slightly, as if the abbreviated name bothered her, and turned to fully face Cohen again.

"What is happening today?" he asked one more time.

"I'll be making some deals today," she replied in the same casual voice.

"Am I included in that?"

Luminita considered him. "Why should you be?"

Andrew flexed his scabbed knuckles, cracking them open again. He could have drawn on the lab geek's anxiousness to heal, but…he wanted these wounds. They reminded him of what was important, even though punching the wall had become increasingly less satisfying.

"How long are you going to keep me in here?"

Luminita tilted her head, further appraising him. "You've yet to give me a reason to release you."

"What do you want from me?"

The woman's brow wrinkled. "I already gave you the answer."

"Lilith and Chance." Cohen pulled the wet shirt from his slumped shoulders and flung it in the sink. Defeat was a physical entity weighing him down. He sank onto the cot and rubbed a hand through his wet hair.

"Yes…" Luminita moved closer and crouched before him. "But in Lilith's case…it really is in her best interest."

"Why only in *her* case?" Cohen narrowed his eyes to suspicious slits. "I mean, if I infected her, surely Chance is also infected."

"Of course, he is." A condescending laugh bellowed from her, further stoking Cohen's anger. "However, once cured, I have tests for Chance. Some of them are…rather painful. His remaining life will not be a happy one, I'm afraid."

Conflicting emotions roared to the surface in Cohen's brain, and so did the demon.

Admit it. It's the future you desire for him. You want him to suffer for possessing what you covet more than anything else in this miserable world. You want to take what's his.

No. That would hurt her. I never want to hurt her again.

But what if that's not up to you? What if Chance's future is inevitable? It won't be your fault. She'll need you to help her cope…help her forget.

The unshakeable dream from the cabin surged to the forefront: Chance lying in a sea of blood; Lilith in her lavender nightgown, weeping over his corpse; the warmth of her body when Cohen pulled her away; the petal softness of her quivering lips; the desperation in her shining olive eyes when she *begged* him to help her forget; the salty taste of her tears when he gave in and kissed her.

"Andrew?" Luminita's voice shattered the memory before the horrific appearance of Alexis tainted the dream. "Are you okay?"

"Fine," he grumbled, smoothing his hair against his scalp. The memory of the nightmare's kiss warred against the recollection of the real one he had stolen in Duncan's basement. The pliant tenderness of her lips still haunted him. "What do you plan to do with Lilith?"

Luminita's eyes warmed, and she moved close enough to touch his cheek. "I only require small blood donations from her. Once she's cured, I can keep her comfortable here, safe, protected."

His instinct urged him to pull away and scream "liar," but he didn't. The simple touch soothed his raw soul. He desperately wanted to believe Luminita, to believe she would keep her word.

"You already feel cooler. I think your fever is breaking."

He ignored the comment, even though she was right. The room already seemed more bearable, and the chills weren't as severe.

"Why? Why would you protect her?"

Luminita took another crouching step, cradling his face between her palms. "For two reasons. She is the last of Gregor's line, my last hope of recreating Ashcroft, but"—she angled her head to lock eyes with him—"also for you, *fiul.*"

"For me?" Cohen stared at her in stunned confusion.

"Yes. You love her, don't you?"

Although he had said it before, for some reason, admitting it now, like this, felt like a betrayal. It seemed more real when he wasn't hurling the words like a weapon to wound Luminita or Alexis.

*Alexis…God. What I did to her…*It still soured his stomach.

"Andrew. Do you love her?"

"Yes," he whispered. Shame coiled in his guts.

"*Fiul.*" Her voice almost sounded compassionate, and for a selfish moment, Cohen leaned into her touch. "You are young and have always been a very deep well. You've skillfully hidden your nature for so long— you had to, or Farren would have killed you—but you *feel* so deeply. Do not be ashamed."

Cohen locked his misty eyes on hers. "But…emotions of any kind are a weakness. *You* taught me that."

One corner of her mouth lifted. "Yes, well…It is difficult to achieve and even more challenging to maintain. None of us are perfect."

A deep frown pulled at Andrew's features. "What?" Cohen jerked away from her touch but remained seated on the cot. "*You* are the one who preached constant vigilance, who scoffs when anyone shows the faintest sliver of affection, who lectures about the dangers of impetuous youth! Always prepared, always in control. Remember?"

"And all those things are still true…*for me.* And maybe for you in the future. I believe that driving yourself mad, trying to throw your life away for a vampire, is ludicrous. I…have some expertise in that matter."

Luminita reached out for him again, as if he were a skittish yet feral animal. Perhaps the comparison wasn't far off.

"But…if she is what brings you back to me…what heals you, then she is yours."

"Mine?" His growl made her hand stop in midmotion. "She *isn't* mine. She'll *never* be mine." Andrew's slitted eyes bored into her, and her arm fell to her side. "Lilith isn't a prize, a distraction, a fucking pet!"

Luminita stood and retreated a step. "That is not what I meant."

"Why do you even care? You love *no one*. You desire *nothing* but your power…your plans. You aren't capable of anything else. Why waste your time trying to save me? What value could I *possibly* have?"

Luminita stared hard at the floor. "It isn't true," she said in a small, almost unrecognizable voice.

"What isn't?"

"I *do* care. I tried to cut ties…to leave you behind, but…I couldn't."

Andrew snorted in disbelief. "Enough games. I'm tired."

When Luminita met his stare, her ocean-blue eyes glistened with unshed tears, catching Cohen completely off guard. However, a quick flashback of the medical center last year was all it took to snap him out of her manipulative spell.

"Familiarity and finding excuses to make me useful are not the same thing as caring. What you did to me…I *cannot* forgive that, and if you truly cared, you wouldn't have been able to do it."

The sadness seeping from her appeared genuine. Hell, she might even have believed it herself, but it didn't change things. No amount of supposed heartbreak could undo what she had done.

"Find some other fool to lap up your lies. Maybe your partner, Aaron, is available."

At the mention of Aaron's name, a vicious rage saturated the air like thick smoke.

"So, you do not wish to help me save Lilith?" Like the flick of a switch, all the tender compassion vanished, leaving malice in its wake. "I could always lock her in a cell and bleed her almost dry every few weeks. I'm sure the isolation would eventually drive her insane."

Andrew surged to his feet and snatched her arms, towering over her petite form. "You will *not* touch her!"

The same emotionless face Luminita had worn when she sliced him up stared back at him now. "You are my only incentive to treat Lilith well. If you refuse to cooperate, I'm free to do as I please. Do you think a medically induced coma sounds more humane?"

Cohen shoved her away, as if just touching her might somehow infect him. Nausea and loathing twisted his insides in equal measure. The very thought of either of those futures for Lilith made him want to tear the Romanian limb from limb.

Wormwood

Luminita smoothed out her long-sleeved blouse and slacks, regaining her composure. "All you have to do is help me, Andrew. We do not have to be enemies."

Cohen stared at her, the sick feeling only spreading.

"Come with me to the lab."

She held out her hand, but he just swallowed hard and studied it.

"We can both have what we want and save Lilith's life in the process."

When Cohen still didn't take her hand, she sighed and tried again.

"Do you want Lilith to die? Because without the cure, she will."

The words cracked his already fractured heart.

"I promise, on my own life, as long as you help me, I will treat Lilith fairly and give you both a good life."

Despite the overwhelming shame drowning out the nausea, Andrew took Luminita's hand.

Chapter 35

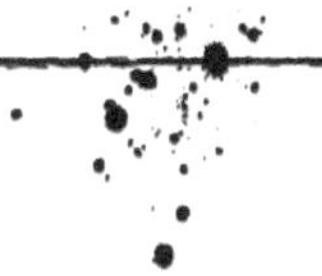

Lilith stared down the modest colonial on the edge of Brooklyn. Her heart thumped heavily in her throat. She hadn't been this nervous to knock on the red door since the night she had come here for help over eight months ago.

This time, her anxiety didn't stem from a fear of Gloria slamming the door in her face. Instead, the gut-wrenching idea of Gloria waving off her concerns consumed Lilith's thoughts.

The odds of a professional hitman making the connection to her late partner's family and taking advantage of that leverage was high, but what if Gloria refused to leave? It was bad enough that Lilith had gotten her husband, Felipe, killed. The least she could do was protect his family.

Lilith glanced up and down the quiet street. Gibson had parked the RV several blocks away, just in case, but everything seemed peaceful beneath the warm morning sun.

With a resolute sigh, Lilith raised her hand and rapped her knuckles against the door. A voice yelled deep within the house, and stomping footsteps approached. The door was yanked open, and seventeen-year-old Erica's sour frown transformed into utter shock. Her jaw nearly hit the floor.

"Auntie Lil? What…happened to your hair?" The girl sounded outraged, which suddenly made Lilith feel stupidly self-conscious.

"I heard blondes had more fun."

Erica snorted and rolled her dark eyes. "Did you drag that joke back from the Paleolithic era with you?"

A smirk pulled at Lilith's lips. The girl had more than her fair share of spunk and constantly kept Gloria on her toes.

"Hey, I'm not even thirty. Where's your mom?"

A heavy sigh escaped the irritated teen, and she held the door open wider. "Kitchen."

"Thanks, kid."

Erica groaned. "I am *not* a kid."

Lilith held up her hands in surrender. "Sorry, but could you do me a favor? Occupy Sophia and Rose for a few so I can talk to your mom in private?"

Erica stopped on the bottom step, narrowing her eyes. "Boyfriend trouble?"

Lilith chuckled. "No. Just the regular kind of trouble."

"*Fine.*" The teen rolled her eyes again and stomped up the stairs.

"Erica! Who was at the door?" Gloria's commanding voice boomed from the kitchen.

"Auntie Lil!" Erica shrieked with a heavy dose of attitude.

Gloria instantly appeared in the kitchen doorway with a huge smile. However, when her eyes truly settled on Lilith, they widened in an expression resembling horror.

"*Bonita,*" she whispered, slowly pacing forward. "Your hair…Your beautiful red curls!"

Wow. Between Erica and Gloria, Lilith was really starting to feel self-conscious, which was idiotic considering their dire circumstances.

A severe frown wrinkled Gloria's face. "What's wrong? Did Chance hurt you? I swear to God, *bonita*. I will end him."

Lilith blinked at the odd turn in conversation. "What? No! Why would you ask that?"

Gloria raised her eyebrows, clearly unconvinced. "I don't believe you. No one changes their hair *that* dramatically unless something's wrong— typically a breakup."

"Or if you're on the run," Lilith supplied. "It was a necessary precaution." When the woman continued to stare her down, she elaborated on her love life. "Chance and I are…" Lilith paused, realizing she hadn't told Gloria yet. "We're engaged, actually."

Gloria's dark eyes glittered and immediately fell to Lilith's naked ring finger. "Are you sure? Your finger says otherwise."

Lilith chuckled. "I'm very sure. Our mission down in Alabama went sideways, and we've been hiding out since then. Not really a good time to go ring shopping."

"So, the rumors are true? You're dodging the Elders?"

"No," Lilith quickly replied. "We've been communicating with Antonio the entire time. We're dodging Aaron and his psychotic partner. And now…" Lilith exhaled slowly. "There's a contract out on my life."

Tension filled the air, increasing with each passing second while Gloria studied her. Finally, it became too much.

"I'm here because I'm worried about you and the girls. I'm working with an FBI agent, and she—"

"Stop." Gloria held up a hand. Her face was set in stern lines. "Why is there a contract on your life?"

Lilith swallowed and blew out a breath, trying to mentally condense the story. "I…had a boyfriend in college. He was emotionally and physically abusive. It was bad…and then it got worse. His dad tried to buy me off. He's a powerful real estate mogul with his hands in a lot of corrupt pies. I didn't want money. I just wanted David Boston gone."

Gloria opened her mouth, but Lilith barreled ahead.

"Anyway, this ex showed up here a little over a week ago, looking for his FBI partner, convinced I was behind her disappearance. The man almost killed me. He held me at gunpoint and would have shot me if not for Agent Hersch. Chance refused to let Boston have another opportunity to hurt me."

Lilith lowered her eyes to the floor, unable to meet Gloria's stare.

"Chance killed him."

"*Dios mio*," Gloria whispered.

When Lilith looked back up, Gloria had tears in her eyes, and her hand covered her mouth.

"*Bonita*, I am so sorry."

Lilith hadn't allowed herself to dwell on the moment. After the siren, Lilith had no room to point blame. Knowing Boston could never touch her again had lifted a weight from her shoulders, but the way Chance had done it, with no hesitation…

That side of Chance had scared her ever since he took down her cousin Spencer. In those moments, it was like someone flipped a switch on his humanity.

Lilith shook off the thoughts. Now was not the time to explore those emotions. She needed to stay on topic.

"Boston's father is the one who issued the contracts. It's not just me. He wants my whole team dead, except Chance. The bastard wants him alive." The reasons why made Lilith's throat tighten.

"How can I help?"

A faint smile pulled at Lilith's lips. "That's not why I'm here."

Gloria crossed the room and flung her arms around Lilith, squeezing her tightly. Tears prickled Lilith's eyes. She had endured so much since the last time she had been here. God, she had almost lost Chance.

No. *Had* lost Chance. He'd coded twice during surgery.

Lilith wanted to spill everything, unload each painful moment, but that wasn't the reason for her visit. There were important things to handle. After hugging Gloria, she pulled away.

"I need you and the girls to pack a few things. I have to get you out of here. My connection to you is too public. Eventually, someone is going to show up, intent on using you as bait."

"Where will we go? Solasta?"

"No. They've already been breached once, and I'm just as publicly connected to Solasta, if not more. Agent Hersch called in some favors. There's a safe house in the city, and she'll have FBI agents stationed there to guard you."

"A *human* FBI agent?"

Lilith bit at her lip. The next part was risky, but ultimately, she trusted Gloria. "Agent Hersch knows everything. Her men won't, though."

Gloria stepped back with her eyebrows raised. "Everything? As in *us*? Vampires?"

"Yes. Have you heard about the virus down south?"

Gloria appeared suspicious but nodded.

"It affects vampires. In fact, the people who released it were targeting us. We won't be able to hide much longer."

"And Antonio knows all this?"

Lilith slumped her shoulders. "We're working on that."

Gloria still appeared skeptical.

"We can revisit all of this in the RV."

"RV?"

"Yeah." Lilith chuckled. "Agent Hersch 'procured' one so we could all travel together. Please, Gloria. I can't let you and the girls stay here. It's too dangerous."

Once again, Gloria considered her for a while. "All right." The woman turned toward the stairs. "Girls!" she bellowed, so loud Lilith swore the house shook.

Nine-year-old Sophia peeked down from the top of the stairs seconds later. "Yes, Mom?"

"All of you!"

Sophia swiveled her head, French braids flying, and yelled for the others. "Erica! Rose!"

Little Rose, who was only six, appeared beside her sister and smiled down at Lilith. She was the quiet one of the bunch.

"What?" Erica groaned when she joined her sisters.

"Erica, you all need to pack some clothes for a few days. Help your sisters and make it fast!"

"Are we going on vacation with Auntie Lil?" Sophia practically danced with excitement, and Rose's eyes widened to saucers.

"Kind of," Lilith answered, smiling. "It's a top-secret assignment."

"Woah," Sophia and Rose whispered in unison, both wearing excited smiles.

Erica, however, performed another epic eye roll and shooed her sisters away from the stairs. "Fine. Come on."

Thirty minutes later, they were all climbing into the RV. Sophia rambled on about how cool the vehicle was, and Rose stared in silent wonder.

Erica seemed perpetually irritated until she caught sight of Keller lounging at the table. Then she was all shy smiles while tucking her long dark hair behind her ears. *That* was disturbing, considering Keller was over twice her age.

"Erica, couch!" Gloria snapped with authority.

The moody teen dropped to the seat immediately but kept her eyes on the table.

"Gloria! Good to see you." Chance flashed a bright smile and strolled up to give her a hug, which Gloria returned, but only for a moment.

She stepped back and grabbed his face with a stern expression. "Chance Deveraux. I have two things to say to you."

His panicked eyes darted to Lilith, who merely shrugged. She had no idea what the woman was about to say.

"It's not an engagement until you put a ring on her finger."

Both Lilith and Chance grinned.

"And..." Gloria placed a kiss on his cheek. "Thank you for taking care of my *bonita*. For making sure that *pendejo* can never hurt her again."

Chance's throat bobbed a few times when he straightened. "I'll always take care of her." The words left his mouth like a solemn oath, which it was to him.

"You'll make a good husband." Gloria patted his blushing cheek before moving to sit next to Erica. "But get the woman a ring."

Chance made eye contact with Lilith, and all those haunting thoughts from earlier evaporated. The cold, calculating side of him only existed to protect the people he loved. He would never hesitate to keep them safe, to keep *her* safe.

How could Lilith ever fault him for that?

Chapter 36

Luminita strode inside the central lab with confidence, but Cohen stopped in the doorway. It wasn't the scope or sophistication of the equipment halting his steps. His gaze roamed from the brunette zip-tied to a chair to the two men standing with Aaron, one of whom held a little girl.

Trepidation made Cohen's pulse skitter. Whatever Luminita had planned wasn't good, not that it ever was.

"Andrew?" Luminita stood in the middle of the lab, eyeing him expectantly.

He didn't want to comply, didn't want to do anything she would ask of him, but the cost of refusing was too high. Lilith's life was worth more than his pride, morality…Everything, really.

The brunette woman peered over her shoulder at the sound of his name. Recognition blazed in her hazel eyes, but Andrew had no idea who she was. When the woman didn't notice the same familiarity in his face, sad defeat surrounded her, like a suffocating blanket.

Luminita's heels echoed off the tile, drawing Andrew's attention. When she approached Aaron and his guests, an odd smirk crept over Aaron's face, one which Luminita purposely ignored. She pivoted sharply and stood beside the taller mystery man—the one without a child.

"We've been waiting on you, Nita." Aaron's harsh tone earned him a scathing glare from her, but it only broadened the man's grin.

Luminita drew in a breath, reining in her tendrils of anxiety, and settled her focus on Andrew. "Join me, please."

It was the "please" which caught his notice. Luminita rarely used the word, but she had already said it multiple times this morning. Perhaps it had something to do with the odd interaction with Aaron. Was it a new dynamic, a paradigm shift, or had their partnership always been this tumultuous?

After briefly considering his options—which admittedly weren't many—Andrew joined her. He still had no idea what was going on or who these people were, but the situation brought back memories of Farren's courtroom.

Of course, he had been on the receiving end of *that* nightmare.

Luminita smiled up at Andrew when he took his place beside her, invoking a host of mixed emotions. He wished he could forget his life before the medical center, forget the ways Luminita had helped him through so many things. Cohen wanted to burn away all the good so he could simply hate her, as he should.

Hate was easy. Everything else was hard.

"Andrew, I'd like to introduce you to Orchid, although I've heard you met briefly." Luminita waved a hand at the brunette strapped to the chair. "Otherwise known as Helena Vieux."

Andrew's jaw dropped. "Vieux? You told me she was dead." The disbelief quickly transformed into rage at yet another lie.

"A necessity at the time, I assure you," Luminita informed him. "Exposing her identity when you called would have been…problematic." A soft chuckle spilled past Luminita's lips, but it was far from friendly. "Of course, complications arose regardless. Didn't they, Helena?"

The prisoner met Luminita's gaze with a chilling stare full of venom. "Let my family go. You have me. You don't need them anymore."

Family? Cohen looked over at the man and child, both clinging to one another with tears in their eyes. The little girl couldn't have been more than six or seven years old.

"I'm afraid you're mistaken." Aaron's smugness bordered on sadism. He was enjoying this.

"What happened in Duncan's basement?" Luminita asked firmly, side-eyeing Aaron.

Is that why I'm here? As a damn witness?

"I already told you. Ashcroft bested my men, and I ran. I don't know where Ashcroft is."

"She's lying." The unfamiliar voice might have drawn Andrew's attention, if not for the horrified expression on Orchid's face.

"No!" She shook her head, panic oozing from every pore. "Noah! Be quiet."

"Let him speak," Luminita chided.

Finally, Andrew dragged his gaze to the man gripping the little girl. Pain, anger, and desperation all glistened in his eyes.

"I'm sorry, Lena, but I have to protect Desi." The man tightened his arms around his daughter. "She said she'd let us go if I helped her."

"She's lying!" Orchid screeched through a sob. "Please!"

The man's throat bobbed, and tears streaked his cheeks, but he turned to face Luminita as if he could no longer look at Orchid. "Ashcroft, the one you asked about…she told me she killed him…that she couldn't let you have another killer."

"Noah!" Orchid's heart-wrenching cry of betrayal struck Cohen right to his core.

"Tsk, tsk." Luminita stared hard at Orchid. "I wanted no lies between us."

"*Lies*? You want to speak about lies! You told me Chance died in that wreck! You *stole* my fucking son!"

Andrew paled, but Luminita didn't seem the least bit affected. *God, how many lives has this woman destroyed?* Sickness and hatred burned in his gut.

"Dramatics." With that, Luminita focused on Noah. "Is there anything else that may be of use?"

The man swallowed hard, hedging a look at Orchid before answering. "She has a phone—"

"Stop!" Orchid shrieked. "Don't do this! Please!" The woman rocked against her restraints with sudden desperation.

Noah paused. He closed his eyes for a moment. When he opened them, he didn't look in her direction again. "She said I could use it to contact people who would protect us." He paused again but finally conceded. "It's under the driver's seat."

"No!" Orchid wailed, dissolving into wracking sobs. "Why? *Why* would you do this? She's fucking lying to you."

"Mommy!" The little girl wiggled in Noah's arms, but he held on tight, still refusing to look at Orchid.

"I'm sorry, Lena, but I had to take that chance. *Someone* had to put Desiree first." Then he turned his attention back to Luminita. "I did what you wanted. Are we free to go?"

"May I?" Luminita stalked toward them, holding her arms out to the child, who merely blinked her teary eyes in confusion.

"I'd rather leave now." Noah clutched his daughter closer and turned away.

Luminita flicked her gaze to the other man beside Aaron. Apparently, that was the only command he needed.

"Hand her the girl." The man's Irish accent was prominent, but his tone didn't seem all that commanding.

To Andrew's surprise, Noah immediately complied, without hesitation. *What the actual fuck?*

Luminita pivoted away from Noah before putting Desiree down. She crouched, meeting the little girl at eye level, and ran her fingers through her silken hair. "Such a pretty little thing."

"Luminita, please! I beg you…Don't hurt her, *please*," Orchid pleaded between uneven breaths.

"Goodness. I don't intend to harm a single hair on her head. Do I, sweetness?"

Fear swam in Desiree's glassy eyes, but she stared right back at the Romanian without saying a word.

"Andrew." Luminita peered up at Cohen. "Your hands are injured." She inclined her head toward Noah. "Heal yourself…*completely*."

Andrew balked at the unexpected request. "I—"

"No!" Orchid shouted. "Just let him go."

Luminita lifted a brow. "After he betrayed you?"

"Stop playing games. Just let them go and I'll do anything you ask."

The sly grin slithering across Luminita's lips made Andrew's heart sink. "Oh, Orchid…I know you'll do anything I ask." Then she fixed her stare on Andrew with commanding authority. "Do it now!"

Flashes of Alexis played through his head—her choking gasps, the light draining from her emerald eyes, her body growing cool beneath his touch. The vivid memories sent his heart racing until only his pulse roared in his ears.

"Andrew." Luminita rose, keeping one hand on the girl's shoulder. "You are either with me or you are not. Remember what is at stake."

"Please!" Orchid's tear-drenched voice tore at Andrew's heart. "Don't do this! He's innocent, please!"

Agony twisted Cohen's guts, and he fought back the bile climbing his throat. Killing Alexis had been a desperate act, but this…He couldn't explain away cold-blooded murder.

"If you want to help your precious Lily, you will do as I command."

Cohen closed his eyes. A tear slipped down his cheek. *She* was what mattered, and he *had* to help her, to right what he had done. If that meant taking this man's life, further darkening his soul, he would be the villain if it saved Lilith. He had sworn that once before.

Andrew forced himself to step forward and turn toward Noah. The man's eyes went wide, finally comprehending the situation, and he started to move.

"Stand still and don't speak," the Irishman commanded.

Noah halted like a damn statue.

"Andrew Cohen! I saved your life. Don't do this!" Orchid spat every word with heartbreaking conviction.

"And you shouldn't have. I told you that." Andrew's shoulders slumped, but he put one foot in front of the other.

"Luminita! Please! Don't make my daughter watch this." Orchid's sobbing plea halted Cohen's steps, shaking his resolve.

Andrew tried to speak, but the words died in his mouth. All he could do was stare at Luminita, a silent prayer in his eyes. To kill this man in front of his own daughter…He would be no better than Ashcroft.

"Killian." Luminita didn't take her firm attention off Andrew while she spoke.

The Irishman crouched to meet Desiree's panicked eyes, and his warm smile made his cheeks dimple. "Would you like some ice cream, little lass?"

Desiree peered around the room. "No," she said quietly.

"Ah, but the adults need to talk, and my friend over there"—the man nodded toward one of the guards—"he needs some cheering up. Do you prefer chocolate or strawberry?"

A soft smile tugged at the girl's lips. "Strawberry?" she whispered with excitement.

"Aye. You can have your fill." Killian flashed a wink and led her over to the guard. "Off you go."

Desiree peeked back with a confused frown before taking the guard's hand and walking out of the room.

The whole exchange had seemed surreal, but when the second the door closed, Luminita's snapped order stole Cohen's attention.

"Proceed."

Andrew turned back toward Noah, who stood still as stone, except for his wildly roving eyes. The man couldn't move but was conscious. He knew what was about to happen—or the end result, anyway. Cohen realized then that Luminita had wanted the man to betray his wife. This *Killian* could have forced the information from Noah, but he hadn't.

Luminita had manipulated the man into choosing darkness just as she was doing with Cohen now.

Thoughts of the cabin drifted through Andrew's mind, specifically the morning after his nightmare. He had told Lilith the truth about his feelings, and she had reached toward him instead of pulling away. Her words still echoed through his head.

You are not your past or your darkest moments. Those are not what define you.

He had asked her what did define him, and she had replied simply, *What you do next.*

Doing this, taking a life in this manner, he would be stepping over a line he couldn't uncross. Andrew would become a monster Lilith would pull away from. There would be no forgiveness for him this time. She wouldn't reach for him again. He would lose everything.

"Andrew." Luminita's voice snapped through the air like a whip. "I *will* let her suffer."

That was what undid him.

He couldn't allow Lilith's suffering, not when he could prevent it. Andrew owed her *everything*. The darkness of his soul didn't matter. He had seen the light, basked in its warmth for a few precious moments. As much as he craved more, it didn't belong to him. It had been borrowed, a stolen moment of selfishness, but he could ensure the light in Lilith's soul persisted.

Cohen blocked out Orchid's incoherent sobs. He focused on his purpose, summoning the image of Lilith from his last dream. She had seemed so real, as if she had cut through time and space to reach him.

You matter. Your life matters, she had said. Would she still think that if she knew how he had cursed her with one selfish kiss? Even if she did, the truth of *this* moment would forever change things.

Andrew's hands trembled when he reached up and gripped the man's face. Orchid's desperate wails haunted the background, and Noah's wide eyes flooded with tears.

"Release him." Luminita's words came as a shock.

An almost euphoric relief flooded Andrew's body.

Was she simply testing me?

Cohen peered over his shoulder, pulling his hands away.

But the Romanian wasn't speaking to him. She was giving Killian the command. The brief glimmer of hope transmuted into a ball of lead, sinking in his stomach.

"No," Andrew whispered in horror, his gaze snapping back to Noah.

The man tensed, and his panicked terror soured the air.

"Why?" Andrew shouted with sickening anger. He didn't need to specify.

"You must prove your dedication," Luminita replied with calm detachment. Then she turned her attention back to Killian. "Release him."

The Irishman did as commanded.

"Please, don't." Noah's ragged words constricted Andrew's throat until he could barely drag in a breath. The man vibrated with paralyzing fear. Andrew's hands hovered above the skin, but the man didn't move, didn't run.

For Lilith, Cohen reminded himself.

With fierce determination, Andrew gripped Noah's face. Each fractured bone screamed in answer, but he held firm. He closed his eyes, unwilling to watch the light fade from Noah's. After steeling his resolve, Andrew latched onto the man's torment, heartbreak, essence, and drew it all in.

The heady rush made his stomach clench, and the acrid taste of bile filled his mouth. Andrew shoved it all down, ripping at Noah's energy, devouring it while the man started to flail. Hands struck his face, arms, shoulders, but the force grew weaker with each hit.

"Please…" Noah's weak voice cut into Andrew's consciousness, but he desperately held on. "My daughter…needs me."

Tears streamed down Andrew's cheeks, as if his soul had been flayed open. Perhaps it had. But he maintained his grip and tore away every bit of power until Noah went limp beneath his hands.

Disgust burned everything else away, and Andrew stepped back, to frantically wipe his palms on his pants. The room spun, and Andrew doubled over, gripping his knees.

Noah collapsed to the floor. Orchid's heart-wrenching shrieks reached a fevered pitch—a sound which would forever haunt him.

Andrew cast Luminita a hateful glare. He had never believed in Christian mythology, but if the Devil existed, it was this woman. "Take me back to my cell." The raspy words barely clawed their way past his constricted throat.

The Romanian said nothing.

"Guards. Take Orchid away." Aaron stared Cohen down while he gave the order.

Footsteps shuffled behind him, and muffled cries echoed off the walls.

"What more do you want from me?" Andrew asked.

A vicious sneer pulled at the man's lips. "I still fail to comprehend your usefulness." Aaron moved forward while mercs dragged Orchid past him. "All you are is a distraction." He took another step.

"Aaron." A clear warning resided in Luminita's tone, and the man halted.

"*He* is your weakness…the thing holding you back."

The lethal glint in Aaron's stormy eyes obliterated Andrew's self-loathing. He was now keenly aware of how tentative his survival was. Luminita wasn't the only one with control here.

I can't help Lilith if I'm dead.

"I *need* him to secure Lilith." Luminita spat the words through gritted teeth.

Aaron expelled a repulsed groan. "A useless endeavor. There is nothing special about my meddlesome niece. She's a nuisance, a fucking albatross that has cost us at every turn. And you don't need this"—Aaron raked his gaze over Cohen with revulsion—"pathetic, love-sick psychotic for anything. His mind is already broken."

Anger bubbled to the surface with every word, but as much as Andrew wanted to rise to Lilith's defense, convincing Aaron of her value would be counterproductive. *Let Aaron underestimate her.*

"That is enough!" Luminita snapped. "Guards, take Andrew to his room." She turned to square off with Aaron. The man loomed over her by a foot, but she didn't seem to care.

Whatever she said to Aaron made the man's jaw tick, and he balled his hands into fists.

A guard shoved Andrew toward the door leading back to his cell, and Cohen breathed a little easier. Hopefully, Luminita could keep her *partner* in check.

Once Andrew entered the hall, everything crashed over him again. The feel of Noah's stubbled skin lingered on his palms, twisting Andrew's stomach. He flexed his healed hands, missing the burn of cracked skin and the ache of fractured bones.

In all his years, he had never drained a person, not completely, until Alexis and now Orchid's husband—a father. He had taken lives before, of course, but not like that, not by stealing every shred of vitality, by devouring their soul.

But what scared Andrew most was the exhilarating rush, like a goddamn drug. The dark temptation the act offered could easily slip into an addiction.

Part of him wanted to declare to the heavens and every higher power that he would never do it again, but if it meant saving the woman he loved…

She was worth *any* price.

Chapter 37

Tim ran through the plan for the twentieth time and carefully wiped his sweaty palms on his jeans, avoiding the still-tender wound in his thigh. A version of the truth was always best. He would use that for Jill, but the staff…Tim definitely couldn't use any variation of the actual story with them.

"Are you okay?" Eileen asked.

"I don't care for lying. Part of the reason I never dated."

Eileen raised an eyebrow, but the smile gracing her lips was playful. "Are you planning on lying to me?"

"Never, Pixie." Tim flashed a lopsided grin. "You read me too well anyway. It'd be pointless."

"Smart man." Eileen patted his cheek with a radiant smile that did things to him, but he quickly reined in his response.

Now was *not* the time.

The RV came to a stop, and Gibson hollered from the driver's seat. "We're here."

Tim drew in a deep breath and exhaled slowly. "Showtime."

"Are you sure you want me to go in with you?" Eileen rubbed the thumb of one hand against the palm of her other, as if suddenly nervous.

"Of course," he said with a frown. "I mean, unless you aren't comfortable—"

"No." Eileen pulled on another smile, but this one didn't quite reach her vibrant blue eyes.

Tim stood and offered his hand, which she took without hesitation, much to his relief. "Come on, pixie warrior. My sister isn't scary."

A skittish laugh confirmed his suspicion. But Eileen had *nothing* to worry about. Getting Jill out of the facility was their goal. They weren't there for a formal inquisition about their love life. Although, he had no doubt Jill would love Eileen. His sister harped on him every week about getting out there, finding a nice girl, and settling down.

Tim turned his attention to the table, where Lilith and Chance sat with Keller. "This might take a while to clear with the facility. Shouldn't take more than half an hour, though."

Chance passed him a walkie, which Tim clipped to his belt. "Call us if you run into trouble."

"Will do."

Tim led Eileen down the steps and across the modest parking lot. When he reached the front door, he pressed the call button, like he'd done thousands of times. For some reason, the familiar action felt different this time.

"*How can I help you?*" an unrecognizable voice rattled through the speaker.

"It's Tim. I'm here to see Jill Dayton."

A buzzer immediately followed his response. Tim pulled the door open and held it for Eileen. It was pure habit drilled into him by a mother who had refused to have an unchivalrous son. Eileen raised one brow and eyed him when she walked inside. The neutral expression left him confused over whether he should keep opening doors for her.

Shit. Maybe she finds it insulting.

However, when they reached the inner set, Eileen stopped and peered over her shoulder with an impish yet expectant look.

Tim snorted a laugh, reached around her, and opened the door. "After you."

"Thanks, handsome." Eileen winked.

Tim rubbed his jaw and reminded himself they were sharing an RV with far too many people to entertain his current thoughts.

"You coming?" Eileen asked with a smirk.

"That's a loaded question," Tim mumbled under his breath. Once he caught up to her, he slid his fingers between hers. He simply needed to touch her. Eileen just had that kind of effect on him, pulling him toward her like a magnet.

"Tim!" Meg, the usual receptionist, rose from her seat, beaming at him. "You had us worried when you didn't show up last Thursday."

"Hey, Meg. Sorry. Something came up with work."

The middle-aged woman's studious gaze shifted to Eileen. "And who is your guest? For the sign-in log, of course."

The two had discussed whether to use real names. In the end, they had decided to keep everything possible aboveboard. If someone linked Tim to Jill, giving their names to Meg wouldn't really be new information.

"This is Eileen Hersch, my girlfriend."

Eileen's hand tensed in his. He gave it a squeeze but kept his eyes calmly fixed on Meg.

"Oh." The woman glanced between them several times before smiling again. "Sorry. You've just never brought a *female* guest before."

The odd way she stressed *female* made him pause. He had only ever brought Chance and Gibson to visit with Jill. Yeah, the guys would get a kick out of that.

"First time for everything. Actually, Eileen and I want to take Jill with us for a few days. We have an RV, and Jill has always wanted to take a road trip."

The woman drew her dark eyebrows together. "Well, I can page the nurse on duty to meet you in the visitor's room. Usually, we have a bit more notice for extended trips."

"I apologize, but the opportunity just popped up."

Meg's expression softened. "Well, I don't see it being an issue."

"Thanks, Meg. I appreciate it. Can we go back?"

"Of course. I'll have someone bring Jill out to you."

Tim flashed the receptionist a grateful smile and led Eileen down the hall.

A light chuckle caught his attention.

"What are you giggling about?"

"Nothing. I'm just…not used to it. *Girlfriend.*"

"Should I not use that term?" Tim asked with genuine curiosity, trying to ignore the weird fear twisting his gut.

"Oh, no. I like it. It's just new…different." Eileen's cheeks turned bright pink.

Tim stepped into Eileen's path, making her stop short. "Hey, if it makes you uncomfortable…if I'm getting ahead of myself, tell me. I don't want to be some pushy asshole." Tim tilted her chin up with his thumb. "You've dealt with enough of those."

Eileen's face lit with a wide smile. "You aren't a pushy asshole. You are the farthest thing from that. I only meant it's been a long time since I was someone's girlfriend." Eileen leaned up on her tiptoes and drew him down for a quick kiss, sending a jolt through him. "I'm happy to be yours," she whispered against his lips.

Tim had to fight the urge to pick her up and pin her to the damn wall. Everything she did drove him wild—a wholly unfamiliar sensation.

"Eileen," he whispered back.

"Yes?" Her breath warmed his lips.

"I need you to back up. We *really* don't have time for bathroom sex."

Eileen slowly retreated. Her blue eyes sparkled, and her teeth raked across her bottom lip.

That definitely did *not* help matters.

Tim averted his gaze to the ceiling and willed certain parts of his anatomy to calm the fuck down. "Dear God, woman. Take pity on me. This is not the place for me to have a raging hard-on, especially when I'm here to see my sister."

A bubble of laughter escaped before Eileen covered her mouth and backed away from him some more. "I'm sorry," she squeaked out from behind her hand, but there was zero remorse in her tone.

Tim stretched his neck and took a few calming breaths. "Don't apologize." He sighed. "I haven't had this sort of reaction to someone in…well, ever, if I'm being honest."

"That really makes me want to kiss you more."

The radiant grin made his blood heat, despite Eileen's attempt to hide it behind her hand.

"You're gonna be the death of me." Tim shook his head but couldn't hide his smirk either. "All right." He huffed and grabbed her hand. "We need to get Jill and get out of here before I maul you in the hallway and get us both arrested."

The barely restrained giggles from Eileen made his heart swell, but he strode forward, determined to get through this.

The visitation room doubled as the dining area. A few residents still sat at tables, finishing their breakfast. Tim headed for an empty table beside the tall windows.

Jill loved staring out at the small garden. Before her piece-of-shit husband beat her into a coma, Jill had loved growing peonies—or "fluffy roses," as she called them.

Tim sank into a chair across the table from Eileen and rubbed his hands over his face. Now that he had his body and libido under control—mostly, at least—the nerves set back in.

"Timothy!" Jill's excited voice made his head snap up with a broad smile. His sister always used his full name. Just one of her quirks.

"Jillybean!" Tim rose from his seat as the tech pushed Jill's wheelchair up to the table. "They cut your hair."

Her light blond hair didn't even reach her shoulders now. He brushed the strands from her face and placed a kiss on her cheek.

"Do you like it?"

Jill preened, her grin brightening, and for the millionth time, Tim thanked God the stroke hadn't stolen that smile. The left-sided paralysis hadn't extended to her facial muscles.

"You always look gorgeous, Jilly."

"And who's this?" Jill moved her gaze to Eileen, brows lifting.

Pink tinged Eileen's cheeks when Tim glanced over at her. "My girlfriend, Eileen."

"*Girlfriend?*" Jill asked incredulously. "You ended the dry stretch? I gave up hope *years* ago." Jill's tinkling laughter eased his nerves.

Although, he wished she hadn't mentioned the dry stretch. Tim had told Eileen it had been a while but never specified a precise timeframe.

"Years?" Eileen asked with an amused expression. "Exactly how long was this *dry stretch?*"

Well, fuck. "I told you I was rusty. Can we just leave it at that?"

"Well over twenty years," Jill blurted without remorse. "The last time he went on a proper date, if you can even call it that, was taking a coworker with him to chaperone my sophomore homecoming dance."

Eileen's eyes went wide while she stared up at him.

Tim sank back into the chair, cheeks burning. "Thanks for that, Jill," he muttered.

"Wow. That is *definitely* more than *a while.*" The teasing tone in Eileen's voice eased some of his embarrassment, but not all of it.

"Oh, come on, Timothy. Girls never freak out over that kinda thing, right, Eileen?"

Eileen cleared her throat, probably to keep from laughing. "It's… sweet and explains a lot."

Tim peered up at her from beneath his brow. "Can we talk about this later?"

After considering him for a moment, Eileen nodded. "Of course, handsome."

Jill's gaze bounced between them, her smile growing brighter. "I really never thought I'd see the day. My brother, the eternal bachelor, in love."

"Jilly." Tim turned to her with a fierce need to redirect the conversation.

It was *far* too soon to be venturing into love territory. The last thing he wanted was to scare Eileen off completely. Bringing up his past had been bad enough.

"We're here for a reason, not just a visit." Tim scooted his chair closer and lowered his voice. "Some things went south with a job, and you might be in danger. Eileen is an FBI agent. We're gonna take you someplace with a few other people until it's safe for you to come back."

The radiant smile fell away, leaving a concerned frown. "Are *you* in danger?"

"Yeah." Tim rubbed at his jaw. "A lot of us are, but we can't tell the staff. As far as they're concerned, Eileen and I are taking you on a road trip in the RV outside."

After a thoughtful nod, Jill met his eyes. "So, we're all going to hide out…together?"

Tim drew in a deep breath, released it slowly, and took her hand. "No, Jillybean. Some friends of mine are going to take care of you, but I've got to neutralize the threat."

"He means *we*," Eileen corrected. "Tim isn't doing this alone. We have a whole team."

Her words seemed to reassure Jill, but tears still welled in his sister's eyes. "Okay."

"Hey, Tim. Meg said you wanted to speak with me."

Thank God. He hadn't known who was on duty, but he'd hoped it was Sarah.

Tim patted Jill's hand while he stood. "It's gonna be okay. Now, look like you're happy to see me."

Jill managed a smile and shook her head. "Fine."

Tim flicked his eyes to Eileen for a moment.

"We'll be okay," she reassured him.

Seeing the two women seated at the same table made Tim's chest glow. It was a sight he thought he would never actually witness. He had given up a long time ago, even before that stupid dance.

"Go on, weirdo," Jill prompted him with a chuckle.

Tim turned away to face the facility's most reasonable nurse. "Can we talk over there?" Tim lowered his voice. "I don't want to ruin the surprise."

Eileen watched Tim wander off with the nurse. *Twenty damn years.* Not a single woman had interested him in all that time, but somehow, *she* had broken that spell? It was insanely flattering but also scary as hell. Eileen didn't consider herself *that* special.

"So…" Jill's hesitant voice drew Eileen's focus. "How did you meet my brother?"

Eileen relaxed into her seat with a warm smile. Making Jill feel comfortable was her top priority, and showing confidence would help reassure her.

"We met on a case, actually. Tim was helping Chance and Lilith."

"I know Chance. He visited a few times with Tim. I've only heard stories about Lilith. She sounds nice, though." A soft melancholy pulled at her features.

It was understandable. Jill was still young, perhaps mid-thirties, and being confined to a group home, no matter how nice, had to get lonely.

"Well, you'll see them both. They're out in the RV."

Jill's mood seemed to improve a bit, but she shifted her gaze to Tim with a worried expression.

"So…twenty years, huh?"

The diversion worked. A happy grin curved Jill's mouth. "Yep." She made the "P" pop. "Honestly, even before that…he has never introduced a girl to the family."

"Well." Eileen rubbed her heated cheek. "I mean…this is a bit different. We needed to make sure you were safe. I'm not sure this really qualifies."

"Of course, it does!" Jill stared at Eileen as if the answer couldn't have been more obvious. "How many people are in the RV?"

"Uh, a lot."

"Including Chance, who I've already met?"

"Yes."

"Timothy could have chosen anyone to come in here with him. He also could have just introduced you as Eileen, but he started with 'my girlfriend.' Trust me. That's a 'meet the family' moment. Timothy and I are the only ones left, after mom passed five years ago."

Eileen peered over at Tim, who was animatedly talking with the silver-haired nurse. The man kept finding ways to surprise her, and they didn't even seem intentional.

"I don't need to question your intentions, do I?"

Eileen turned back to Jill with a chuckle. "Your brother is the best man I have *ever* met. He's a damn unicorn. I have zero intention of hurting him, especially after he's saved my life in countless ways."

Jill positively beamed at her. "I like you. I always wanted a sister."

"And I always wanted one that liked me."

They both laughed.

"What's so funny?" Tim asked in his nervous-but-trying-to-sound-casual voice.

"I was telling her *all* about that powder-blue tux you wore to that homecoming dance…with the white frills."

"Jilly," Tim growled.

Eileen covered her mouth and bit back a laugh.

"Oh, come on! I have literally *never* been able to embarrass you in front of a girl. It's a rite of passage!"

Tim scratched his neck and ignored the subject. "Sarah's packing up a week's worth of meds for you. Should we go to your room and pack some clothes?"

"Eileen can take me."

Eileen sat up a bit straighter, surprised by Jill's answer.

"Jilly, let it go." Tim huffed.

"I'll behave," Jill said in a singsong voice. "No more embarrassing stories. I like her, and I'd feel more comfortable with her handling my unmentionables."

Tim held up his hands and stepped back. "All right, Jillybean. You win."

When his warm brown eyes met Eileen's, they held a weight which made her chest tighten. He smiled at her like she was the most precious thing in the world and still couldn't believe himself worthy. She *really* wanted to kiss him. No one had *ever* looked at her like that, not even on her wedding day.

Yep. I'm definitely a goner. Head over damn heels.

Chapter 38

Once Luminita settled into the chair behind her desk and collected herself, she grabbed the phone. Balance had to be restored, or rather, she needed to reclaim her power. Since Aaron's little performance last night, he had grown far too bold.

With a resolute sigh, Luminita jabbed the button for security.

The nameless man responded within two rings. "Yes, ma'am."

"Inform Mr. Bogdan he is to come to my room immediately. Ensure he knows it is *not* a request."

After setting the phone down in its cradle, she drew in a deep breath. Aaron was right about one thing: Allowing him to drink her blood had given him an advantage. She had spent so much time ensuring he never drank it but then had demanded it in some pleasure-fueled moment of weakness.

Why had she asked him to bite her? She refused to believe she actually *wanted* him to know her feelings, to know how he affected her without having to say it. The moment his fangs pierced her skin had been freeing and euphoric on some level, but had it been worth the price? No.

Aaron's very vocal opinion of Cohen made it clear what allowing this to continue would cost her. Perhaps the man was correct about Cohen being her weakness, but every time she tried to sever the ties between them, Andrew's fractured soul, his emotional torment, dragged her back.

Luminita wasn't willing to let go. The man truly felt like a son to her. She had only experienced the sensation once before and couldn't allow both stories to end in tragedy.

No. Luminita needed to snatch the reins from Aaron's hands and make his role perfectly clear. Stifling her emotions was critical to her plan.

The effects from the Durand blood would only last a few days, and until then, it was only an advantage if she had emotions to sense.

Last night, Aaron had gained the upper hand by making her wait at the door, stoking her anger into rage, which had left her emotionally open—a moronic error she would not repeat. Instead, she would force *him* to come to her. He was hers to command. She had made that claim many times in the distant past. She needed it to be true once more.

Luminita smoothed her slacks, trying to let the irritation go. She hated the infernal things, but Aaron was far too fond of her skirts, and this game required every possible advantage.

She had chosen Aaron centuries ago in Romania for his bloodthirsty, primal nature, but the man wasn't stupid. His years of blending within the vampire Elders had given her many points of manipulation, but now that the charade was over, her leverage was waning.

Luminita's mind worked furiously, combing through every possible angle, but Aaron's only desire was Ashcroft. He had never seen the value in Chance and Lilith. How could she bring him to heel if the only thing he wanted was an impossibility?

There has to be something else he craves. When Luminita glanced down at her slacks, a thought occurred to her, and a wicked grin curled her lips. It was a dangerous play, but if it worked…

Perhaps I've been looking at this all wrong. There *was* something else Aaron desired. What if, instead of cutting off her emotions, she fully embraced the ones he *wanted* to see. What if she offered him the one night he had craved so intently—the night she had broken them both? It would blind him, distract him long enough for her to make her move.

Luminita pushed away from the desk and crossed the room to her closet. After shoving aside all her designer clothes, she reached for a garment tucked in the back. When she pulled out the dress, her grin widened, but a small voice screamed in protest.

She ignored it, like always.

Aaron stormed down the hall, fuming at the audacity of being forcibly summoned. Luminita seemed to love nothing more than pushing buttons, except perhaps for Andrew Cohen. Why the woman hadn't cut the virtually suicidal man loose was beyond him, beyond logic. For such a rational and devious mind, Cohen was an obvious blind spot.

He had watched enough of the footage from the cell to recognize a man unhinged. Cohen was a ticking time bomb, and Aaron had no interest in getting caught in the blast. He hadn't survived nearly eight thousand years to be taken out by something so trivial.

When Aaron reached Luminita's door, he straightened his dress shirt, rolled his shoulders, and released an aggravated sigh before knocking. Of course, there was no answer.

Turnabout is fair play, I suppose.

Aaron gripped the door handle, surprised to find it unlocked, and barreled inside. "Nita!" he growled past gritted teeth. "I am not one of your lackey's to be summoned whenever—"

The words died in his throat, and he came to an abrupt halt, hand still gripping the door.

Luminita lounged on the desk, one leg dangling over the edge, draped in familiar swaths of scarlet gossamer like a goddess. The fabric barely covered each breast and left a wide "V" of flesh exposed to her navel. The high slits rode all the way to her hips, allowing the ethereal fabric to spill between her thighs.

That *particular* dress had been burned into Aaron's memory with conflicting emotions: both ravenous desire and his first heartbreak.

The raven curls she typically tamed into complicated braids fell wildly down her back, shimmering in the light like they had that fateful night. Intricate designs graced the delicate gold bands at her arms and neck, with a matching belt slung low on her sensual hips.

The sight sent Aaron right back to the night of Dragobete and her infernal ritual. He had stared at her in such lustful adoration, ready to fall at her feet, to worship his goddess. She had stolen the moment from him, twisted it up. The woman drugged him with Datura Seeds until only the beast remained and he had no recollection of their union.

For one fleeting day in all his years of life, Aaron had truly believed in a brilliant soul, but her actions both that night and in the years which followed left nothing but tattered remnants festering over the centuries.

"You were saying?" A salacious grin curved the woman's ruby lips.

Aaron forced his eyes away from her, turning to close the door to give himself a moment. No doubt, Luminita wished to reclaim the advantage. This was merely another tactic, nothing more—a chess move in a much larger game. Of course, knowing that only made the action hurt worse. The pang in his chest was downright torturous.

"I was saying," he began, facing her again. "I am not *yours* to summon."

Luminita tilted her head with an amused expression, echoing the emotion emanating from her. "You are not mine? Hmm."

Her ocean-blue eyes stared off into the distance for a moment. When they returned to him, her stare held him in place. She slid off the desk, the fluid motion accentuating every exposed curve of her body. The woman was hypnotic, just as she'd been the night they'd met.

Luminita sauntered closer, and every one of Aaron's muscles stiffened, including the traitorous one between his legs. She had always had that maddening effect on him.

"It's an odd thing for *you* to say." Luminita came to a stop, just out of reach, and raked her eyes over him with unfiltered desire. "Especially after I've claimed you."

Once her words finally registered past the lust thrumming through him, suspicion narrowed his eyes. "I believe it was *I* who did the claiming."

The laughter which escaped Luminita made his blood heat, but Aaron wasn't certain if it stemmed from anger or raw attraction—maybe both.

"I'm not speaking of yesterday, *Sălbatic meu*." The Romanian endearment rolled off her tongue like a lover's whisper, making his breaths rapid.

"What do you mean?" He forced the words out while his mind scrambled to think of something besides his fierce craving to lick the expanse of exposed skin between her breasts.

Luminita followed his gaze and trailed a delicate finger down her porcelain flesh, to the gold belt cinching the fabric below her navel. "There was a time when you were quite"—Luminita's fingers danced over the clasp—"devout. I claimed you as mine on Dragobete."

Aaron dredged up every remaining shred of his restraint and glared at the infuriating yet undeniably seductive woman in front of him. She was the only one who had ever truly drawn out his passion. It hadn't even existed before her.

"You claimed my body, *not me*, remember? I wasn't what you wanted, wasn't enough. And why are you bringing that up now, I wonder?"

Luminita took one sensuous step forward. The translucent fabric swayed between her thighs. If he reached out, he could touch that porcelain skin, but he willed his body to remain still.

"Sălbatic, *you* chose to play this game, and I intend to finish it."

Wormwood

The violent light in her eyes cracked his restraint, and he stepped forward, looming over her close enough to inhale the heady scent of snowdrops and crocus. The familiar smell conjured flashes of Luminita's Dionysian rite, the one night he had desperately wanted to change.

He recognized every dirty trick, but unbridled lust scattered his logic to the furthest recesses of his mind. Aaron detested the modern world, and every single atom in his body wanted this reprieve, this opportunity to return to his primal nature, to take what he *truly* desired—the goddess he had first met, the one he had worshipped.

Aaron dropped his hooded eyes to Luminita's navel and brushed the backs of his fingers against the exposed skin. Goosebumps and fervent heat rose, following his fingers while they glided up her body in a faint caress. By the time he reached the valley between her breasts, he had fixated on her pebbled nipples pressing against the almost sheer fabric.

Luminita took a step back, teeth sinking into her bottom lip. A delighted grin formed. "Are you quite certain you aren't mine?" She retreated another step. "You seem rather intent on worshipping me."

After a few more backward paces, Luminita leaned against the desk. Every line of her body dared him to deny her words.

Aaron closed the distance and curled his fingers around her slender throat. "Is that what you truly want from me? Worship? You weren't content with it that night."

Luminita met his heavy gaze without a flicker of doubt but didn't say a word. The last time they had been in this position, she had wanted his savagery, and her pulse racing beneath his palm indicated that hadn't changed. She claimed this was a game, but it didn't feel like one. There was something true in her, lingering beneath the callous surface.

Aaron hovered closer. Her soft exhales warmed his skin.

"I don't think you really desire tender devotions, Nita."

The woman leaned into his hand, her lips almost touching his. "There are many ways to worship, even violent ones."

The intoxicating words and her hypnotic scent tested his control, but the wild hunger in her sparkling eyes snapped it. He tightened his grip and brought her closer. The air crackled with an acute anticipation, which ignited when his mouth met hers. The brutal kiss nearly wrecked him. It reminded him so much of their first one, their collision of souls.

When he captured her bottom lip between his teeth, he bit down until the coppery taste of blood danced across his tongue. It was the only missing component—the blood, even if it hadn't been hers that night.

Luminita didn't pull back, didn't try to escape. To his surprise, a moan vibrated beneath the hand still clutching her throat, and it sent a deviant thrill racing through his bones.

Aaron released her. Both hands rushed to grip her ass and lift her onto the desk. If depraved adulation was what she craved, he would draw every ounce of painful pleasure from her provocative body, show her what she had given up that night and every day since.

Luminita fisted his shirt and ripped it open, her nails biting into his sides. The rapturous sting made his erection strain painfully against his slacks while she forced him closer. As soon as he settled between her thighs, she shamelessly rocked her hips against him, only making matters worse.

This was how he had always wanted her—driving his savagery with her willing body instead of her sharp words—but with Luminita, there was always a price. He had learned that far too many times.

Aaron broke the bruising kiss with a feral growl and shoved her down against the desk. Her inky hair splayed out around her in wild curls, and her chest heaved beneath his hand. He studied her with his last tentative shred of logic.

"What do you really want, Nita? What is this?"

Luminita stared up at him with such weight and significance, it stole the air from his lungs. He was only distantly aware of her hands traveling to her belt. "For you to fulfill your purpose." She unlocked the clasp. "For you to take your place as my true consort, Sălbatic, like you always should have been." She ripped away the belt, letting it clatter to the floor. "For us both to finally give in to the inevitability and rewrite the past."

The words were the exact ones he had wanted to hear for nearly eight hundred years, which was reason enough *not* to trust them. But the sensations beneath his touch, her deep desire, the tired relief that came with giving in, the tinge of sadness when she referred to that night…The truth of those sensations shook his tattered soul.

Nails scratched down his arms with a satisfying burn, and she gripped his hand on her chest. Curious, Aaron allowed her to drag his hand up her body until it once again rested on her throat.

"Prove your savage devotion, *if* you still carry it with you. I want *your* frenzy."

The challenge didn't contain the venom he was accustomed to, and it wasn't an order either. This was a plea, and it stirred long dormant desires. Blood pounded in his ears like the rhythmic drums of his youth, pulsing in time to his raging heart.

His fingers encircled her throat, tightening until a breathy gasp escaped. The thin veneer snapped.

Aaron used his free hand to rip off his belt. The snapping leather elicited a shiver from his goddess, but he let the belt fall to the floor. His desire wasn't to mar her porcelain skin with crude welts. He would *never* be Vlad, never cover her back with hideous scars inflicted with hate. Aaron wanted to mark her with his hands and teeth, patterns no one else could reproduce, claiming her in divine worship.

Inevitable. The word swam in his veins. A collision of souls which had begun centuries ago. One that could easily destroy them both.

That realization ripped through the intoxicating moment.

Aaron released her and tried to step back, but she locked her legs around him. This was precisely what she wanted, a ravenous man lost to his one true desire, but why? To what end? Luminita always had plans, fucking games, and he no longer desired to merely be a pawn on her chessboard. If this wasn't real...If she didn't mean it...

Luminita, sensing his hesitation, rose off the desk, pressing her chest firmly against his, and tilted her chin to stare up at him.

"I'm tired of games...at least, where *you* are concerned." She allowed her fingertips to drift down his stomach. "You were right. I *do* crave you. I have *always* craved *you*." Her deft fingers unfastened his slacks. "You've had enough of my blood to know I speak the truth, but if you require further proof..."

Luminita grabbed his hand and guided it past the sheer fabric between her thighs.

The feel of her velvety skin slick with arousal fueled his carnal beast. Logic wilted under the heat roiling between them, as hot as the surface of the sun. With a feral growl, Aaron snatched her wild curls and pulled her head back. A sharp inhale preceded the flush of pink creeping up her neck, and Aaron chased its path with his tongue.

When he reached her mouth, his lips hovered over hers, stealing each exhaled breath. "If you're fucking with me, Nita...I'll burn it *all* down, and you with it."

Nails bit into his shoulders when she impatiently leaned up to erase the distance. Her tongue danced across his lip, coaxing him, and he gave in. Aaron wanted to taste each inch, claim every piece of her, feel her shatter over and over until she lost herself in the abyss, unable to plot, content to simply be for a few blissful moments.

He returned her fervent kiss with a ferocious demand, his tongue claiming her mouth. A tender moan traveled up her throat, and he devoured it like a starving beast.

Hands slid beneath his slacks and boxer briefs, shoving them down his hips and freeing him with an addictive rush. A sudden need to shed everything overtook him. After pulling his hand from her hair, he yanked off his ruined shirt and made quick work of everything else.

Luminita lounged back against the desk. Her hooded eyes watched every motion. It wasn't the calculating stare he usually experienced.

She is here, in the moment, not ten steps ahead, and fuck…I forgot how much I wanted it.

Aaron placed his palms on the desk, caging her body beneath him, and dropped his lips to the delicate skin below her navel. She shuddered at the light touch, but the press of his teeth made the woman's entire body hum with raw desire. It was goddamn delectable.

With his heart still racing, Aaron prowled over her, leaving bites which faded as soon as he released the skin. The woman healed too quickly, eradicating every claiming mark, wiping the slate clean.

Frustration itched within him by the time he reached the delicate curve of her neck. When his teeth savagely sank into it, piercing the surface, Luminita arched off the desk and pressed against him with a mewling moan, soothing his irritation.

Blood surged across his tongue, flavor exploding over his taste buds. It was like none he had ever tasted, pure magic. Vlad had indeed been right about that fact. The amplified crackle of carnal energy arcing between them made his head swim. Aaron moved his body against hers, and she met every motion, spurring him on with intoxicating moans.

When Aaron extracted his teeth from her neck, blood trickled from the crescent-shaped wounds. He lapped up every delicious drop. A euphoric haze overtook him. Reality blurred, but it wasn't the Datura Seeds stealing the moment this time. It was pure bliss, as if everything was suddenly the way it always should have been.

Luminita, taking advantage of his blood-drunk state, locked her legs around his waist and rolled him onto his back. Aaron's gaze roved up her body and fixed on *her*. She straddled him like the chaotic goddess she was—unruly midnight-black curls framing her exquisite face, ocean-blue eyes blazing with unbridled passion, her flawless skin flushed. The air seized in his lungs at the sight, one he had envisioned so many times.

She rocked her hips against him teasingly, and the desperate ache became more acute.

"Draga." The old name left his lips as a prayer, a plea.

Luminita tilted her mouth in a devious smile, but a twinge of sadness accompanied her touch. With one hand, she reached behind her neck to undo the final clasp, and the gossamer fabric fell to his stomach, revealing her full majesty.

Aaron glided his hands up her thighs while she tossed the dress aside. He needed to be inside her, to hear her screams fill the room—loud enough to drown out the pounding in his ears—to feel her reach the agonizing peak of pleasure only he could elicit.

Aaron gripped her hips with bruising force and lifted. Her eyes glimmered with the same dark hunger, and she kept them firmly trained on his. After positioning himself beneath her, he brought her down hard and thrust upward. The violent motion ripped a cry from them both.

Luminita curled her nails into his chest, breaking the skin. The sudden sting only made him more ravenous, and he wasn't the only one.

Her hips rolled erotically, demanding more. He would gladly give it.

Aaron scooted them back on the desk, enough to brace his feet on the edge, and drove into her so hard she tipped forward. A feral cry tore from her throat, and her hands slapped the desk, bracing herself. He needed more of those sounds—unrestrained screams where logic and plans had no place.

Aaron banded his arms around her and crushed her to his chest while he continued to drive into her. Each cry sounded more delicious than the last, becoming far too tempting. He sealed his mouth roughly over hers to steal those cries, to swallow them.

Fingers sank into his hair, twisting and pulling, until nails bit into his scalp. Every sear of pain, every violent devotion, made him thrust harder.

Luminita broke away, her unfettered shout of elation washing over his face. She was *so* close to the edge, to breaking. Aaron could feel it in her tensing muscles, taste it on her sawing breaths, hear it in the gathering crescendo of her screams, sense it in her growing euphoria. Every bit of it engulfed him, an absolute heaven he had never truly known.

Steel pressed to his throat, and Aaron froze with a dart of blind panic. His mind screamed in protest, furious that she intended to steal this from him *again*.

Luminita's face hovered over him. She gasped for breath, sweat glistening on her rosy cheeks, ringlets of her black tresses clinging to her face and neck. A storm raged in her deep blue eyes, and it held him captive.

The woman is a fucking vision, even with a knife pressed to my skin.

"I didn't tell you to stop." She bit her bottom lip and trailed the blade down to the center of his chest in a faint touch.

Everything amplified the primal *need* to break her, and when Luminita swiveled her hips again, demanding a response, he complied like a man possessed by a singular mission.

Aaron pistoned into her with every ounce of strength, his bruising hands forcing her down. Her ragged screams resumed, sweet music to his ears, and the blade bounced against his chest. A few times it broke the skin with a satisfying burn, heightening his pleasure.

Then the knife clattered to the floor. Luminita gripped the desk's edge, and a deafening shriek split the air. She shattered, her muscles quivering, her walls pulsating with a death grip. The absolute nirvana detonated through him, pulling him right over the edge in a rapturous high which thoroughly destroyed him.

The world stilled. The universe stopped in those precious seconds. A true collision of souls, just like he *knew* it would be.

Luminita collapsed against his chest while they both fought for each gasping, exalted breath. In that unguarded moment, he felt something entirely unfamiliar in Luminita—contentment, peace, fulfillment, like the final piece in a puzzle snapping into place.

Aaron lowered his eyes to the graceful line of her neck. His savage bite was nothing more than light pink crescents on her otherwise unblemished skin. Even that last vestige of their violence would disappear in minutes. He coasted over the fading marks with the pads of his fingers, and Luminita stirred, but Aaron kept his focus locked on the bite mark.

A flicker of emotion slid over her too fast for him to identify, and a sharp pain flared in his upper arm. Aaron whipped his head to the side, noticing a syringe in Luminita's hand.

Absolute rage flooded him. His eyes snapped to hers. "What did you do?" His voice trembled with the memory that question summoned: the first time he had truly cried.

Luminita looked to the syringe with something akin to deep regret. The thing fell to the floor, and the delicate column of her throat shifted.

When her stormy eyes met his again, tears flooded them, just as they had on Dragobete.

"Wormwood," she whispered in a haunted tone.

Aaron shoved her off him and surged to his feet. Red blurred his vision, and an old hatred burned through every vein. "You tried to infect me with the fucking virus?" he snarled.

Luminita kept her gaze fixed on the floor and pulled the iridescent fabric around her, shielding her body, falling in on herself with a million emotions. She didn't utter a single word while fastening the clasp at her neck.

"Nita!" Aaron stormed up to her and snatched her arms. "You *know* it takes far more than one exposure to infect a pureblood. What the hell are you doing?"

Bitter remorse flooded the air around her, but she still refused to meet his eyes.

He gripped her chin, forcing her to look at him.

"Not when it's tailored to your DNA."

The sentence struck him harder than any physical blow ever could. "Why?" he asked, unable to form any other words.

Tears lined her lashes, and he sensed the contrite panic swirling beneath the surface. What they shared had moved her as much as it had affected him. It had meant something to her. He knew it with certainty. It had *changed* them.

"I needed you under control…on *my* side. I needed insurance." Desperation warred with her lack of confidence in those words.

A snarl lifted his lip, and he tightened his hand around her jaw. "I am *not* one of your blind lackeys, here to follow every order. I'm your *partner.* I'm on *our* side. I challenge you, I question you, and your response is to fucking condemn me?"

"I have the cure," Luminita said quickly, as if that made everything okay.

"You engineered a virus to attack *me*. Then you lured me into thinking we *finally* had a true partnership, seducing me with the night I desperately wish to change…"

Luminita's breaths quickened, and beneath the sorrow, fear tainted the air.

Absolute fear.

Luminita, this Goddess of Blood and Chaos, was *terrified of him*. Aaron leaned in close enough to taste her heavy exhales.

"Why are you scared of me?"

Defensive anger reached her eyes, and she pulled away from his grip. The crimson fabric swirled around her.

No. She doesn't get to walk away. Not this time.

Aaron closed the distance in three long strides and locked his arms around her, pulling her back against his chest. He hovered his lips over her ear.

"You came undone on top of me, Draga. You felt it. The euphoric rapture. You were there…in the moment, not plotting ahead. You were *with* me. Is that what scared you?"

Luminita didn't speak. She didn't need to. The longing ache emanating from her sent forgotten thrills racing through him. Centuries-old regret and heartbreak—he felt it all.

"Why do I scare you?" he whispered.

She still refused to answer.

With a growl, Aaron released her and stormed around the desk. He scooped up the discarded knife. Luminita's eyes widened when he strode back to her with the weapon.

"You can't get the cure without me," she said. "I'm the only one with access."

Aaron continued on his path, undeterred, and stopped before her. "You want leverage? The upper hand? Will that make you comfortable?"

Before she could answer, Aaron sank to his knees before her and grabbed her hand. He wrapped it around the knife's handle and brought the point to his chest.

"*You* are *my* goddess, and *I* am *your* consort. If you pledge to stop plotting against me…to stop pushing me away, I will give my loyalty and my life to you. It's always been yours anyway."

Shock gave way to true confliction while Luminita stared down at him. "Andrew is non-negotiable."

Disgust and envy churned his gut. She was willing to destroy him to save *Cohen*? The knowledge caught in his throat like a bitter pill. However, if suffering the man's existence gave him true divinity with *her*, it was a worthy trade.

"I will not harm him," Aaron swore with a heavy heart.

Studious eyes gauged the weight of every word. "And I have a plan for Orchid."

"I will not interfere, but *only* if you include me in your plans. *True partners*, Nita. Equals!"

A warm drop of blood trickled down his chest from the blade's point, but he didn't pull away.

"Orchid is the best assassin I have, and she won't refuse the mission."

"Why?" he asked simply. "Who's the target?"

"David Boston, Sr."

"Why not send Killian? He's gifted with humans."

No animosity lingered in his tone. Luminita drew her brows together, as if truly seeing him for the first time in a long while.

"I need Killian. There are too many humans here to let him leave for this." Luminita tossed the dagger to the ground.

Relief and hope sprang to life in Aaron's chest. He pulled her down to her knees, and she let him. Perhaps Luminita really was tired of fighting their connection.

"I'm…" She had trouble finding her voice. "…sorry."

Luminita didn't only mean the virus. He could tell that much. Aaron wrapped a fist in the ethereal dress. He tugged her against him, his mouth claiming hers fiercely.

There was no hesitation. She glided her tongue against his in urgent demand and dove her fingers into his hair.

In truth, he would have worshiped her indefinitely without the incentive of a cure. Her violent passion stirred things nothing else had.

If only he had made her understand sooner, shown her the power she held over him, fell to his knees before his goddess on Dragobete with the same oath, perhaps they might have avoided the cataclysmic events which had shredded and tainted their souls.

Aaron pulled away just enough to whisper one thing before claiming her mouth again. *"Draga meu."*

My Beloved.

Chapter 39

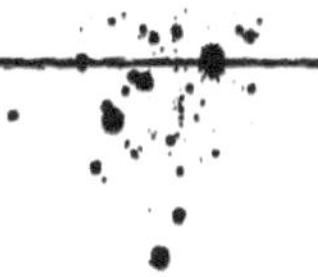

"Nic, are you sure you don't want me to go with you?"

Nicci smiled over at Tim, who sat beside Eileen on the bottom bunk. "No offense, big fella, but I don't think your presence would help matters."

"I could go with you," Lilith offered.

"I appreciate it, partner, but I think bringing you would only piss Alicia off more. She...isn't your biggest fan. Besides, this is something I have to do on my own."

Nicci's heart felt like a lead weight in her chest. The breakup had *not* gone well. Alicia hadn't believed any of her very valid reasons, and the woman had argued every point, demanding a truth Nicci could never give her, not even now.

Of course, the virus might change things. She might not have to hide that side forever. But her gut said Alicia couldn't handle the truth. Being a vampire, a pureblood, a different damn species, was a huge lie to swallow.

Tim made it work. She gazed over at her bestie, whose arm was draped around Eileen. The woman's smile when she spoke to him was absolutely radiant. But their situation was different. Tim was only a half-blood, basically one tiny step from human, and Eileen had known who and what he was *before* they got together. Nicci had been lying to Alicia for almost three years.

The RV came to a stop in Murray Hill along a row of brownstones, and Nicci's pulse rocketed.

This is not going to go well.

"The address you gave me is a few blocks up."

Nicci nodded her thanks to Gibson and stood. After checking her walkie, she strode to the steps.

"Good luck. Call if you need backup," Tim hollered.

Nicci joked around with him a lot, but Tim truly was one of her favorite people. The man was all heart and plain truth, something she could relate to. Well, at least the last part. Nicci had zero problems doling out truth, except to the one person who wanted it most.

"Thanks, big fella." She flashed a hollow smile and stepped out onto the sidewalk.

Nicci jammed her hands into her jean pockets and focused on the concrete while she walked the familiar route to Alicia's house. She *still* had no clue how to do this.

What if she slams the door in my face? What if she refuses to talk to me? What if she won't leave without the truth? What if I give it to her? What if she runs screaming?

The worst part of all of it…She *wanted* to be with Alicia. Perhaps all this would have been easier if she didn't. It had taken every ounce of Nicci's strength not to give in the night she had ended things, to just walk away while Alicia shed furious tears in the kitchen. Nicci had thought by cutting ties she would be keeping the woman she loved safe, but obviously, her logic was flawed.

Nicci crossed one side street, then another, still emersed in her chaotic thoughts. Each step closer tightened her chest more.

"Come on, breathe. You can do this," she muttered to herself.

"Nicci?"

Fear ripped through her chest, and she snapped her head up. Alicia stood in front of her, with grocery bags hanging from her arms. The morning sun gave her near-black waves an ethereal shimmer, and a thin sheen of sweat glistened on her sun-kissed skin. Nicci's throat tightened.

"What are you doing here?" Alicia's shock quickly transformed into guarded anger, but a fragile hope lingered in her dark eyes.

It broke Nicci's heart all over again.

"I…uh…" Nicci cleared her throat and tried to get her head straight. "I need to talk to you. It's important."

"It's always important to *you*. More than our relationship, right?"

A heavy sigh left Nicci deflated. "I'm trying to keep you safe."

"By lying to me? By keeping things from me? By running off to who knows where with your fucking partner? I don't want your protection, Nicci. Just go."

Every word hit like a physical blow before Alicia stormed toward her house. But no matter how much Nicci wanted to listen, to walk away and leave Alicia in peace, she couldn't.

It's my fault she's in danger.

Nicci jogged up the path, her ponytail swinging like a pendulum, and reached the stairs before Alicia found her keys in the bottom of her monstrous purse.

"Look, I know you're mad. You have every right to be. You can hate me all you want, but…" Nicci swiped the keys from Alicia's hand. "I *need* to talk to you."

Although a deep crease formed between Alicia's brows, her dark brown eyes studied Nicci carefully. After several riotous heartbeats, the woman released a sigh.

"Fine." She snatched back her keys and unlocked the door.

Nicci scooped up the grocery bags with a faint smile. "Thank you."

Alicia watched her with an unimpressed scowl. "This better be serious, and you *better* tell me the damn truth."

"I will." *A version of it*, Nicci thought sadly. She *hated* lying to Alicia. That was why she had refused to live together.

Sure, Solasta provided various means to disguise blood—herbal supplement bottles with a medical prescription were the most popular— but so much of Nicci's life consisted of lying to the world. Home was the one place she could be herself. If she lived with Alicia, she would have to wear that mask twenty-four seven. It would eat away at her, and eventually, she would resent the constant act.

Nicci followed Alicia through the hallway, back to the familiar kitchen, and set the bags on the counter, trying to push away all the irrelevant thoughts about their relationship. None of it mattered. She wasn't here to win her back. Nicci was there to ensure Alicia's safety.

"Okay, Nicci. What's this about?" Once again, a hopeful glint lit Alicia's stare, and it sliced right into Nicci's heart.

"I'm in some big-time trouble. Things went insanely south on a case."

Concern drew Alicia's brows together, and she stepped forward, placing a hand on Nicci's arm. "Shit. How can I help?"

This. This was why she had fallen for the woman—her fierce compassion, no matter the circumstance. It sure as hell hadn't been Alicia's horrific taste in movies.

A damn ocean of lies and heartache flowed between them, but in that moment, they were all forgotten.

"I appreciate it." Nicci patted her hand before pulling away. She didn't want to, but sending mixed signals wasn't fair. Nothing had changed. Being together was too dangerous, too hard. "That's not why I'm here, though."

Alicia straightened, trying to hide her disappointment. "Why *are* you here?"

"There are people…hunting me and my team. These people will find any pressure point to flush us out, especially people we care about."

A sardonic huff escaped Alicia's chest. "What the hell is this, Nicci? You already told me it's *too dangerous to be together*, which I think is a *bullshit* excuse."

"You're right!" Nicci held up her hands. "Sort of…" she corrected. "There's stuff I *couldn't* tell you, and I hate that, *but* you are in real danger. I want to take you to a safe house."

"Why?" Alicia's stare hardened, but her eyes misted. "We aren't together, remember? I'm not your problem."

"I still care, and this is *real*. A team of guys attacked my people at our last hotel with semi-auto rifles."

Alicia's calculated stare made Nicci want to crawl under the damn table.

"What things couldn't you tell me?"

Nicci blinked. "Seriously? That's your takeaway? Not the fact that people are turning hotels into Swiss cheese, trying to get to us?"

Alicia crossed her arms over her chest while she pinned Nicci with a glare. "What things couldn't you tell me?" she repeated firmly.

Nicci sighed and slumped against the counter. "I still can't tell you."

"Why?"

"Because…" Nicci expelled a heavy breath. "It's too dangerous."

The woman raised her eyebrows nearly to her hairline. "More than a surprise death squad?"

Nicci froze. *Shit. That's an excellent point.* "Um…probably not."

One corner of Alicia's mouth twitched, almost forming a smile. "Care to try again?"

"Can we talk about this later? I really need to get you out of here."

"No. Now. If you can't give me a real answer, I'm not going anywhere."

"Alicia, this is not a joke." As soon as the words left Nicci's mouth, she knew they had been a mistake.

Outrage flooded Alicia's eyes, and she straightened again. "Do you see me laughing?"

"Come on." Nicci huffed. Dread twisted her insides. "Don't make this harder than it needs to be."

Alicia locked her eyes onto Nicci's with breathtaking ferocity. "Give me a reason to trust you. Why can't you let me in?"

Nicci lowered her gaze to the floor, her heart cracking. "Because…if you truly knew me…*all* of me…it'd terrify you." The words hung between them like a palpable entity until Alicia drew in a shaky breath.

"What? Are you some kind of serial killer or something?" The feeble attempt at a joking tone failed.

"No, but…I can't talk about it…definitely not here, not now." Tears prickled at Nicci's eyes. Fear and panic warred for domination. "I just need to make sure you're safe."

Hands brushed her cheeks. Nicci peered up at Alicia's teary eyes, and for the millionth time in the past three years, Nicci wished she had a simple human life, one she could share.

"Talk to me, Nic."

The strained words pulled on every heartstring, and Nicci told her the truth. "I *really* wish I could."

Alicia frowned but refused to give up. "Nic." She stepped closer, cradling Nicci's face in her palms. "You *can* talk to me. I love you. Whatever you tell me won't change that."

Nicci's face fell, and tears rolled down her cheeks. *If only I believed that.*

"I know you think it won't, but…" Nicci gently took Alicia's hands and guided them away from her face without letting go. "Even *if* you believed me…you would never see me like this again."

After glancing down at their connected hands, Alicia met her eyes. "I don't believe you. I think you're scared."

Nicci shook her head and tried to suck in a breath past the boulder wedged in her throat. "I am *absolutely* scared. I'm terrified, Alicia. The night my apartment was tossed…if you'd been there, you'd be dead. Hell, right now, you're in danger because my name is on the list of every professional hitman in North Ameri—"

Before Nicci finished, Alicia's mouth crashed against hers, burning through Nicci's defenses. After a brief shocked pause, everything else fell away, and Nicci returned the urgent kiss. She pulled Alicia closer, fingers delving into her silky curls, desperate to disappear in the moment.

If only I could share everything and still *have this.*

Alicia broke the kiss with a breathless smile. She leaned her forehead against Nicci's. "This is real. This is what I want, no matter how scary you think it is."

Reality crashed into the moment, souring it. "You only say that because you don't know."

"Then tell me."

Nicci swallowed hard and closed her eyes. "Can I please get you someplace safe? We can talk about everything else when we're out of danger, okay?"

Alicia leaned back, fierce determination blazing in her expression. "Promise me."

"I promise." Nicci avoided her gaze and lied with a heavy heart.

"No. Look at me." Once she complied, Alicia continued. "Promise me you won't try to break up with me again over this shit. Promise that you'll tell me *everything*. It should be my decision what happens after that."

When Nicci hesitated, Alicia shook her head.

"Three years. We've been together three years despite the fact we never spend more than two days together at a time, that you don't want to live together, that you keep secrets. I'm *still* here. You owe me a damn choice."

Fuck. If I don't promise…really promise, she'll never leave here with me, and if I do…if I tell her everything…

"I promise," Nicci said with firm resolve. "Once this mess is over, I'll tell you everything." *Eileen didn't freak out. Maybe Alicia wouldn't either. At this point, I can either dump her and never look back or confess. Only one offers a possible future with the woman I love.*

Alicia closed the distance again and wiped the tears from Nicci's cheeks. "I missed you."

Nicci wrapped her arms around Alicia's waist, leaning up to kiss her petal-soft lips. "I missed you too." For one selfish moment, she soaked in every sensation, just in case she never got another chance. "We do need to go. Can you pack a week's worth of clothes? Nothing crazy."

Alicia arched a brow. "Crazy?"

"Yeah." Nicci chuckled. "No five-pound hair dryer. No stilettos. No fifteen outfits for one possible occasion. You'll be hiding out with two other women, a teenager, and two kids."

Alicia smirked and slid out of Nicci's arms. "Fine. Just the essentials." A bright smile lit her luminous face, and she sauntered toward the stairs. The hypnotic sway of her hips made Nicci grin. "Give me five minutes."

"So, you mean twenty?" Nicci called after her.

Alicia paused, peered over her shoulder, and rolled her eyes. "Very funny."

Nicci laughed before hopping on the counter, letting her legs dangle. When she had strode toward the brownstone, this was *not* the outcome she had expected. Honestly, she had thought getting Alicia to listen at all would be a stretch. Still, a large part of her feared it wouldn't last once she kept her word.

Alicia was right, though. She deserved an informed choice. The woman had earned that, and with the virus forcing their hand toward public exposure, it looked like the truth was actually possible.

The faint squeak of the mudroom door sent an instant jolt up Nicci's spine.

She whipped her head toward the back room while she slid off the counter. Blood instantly pounded in her ears, and she crouched, hiding behind the island and drawing her gun from its holster.

A soft footstep sounded on the tile, then another. A shadow fell across the threshold.

Nicci's pulse went wild. She trained her gun on the doorway, waiting with measured breaths. If this was an entire squad, like the one at the hotel, they could be approaching from all entry points. There could be someone on the fire escape.

Fuck. Nicci pushed the panic down. All she could do was handle the threat in front of her. Freaking out over all the possible scenarios would only distract her, and she couldn't scream a warning to Alicia or use the walkie without giving away her position.

A man appeared at the kitchen's rear entrance. He didn't seem imposing, dressed in khakis and a polo, but he held a gun.

No, she realized, spotting the holster of darts and the odd shape to the pistol. *A tranquilizer gun. Must be someone on Luminita's side.*

Being captured and delivered to Luminita wasn't much better than death, but it gave Nicci an edge if the perp's mission was to take them alive.

The man stepped into the kitchen. His eyes scanned the room.

Fucking amateur. Nicci lined up her shot. It was a risk. If there were others, firing her weapon would alert everyone, but her gut said this was a solo job.

After exhaling softly, Nicci squeezed the trigger. A loud crack echoed through the house, and the man's head snapped back before he crumpled to the ground.

Nicci hustled out of her spot while feet pounded upstairs. Once she reached the perp and ensured the shot between his eyes had done the trick, she swung her gun toward the open back door.

No movement.

Feet raced down the stairs, but only one set. The rest of the house, including the backyard, was silent.

"Nic!" Alicia's panicked voice came from the stairs, but Nicci kept her studious gaze on the backyard.

"I'm okay! Stay there! Don't come in the kitchen."

The footsteps halted, and Nicci peered outside, checking the rear fire escape and scanning the rest of the small yard.

Nothing.

Nicci holstered her weapon and jogged back into the mudroom, avoiding the erratic splatters of blood and brain matter. She paused at the body, stripped off the holster of tranquilizer darts, and snatched the gun from the man's hand.

"What's happening?" Alicia called. Her soft steps accompanied her words.

"Don't come in here. Grab your shoes. We have to go now." If one merc had already had this idea, there would be more, and not all of them wanted to take prisoners.

"Oh my god!"

Alicia stood at the island, hands covering her pale face.

"Damnit. I told you not to come in here." Nicci sighed, jamming the perp's gun in her back pocket.

"Is he…" The words trailed off. Alicia's wide eyes roamed over the body to the trail of blood and brain matter.

"Shoes, purse! Let's go!" Nicci jogged around the island, but Alicia didn't move. Once she reached her, Nicci gripped her face, forcing Alicia to meet her eyes. "Ali, I need you to put your shoes on and grab your purse. We have to go *now*. He won't be the last one to come looking for you."

"What about…" She looked back to the dead man in her mudroom.

"We don't have time. *We have to go.*"

A tear jostled free when she nodded. "Okay."

Finally, Alicia launched into action, scooping up her keys and purse before running for the front door, where she kept her sneakers. Once she slid them on, Nicci held out a hand.

"Let me check the front first."

After another nod from Alicia, Nicci eased the door open and peeked through the crack at the empty sidewalk. She grabbed the tranq gun, holding it at her side, and opened the door a little wider to inspect the street.

Nothing.

"Okay. The vehicle is four blocks away. Follow me and stay close."

Alicia swallowed hard but nodded again.

They jogged out into the late morning sunshine. Nicci constantly scanned the area, but it seemed her gut had been right. The perp didn't appear to have any partners.

When the RV came into sight, the panic searing through Nicci's veins started to recede. A close call. If she hadn't gotten there when she did…If Alicia hadn't listened to her…

The door swung open as they approached. Tim greeted them with a worried expression.

"Everything okay?"

Nicci shook her head and ushered Alicia past him. "No. We had company. Thankfully, just one guy."

"Are you okay?" Lilith asked when Nicci reached the top of the stairs.

"We're fine, partner."

Gibson wasted no time pulling away from the curb and heading toward Grand Central Parkway. Meanwhile, everyone else focused on Nicci and Alicia with curiosity.

"Alicia, let me introduce everyone. The big guy there"—Nicci pointed to Tim—"is Timothy Bardow, one of my best friends. Our driver is Gibson." She gestured to the table. "This is Keller, Chance Deveraux, and my partner, Lilith Adams."

Nicci didn't miss the hard edge to Alicia's expression when her eyes fell on Lilith, but she wasn't ready to tackle that problem.

After turning around, she introduced Gloria, Erica, Sophia, and Rose, all piled on the couch. Then she smiled over at Tim's sister, who sat in her wheelchair parked by the bunk beds.

"This is Jill. You'll be bunking with her, Gloria, and the girls. Lastly"—Nicci gestured to the bottom bunk—"this is Special Agent

Eileen Hersch. She's the one who pulled strings to get us a safe house. Everyone, this is Alicia."

A tense silence filled the vehicle until Alicia chuckled lightly. "Well, it's nice to finally meet *anyone* from Nicci's life." She rested her dark eyes on Nicci with an indecipherable expression. "Only took you three years, a breakup, and a dead man in my kitchen."

Nicci swallowed hard. Her panic reared back to life until Alicia's mouth relaxed into a smile.

"It's a start."

Chapter 40

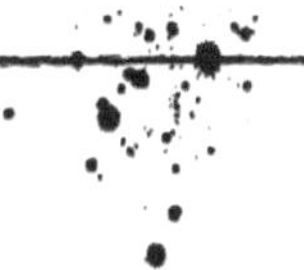

Dread weighed heavy on Eileen's shoulders while she stood at the front of the RV. Her gaze roamed over the expectant faces. If she was wrong about Agent Hernandez and her team, Eileen would be endangering every single one of them, including Jill and Tim.

But there was no other option. Leaving them at some random hotel was far too dangerous. These people needed protection. The team certainly couldn't drag them along. Six adults fit comfortably in the RV, but nine adults, a teen, and two children? Not to mention, they were innocents who didn't belong anywhere near a fight.

Eileen focused on Tim's confident smile. He trusted her with not only his life, but also his sister's. Just the idea of letting him down, failing, hurt like a gaping wound in her chest.

"Okay." Eileen drew in a deep breath, letting it stretch her lungs, and released it in a huff. "I don't want to overwhelm the FBI agents, and the safehouse is four blocks away. I suggest you relay any messages now, before we leave."

"I'm going with you," Tim added in a resolute voice.

A smile tugged at Eileen's mouth, and she nodded. She had expected him to insist, but it still summoned a warm glow despite their previous argument. Eileen understood why he wanted to go with her, and it wasn't because he didn't trust her to handle things. He just wanted to be there.

"Tim and I will escort the civilians. My contact should be there soon, so we'll leave in ten to fifteen minutes." Eileen turned to step outside and give the others a few moments of privacy.

"Pixie."

Eileen smiled at the nickname and peered over her shoulder.

"Can you grab Jill's wheelchair?"

Tim scooped up his sister, who draped her right arm around his neck with practiced ease. Her left dangled uselessly at her side. Outrage flared at the injustice of it all. Jill was far too young. If it hadn't been for the woman's asshole husband, she would have been living a normal, healthy life.

Eileen had been lucky. Her abusive ex, Karl, had avoided hitting her in noticeable places, including her face.

"Sure." Eileen hurried forward and deftly folded the chair in two quick maneuvers. Once she carried it outside, Eileen unfolded it and locked the wheels.

"She's a pro." Jill grinned and winked.

Eileen couldn't help but admire the woman. Despite what had happened, despite losing control of half her body, despite life stealing her independence, Jill radiated an infectious light.

"I got used to one when…" she blurted out before considering where that story led. "I fractured my right ankle and dislocated my left knee. Had to have minor surgery on both." Eileen hurried through the rest and hoped no one asked questions because it already felt like a lie. It hadn't been her fault, and it hadn't been an accident either.

About a month after she graduated from Quantico and married Karl, he had lost his temper and pushed her down the concrete steps. She should have left him then, but he had apologized so much. The man had seemed honestly distraught. *Such a fucking lie.*

"Ouch! How the hell did you manage that?" Jill asked while Tim settled her into the wheelchair.

Of course. I had to open my mouth. "I…uh, fell down my front steps. Bones plus concrete isn't a great combination," Eileen said with a dark chuckle.

Tim caught her eyes, clearly seeing through her bullshit, and a muscle in his jaw ticked.

"It was a long time ago."

Jill's gaze bounced between Eileen and her brother. "Did I miss something?"

Well, shit. Apparently, Jill is incredibly perceptive too.

"It's nothing." Eileen flashed an uneasy smile and turned to stare down the quiet sidewalk, hugging her midsection. She hated the odd embarrassment which still accompanied the faded memories. Eileen couldn't even recall why Karl had been mad, just the furious lines of his face.

Tim's hands slid over her shoulders, and his breath caressed the shell of her ear. "It's *not* nothing."

Shivers danced down her spine, and she leaned back into him before peeking over her shoulder. "Okay," she whispered. "But it's not worth talking about either. It's in the past."

Detailing Karl's sins wouldn't change anything, and honestly, she couldn't remember half of what had transpired. When trauma first happens, people think it will be permanently etched in their mind—a crystal-clear memory of each time they were broken. In truth, the moments fade and blur. They jumble together, becoming less important, less relevant, until certain circumstances dredge them up from the depths.

"Hmm. That makes sense."

They both turned to face Jill, but Tim spoke before Eileen found her voice. "What does?"

A knowing smile brightened Jill's soft face. "Let me guess. You married the wrong guy young, and it turned into a revolving door of pain and apologies?"

Eileen chuckled in amusement. "Looks like blunt honesty runs in the family."

Jill relaxed in her chair. "I spent enough of my life lying to family, friends, and myself about what happened in my house. Now I just speak the truth."

A sudden burning question overcame Eileen's polite logic. "Can I ask you something?"

A curious grin reached all the way to Jill's eyes. "Sure."

After a quick glance at Tim, who seemed equally intrigued, Eileen settled her focus back on Jill. "Why did you keep his last name?"

When Jill's eyebrows shot up and Tim stiffened beside her, panic seized her chest.

"Shit. Sorry. You do *not* have to answer that." Heat blazed across her cheeks like a brand.

"No. It's fine. Most people don't have the balls to ask." Jill turned her smile on Tim. "I *really* like her. Don't fuck it up."

Tim nodded with a lopsided smirk, and Jill shifted her attention back to Eileen. "My husband disappeared. It's been over seven years, and the court declared him legally dead, so I *could* go back to my maiden name, but…"

For the first time since they had met, a haunted expression dimmed her brightness to a flicker.

"Sometimes, it feels like I dreamt the whole thing…or like the memories belong to someone else, ya know?" Jill's misty eyes searched Eileen's, as if looking for a kindred spark.

"Yeah, like it happened in a past life."

The tension left Jill's shoulders, and she smiled, the light returning to her features. "I never want to forget it happened to me. Forgetting means giving someone else the opportunity to fool me again."

Eileen lifted a corner of her mouth. "That makes a certain sense. I filed paperwork the day Karl was arrested. Then I just avoided men for the next decade."

Jill laughed—a bright, bubbly sound. "Me too…although admittedly not by choice." The woman flashed Tim a mischievous smile. "You could at *least* bring me some handsome *single* visitors to talk to…like Gibson."

Tim snorted a laugh. "That's a *hell no* from me. I'm not setting guys up with my *sister.*"

Jill rolled her eyes and huffed. "You're no fun. What about you, Eileen? Any single friends?"

"Unfortunately, I currently live in Knoxville, but…" A slight smile pulled at her lips. "I'm planning to relocate."

Although Jill's knowing smile widened, she didn't push for details. "What about the agents guarding us at the safe house? Any eye candy?"

"I, uh…" Once again, Eileen's cheeks blazed hot. She didn't like admitting that she didn't know the members of Hernandez's team. "I don't know. Hernandez and I went through Quantico together, and I *do* trust her. *Plus*, she owes me big time for taking the Cappalletty case."

"Relax, pixie warrior." Tim squeezed her shoulder and tugged her against his side. "Jill's just giving you shit." He pressed a kiss to her temple, and it instantly soothed her nerves.

Eileen still marveled at how *easy* things felt with Tim, like she had known him for years.

"Um, excuse me, but I'm completely serious. I'm half paralyzed, not dead."

While Tim paled, Jill flashed Eileen a conspiratorial wink which made them both laugh.

"Jillybean, there's some things I never need to know," Tim groaned.

"Well, thankfully, I have Eileen for girl talk now."

The radiant smile on Jill's face warmed every inch of Eileen's heart.

"Mia." Eileen jogged well ahead of the others, coming to a stop in front of a tall brunette.

The curvy woman was over six foot, with more than her fair share of muscle—the primary reason Hernandez had dominated most of their class in hand-to-hand combat.

"Eileen." The woman cracked a warm smile and pulled Hersch in for a side hug. "It's nice to see you."

"Yeah, well. There's a good chance you'll be seeing more of me."

"Oh?" Mia raised her eyebrows. "Thinking of making a change?"

"Without John, Knoxville just doesn't feel like home anymore." It wasn't a lie. She still couldn't purge the image of her partner's body in his bathtub, blood discoloring the water.

The woman rested her hand on Eileen's shoulder. "I'm sorry. No one should lose a partner like that."

Eileen simply nodded.

She couldn't correct her about John's murder without launching into an unbelievable story that wasn't really hers to share. So, for now, she had to embrace the lie of John's suicide.

"Anyway, I'm looking into a transfer here once I'm off bereavement and this situation is over."

A wide smile lit Mia's face. "We'd be lucky to have your brains, Hersch. I'll put in a good word with the director."

"Thanks."

Footsteps sounded behind her, and Mia focused past Eileen to the motley group, studying each one.

"Everyone, this is Special Agent Mia Hernandez."

Tim, who was pushing Jill's wheelchair, stopped beside Eileen, his arm brushing hers. Mia stared at him for a moment before addressing the entire group.

"Welcome. We'll do proper introductions inside, but it's only civilians from this point. You said *three* adults, one teen, and two children, correct?" Mia's black eyes settled on Tim again.

"Yes," Eileen replied quickly.

Mia nodded, but the look she gave Eileen indicated she definitely had questions. Although Mia had been stationed in a different state after graduation, they had kept in touch, especially during the end with Karl.

"Well, I will have two agents on-site at all times, four in total, rotating in twelve-hour shifts."

"People you trust implicitly?" Eileen asked. "Boston is *very* well connected and has already pulled a lot of strings in the FBI."

Hernandez gave a firm nod. "I've worked closely with all four and thoroughly vetted each one myself for a high-security taskforce. Plus, I will be on-site from ten to six every day to oversee things."

Eileen could almost feel Tim relax beside her. He trusted her, but hearing the plan helped. "Thanks, Mia. I really appreciate it."

"It's the least I could do after you carried my ass through national law."

"I'm fairly certain you settled that debt in Hogan's Alley."

Mia chuckled. "That was my job as team lead. Doesn't count. Although…if you go through with the transfer, I'll have plenty of chances to pay you back."

Eileen sensed Tim and Jill's eyes on her, but she kept her focus on Mia with a smile. "I look forward to that."

"Agent Hernandez," Tim said. "Two of our people have health conditions that require refrigerated prescriptions. It's important the bottles remain air-tight until use."

"Understood. That isn't a problem."

"We have a week's supply," Gloria added.

"If things drag out longer, we will need a way to deliver more."

Mia nodded at Tim. "You can use my cell as a contact. Eileen can give you the number."

"Thank you, Agent Hernandez." After flashing a grateful smile, Tim stepped away to crouch in front of Jill. "Hopefully, it will just be a few days, Jillybean." He tucked a blond lock behind her ear.

A few tears glistened on her pale lashes, but Jill wore a bright smile. "I know, Timothy. Just *be careful* and take care of my future sister-in-law."

Tim's face turned a glowing shade of red, and Jill covered her mouth to keep from laughing. Of course, Eileen's cheeks burned like a damn four-alarm fire too.

"You just *can't* help yourself, can you?" Tim asked, shaking his head.

Jill leaned forward to whisper something, and Eileen peeked up at Mia. An amused smile graced the woman's face, and she waggled a finger between them—their signal from college when Mia needed an explanation.

Eileen moved over next to her, trying not to grin like a damn idiot. "Before you say anything, it's brand-new, and he is"—she slid her gaze back to Tim—"…amazing."

"I can see that…on both counts," Mia whispered.

"One thing I forgot to mention. Jill, Tim's sister, she can't move her left side, so she needs a little help. Gloria and her daughter Erica have agreed to take care of her, but I wanted you to be aware."

"She's awful young. Accident?"

"Of the Karl variety."

Mia swallowed hard. "Please tell me the fucker at least got jail time."

Eileen hesitated. Telling her the truth would endanger Tim, something she would never do. For now, she needed to stick to verifiable facts, even if she did trust Mia.

"Got off on a technicality and disappeared." Eileen sighed heavily.

"Is he a security risk?"

"Doubtful. It's been over seven years. I don't think he's coming back."

"Shame."

Eileen peered over at Mia. The intimidating woman stood with her arms crossed, staring at Jill with a soft frown.

"I would have enjoyed putting a bullet or two in the guy." Then she snapped her gaze to Eileen. "Same goes for Karl, if he ever gets out."

Chapter 41

"Where's Dad? Why isn't he here?" Desiree cried angrily. Her little chest heaved, and tears gathered in her hazel eyes.

Helena's heart cracked in two. The air seized in her lungs. "Baby, Dad…" She couldn't do it, couldn't say it.

Desi's watery eyes stared up at her expectantly. They had more brown than Noah's vibrant green, but still reminded her of him so much. How was she supposed to sit in this cell and tell her little girl she would never see her father again?

"I don't know, Desi. I'm sorry," she whispered, caving to her cowardice. Helena couldn't steal the hopeful glint from her eyes.

The little girl frowned and peered around the room. "I don't like this place. I want to go home."

"I know, sweetheart. I want to go home too." Helena tugged Desi close, wrapping her arms around her, and sobbed against her shoulder. She couldn't get the image out of her mind.

Cohen had killed Noah, drained him right in front of her, stole all his essence, and left an empty husk.

Noah is dead. The thought twisted her stomach into painful knots. *And he's dead because of me.* That was the part she wasn't sure she could live with, but Desi needed her now more than ever. Helena *refused* to leave another child alone in the world. She had to figure a way out of this.

There *had* to be a way. Luminita hadn't killed her yet, which meant she wanted something. Hopefully, it wasn't simply Ashcroft's location. The abomination was never coming back to life. Helena had ensured that by tossing the head and burning the body.

"I want Dad," Desi whispered against her shoulder.

Fresh tears prickled Helena's eyes.

"I know, baby." She stroked her daughter's hair and pressed kisses to her temples, but it would never be enough. Desi adored her father. They had always had a closer relationship, like two peas in a pod.

Part of that had been due to Helena's job as a pharmaceutical rep. She traveled a lot, partly by design. It wasn't that she didn't love Noah and Desi; she did, whole-heartedly, but that only made things harder. The secrets, the lies…They weighed heavy on her, and it was easier to bear if she had more time alone.

When she'd been home, she was present, involved, loving, but the time away gave her space to release all the sadness, guilt, and grief she kept bottled inside—the stuff she had never wanted her family to see.

"I love you, Desi." Helena squeezed her tighter, and Desi returned the hug.

"I love you too, Mom. Don't be so sad."

The words made her chest ache. One day—assuming they both survived this—Desi would uncover the truth, and she would never say it again. Of course, that had always been a ticking time bomb. Once Desi truly started developing her abilities as a half-blood Durand, it would force the truth. The girl already sensed far too much for her age.

Helena desperately wanted to regret taking Luminita's deal, but had she stayed with Bastien, continued that life, she would have died of an overdose if Bastien hadn't beaten her to death. Then Chance would have been alone with *him*.

Chance had admitted he'd suffered in the foster homes and the children's hospital, although not to what extent. Still, she could hazard a guess. But life with Bastien…It would have been worse, if Chance had even lived long enough to find out. Farren would have found them eventually, and he had been a stringent believer in maintaining the purity of the bloodlines.

No. As painful as it might have been, taking Luminita's deal had been her only choice. Although, Helena never should have involved others in her life. She should have turned Noah down the first time he asked her out.

Desi nestled her cheek against Helena's chest.

No. She couldn't regret that choice either. Without Noah, there would have been no Desiree.

Helena closed her eyes, sending fresh tears down her cheeks. There was no magic answer which would have erased what transpired today.

Even if there were, it wouldn't change things now. Noah would still be dead. Desiree would still be without a father.

Helena had no idea how much time had passed while they sat there, clinging to each other. The cells didn't come with clocks, but the light from the small window had shifted a decent amount.

Perhaps early afternoon?

Desi hadn't moved much or spoken in what felt like hours. Every now and then, her little shoulders would shake with a few muffled cries, and Helena would hold her tighter.

The girl was seven. She knew things were bad, that they were in trouble of some kind. She could sense all the grief and sadness. Helena couldn't shield her from that. But at least Luminita hadn't made her daughter witness what happened to Noah. It had been a small mercy, but it gave her hope.

Metallic clicks preceded the sound of metal grinding against metal, and Helena's arms instinctively squeezed her daughter.

Aaron Bogdan stood on the threshold, flanked by two of the nameless mercs. A violent glint lit his eerie grey eyes, and a devious grin stretched his lips. Her hope withered beneath them.

"Take the girl," he ordered, keeping his stare locked on Helena.

Her heart dropped, hitting every single rib on the way down. "No," she said breathlessly.

The two men moved past Aaron, entering the cell, and Helena scrambled to her feet, clutching Desi close against her.

"No," she said more assertively this time.

The men hesitated. Of course, it had nothing to do with their questionable morals. These men knew who she was, what she was capable of, and how badly she could hurt them.

"Take. The. Girl," Aaron repeated in a forceful cadence.

The mercs resumed their march toward Helena, and every instinct told her to fight, to tear these men apart, and to destroy the smug bastard still standing in the doorway.

"Mom, I don't want to go!" Desi squeezed Helena's neck, burying her face.

She couldn't fight, not with Desiree here. *Fuck.*

"Hand her over, Helena. It's for the best. I assure you."

Luminita's voice drew Helena's attention back to the door. The petite woman stepped around Aaron, her fingers skimming over his arm. The man dipped his chin toward Luminita, and the corners of his mouth lifted.

"Promise you won't hurt her," Helena blurted in desperation. Why, she didn't know. Luminita's word meant nothing—*less* than nothing.

"I do not intend to harm the child if"—she paused for effect—"you cooperate."

Helena shifted her attention from Luminita's pleasant smile to the dark expression Aaron wore, then to the guards hovering nearby. What choice did she have? If there was any hope of escaping the situation, it would have to start with her cooperation.

"Okay," she stated on a shaky breath.

"No, Mom! I don't want to go!" Desi clung to her, refusing to release her grip.

With slow gentle movements, Helena put her down, unclasped the little girl's arms, and crouched in front of her. "Desi, sweetheart…" She cradled her daughter's face in her palms. "It's gonna be okay."

When a fat tear rolled down her little cheek, Helena wiped it away.

"Be brave for Mommy. I need to talk to these people. That's all, okay?"

"Then I want to be with Dad."

The words stabbed into Helena's chest like a dagger. "You can't, baby, not right now."

Desi's face crumpled. "Why? You said you didn't know."

Breathing past the boulder-sized lump in her constricted throat was almost impossible. She still couldn't say it.

"You just can't right now. Go with them. They'll watch you, okay? It won't be long."

Once Desi nodded with a fearful frown, Helena turned a glare full of white-hot rage on the two men standing before them.

"If *anything* happens to her…"

She didn't have to finish the sentence. They knew her reputation. The merc on the left silently nodded his understanding. The other remained stoic.

Helena pulled Desi into a tight hug and pressed kisses against her cheek. "I love you, baby. I'll see you soon."

Her daughter didn't respond. Another crack manifested in Helena's already fractured heart.

While trying to keep her tears at bay, Helena guided Desi toward the man on the left. Every step hurt. Every instinct screamed. Every fiber recoiled at voluntarily giving her daughter to them.

The merc softly gripped Desi's hand. "Come on. There's a puzzle I need help with." The man flicked his gaze up to Helena with sympathy, which surprised her. "She'll be all right."

While the guard led Desi away, the little girl peered over her shoulder, watching her mother with a deep frown. Helena sank to her knees and tried to put on a brave smile despite the utter carnage churning inside her aching chest.

"Very…touching." Aaron's condescending voice grated down Helena's spine. He stepped aside, allowing the guard and Desi past him.

The second merc still stood in front of Helena, watching her blankly.

Luminita's heels echoed off the walls when she wandered further into the cell. "Ah, Helena. You've made quite a mess of things."

How could the woman speak so casually after executing Noah?

"*I* didn't make the mess." The words emerged in a growl, but Luminita obviously wasn't intimidated.

"I gave you rather simple instructions." Luminita lowered herself onto the cot, but the sound of the door closing drew Helena's focus.

Aaron strolled closer until he stood beside Luminita. It seemed they had resolved whatever animosity lingered between them. Either of them separately was a problem, but together, cooperating without dissention?

Helena swallowed hard.

"I will only ask this nicely one more time, Helena." Luminita's ocean-blue eyes turned arctic. "What happened to Ashcroft?"

"Let my daughter go, and I'll tell you." It was the one bargaining chip she had.

A weary sigh rushed past Luminita's lips. "We have a video feed with sound in this room. The guard watching your daughter has explicit instructions to snap her neck if you harm a single person in this cell."

"What makes you think he'll obey?" Helena challenged.

The man had seemed bothered by what was happening. Maybe there was a chance he would ignore the order.

A wide grin split Aaron's lips, and a hollow pit formed in Helena's stomach. "Killian is with them."

The sentence confused her at first until she recalled the Irishman from this morning. Dread began to weave its way through her bones.

"Killian Byrne is a special creature. Can you guess his talent?" Luminita cradled her chin in her palm and leaned against her knee.

"He can influence people?" Even as the words left her mouth, Helena realized he was more than that. Noah hadn't been *influenced* to stand still.

Luminita hiked a brow. "I think you can do better than that."

"He commands people," Helena amended.

"Now she's learning." Luminita grinned. "Humans, specifically. He gives a verbal order, and the subject carries it out. Quite simple and effective. Now…what happened to Ashcroft?"

"Please. She's just a kid," Helena pleaded.

Aaron turned his attention to the merc and nodded.

With the flick of a wrist, the man extended a telescoping baton. There was a precious second where Helena could have fought, but Luminita's threat kept her still.

He reared back and brought the baton down against her shoulders with brutal force. The sharp sting warred against the deep, bruising ache for dominance, and a small whimper escaped.

"Ashcroft," Luminita demanded.

"He's dead." Helena raised her glare to the Romanian with seething hatred. "You can't bring him back this time."

Luminita narrowed her eyes to slits and assessed her words. "What did you do?"

Helena merely stared back at the woman defiantly.

Aaron dipped his head, and the metal rod struck Helena's ribs a second later. Once the initial pain ebbed, fire infused each labored breath.

Fucking rib fractures.

"Fine," Helena spat. "I decapitated him, tossed his head in the river, and burned his body. I'm sure you saw the news reports about the house fire…how hot it got…how badly the victims were burned."

While Luminita maintained her calm façade, a muscle ticked in Aaron's clenched jaw. He nodded toward the guard without taking his furious eyes off her. When the man hesitated, the full weight of Aaron's glare swung to the merc.

He didn't hesitate a second time.

The vicious blow hit Helena's left shoulder, making the whole joint explode in pain, which traveled down her arm.

"And Chance? Lilith?"

Helena swallowed hard. "I didn't find them."

Aaron gave the signal, but Luminita held up a hand. "They were there at Duncan's, though. Were they not?"

Helena drew in a sharp breath despite her fractured rib. That information couldn't hurt them. "Yes."

"Hmm. And how, exactly, did they escape?"

This time, Helena frowned. "You told me Chance, Cohen, and Ashcroft were the primary targets. You instructed me to let Lilith leave."

"And yet you only brought me Cohen."

Helena nodded, trying to figure out what she could and couldn't say. "Chance was…badly injured. If we had taken him, he would not have survived the trip. You wanted him alive. I decided to let them leave to improve his odds of survival."

Luminita tilted her head. "You are a Durand. Your blood could have healed him. You obviously were aware of this since you did just that to save Andrew. In fact, by not giving your blood to Chance, you further endangered his life."

The argument died on her tongue. Luminita was right, but the thought of handing him over to these monsters…

Tears flooded Helena's vision. "Please. He's my son." The words spilled from her trembling lips in a plea.

Luminita straightened and smoothed her skirt, a cool confidence washing over her. "Which is why you will accept my offer."

Helena drew her brows together in confusion. "What offer?"

"One more job. An assassination, to be more specific."

Trepidation flooded Helena's system. "Who's the target?"

A triumphant smile curved Luminita's mouth. "Oh, I think you'll like this one…David Boston, Senior."

Understanding suddenly hit Helena. Luminita wanted the threat removed against Chance and Lilith's life. She couldn't use them if they were dead.

"And in return?"

Luminita pivoted and peered up at Aaron, who reluctantly nodded. Then the woman's weighty stare fell back to Helena. "Desiree's freedom."

The words echoed in her skull. Desiree's…Not hers.

"Your life is not negotiable, Helena. Make no mistake, this will be the final mission for Orchid. I can no longer trust you, except in this."

Because killing Boston means saving Chance's life. The longer he's allowed to live, the more danger my son is in.

"Take out the target, return here, and I will set Desiree free."

The empty ache in her chest hurt more than the blows from the merc's baton. "She'll be alone." Helena's stare fell to the concrete with heavy tears.

Fingers lifted her chin until Helena met Luminita's crisp blue eyes. "But she will be alive. I'm offering you an opportunity to save both of your children, Helena."

"What are you going to do to Chance?" She barely got the shaky question out before her breath hitched.

"As long as he cooperates, I will treat him fairly."

Helena knew better than to trust this devil's words, but what choice did she truly have? Boston needed to be taken out and fast. Doing so would at least eliminate one threat and save her daughter's life.

Luminita was right. The Romanian *could* trust her with this mission.

Her life had to end someday. It might as well mean something.

"I'll take the deal. Boston's life and mine in exchange for Chance and Desi."

Luminita looked up at the merc and nodded toward the exit. After retracting his baton, he hustled over to the door and opened it.

"You've made the right decision. I'll have a team prepare you tonight." Luminita rose to her feet.

"Can I…see my daughter?"

The woman considered Helena for a moment, but Aaron was the one who spoke.

"You can see her when the mission is complete." He placed a hand on the small of Luminita's back and guided her toward the door.

Luminita only held her gaze for a second longer. Then they walked out of the cell, locking the door behind them, leaving Helena alone in her misery.

Chapter 42

Andrew paced the cell, his mind caught between horror and hope. He had crossed a line. It was one he could never uncross. Killing a perp in self-defense—hell, even killing Alexis while out of control—was a far cry from what he had done to Noah. He stared down at his unblemished hands and once again felt sick.

The man had been innocent—a husband, a father. He *mattered* to people, people who would miss him. In a few horrible moments, Andrew had stolen that life, stolen him from his loved ones, left that little girl fatherless. But what disturbed him the most was his lack of true remorse and the reassurance that Luminita would let him help Lilith.

The man's death had given Cohen hope.

He didn't buy into Luminita's bullshit about Lilith being his. Even separated from Chance, it would never happen. He knew that. This wasn't about him and his useless desires. It was about her and righting a horrible wrong. Once Lilith was safe, healthy, he would no longer have a purpose. He could end this miserable existence.

Perhaps there was another universe where stars aligned just right. Maybe there was a version of them who had found each other. It was a pretty thought, but the way she looked at Chance…Cohen would never have that in this life.

Of course, to ensure her safety, he would have to eventually get her away from Luminita and Aaron. That would take time, planning, and an insane amount of luck. So, for now, he would continue to suffer, cut off from the only person who made him feel truly seen.

Andrew paused in front of the cinderblock wall and stared at the blood stains littering the surface. Physical pain eased the emotional torment, and he desperately wanted to punch the wall until his fists were raw and bloody again.

There was a tipping point. He recognized the fact now but hadn't before. There had been a time when the pain he felt made him stronger, made him whole, but now the same pain which had made him feel alive had broken him.

He couldn't pinpoint exactly when it had happened or whether the cause had been Lilith or Luminita, but he no longer recognized himself or his thoughts. The very idea of taking his own life would have disgusted the man he had been a year ago, but at the same time, he had no desire to go back to being that man. He had been sleepwalking through life, surviving his grandfather, playing the dutiful cop, acting like a real person.

Andrew pressed his palm against the largest bloodstain, letting the concrete cool his skin. If he truly wanted to save Lilith in every way, he had to pull himself together. Cohen had to find a way to reconcile two versions of himself—the strength of who he had been with the awareness of who he was now. He could mull over what should happen next once he'd ensured Lilith's safety.

With a calming exhale, Andrew slid his hand away from the wall and paced over to the cot. When he sank onto the mattress, the image from his first dream here flitted through his mind. Lilith had crouched beside his bed, whispering for him to wake up.

Like the dream last night, it had felt real, as if she had truly been in the cell with him. It was different from anything he had experienced prior.

Perhaps it was his strong connection to the woman, his vision of her as his personal savior, but it kept nagging at him. There were myths among the Durand of the ability to walk dreams, to connect to another person while sleeping, but that's all they were—myths. Cohen didn't have that ability, and Lilith was a vampire, not Durand. Besides, if a dream-walker existed, Luminita would have had that in her arsenal.

Speaking of arsenal… The Irishman, Killian. Cohen had never met him, but the man obviously had a unique talent. His persuasion was only outmatched by Peisinoe.

The Siren had checked two boxes—control over males and as a spy to funnel information about Farren and his movements. Cohen wondered if Killian's powers were limited to males as well? After all, Killian had resorted to bribery with the girl. Cohen needed more information before making any sort of move. Luminita probably had a few surprises tucked away here.

For the time being, Cohen needed to find the balance between being a loyal subject and a broken man. It was a role he had played before with Farren and should be able to pull off again. Luminita already wanted to believe him. She had demonstrated that by standing up to Aaron, defending Cohen and his purpose.

Andrew rubbed his face with a heavy sigh. He needed out of this goddamn cell. Now that the fever had broken, he felt clearheaded. Well, relatively speaking, anyway. The silent monotony of the room was starting to wear on him, especially without the demonic inner voice to fight against. If only he could talk to Luminita, get some answers…

The lock clicked. Andrew snapped his head up at the sound.

Speak of the devil.

The door swung open, and Luminita strode inside, wearing her usual pencil skirt. But there was something different about her. He recognized it immediately, like a change in the air's scent before a storm.

Luminita had always been reserved, cut off from her emotions. He had sensed the leaks earlier, but now, it was like the dam had burst and she vibrated in full color. Despite that fact, the confidence she wore seemed impenetrable.

All Andrew could do was stare and blink.

"Andrew." The name rolled off her tongue affectionately. "I have something for you."

Cohen raised one eyebrow and continued to watch her.

Luminita pulled a phone from her pocket and tossed it on the bed next to him. "This is the cell retrieved from Orchid's car. The last call was to Lilith."

Andrew scooped up the device. He stared at it for a moment before meeting Luminita's eyes again. "You're giving me this?"

"Yes. We are on the same side, remember? We both want Lilith healthy."

Meaning the woman knew he wouldn't undermine her plans because it would endanger Lilith. *Point made.*

"What do you want me to do?"

Luminita crouched before him. "We need to convince Lilith to meet you, preferably without all her friends."

Cohen shook his head. "Chance won't let that happen. Hell, none of them would, even if I told her what's at stake."

"Hmm. It *is* a conundrum, is it not? She probably wouldn't believe you infected her either. She knows I have you." Luminita looked away, working the problem.

"None of them will allow her to endanger herself, not after Ashcroft."

"But Lilith is a strong woman capable of making her own decisions. She seems to have a penchant for saving others. What if she believed your life was in danger."

"Is it?" Cohen carefully gauged her reaction.

A small sound like a huff escaped, and she tilted her head. "We are on the same side. I told you that."

"Aaron doesn't seem to agree with your assessment of the situation."

Luminita's lips twisted, as if trying to hide a smile. It was an odd expression Cohen had never seen on her.

"Aaron and I have come to a mutually beneficial understanding."

Dread blossomed in Cohen's chest. If that were true, dissention in the ranks would no longer be a useful tactic. The thought of Luminita and Aaron on the same page was…terrifying.

"What sort of understanding?"

The woman pressed her mouth into a firm line before she stood and wandered toward the wall. "It's of a personal nature, but I made it clear you aren't to be harmed." She trailed her fingers over the dried blood, almost caressing the stains.

"And what did you promise him in return?"

As soon as the question left his mouth, Andrew wished he could snatch it back. Luminita wasn't his friend, far from it. Why should he care what the woman had sacrificed to keep him alive? She owed him, after the medical center.

Inky black curls spilled down her back when she peered over her shoulder at him in surprise, but she quickly schooled her reaction.

"Would Lilith meet you if she believed your life is in danger?" she repeated, ignoring his question.

Andrew considered her words. *Would she?* "I…don't know. I'd like to think she would, but the others…"

His thoughts drifted to Chance with rising ambivalence.

Knowing the man was half-Durand had changed Andrew's view of him. He couldn't shake it, especially after learning Chance had been in love with Lilith for thirteen years and never said a thing. Some might call it romantic, but to him, it screamed *stalker.*

Not that Cohen had handled things any better by banging Lilith look-alikes for the past eight months.

"Hmm. Then perhaps a more…innocent life? One Chance deems worthy of the risk? Desiree?"

Cohen peered up at her while she continued to trace the various bloodstains. "Orchid's daughter?" The thought of putting the little girl directly in harm's way twisted his stomach.

"She is his half-sister, after all." Luminita turned to lock eyes with him. "If you asked Lilith to meet you alone for the sake of the girl's life, would she?"

"Yes, but…Chance, Tim, Nicci…They'd never allow it. Even if she agreed, they'd form a plan, just like they did with Ashcroft until your men crashed the party."

A sparkle lit her blue eyes. "My men were always part of the plan."

"What?" Cohen frowned, unable to make the connection.

"Hmm. It appears he kept that secret." A smile crept across her face, and she leaned against a clean section of the wall. "Chance called me before you left the cabin and made a deal—He would lead me to Ashcroft and surrender to my men in exchange for Lilith's freedom."

A twisting vortex of hatred burst to life in his chest.

That's why the fucker calmly went along with the plan, why he didn't protest. Chance lied to us, lied to her. The bastard should have known Luminita would never hold up her end of the deal. All he did was ensure Lilith would be left unprotected. The fucking idiot.

Cohen swallowed his rage with difficulty and focused on the current issue. "No matter what I say, you should plan for their entire team to be present, *if* she agrees to meet me."

"And who comprises Lilith's *team*?"

Every instinct told him to keep his mouth shut, but he reminded himself this was *for* Lilith, to save her.

"Chance. Tim and Gibson, who are half-bloods. Nicci—a pureblood. Plus Keller and Agent Hersch, who are both human. That's assuming they haven't picked up any other stragglers."

"They have humans with them?" Luminita hiked her eyebrows.

Cohen nodded, his head hanging low. "Yes, and they are both aware of vampires and the Durand. Agent John Gorman knew as well, but your assassin took care of him." An accusation lingered in his tone.

Luminita merely smiled before staring off in thought. Then she pushed away from the wall and wandered toward the door.

"Call Lilith. Tell her whatever you like, as long as she agrees to meet you somewhere in Elkins, West Virginia."

"What about the rest of them?"

"I have a plan." She sauntered through the door, not bothering to close it behind her.

Andrew surged to his feet. "Luminita. You're leaving the door open?"

She paused on the threshold and glanced over her shoulder. "You've earned a little freedom, unless…you'd rather I close it."

"No," he replied quickly.

"Take your time, consider your words, and remember what's at stake." Luminita held his gaze, impressing the weight of her statement, before turning and walking away. The click of her stilettos on the concrete echoed into the room, fading with each step.

Andrew stared at the phone resting in his palm. He could talk to her, *really* talk to her. Knowing that made his chest ache. But realizing that also meant lying to her, convincing her to fall into a trap, even if it was for her own good…

He collapsed on the mattress again, his shoulders impossibly heavy.

You could tell her the truth. Confess your sin. The inner voice spoke in an almost compassionate tone, making Cohen's eyes mist.

"No. Luminita is right. She wouldn't believe it. The woman will not take a risk for her own safety."

Are you certain that's why you don't want to tell her?

Cohen rubbed a hand over his mouth. The dark truth vibrated in his bones. He had to be honest with her eventually, and he would, but he selfishly wanted some time where she didn't hate him. That didn't make him a monster. He had already sacrificed his soul for her. Was a little time to bask in her good graces too much to ask?

Fuck. I have no right to ask *for anything from her.*

Then don't ask.

Although the words only existed in his head, they seemed to echo through the now open room. He needed to organize his thoughts, figure out what to say, brace himself to hear her voice.

Andrew rose to his feet again, slipped the phone in his pocket, and strolled toward the hallway.

Chapter 43

"Are you sure this is necessary? We're not raiding a Durand stronghold." Lilith tugged at the Kevlar vest, trying to get comfortable. Of course, once she stepped out into the glaring afternoon sun in jeans and the heavy bulletproof vest, her discomfort would only get worse.

Chance pressed his mouth into a firm line, immediately giving away his answer. "And we were *just* staying in a hotel when a team of mercs attacked. Nicci was *just* picking up Alicia when someone tried to abduct them. *Yes.* It's necessary."

The man wasn't wrong. With a resigned sigh, Lilith tightened the last strap on her vest.

"You said the hidden drive is in his office?" he asked.

Chance already knew the answer. They had gone over this a hundred times. He was just trying to keep her focused on the task at hand.

"Yeah. It's off the main lab."

"Okay. It's me, you, and Nicci. Tim and Gibson are gonna stay behind with Eileen."

"That makes sense." For some reason she couldn't comprehend, things just felt *wrong*. Maybe it was the weird change in her dreams or the fact that Chance seemed…Lilith didn't know how to finish the thought.

The news of Cohen's survival had affected Chance on an almost cellular level, but she thought she had at least squashed his insecurities about her loyalty. Still, Chance seemed…distant today. Perhaps that was the right word.

"Do you have your sidearm?" Chance asked, pulling her from her thoughts.

"Uh, yes, and a spare clip."

"Knife?"

Lilith hiked an eyebrow, but Chance was busy stuffing the walkie and other equipment into his vest on the bed. She peered down at the tactical knife strapped to her jean-clad thigh and waited.

When she didn't answer, he finally peered up at her, following her line of sight.

"Do you want to talk about what's bothering you?" Lilith asked. The voice inside her head was screaming for her to let things go. Maybe one day, she would learn to listen. It apparently wasn't today.

Chance drew his brows together but appeared more concerned than confused. "What do you mean?"

Lilith swallowed hard at the obvious evasion and sank to the mattress. She looked around the RV's small bedroom while she figured out what to say. "I can just tell something's wrong."

Chance stood tall in her periphery, abandoning the tac vest. "About going into Solasta? We could have someone else—"

"No." Lilith huffed, rubbing her face. "With you. Something is wrong with *you*."

He didn't answer.

Lilith closed her eyes for a deep breath and braced her palms on her knees. "Talk to me, *beau*."

Chance flicked his hazel eyes up to meet hers. "Nothing is *wrong* with me." The sentence seemed to offend him, as if she had inferred he was somehow damaged.

An exasperated sigh rushed past Lilith's lips, but before she said anything, Chance stepped around the bed and knelt in front of her.

"I had a weird fucking dream last night that kinda threw me, and then Gloria's comment…"

Lilith frowned, tilting her head to the side. "Gloria's comment?" It took her a second to figure out what Gloria could have possibly said to bother him. "About the ring?"

When pink tinged his tanned cheeks, she chuckled.

"She was giving you a hard time. It doesn't mean anything."

A serious expression hardened his features, and Chance held her gaze with a fierce intensity. "It means everything. *You* mean everything."

The conviction in his voice made butterflies dance in her stomach.

"That's not what I meant, and you know it. I don't need a ring to prove who you are to me." She slid her fingertips through his tousled hair, and a smile tugged at his lips. "Now…what was this dream?"

The concern instantly returned. "It's nothing. I just need to shake it off."

Lilith gripped his chin, refusing to let him look away. "Talk."

Chance closed his eyes and sighed. "It'll only make you mad."

"Cohen," Lilith said in a huff. "We're back to this again?"

"No, *cherie*. I'm not questioning you or us. It's…"

A growl rumbled from his throat. Although it stemmed from frustration, the sound still sent giddy shivers skittering down her spine.

"Hey." Lilith waited until he met her gaze again. "Tell me. Maybe talking about it will help you out of your funk."

Chance sat back on his heels and shook his head. "Fine. In my dream, I saw Andrew kneeling on the floor of Duncan's basement, sobbing …Then I saw you standing a few feet away, dressed in your nightgown. You said his name, walked over to him, touched his shoulder, and asked if he was okay."

A familiar feeling crept into her mind while he spoke, as if she had seen this.

"Andrew shook his head. The man was a complete wreck, and I could feel the hopelessness rolling off him in waves big enough to drown in. But you…" His gaze fell. "You wanted so badly to help him. And you asked, but he didn't want your help. He said he's still selfish…still wants you."

Everything clicked into place at those words, and Lilith's body stiffened.

That's not possible.

A miserable grumble sounded before he continued, still avoiding her gaze. "You told him to stop punishing himself and touched the man's raw knuckles."

Every time Chance spoke, the stab of anxiety twisted deeper.

No. It's. Not. Possible.

"You told Cohen that you could start over…be friends…that you just needed to find him."

"Stop," Lilith whispered on a shaky breath.

Every shred of her sanity rebelled against what he was saying. He *couldn't* know those things. It wasn't possible.

Chance snapped his gaze up to hers, finally taking her in. "What's wrong?"

Lilith shook her head, still struggling to put her thoughts into words that wouldn't sound completely insane. "You're…describing the dream *I* had last night. How?"

"What?" Chance frowned. "No. Maybe they were similar, but—"

"I don't want to lose anyone else. Please. *You* matter. *Your life* matters." When she spoke the lines from her dream, Chance's eyes widened. "Cohen said, 'It doesn't,' and I said, 'It does to *me*.' Then I woke up."

"That's exactly what happened." Chance swallowed hard and held her steady gaze.

"*How* is that possible?"

"It's not," Chance replied, utterly lost. Then his frown deepened, as if something had occurred to him. "At the hospital, when I woke up…you mentioned a dream you'd had about Ashcroft. I swear I saw it happen."

"What do you mean?"

"When I was under, I was stuck in a continuous loop, reliving the worst decision of my life…the one that almost cost me *you*—making the deal with Luminita." The guilt he still felt made her stomach twist.

"I'm still here," Lilith said softly.

Chance dipped his chin and exhaled. "After speaking with her, I'd fight Ashcroft, lose…and then I'd see you weeping. You were so angry at me…You wouldn't forgive me for what I'd done." Chance cleared his throat, and tears filled his glassy eyes. "But once…there was something different. One time, during my fight with Ashcroft, I turned to see you kneeling in front of him. Cohen's corpse laid to one side and mine to the other. You asked Ashcroft what else he could take from you, and—"

"Slit my wrists," she whispered in a shocked tone, trying to make sense of it. "Maybe it's…because I had your blood?" Though that didn't seem to make much sense either.

Lilith had drunk Andrew's blood several times, and although she'd had side effects, they had been limited to drawing on other's emotions. It wasn't like her eyes had started changing color.

"I don't know." Chance's shoulders fell, along with his gaze. "Maybe it's me. Maybe I'm just…different."

The misery etched in his expression tugged at her heart, and she slid off the bed to cradle his face between her palms.

"Stop. Whatever is happening, we'll figure it out. *We always do*, remember?"

Chance's throat bobbed, but he nodded. "If you and I are aware…sharing dreams, do you think…" The words trailed off, and

Chance cleared his throat before trying again. "Do you think Andrew is really there?"

Lilith frowned, seriously considering his question. "I don't know. I mean…he's popped up in my dream a couple of times now, and when he does, it feels…different, more real." She didn't miss the subtle flinch from Chance and hated how all this hurt him. "I just feel bad for him, Chance. He's in pain…a *lot* of pain."

"And you don't think he deserves it?"

Lilith could tell how much the answer meant to him. "He does," she reluctantly agreed. "In part, at least."

A muscle ticked in Chance's jaw. "The man kissed you while Ashcroft ripped me apart. I still feel his fucking talons in my flesh."

Thrown out in black and white like that, it *did* seem unforgiveable.

"I know, and it was wrong. *Very* fucking wrong. I won't forgive him for that…for almost losing you." She caressed his stubbled cheek.

"But…" he prompted with a guarded tone.

"But I don't want him to die. The guy is lost."

"I don't think he is."

"What?" Lilith asked, completely confused.

"He has a purpose, remember?"

Lilith glared at his sharp tone.

"Look, Lily. I know you love me. This isn't about that. Cohen is dangerous. That's all I'm saying. I know what you two went through in the medical center last year forged a bond, but his obsession with you…it isn't healthy."

"I only want to help him."

"I know." Chance sighed and tucked a few strands of hair behind her ear. "But, *cherie*…what if you can't? What if *that* is the thing that gets you killed?"

The thought didn't sit well with her, but once again, Chance wasn't wrong. What if Cohen *couldn't* be helped? What if he was too far gone? What if he dragged her down with him?

"All I'm asking is for you to be careful where he's concerned, even in your dreams."

Lilith didn't trust her voice, so she settled for a nod.

Before she could move, Chance drew her into his arms and rested his chin on her head, holding her tight. "I love you, and I can't lose you, *amour de ma vie*. None of this means anything without you."

"I love you too," she whispered against his chest.

Memories of those torturous days sitting by his hospital bed flooded her mind. The very *idea* of losing Chance almost broke her. He was her future, the person she had chosen to spend her life with, *her* purpose.

"I'll be careful. I'm sorry."

Chance placed a soft kiss in her hair. "Don't apologize, *mon petite cherie*." He leaned back enough to tilt her chin. "You care deeply about people, even the wrong ones."

The last phrase hurt, reminding her of the argument with Cohen in the cabin. He had accused her of trusting bad men and had lumped Chance into that group, along with himself.

"I love your heart, *cherie*. Just be careful with it."

His lips touched hers in a faint caress, making her forget the knot of worry in her stomach. The undeniable current between them overpowered everything else. It always did.

When her tongue flicked against his, Chance broke the kiss. His thumb ghosted over her bottom lip.

"You can't kiss me like that right now." A lopsided grin lit his face. He looked more like himself than he had all day. "We have things to do."

As if on cue, someone knocked on the thin door. "You guys about ready? You better not be making out in there. It's rude."

Both Lilith and Chance bit back a laugh at Nicci.

"Almost ready," Lilith managed to say in a passably normal voice.

Chance rose to his feet and held out a hand to help her up, which she gladly accepted. "Go ahead and keep Nicci company. I'll be ready in a second."

Lilith stole one more kiss before opening the door.

Chapter 44

Lilith shielded her eyes from the afternoon sun and stared up at the familiar building in New Rochelle. Over the past seven years, she had spent as much time in this concrete and glass building as she had at her apartment, especially when she'd interned at the lab with Dr. Scott. Solasta was her second home and had always felt welcoming—until they'd placed her on suspension.

It felt weird strolling down the same sidewalk when she wasn't the same person. In less than a year, everything had changed. She tugged at the stifling Kevlar vest—physical proof of how different her life had become.

Lilith glanced at Chance, who continually scanned the immediate area with his Beretta loose at his side. All vampires in the city and surrounding areas came to Solasta for blood supplies, but very few ever ventured beyond the blood bank and emergency services.

Chance had probably been to the offices and labs thousands of times with Gregor. When her father had been alive, he had touched base with current projects and received reports from the various departments each week, usually in person. Still, it felt odd to have Chance with her for the first time in such a familiar place, as if she was showing him another sliver of her life.

Of course, this was not a normal visit by any stretch of the imagination. Lilith wasn't here to file reports, drop off trace evidence, analyze results, or even run errands. She needed to get in Dr. Scott's office, retrieve the ghost drive, and get out.

Nice and simple.

Dread balled in her stomach. Nothing had been *nice and simple* lately, and she doubted this endeavor would be any different.

When they neared the entrance, Lilith dug her badge out of her wallet. She stepped up to the smoky glass doors and swiped the plastic card over the electronic box.

Nothing happened.

The door was supposed to pop open. Lilith swiped it again, but the doors remained locked.

"Chance? I thought you said Antonio reinstated our credentials." She tried again.

Nothing.

"That's what he told me."

"Well, this is gonna be a real quick trip because my badge isn't working."

"What?" Chance whirled away from the open area to face her. "There has to be a mistake."

Lilith glared at him and dramatically swiped her badge for the fourth time. The door didn't budge.

"Please wait. An escort will accompany you to the department you wish to see," an automated voice reported from overhead.

Lilith tilted her head back. A camera and speaker had been installed several feet above the door.

Huh. That's new.

"Probably added security because of the break-in and kidnapping," Chance said, as if reading her mind.

A few seconds later, the door unlocked with a thunk.

Lilith grabbed the handle and pulled, then proceeded inside like normal. She quickly came to a stop after two steps.

Typically, only a few fake trees and empty armchairs dotted the vacant lobby, but today, four men in full head-to-toe tactical gear lined the room, their assault rifles trained on the door.

"Names!" one of the men shouted while the door swung closed behind Nicci.

"CSI Lilith Adams, Security Specialist Chance Deveraux, and Detective Nicci DeLuca." Chance holstered his weapon and held up his open palms.

The man on the left lowered his gun and marched straight toward Lilith with what looked like an overgrown laser thermometer. "We need to confirm your identity via retinal scan." He held it up. "Just look straight into the lens."

After a few seconds, he tucked away the weird device.

What the hell?

Once again, Chance seemed to read her mind.

"You don't look like your security ID photo," he said.

Chance had reworked all the security protocols for the labs. Of course, he would know their procedures. He had written them.

The blond hair. Right. Part of her just wanted to grab some dye and get back to normal, but nothing boxed would match her natural red.

"Who are you here to see?" The man who had spoken first—she assumed he was in charge—used a brusque tone, as if all this was a massive inconvenience to his fun-filled day.

Lilith seriously doubted this part of the facility saw much traffic. Hell, this was the first time she had seen anyone else in the lobby, including the men working security.

"Claudia, Dr. Scott's intern. She should be in the research lab."

The man dipped his chin and turned on his heel. "Follow me."

"I know where it is," Lilith stated, trailing behind him. "This isn't necessary."

Chance nudged her, drawing her attention, and shook his head with a firm frown. Lilith shrugged at him with a half-smile. But she hadn't noticed the man in charge stop abruptly. Lilith ran right into his back.

A loud groan echoed through the space. When the guy finally turned around, his pockmarked face pulled into a stern glare.

"Miss Adams. We had a massive security breach. Protocols have changed. And please…watch where you're going."

"Sorry." She grimaced, and Chance nudged her again.

This time when she looked at him, he wore an amused grin which was entirely too sinful to be fair.

"Stop distracting me," she hissed, jamming her elbow into his side.

Naturally, his grin widened.

The man led them to the elevators and pressed the call button.

"Has there been any word on Dr. Scott?" Lilith asked, too curious to not ask.

"No," was the quick reply.

Okay. So much for small talk.

"Is it being handled internally, or was it kicked over to missing persons?" Nicci asked when the elevator dinged.

The man exhaled a heavy sigh. Clearly, he disliked escorting civilians around the building. His heavy steel-blue eyes assessed each of them.

"I'm sure it will come as no shock that, with Gregor and Duncan's deaths and Aaron's disappearance, things are…disorganized. The short answer is, I don't know."

Shit. It hadn't dawned on Lilith that, with Aaron missing, there was no one to oversee Solasta. Sure, there was a director of operations, but with the way Solasta had been built, the bylines clearly stated that the final say in all significant matters had to pass through the owner. After Gregor's death, the board had appointed Aaron as his replacement, and now…

"Has the board appointed a new CEO, or are they waiting to see what happens with my uncle?"

Once again, the man considered her before speaking. "Not officially." Something about his tone seemed significant, like it was an inside joke she should know.

Lilith was about to ask, but the elevator doors opened, and the guy strode down the hall in a clipped cadence. His three guards ushered them out, keeping pace behind them until they reached the bank of frosted glass.

"Here you are. The main research lab. Two of my men will stand here and escort you back when you're finished." While he rattled off his instructions, the man headed back to the elevators.

"Wait, who are they unofficially appointing?" Lilith asked his retreating back.

The man didn't answer.

"He's a big ole ball of sunshine," Nicci grumbled.

One of the guards choked on a laugh.

"Come on. Let's just get this done." Chance shook his head at Nicci but still wore an amused smile. At least he seemed to be in a better mood since their talk.

Lilith knocked on the glass, and a few minutes later, a brunette with thick bangs and a messy bun appeared.

"Can I help you?" A puzzled expression pinched her brow until she caught sight of Nicci. "Oh, Detective DeLuca." Then her red-rimmed eyes shot back to Lilith. "Ms. Adams. I'm so sorry. I didn't recognize you."

"I've been getting that a lot," Lilith replied in a huff. That settled it. First chance she got, she was dying her hair. "This is Chance Dever—"

"Oh, I know." Pink colored the woman's full cheeks, and the air immediately froze in Lilith's lungs. "Nice to see you again, Chance."

Claudia's shy smile felt like a damn knife to the ribs.

I will not choose violence today, Lilith thought to herself. Despite that mantra, her mind whirled through a hundred reasons why this woman would know him.

Chance settled his hand on Lilith's shoulder. "I was here a few months ago, installing the security upgrades, *mon fiancé.*"

As soon as the last word left his mouth, Claudia's smile dimmed. "Fiancé?"

"Yep." Lilith let the "P" pop while the woman's cheeks turned crimson.

"Uh, I'm sorry. I…hadn't heard." Nervous tension filled the space, but Lilith was in no hurry to ease Claudia's discomfort. "Uh…I guess you're here to see Dr. Scott's office?" she finally asked, keeping her eyes fixed on Lilith.

"Correct again," Lilith answered in a flat tone.

The last time she'd been here, she had felt sorry for the girl. Dr. Scott was an uncompromising, demanding asshole to his interns and assistants. Now, however… Lilith tried to keep her territorial Scorpio side in check, at least enough to accomplish their mission.

Claudia chewed at her bottom lip and swung the door open.

"Thanks. I know where it is." Lilith stalked past her, heading directly for Dr. Scott's office.

It only took a few steps for Chance to catch up.

"I think you enjoyed that a little too much," he teased in a low whisper.

Lilith shot him an answering glare. "That is *not* the word I'd use."

"*Cherie.*" Concern edged into his voice.

After glowering at him again, Lilith peeked over her shoulder. Nicci was still at the door, talking with Claudia. Either her partner felt they were better off retrieving the drive alone or didn't want to be present for the sharp words on the tip of Lilith's tongue.

No one had ever accused her partner of being dumb.

Lilith stormed into Dr. Scott's office and contemplated closing the door in Chance's face. It was completely illogical. The girl was probably just smitten. Chance was more than easy on the eyes. But none of that quelled the ridiculous anger burning in her chest.

Lilith's hand almost shook on the knob while she forced herself to keep the door open until Chance jogged inside. Then she slammed it shut, indulging her irrational fury, and took several breaths.

"Hey, *cherie*. Nothing ever happened with Claudia, if that's what you're thinking."

He went to step closer, but Lilith held up a hand, still trying to control her breathing.

"I know," she managed to grind out.

"Then what is all this…"

Lilith expelled a slow breath, willing the stupid anger out of her body. "I don't know." She sighed heavily and stalked past him toward the map of Scotland behind Scott's desk.

"You do realize you have nothing to be jealous about, correct?" A trace of amusement colored his words. "I'm fairly certain my tattoo has *your* name on it, no one else's."

"I know." Lilith's hands paused along the frame's edge, and she peered over her shoulder. "It wasn't that. Jealousy implies I don't trust you. I do…It was more like"—Lilith frowned at the floor—"a territorial response. When she flashed that shy smile at you, I swear to God, I wanted to scratch her face off."

When Lilith turned back to Chance, his lips twitched. He lost the fight and *grinned* at her. A full-on, beaming, Cheshire cat grin.

"You've told me a lot of pretty things, Lily, but I think *that* is my favorite." A deep chuckle rumbled in his chest.

Lilith snatched the stress ball off Scott's desk and chucked it at Chance with a little growl. He easily ducked the shot, letting the ball ricochet off the wall.

"Don't be an ass."

Once again, Chance's grin only widened.

Lilith refocused on the task at hand. She slid her finger down the frame, searching for the slight bevel.

"*Amor de ma vie*," Chance whispered against her ear, causing Lilith's heart to leap into her damn throat—she hadn't even heard him move. "It doesn't matter who smiles at me or bats their eyelashes." His hands coasted around her waist with excruciatingly slow movements. "You're the only one I *ever* want to touch." He tugged her back against him and nuzzled a kiss against the sensitive skin of her neck, sending sparks through every cell.

Well, now I feel completely ridiculous. The thought made her defensive, which always drew out her sarcastic humor. "Are you sure? I mean, once we exchange vows, you're stuck with me."

Chance spun her around, his hand cradling her nape, and pulled her into a dizzying kiss full of promises. A thrill rocketed all the way to her toes. It didn't matter how many times she kissed this man; it was never enough.

When he broke away, touching his forehead to hers, he whispered against her lips. "We've already exchanged the vows that matter to me. You are mine, and I am yours, remember?"

Lilith struggled for a breath, and tears blurred her vision. "I know." The shaky words barely made a sound. She cleared her throat and tried again. "I'm sorry."

The corners of his mouth lifted, and he stroked his thumb lightly over her cheek. "Don't apologize. I like your feral side," he teased.

Lilith's cheeks heated, and a nervous laugh escaped. "You would, perv. Can I…get back to work now?"

Chance hesitated but finally let her go and stepped back. He leaned against the desk with a rakish smirk, and Lilith drew in a steadying breath. As much as she would have loved to climb him like a damn tree, they were there for a reason.

After closing her eyes and exhaling slowly, she turned back to the map. She ran her fingers along the frame's right side, eventually catching on the tiny bevel of a button. Lilith pressed it, and the map swung away from the wall, revealing a specialized safe.

"Hopefully, Gerard hasn't changed the code." She typed in the familiar eight digits, and a green LED lit. "Thank God," she whispered.

Lilith cranked the handle and opened the safe. On the bottom shelf was a collection of files, passports, stacks of money—everything Dr. Gerard Scott would have needed to start a new life. On the second shelf sat a black box with green lights connected to a large battery-operated power supply.

The ghost drive.

Relief washed through her body like a calming wave. As long as Nicci could access the files, they should have everything they needed.

Lilith grabbed both devices from the top shelf and handed them to Chance before closing and locking the safe. Once she swung the map back in place and pressed until it clicked, Chance handed the drive and power supply back to her.

"Okay, *cherie*. Let's grab Nicci and get out of here."

She nodded but stared at the door with rising dread. Claudia probably thought she was a crazy person after the way Lilith had acted.

Chance peered back at her while reaching for the door. He chuckled. "Come on, my little Scorpio. Carrying the drive will keep you from scratching Claudia's face off. Let's go."

Lilith shot him an unamused glare—mostly for show—and followed him through the door.

When they strolled into the lab, Nicci glanced up. Her partner's nervous expression quickly faded. "Well, thank you, Claudia. I appreciate your account of what happened."

"And thank you for letting us borrow some of Dr. Scott's equipment," Lilith added with a forced smile.

The woman's eyes went round beneath her heavy bangs. "Oh, of course. I…uh, apologize about earlier. I didn't know." She darted her brown eyes to Chance but, thankfully, didn't allow them to linger.

"It's okay, Claudia. We haven't told many people yet. Have we, *mon petite scorpion?*" Chance bumped Lilith's arm lightly, flashing an enigmatic smile.

"You are *so funny,*" Lilith whispered with scathing sarcasm. "Keep it up." She let the threat dangle between them.

Chance stifled a laugh behind a cough and cleared his throat.

"I warned you," she said, loud enough for only him to hear. Then she turned her attention to Claudia. "It can be confusing"—she glanced at Chance with a sharp smile—"when I don't have a ring."

That sobered him up quickly. The humor drained from his face.

"It's a good thing I love him. Plus…" Lilith held his gaze with a softer expression. "I never cared for diamonds anyway. Boring and gaudy."

When she winked, the growing concern on Chance's face eased.

"Yeah. Well." Nicci shot them both a what-the-fuck look. "We should get moving. Thanks, Claudia." She grabbed the door and ushered Lilith and Chance out into the hall.

"Do I need to ask?" Nicci snapped once they were out of Claudia's earshot, although their armed escort still trailed behind them.

"Everything's fine," Lilith said quickly.

Nicci's glare lingered on her, one eyebrow rising.

"Seriously. I just…had a moment." Lilith could almost feel the chuckle brewing in Chance's chest. *God.* He found the situation far too amusing for his own good.

"Is it over now?" Nicci asked, pressing the down button for the elevator.

"All good," Lilith answered.

Her partner turned on Chance.

"Fine here. Thanks."

Suspicion hooded her gaze while she looked back and forth between them. "Better be. We still have people stashed in a safe house, waiting on us, and we haven't even discussed what to do about you-know-who's father."

Lilith nodded solemnly. Nicci was right. Too much was riding on their shoulders—an unrelenting fact haunting her life for the past year.

Damn. I'm tired.

They filed into the elevator with their armed escort, and Nicci jabbed the lobby button, clearly still pissed.

"I'm sorry, Nicci. We'll figure it out. I promise."

Nicci peered over her shoulder at Lilith, and her anger transformed into pure pain. "No. I'm sorry for snapping. We're all doing our best." Her shoulders sagged, and she blew out a breath. "I'm just upset about Alicia. I shouldn't be taking it out on you."

Lilith placed a hand on her partner's shoulder. "We'll get her home safe. This is only temporary."

"I know. It's not that. Alicia—" Nicci paused and glanced around as if she'd forgotten they weren't alone. "We can talk about this later."

The elevator doors opened before Lilith said anything else. Nicci unholstered her weapon. Lilith and Chance followed suit, their escort trailing behind them.

"I trust you found what you needed?" the head guard asked when they approached.

With a smile, Lilith lifted the external hard drive and power supply. "Yep. Thank you for your time. And I'm sorry about earlier."

A wry expression darkened his craggy face, and he turned to the door, unlocking it without another word.

Super friendly.

Nicci stepped through the doors first, marching out into the hot summer sun. Lilith trailed behind her, followed by Chance, who once again held his berretta loose by his side.

The temperature had already risen by several degrees, and without a breeze to break up the stifling heat, sweat beaded on Lilith's skin in seconds. Within a few steps, she was desperately looking forward to the RV's air conditioning.

When Nicci neared the first crosswalk, screeching tires drew their attention. A panel van careened around a corner a few blocks away.

Everyone froze.

"Get back inside!" Chance yelled, grabbing Lilith by the collar of her Kevlar vest to spin her around. "Now!"

Nicci sprinted past them like a rocket, waving her hands at the glass doors in the hopes the cluster of guards were still watching. Lilith raced after her, blood thundering in her ears.

The roar of the van's engine grew closer, and Lilith thought her heart might beat right out of her damn chest. Nicci was at the building's entrance, repeatedly bashing the call button, but the door hadn't opened yet.

Fuck.

In midstride, Lilith was tackled sideways, and she clutched the drive tight to her chest. Even landing in the grass didn't soften the blow to her shoulder—the same one she had broken last year. Pain flared, making her fingers go numb, but she held onto the drive for dear life.

Shots rang out, the sound ricocheting off the buildings. Glass shattered.

"Stay down, *cherie*," Chance whispered against her ear before his weight lifted off her.

Lilith glanced at Solasta with her heart sinking. Nicci was nowhere to be seen, and one of the glass doors had shattered.

Chapter 45

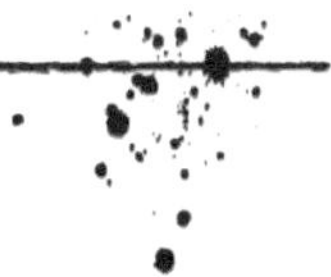

Splinters of concrete exploded in dust clouds, and an unrelenting barrage of bullets pelted the low wall with a deafening racket. Lilith put the equipment down and curled into a ball in the grass a few feet from the barrier, hands clamped over her ears.

Memories of the firefight in New Haven overcame her: shattering glass, the merciless barrage of automatic gunfire peppering the rental car, mercenaries circling the wreck, hands digging into her hair to pull her through the window…When Farren's men had attacked, Cohen and Lilith had barely survived, and there had only been four of them. This sounded like more.

"Lily!" Chance's shout hardly registered over the gunfire. He inched further toward her, and she locked her eyes onto his. "When they reload, I'll lay down cover fire so you can run."

Lilith heard every word, but her brain didn't comprehend their meaning past the haze of traumatic memories and blaring panic.

"*Cherie!*" Chance yelled. "I need you to run when I start shooting! Get inside as fast as you can! Do you understand? I need you to run!"

Run. The word finally registered. *He wants me to run…to leave him behind.*

Every breath became labored, and her heart thrashed against her ribs. The panicked fog evaporated, and she drew her gun. Lilith couldn't abandon him, couldn't leave him to fight these men alone.

"No!" she shouted back, shaking her head. "I'm *not* leaving you."

"Lilith. Now is *not* the time to make a statement."

She pinned him with an icy stare and crawled toward the wall. "I'm staying!"

Chance clenched his jaw, his mouth forming a firm line, but his hazel eyes glistened with unshed tears. "Don't do this, Lily. Please! I need you safe!"

It was a familiar argument they'd had a dozen times, and Chance should have known it was one he would not win.

"And *I* need *you* safe!" Lilith reached the space beside him, put her back to the wall, and clicked off the safety on her gun.

"*Bon Dieu*, Lily! Why can't you just fucking listen?" Frustration and tears made his voice waver, but it didn't deter her.

"Because I love you, asshole. Would *you* leave me alone out here?"

"No," he uttered on a heavy sigh, conceding defeat.

"Then shut the fuck up."

Chance opened his mouth to say something, but the thunderous onslaught of bullets stopped. Time froze for a second when their eyes met.

Almost in unison, they whirled around to peer over the concrete and assess the situation. Lilith spotted at least six mercs scattered around the courtyard, near the street, and behind the white panel van.

Most of them were in at least partial cover while reloading. From what she could observe, they were decked out from head to toe like pros, similar to the Solasta guards. However, true professionals would have staggered their fire to avoid reloading at the same time—something Tim had taught her during her weapons training.

So far, none of the hitmen they had encountered had been top of the line, but that wouldn't hold true for long. The group needed to take care of Boston before the true threats closed in. Things would only get worse until they did.

Chance popped off a few rounds, one striking a perp in the kneecap. A shriek of pain split the air, accompanying the mechanical sound of clips loading.

Lilith lined up her shot, exhaled, and squeezed the trigger. The first bullet struck the merc's vest when he hopped up, and he stumbled backward a step. The second sent a spray of blood from below his right eye, and the perp crumpled to the ground.

Chance peeked over his shoulder at her with an actual smile right before the mercs opened fire again.

Lilith crouched when the onslaught resumed chewing up the concrete. Glass crashed behind them once more, and Lilith glanced over at the front doors. Most of them were shattered now, and she spotted movement inside.

Hopefully, it was Solasta security coming to their rescue. The fight was on their property. They would want to clean this up fast to mitigate police involvement—or at least, she hoped so.

When she turned back, Lilith noticed the debris from the wall flying at different angles. *The mercs are moving. Shit.* There were still at least four perps out there, and if they flanked them…

"Lily. We need to get inside!" Apparently, Chance had detected their movement too. At least he had said *we* and not *you* this time.

Gunfire erupted behind them, and Lilith curled into a ball, covering her ears. For one panicked breath, she thought the bad guys had them surrounded, but Chance yanked on her Kevlar vest.

"Lily! We need to move! Now! Grab the drive!"

Solasta guards were laying down cover fire. A few screams came from the van's direction, but the overwhelming noise made them impossible to pinpoint.

Lilith crawled out as far as she could and snatched the thin box, pulling it away from the power supply. She stuffed the drive into the front of her vest and retreated to the wall. Hopefully, Nicci could still make it work, but Lilith needed both her hands.

"Lilith, listen to me." Chance grabbed her face and locked eyes with her. "I *need* you to go first. Run as fast as you can. I'll watch your back and be *right behind you*. I promise."

She studied his green-flecked eyes, hesitating. Every instinct screamed *no*.

"Please. Don't fight me on this. Run."

Lilith swallowed hard, her eyes stinging, and stole a quick kiss. "You better be right behind me."

He nodded and released her, readying his weapon. The staccato pops of gunfire started to ease, and Chance screamed, "Now!"

Lilith jumped to her feet and raced for the building with every bit of speed she had. Shots sounded behind her. The guards inched out of the shattered windows, firing at their attackers. Air burned in her lungs almost immediately, and her muscles screamed in protest, but Lilith pushed harder, sprinting for the ruined lobby.

The moment her sneakers touched the marble, something hit her from behind and sent her careening forward. She had just enough time to twist so she didn't land on the drive. The same shoulder collided with the unforgiving floor, but the sharp pain in her back was worse, accompanying every shallow breath.

"Fuck. You're hit!" Nicci screamed while running over to drag her partner to safety.

"Chance," she managed to croak out past the stabbing pain. It felt like a red-hot poker between her ribs.

Lilith grimaced through the burning agony to stare back at the doors. The passing seconds made her chest constrict until Chance finally barreled inside.

He skidded to his knees beside them and reached for her. "Lily!" Desperation pulled at every line in his handsome face.

"Help me get her to the elevator!" Nicci barked.

Chance scooped her up. Each movement made the pain worse, like a knife digging deeper into her back.

Shit. Lilith clamped down on her bottom lip, trying to keep from screaming, but a whimper still escaped.

"Hold on, *cherie!*"

Nicci raced ahead to call the elevator. Chance moved slower, trying not to jostle her. By the time he caught up to Nicci, the elevator had arrived. The three of them rushed inside, and Nicci repeatedly mashed the button to close the doors.

Once they'd shut, blocking out the riotous sounds of the lobby, Chance gingerly sat Lilith down and ripped off the vest's straps. The drive clattered to the ground, forgotten, while he gently removed her Kevlar.

The pain lessened a little without the pressure of whatever had been digging into her back, but breathing still hurt like a son of a bitch. Chance guided her forward and shoved her shirt up.

"Oh, thank fuck," Chance muttered with a pained sigh. "The vest caught it."

Nicci had been right. Lilith had taken a bullet. If it hadn't been for the vest...

Lilith groaned and winced while Chance lightly palpated the area to the right of her spine. "Still hurts like hell."

"Probably a fractured rib." He increased the pressure slightly, and Lilith cried out, jerking away from his touch. "Definitely a fractured rib."

"Better than dead." Nicci paced back and forth in the small space, shaking her head. "This was a fucking ballsy move. Attacking us *here*...in broad daylight?"

"They…" Another sharp jolt shot down Lilith's back, like damn fireworks across her nerves. "They don't know what this place is."

She paused again, struggling to inhale. It was getting harder to drag in air.

"Don't talk." Chance appeared in front of her, tilting her chin. Tears welled in his eyes while he searched her face. "The Kevlar may have stopped the bullet, but that doesn't mean a rib didn't puncture your lung. Slow, steady breaths. Keep them shallow for now."

Lilith nodded with a grimace and tried to quell her rising panic. It felt like breathing around shards of glass, with a vise compressing her rib cage.

"In for one, two…Exhale one, two." Chance coached her until she reached a sustainable rhythm. Then he grabbed the knife sheathed at her thigh and pressed it to his wrist.

"Wait." Lilith placed a hand over his. "Don't. I'm okay."

It was a lie. Her chest became more restricted every time she took a breath, making each one more difficult than the last.

"You are *not* okay, and I can help you."

"Lil, don't fight him on this," Nicci said. "We need you at full capacity here."

Lilith tried to inhale again, but the stabbing sensation stopped her short, trapping the air in her lungs. Chance shook off her hand and sliced through his skin. As soon as the blood welled to the surface, he placed the wound to her mouth.

"I swear to God, Lily. Don't be stubborn. I'll open every goddamn artery if you don't drink."

The torment in his expression alone was reason enough to comply.

The blood exploded over her tongue in a subtle myriad of flavors, and in seconds, its soothing effects eased the pressure to an almost tolerable level. Chance caressed her hair in soft strokes, releasing a heavy sigh of relief when her breathing became steady.

The slice closed, and Lilith pulled his arm away from her mouth. Taking anything from him after what he had barely survived bothered her, but he and Nicci were right. She had needed it.

Pain still flared across her back, but it lessened with each breath.

Chance pulled her into his arms, tucking her head against his chest. The rapid beat of his racing heart began to slow.

"You should have listened to me. Why didn't you run when I first told you to?" he whispered against her hair.

"You know why. I'm okay. We're *both* okay."

He tightened his arms as if he might be scared she'd disappear.

No.

Chance *was* scared.

She felt it like her own fear was haunting the deepest recesses of her bones, pulling at her sinew, consuming her.

"I can't lose you." His haunted tone summoned memories of him in that damn hospital bed, and tears blurred her vision.

"I'm okay." Lilith placed a kiss at the center of his chest, and he hugged her closer. "Okay. Ow. I'm still tender."

"Shit. I'm sorry." Chance immediately loosened his grip on her. His arms rested against her while his cheek nuzzled her hair.

For a moment, Lilith lost herself in every chaotic emotion humming beneath his warm skin. There were *so* many and then ran impossibly deep.

The elevator dinged, and in a split-second, Nicci and Chance had their guns trained on the doors. But when they opened, the Solasta security lead's pot-marked face loomed into view.

"Everyone okay?" Genuine concern filled his voice.

I suppose letting the former owner's daughter die in the building would hamper his career.

"We're fine," Lilith said while Nicci and Chance lowered their weapons.

"The targets have been neutralized, but authorities are already in route. You should leave before they get here. We'll clean up this mess."

"Thank you." Lilith flashed a grateful smile and tried to move, but Chance held her in place.

"I'll carry you," he whispered.

Lilith leaned back enough to meet his eyes. "You will not. I can walk. Besides, we don't know if there are any other surprises waiting for us. You need your hands free."

"She's right." Nicci scooped up the drive and tucked it into her vest. "We need to get back to the others. She can walk, and you carrying her will just slow us down."

Chance held Lilith's stare for a long moment. Tumultuous emotions flickered through his eyes. After brushing the blond strands from her face, he reluctantly let her go.

Lilith got to her knees and cradled his face in her palms, but he avoided her eyes this time. "Chance."

A slow exhale washed over her lips before he met her gaze again. "I can't keep failing you."

The pained words made her brow wrinkle. "You didn't fail. I'll be fine. See? I'm already breathing better...because of you."

Chance didn't appear convinced. His eyes were still glassy, but he nodded.

Lilith captured his lips in a searing kiss, hoping to ease his illogical guilt. Then she rested her forehead against his. "Let's get back to the RV and figure this out. Okay, *beau? Mo laime toi.*"

"I love you too." A smile cracked through his misery, and he rubbed his thumb over her left ring finger.

"Come on, you two. You can profess your undying love in the damn RV," Nicci playfully grumbled.

Lilith swore she heard a snicker from the Solasta guard before she grabbed her vest off the floor. When she flipped the thing around, her stomach clenched.

A bullet was deeply lodged in the fabric a few inches below the white letters which read "CSI." If the Kevlar had been any thinner or if the shot had struck an inch or two higher, it wouldn't have stopped the thing.

Lilith tried to push the bullet out, but it was firmly lodged in place.

After a moment's consideration, she slid the vest back on. Although the thing dug into her sensitive flesh, it was better than venturing outside without one. She left the straps a little loose to cut down the discomfort, and Chance helped her to her feet.

"Stay close to me, *mon fiancé.*"

"Always." She smiled up at him.

Chapter 46

Too many thoughts weighed on Luminita's mind. Distracted, she went through the motions, passing the multiple security checks to Dr. Scott's lab.

"Wormwood," she uttered with a pang of guilt.

When she'd requested for Dr. Scott's first test of Wormwood's DNA-specific strain to be tailored to Aaron, it had seemed like a solid plan. Utilizing the cure to keep Aaron in line made sense—right up until this afternoon.

Embodying her past self, embracing her role as his Goddess of Blood and Chaos to draw Aaron in, wasn't supposed to affect *her*. It was a guise, a ruse, a way to manipulate the man and throw him off guard, to take back control. At least, she had thought that's all it would be.

Yet, something in his eyes, in their connection, had shifted in those moments. Her words had unintentionally emerged with meaning, weight, regret, as if her soul had been waiting for that moment, seeking an excuse to make it happen. Then their violent abandon had stripped away the masks and left her bare to him, like she had been on that night in Oarzina long ago.

After Luminita injected him, the regret had immediately clenched her insides, but she still couldn't comprehend the reason. Or perhaps she had chosen to ignore why. After all, the only regret she had harbored over the years was Vlad.

The tiny voice she typically ignored spoke louder this time.

The Datura Seeds.

Luminita swallowed hard while the memory of her panicked desperation to undo what she had done returned to her. The moment he had drained the chalice she pressed to his lips, she had felt regret, wanted to take it all back, just like she did now.

However, Aaron's reaction was not the same as it had been the spring of 1241. Once the initial fury passed, he had *still* wanted to worship her, prove himself a true partner, and had asked her to do the same. The man had put a dagger to his chest and begged for trust, for equality.

Why would he do that after what she had done? After everything they had both endured? After all the ways they had hurt each other?

The door unlocked, and Luminita swung it open, stepped inside, and closed it behind her. The confusing thoughts still whirled in her mind.

"To what do I owe the pleasure this afternoon?" Dr. Scott's greeting held no warmth, not that she had expected it to. He was her prisoner, after all.

Luminita shook off her internal conflict, straightened her asymmetrical jacket, and focused on the large man hunched over a microscope. "For two reasons: I need another dose of the cure, and I require another DNA-targeted strain."

Dr. Scott swiveled on his stool and took her in with a tapered gaze. "Is that all?" He scoffed.

The glare she leveled at Dr. Scott had made stronger men break.

"All right." He released the words on a huff. "Do you have the DNA for the target?"

"Not yet. What *precisely* do you need?"

"A vial of blood or several hair follicles…Saliva would work…or semen, even tissue. I need enough for four or five samples."

"I'll make sure it's done. How many doses of the cure do you have ready?"

"It's not a cure." The man chuckled derisively. "It's a vaccine, which also provides immunization."

"I don't need a lesson in scientific semantics. How many doses?"

"So far…three. The process is quite lengthy and tends to destabilize when made in large batches. Also, I would like to point out that I have not tested it. In theory, it *should* work, but…Cohen was the only one who's received a dose, and he wasn't infected."

Luminita considered his words. "What if it doesn't work?"

Dr. Scott bunched his bright red eyebrows together. "Then it doesn't work."

Luminita stretched her neck, trying to control her irritation. "Are there possible side effects?"

Wormwood

The man pressed his mouth into a firm line and clenched his jaw for a moment. "I don't know since *I haven't tested it.*"

"I've provided you with a wide range of test subjects. Have your assistant administer them to the vampires first, specifically the pureblood ones."

"Does this have anything to do with the DNA-tailored virus I made you?" Suspicion hummed over his pale skin.

"That is none of your concern. Do as you're instructed and continue making doses of the cure. I'll get you the DNA for the next target."

Luminita spun on her heel and stormed toward the door. Her mind raced through her options. Obtaining the samples would be tricky but not impossible for the right agent. But if the cure didn't work…

When she had hatched her plan to infect Aaron, she hadn't really cared if the vaccine worked. Between his pushback in all matters and his little display in his room, she'd seen his survival as optional. Or at least, she had desperately tried to convince herself of that. But now, old fears crept into the back of her mind, ones she had forgotten.

The possibility of the vaccine being ineffective or causing side effects bothered her on a frighteningly deep level. Testing it on others first seemed prudent.

It was only a consideration she made now, not before she had administered it to Andrew. Perhaps the reason stemmed from her resentment of his shift in loyalties. Maybe Aaron's pledge had simply moved her.

When she locked the door behind her, Luminita's shoulders drooped. It hadn't been the pledge. She had regretted her actions the moment the needle broke his skin. Hell, she almost hadn't gone through with it.

When she had held the knife to his throat, his shock had been tempered by her words. He hadn't retaliated, hadn't pulled away.

No.

Aaron had tightened his hands on her hips, fingers digging in until they bruised her skin, and viciously thrust until they had both unraveled.

Trust…

In that moment, he had trusted her, and even after her betrayal, he'd sought equal ground.

What if it was all an act? Every wild emotion had felt real, and maybe they were at the time, but would he keep his word? Once Aaron had the vaccine, would his loyalty shift?

None of it matters. Plan for every contingency.

Luminita inhaled deeply and shoved everything down. She hadn't survived over a thousand years by relying on others or trying to divine their motivations. Manipulating the odds, planning her strikes far in advance, unraveling the patterns to reknit them in her favor…That was what kept her alive, kept her from falling into the hands of others, like she had with Vlad.

While she walked toward the main lab, Luminita took out her phone and scrolled through her contacts. This job required a delicate touch. Luminita hovered her thumb over several names before a smile split her lips. She tapped the contact.

"Luminita," a gravelly voice rumbled from her speaker. "I didn't expect to hear from you, especially after things came to light at PMIC."

"I'm calling in a favor." She didn't have the time or energy for small talk.

"Are you now?" Amusement colored his words.

"You owe me," Luminita growled. "You wouldn't have your seat on the Council without me."

"A fact you frequently enjoy reminding me of. And you couldn't have hidden your experiments in our building without my help. I think that makes us even."

"I need this favor."

The man released a heavy sigh. "I'm assuming this is about the Cohen situation?"

Luminita paused with her hand on the door to the central lab. "Why would you think that?"

"Mannix wants him brought in…You too, actually." His disapproving tone eased her sudden apprehension.

"Of course, he does. No. That is not why I'm calling."

"Then do tell."

"Has Mannix returned to the building yet?"

"How do you know he left?"

"I have my sources. You aren't my only ally."

"No," the man replied, hesitating. "His plane isn't landing until tomorrow."

"Excellent. I need you to get someone in and out of his apartment."

"Ethan's apartment?" Luminita could practically hear his eyebrows hit his hairline. "You have got to be joking."

"You run security for the building, and you know his place better than anyone."

"And *you know* Mannix has his own separate system. Not to mention, my role in your little experiments have put my reputation in question. Ethan isn't exactly happy with me at the moment. I have people watching my every move."

"Obviously, not too closely, or you never would have answered my call."

"What makes you think I'd help you? I may *owe* you and dislike Ethan's politics, but I won't hurt him."

"Asher, I need your help. If you refuse, I'll find someone else, and I can't guarantee they'll act in Ethan's best interest."

A long moment of silence stretched out. Luminita wondered if her gamble would pay off.

"No. I'm done." The man hung up.

Luminita's smile broadened while she crossed the lab.

Asher would report her call to Mannix, who would insist on a full security sweep of his apartment. His focus would be on the PMIC building, and as a result, he was more likely to drop his guard outside of it. Even if Asher didn't relay the threat, he would try to keep Mannix away as long as possible, as a precaution.

Luminita brought up another contact and pressed the call button. The man answered on the third ring.

"Dragaica, two calls in a matter of days. You must be quite busy. Who's the contract on this time?"

"It's a specialized job. I need *you* on it personally."

"I'm quite pricey."

"You're worth it."

"Flattery doesn't support my lifestyle. What's the job?"

"I need DNA samples from Ethan Mannix."

Silence filled the line.

"You won't even have to set foot in PMIC," she coaxed.

"Why is that? The man rarely leaves the building."

"He took a trip to Philadelphia, and his private plane doesn't touch down in Huntsville until tomorrow. I'm sure you can find the flight details."

"What *exactly* do you need?"

"I need enough DNA for five viable samples. The source doesn't matter, as long as you are certain it belongs to Mannix."

"$200,000."

"For DNA samples?" Luminita chuckled. "Fifty sounds more appropriate."

"If you want my finesse and discretion to procure DNA from the leader of the Durand Council, that is my price."

Luminita entered the hall leading to her apartment and considered the offer. The price was outrageous, but so was the risk.

"You know…assassination would be cheaper," he offered.

"No. I want to send a very specific message. $200,000. I'll text you the drop location and who you'll be meeting for the exchange."

Luminita hung up and slid the phone into the pocket of her skirt. When she finally raised her eyes, they landed on Aaron, who leaned against her door with a sinful smile.

Despite her determination to keep everything buttoned down, the subtle curve of his lips made her core clench.

"And what specific message are we sending for $200k?"

A few days ago, that question would have been steeped in snide sarcasm, but now, he sounded playful, almost like the man she had first shared a room with over a busy tavern.

Luminita stepped up close, watching his grin stretch. That alone felt surreal. The man typically scowled, and on the rare occasion he *did* smile, it was usually out of malice. The one he wore now reminded her of the alluring expression of bliss he had worn while presenting his first gift to her.

The thought of the ruby pendant tugged at her, but she brushed it aside. Dwelling on the necklace was pointless. Aaron had thrown it away in a fit of rage centuries ago.

When she was close enough to feel his body heat, he straightened but didn't touch her, as if denying himself was just as much fun.

A sudden need to test his limits rose to the surface.

Luminita leaned up on her tip toes, lips hovering over his neck, and reached past him to turn the doorknob. Without a word, she slid by him and sauntered into her apartment but left the door open.

"Nita." Concern and desire warred for control within that one word.

She continued toward the divider screen with slow steps. Her grin widened when the door closed and his footsteps quickened behind her.

Aaron gripped her arm and spun her around to face him. "We have a deal, Nita. True partners. And as such, we share information." Beneath the heat and attraction, she sensed an old tension which almost felt

…sad. The longer she remained silent, the stronger that sensation became. "Is that not what we are?"

Aaron studied her face for an answer.

Part of her wanted to end this now, to remove this complication, but the energy crackling between them drew her in, like it always had. "$200k is the cost of obtaining DNA from Mannix."

Although the anxiousness beneath his skin eased, his expression turned serious. "For the Wormwood virus?"

Luminita nodded, carefully assessing him.

"You want him to die from the virus he refused to acknowledge when Cohen brought it to the Council."

"You *have* been paying attention," Luminita teased.

He tightened the grip on her arm and drew his brows together. "Of course, I have."

"Well, you haven't always been this"—she raked her gaze over him from head to toe before meeting his eyes again—"attentive."

One corner of his mouth lifted while a seductive growl rumbled from his chest. "I've always paid attention."

Luminita slid her fingers over his dress shirt, lingering at the center of his chest, and Aaron drew in a sharp breath. The cut from his oath earlier hadn't fully healed, though it would soon. The thought summoned a melancholy feeling.

"For the past several centuries, you've prioritized your position within the vampire Elders over everything else."

"For the resources it afforded us, not because I value my race as it is now. Evolution, dominion over humans, control…Those are the things we are striving to achieve."

Her nail caught on the button, and she worked it through the buttonhole. "And Eden…Was she a *resource?*"

A delicious jolt of shock tore through him, and he gripped both her arms. "A necessity."

Luminita peered up at him, arching one brow. "The Elders forced you to take a wife?"

"Why are you asking about her?" His grey eyes hardened.

"I'm curious how much was an act," she replied simply.

It wasn't the full truth, of course. For a long time, she had been the only woman his body responded to, the only one he desired. Then, there was Eden.

He carefully weighed her words before he answered. "Attempting to procreate is an expectation among the older purebloods. I wanted to blend in, keep suspicion off our endeavors, Nita."

"There is one problem with that explanation." She fiercely held his gaze again. "You married her before approaching me to rekindle our partnership."

"But the mission has never changed. Even when we weren't speaking, I was working toward our goal. What is this really about?"

On some level, Luminita knew she should drop the subject, but a burning need to understand overtook her. Pureblood vampires did not reproduce easily, which meant a lot of sex, and the thought disturbed her. It always had, no matter how much she tried to shove it from her mind.

"Did you love her?"

Aaron's face pinched in a frown tinged with disgust. "No."

"Did she know?"

"Where is this coming from? You've *never* asked me about Eden." Aaron searched her eyes once more but didn't seem to find what he was looking for.

"Curiosity. *You* are the one who wanted a true partnership."

"It was a role we were both forced to play. Yes, she knew I didn't love her. She didn't love me either. It was a marriage of convenience for us both."

"With certain perks, I'm sure. Enough to spawn a child." The words emerged with far more animosity than Luminita had intended. *I should have more control than this.*

"*Duties*, not perks. Had she lived through Michael's birth, she intended to leave with him."

He spoke the words so calmly, so unemotionally.

"And you would have let her walk away?"

"Yes," he said without hesitation. "We'd agreed on it. I'd only entered my *arrangement* with Eden because the Elders expected an heir from me."

"And what do *you* truly want?"

Aaron stared down at her with an expression so open, so free of pretense, it made her breath hitch. "What I've always wanted—*our* vision for the future. I'm tired of hiding, cowering behind weak men. None of them see the world the way you and I do." He released her arms, his fingers trailing up her to shoulders in a shiver-inducing touch.

"Why haven't you asked me for the vaccine?" Luminita studied every single emotion flickering beneath his skin, searching for any possible deception.

"Draga." He stroked his thumb over her cheek. "You infected me because you needed control in order to trust me…to bring me to heel." He leaned down, brushing the raven curls from her shoulder. "I felt your fear and regret in my very viscera. If living with this…waiting for you to offer me the cure…is the price of your trust, I'll gladly pay it."

His lips brushed against her sensitive ear, and she fought off the warmth seeping into her core.

"And if I think this is all an act? If I never give it to you?"

Aaron slid his hands around her waist and drew her against him. "You will. You let me in. You *finally* let me in after centuries."

Luminita stiffened as if the words were abrasive, but they affected her unexpectedly. "Sentimentality does not suit you."

A thrill skittered across her nerves when his teeth grazed her neck.

"Now *you* are the one acting. I think you need to let go. You crave the loss of control, but that requires trust, and for a moment…I had that."

"You are making wild assumptions," Luminita snapped. "You don't know what I want." She pulled away from him, but he gripped her arms, drawing her right back.

"Yes, I do." His grey eyes burned into hers with absolute conviction. "When I arrived here, you pushed and pushed until I ripped away your control, but today…" The intense heat in his stare turned her molten. "You *gave* it to me. You weren't plotting or scheming. You were right there in the moment with me."

Every survival instinct screamed for her to break his hold and run, but their connection kept her rooted to the spot. Luminita might have orchestrated the circumstances, but he was right. Somewhere in the seduction, she had gotten lost in her role, beguiled by her own design. Perhaps, subconsciously, she had wanted to recreate that night as much as Aaron did and had made every excuse to make it happen.

However, conceding was not in her nature.

"No. I played a part. I gave you what you wanted to gain the upper hand. I infected you."

None of those words seemed to faze him.

"It may have started that way, but it didn't *end* that way."

"But it did. I accomplished my mission."

A knowing grin pulled at his lips. "I felt every ounce of your regret, Nita. You only followed through because you were afraid. You don't have to fear me, not now." Aaron stalked forward, backing her up until her legs hit the bed.

Desire made her heart race, but she still couldn't give in. She *refused* to. Luminita was the master of her own destiny. She had sacrificed *everything* to ensure that, and she couldn't grant Aaron the power to hurt her like he had in the past.

"No. I don't want you." Luminita forced the lie past her gritted teeth.

The man's grin broadened. "I don't have to slide my hand between your slick thighs to know that's a lie." He shoved her onto the bed, and before she could scramble to her feet, Aaron gripped her tight skirt and ripped the fabric up to her hip.

"Physical attraction is *not* the same thing." Luminita scowled at him with all her righteous fury, but still, the man didn't waver.

Aaron leaned down and prowled up her body until his lips almost touched hers. "I've had your blood, Draga. I know the truth. Fight it all you want. I welcome the challenge."

While Luminita was trying to comprehend those words, Aaron's knees hit the carpet, and he gripped her thighs, dragging her to the bed's edge.

"What are you doing?" she growled when he draped one leg over his shoulder.

"Not asking permission."

Chapter 47

Chance led the way back to the RV, keeping his focus solely on their surroundings and blocking *everything* else out. He *had* to. If he allowed himself to think about Lilith, about what had happened, how he had almost lost her *again*, he would make another mistake.

As if summoned, the scene outside Solasta started to replay, but Chance quickly shoved it away with steely resolve. He refused to fail her again, and he couldn't afford to dwell on things while they were out in the open.

The air filled with tumultuous emotions which didn't belong to him. Chance jogged ahead, putting some distance between Lilith and himself. Sensing her undulating fear and concern only made it harder to focus.

Once they made it to safety, he could accept her reassurances, not that he would take them to heart. He could fall apart later, but not now.

No distractions.

Chance rounded the last corner and slowed to a walk when the RV came into view a few yards ahead. *Almost there.* He waited for the relief to set in, but it never came. They weren't safe yet.

By the time the girls caught up, Lilith's breathing was almost normal. Knowing that should have eased the panicked guilt squeezing his ribs, but it didn't.

Lilith fell in step beside him, and he sensed her eyes on him, studying him. She'd had his blood. Lilith recognized all his turmoil just below the surface.

"Chance?"

With one word, she summoned everything he had been struggling to suppress. He couldn't respond when the memory tore through his head, and he couldn't stop it—Lilith sprinting for the building, the unexpected pop from a merc Chance hadn't seen, Lilith hitting the marble with the shot's force.

In that moment, Chance's entire world had ground to a halt, the air had frozen in his lungs, his heart had stopped, and his brain had screamed…*Everything* had narrowed to Lilith sprawled out on the floor.

When he'd finally seen her move, the universe had sped back into action, and he'd blindly raced for her. He *had* to get to her, make sure she was okay. Nothing else mattered to him—would *ever* matter to him.

Even with the vest, it had been a close call. *Too* close. An inch or two higher and the bullet would have missed the plate. Hell, she had still suffered a punctured lung and couldn't breathe.

What if he hadn't gotten to her in time? What if he'd been pinned down by the mercs? What if he'd been hurt and couldn't get to her? All those questions scared him, but one terrifying truth topped them all.

They hadn't seen the true professionals yet.

This had been another band of loosely trained militia looking to make a name for themselves. A truly organized hit would have ended the game, taken them all out from a distance. They needed to get their names off the damn hit list and fast. Luminita's offer hadn't seemed effective so far, or perhaps that was why they hadn't seen a true pro yet.

When Chance, Lilith, and Nicci approached the RV, Tim jogged down the steps to meet them.

"What the hell happened? There's all kinds of chatter on the police scanner."

"Ambush," Chance answered stiffly.

"Anyone hurt?" Tim carefully scanned each one of them.

The words caught in Chance's throat. He couldn't say it, couldn't admit it.

"We're all in one piece." Lilith flashed an uneasy smile. She tried to hide it, probably for Chance's benefit, but the ordeal had shaken her, and his emotional lockdown wasn't helping matters. "I'll let Chance fill you in. I need to get this vest off. The bullet is still digging into my ribs."

Lilith spared a quick glance at Chance, but when he didn't meet her eyes, she hurried up the RV stairs.

"Bullet?" Tim raised a blond eyebrow and directed his gaze to Chance.

"I'm gonna give Lil a hand," Nicci muttered, jogging after her partner.

Either the detective wasn't eager to rehash things or recognized Chance needed a moment. Probably both.

"We were on our way back…hadn't even left the courtyard. A van screeched around a corner, barreling toward us. Nicci was faster. She made it back inside. But Lilith and I were stuck behind the low wall. I counted six…"

Chance heaved a sigh. He had miscounted, made a critical mistake.

"They started circling, trying to cut us off from Solasta. We *had* to move. We didn't have a choice." Chance finally allowed the full weight of his guilt to settle across his shoulders.

The moment whirled through his mind again. Lilith running, *pop*, her body flying forward, hitting the marble.

I almost lost her…again.

"Brother." Tim clapped a hand on Chance's arm, pulling him from the loop. Concern filled the man's touch, but it just made the failure more poignant.

"When Lilith ran for the building, she took a bullet to the vest." The memory constricted Chance's throat, and he had to force a swallow before he continued. "I *tried* to cover her, but…I didn't see him…the seventh man. I *should* have seen him."

"Hey, you're both here, breathing and alive. Cut yourself some slack, man."

Chance glared at Tim from beneath his brow. "I'm a professional. I *should have seen the threat.* It's my damn job."

"No one is perfect—"

"You don't get it. These weren't even fucking pros." Chance interrupted. "What if…" He lowered his gaze to the cracked concrete. "What if I'm not enough? I couldn't protect her from Ashcroft… couldn't protect her today."

"Stop," Tim ordered. "You can't dwell on that shit. You're only one man, but you are *not* alone. Lilith is okay."

"For now." Chance appreciated the sentiment, but it didn't ease the hollow ache in his chest, didn't quiet the inner voice screaming that he was doomed to fail. "What happens when the true players come after us?"

"We have to get rid of the fucking contract," Tim stated, as if it were that simple.

"And how are we gonna do that?"

Tim shrugged. "Step one is calling the Elders. You know that."

Chance nodded. He would have to make Lilith see reason. They couldn't put off the call to Antonio. The man needed to know what was going on, and they needed his help.

"In the meantime, worrying yourself into a damn coma isn't gonna do anyone any favors."

"I know." Chance had to do better. It was that simple.

"Come on, man." Tim patted his shoulder again and turned him toward the RV. "We shouldn't stay in one place too long."

"You're right." Chance followed Tim up the RV steps, with the weight of too many things on his shoulders.

"Keller, head toward I-95 South for now," Tim directed before heading toward the back.

As soon as Chance ascended the stairs, his eyes found Lilith's, as if his gaze had been drawn there by an irresistible force. She stood in the rear bedroom's doorway, breathing normally, but fear and tension writhed beneath the surface, echoing his own turbulent emotions.

"Lil, I'll take a look at your vest."

She focused on Tim before glancing down at the vest in her hands. Once she tossed the thing to him, Lilith settled her stare back on Chance, as if maintaining eye contact helped quell the chaos in her head.

It wasn't enough for him. Chance needed to touch her, hold her, truly believe she was okay. The RV door closed, and the vehicle started moving, but he ignored all of it. Every cell rioted with the need to feel her, but Tim was still blocking the damn aisle.

"Tim," Chance said with measured breaths. "Please…move your ass."

After an amused smirk which crawled under Chance's skin, the man finally sat down on the bunk next to Eileen, leaving the aisle clear.

Chance hurried toward Lilith. He *had* to close the distance, feel her warmth, listen to her heartbeat, remind himself she was alive. It was an overwhelming compulsion now that they were safe.

When he reached her, she wrapped her arms around his neck with the same urgency, and Chance squeezed her against him.

She's here…alive…in my arms…breathing.

"I'm so fucking sorry, *cherie*," he whispered against her hair.

Lilith tightened her arms and released a soft sigh. "Stop. *You* saved my life…again. We have to get off that damn hit list. I can't…lose you."

A surge of panicked fear and overwhelming sorrow raged beneath her skin, and he instinctually knew which memory haunted her thoughts—

the van after Ashcroft's attack, fighting to save Chance's life and almost failing.

"I can't lose you either, *mon fiancé.*" Chance nuzzled the curve of her neck and placed a soft kiss on the delicate skin. All he wanted to do was back her into the bedroom, hold her in his arms, and do everything in his power to erase the sadness lingering beneath the surface.

As if sensing his desperate desire, Lilith turned her head slightly, her lips grazing his ear. The faint touch sent a shiver down his spine.

"Later, *beau.* We have work to do."

Despite everything, a chuckle rumbled from Chance's chest. "Seductively whispering in my ear like that makes me *less* patient, not more."

Lilith pulled back, wearing a radiant smile full of suggestive things. That's all it took. One smile from her and the rest of the world disappeared, along with the panic in his head.

Fucking magic. The woman is pure magic. Chance traced the slight dimple in her cheek, reveling in the silkiness of her skin.

"What's the plan?" Keller hollered from the driver's seat.

Lilith winked up at Chance before peering around him. "We head back to Knoxville."

"When we get close, we should stop outside the city and take public transport to the hospital," Eileen suggested. "Less likely for the RV to be reported."

"Good point." Tim smiled at the agent before returning his attention to Keller. "We should take a less direct route too. Stop at a different campground, change plates again if possible."

"Meanwhile…" Lilith turned to Nicci, who sat at the dining table with her laptop and Dr. Scott's ghost drive. "Can you crack the encryption on the drive?"

"Slight problem there." Nicci frowned at the black box. "We lost the power supply in the chaos. I can't do anything without it."

"Can we get a new one?" Tim asked with an irritated sigh.

"Of course. We can stop by a Best Buy or something on the way."

"Okay. Nicci, coordinate with Keller. We'll stop at the closest place." Lilith was already in problem-solving mode.

"Lily." Chance tried to capture her attention, but she kept talking.

"We need to see if the drive is still viable as soon as possible."

"Lilith." Chance tugged her back to face him. "I have to call Antonio. We can't wait…not after what just happened." He braced for an argument, but to his surprise, Lilith nodded.

"You're right. You should call him now. He needs to know what's going on…*everything*." Although her words sounded confident, nervous energy thrummed beneath them.

"What do you mean by *everything*?" Tim surged to his feet with a swell of guarded panic.

"I mean…all of it," Lilith said quietly.

"*Not* Eileen." The man went rigid, crossing his arms over his chest. "He doesn't need to know about her."

Chance opened his mouth to say something, but Lilith spoke first.

"We have no choice, Tim. She is part of all this. If I leave her out, how do I explain Dr. Preston? Why we can trust him? How do I convince him our plan for the virus is viable? How do we sway him toward taking things public? She is an FBI agent with a clean record, and she's on our side."

"No," Tim stated with an iron resolve.

"No offense, but…" Eileen rose to her feet and placed a hand on Tim's arm. "Shouldn't it be my decision?"

Tension made the tight quarters seem even smaller while Chance waited for Lilith's answer.

She hadn't been wrong about her response to Tim. Eileen had played a critical role in their story's credibility, but Chance also understood Tim's urge to protect her. Antonio was one of the most reasonable and level-headed of the Elders, but Eileen's safety wasn't guaranteed. She was a human with intimate knowledge of their kind.

Even if Antonio understood the desperate circumstances and didn't fault Lilith's judgment, most Elders strictly upheld their law of secrecy, no matter how honorable the cause. Breaking that covenant typically carried a heavy sentence for both the vampire who had revealed secrets and the human who knew about them.

"Yes," Lilith finally replied. "It should be up to you. You've earned that right."

Eileen turned to face Tim and rested her palms on his crossed arms. "I know you want to protect me, but Lilith is right. Without me…the narrative doesn't make sense."

Chance watched his friend's face crumple.

"You don't understand what you're risking." The heartache in the man's voice was stifling.

Chance slid his arm around Lilith's shoulders with a sudden need to hold her close. Telling Antonio everything would put them both at risk.

"Yes, I do," Eileen stated simply. "But protecting me puts you *all* in danger."

Tears filled Tim's eyes. The agent smiled softly and caressed his cheek. In all the years Chance had known him, he had never seen Tim like this—at least not since Jill's husband put her in the hospital.

"*Mon frère*, we won't let anything happen to her or Lilith. You know that. If the Elders come for either of them, we'll fight. You aren't alone either."

Tim moved his watery gaze to Chance with a silent plea.

"It's the right choice," Chance reassured him. "We'll *make* Antonio understand."

Slowly, Tim's posture softened, and he allowed his eyes to drift back to Eileen. "I won't let anything happen to you…not while I'm still breathing."

A bright smile tipped the corners of Eileen's mouth. "I know. I feel the same way. That's why I have to do this."

Tim swallowed hard. He stared at her for a long moment before giving Chance a firm nod. "Make the call."

Chance dug the burner out of his pocket and dialed before they all lost their nerve. It was now or never.

"Who is this?" Antonio's deep voice held more than a little irritation. *Not a good start.*

Chance pressed the speakerphone icon and placed the cell on the table. "Deveraux, sir. We're all here."

"Adams?" The firm snap of the man's voice summoned a chorus of apprehension from the entire group.

"Yes, sir. I'm here," Lilith replied.

She fought to keep the tremble from her voice, but Chance felt it.

"What in the hell is going on? I just got a call from Solasta Security. You had a damn shootout in public? They said you were hit."

Chance took over, quickly summing up the events. "She's okay, but yes. DeLuca, Adams, and I were attacked outside the building."

"Why?" The question held a firm command, one which could no longer be ignored.

Chance stared down at Lilith with a silent question. He would tell the story if she couldn't.

"Antonio, I need to fill you in. It's a lengthy story," Lilith stated, leaning into Chance's side.

He tightened his arm around her shoulders.

"Okay, Adams. I'm all ears."

The man sounded less hostile now, but the column of Lilith's throat shifted with a heavy swallow. She launched into a full account, starting with a brief description of her relationship with David Boston, Jr. Lilith didn't exclude a single pertinent fact while Keller navigated the RV through narrow streets.

When she reached her tell-all at the cabin, she paused.

"I need you to know…we didn't have a choice, Antonio." Her eyes darted to Tim and Eileen with nervous tension. "I had to tell Agents Hersch and Gorman everything. They'd seen too much, witnessed the impossible, and we needed allies. Aaron tried to pin everything on me, the Durand Council was hunting us—"

"You revealed our secrets to human FBI agents?" Guarded caution filled the man's voice, but at least Antonio didn't seem to be condemning her just yet.

Tim stiffened on the bunk bed and wrapped an arm around Eileen. This was the moment of truth. No turning back.

After a nod from Eileen, Lilith finally answered. "Yes, sir."

"And where are these agents now?"

A spike of fear emanated from Tim, but the question sounded more practical than threatening. Hopefully, that was a good sign.

"Agent Gorman was…killed, but Agent Hersch is here with us."

Tense silence filled the space while everyone collectively held their breath.

"I'm guessing there's more to this story of yours?" Antonio carefully replied. Apparently, he wanted the full account before showing any hints of judgment. At least that meant the man was listening.

"Yes, sir."

"Continue," he commanded, his tone business-like.

Lilith did just that, explaining everything which had occurred at the cabin, minus Cohen's mental breakdowns. However, when she reached the fight at Duncan's, her words faltered, lost in the undertow of the memory.

"Breathe, *mon cherie*," Chance whispered.

Tears welled in her olive eyes. Conflicting emotions warred behind them.

This was the tipping point, not simply because it was the most painful of her memories, but because it had led to the most dangerous breach of secrecy. Confessing to human law enforcement was one thing. Handing over scientific evidence of their existence to a human scientist, however …Not to mention, her plan concerning the virus. It was all dangerous territory.

Lilith drew in a deep breath, wiped her eyes, and exhaled heavily before speaking again.

Chapter 48

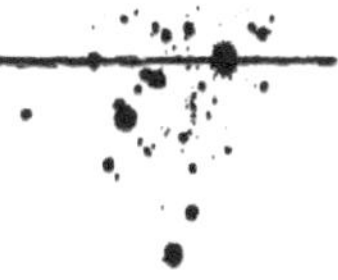

"Lilith, I need you to continue," Antonio gently prodded.

Lilith peered up at Chance while the memories of that night tightened her throat. She hugged his waist, reminding herself he was here, alive and breathing, sitting at the table beside her.

I can do this.

After a slow exhale, Lilith focused on the burner phone. "We fought Ashcroft at Duncan's house in Madisonville. Both Chance and Cohen were gravely injured in the attack. We managed to get Chance out, but…"

Vivid memories haunted her: Chance's blood seeping between her fingers, an ocean of red dripping to the floor and soaking her jeans, her desperate pleas for him not to give up, Chance apologizing, saying goodbye.

Lilith swallowed down the instinctual panic those horrific memories always summoned.

"He needed medical attention," she finally managed to say. "Luminita had control of Goditha. She'd slaughtered the entire staff. Driving to another of our medical facilities would have taken too long."

Despite her resolve, tears spilled down Lilith's cheeks. When she found her voice again, it wavered and cracked under the strain of her worst memories.

"He was dying, and I…I couldn't…" The words wouldn't come out. She opened her mouth but was unable to make a damn sound past the tears constricting her throat.

"Agent Hersch suggested a colleague," Nicci said with a sympathetic smile. "A research doctor in Knoxville she's worked with for years."

"DeLuca?"

"Yes, sir. Chance was near death…He's a half-blood…and we *all* felt the risk was worth it."

Gratitude made Lilith's heart swell. With that one statement, Nicci had diffused the responsibility, refusing to let her partner face the music alone.

"The risk of taking him to a human hospital?" The man's tone remained neutral, as if merely clarifying the implied fact.

For once, Lilith wished the Durand ability to sense emotion worked over the phone. Antonio's guarded and measured responses gave no clue to his mindset.

"Yes," Nicci answered quickly. "Even then…he coded twice during surgery and was in ICU for three days."

"And what were the repercussions of this hospital stay? Were you able to maintain secrecy?" Antonio wanted a damage report.

Fear tainted the air, emanating from everyone in the RV. This was the moment of truth, the one which would make or break them, and Lilith refused to let anyone else take the fall.

"*I* made a judgment call," Lilith stated clearly. "Chance was in ICU. Luminita, the Durand, Aaron, and the Elders were all searching for us. The doctor needed to be aware of certain medical facts and required an explanation why our anonymity was so important. *I* did what I had to do."

"What are you saying, Adams?" A clear warning filled his question, shaking Lilith's resolve, but she couldn't turn back now.

"I gave Dr. Preston the truth about us…about Chance."

A heavy sigh rattled through the speaker. Lilith's pulse raced.

"Dr. Preston is trustworthy. He'll make an excellent ally when we go public." Lilith rushed through her explanation, praying Antonio would understand, see the logic.

"*If*, Adams. *If* we go public."

"The virus will force our hand. It's spread to three other states—"

"Six, actually," Antonio interrupted. "As of this morning, Georgia, North Carolina, and South Carolina have reported multiple outbreaks of Parvo B-20. Lockdowns in those states are eminent." The weariness in his voice gave Lilith hope. "Between the attacks on our facilities, Aaron going MIA, and this damn virus…things are absolute chaos."

"Antonio, what if I could deliver a way out…a way to take vampires public in a positive light?"

"What are you talking about?"

Lilith heard it—the guarded optimism in his question.

"Before Dr. Scott's abduction, he was working on a vaccine for the virus. I believe the computers recovered from the cult's compound were key. The leaders may have been delusional, but they wouldn't have risked releasing a virus if they didn't have a failsafe for their members."

"Yes, but as you mentioned, he's been taken, along with all his research."

"Perhaps not all."

"Spit it out, Adams. I don't have time for games and riddles." Antonio's irritated order rattled the phone's speaker.

"I interned with Dr. Scott. He trusted me. The reason we were at Solasta today was to retrieve the hidden drive that automatically backs up all his work. If Dr. Scott had a cure formulated before he disappeared, it will be on this drive."

"But," Nicci cut in with a steely glare, "I need to decrypt it first, assuming it wasn't damaged during the attack."

"And if the drive has what you need? What's your plan, Adams? I know you have one, or you wouldn't have called."

Lilith forced a swallow past her suddenly dry throat. There was a very good chance Antonio wouldn't go for this. It went against every rule they had ever lived by.

"Dr. Preston recommended a virologist he knows and trusts—"

"A human?" Antonio interrupted sharply.

"Yes, but—"

"You've already exposed us to three humans. Now you want to not only add to that problematic collection, but hand over evidence that could make us culpable for a damn pandemic?"

Lilith's heart pounded in her throat. She had to make him understand, but how?

"I can assure you. The evidence from those computers will clearly identify Dr. Rachel Thomas and Dr. Kelley Wolfe as the terrorists responsible for the Pandemic."

"Who is this?" Antonio snapped.

"Special Agent Eileen Hersch, sir."

Tim stiffened beside her with a horrified expression. Lilith could almost swear she felt the man's terrified heartbeat.

"The *human* FBI agent?"

Eileen bristled, but the woman kept her voice polite. "That's correct. I worked the Cappalletty case with my partner. I was the one who discovered the cult's compound and handed the computers over to Solasta for independent study. The simple fact is…you needed my help. Without my cooperation, Goditha would have been held responsible for the virus. I supplied the proof that identifies your race as victims and not suspects."

Lilith couldn't help but be impressed by Eileen's calm confidence and how easily she asserted both her usefulness as an ally and her trustworthiness.

Silence descended, but Eileen wasn't content to let it stretch out for too long.

"Also, as a *human*, I believe Lilith has formulated the best possible plan, given the circumstances. First, you don't have a virologist capable of working on a vaccine nearby. Second, handing the information over to a human to formulate fosters trust.

"If you were to go public with a working vaccine in cooperation with humans, the general public will be more likely to trust it. Last but not least, a human virologist will have plenty of incentive to work fast with how quickly the virus is spreading through the human population."

Tim squeezed Eileen's hand. His smile brimmed with pride and fear in equal measure.

After a quiet moment, Antonio finally spoke. "Adams. How certain are you about all this?"

Relief flooded Lilith's entire body. He hadn't agreed to anything yet, but he was listening. Antonio seemed to understand the validity of Eileen's speech, thank the powers that be. Of course, that didn't mean they were out of the woods yet.

"If the drive isn't damaged…I'm very certain, sir."

"And if it is? What's your plan then?"

"Luminita has Dr. Scott. We'll find her research facility and do whatever is necessary to recover our virologist."

"That needs to happen regardless at some point. The Durand are a problem." Another heavy sigh reverberated through the speaker. "I'm going to be blunt, Adams. This situation is a goddamn catastrophe, but…we should have seen it coming. If you can give me hard proof on any of your claims about Aaron, I don't see how the Elders can fault your decisions. I believe your plan has merit, and with the acceleration of this virus, we don't have much time until our hand is forced. Controlling the manner in which we are exposed makes sense, and Agent Hersch made some excellent points."

Lilith started to truly relax for the first time since the mercs had attacked them outside Solasta.

"But." The word rang through the RV with an impending sense of doom. "I have to take all of this to the Elders. I believe, after Michael's death, we have the majority on our side, but I can't guarantee that. I will have to uphold the Elder's decisions…no matter the outcome."

"What if we can prove Aaron's involvement with the database?" Nicci asked hurriedly. "Will that be enough? I'm close to cracking the user list."

Antonio seemed to consider that for a minute. "It's a start, DeLuca. At the very least, it will prove Aaron has been gathering illegal information on our citizens that directly led to our exposure, assuming you can also prove that humans infiltrated that database."

"We already have circumstantial confirmation of that, with the inclusion of Lilith's recorded therapy sessions and the identification of the microphone's origin, but as soon as I have that user list, I will have definitive proof, sir."

"You have your work cut out for you, DeLuca. I'll give you forty-eight hours to gather as much proof as you can before I take all this to the Elders. That's all I can give you."

A massive weight lifted from Lilith's shoulders.

"Sir, there is another problem."

Lilith peered up at Chance. Fresh trepidation blossomed in her chest. *That didn't last long.*

"What is it, Deveraux?"

"David Boston, Sr. He has all our names on a hit list, and it's only a matter of time until the professional hitmen descend on us."

"Bringing that to the Elders before you have proof against Aaron is…problematic. They will want an explanation, and Agent Hersch's name is on that list."

Once again, silent unease seemed to steal all the oxygen from the RV. Forty-eight hours, plus however long the Elders took to deliberate, assuming the decision went in their favor…It was too long, and Lilith knew it.

Hell, everyone in the RV did.

"This situation with Solasta might give me some leeway. I'll see if I can send a team to Philadelphia, along with a few of my own men. However, if Boston is as powerful and resourceful as you claim, Adams, it may not be enough."

"I understand, sir. We appreciate any assistance you can provide."

"Lilith, one more thing." The business tone fell away with the use of her first name. "I owe you an apology. I thought appointing Aaron to take Gregor's place would appease the man, make him more cooperative with our cause. I admit when I make mistakes. I'll do what I can on your behalf. Just get me the proof I need."

"Thank you. We will, sir."

Lilith reached forward to press the end call icon, but she couldn't tear her stare away from the cell. Her thoughts wandered. All things considered, the call had gone better than expected, but a sour weight still sat in her stomach.

Everything hinged on that ghost drive. If she was wrong, if it was damaged, if Nicci couldn't decrypt it…

"Once I have the power supply, we'll have a better idea of what's possible," Nicci said, as if reading Lilith's mind.

Of course, it wasn't a very far leap in logic.

"Should be at Best Buy in about twenty minutes," Keller reported from the driver's seat.

"What about the database?" Lilith asked tentatively.

"Honestly? I haven't had time to work on it since we left for PMIC, but I'll get working on it right away."

Lilith nodded and flopped back in her seat. There had to be something else, some other angle, some other proof, but if it existed, she had no clue where to look.

"We'll figure it out, *cherie*. We always do, remember?"

Lilith desperately wanted to believe Chance's whispered words, but it felt like they were balancing on a knife's edge, one wrong move from falling into an inescapable abyss.

So many things could go wrong.

Chapter 49

Helena watched the light from the small window slowly stretch and travel her cell while the hours crawled by.

Noah is dead, she reminded herself over and over, clutching her knees tighter to her chest. *But...I can still save Desi and perhaps Chance.*

David Boston, Senior.

The size and scope of the contract he had placed, especially including FBI agents, indicated a man of wealth and power. It wouldn't be an easy mission. Typically, she would have weeks to plan, study routines, learn the layouts of his favorite places, and plot the best technique. Chance didn't have weeks.

Hopefully, Luminita had enough intel to give Helena a jump-start. If she had to go in blind, too many things could go wrong.

Although Luminita had made it quite clear Helena's life was forfeit, she still had to make it back alive to satisfy the terms of Luminita's deal. If she died on this mission, so did Desiree, and if she failed the mission, Chance would too.

The rectangle of light turned pink, orange, crimson, and then purple. By the time it began to fade, the last ten years seemed like the distant memories of a past life or an alternate reality. Helena had deluded herself into thinking she could start over, cut ties with the Durand, and live a normal life.

None of it had been real. Noah had died for a cruel fantasy.

Helena's husband had never truly known her. Lena was a lie, a fabrication. She had kept secrets and played the role of a dutiful wife for ten years, but what bothered her most...He had seemed happy with the lie.

Had she been that convincing? Or perhaps Noah had simply never wanted anything deeper.

The thought twisted her guts. Noah had never pushed. He'd freely given her space without complaint. The man had never insisted on learning about her past. Had never probed her inner thoughts. Noah hadn't even balked when she didn't invite a single soul to their little wedding.

Helena had always found comfort in that. But she now realized Noah had made it easy to lie because he'd never wanted the truth. Maybe their love story wasn't as grand as she'd thought. Perhaps it hadn't been love at all.

Some part recognized she shouldn't place the blame on Noah. He had suffered and ultimately died because of her. Still, in the end, Noah had betrayed her. He'd used their talk—the one time she had bared her soul to him—to gather information and had handed it all over to Luminita.

To save Desi, she told herself. But was that the truth? Helena didn't even know anymore. The only *love* she had known was either abusive and toxic—Bastien—or superficial and convenient, safe.

Of course, it didn't really matter, not anymore. Noah was gone. Even if their marriage had been nothing more than a comfortable façade, it was over now anyway. Desi was all that remained of their life together, and soon, she would be alone in the world—an orphan, just like Chance.

The heavy door to her cell unlocked, pulling Helena away from her morose thoughts, and Orchid slowly rose to her feet. Lena Carter and Helena Vieux were dead. One more mission, and Orchid would finally join them. The certainty of that was oddly comforting.

Two guards entered the cell, weapons at the ready, but Orchid stood with her hands raised like a good soldier, awaiting orders. Any attempt to fight would result in deadly consequences for Desiree. The guards didn't need to voice the threat.

"All the arrangements have been made." The man on the left lowered his weapon, pulled a thick manila envelope from his tac vest, and handed it to her. "That's everything we have on the target."

Orchid accepted the file and cracked it open. Philadelphia. Unfortunately, she didn't have any contacts there.

"If you'll follow me." The same man turned and stalked into the hall while his partner stood by the door, waiting for her to follow.

Orchid suppressed her instinctual desire to snap the merc's neck. The straggler predictably fell in step behind her when she walked into the hall.

Orchid forced her gaze away from the doors to the other cells. Desiree was probably behind one of them, but knowing which one would only torment her. Instead, she concentrated on the information in her hands.

David Elias Boston II was a founding partner at B&A Realty, an ultra-successful conglomerate specializing in commercial and luxury properties. Divorced. One son, David Boston, Jr.—although technically, he should have been David Boston III—deceased. No other living family. He owned a penthouse on Rittenhouse Square at The Laurel and worked in a high-rise in Philadelphia's Central Business District.

In other words, lots of security on both fronts.

Orchid frowned at the headshot pulled from the company's website. The man didn't appear all that intimidating. Gray sprinkled his dark curls, a few extra pounds made his cheeks plump, and his brown eyes seemed too small for his face. He was mildly attractive, but if it hadn't been for the swanky custom suit, she would have pegged him as a mid-tier lawyer or an accountant at a big firm. The man certainly didn't look like a corrupt business mogul capable of issuing multiple high-level contracts.

Of course, money opened all kinds of doors and covered all manner of sins.

The police reports caught her attention next. All of them—every single one—had ultimately been recanted. There were at least a dozen leveled against his son and triple that for the man himself. They held common themes—domestic violence and sexual assault. Only one had resulted in a charge, which had later been dropped.

An assault in Los Angeles on the UCLA campus almost ten years prior. The perpetrator was identified as David Boston, Jr., and the victim was…Lilith Adams.

Orchid came to a halt, and her heart pounded. She scoured over every single detail in the report.

Boston had been accused of severely beating his girlfriend in the parking lot. The list of injuries made Orchid's stomach sour until bile rose in her throat.

Nasal fracture, lacerations around the eyes, split lip, multiple contusions, orbital fracture, two broken ribs, periorbital hematoma, fractured wrist, a near rupture of the spleen, dislocated shoulder, and a hairline skull fracture.

If Lilith had been human, David Boston, Jr. would have been facing murder charges. Judging by his father's track record, he would have evaded that jail sentence.

Suddenly, everything made sense.

Chance had killed the man who had abused and nearly killed the woman he loved. Of course, he did. Prideful tears flooded her eyes. Lilith was right. Despite everything Chance had endured, he *was* a good man, a just man, a protector.

"Ma'am." The guard's irritated voice drew Orchid's attention away from the file. "This way."

Orchid quickly wiped away the tears threatening to spill, closed the folder, and nodded.

After a curiously long look, the merc turned around, leading her to the outside door where another pair of men stood guard. She looked at the table where she had relinquished all her weapons, but it was empty.

Orchid stepped out into the night. A breeze rustled the leaves and made the humid air tolerable, but the hum of machines and the whir of generators were the only sounds. It was eerie facing the woods without the serenade of crickets and frogs, like the forest creatures knew something evil and unnatural lurked among them.

Orchid followed the merc who ventured toward her vehicle. Security lights harshly illuminated the area, casting stark shadows which stretched into the trees like devilish talons. Luminita stood beside the SUV, wearing her typical business attire, although she had opted to forgo the leather jacket she usually donned when venturing outside.

"Orchid. I see you received the information I gathered for you." The woman's stare landed on the file in Orchid's hands. Something sharp lingered in her smile. "I trust it has everything you need?"

Orchid stopped a few feet away and schooled her expression. Every fiber of her being wanted to gut the Romanian for her cruel lies and vicious games. No doubt, including Lilith's police report was yet another emotional torment Luminita had planned.

"I haven't had an opportunity to look through everything, but I'm sure it's enough to get started."

A little of the amusement faded from Luminita's Caribbean-blue eyes. "Well, you'll find an array of supplies and weapons in your vehicle, including your knives."

"And my phone?" Orchid resolutely held the woman's stare.

A slow grin unfurled across Luminita's lips. "No. Your job does not require communication with Lilith or Chance. Take out the target and return here. It's that simple."

Orchid struggled to keep the disappointment off her face. She had hoped to at least let them know she was going after Boston, to give them a little peace of mind. Although, if Orchid was being honest, she just wanted to speak to her son one last time.

"Do I need to remind you of the terms?" Luminita folded her arms over her chest, her eyes narrowing.

"No. Once I've completed the mission, I return here, and you let Desi go. I have your word on that?"

"Of course." The same sharpness edged into the woman's smile, and Orchid's heart sank.

What good was the demon's word? She had lied before, lied about *everything*.

What choice do I have? I can't take this facility by myself. If I don't go, Desi will die. Luminita might not keep her word, but there was at least a chance she would if Orchid followed the rules. Besides, Chance needed Boston dead. If she could take away this threat for him and his fiancé, perhaps it would at least earn her a tiny place in his heart.

"I'll make contact when the target is neutralized." Orchid stepped around her and reached for the door, but the vehicle was locked.

"One last thing." Luminita almost purred the words while she held out the key fob. "Make it bloody...brutal. I want this to be a very clear message. Am I understood?"

Orchid frowned and reached for the key, but Luminita pulled her hand back.

"Bloody increases the risk of being caught. It's more of a challenge."

A cruel smile graced the woman's mouth.

"As long as you make a clean exit, being caught isn't a concern, is it? Only one fate awaits you, Orchid."

The truth of those words lanced through her heart. One last mission. Desi would be free, and in a way, she would be too.

Once Orchid nodded in understanding, Luminita handed her the key and pushed away from the vehicle with a confident stride.

The hardest part of all this was watching that devil walk away.

Luminita deserved to be destroyed for all the pain and havoc she had caused, and now, Helena and Lena would never see justice for what Luminita had cost them.

All Orchid could do was beg the higher powers to exact the karmic retribution she couldn't.

Please...make her suffer.

Chapter 50

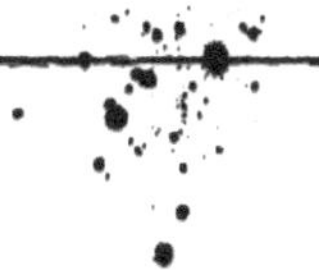

Blood. There was so much blood. Lilith stared down at her hands. Crimson seeped between her fingers while she pressed evidence bags against the deep lacerations in Chance's chest. His heartbeat was so faint, and each gurgled breath came slower. She was losing him.

It wasn't enough. *She* wasn't enough.

"Stay with me!" The desperate scream tore from her raw throat, and the world blurred with her tears. She used her forearm to wipe them away and tried to breathe past the sheer panic tensing her body.

A gargled cough captured her attention, but when she peered up, it wasn't Chance's face she saw. Shock jolted down her spine, and she immediately gazed at her hands.

Hot, sticky blood still gushed around her fingers, but instead of three deep cuts across the chest, a gaping hole lay in its center.

"Lilith…" Andrew whispered her name, but she couldn't tear her attention away from the mangled heart beating beneath her fingers. "I'm sorry."

Lilith shook her head vehemently and pulled away. "No. This isn't real. It isn't right."

Andrew relaxed against the van's seat. His golden eyes flooded with tears while he watched her. "It's okay."

The peace in his expression terrified her.

"No, it's not," Lilith whispered, her voice cracking.

One corner of his mouth lifted, and a tear fell against the seat. "It only beats because of you."

The guilt crushed her chest, stealing her breath. Lilith clamped her hands over her ears and squeezed her teary eyes shut.

"No. Stop! It's not real! None of this is real."

A whisper reached her ears regardless of what she did.

"Oh, but it is." Luminita's Romanian-flecked voice sent chills down Lilith's spine. "If you could only save one…"

Lilith opened her eyes to the familiar cave of horrors which frequently haunted her nightmares. Luminita stood between two gurneys, a bloody scalpel in her hand. Cohen lay on one side and Chance on the other.

"They both wear your scars." Luminita's grin stretched, and her heels clicked against the cold stone. She strolled toward Cohen. "Would you like to see?"

"No! Stop!" Lilith screamed, but the woman ignored her.

The flickering lamplight glinted against the blood-drenched blade hovering over Andrew's chest.

This is just another nightmare, Lilith tried to tell herself, willing her heart to stop racing.

But was it? After her conversation with Chance, she wasn't sure anymore. What if Luminita was torturing Cohen again? Of course, if that were true, Lilith was powerless to stop it. Just like before, in the medical center, all she could do was bear witness.

Horrific screams tore through the air, and Lilith curled into a ball, covering her ears.

It didn't matter.

Every ounce of pain poured into her skin, as if the scalpel were cutting *her* flesh and not Cohen's. She felt the blade travel up until it nicked the sternum, wrenching a shriek from Lilith's raw throat.

Then it stopped.

"Choose!" Luminita commanded.

Lilith watched in horror while the woman stalked toward Chance.

"Choose or I kill them both!"

"Chance!" Lilith screamed. "It will *always* be Chance." The words were true, but the moment they left her mouth, she turned to stare at Cohen's tear-streaked face. "I'm so sorry."

The rest of her words died in her throat. That peaceful expression blanketed Cohen's face again.

"It's okay. It only beat because of you."

The words cracked something in Lilith's heart and tears fell. "You *deserve* more. I'm sorry I can't give it to you."

Luminita paced back to Andrew's gurney, but Lilith kept her eyes locked on his.

"No," he whispered. "You gave me more than I deserved. Always."

The scalpel was raised over his neck, and still, Lilith couldn't look away. She refused to. That was the least she could give him.

A flash of silver arced down, and a beep pulled her from the dream.

Lilith startled awake with tears still flooding her eyes. She whipped her head around. Chance slept peacefully beside her. His chest rose and fell with calm, even breaths.

It was just a nightmare, Lilith reminded herself again.

She sat up, wiping her cheeks. Then she remembered the beep which had woken her. A light flashed on the burner phone, and she snatched it off the small nightstand.

A text message—from Orchid.

Lilith. I need to speak to you in private. Call me when you're alone.

Lilith frowned at the screen, rereading the message. What could Orchid possibly have to talk about in private? If it was about Chance, Lilith had made her stance very clear. Orchid needed to have those conversations with *him*. Lilith refused to harbor secrets.

About what? Lilith sent the quick response before climbing out of bed.

The RV wasn't moving, which probably meant they had stopped for the night. Lilith crept out of the bedroom as another ding sounded from the burner.

"Who's texting you?"

The whispered voice nearly made Lilith's heart jump right out of her damn chest. She squeezed her eyes closed for a moment, trying to breathe, and then glared over at Nicci.

"Dammit, woman. Are you trying to scare me to death?" Lilith whisper-screamed.

Nicci smirked from the dining table where she sat, typing away on her laptop. "So, who's texting you?" she repeated.

"Orchid." Lilith unlocked the screen and stared at the new message.

Please. It's important.

"About what?"

"I don't know." Lilith stared at the message. "She wants to talk in private."

Nicci raised one brow.

"I'll make the call outside. I don't want to wake anyone anyway."

"Just stay close by."

Lilith nodded and tip-toed through the RV, past Tim and Eileen sleeping on the bottom bunk, Gibson on the top bunk, and Keller sprawled out on the couch.

A moderately cool breeze greeted her when she stepped out into the night. This campground wasn't as nice as the previous one, but it had a few benches in the center. Lilith wandered toward the closest one while pressing the call icon. The phone rang until it went to a generic voicemail.

"Oh, come the fuck on." Lilith growled in frustration, sank onto the park bench, and dialed again.

This time, the line picked up on the third ring.

"Orchid," Lilith said on a sigh. "What is this about?"

The line was silent. The longer it stretched out, the stronger her sense of dread became.

"Orchid?"

"No."

Lilith nearly dropped the phone in shock. A tidal wave of emotions dragged her under. "Andrew?" she whispered on a shaky breath.

"Yes." Misery seemed to saturate that one word.

"You're really alive?" Tears filled her eyes with an unexpected and overwhelming rush of relief.

Orchid had told her Andrew had survived, but on some level, Lilith had been scared to believe it.

"Yeah." His voice broke, and he cleared his throat before speaking again. "Are you okay?"

The question tore at her heart. He was the one in Luminita's clutches, at her non-existent mercy.

"I'm all right. Are *you* okay?"

Silence filled the line again.

"Andrew?"

"No. Not really, but that's not new."

Lilith opened her mouth to say something, but he quickly continued.

"I'm so sorry, Lilith. I…" His voice broke again, heavy with tears. "I can't tell you how fucking sorry I am."

Her heart raged against her ribs. "For what, Andrew?"

He swallowed hard and released a pained sigh.

"You…" He drew in another deep breath. "You offered me your friendship, and I…"

When his voice broke again, Lilith wiped the tears from her cheeks. "It's okay," she said softly.

"No. You gave me more than I deserved, and I was…selfish."

His words echoed her nightmare, and Lilith's trembling hand covered her mouth to keep from sobbing. For a moment, all she could picture was Andrew strapped to that table, eyes locked on her, while Luminita's blade was poised to strike a fatal blow.

"I never should have hesitated. I *never* should have kissed you."

After a hitched breath, Lilith forced words past her constricted throat. "You saved me…saved Chance."

"He's alive?"

To Lilith's surprise, hope infused his tone.

"Yes, because of you. Andrew…what you said that night—"

"Forget it, please," he interrupted.

"I can't," Lilith admitted. "I know you think I saved your soul, but…" This time, it was her voice which broke. "Everything that's happened to you…it's all my fault. You almost died because of me…*for* me. That's not salvation."

Another heavy pause weighed on her heart.

"Don't do that, *please*. My life before…it didn't mean anything."

"Pain and misery? That's not meaning."

"Lilith, you are the only one who has ever wanted to see me for who I am…who cared too much to pull away. I know…Chance is it for you, but you taught me what love looks like. That *means* something."

The ache in her chest only worsened. How was she supposed to respond to that? What hurt even more was the fact she knew it was true. Lilith did love Andrew, just not in the way he truly wanted, not in the way she loved Chance.

"Don't feel guilty. I know who I am to you, and I'm okay with that. I wouldn't take back a single moment…except perhaps the kiss I stole from you."

Lilith wanted to be angry. Chance was right. While he was losing to Ashcroft, Cohen took precious seconds to say goodbye. Perhaps if Chance hadn't made it, she would be angry, but she simply didn't have it in her heart to pass judgement on Cohen for that moment.

"You didn't—"

"I did." He cut her off again. "I took advantage of your friendship in that moment, and I *am* sorry. Lilith…I swear…I just want to keep you safe."

The last word cut through the haze with alarming clarity. "Andrew, how did you get Orchid's phone?"

He hesitated, as if the abrupt subject change had stunned him. "She gave it to me."

"Orchid's there with you?"

"No. Not anymore."

Panic flared in Lilith's lungs, making them burn. If Orchid was dead, Lilith couldn't handle telling Chance one more life-shattering thing right now.

"Luminita sent her on a mission. I don't know what. She refused to tell me when she got me out. Her daughter is still being held in Luminita's compound. We...weren't able to get to her."

"Where are you?"

"Elkins, West Virginia. I know I have no right to ask, but...can you meet me...alone?"

Alarm bells blazed to life in Lilith's head. "Alone? Why?"

Another pained sigh rattled through the phone. "Several reasons. I'm sure I'm not...welcome among the others right now, and a bunch of strangers infiltrating the town would draw attention."

"But I don't see how I—"

"Orchid and I are going in for her daughter when she returns."

"Then let us help. We need to take Luminita down."

"No. I can't endanger their lives again or *yours*. I just..." Tears strained his voice again. "I want to say goodbye the right way."

"Andrew..." Even if Lilith had known what to say, his name was all she managed to get out before her throat tightened with tears again.

"I don't want your last memory of me to be a selfish one." Andrew cleared his throat before a derisive huff escaped. "And here I am...making a selfish request. I keep trying...but I can't seem to be unselfish when it comes to you, Lilith."

She couldn't hold back the tears this time. One soft sob escaped before she clamped her hand over her mouth and tried to breathe through her nose.

"Please...don't cry. Not for me."

Naturally, that only made things worse.

Lilith tilted her head back, dragging in shallow breaths until she could speak again. "Don't do this, Andrew. Let us come get you. We can make a plan. Work together."

"No," he responded with another weary sigh. "I just want to say goodbye. Please. Do this one thing for me."

"Andrew...I can't just leave. My name is on the list of every hitman in North America. A militia attacked us in front of Solasta today...in broad daylight. The others won't let me out of their sight."

"Are you okay?" Sudden concern filled his voice.

"Yes, but…I did take a bullet to the vest. It collapsed my lung. If Chance hadn't been there…"

"Fuck."

Lilith listened to his heavy inhalations, uncertain what to say.

"Fine. Meet me in Elkins. Bring the others if you have to."

"You'll let us help you?" A fragile hope sprang to life in her chest.

After several excruciating seconds, Andrew finally answered.

"Yes." The word seemed saturated in a heartbreak she couldn't understand.

"When should we meet you?"

"Can you be here by tomorrow evening? Six o'clock?"

Lilith had no clue where they were, how long they had been driving. After the call to Antonio, she had collapsed on the bed, exhausted. She glanced at the clock on the phone: 11:17. They couldn't be *that* far from West Virginia.

"I think so."

"Text me at this number if anything changes, okay?"

"I will, and Andrew…thank you for letting us help."

"*Don't* thank me. Just stay safe." He hung up before she could say anything else.

Lilith stared down at the phone, lost in an entire novel full of conflicted feelings. The thought of Cohen running headlong into a suicide mission terrified her.

The memory of that nightmare flashed through her mind—the one where he had given up. She had told him the truth in that dream. Lilith didn't want to lose anyone else. Andrew's life mattered. *He* mattered.

Now she just had to make everyone else understand it, especially Chance. Her guts twisted at the very thought.

This is not *going to go over well.*

Chapter 51

Cohen stared at the phone in his hand, and abject misery strangled his heart. As much as he had tried to brace himself for hearing her voice, for facing her wrath, *nothing* could have prepared him for what had happened.

Lilith hadn't lashed out, screamed at him, hung up…To his utter shock, she had sounded *relieved* to hear his voice, to know he was alive. Cohen hadn't anticipated that. And when she'd cried…That moment had struck him right to the very core.

All that brutal, breathtaking honesty from her, the raw emotions he didn't need to feel to know they existed, and *he had lied.*

Andrew's shoulders slumped and he wiped at his eyes. He had spun a story he knew she would believe, played on her sympathy, and taken advantage of how she felt.

Only to save her, he reminded himself, but it didn't assuage the guilt. No matter how noble his cause, he had manipulated the woman he loved in her moment of vulnerability. Andrew had betrayed that fragile trust she extended to him yet again.

Of course, not everything had been an outright lie. Cohen truly felt every word he'd said, even if he had constructed them into a fictitious situation. He *did* want to say goodbye the right way, make up for his moment of selfishness. To do that, however, he had to save her life.

Still, the lies remained a bitterness on his tongue, souring his stomach.

He'd heard it in her voice. Lilith wanted to see him, wanted to rescue him, wanted to know he was okay. Despite his selfish declaration and the irreplaceable kiss he had stolen, she was still fighting to draw him closer instead of pushing him away.

Why? What makes me deserve such generous devotion? What makes me worthy of even a slight sliver of her heart? What could possibly be left in me to love?

Andrew dropped the phone on the bed and smoothed his blond hair to his scalp. His chest tightened to the point of agony. If Lilith knew the full truth, the cost of that kiss, how he had condemned her, she wouldn't have been so desperate to save him. Lilith deserved to know, but he couldn't tell her.

The logical side argued that if he had, she either wouldn't have believed him or wouldn't have trusted Luminita. The truth would have irrevocably linked him to the Romanian, and Andrew would have never been able to talk her into meeting. It was all a sound assessment, but it wasn't the deepest truth.

Cohen wasn't ready.

Once Lilith knew he had infected her in that moment of weakness, he would lose her completely, and he just wasn't *ready* to let go. Knowing she cared about him the way she did was his lifeforce, the one thing keeping him going, and if he lost it right now...

Of course, the moment she realizes I set her up for Luminita, that will happen anyway.

Just picturing Lilith's horrified face and her inevitable expression of utter betrayal almost had Andrew picking up the phone. But if he backed out, if he confessed now, she would die a painful death. Luminita was the only way to save her, and Lilith deserved salvation more than he deserved her presence in his life.

Life. Is there life after her?

Andrew honestly didn't know the answer to that question. If there was, he couldn't see it. The very thought of trudging through the dreary world without her spark seemed hopeless and exhausting. He would rather live in constant pain if it meant staying in her orbit, but soon, he doubted he'd have that choice.

With that one phone call, he had severed the tie between them. Lilith just didn't know it yet. The end was inescapable, especially since Andrew had been unable to convince her to meet him alone.

That doomed attempt hadn't been for Luminita's sake. Being present would put the others in danger. Cohen held no illusions about Luminita and Aaron. They were ruthless creatures, and Chance was the only other asset among their group. They wouldn't hesitate to eliminate a threat. Blood would be spilled.

The only thing he could do now was try to minimize the damage. If he plotted things out with Luminita, perhaps he could keep most of them safe.

Fuck.

Cohen dragged himself off the mattress and stalked out of his cell. Luminita hadn't locked the door since she'd given him the phone. Most of the time, he merely paced the guarded halls, but tonight, he had a mission.

The merc guarding the central lab blocked the door when Cohen passed his typical turning point.

"I need to see Luminita. Now." Despite the hollow ache in his chest, Andrew spoke with brusque confidence.

The guard's stare lingered on Andrew. The small throat mic transmitted his message as the man spoke. "Patch me through to Miss Dragomir's quarters."

Cohen withstood the awkward silence, wearing his familiar mask of indifference while steeling his nerves. He *had* to make Luminita see reason and limit the possible carnage.

"Yes. Detective Andrew Cohen is requesting to speak with you… Understood." The guard's posture relaxed. "If you'll follow me."

The man turned, grabbed a keycard dangling from a badge reel, and swiped it across the little black box. A green LED lit up, and he opened the door.

Andrew followed the guard across the lab, pointedly staring at the floor. The memories of Noah's death were haunting enough without seeing them play out in this place. It had been a defining moment, an action he couldn't take back, but Cohen had only done it for *her.* Lilith's life was worth any cost.

His soul probably wasn't worth much anyway.

The guard repeated the procedure with the keycard and led Andrew into a nearly identical hall.

"She's expecting you." The man gestured toward the ornate door at the end.

Cohen gave a curt nod and strode toward Luminita's quarters, trying to suppress the anxious energy churning his gut. He needed to remove his emotions, like a snake shedding its skin. Luminita would not respond to sentimentality. She only cared about the next play, how things would impact her plans, and what would benefit her cause.

When he reached the door, Andrew drew in a deep breath, smoothed his hands down his cotton shirt, and slowly exhaled. He couldn't suppress his feelings about Lilith, but Luminita would expect those. She had witnessed their terrifying depths, and even if he could smother them temporarily, it would only make Luminita suspicious.

A dark chuckle escaped at the very thought.

If he had been able to suppress his feelings for Lilith, none of them would be in this mess.

But nothing could disguise the gaping hole in his chest. It had started as something small, an itch he couldn't help but scratch, but over time, he had dug deeper in compulsive desperation until nothing remained of his heart but a raw, bleeding wound.

With one last calming breath, Cohen raised his hand and knocked on the door.

"Come in," Luminita's voice carried from inside.

Andrew didn't hesitate. He twisted the handle and marched through the doorway with purpose. Luminita's desk sat empty, with a few soft lamps providing a dim light. He frowned, gaze traveling the vacant room.

"It's rather late."

Luminita appeared beside the divider screen, tying a silk robe closed.

Cohen quickly schooled his surprised expression. "I spoke with Lilith. I thought you'd like to know."

She arched one dark eyebrow and sauntered barefoot to her desk. "And? Will she meet you?" Instead of sitting in her chair, Luminita perched on her desk with an almost excited smile.

"Yes, but…not alone."

While Luminita nodded slowly, Andrew studied every flicker emanating from her, and there were *a lot*. He knew how to handle the cold, calculating version of Luminita, but this, the version she had been the past few days, he barely recognized.

"Well, that is disappointing."

"A group of mercs attacked them outside of Solasta today. Lilith was shot."

Luminita snapped her eyes up to his. "But you said you spoke with her…"

"Yes, Chance helped her recover."

"How fortunate for us." Luminita pulled her robe tighter. Her gaze drifted off as if she were lost in thought.

"The others *will* be present. We can't avoid that without risking Lilith's safety."

Luminita nodded absently.

"It's in our best interest to apprehend Lilith with as few casualties as possible."

"And why is that?"

Cohen whipped around at the sound of Aaron's condescending voice. The man stood beside the screen, dressed only in a pair of black satin pajama pants. Andrew had been so intent on persuading Luminita, he hadn't noticed a second signature in the room.

The tendrils of desire snaking out from them completed the unexpected picture. Aaron and Luminita were *more* than partners, but it was a new development, a tenuous bond prone to control issues.

That explained their shifting dynamic and odd behavior. Luminita *never* let people in. No wonder she had been off her game. For some inexplicable reason, Aaron made the woman *feel.*

With that realization came a disturbing stab of jealousy. Aaron was able to *reach* Luminita, slip past her obsidian walls of logic and control. If Cohen had been able to get through to her like Aaron obviously had, perhaps she wouldn't have been able to carve him up, torture him, use him.

When Andrew didn't answer, Aaron folded his arms over his broad chest, stern expression darkening. "Well, *detective?*"

The title sounded like an insult, but Cohen ignored the snide tone. "Elkins may be remote, but drawing attention is detrimental to our cause."

"*Our* cause?" Aaron scoffed, his eyebrows hiking nearly to his hairline. "Since when are *you* part of *our* cause?"

Cohen ignored him and turned back to Luminita. "Nita. Are you starting a war or securing an asset?"

She silently considered the question, but Aaron answered without hesitating.

"They are one and the same. We are abducting an Elder's daughter. Not just any Elder, but the former leader of the American territories. Do you really think they won't retaliate if we play nice and spare a few insignificant vampires?"

Andrew kept his eyes on Luminita, refusing to acknowledge Aaron. The man made a point, but Cohen refused to accept his answer. *Luminita* was the brains of the operation. He had to make *her* see that leaving the others alive would benefit them.

"There is a distinct difference between abduction and a massacre, especially with an FBI agent present. You *know* that."

While Andrew spoke, Aaron slowly paced over to stand behind the desk. Irritation and suppressed disgust hovered around the man like a dark cloud.

The feeling was mutual.

"Not to mention," Cohen continued, returning his focus to Luminita. "Any drastic measures will endanger your second target—Chance Deveraux."

"It sounds more like sentimentality for my *niece*."

Andrew finally met Aaron's sharp stare.

"Are you trying to minimize the damage?" Aaron asked. "Finding excuses to spare her friends in the hopes she'll overlook everything else?"

Cohen kept his impassive mask in place, but just barely. The truth of Aaron's words rang through his bones.

"Let me tell you something about my *niece*." Aaron leaned forward, pressing his curled fists against the wood. "No amount of backpedaling or heroics will be enough. She will *not* forgive your betrayal this time."

Rage broke through Andrew's calm. "You know *nothing* about Lilith. This isn't about her. This is about preventing unnecessary complications."

A dark scoff escaped the man, but Cohen averted his attention to Luminita again.

"If you want Chance alive, keep things civil. Once Lilith is healthy, he may even honor your deal for an exchange. Surely, Chance is the better specimen."

"And there it is!" Aaron barked a laugh and slapped the desk. "Hand over the man in your way so you can run off with the girl."

A snarl curved Cohen's mouth, but once again, he wondered if those words were true. Even if they were, he would never give Aaron that satisfaction.

"Chance is the progeny of two purebloods. This has nothing to do with who he is to Lilith…or me. He's the best choice!"

"Stop," Luminita commanded calmly. For the first time since Andrew had entered her apartment, a shrewd expression lit her face. "Chance is *not* necessarily the best choice. If we are correct about Lilith's blood holding the key, we could use her to create an army. Chance is only one man."

Cohen blocked the mental image of a horde of Ashcroft-like creatures before the shiver could run down his spine.

Stay focused. I can't argue that the repeated exposures to Durand blood may have tainted any special properties her blood contained…or point out that she'd almost bled out multiple times. Downplaying Lilith's importance would only give Luminita less incentive to save her.

"Chance is unique," Cohen countered, trying to assemble a plausible argument.

"A half—" Aaron started, but Luminita raised her hand, stopping him short.

"Let him speak," she said over her shoulder, though her voice held less commanding force than Andrew had expected.

Cohen glanced at Aaron only long enough to see the barely contained rage flashing in his grey eyes.

"Andrew. What makes him unique?" To his surprise, Luminita's tone was patient, almost gentle.

"You and Aaron stalked him for twenty years, kept him secret, hid his lineage. If a child of a pureblood Durand and a pureblood vampire were common, you wouldn't have exerted so much effort. Surely, I'm not out of line here."

A disappointed sigh escaped Luminita's full lips. "True, but so far, he has only shown common Durand abilities…weaker ones at that." A soft swallow followed her words, and one shoulder shrugged.

Luminita didn't believe what she had said. She was lying. Granted, she lied constantly, but this time, she wanted him to notice.

"That you know of."

A faint smile stretched her lips at Cohen's answer. She wanted *him* to convince Aaron of Chance's worth.

"Wouldn't it better serve your purpose to dispose of Chance? Eliminate your romantic rival so she doesn't pine over him or try to rescue him? Or is this disgusting, lovesick brooding an act?" A devious grin curved Aaron's mouth, and Andrew struggled to keep his anger in check.

"This isn't about what I want."

"It's not?" Aaron raised his eyebrows in amusement. "*You want* to save my niece. *You want* her treated fairly. *You want* the others spared. What *you want* is all I've heard thus far."

Frustration burned through Andrew's flimsy masks, and he dragged a hand through his hair. "No one asked for your fucking insight, Aaron."

Andrew's clipped words only broadened the man's smile.

Fuck. Aaron was picking a fight to throw him off-balance, and he knew precisely where to hit.

I need to rein things in…gain control.

"Fine. Let me clarify for you, Aaron. I want Lilith here, safe and healthy. I don't want the involvement of law enforcement, either local or federal. I don't want outright war with the Elders. Mannix and the Council are enough to contend with. And as for Chance—"

Luminita interrupted with a calm request. "Andrew, tell me about the moment you realized what Chance was."

Cohen had explained it to her on the phone that night. This request wasn't for her benefit. It was for Aaron's.

"Chance was hurt…bad…during Orchid's attack. I let him draw on me to heal."

Aaron was surprised by that. He stood tall, crossing his arms over his chest again.

"When he took my hand…it was like touching a live battery, entirely different than any Durand I've come into contact with…except one—Ashcroft."

The smug expression fell from Aaron's face, and something like hunger burned in his eyes.

"It wasn't precisely the same. Ashcroft was like touching…an atom bomb of hatred and depravity, but still…Chance is *not* a common Durand."

"And has Chance shown any signs of a signature gift?" Luminita studied him, curious.

Signature powers varied greatly among their kind, from something as innocuous as Cohen's shifting eye color to Isadora's horrific ability to control the dead with her voice. Luminita loved to collect the rare ones.

"No."

Cohen paused as soon as the word left his mouth.

"Actually…" The recent nightmares popped into his head. The odd moments of realism, the way Lilith spoke to him, as if she were really there. It all started after Chance had given her his blood.

What if I'm not losing my mind? At least, not completely. What if…

Andrew snapped his gaze up to Luminita. Even if he was wrong, it would at least distract her for a while.

"I think Deveraux is a…dreamwalker." Once the impossible words tumbled from his mouth, the certainty of them rested in his gut.

Luminita straightened, her sea-blue eyes widening, and desire perfumed the air in a cloying cloud.

"What?" Aaron snapped. "Impossible. They are a myth. They don't exist."

Once again, Luminita held up her hand to silence Aaron. She slid off the desk and stepped closer, never taking her eyes off Andrew, as if he would disappear if she did.

"Tell me."

A moment of indecision struck, but it was too late. He had already said the word. Luminita wanted Chance before, but now…

This went beyond Luminita's compulsion to collect oddities.

Aaron was right about one thing. Dreamwalkers *were* a myth. They only existed in oral histories, never recorded. An opportunity to study a mythical creature meant Luminita would ensure Chance's survival, even after capture. The man was her holy grail, her white whale.

"Andrew." Luminita gripped his chin, her features hardening. "Tell. Me."

He nodded awkwardly, and she released him but didn't back away. Instead, she studied his eyes intently, waiting for any sign of deception.

"My blood activated his dormant Durand side in Phipps Bend. Then, at the cabin, Chance gave Lilith his blood when we were unable to secure units from Solasta. Ever since then, Lilith has been appearing in my dreams, stronger and more realistic each time."

"That's called obsession." Aaron scoffed.

"I thought so at first too," Cohen admitted.

The vivid memory came back to him, making his eyes mist. *Your life matters. You matter.* Lilith had said those words to him in a dream with genuine tears in her eyes. It had been real. He knew that with unwavering certainty now.

Andrew couldn't hold back the heart-wrenching emotions coursing through him, even if he wanted to. He embraced them, letting the sorrow permeate the room.

"She didn't torment me the way my nightmares always do. She wanted to find me…wanted me to hold on and not give up…just like she did on the phone tonight." Several tears escaped when he met Luminita's wild stare. "No vampire has that ability. It has to be Deveraux…his blood connecting us."

Chapter 52

After completing another line of code, Nicci looked from the laptop's clock to the RV door. Lilith had stepped out twenty-two minutes ago to call Orchid, and every second since had ratcheted Nicci's anxiety.

The campground was nearly vacant, and the likelihood of any hitmen finding them out here was remote, but Nicci couldn't shake the image of Lilith struggling to breathe in the elevator at Solasta. If Chance hadn't been there, things could have gone wrong fast.

Thirty minutes and I'm going out there to check on her.

Nicci forced her attention back on the computer screen. A few more clicks, and *voila!* She was in the ghost drive from Dr. Scott's office.

The encryption had been adequate but barely. Nicci had expected more out of a paranoid person like Scott. Once things were over, she would have to give Solasta a few pointers on programming upgrades.

A heady little rush tingled her nerves while Nicci browsed the drive's contents. A folder labeled "Wormwood" caught her attention for several reasons. Not only was it the most recent folder accessed, but the name also stuck out compared to the others, which were mostly odd number and letter combinations.

Wormwood was a hallucinogenic herb, the active ingredient in absinthe. And thanks to her discussions with Agent Gorman, who had been an insanely detailed history buff, Nicci also knew it was closely tied to Apollo and Artemis—the deities the cult had worshipped.

Nicci wondered if Dr. Thomas and Dr. Wolfe had been aware of the Judeo-Christian history. The name of each angel from Revelations had been drilled into Nicci's head during her Catholic education, and Wormwood was a difficult one to forget.

If the Grecian cult psychos had been aware of the angel's role in the apocalypse, naming the virus after him made a certain sense. Although Wormwood poisoned the water in Revelations, it was still a reckoning to destroy the wicked and unfaithful. The cult had tried to purge the world of vampires, but the virus itself had turned out to be less selective.

Of course, if the cult created an antidote, perhaps they had anticipated the virus crossing into the human population.

Nicci glanced at the clock. *Thirty minutes. Time's up.*

Nicci crept around the dining table and past the others while they slept. Tim grunted softly, and Nicci froze for a moment. Eileen shifted, draping an arm across his chest, summoning a smile from the sleeping man's face.

Nicci couldn't help but grin at them. They gave her hope. Perhaps when the dust settled, she could still work things out with Alicia.

When neither of them moved again, Nicci continued her stealthy exit into the humid night. She spotted Lilith right away, and the anxious tension pulling at her muscles eased.

Lilith didn't appear to be on the phone, but Nicci couldn't be sure. The woman was sitting at a bench, facing away from the RV. Nicci didn't hear voices, though. The breeze simply ruffled Lilith's moonlit hair while she sat in stoic silence.

"Lil? You okay?" Nicci asked when she approached.

The woman's spine stiffened, but she didn't respond.

Nicci strolled around the table and sat on the bench beside her. For a moment, they both stared out over the campground. The songs of crickets filled the void.

"Partner? Are you okay?" Nicci tried again. When Lilith still didn't say anything, Nicci stole a quick peek at the woman's face, which gave her the answer. "What happened?" she asked quickly, her chest tightening.

Lilith wiped at her red-rimmed eyes and cleared her throat, but when she opened her mouth, nothing came out. She merely leaned forward, covering her face, and drew in sawing breaths.

Nicci rubbed Lilith's back in soothing circles, just like she had done the night Chance was rushed into surgery, the night he had almost died.

"Lil. Talk to me. What's wrong?"

After a heaving sigh, Lilith straightened. "It wasn't Orchid." She barely managed to get the raspy words out and drew in another deep breath.

Nicci's brow furrowed. "Someone else had Orchid's phone?" Then it hit her. "Oh my god, is she…"

Nicci let the implied question linger in the air.

"No," Lilith answered, roughly rubbing her face. With one last cleansing inhale, Lilith changed the subject. "Any luck with the drive?"

Back to avoidance. Nicci raised an eyebrow but finally relented. "Yeah. Just cracked it. Seems like it survived the shootout."

"Did you find the cult's files on the virus?" Hope lit the woman's teary eyes, but desperation clawed around the edges. Whatever had Lilith upset, she wasn't ready to talk about it yet.

"I think so. There's a folder named 'Wormwood' that looks promising. It was the last one Dr. Scott accessed. I haven't checked it out yet."

Something seemed to click in Lilith's mind, her stare going distant for a second.

"Nicci, about the database…I had a thought. Is there a way to isolate an entry's history? Who altered it and when? That kind of thing?"

"There should be since it's a shared file. Why?"

"Just identifying Aaron as a user may not be enough, even if we can prove how long he's had access. It was created by one of our scientists at Goditha. He could reason his knowledge of it away. But…if we can prove Aaron changed the info on Chance and his father…"

"Yeah, but couldn't Dr. Nichols have changed it? I mean, we already know Aaron threatened Nichols into silence…Probably had his daughter killed as a message."

"It's possible," Lilith said. "But I don't think so. Aaron doesn't like sharing info, and he obviously kept Chance a *deep* secret. I bet my paycheck Aaron altered the file himself before Nichols noticed the connection."

"Okay, but then why leave Chance's lineage as 'half-blood' and 'unknown'? Why not get rid of the mystery?"

"If Dr. Nichols ever tested Chance's blood against the database, it would throw up red flags. He'd know someone tampered with it. Bastien was already dead at that point, so changing his entry from pureblood to half-blood wouldn't be contradicted."

Nicci considered it for a moment. It made sense.

"All right. I can take a look. I should finally have the user list by morning. Then I can view all the changes by particular users. If Aaron altered anything, I'll see it."

The corners of Lilith's mouth lifted into a weak smile. "Okay." She nodded resolutely and moved to stand. "We should take a look at those Wormwood files."

Nicci laid a hand on her arm, stopping her short. "Wait. Sit."

Lilith slowly lowered herself back onto the bench with clear apprehension.

"Lil. I know you want to run headfirst into problem-solving mode, but…you're clearly upset."

The woman's flimsy veneer cracked. Lilith turned the burner phone over in her hand and stared at it with fresh tears in her eyes.

"I can't talk about it, Nic. I mean…" Lilith swallowed hard. "I *have* to, eventually. I know that, but…I'm not ready for the fights and arguments."

Nicci frowned. "The fights? Lil, we are all on *your* side. Who did you talk to?"

Lilith cast a nervous side glance at Nicci. "It was…" She hesitated and cleared her throat again before refocusing on the phone. Tears filled her eyes nearly to the brim. "Cohen," she finally admitted, her cheeks flushing a faint pink.

Nicci pulled back with a growing sense of apprehension. Her own feelings about Cohen were conflicted at best, but what truly worried her was that Luminita had her claws in him and could easily use him like a puppet. Especially, considering the mental shape Cohen had been in.

"I know you hate the guy…" Lilith uttered on a sigh.

"I guess I've never been subtle about that fact." With a little effort, Nicci cracked a grin and bumped Lilith's shoulder, hoping to break some of the tension.

Her partner smiled briefly. "You aren't subtle about much."

Nicci shrugged. "True. So, what did Cohen say?"

She tried to keep the judgment and fear out of her voice, despite her ambivalent feelings on the subject. Whatever Cohen said, it had hurt her, and Lilith needed someone to talk to who wouldn't fly off the handle.

For Lilith, her partner, Nicci could at least play the role temporarily.

"I don't want to get into logistics. It's something we'll all have to discuss. But the others should sleep while they can."

"Forget logistics, then. Why are you so upset? I'm your *partner*. I'm here for *you*."

Lilith raised one eyebrow in skepticism, and it felt like a slap to the face. Granted, Nicci could be a bull in a china shop when it came to dispensing truth, but she thought Lilith trusted her more than that. Maybe she had been a little too blunt and harsh when it came to Lilith's feelings.

"No judgment. Promise. Just talk to me. Please."

They stared at each other for a moment before Lilith frowned at the burner phone again. A few tears jostled free.

"I realize no one understands, but…" Her watery eyes met Nicci's with a silent plea to keep her promise. "I *care* about him. We have this…" Lilith struggled to find the right word. "…*bond*. It's not like how I love Chance, but it runs deeper than simple friendship. I can't explain it, Nic."

Lilith expelled a pained sigh, and her hands trembled around the phone.

"I *hate* that he's suffering, that he wants to just…give up. It breaks my heart, Nicci." Her breathing hitched, and she angled her head back to keep from sobbing.

Nicci's instincts screamed to blast her partner with unfettered truth in the hopes she would finally see Cohen for who he was, to recognize how untrustworthy he could be. But was he? The man had tried to sacrifice himself to protect Lilith *and* Chance.

Maybe Lilith saw a part of Cohen no one else did, or maybe his acting had simply improved. Either way, Lilith didn't need a lecture or a solution right now. She needed a safe space to unpack her feelings. It wasn't Nicci's area of expertise, but she would do her best.

"Lil…it's not your fault. You didn't break him," she stated quietly.

"It's not just the guilt." Lilith leaned forward, resting her elbows on her knees. "I…" Her voice cracked, and she wiped her eyes again. "I know it sounds stupid, but…"

A frown formed, and she turned to meet Nicci's stare.

"I don't want to lose him. He thinks he has nothing to live for…nothing to offer." In that moment, Lilith lost the fight with an expression of pure heartbreak. Tears freely streaked down her cheeks. "I don't think my friendship is enough, and that…*hurts*."

Nicci had to fight back her own tears when she wrapped an arm around Lilith's shaking shoulders. The words hit close to home, *too* close. She was still fumbling for something to say when Lilith continued.

"He said…" The woman cleared her throat. "…he wants to say goodbye the right way this time."

The last two words caught Nicci's attention. "Wait. What did he mean by *this time*?"

A deep pink flushed Lilith's cheeks, and she stared at the grass. "In Duncan's basement...before Cohen went after Ashcroft to save Chance..." Once again, Lilith paused, collecting herself. "He confessed some things."

Lilith looked to Nicci warily.

"Like what?"

"That he loves me. That I saved his soul. Then he asked me to forgive him for being selfish, and..." The pink in her cheeks turned scarlet. "He kissed me." Lilith swallowed hard at Nicci's shocked expression. "He told me to *live and be happy*, then threw me in your direction."

"Jesus, Lil." Nicci couldn't hide the myriad of emotions in her voice. Of course, Lilith probably sensed them all anyway, after drinking Chance's blood earlier. "He kissed you while Ashcroft was tearing Chance apart?"

Despite her promise, judgment leaked into Nicci's voice.

Lilith's shoulders slumped. "I know. I should be furious, and if Chance hadn't made it...I would be, but...I just can't hate Andrew. He risked everything to save the man *I love*. Despite his own feelings, Nic. And now...he's torturing himself over that moment of selfishness. He just wants to make things right."

"That's why he called? To say goodbye the right way? To apologize?" With some additional effort, Nicci managed to keep her voice soft and neutral this time.

Lilith stiffened. "Yes and no."

The alarm bells blared in Nicci's head, but she stifled them for now. Lilith had said she would share the specifics with everyone. There was no sense in pushing her yet. The woman needed a compassionate outlet, a way to relieve the pressure. There would be plenty of time for lectures later.

"Did I ever tell you how I met Alicia?"

Lilith frowned at the abrupt subject change. "No."

Nicci summoned the painful memories she had kept buried for years. "I met her in a support group. It was for people who'd lost loved ones to suicide."

Lilith blinked and sat up a little straighter. "Nic, I'm sorry. I didn't know."

"It's not something I talk about. Alicia and the people in that group are the only ones who know." A steadying breath rushed past Nicci's pursed lips. "My cousin Olivia and I were really close...best friends

…sisters. We knew *everything* about each other, or so I thought. Four years ago this September, Livi swallowed a handful of sleeping pills and slit her wrists in the bathtub."

The memories surged to the forefront, the ones Nicci had tried to block out, the ones far too similar to Agent Gorman's murder scene, which had been staged to look like a suicide.

"Livi didn't write a note. No one knew why she'd taken her life, especially me. She always seemed so happy, never got in trouble, no history of drugs…It didn't make sense."

"Did you ever find out why?"

Nicci nodded and cleared her throat. "Emails surfaced a few weeks later. Livi had been hiding her mental health issues with the skill of a damn Durand. She'd been seeing a shrink for a few years, and the guy…took advantage of her fragile mental state. They'd been seeing each other in secret for five months, and when he broke things off, she…snapped. She killed herself that night and emailed him her suicide note."

"That's awful. God, Nicci. I'm so sorry." The misery in Lilith's voice only amplified her own.

Nicci waved off her concern. She didn't want to drag this out. Talking about it was still painful.

"*The point is*…you can't save someone who doesn't want to be saved. I spent a lot of time trying to learn that lesson…I'm *still* trying. Livi never reached out, never told me what was going on. For a long time, I blamed myself. If I'd been a better friend…maybe she would have come to me. If I'd tried harder, looked deeper, been more understanding…"

It took a moment for Nicci to breathe past the shadow of guilt which still lingered.

"But the truth is, Livi didn't come to me because she was ashamed and didn't want me to talk her out of anything, not even at the end. She thought taking her life was a gift to the world. She'd no longer be a burden that dragged everyone down with her."

Lilith lowered her head when she made the connection to Cohen's situation. "He feels so guilty…I keep trying to tell him he matters, but…he doesn't believe me. I don't know how to get through to him."

Nicci gingerly touched her shoulder. "He called you. He reached out. That's more than Livi ever did. But, Lil…there's a possibility that nothing you say will make a difference."

The heartbroken expression on Lilith's face transformed into a glare. "That doesn't mean I shouldn't *try*."

Nicci quickly held up her hands. "I never said that."

Once again, Lilith raised a skeptical eyebrow.

"Okay, okay. I'm not saying that *now*. Cohen is your friend. You're allowed to care."

A defeated huff escaped Lilith's throat. "Pretty sure Chance won't agree."

"Does he know?" The question popped out before Nicci had thought it through.

"About Duncan's? Yes. I told him." Nervous tension keyed up every muscle.

"How did that go?"

Lilith expelled a heavy breath. "About as well as can be expected. He wants to tear Cohen's throat out."

"Can you blame the guy?" When Lilith's expression hardened, Nicci quickly explained. "I am not passing judgment. I mean, Lil…just look at how you reacted to the intern at Solasta. She was a stranger with a crush. If Chance had a close female friend who was head-over-heels in love with him…you'd be in jail, and I'd be bailing you out."

Lilith blinked and sat up straighter. The blood drained from her face. Then a pained laugh surprised Nicci.

"You're absolutely right. Shit."

"Maybe cut the handsome guy a little slack?" Nicci nudged Lilith with her elbow. "And as for Andrew…" She swallowed all her personal opinions and just spoke to her partner. "All you can do is be his friend. If that's not enough…that's not on anyone but him. You can only save someone who *wants* salvation."

A corner of Lilith's mouth lifted, but it wasn't quite a smile. "Salvation means different things to different people. What if he views death as salvation?"

Nicci wrapped an arm around Lilith's shoulders again and let out a soft sigh. "Then that's *his* choice."

Lilith stared down at the phone, her thumb caressing the screen.

"Come on," Nicci said, hopping off the bench.

"To do what?"

"Let's look through the Wormwood files and see what we can find in the database until the others wake up."

She needed to get Lilith's mind off Cohen for a while. Whatever the logistics were about the phone call, Nicci had a feeling Lilith was correct in her assumption. There would be fights, arguments, lectures, and her partner needed to mentally recoup before that.

Lilith's hesitant smile broadened. "Sounds like a plan, partner. Hey, Nic. Thank you…for sharing, for caring enough to let me talk…I mean that."

"Of course." Nicci smiled wholeheartedly. "We're partners. I know I can be…brutally honest, but…thank you for trusting me enough to open up. I'm always here for you."

Lilith wrapped Nicci up in a huge hug which ate away at the pain from failing Livi. Nearly four years later, Nicci was still trying to assuage the guilt, despite what she had told Lilith. At least, she hadn't failed her partner.

Chapter 53

The second Cohen stepped out of Luminita's quarters, Aaron slammed the door and flipped the lock. Seething anger boiled his blood, tensed his shoulders, and curled his hands into fists.

Luminita was *still* keeping secrets. On top of that, she had dismissed him several times during her little exchange with Cohen. Apparently, she required another reminder of his role in this endeavor. He was *not* some lackey to be silenced by a simple gesture from his mistress.

The rational side argued that the woman hadn't trusted a soul her entire life—which spanned a damn millennium—but he had to get through to her, force her to see his value. They were better together, on equal footing.

Equal, he thought derisively. They had *never* been equal. Even the recent moments when Aaron thought he had taken control had been nothing more than manipulations if the woman was *still* hiding things.

"Aaron." Luminita released his name on a sigh.

The tone sounded tired, but nervous tension leaked through the room. The Durand blood gifted him with the ability to see past her charades. He wasn't so easily fooled anymore. She would have to try harder than that.

He continued to stare at the door, letting the rage flow through his veins until it finally ebbed enough to unclench his fists. Once he had things under control, Aaron turned and faced Luminita with a determined stare.

"You gave me your word, Nita. Partners. *True* partners. Remember?"

Luminita slid back onto the desk with a closed-off expression, but she couldn't hide the conflicted feelings churning beneath the surface—not from him. Every single one tingled over his skin in quick succession, which only hardened his resolve.

"You've been holding things back."

She lifted her eyes. They were a brilliant shade of blue, like the crystal-clear waters of the Caribbean. The woman studied him carefully before answering.

"Yes."

The calm admission was progress, a step in the right direction, but he found himself oddly disappointed. Aaron had anticipated a fight, and the savage within him craved the confrontation.

He clasped his hands behind his back and paced forward with slow steps. "Why did Cohen say he wanted Lilith here safe and *healthy*? It was an unusual choice of words."

A slight grin slithered across her full lips. "Very perceptive, Sălbatic." She took in his tense form, gaze lingering on his bare torso in appreciation while he stalked closer.

"Are you going to answer my question?" The threat in his words widened her sensual grin.

"If I don't?" Luminita arched one delicate eyebrow in clear challenge.

Apparently, he wasn't the only one craving a fight. The thought of teasing the information from her supple flesh quickened his pulse.

"You will." He spoke with confidence when he drew nearer and noticed her rapid breaths. "I'll make certain of it."

"And how, precisely, will you accomplish that?" Luminita slowly crossed her legs and watched him intently.

The black satin sleep pants did little to hide his arousal. "Nita…"

A soft blush traveled up her neck. He took the last few steps.

His fingertips ghosted over her neck, denying her the choking hold he knew she craved. When he slid his hand into her raven-black hair, Luminita's light shiver brought a smile to his face, but it wasn't the response he truly wanted. Aaron gripped her hair roughly and yanked her head back, forcing her to meet his eyes.

Luminita drew in a sharp breath, and her heady desire seeped into his skin.

That was the sensation he craved.

Aaron hovered closer until their lips almost touched. His breath mingled with her heavy exhales.

"You don't have to withhold information. I'll bite, mark, and claim every inch of you regardless."

He pulled back enough to crowd her vision. Her pupils dilated with an intoxicating rush of primal lust.

Even better.

"Now." He twisted his fingers in her hair until she winced. "Answer the question."

This time, Luminita didn't toy with him. "He believes Lilith is infected with the Wormwood virus."

Aaron lifted his brow in surprise and loosened his grip, but he didn't release her. "And why does he believe that?"

Luminita carefully uncrossed her legs, allowing him to move between them. Still, she kept her piercing stare trained on him, always assessing. "Because I told him *he* infected her."

Cohen's overwhelming guilt now made sense. He was desperate to correct his *accidental* betrayal.

Luminita has a cure. She's the only one who has it. One she has yet to give me. Aaron shoved the last thought down deep.

"It's not true, of course," Luminita continued. "In fact, Andrew himself isn't infected."

Aaron withdrew his fingers from her hair, and he watched them trace down the edge of her robe, sinking toward the sash. "Any why would he think he's infected?"

Luminita's thighs tensed against his. "I kept him in isolation to aggravate his crumbling mental state. Then I instructed the guards to gradually increase the temperature of his cell to enhance the illusion. When I entered the cell to give him the cure—a placebo, of course—they rapidly dropped the cell's temperature to induce chills that would eventually subside as his heated skin adjusted. Believing in both the virus and the cure were necessary to properly…motivate him."

Aaron couldn't help but be impressed. Both the woman's precise tactics and ruthless thoroughness were commendable, when they weren't aimed at him.

"So." Aaron tugged at the loosely tied sash and dragged his heated gaze back up to her eyes, though the act took a tremendous effort. "Emotionally torturing the man is not off the table. Good to know."

No judgement existed in his words—quite the opposite—but the woman still flinched.

"I'm doing what is necessary." An icy chill flooded her eyes. "It was the only way to gain his cooperation in time to act."

"Hmm." Aaron ran his nails up her thighs with purposeful pressure. The way her porcelain skin reddened only heightened his desire, and he pushed closer. "And the FBI involvement?"

Changing the subject eased the defensive tension from her.

"Special Agent Eileen Hersch. I only recently confirmed that she's still working with Lilith…traveling with them. Orchid used her to track them down at the cabin, but when I didn't see her there during my visit, I'd assumed she'd left."

Aaron's touch turned soft, barely grazing her upper thigh, leaving her wanting more. "That complicates things."

"Actually," Luminita whispered, her eyes fluttering closed. She tried to regain control, to bank the growing heat he felt between her thighs.

That was the last thing he wanted.

With one quick motion, he gripped her hips and yanked her to the desk's edge, crushing her lithe body against his. "Why is that not a problem?" he asked in a gravelly voice.

Luminita tilted her chin up. Her sparkling eyes were wild. "Eileen and one of the others, Brian Keller, are human." A devious grin split her full lips. "It just so happens, there is a solution for that."

"Killian," Aaron supplied, quickly making the connection.

"Yes." The word slipped out on a soft moan while Aaron pulled the robe from her shoulders.

"And if Cohen is correct about Chance's ability?" He forcefully tore his hungry gaze up to witness the blazing obsession in her eyes.

"Then we *must* have him."

We. That one word did unspeakable things to him. "Should he be our priority, then?"

While Luminita carefully considered his question, Aaron succumbed to his desire. He rolled his hips, reveling in the slight friction the satin provided—a thin barrier between them.

A soft groan escaped her throat, and she locked her heated stare onto him. "You are distracting me. Do you want an answer or not?"

Aaron stilled but refused to back away. "I wasn't aware you were so easily rattled. I don't recall that ever being the case."

Luminita narrowed her stare on his slow grin full of dark promises.

"No. Recreating Ashcroft's abilities is our primary focus." The woman ignored his taunt, but pink still flushed her cheeks. "That is the way we advance our species…the way we gain the upper hand. Cohen is correct about one thing: As long as we have Lilith, capturing Chance is an inevitability."

Aaron flexed his hands and gripped her hips tighter, fighting his instinctual desires. As intoxicating and alluring as his goddess was, he needed to find out what he could while she was in a talkative mood.

"And if Lilith's blood doesn't work?"

"Then her only use will be to secure Chance."

He pressed his nails into her skin, and her thighs clenched tighter. "And once we have Chance?"

"She will serve as an effective motivation for Chance's continued cooperation."

Aaron strongly disliked that answer. His niece represented the weakness infecting their kind, and as a pureblood of her stock, it sickened him. On top of that, it was her birth which had motivated Gregor to push for taking vampires public. She was the reason they were running out of time.

"Is that to benefit *us* or *Andrew*?"

"Us," she stated boldly, but for some reason, he didn't trust her answer.

Aaron guided his hand up to her neck with a gentle caress, which she found infuriating. "What about Andrew? Once we have Lilith—"

"No," she snapped. "I told you. He is non-negotiable."

Sifting through Luminita's emotions on the subject proved…difficult. He couldn't tell if her protectiveness stemmed from genuine affection or familiarity, and Aaron found himself wondering if she would defend *him* so adamantly.

After capturing her throat in a firm grip, Aaron lowered to whisper against her lips. "He isn't Andrei."

She flinched at that statement.

"You have his cooperation now, but what happens when he discovers your little deception about the virus? What happens when you exploit Lilith—the woman he supposedly loves—to capture and study Chance?"

The delicate column of her throat shifted beneath his palm.

"At best, the man will turn his back on you again."

A sudden swell of unexpected rage burned into Aaron's skin, disorienting him. Luminita snatched his wrist in a tight hold.

"You did the same! Multiple times."

Shock and confusion raced through his mind while Luminita's anger continued to build. When she wrenched his hand from her neck, Aaron pulled back to meet her accusatory glare.

"What are you talking about?"

As quickly as it had appeared, the fury cooled, tempered into something far more dangerous. Her fingertips glided over the light patterns of hair on his chest.

"You left me…to wage war on Vlad…"

"I did that *for* you. You know that."

Luminita narrowed her eyes to slits. "No. You did it for you! You did it because I couldn't give you what you wanted *when* you wanted it."

His mind stammered over her confession, but she didn't wait for a response.

"Then you abandoned me to play your *vampire* games." Her nails trailed down his abdomen, but it was the shocking soul-deep pain accompanying her words which made his heart race.

"You…" Luminita caressed her palm over the black satin, tracing the hard length of him, and Aaron swallowed hard, trying to think past the fog of lust she had summoned. "*You* turned your back on me, *Sălbatic…over and over.*"

A flash of ancient wrath was his only warning before her fingers clenched painfully tight around him through the fabric. He sucked in a hissing breath. She dug her nails into the satin, threatening a worse punishment if he moved.

"No," he managed to say, but she ignored him.

"You claimed to worship me…to *love me*. Still, you walked away for vengeance and then to *lessen* yourself…to cower to the expectations of weaker men. Precisely the same reason you despise your niece so much. Did I truly mean so little to you?"

"Nita." Despite her excruciating grip on his cock, her question shifted something in his chest. *So little? How could she ever think that?* "I did what *we* needed to ensure the future. I built resources for *us*…for *our* cause. This facility, standing on the cusp of our dream, would not have been possible otherwise."

Although Luminita loosened her fingers, her calculating stare still fixed him in place.

"If that's true…if that were your only reason for walking away…then why leave without a word after Bathory? Why sneak away in the middle of the night, like a coward, and sever all contact for centuries? Why throw me away?"

The mounting agony and anger emanating from her confounded him. But the longer Aaron stared down at her searching eyes, the more the impossible reality sank in. Even without the Durand blood, the answer was obvious in every line of her furious face.

He hadn't seen her this open since the night she had pleaded with him not to leave Oarzina, the only time she had claimed to love him. *Luminita Dragomir*, Goddess of Blood and Chaos, *Drăgaica*, Lady of Flowers, *Draga*, his beloved, *needed* the answer.

Aaron thought that part of her had died long ago, but here it was. The stunning realization pulled the unvarnished truth from him.

"Because I couldn't bear to see how little you cared when I left."

In one heartbeat, the woman's anger evaporated, and she stared up at him like a mystifying puzzle.

"I…" Aaron shifted uncomfortably. He wasn't accustomed to these types of conversations anymore, but this wasn't just anyone.

This was Luminita, *his Draga*, the goddess he had still worshipped from afar all these years. Suddenly, he missed the familiar weight of the small gem he always carried in his pocket.

After a slow exhale, he started again.

"I tried to crack your mental walls for *so long*. For a time, I thought I'd gotten close, but…perhaps I never truly made a scratch. And after Vlad's death…you pulled farther and farther away."

Aaron cradled her nape and spoke the words he had never uttered to a single soul—the secret he had buried and left for dead centuries ago.

"I had to leave after Bathory to protect you. Radu warned me the Elders were close to discovering you, and I couldn't allow that. But if I witnessed the cold, callous expression you'd perfected…if you didn't care about me leaving…if it made no difference to you…I'd have either lost my resolve or broken completely."

Luminita released his hard length to grip his jaw, her fierce stare boring into him. "Of course, I cared. You were *mine*, Sălbatic. That is why I begged you not to go after Vlad, to stay with me, to give me time. I loved you."

Loved. Her uttering the word in the past tense felt devastating.

"You knew my goals, my secrets…more than anyone ever has. I've collected many unique specimens, but none of them—not even Andrew—are *my Savage*. None of them were *you*."

The entire world seemed to tilt on its axis. Everything she had said rang true to each sense, but some distant part of him screamed it was all an act, a manipulation.

But he *wanted* to believe it.

Aaron allowed every flicker of jealousy, possessiveness, pain, and deep-seated desire from her to suffocate his paranoid logic.

"And *you* are the only goddess I have *ever* worshipped. I only wanted to keep you safe, and until the Elders trusted me…any contact would endanger you. But…the truth is…" He swallowed hard and forced the painful words. "I didn't reach out to you because it hurt too much. Seeing you in Ahnenerbe…witnessing the cold expression on your face that barely held a trace of recognition…it almost broke me, Draga."

Tears misted her eyes with a flood of heartache. "I had to protect myself. That's why I pulled away after Vlad, but you still managed to wound me. When you left after Bathory, abandoned me to the world and disappeared…that hurt more than any of Vlad's torments. Then you appeared in Ahnenerbe, disgusted with what I had become. And when you finally came back to me…" Her teary gaze fell to his chest with a heart-rending shiver. "You belonged to someone else."

The unvarnished truth tumbling from her lips was his absolute undoing. "No, Draga." He tipped her chin up until her eyes met his again. "I have never belonged to anyone but you."

In a heady rush of unfamiliar emotion, Aaron captured her mouth with a rough, insistent kiss. The fire was instantaneous, consuming them both. At the urge of his tongue, she parted her lips, granting him access. Aaron thoroughly claimed her mouth while lifting her off the desk.

Luminita clung to his neck, meeting every writhing motion of his tongue with equal passion. Compulsive need tore through every cell on a level he hadn't experienced in centuries. No, more than that. Their combined frenzy amplified everything.

The kiss wasn't enough. He needed all of her, and he needed it now. Aaron surged past the desk and didn't stop until Luminita's back hit the wall.

The force expelled the air from her lungs in a heavy moan, making him positively ravenous. His urge to claim every piece of her in violent worship was undeniable. It drove his hips forward, seeking the friction of her body, and flooded the room with animalistic lust. This was his heaven, the only one he ever wanted to know.

Wormwood

Nails scratched at his waist in Luminita's hasty desperation to get rid of the satin barrier between them. Her teeth caught his bottom lip, and the sound of tearing fabric barely registered over the blood pounding in his ears.

The carnal energy reached a fevered pitch bordering on insanity. Nothing had *ever* felt like this. Aaron broke the insatiable kiss, his head spinning. The curse growled past his lips.

"Fuck, Nita."

The whimpering moan she released between panting breaths sounded divine. He found the graceful curve of her neck, and she locked her legs around his waist, hips rocking against him.

They had been in this position centuries ago in Beszterce. Unlike that night, when his lips coasted along her neck, there was no pretense, no hesitation, no blind panic. Here, Aaron had the ability to reclaim another night which had haunted him—the night her vicious words had chased him away to Belgrade.

This time, Luminita wanted her savage, and that's exactly what he would be. Aaron pierced her blushing skin with his delicate fangs, and his teeth followed suit, biting deep.

A ragged cry soaked in ecstasy tore from Luminita's throat and reverberated through the room. Her nails dug into his shoulders, drawing blood, but he barely felt it past the blazing heat raging between them.

Now.

He needed her now. All of her.

Aaron grabbed her hips and pulled her down, burying himself inside her with one vicious thrust. Luminita's blissful scream drowned out his own, and her back arched off the wall.

"*A mea! Sălbatic meu!*" Luminita gasped breathlessly, clinging to him.

Mine. My savage. Those words from her lips in her native tongue were the ultimate aphrodisiac. He had craved them for centuries but had never thought he would hear them again, not like this.

"Don't hold back," she groaned with raw vulnerability, making him pull out and drive inside with bruising force, eager to meet her demand.

When Luminita arched her back again, taking him deeper, Aaron released her neck and captured her nipple between his teeth. Her breath hitched, but her walls pulsed around him in immediate answer to the sharp pressure, and he almost broke. He dug his nails into her hips and held on, determined to make her shatter first. Aaron needed to feel her come undone more than he needed his next breath.

He railed into her like a desperate man until her moans and screams were the only sounds that existed. They were his lifeblood, his mana from heaven. Aaron sensed the mounting pressure, not just in her taut muscles, but in the euphoria rising beneath her skin, twining around his corded muscles, dragging him closer.

Luminita arched off the wall one more time, her entire body clenching with a rapturous scream. It broke him, shoving him off the edge with her.

The pure ecstasy pulsing through his body was like nothing Aaron had ever experienced. Even yesterday paled in comparison.

The raw moment on the desk might have opened his eyes, but *this*, the truth of her feelings and this raw moment between them…This had shattered his previous existence, torn him wide open, and utterly destroyed what he thought he knew about the world.

She had truly loved him once. It hadn't been a manipulation. It had been real, which meant he could reach her again, bring her back to him. He *had* to believe that.

They both struggled to drag in air, hearts galloping at a frightening pace, drenched in sweat. The euphoria began to dwindle. He curled his fingers in her damp hair, lips hovering above hers, tasting each sawed breath.

"You are the only one, *Zeita meu. Draga meu.*"

Even now, after what they had just experienced, created, Luminita's sea-blue eyes searched his for the lie, but she would find none. She had been his goddess since the moment they had met over eight hundred years ago. His soul only existed because of her. It belonged to her.

Now, Luminita had not only revived the tattered thing, but she had finally claimed it in full.

Chapter 54

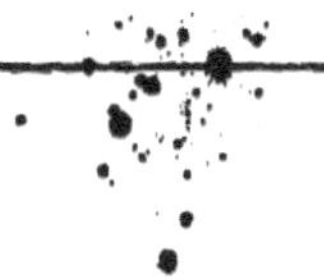

Chance's heart thrashed against his ribs like a rabid animal. He couldn't find Lilith.

The scenes around him changed in disorienting swirls of smoke and misery, but Lilith wasn't in any of them. Mariah's office, Goditha, Phipps Bend, a blood-soaked hotel room, Farren's courtroom, the medical center in New York City, the PMIC lobby, Ivanov's lab, the cabin, Duncan's basement…They were all vacant. He couldn't find a single trace of her.

Panic seared through his nerves, threatening to consume him, to drag him into madness. Chance ran faster. His lungs burned from the effort, worsening the pain in his chest. He couldn't lose Lilith, refused to face a future without her.

His bare feet hit packed earth, and he came to a stop. These weren't the familiar woods around Cohen's cabin or anything he remembered from his youth. Thick spruce trees, yellow birches, and red maples created a cornucopia of color muted by moonlight. Honeysuckle accented the humid night air, and its sweetness seemed deceptive. Chance didn't know this place.

A shot echoed through the silent night with chilling finality. His pulse rocketed. Several pops of automatic gunfire quickly followed, and Chance took off, racing toward them.

He tore through the moonlit forest, his foot catching on a root. The ground rushed up to meet him.

The pain never came.

Chance's eyes flew open, and he lashed his arms out to grip the bed. The sensation of falling made his stomach sink.

It was a nightmare. It wasn't real. The mantra didn't eradicate the desperation in his bones, but his thundering pulse slowly began to calm. He dragged in a cleansing breath and slid his palm across the bed. When only the cool sheets greeted his touch and the emptiness registered, the all-consuming panic from his dream returned.

Chance sat bolt upright and scanned the dimly lit bedroom of the RV. Lilith wasn't there, but the vehicle wasn't moving either. There was every possibility she was in front with the others or outside.

After a few seconds, Chance managed to quell the riotous emotions seizing his chest and stretched his senses. He picked up four subtle signatures—most likely people sleeping—and two brimming with excitement.

The numbers match. No one is missing or injured. She's okay, he tried to tell himself, but he wouldn't truly believe it until he saw her, held her. The nightmare still had its venomous claws in his soul. The simplistic torture of it had embodied his greatest fears—losing her, not being enough, failing her.

Chance hurried off the bed, tugged on a shirt and a pair of sleep pants, reached for the door handle, and paused. He couldn't barrel in there like a damn madman. With a concerted effort, he drew in one more breath to still the irrational vortex of panic.

The light from two laptop screens illuminated radiant smiles on both Lilith and Nicci's faces.

"This is perfect," Lilith whispered excitedly.

Chance stood in the doorway, watching her for a moment. A smile snuck across his face. Seeing her like this, happy, elated…It eased all the pain in his chest from moments ago.

"What are we celebrating?" Chance asked, quietly padding closer.

When Lilith's gaze snapped up to him, her smile faltered and quickly faded. Nervous fear bled into her excitement until it permeated the room.

Chance came to an abrupt halt, stunned and devastated by her response.

Before he could open his mouth, Lilith forced the smile back in place, but her fear was still palpable. "We got him."

A frown creased Chance's brow while he struggled to comprehend the cryptic words past the panicked confusion tearing his chest apart. "Who?"

"Aaron." True joy leaked into her expression, overpowering everything else. "Nicci identified him as a user in the database, but she also found every change he personally made…complete with dates."

Lilith slid away from the table and paced toward him, still smiling. The inexplicable fear lingered beneath the surface, but her excitement surged to the forefront.

"We have the proof we need. The Elders will *have* to listen."

Chance decided to focus on facts instead of trying to decipher Lilith's odd behavior. She didn't seem to be in a hurry to discuss whatever was bothering her.

"How many users were there? Who were they?"

"Aaron, Dr. Nichols, Dr. Thomas, Dr. Wolfe, and a few other doctors I don't recognize, and…" Nicci paused for a moment. "Bastian Deveraux."

"My father?" Chance failed to see the connection. "Why would he be listed as a user? He died over twenty years ago."

Lilith bit at the corner of her lip, drawing his attention. "When I spoke with Orchid…in the hospital while you were…" Her words trailed off, as if she were incapable of saying it out loud. "Your father was one of Aaron's scientists in his secret lab near New Orleans. He was let go before you were born. That's how he met Orchid…at the facility, working an espionage mission for Farren. The database shows the entire history of the file from the time it was created…thirty years ago."

Lilith took a tentative stop forward.

"I'm sorry, Chance. There was so much going on. I wasn't trying to keep it from you, I promise."

Is that why she's so afraid? Did she really think I'd hold that against her?

As soon as she was within reach, Chance tugged her against him and wrapped his arms around her. "Shh, *cherie*. Don't apologize. It doesn't matter. I know who my father was to me, and that's all he'll ever be."

He nestled his cheek against her hair and memorized the feel of her in his arms. If he held her long enough, maybe he could forget the haunting desperation from his nightmare.

"Chance? Are you okay?"

The nervous fear returned, but Chance couldn't understand why.

"I am now," he said on a sigh. "Just another bad dream."

Lilith stiffened in his arms, her fear spiking. "About what?"

"I…couldn't find you. I ran through every place I could think of, but you were nowhere to be found. When I woke up and you were gone, I was…worried." He tightened his arms around her, trying to ease the dark emotions still emanating from her.

Lilith leaned back enough to meet his eyes. The pain in her expression made his chest tighten.

"I'm okay, but…we need to talk…in private."

Panic shot through him like a bolt. Nothing good ever followed those words. "Okay," he managed to say around the sudden lump in his throat.

Lilith caressed his cheek, holding his gaze, and flashed a soft smile which didn't quite reach her eyes. "I love you, *beau*. There's just some things you need to know before the others wake up."

The words helped but not nearly enough. While Chance struggled to wrangle his spiraling thoughts, Lilith turned back to Nicci.

"Can you send everything we found to Antonio?"

Nicci nodded with a sympathetic smile bouncing between Lilith and Chance, which only deepened the sour pit in his stomach.

"Sure thing, partner."

"Thanks, Nicci." Lilith inhaled deeply, the hum of anxiety increasing, and grabbed his hand. Without another word, she led him back to the bedroom.

By the time Lilith closed the door, she was practically shaking. Dread bled into her fear and anxiety. This couldn't just be about his dad. There had to be something else, something big.

"*Cherie. Amour de ma vie.* What's wrong?"

Lilith swallowed hard and visibly braced herself before she turned to face him. "This is something that concerns everyone, but…" Her words faltered, as if she had lost her nerve.

Concerns everyone. A brief sense of relief allowed Chance to exhale deeply. Whatever this was, it wasn't about them, their relationship.

"I didn't want to blindside you in front of the others. You deserve better than that."

Fuck. Maybe I'm wrong. "Blindside me?" His frown deepened. "With what, *cherie*?" Chance reached for her with urgency, but she slid away from him.

"Chance, please. Just let me say this first, okay?"

That same fear and dread thrummed between them like a physical presence, like a black hole in his chest.

Chance sank onto the bed, trying to breathe. *What the hell is happening?* His mind raced through every worse-case scenario, which, considering the past week, were pretty damn horrific.

"I got a call late last night." Lilith's voice trembled, and she rubbed at her palms, clearly agitated.

"Just tell me, Lily." Chance couldn't take much more of the torturous anticipation. Drawing it out only made things worse. At this point, not knowing was probably worse than whatever she had to tell him. Or at least, that's what he tried to believe.

She finally peered at him, *truly* looked at him. Even without his Durand abilities, he could tell she was terrified.

But of what? Of me? That's ridiculous. I'd never hurt her.

"I recognized Orchid's number, but…it wasn't Orchid." The column of her throat shifted, her fear reaching a fevered pitch that flushed her skin. "It was…Andrew."

Everything—every emotion, every thought—went still, as if his entire being had come to a grinding halt on that one name.

"He said Orchid got him out and gave him the phone before she went on a mission for Luminita. She was okay the last time he saw her." She rushed through the explanation, as if *Orchid* was his concern.

Lilith obviously hoped the news would make him feel better. Orchid was still alive. But the truth was, he didn't care what happened to her. The woman had made her choice, and once again, it wasn't him.

No.

Orchid's fate wasn't what made his chest feel like a nuclear blast zone.

Andrew Cohen had called her, and now she was afraid, full of dread, and avoiding his touch. It didn't take much imagination to make the leap in logic.

"He wants you to meet him," Chance uttered on a pained sigh before rubbing his face.

Lilith bypassed his assumption. Her fear thickened the air like molasses. "He's waiting for Orchid to return. Then they're going back in for her daughter."

"And they want our help?" Chance kept the question as neutral as he could. The feat was downright miraculous, considering the pain shredding his heart. No matter what horrible things Cohen had done, what sins he had committed, he called and she wanted to help.

"That's not why he called." Lilith's voice practically vibrated with apprehension, drawing his focus. Her tear-filled eyes only held his for a second before she lowered her gaze to the floor. "Yes. He wanted me to meet him but to say goodbye the right way."

The white noise and heart-rending pain gave way to white-hot rage in an instant, surging through the room like a damn tidal wave.

"What the fuck does that mean?"

Lilith took several steps back. Her eyes widened when they rose to meet his. "He…regrets what happened…what he did…the kiss."

Chance blew out a terse laugh and shook his head. "Yeah, I'm sure he does." The sarcastic words emerged sharper than he had intended. *Fuck.* Chance curled his fists in the sheet to keep from punching the wall.

"Chance…" Her voice shook again and broke. Lilith was clearly terrified. Her hands trembled, and she took another shaky step away from him.

He dropped his chin and forced his anger down. Chance refused to be someone she feared, refused to be Boston. She wasn't the target of his rage. That rested solely on Andrew Cohen.

Once he finally trusted his voice, he glanced up at her. Lilith studied every single muscle, every movement, while her chest rose and fell with rapid breaths.

"Goddammit, Lily. You know I'd *never* hurt you. Don't look at me like that."

She didn't say anything or move closer, but the tension in her muscles eased.

Chance dragged a hand down his face with a pitiful chuckle. "Andrew's the one who fucked lookalikes, brought chaos into our lives, almost got you killed, *nearly* got me killed, and *I'm* the one you're scared of?"

"That's not true," Lilith stated in a firm voice.

"Which part?" Chance asked darkly. He wiped his hands over his face again to keep the tears at bay.

Fingertips touched his arms, pulling his hands away from his face. Lilith crouched before him, tears glistening in her olive eyes. She cradled his cheeks in her palms and fiercely held his gaze.

"I am not afraid of you. I know you'd *never* hurt me, *beau*."

"I could feel it, Lilith…from the moment I walked out of the bedroom."

Chance tried to pull away, but she held him in place.

"I need you to listen. I was scared of your reaction…scared of hurting you. I was never scared of *you*. The last time we had a conversation like this, you almost turned your back on me. I can't do this alone."

Chance drew his brows together and gently slid her hands away from his face. "Lily, I told you before…I will *never* leave you. You are my everything, the love of my damn life."

"And you are mine."

"Are you s—"

Lilith clamped a hand over his mouth with a determined scowl. "Do *not* finish that question."

With a firm glare, Chance pulled her hand away. "Fine, but how many times does the man have to fuck up before you walk away? What is it gonna take, Lily? What are you fighting to save?"

Her face fell, and she sat back on her heels. "You're right. I don't know. He just…sounds so broken."

"And that's not your fault. It's also not your responsibility to fix."

"I know, but…what if I'm the only one who can? I'm tired of losing people I care about."

Chance bit back the jealousy and bitterness her words summoned. Cohen had some small sliver of her heart, and it was far more than the man deserved.

"What are you willing to sacrifice in the process?"

It felt like his entire world hinged on her answer. Probably because it did. She *was* his world. If she put Cohen first, if saving him was worth losing everything, then it didn't matter how many times they had claimed each other or what vows they had made.

Just the thought of that outcome made the air in his lungs burn and his blood pound in her ears. The painful seconds seemed to stretch into excruciating hours while he awaited her verdict.

Tears streaked down her cheeks, and she held his pleading gaze. "Not you…*Never* you."

The air rushed from his lungs in an almost painful sigh of relief.

Lilith scooted closer, caressing his face again. She pressed her forehead to his with sawing breaths. "I *love you*."

"I love you, *mon fiancé*." His voice nearly broke in a soft sob. The urgent need from his nightmare resurfaced. He had to touch her, hold her.

Chance pulled her up into his lap, wrapped his arms around her, and breathed.

"I'm sorry." She whispered the apology so softly he almost didn't hear it.

"About what?"

Lilith sat back, locking eyes with him. "I know the bond I have with Andrew hurts you. Hell, after the way I acted at Solasta, I'm absolutely positive you have *far* more restraint than I'd have if the roles were reversed."

A smile graced his lips at the thought of his feral Scorpio, but the fact that she finally recognized his struggle meant far more to him.

"I care about what happens to him," Lilith said. "I care about him."

Conflicted emotions tightened Chance's throat.

"But…" she continued. "I will always put you first. I never want anyone else, just you, because you are mine and I am yours. Always."

He tightened his embrace while those words soothed the raging fire in his soul. They were a balm to his battered and abused heart. Once his pulse slowed to a normal rhythm and the white noise in his head finally subsided, a nagging thought rose to the surface.

"*Cherie.* Did Cohen ask you to meet him alone?"

"Yes," she answered softly, still clinging to him.

"You realize that means it's a trap, right?"

Lilith sat back enough to meet his worried stare, but there was no defensive anger, no shock, no confusion in her signature.

"It's absolutely a trap."

Surprise made him arch his brow, and Lilith cracked a smile.

"I'm not a complete idiot. Andrew said every perfect thing to convince me…everything he *knew* would convince me."

"And what did you say?"

"I told him about the attack at Solasta. I said it was too dangerous for me to be on my own."

"So, you're not meeting him?" It sounded more like a demand than a question.

"*We* are."

"Lily—"

"Stop," Lilith interrupted. "We need to discuss the details with everyone present."

"Okay, but tell me one thing. If you know it's a trap, why go at all?"

Lilith straightened her back. She had prepared for this.

"Something is seriously wrong if Cohen is that desperate. He wouldn't set us up to simply save his own skin. The man has zero sense of self-preservation right now. There's something else at play, and we need to know what. Besides, we need information on Luminita, and Cohen was probably telling the truth about her having Orchid's daughter."

Wormwood

"*Cherie.* You are placing an awful lot of faith in the man. He's a Durand, capable of anything. What if playing the victim is a predatory tactic to lure you in? Saving his skin was all he cared about when we first met him."

"Luminita changed that. The medical center destroyed some vital part of him. Chance, I'm telling you…I *know* him. Please, trust me."

Chapter 55

Luminita woke to sunlight streaming through her window. The rays cut across the floor, illuminating spatters of blood near the wall—the only remnants of their violent passion. Her gaze drifted to Aaron sleeping soundly beside her. She hadn't realized how much resentment and anger she had still carried all these years.

That was the problem with burying emotions. She had forgotten they existed. Apparently, they had thrived and festered in the dark pit she had sequestered them to.

*Apa linǎeste adânеǎ…*Still waters run deep.

They had been slowly escaping since she'd pressed the scalpel to Andrew's skin all those months ago, but after last night, the pit ceased to exist. Every emotion she'd suppressed had flooded her at once in an apocalyptic torrent until each nerve ending ached and she spewed more truth than she had in centuries.

Now, Luminita's chaotic feelings swirled around her constantly, overwhelming but undeniable. They refused to be ignored any longer, and that terrified her.

Her survival had always hinged on her ability to remove emotion from every equation. As a woman in ancient Romania, life had been violent and dangerous, even more so as a Durand. The turbulent political and religious situations had made the outcomes difficult to predict. Her father had depended on alliances and the bonds of family. Those choices had cost him everything but taught her a valuable lesson.

After his death, Luminita had approached things logically, with no allegiance to hinder her progress. She rebuked ties to others which might complicate her life. Instead, she used their loyalties against them, plotting and planning with precision.

Aaron had been an exception—one which had already cost her dearly.

Vlad Dracul was the biggest mistake she had ever made. In 15th-century Romania, women had had no power at all, except through marriage. Luminita had thought manipulating a half-blood vampire in position to be Voivode of Wallachia would be an easy task.

She had been so terribly wrong.

The moment the monster had tasted her blood and knew the truth of her feelings, he had tormented her mercilessly in every way possible. For a long time, Luminita had thought her blood was the source of his madness. It wasn't. Vlad was already a monster when she'd met him, and when he'd realized she didn't love him, he had stopped hiding it from her.

That was the truth.

Lashing out against him to protect herself had real consequences back then, ones she hadn't been willing to risk. Her life and Aaron's were a constant threat Vlad used to maintain control over her, to abuse her for years, until she viewed death as her only means of escape.

Aaron had saved her from a horrific fate. He had nursed her back to health in Poiana Negrii, and for a time, they had shared some semblance of a life. Aaron had called her Draga back then—Beloved. He hadn't called her that in a *very* long time.

Since they had rekindled their partnership to advance their kind some sixty years ago, the only nickname he'd used was Nita. Until now.

That name spilling from his lips while pure ecstasy still swam in their veins had felt surreal, as if Luminita had been thrown back in time to the little house in Oarzina. That was the true moment which changed things between them.

That fateful night, she had begged, pleaded, even commanded Aaron to stay. She'd laid her emotions wide open, told him the truth of things, and he had still left her. Aaron had felt raising an army and taking down Vlad was the only way she could truly heal, but Luminita saw it for what it was—rejection. She was too broken, and he could not fix her fast enough for his satisfaction.

Luminita had never let him in again after that, not truly. She'd tried for a time during their trek to Visegrád, but he'd betrayed her confidence yet again when he'd accidentally given Vlad valuable information with which to torment her further.

Deep connections and trust led to weakness, susceptibility, vulnerability, and she had no interest in those things after Visegrád. They were too painful when exploited, more excruciating than even Vlad's vicious psychological and physical abuse.

Luminita traced the unblemished skin of Aaron's shoulder. She missed the half-moon cuts her nails had formed last night. As long as she allowed him to drink her blood, she could never truly mark him.

A slight frown pulled at her features.

Attachment was dangerous. She had allowed it in Romania, and horrible things had befallen them both. *Prostul moare de grija alutia*—The fool dies worrying about someone else.

Keeping him in the dark, never embracing their nature together again, always pushing him away…It all boiled down to self-preservation. If she didn't allow him close, he couldn't hurt her again, couldn't betray her. Of course, that hadn't been true. Even with the distance she'd put between them, it had destroyed her when he left Trenčín and disappeared for centuries.

The irony was quite poetic. All her modes of self-preservation—drugging him, refusing her own attachment, lying about the way he affected, hiding how important he was to her, keeping the distance between them—those were the things which had forced him to abandon her. Luminita swallowed hard at the thought. The bone-deep wound of Aaron leaving after Bathory had ultimately been self-inflicted. She had given him no reason to stay in the end.

A frustrated growl escaped her throat, and she rolled off the bed, snatching her robe from the floor. Attempting to reconcile two opposing sides of herself made her veins itch. It was bad enough Aaron could sense her true feelings, but last night, he had told her plainly how much she meant. His truth and trust had coaxed the same from her. She had confessed and could not take it back.

Fuck.

Care about no one…That had kept her alive, but the exceptions she had allowed could ruin her. Losing Andrei had been painful enough.

Aaron's question about Andrew from last night came back to her.

What happens when he discovers your little deception about the virus?

Luminita had never allowed herself to ponder that thought for too long because she knew the answer. Once Andrew learned the truth, it would end. She would have no choice. No amount of bribery or placating would redeem Luminita in his eyes. Her only hope of keeping the boy alive was ensuring he never uncovered the truth.

Lilith would correct his assumptions about the virus and her ability to be infected. That was inevitable. Luminita's only recourse was to present proof of her illness, to convince both Cohen and Lilith that she was indeed infected.

Not an easy task.

Lilith was a woman of science and would not be easily fooled. But this was a practical problem which had an answer, unlike Luminita's romantic existential crisis.

She stalked over to her closet and selected her favorite items, ones which instilled confidence and power. Her attire acted as a shield—her metaphorical war paint. They imbued certain attributes with their crisp, modern lines and bold colors.

Once she had slipped into the dark green pencil skirt, lavender blouse, and black stilettos, she snuck out of the room and headed for Dr. Scott's lab.

She made it to the central hub before her cell phone rang.

"*Drăgaica.* I've secured the samples you requested."

"Were you discovered?"

"No. I retrieved some from the plane and utilized a stewardess to secure the others. Mannix is not aware. He is en route to PMIC as we speak."

"Excellent. I'll text you the drop information. Once my agent has possession, half the agreed sum will be wired to your account. You'll receive the other half after my scientist ensures the samples' viability."

"Understood."

Luminita ended the call, feeling a little lighter. One problem would soon be solved. Mannix and his reign over the Council would come to a justifiable end.

She would lose Asher's support, of course, but she had always known that day would come. The man's love and devotion had always outweighed his disagreement with Mannix's beliefs. The heart wants what the heart wants, frequently to its detriment.

Aaron flashed through her mind. *Is that what my heart wants?* She had never considered the possibility with anyone else. Luminita had taken lovers, but none of them had reached her. They were tools, dalliances, indulgences, all of which quickly became cumbersome. No one challenged her, pushed her, forced her to *feel,* affected her on such a deep level. She had never uttered the words *I love you* to any other suiter—only Aaron.

A groan escaped, and she continued toward her destination.

*This…*was precisely why she avoided entanglements. They distracted her from her mission.

Luminita squared her shoulders and drew in a deep breath while she took the last few steps toward the door. Her mental energy needed to remain focused on the path ahead. Too many things could go wrong if she allowed herself to linger on personal matters.

She forced those obsidian walls back into place and dug a new pit.

Luminita went through the security protocols. The lock thunked loudly in the wall, and she stuffed every single irritating emotion into the dark hole she had formed. This was how she survived. This was how she stayed ahead.

Always prepared, always vigilant.

An apathetic calm settled over her, and she sighed in relief before opening the door.

"Finally," Dr. Scott grunted from his workstation. "I was starting to think you were ignoring my messages."

A frown formed on Luminita's face. "What messages?"

Dr. Scott peered up from his notebook and arched a fiery brow. "The ones I left last night."

Irritation seared through her body, reinforcing her need to sever her romantic distractions. Luminita had missed his messages because she was too busy allowing herself to be weak, delving into emotionally deep waters which threatened to drown her, granting Aaron the ability to hurt yet again.

"Tell me."

The man set his pen down on the paper with an aggravated huff. "The preliminary tests of the vaccine are showing promise in the pureblood vampire subject. You wanted me to notify you as soon as I saw progress."

"And side effects?"

"It's one subject, and it's only been a day. No immediate side effects, but I can't make guarantees based on such *excessively* limited data." Dr. Scott ran a thick hand through his fire-red hair. "I need months…years to study both the virus and its counterpart properly."

"A luxury you do not have," Luminita said in clipped tones. "Continue to monitor the pureblood. In the meantime, I have other tasks for you."

"Such as?"

Anger slithered through the air, but she ignored it.

"You will receive DNA samples later today to tailor the virus. Once you've verified the samples are usable and that you have enough, you are to notify security of this. The second project is…more of a challenge."

Curiosity overpowered his anger, as she knew it would.

"A target needs to believe she is infected with the Wormwood virus."

A crease formed between his brows. "Then why not simply infect her?"

"Because her blood is valuable, and I will not risk contaminating it. However, this woman of science must be convinced she is suffering from Wormwood."

"Woman of science?" Dr. Scott huffed a laugh. "I need more specifics than that."

"Lilith Adams."

The hefty man stilled on his stool. His glare narrowed to points. "She knows too much about its transmission. She won't be fooled. Regardless of delivery, it would take hundreds of exposures to infect someone of *her* lineage."

"Which is precisely why I need *you* to convince her otherwise."

Dr. Scott folded his thick forearms across his chest. "And *why* would I do that?"

Luminita rubbed at the bridge of her nose, already weary of the conversation. "You work for me."

"Not by choice, and you won't kill me. You need me for your projects. So, what is my incentive?"

Luminita dropped her hand and hardened her stare on the infuriating man. She took a step forward, her heels clicking sharply against the tile.

"Dr. Scott, do you know a vampire's limitations when it comes to regeneration?"

The smug grin on his broad face faltered.

"I can tell you from *personal experience*. Even a pureblood, such as yourself, cannot regrow limbs, not even a finger." Another slow step and another harsh clack of her heel. "I need your mind. Everything else is negotiable. Fail me, and I'll remove a leg. *Defy* me, and I'll mangle the thing into an unrecognizable mass of flesh and bone. If it starts to heal, I'll repeat the damage, daily if necessary, until it falls off on its own. Do *not* test my patience!"

Dr. Scott's pale complexion turned deathly white, and he nodded.

"*I* control your fate, Dr. Scott." Righteous indignation narrowed her eyes to slits. "You *will* convince Lilith beyond doubt. Say the words!"

"Yes. I will find a way. You have my word."

"Ensure *your word* is an unbreakable vow, or I will see how breakable your limbs are."

The man's Adam's apple bobbed, and he nodded emphatically. "Understood."

"Then I will leave you to your work." The harsh warning still lingered in her tone.

Once he dipped his head again, she turned and marched out of the lab, locking everything securely behind her.

Luminita surged forward in a sea of anger which refused to be stifled. This was not her. Allowing these powerful emotions to riot through her system felt beyond unnatural, but control seemed impossible for long.

Had it abandoned her completely? Was this the price for connection? She didn't recall it having been this way back in Oarzina.

Perhaps the reason was because it wasn't just Aaron. The hatred and jealousy churning her gut over Andrew's loyalty to the vampire preceded Aaron's true return. The domino had fallen long before.

Was it when she took Andrew under her wing, or had she been fooling herself all these centuries?

What she had admitted to Aaron—how his departure in 1610 had wounded her—suggested her fall had begun far earlier than Andrew Cohen. Although, if she was being honest, they pre-dated that disaster. The Dragobete ritual…The regret and sickness she had felt for her actions…That had been the true start of her decline.

What if her feelings were a tidal wave she could no longer fend off? How could she remain clear-headed, keep her balance, and plot every move if these things consumed her?

Why did she have to push Aaron that first night? All this could have been avoided.

No, not avoided, but manageable.

Unfortunately, Luminita knew the answer in her very sinew. She had missed her Savage. When he had stormed into her room, chest heaving with fury, it had dredged up memories of their first encounter and everything she loved about him. Luminita craved his power. She craved *him*, *always* had, no matter how much she tried to deny it.

"Nita?"

Andrew's voice drew her attention away from her thoughts, and she glanced up at her surroundings. She had wandered into the prisoner's wing.

Why had she come here? Had she been *that* distracted once again?

"Are you okay?"

Luminita smoothed her silk blouse and pulled on a smile. "Of course. Have you heard back from Lilith?"

Andrew studied her carefully, like a cop eyeing a suspect. "No. Not yet."

"Well, inform me when you do." After flashing a pleasant smile, Luminita turned back toward the central lab.

"Nita. Something is wrong." His words halted her steps. "You've been…different. I'm not sure if that's a good thing or a bad thing, considering our past, but…if you're not in control, things could end very badly today."

Luminita glared over her shoulder. "Just do your part. Do not feign concern for me. It's a waste of your time and mine."

Andrew blinked with a spike of pain before he smothered it behind his impassive mask. She had taught him better than that.

Luminita swiped her keycard and continued forward with determination. She *would* regain control of herself and the situation. Once they had Lilith, the true work could begin, and she could bury herself in it, detach herself from the tangled web of feelings plaguing her.

With every step toward her apartment, Luminita shoved the overwhelming things deeper into the pit. By the time she reached her door, she felt nothing, and it was blissful.

Chapter 56

Tension permeated the RV, and Lilith looked from one anxious face to the next.

After she had spilled the details of Andrew's call, everyone had fallen silent. Confusion, anger, outrage, disbelief...They all blended into a suffocating mess growing stronger while the seconds stretched into minutes. By the time Tim finally broke the quiet, Lilith's chest felt impossibly tight.

"It's a fucking trap, Lil."

Lilith expelled a breath, which relaxed her constricted lungs. She had expected that response. "I know."

A brief glimpse of surprise transformed into a weighted stare. Tim swung his attention to Chance. "Please, tell me we aren't actually entertaining this ridiculous idea."

Lilith peered at Chance, who was already studying her. Even from across the aisle, she could feel his reluctance like a second skin. For a moment, Lilith thought he would cave, give in to his fear, and side with Tim.

What if they all refuse? Am I willing to venture out alone? Her heart thudded violently at the very idea.

"*Cherie*, why don't you explain?"

The tightness in her chest loosened again. He might not like it, but so far, Chance was onboard.

"Fuck." Tim huffed and sat back, stretching his neck.

"Lil, I know you care about the guy, but..." Nicci started strong, but her words trailed off.

"It's not about that, Nicci. It's the opposite that's important." Nervous tension writhed in her guts, and she stood up to pace the aisle, hoping it would alleviate the pressure. "While we were at the cabin, I asked Cohen how the cult convinced him to betray the Durand. They tried torture him at first but quickly learned it wasn't an effective motivator."

Lilith darted her gaze to Chance nervously. She hadn't shared this particular detail. It simply hadn't occurred to her.

"The cult threatened to infect me with the virus if he didn't get them inside PMIC."

A muscle ticked in Chance's jaw.

"Cohen baited a trap for me with that phone call. He wouldn't do that to save his own hide. He's proven that."

"Proven?" Tim scoffed, and Lilith came to a halt. "First off, you have no proof his story about the cult is actually what happened. The man was one minor setback away from a full psychotic break. He may not even know what's true. On top of that, Luminita has had her claws in him for *days*, and we all know how depraved that woman is. In the shape he was in, he wouldn't be difficult to manipulate."

Irritation itched beneath her skin, and Lilith resumed pacing. "You aren't completely wrong, but…my gut says there's something more going on. Andrew didn't sound confused—"

"Just suicidal," Tim interjected.

"Not helping," Nicci threw him a chastising scowl.

Tim rolled his eyes and sighed heavily. "Look…I'm all for helping the guy, but not if it puts us all in danger."

"He didn't have to help with Ashcroft. I gave him an out…told him it was okay to walk away." Lilith leveled Tim with a glare, but the man stared right back, unaffected.

"Lil, he had his own selfish reasons. *That*…he did prove. Chance almost died because of it. This is not the same thing."

The mounting anger from Chance slid over Lilith's skin, tingling and crackling like a thunderstorm.

"We're getting off topic," Lilith said, trying to quickly correct course. "We know Dr. Scott and his research were abducted by someone with impressive resources. We also know Luminita swiped all the infected blood from Goditha. Now Aaron has gone AWOL. It doesn't take a huge leap in logic to connect the dots. What if this isn't about *me*? What if Andrew wants to meet because he knows there's more at stake?"

"Lil, no offense, but I call bullshit on that one," Nicci stated in a flat tone. "Cohen might *care* about you, but he doesn't give a shit about anyone or anything else."

"That's not true. He came to us about the virus because it was killing his people."

Nicci tilted her head with a stern frown. "I don't think he feels the same way anymore."

"Why do you say that?" Lilith paused and frowned at her partner.

"At the cabin, Tim overheard a conversation he had with Alexis. He told her, and I quote, '*All Durand deserve destruction, myself included.*'"

An inkling of doubt wormed its way inside Lilith's head. *Am I reading this all wrong?*

No.

"Even if you're right about that…if I'm the only thing important to him…he wouldn't put me in harm's way unless he had a *very* compelling reason."

"Or because he wants you," Chance countered.

Lilith rounded on him, hurt and confused by the suggestion. "What?"

Chance exhaled slowly, reining in his tumultuous emotions, and locked eyes with her. "What if Luminita promised him…a future with you…a way to separate you from me?"

The questions hurt him to say out loud, but when he released a pained sigh, Lilith realized what came next cut him even deeper.

"The man told you he loves you, *cherie.*" His hazel eyes misted, and he dropped his gaze to his hands. "Love will drive a man to do a lot of things…not all of them good."

Lilith swallowed hard. Her throat felt like the damn Sahara Desert. With a heavy heart, she stalked over to him and tipped his chin up until he met her stare.

"It's impossible to truly separate us. I am *yours*, and you are *mine*, no matter the distance. Always."

Chance's eyes softened. "*You* and *I* know that…"

"And so does Andrew. He know how I feel. Besides, kidnapping me or hurting you would only end our tentative friendship. I'd hate him. He wouldn't do this for himself."

Lilith couldn't tell if her answer made Chance more anxious or relieved, but Tim didn't wait for him to respond.

"I say we continue to Knoxville as planned." Tim narrowed his eyes on Lilith when she turned, as if his stare alone could intimidate her into compliance. "This is an unnecessary complication."

The words hurt. Andrew was still a person. He had risked his life for her happiness. On some level, she knew in her gut that it was still his goal. However, that argument wouldn't earn her any allies.

"We don't know Luminita's plan for the virus. There's already a damn pandemic spreading like wildfire."

"Which is *why* we need to get the ghost drive to Knoxville ASAP," Tim argued. "Fuck Luminita's plans. We have a formula for the vaccine, right?"

"We don't know that for sure. I'm not a fucking virologist, and even if we do, we don't know it will work. We also don't know what Luminita is up to. She didn't just take the research and the blood. She took Dr. Scott. There's nothing to stop her altering the damn thing."

Tim refused to budge. "Getting the drive into the right hands should still be our priority!"

"Fine. Nicci can deliver it while the rest of us go to the meet."

That made the most sense. Nicci knew the drive. She had met with Dr. Preston…

"Oh, no you don't!" Nicci surged to her feet. "*You* are *my* partner. I go where you go. Period. Send Gibson."

"Dr. Preston knows you—"

"I don't care. He's met Gibson. I'm *not* going anywhere without you!"

It took a second for the subtext to sink in. Nicci was onboard, just not about sending her to Knoxville.

"Damn it, Nic," Tim growled. "Please tell me you aren't siding with her on this!"

"The real question is why aren't you?" Nicci snapped. "You were all for being the man's therapist. Lil's right, and you know it! Cohen wouldn't put her in danger unless the stakes are really fucking high. Whatever Luminita has planned, we *need* to know."

"And you think playing into a trap is gonna get us answers?" Tim clenched his hands into fists. "Lilith isn't the only one in danger here!"

All eyes shifted to Eileen, including Tim's.

"Back me up here. This is insane," Tim pleaded with her, but the petite woman hesitated.

"Tim." Eileen placed a hand on his tense bicep. "We *know* it's a trap. That gives us an advantage. We don't have to go in blind."

Tim shook his head in disbelief. "You are all fucking nuts."

Eileen ignored his muttered comment and moved her focus to Lilith. "Has Cohen set the location?"

"Elkins, West Virginia, but not a specific address or anything. I'm supposed to text him if we can meet by six tonight."

Eileen nodded with a soft smile. "Good. We'll look at maps of the area and find a spot that gives us the upper hand. Tim is a sniper. He can cover us."

Tim clenched his jaw so hard a muscle ticked in his cheek, but Eileen kept going.

"Once we find a suitable spot, you can text Cohen with the location. Set the expectation that this meeting will *only* happen on *your* terms."

Tim turned to Chance with an imploring look of desperation. "How can you be cool with *any* of this?"

"I'm not."

Lilith's heart jumped into her throat when the fight in Chance's loft popped into her mind. The hurt and dejection she had felt when he appeared to turn his back on her returned full force. Was this the final straw? His line in the sand?

"But…" Chance continued. "We need information, and this is our best opportunity to get it."

The air trapped in Lilith's lungs escaped in a subtle sigh of relief.

"By using your fiancé as bait?"

Chance met Lilith's eyes again, studying her. An entire novel passed between them with that one look.

"Lilith thinks it's worth the risk, and she asked me to trust her." A faint smile tugged at his mouth but never fully formed. "Besides, there's a possibility some of his story isn't fabricated. Luminita has Orchid's family. That's why she left. If Cohen is using her phone, I doubt she was able to free them."

Tim released a weary sigh and dragged a hand roughly over his face. "I don't like this."

"You don't have to go."

Tim shot Chance an ambivalent glare full of dark memories. "Fuck you. The last time I let you two traipse off without me, you died. You coded two fucking times! Don't spout that bullshit to me, asshole."

"Then stop bitching and help." Chance tossed Tim one of the burner phones. "Cool off and then call Antonio. Give him an update."

Before Tim opened his mouth to say anything, Chance moved on. He passed Eileen another burner.

"Call Dr. Preston. Fill him in on the change in plans. Gibson will drop off the drive, so tell him to have that virologist ready to go."

After she nodded, Chance shifted his focus.

"Gibson, you're gonna need wheels, and Keller, we need maps, preferably topographical ones. Help Gibson and see if you can find some physical ones in the closest town. They'll be easier to use than squinting at a screen."

Tim was still grumbling when the four of them filed outside.

"I'm gonna try to calm the big fella down." Nicci hurried after the others, leaving Lilith and Chance alone.

"Thank you." Lilith smiled and paced to stand in front of him.

Chance slid his arms around her waist and pulled her onto his lap. "Don't thank me," he whispered. He tightened his embrace, crushing her against his chest while he nestled into her neck. "I'm terrified, *cherie*. A lot can go wrong. And I wasn't able to protect you last time."

Lilith held on tight and memorized his warmth, his scent, the tears wetting her shoulder—everything. She had come so close to losing him during her last crazy plan.

Lilith found herself wondering if the world was worth it, worth risking Chance's life yet again. But in the end, if the virus devastated everything, they would be dead too.

"I *cannot* lose you, *cherie*. I just can't." His tear-drenched confession trickled over her skin.

Lilith leaned back and met his watery eyes. "You won't. You can't. Even if the worst happens, you'll never lose me, Chance. Because this"— she placed her palm over his chest—"is my home."

Chance's face crumpled. He moved his hand up to cradle her nape. For a moment, he simply stared at her, studying every line of her face. Then he drew her close, his lips crashing against hers with a fervent need to chase away all his dark thoughts.

She melted into the kiss, memorizing that too.

Chapter 57

Tim hesitated once he set foot outside. He watched Eileen hurry around the RV, burner phone in hand, and somehow knew he shouldn't follow. An unfamiliar mix of fear and anxiety made his chest ache.

Shit. I am fucking this all up.

Lilith's reasons for wanting to meet Cohen made sense, and a few weeks ago, he probably wouldn't have been so dead set against it, but now...

"Hey, big fella." Nicci rested a hand on his arm, but he couldn't tear his gaze away from where Eileen had disappeared. "Let's take a walk. Come on."

Nicci tugged at his arm, and he expelled a heavy breath, still staring at the front of the RV.

"That's not gonna help."

The petite detective walked around to block his line of sight. "The *last* thing you need to do right now is pull some caveman macho bullshit with Eileen. You *need* to walk it off. Let's go!"

Tim didn't move. Every instinct told him to go after Eileen, to make her understand. She had refused to listen before Ashcroft, but after almost losing Chance, witnessing him fight for his life in that hospital bed, watching Lilith fade into a ghost of herself at his side...

Nicci shoved hard at his midsection, forcing Tim to take an awkward step backward.

"Now, Bardow!"

"Fine," he huffed.

Nicci led him away from the RV, in the opposite direction from Eileen. The separation became more acute with each step until it felt like a knife in his ribs.

"Jesus fuck, Nic! I don't know how the hell to do this," Tim finally blurted, coming to a stop and raking his hands through his hair. It was all too much.

His friend nodded with understanding. "I get it, but Eileen is tough. I saw the way you two moved like a team at PMIC…like you'd been infiltrating shadow corporations for years together. She took a damn bullet to the vest…*on purpose*! And she's damn smart too."

"But she's still human." Tim rubbed the back of his neck with an irritated groan. He was fully aware of Nicci's points but couldn't seem to think past all the ways he could lose Eileen.

"No offense, Tim, but you're only one baby step away from human yourself."

That sentence caught his attention.

Nicci continued. "That's not a valid argument. It's a fucking excuse, and you damn well know it."

Fuck. She hit that right on-target. "Is it so wrong to want to keep her safe?" Tim frowned down at her. Desperation clawed at his chest.

Nicci locked eyes with him, her cupid's bow mouth set in a firm line. "If it's to the detriment of the mission or takes away her ability to choose, yes! It is! I understand you like her—"

"I don't just *like* her, Nicci," Tim interrupted with a growl. It was the wrong L-word. He had known that since their moment in the cabin.

Hell, probably before that, if he was being honest.

Nicci hiked her eyebrows and took a step back.

"I am fully aware how ridiculous it is. I've never told a woman '*I love you*'—outside of Jill and my mom, of course. I've known Eileen all of what? Two weeks…if that? God…" Tim rubbed his neck again with a derisive laugh, painfully aware of Nicci staring at him like he had lost his mind. "It sounds nuts. I feel like I've known her for years. She feels… familiar, safe, exciting. I'm a fucking goner, Nic."

Tim doubled over, his mounting anxiety skyrocketing to new heights.

While he struggled to drag oxygen into his lungs, Nicci rubbed his back in soothing circles. "Breathe, big guy! Believe it or not, this is all normal."

Tim cast her an incredulous glare. "Normal? It feels like my damn chest is gonna explode."

A wide grin cracked Nicci's face, and the woman *laughed. She's fucking laughing.*

"Yes! When you find your person…the *one*…this is all normal."

"Well, it fucking sucks right now."

"Welcome to the damn club. You know, I knew five minutes after talking to Alicia. Something in my head told me that moment would forever change my life, and it did."

That's how it had felt the moment Eileen showed up at Chance's place. From a distance, the pixie had caught his attention, but when Tim had met those luminous blue eyes the first time, it altered his world. He simply hadn't understood how much until later.

"People like us…the ones that know the real dangers out there…the ones that have lost people, we aren't good at this. We overreact. We try to exert control and minimize the risk."

"So, you think I overreacted?" Tim asked hesitantly, eyeing his friend. He was uncertain which answer he wanted.

Nicci shrugged. "Honestly?"

"Like you're capable of anything else." Tim chuckled and his chest loosened a bit. Somehow, talking about all this was helping.

"Point to you. But to answer your question. No. Not really. It's important to challenge tough decisions. It forces us to step back and look at all the angles. You brought up some valid points in there."

Tim straightened and eyed Nicci carefully. She wasn't done—that much was obvious by the way she stared him down, despite being a full foot shorter than him.

"*But*…if you force Eileen to stay behind…*that* would be a mistake on a lot of levels. The woman cares about you. She wants to keep *you* safe. Taking that away from her will only drive her further away, especially after you took that shot to the leg. Trust me on that."

Tim flashed a half-smile at his friend. "You're a pretty smart cookie, ya know?"

When he ruffled her hair, her resulting glare made him grin.

"About time you noticed, you big lug. Now, call Antonio, update him on the plan, *then* go talk to your girl, okay?"

Tim wasn't sure why, but the tension which had been ratcheting his chest since Lilith started talking this morning finally dissipated. Maybe it was simply knowing he wasn't going nuts, that all this was normal.

"Thanks, Nicci. Seriously, I'm not sure what I'd do without you."

"I do." Nicci chuckled. "You'd all fall to damn pieces. I'm the glue."

Tim released a throaty chuckle while Nicci flashed a cheeky wink and wandered off. The woman wasn't wrong. She wielded the truth like a weapon, but it always helped more than it hurt.

After a few steady breaths, Tim did as she instructed and dialed Antonio.

Eileen hurried around the RV. She was *not* running away from Tim. Well, not exactly, anyway. She just needed a moment.

Tim had been…upset.

Okay, that seemed like an understatement. She had never seen him so keyed up, not even before their tango with Ashcroft, and she wondered how much of it had to do with her. Probably a lot. The man had made some valid arguments but seemed dead set against the meet.

Once she had reached a safe distance from everyone else, Eileen tried to shake off the dread churning in her guts and dialed the cell number on the doctor's business card.

"Dr. Preston. How can I help you?" The man's brusque voice short-circuited her lingering internal thoughts.

"Uh, hi. It's Special Agent Hersch."

For some strange reason, she suddenly felt nervous. Maybe it was because the guy had tried to ask her out the last time they had spoken. It still unnerved her. After five years without a single hint of interest, he made a move now? She was still struggling to understand why.

"Eileen," he stated, as if correcting her. "What can I do for you?"

"There's been a change in plans." Eileen barreled ahead, ignoring his demand for a first-name basis. "We have the info you and your associate need to start working, but we've hit a snag."

"Are you all right?" The unfamiliar and unexpected warmth in his voice was off-putting.

"Yeah, I'm fine…for the time being. Do you remember Gibson? He was with us when we first arrived—dark, shoulder-length hair, salt-and-pepper beard."

"Vaguely. Why?" Dr. Preston returned to his typical clipped tones, which oddly put her at ease. She was more accustomed to his prickly demeanor.

"He will deliver the hard drive. The files you need are already decrypted and ready to go. Hopefully, there's enough information to formulate a vaccine."

"I'll notify Bashir, the virologist I trust. What about you, Eileen?" The man sounded genuinely concerned, and once again, it immediately made her feel uncomfortable.

"Dr. Preston," she said, using his last name to drag the conversation back to professional territory. "I'm fine. We just have someplace else we need to be. It's time-sensitive. Thank you. We'll be in touch."

Eileen hung up before he had a chance to respond. Hopefully, her impersonal demeanor would sink in, and he would stop calling her by her first name, acting like they were friends or anything else.

"You okay?"

Eileen nearly jumped out of her skin at the rich timbre of Tim's voice. She had been so busy glaring at the phone, she hadn't heard him approach. Eileen placed a hand over the racing heart trying to beat out of her chest and drew in a few deep breaths.

"I *was* okay before you scared the hell out of me," she said with a nervous but playful smile.

Tim's grin didn't reach his eyes, though. Eileen *knew* what he was about to say, to ask.

A heavy sigh passed her lips. "I don't want to have this conversation again, Tim." It *wasn't* happening. She didn't care what asinine argument he made. Eileen was *not* letting him sideline her.

Tim furrowed his brow for a moment. "Eileen..." He took a step closer.

"No!" she stated firmly, planting her hands on her hips. "The last time I left, *you* caught a bullet to the thigh. I'm not asking *you* to sit this one out. I know you can't...not after what happened to Chance. So do *not* ask me to sit this out either."

The man merely stared at her, as if confused.

How can I make it any damn clearer?

Eileen marched up to him and grabbed his chin, angling his face down. Once his brown eyes met hers, she spoke each word with firm conviction.

"I see the danger. That's *why* I'm staying with you."

The man's expression softened, but she kept talking, determined to end this argument once and for all.

"When I saw the bodies outside the hotel and Chance said you were hit..." Eileen's pulse raced just thinking about it. The panic that had torn through her body in that moment had left a permanent scar she still felt. "I'm a damn FBI agent—a Special Agent. I've seen team members go down, but *you*...hurt? It sent me into a damn spiral. I freaked out. I'm trained *not* to do that, but *you*..."

Tim's eyes misted, and he coasted his fingertips over her cheek.

Eileen swatted his hand away with a scowl. "No. You need to listen. You aren't the only one who needs to know…*someone* is okay. Asking me to sit in an RV, knowing full well what you're up against, what you might be walking into…it's *not fair*. I *will* be there, Timothy Bardow, watching your back, because there is no other acceptable option for me."

Tim wrapped his arms around her, enveloping all her senses, and rested his chin on top of her head. "I was actually just coming to check on you, Pixie, but…you're right. I'm…not used to any of this."

The cooling relief was instantaneous.

"Dating a woman who can handle herself or one who gives a shit?" Eileen chuckled softly. She already knew his answer, and he didn't disappoint.

"All of it…Dating in general." A warm laugh rumbled in his chest, vibrating against her skin.

Eileen closed her eyes and soaked in the comfortable feel of his strong embrace. It felt like the safest place in the world, like she *belonged* there.

"Can I"—Tim hesitated for a moment before continuing—"ask you something?"

Eileen tipped her face up at him with a wary look. "Yeah."

"When we met with Agent Hernandez…" Tim stared over her head, and a faint blush colored his cheeks. "She mentioned something about a transfer…"

The unexpected topic brought a slow smile to her lips despite the fact he was still nervously avoiding her gaze.

"Yeah. I told her I was considering a transfer to the New York City branch."

"Are you…still considering it?" The slight blush deepened, and Tim finally peered down at her.

Apparently, the blush was contagious. "I, uh…" For a second, her brain halted on one terrifying thought. *What if he thinks things are moving too fast?* Eileen almost couldn't bring herself to say it, but she had never lied to the man, and she wasn't going to start now. "I borrowed the burner before you woke up. I sent the official request to my boss and the New York office this morning."

"Seriously?" The man looked downright scared, and it made her heart thump like a rabbit on speed.

"Yes. I mean, there's always a chance they'll turn it down, but it's doubtful. Mia said she'd put in a good word, and I have the highest test scores in my year at Quantico." Nerves got the better of her while his stare continued to bore into her. "It doesn't have to mean anything, Tim. I'm not pushing—"

Tim's mouth was on hers, and every thought disintegrated in the torrid heat. He broke the kiss too soon, panting, and picked her up so they were eye to eye.

Eileen wrapped her legs around his waist and held on. She was still trying to catch her breath from the brief but searing kiss when Tim cradled her cheek and fiercely met her eyes.

"I know this is gonna sound crazy, but...I fucking love you."

Eileen blinked at the unexpected words, not because they scared her, but because she felt the same way. And *he* had said them first. Her mind kept replaying them, trying to let them sink in.

"Should I not have said that?" Tim asked nervously. His jubilant mood darkened with doubt.

Eileen swallowed the anxious bubble rising in her throat and said the words she had thought she would never utter again, not after Karl.

"I love you too. So...I guess we're both crazy."

The smile that lit his face was downright mesmerizing.

"Maybe we're the sane ones, Pixie, and everyone *else* is crazy."

Eileen slid her arms around his neck and grinned. "Now there's a thought."

"You realize Jill is gonna lose her mind, right? She *really* likes you, and you...moving to New York... She'll insist on being best friends, and she'll *definitely* tell you every one of my embarrassing stories."

Eileen's heart fluttered at the thought, warming her to her toes. "Sounds perfect. Your sister is something special...truly. She's like a ball of sunshine, not because she's oblivious or because life has taken it easy on her. She's experienced the worst kind of betrayal and is determined to make the world a brighter place. I really admire her."

Tim's smile broadened, which Eileen hadn't thought possible.

"Have I told you I love you? I mean...you keep giving me reasons."

Eileen giggled and pressed a soft kiss to his lips. "You can keep saying it. I really love hearing it," she whispered.

"You do?" The deep timbre of Tim's sinful voice made her absolutely melt.

Eileen twined her fingers through his blond curls, and an easy grin curved her lips. "It just might be my favorite thing."

"Might?" he asked, teasing.

"Well…" Eileen sank her teeth into her bottom lip, fighting the coy grin.

Flirting with Tim felt so natural. He drew that side out of her effortlessly—a side she had never known existed.

"When it comes to you, Mr. Bardow, there are lot of things vying for that top spot as my favorite."

Tim's baritone laugh rumbled against her body, proving her point. "Is that so?" An almost feral glint made those brown eyes bore into her.

Her entire body flushed in response. The man had the most intoxicating effect on her.

With an impish grin, Eileen ghosted her lips over his. "Very…" She trailed them along his strong jawline. "…much…" Then she found her way to his ear, barely grazing the surface. "…so."

Tim tightened his hands on her thighs and forcibly cleared his throat. "Are you trying to make me pin you to a damn tree?"

A thrill shot through her, making her shiver in his arms. "Are you threatening me with a good time?"

"Dear God, woman." He groaned with an almost nervous laugh.

"Hey! Lovebirds!" Nicci's voice cut through the moment like a bucket of ice water. "Sorry to interrupt, but Chance wants to talk strategy before Keller and Gibson get back."

Tim turned toward Nicci but didn't loosen his grip on Eileen. "Right now?"

The irritated rasp in his voice almost made Eileen laugh.

"Do you think I'd be here, risking your wrath, if that *wasn't* the case?"

A growl of pure frustration vibrated against her chest, and Eileen buried her face in his neck, struggling to hold back her laughter.

"Fine," Tim said on a sigh. "I'll be right in."

"All right, big fella," Nicci hollered.

"Seems like the tree will have to wait, Pixie." Disappointment saturated each word.

"There will be other trees, I promise." A small giggle emerged, and she pressed a lingering kiss against his warm neck.

"As long as it's with me."

Eileen reared back to stare at him, and his grip tightened to keep her from falling. The comment certainly hadn't sounded like a joke.

"Naturally."

For some reason, Tim didn't seem overly relieved by her answer.

"Um…you did hear the part where I said I love you too, right?"

A devilish grin cracked his grim expression. "I just wanted to hear you say it again."

"You ass." Eileen swatted his shoulder and tried not to laugh, failing miserably.

Chapter 58

Near-scalding water cascaded over Andrew's bowed head while he braced a hand against the shower wall. He tried to let the heat burn away the guilt, but his eyes fixed on the four puckered indents marring his chest.

Luminita's scars had finally healed, only to be replaced by Ashcroft's. At least he knew why.

The kiss.

Andrew closed his eyes, and the moment replayed in his mind, summoning both heartbreaking elation and soul-deep shame. He had spoken the truth. Cohen loved her, but he would never be any good for her. The kiss he had stolen seconds later was evidence of that—the best and worst moment of his life.

Andrew's fingertips traced the angry marks. They weren't light pink and faint, like the ones from Luminita's scalpel. He doubted these would *ever* heal or even fade. They shouldn't. He *deserved* to wear them, especially after last night.

Lilith's tear-filled voice and sobs from the phone call rattled in his skull. He wasn't worthy of them. This was *all* to save her, but the lies still twisted his guts into excruciating knots. Andrew had promised her truth. She had earned that.

For the hundredth time, he considered calling or texting Lilith and just coming clean. Maybe she would see reason. Maybe she would come willingly for the cure…

Sadly, Andrew knew better.

Lilith put everyone else first. Even if she believed him, she wouldn't put her friends in danger—hell, the *world* in danger—to save her own life.

She'd just try to solve the problem on her own. Submitting to Luminita meant possibly enabling the woman to create another Ashcroft.

Of course, if her blood didn't work…

The thought sent a chill down Andrew's spine despite the scorching water.

Treating the viral infection should buy him some time, but he had to find a way to get Lilith out of there before Luminita succeeded or lost her patience, assuming Lilith would even allow him to help at that point.

Andrew angled his face into the hot spray and tried to think past the riotous emotions tearing him apart. Lilith would hate him for this, truly despise him, especially if anything went wrong. Currently, she had faith in him despite every reason why she shouldn't. Once he shattered that…

Days ago, Andrew had nearly strangled Alexis for costing him Lilith's friendship, but it hadn't been her fault. It had *never* been her fault. She never forced him to commit those sinful acts. Alexis had only threatened to expose them.

He was the only one responsible. His obsession, his desperation, his inability to cope…they all led to this inevitable moment.

The water began to cool, and Andrew twisted the knob, allowing the icy blast to shock his system. The air seized in his lungs, and cold seared through every nerve ending until they burned. Andrew shut off the water, shuddering, and reached for a towel.

The extreme temperature change jolted him out of his mind-numbing stupor. He had one mission tonight—safely get Lilith back here with as few complications as possible. Nothing else mattered, especially not *his* desires. He had already irrevocably tarnished the soul she had saved by taking the lives of Alexis and Noah anyway.

The moment on Duncan's porch drifted into his mind when he stared at the mirror—the moment Lilith had healed the scars Luminita left behind. He could still feel the ghost of her arms around his midsection… Her face against his shoulder, wet with tears…The scent of lavender infusing her blond curls…

That one, pure moment of affection given freely would forever be his heaven, not that he deserved any of it.

Andrew expelled a devastated sigh. Today was the day things changed, the day he sacrificed everything that mattered to save *her* life. He would never be painted as a hero, even if things went according to plan, but it didn't matter. Andrew had never been a hero. He was simply attempting to right his mistakes, to find some semblance of redemption.

Wormwood

After fastening the towel around his waist, Andrew scooped up his clothes and slowly made his way down the hall. The excitement of seeing her warred with his dread, despite knowing the outcome. He would have *one more moment* before she realized he had betrayed her.

Andrew blinked back the tears threatening to spill and wandered through his door. There on the mattress sat a crisp medium gray suit, a charcoal dress shirt, and a black belt. The matching boxers, shoes, and socks on the floor below completed the ensemble.

At least he didn't have to meet Lilith in a cotton shirt and grubby scrubs.

When he moved closer, he spotted a note peeking out from the breast pocket. Andrew tossed his dirty clothes into the trashcan and snatched the paper.

Andrew,

I've always found that clothes lend us power. Perhaps this will impart some small bit of clarity and remind you who you are. Help me forge the future.

—Luminita

Andrew crumpled the note in his clenched fist and glared at the suit. None of this was for that traitorous bitch or her maniacal plans. It wasn't even for himself.

Remind you of who you are. He had *no* desire to be the man he had been a year ago.

Sure, that version had never suffered the way he did now, but he had also never experienced anything beautiful. Nothing had moved him. Andrew had allowed Farren to make him numb, cut off from the traumas as well as anything which truly mattered.

He shifted his gaze to the trashcan and contemplated hauling the grimy clothes out and wearing them instead. They felt more…honest.

However, Andrew was smart enough to know his refusal to wear the suit would be seen for what it was—defiance. Staying on good terms with the psycho would benefit his mission. She would be more inclined to listen to him, to treat Lilith well, to leave the others alone.

With a resigned huff, Andrew slid on the dress shirt. Memories of Alexis in a similar shirt resurfaced, and he looked to the spot near the wall where her lifeless body had lain for hours. His stomach soured, and he forced his trembling fingers to work each button.

All these demons were coming to collect, and their retribution was unavoidable. Andrew was on a collision course with fate and karma. Perhaps he always had been.

With a tremendous effort, Cohen pushed everything from his mind and focused on the black boxer briefs, the silky black socks, and the smooth slacks. He maneuvered the belt through each loop, and a calm settled over him.

Andrew didn't want to live as the numb man he had been, but today, right now, he needed a piece of it. His performance *had* to be believable to all parties involved.

If Luminita or Chance sensed his guilt and shame, if Lilith saw it in his face, things could turn disastrous. He hated admitting Luminita was right, but today required he remember who he was and embrace it.

By the time he slid the suit jacket on, he breathed easier. That impassive mask fell into place over his raw and festered soul.

"You owe Lilith this. You owe her everything. Remember what is at stake if you fail."

After a deep, cleansing breath, Andrew turned and exited his cell. Orchid's phone chimed in his pocket, and he halted his footsteps. All his hard work had been undone by that one sound.

With his heart thrashing like a wild creature, Andrew pulled out the phone and tapped the screen.

6pm. Wildwood park. Front entrance. Elkins, WV. We'll be there.

Cohen stared at Lilith's text and read it several times.

She hadn't simply asked for a specific place. Lilith had set the terms. Chance and Tim had probably recommended she do so after scouting a beneficial location.

Good. They are being cautious…as they should be.

Hopefully, Luminita would listen. If they tried to take both Lilith and Chance, it would end in a damn bloodbath. Their smartest move was to take Lilith as fast as possible and lure Chance out later. The man would leave everyone behind to save the woman he loved.

Andrew slid the phone in his pocket and forced the calm persona back into place. He smoothed the lines of his expensive suit and resumed walking toward his target.

Chapter 59

When Aaron finally woke, the afternoon sun sliced across the room in golden hues. A grin tugged at his lips with memories of why he had slept so long.

Mine, she had called him.

He had felt her declaration in every bone of his body. After hundreds of years denying their connection, of building mental walls, she had finally succumbed to their fate.

More than that. She has accepted my true nature, welcomed it, craved it, demanded it, and it was fucking divine.

Aaron allowed his head to fall to the side but found the bed empty. A sudden chill kissed his skin, and disappointment stirred in his chest—an odd sensation he hadn't experienced in so long.

He shifted his gaze to the screen dividing the room. Luminita was here in the apartment. Her emotional vortex told him that much, but he couldn't seem to pick out anything specific.

Her feelings were muddled, all of them bleeding into one another to become an unrecognizable mess. Luminita had *never* been so wide open, exposed. It was both terrifying and breathtaking.

There had been many times in his life when Aaron had wondered if she felt anything at all, for anyone. Since their move to Hungary, every action had served a cold, calculated purpose, nothing more, not even amusement.

But the depth of what emanated from her now was…awe-inspiring.

Aaron slid naked from the bed and glanced over at the wall. His satin sleep pants sat in a shredded heap, bringing a rakish grin to his lips. The woman had been absolutely feral last night.

He scanned the immediate area for something else to wear and found his slacks draped over a chair near the bed, along with his now buttonless dress shirt. It would do for now.

When he slid on his pants, his hand gravitated to the tiny pouch sewn into the lining of his pocket. His thumb brushed over the item hidden there. The tear-drop-shaped gem always brought him a measure of peace.

Aaron padded around the screen. The plush rug kept his steps virtually silent.

Luminita sat at her desk—sadly, fully clothed—with her focus fixed on the laptop in front of her. A line creased the smooth skin between her brows.

"You look worried, *Draga.*"

She snapped her head up, sea-blue eyes narrowing. Irritation surged to the forefront of her internal storm. "Dere is no need to call me dat."

Her Romanian accent was noticeably thicker now, which he found arousing. However, Aaron doubted that was her intended effect. He wondered if it was a conscious move or if her turmoil forced it out of her.

"I disagree," Aaron stated simply, ignoring her mounting anger.

While Luminita's glare turned baleful, Aaron strolled forward and slid into the seat facing her desk.

"Tell me. What's bothering you, *Draga?*"

Luminita leaned back in her chair but kept her blazing eyes locked on him. "And if my answer is *you?*" She arched one elegant eyebrow and set her mouth in a firm line.

Once upon a time, her behavior might have rattled him, but not anymore. He knew the truth, even if she refused to acknowledge it now. Aaron smiled, leaning forward to brace his arms on his knees.

"You truly wish to continue this dance, *Draga?*" Every time he said her nickname, her anger flamed a little hotter, which was admittedly part of the appeal to using it.

Luminita's features hardened. "I don't know vhat you mean."

A light chuckle escaped. "Then allow me to be clear, *Draga.*" He clearly emphasized the name this time and was rewarded with another spike of fury. "Do you want to go back to pretending?"

The woman stiffened but said nothing.

"That's what it is, *Draga meu.* Pushing me away, retreating behind your fucking walls...It's all pretend, and now...we *both* know it. You can't take back what you said last night."

A scoffing laugh erupted from her throat, but her fear slithered through the air, betraying the lie.

Aaron calmly rose to his feet, and her laughter died out. Her glare turned positively arctic when he stepped toward her. This was nothing but the defensive posturing of a wild creature set to run, but Aaron would never let that happen again.

"Do *not* overestimate your value, Aaron."

The words sounded bitter and venomous, but the tone didn't match the nervous thrill coursing through her veins. Drinking the woman's blood had allowed him to sense every shift and miniscule emotion. It acted as a compass, guiding him toward Luminita's True North.

When Aaron stalked around the desk, she started to stand. He stopped her short, forcing her back into the chair.

"Get your hands off me," she hissed, before trying to stand again. This time she used her full strength, but Luminita's blood had provided him several gifts, one of which allowed him to match her physical strength.

He held her firmly in place.

"No," Aaron stated calmly.

"I am not in de mood for games," Luminita snarled like a beast in a trap. In a way, she was.

The woman's viscous sneer faltered when Aaron leaned closer to crowd her vision.

"Neither am I, *Draga*." His sharp tone elicited a shiver which didn't go unnoticed. "You aren't hiding from me any longer. I *refuse* to allow you."

Luminita's fierce eyes bored into him with a clear challenge. "And vhat makes you tink you have any choice in de matter?"

In one quick motion, Aaron snatched her delicate throat and pulled her close. The pounding pulse thudding against his palm and the carnal surge tingling over her skin were confirmation enough.

"Because I am no longer scared to *force* the truth from you."

Luminita's eyes widened, but she remained still. She didn't struggle, didn't claw and scratch. The only thing which fought against his grip was her bone-deep fear.

"*Draga meu*, we are equals now. I know the truth of you, and I will not allow you to force me back into the role of a mere simp. I will rip the truth from you every day if I have to." The ominous tone and implications summoned a sly grin. "Believe me. It's a task I'd greatly enjoy. So, by all means…continue."

He raked his hungry gaze over her purposefully, and her throat shifted with a swallow.

"Now." Aaron eased his grip slightly, allowing her to drag in a full breath. "Tell me why you looked worried."

Luminita shrewdly studied him while drawing air into her lungs. Her breasts rose and fell enticingly beneath the lilac silk of her blouse. When she opened her mouth to speak, her brow furrowed.

"Your hand…" She paused as if struggling to understand.

Panic roared white-hot beneath her skin in a flash, and her paling face mirrored the sensation.

"What is it?" Aaron asked in confusion, releasing her throat. The abrupt and overwhelming shift unnerved him.

"Your hand is warm…*too* warm," she whispered in a haunted tone. "If you're already exhibiting…" Her words trailed off, and her wild eyes searched his. The terror melted away all her rough edges. For a moment, she was the same scared and vulnerable woman who had regretted jabbing a needle into his arm.

The virus. The thought clicked into place with alarming clarity.

Luminita surged to her feet while Aaron stood there, stunned into silence.

A fever. I have a fever. That's why the air is so chilly.

She rushed past him toward the door, but his brain still struggled to grasp the scope of this new revelation.

"Where are you going?" he asked absently, unable to make sense of anything.

Luminita faced him and squared her slender shoulders. "You're right. You are *Sălbatic meu*, and I do *not* wish to lose you. You need to come with me…now." She extended her hand in invitation, and Aaron swore tears glistened along her thick lashes.

When he didn't move, she stepped closer.

"Aaron!" she snapped. "You need the cure now. This cannot wait any longer."

The gravity of his situation finally struck. His body was fighting the virus, and with its modifications, the virus was probably winning. Not even Luminita's blood, with its healing properties, had slowed the progression.

Wormwood

After nearly eight thousand years of life, is this how I end? Aaron rushed around the desk to join her, his own panic mingling with hers.

Luminita kept a brisk pace and led him to the central lab, but his mind still whirled.

"Is there any risk you're infected?" he asked. "Lilith said it can be transmitted sexually, and…it hadn't occurred to me—"

"No." Luminita cut him off but then paused. "Dr. Scott assured me. It was…tailored for you alone. You could only transmit it to someone else with your exact DNA, which is impossible." She didn't look at him, but he felt her remorse like a caress.

Her badge opened the central lab, and she marched across it, heading for the opposite door.

"Nita."

She kept moving, the dread emanating from her in a deafening roar.

"*Draga.*" Aaron grabbed her arm and spun her around. "Are you lying to me?"

Luminita wrinkled her brow in genuine confusion. "About what?"

"Any of it."

"No."

"Then why are you so…unhinged?" The raw emotions were *far* more potent when he touched her. The tidal waves of fear and desperation nearly sent him to his knees.

"The cure. It shows promise in the pureblood vampire specimen, but…" Luminita searched his eyes, as if willing him to understand. "It has never been tested on the DNA-tailored strain. *You* were the first."

That's why she didn't offer me the cure. It is virtually untested.

Luminita shook her head and slid a palm over his stubbled cheek. This time, there was no denying the tears in her eyes. "I *am* sorry, Sălbatic. I did not know it would work so fast. I thought there'd be more time."

The tenderness in her voice seemed surreal, and it made his chest ache, like it had the day on the river, when he had thrown the pendant into the water.

With one tug on her arm, he drew her close, claiming her mouth in a fiery kiss. Everything he couldn't seem to voice or even understand infused that kiss, and she met every flick and caress of his tongue with absolute abandon. In that moment, she was completely open to him.

When his lungs felt as if they might burst, Aaron broke the kiss to drag cooling air into them. "No matter what happens, I don't blame you, *Draga meu.* I didn't give you much reason to trust me."

Luminita jerked back, once again searching his eyes, but she would find no deception. If this was how his long life ended, so be it. Aaron had spent far too long hiding, denying the truth of who he was and what he wanted—what he had always wanted from the day he had set eyes on her.

Her brows drew together the longer she stared at him. "*If* I am capable of complete trust…it would be with you."

The bright grin felt unnatural on his lips. "A conditional admission… in typical Luminita fashion," he teased.

She opened her mouth to say something, but he stopped her with another scorching kiss and crushed her body against his. For a moment, she melted into his touch, providing far more affirmation than her words.

If only he had broken through to her *before* she had turned to such desperate measures.

Luminita braced her palms against his aching chest and pushed away. Heat still stained her cheeks. "We need to see Dr. Scott."

"Wait." Aaron dug his hand in his pocket, fishing out the small gem hidden there. "I…" His voice broke for a moment, but he forced himself to meet her eyes and try again. "I have something that belongs to you."

Luminita shook her head in confusion. "Aaron, this can wait—"

"No," he interrupted, pulling the object from his pocket. He took her hand and laid the small teardrop-shaped ruby in her palm.

True tears flooded her eyes until they flowed freely down her cheeks. Luminita stared at the pendant, and the crippling well of emotions it elicited from her told Aaron everything he *ever* needed to know.

"But you—" A sob broke through, and she clasped a hand over her mouth.

"Threw it in the river?"

She nodded, her teary eyes finally meeting his.

A smile slanted his lips, and he wiped the tears from her cheeks. "It took me all of thirty seconds to regret that decision. I spent hours in the river, searching for it, which is probably why you were gone by the time I returned."

"Why would you do that after…what I did?"

Aaron hung his head for a moment, gathering his strength, before boldly meeting her questioning gaze. "I knew the moment I kissed you…you are an addiction from which I will never recover. Seven thousand years felt like simply biding my time until you arrived. Even after Dragobete, the devastation I felt…was better than feeling nothing."

Aaron brushed the dark curls from her face.

"No one else could be my Goddess of Blood and Chaos, my only challenge, my true equal, *Draga meu*. I've kept that stone with me every single day since as a reminder of that."

Luminita clutched the pendant tightly in her palm and flung her arms around his neck. She captured his mouth in a kiss that was achingly tender, soothing the pain from centuries of emotional wounds. Then she pulled back enough to whisper, "I am sorry, *Sălbatic meu*. For all of it."

Aaron pressed his forehead to hers. "So am I, *Draga meu*. All of it."

After a moment, Luminita stepped away, though Aaron sensed her reluctance. "We need to go. I do not wish to waste time with what's at stake."

My life. She cares about my life. He let that knowledge sink in while she led him toward a hallway he had never explored.

The tile felt frigid on his bare feet, but his focus remained on Nita's sullen form in front of him. She absently caressed the ruby pendant in her palm while she struggled to contain the writhing feelings plaguing her.

They reached the hall's end, and Aaron silently noted all the security measures—retinal and fingerprint scanners as well as a voice-coded password. Heavy bolts clunked in the wall, and the door slowly swung open.

"Ms. Dragomir," a gruff but familiar voice exclaimed from inside. "You've already made your threat quite clear…"

When Aaron stepped into the artificially bright lab behind Luminita, the man's words trailed off.

"Mr. Bogdan?" Dr. Scott's beady eyes widened in surprise.

Aaron had met the man several times over the years when visiting Solasta. Gregor might have owned and operated the company, but Aaron had ensured he held a sizeable number of shares. Keeping an eye on their projects was vital.

The doctor bounced his gaze between Aaron and Luminita with dawning dread. "You work for *her*?"

Aaron found Dr. Scott's assumption more amusing than insulting for some odd reason. "*With*," he corrected.

Luminita stormed up to the bewildered man. "He needs your vaccine, now."

"He's infected?" Dr. Scott's rounded face pinched into a deep frown. "I don't see how that's possible. Not only is he a pureblood, but he's the oldest. I doubt it would ever take root—"

"The DNA-tailored virus you created," she interrupted sharply.

Understanding dawned on the man. "It actually worked?" he muttered in awe. "Are you experiencing symptoms? Already?"

Aaron tried not to take offense to the man's excitement. *Tried* being the operative word.

"Yes, which is why he needs the cure." Luminita's patience was wearing thin.

A scowl marred the man's face. "It's not a *cure*, and I haven't tested it on someone with that strain. There's no guarantee it will even—"

"I'm aware," Aaron stopped the rambling, his own irritation rising. "Unfortunately for us both, I don't have another option."

"Yes, well…" Dr. Scott slid off his stool. "I'd like to take blood samples before and after so I can run tests in the event it…fails."

Aaron nodded, and Dr. Scott patted the now-vacant stool.

"Sit."

Aaron complied to the stocky man's request, and Dr. Scott shuffled around the room, gathering supplies.

"Have you fed recently? That might skew my results if I don't account for it."

Aaron pulled off his ruined shirt, and his gaze collided with Luminita's. "Not on human blood, if that makes a difference."

Conflicting emotions still churned behind her stormy eyes, creating a frothy mess, but regret remained dominant. Aaron wondered if that had to do with the virus or him drinking her blood. That had been the event which had truly tipped the scales.

No. The regret had been there since the moment she realized he was running a fever. It wasn't because of the blood. She hadn't even reacted that way when she first realized her mistake of allowing him to bite her.

Luminita also hadn't emanated that particular emotion around Andrew, despite her supposed misgivings about using him for her ritual. No, she had only exuded remorse around him, only since she had jabbed that needle into his arm.

While he continued to stare at her, he realized the consequences of that action were hitting her full force now.

Aaron hadn't lied earlier. He didn't blame her. Luminita had desired nothing but the ability to control her destiny since she had left Kotor in the eleventh century. Survival meant out-plotting and out-planning the violent patriarchy of every species, not just her own.

For nearly a thousand years, she had refused to put her fate in *anyone's* hands. Luminita *always* maintained firm control of every situation planned for every contingency, with the exception of Vlad.

The unguarded moments between them since his arrival here had scared her. The thought of not always holding the reins, of allowing someone else into her plans, had terrified her into action. Had the roles been reversed, he was likely to have done the same.

Luminita watched the virologist like a hawk while he collected a dozen vials of blood. After moving to the fridge and stowing the samples, Dr. Scott removed a vial of clear liquid.

"I must warn you," the man began. "There might be unknown side effects. It can take months or even years for complications to present themselves. There is also a chance that it will manage your symptoms but not eradicate the virus. Judging by your skin temperature, I'm guessing your fever isn't high grade yet, so hopefully, we have some time."

"Disclaimer noted," Aaron growled. "Get on with it."

"You'll need to come back tomorrow. I'll take new blood samples and track your progress."

"Understood."

Dr. Scott readied the injection and looked to Luminita, as if this were some elaborate scheme to test him.

"Do it now," she commanded in an iron-clad tone.

The man heaved a sigh and shook his head. "Backward science," he muttered irately. Dr Scott wiped an alcohol swab over the deltoid muscle of Aaron's upper arm. "Just randomly dosing subjects blindly." After a steady exhale, he jabbed the needle in and depressed the plunger slowly. "There. Done."

"Aaron."

After sliding on his shirt, Aaron peered up at Luminita. She stalked closer with a more confident air about her than she'd had moments ago.

"Wait for me in the hall, please."

When he didn't move, she leaned close to whisper against his ear. "This is about *his* trust in *me*, not *my* trust in *you*, Sălbatic."

"Of course." Aaron cast a scathing glare at the heavy-set man before rising from the stool. He kept his stare locked on the virologist while he backed out of the room.

Aaron didn't need to voice a threat. The man *knew* who he was, what he was capable of.

Once he was in the hall, their voices were too muffled to understand, even with the door open, but every fiery barb of her rage brought a grin to his lips. The woman was the vengeful Goddess of Blood and Chaos, capable of drowning the world in her fury. Yet she reserved some softness for *him*. The recognition of that felt significant.

Luminita smoothed her dark green pencil skirt when she sauntered out of the lab. With a slap of her hand against a sensor, the door groaned and swung closed. She didn't turn around until the heavy locks thunked into place.

"What was that about?" Aaron asked curiously, matching her quick strides.

"I made my expectations abundantly clear, as well as the consequences of failing." She caught his gaze for a moment. "Concerning you *and* Lilith."

The additional name piqued his interest. "Lilith? What about her?"

Luminita stopped in front of the door to the central hub and faced him. "I want him to convince Lilith she's infected. It's the only way she'll truly cooperate."

"You mean, the only way to save Cohen," Aaron corrected, trying to keep the anger from his voice.

Not that it mattered. She sensed it anyway.

"That as well," she admitted without hesitation.

"You should know…Lilith interned with Dr. Scott after college. They were quite close. He trusted her, and the man is habitually paranoid. Don't be surprised if this backfires on you."

Luminita considered his warning—*truly* considered it. "So…" Her hypnotic sea-blue eyes met his. "If he provides a compelling enough case…she'll believe it?"

Aaron reluctantly dipped his chin. In theory, it was a sound conclusion.

"Then if the man intends to keep his legs, he better be damn convincing." A devilish smile graced her already tempting lips, but the wicked expression vanished as quickly as it had formed. "I should have trusted you sooner, Sălbatic."

Luminita swiped her keycard and stepped into the central lab. She didn't want a response from him, and he complied with her unspoken request. Aaron followed her in silence until they reached the hall leading to Luminita's apartment.

Andrew Cohen leaned against her door with a cool confidence Aaron hadn't seen since the gala. Perhaps it was the suit.

The gala. That had been a particularly irritating experience. He had recognized the man on sight. Luminita kept a few pictures of him in her apartment. She had also talked about him on several occasions, especially when playing the role of his mentor.

But at the gala, Aaron couldn't let Lilith know any of that. Of course, then Dr. Thomas had blurted out his identity, giving him an excuse to express his immediate dislike.

"Detective." Aaron's greeting exuded disdain, but Andrew seemed unbothered.

The man's sea-blue eyes took in Aaron's appearance, from his buttonless dress shirt hanging open to his bare feet. "I suppose this is better than the pajama pants."

A muscle ticked in Aaron's clenched jaw. He wanted nothing more than to rip the smug grin off Cohen's face. "What can we do for you, detective?" Aaron managed to grind out.

"Lilith texted. We have a time and location." Andrew slid the phone into Luminita's hand and started to walk past them. He paused and looked Aaron over again with clear disapproval. "I suggest a shower and a change of clothes."

The man continued down the hall, his hands in his pockets, as if he didn't have a care in the world.

If only staring holes in his back had been effective.

Chapter 60

"It's 16:08. We have just under two hours." Chance slid out of his seat once the RV came to a stop at the entrance to Wildwood Park and Nature Preserve. "The place only has one official entrance, so they should enter here."

The entire meet was a trap. Everyone knew it, so he didn't bother with the illusion that Cohen might show up on his own.

"We should find a place to stash the RV…out of sight, but close enough for a quick retreat," Tim suggested.

"Agreed. Keller, drive around and see what you can find. Tim, you're with me. Everyone else, sit tight." Chance tightened the straps on his Kevlar vest before grabbing the AR-15.

For once, no one argued, not even Lilith. Chance caught her gaze, and the hum of fear in the air crackled between them. She was scared but still not as much as she should have been.

"Stay in the RV until we get back, *cherie*." Chance watched her warily.

Typically, the woman was stubborn to a fault, and he didn't trust her fear to keep her altruistic instincts in check.

"I will. I promise," she replied softly.

Lilith meant it. He could tell. The sincerity of her promise pulsed beneath the nervous self-doubt gnawing at her insides. At least she was aware of how risky this plan was. A lot could go wrong, just like their showdown with Ashcroft in Madisonville—the one he and Cohen had barely survived.

Cohen. Chance tried to stifle the growing hatred the name summoned but ultimately failed. He had loathed the guy enough before, but now, luring Lilith out by preying on her feelings, manipulating her…It made everything worse.

The cold ache of contempt made Chance clench his hands around the assault rifle.

Lilith *still* wanted to save the monster, but that might be the one thing Chance couldn't give her. If *anything* went wrong today, it would *all* rest on Cohen's head.

A frown slowly spread across Lilith's face as she sensed his mounting anger, but before she could comment, Tim clapped Chance on the shoulder.

"You ready, brother?"

Chance flashed Lilith a reassuring smile, which eased her concern. "Yeah, let's go, Tim."

With considerable effort, Chance tore his gaze away from her and jogged down the stairs. Tim followed, hot on his heels. Once the man held up an okay sign, giving the go ahead, Keller pulled the RV out of the lot and back onto the main road.

It didn't feel right, being separated from Lilith, but they needed to scout the area and come up with a solid plan. Still, he felt the physical distance like an ache in his ribs.

"She'll be all right," Tim said, reading his thoughts. "Come on. We'll take the high ground."

Chance finally looked away from the vacant road and followed Tim's line of sight to the gentle hills overlooking the main visitor area. That was the reason they had chosen this place. Not only was access limited to one open spot, but the elevation would give them a clear view of the area, including a good stretch of road.

They both disengaged the safeties but kept the assault rifles loose by their sides while trekking up the first slope.

"I still don't like this plan," Tim grumbled.

"We're all aware." Chance released a heavy sigh. He had hoped to avoid rehashing this conversation. "Trust me. I don't like it any more than you do."

"I should fucking hope not. Your fiancé is the one in the most danger."

Although the knowledge wasn't new, Chance's pulse still sky-rocketed. "Thanks for the reminder."

"There's still time to back out. We could lay low…catch them off guard without using Lilith."

Chance stopped and rounded on Tim. "You think I haven't thought of that? Or a dozen other scenarios that pose less of a risk? I talked them all over with Lilith. She's convinced that Cohen is the key. If she can get through to him, she can find out what he knows."

Tim nodded thoughtfully. "Okay, so we take Cohen as soon as he shows up. Lilith doesn't *have* to be there."

Chance raked a hand through his disheveled hair in frustration. Tim was trying to help, but Chance had already hashed all this out with Lilith, and he still wasn't happy with the result.

"If Cohen doesn't see Lilith, he'll bolt. According to Lily, he knows exactly how much I want to tear out his damn spine."

Now that Lilith wasn't around, Chance let that rage flare from a smolder to a four-alarm fire scorching through every cell. At this point, tearing out the man's spine would be merciful.

Tim marched around Chance and continued up the hill. "All right. Then how *precisely* do you want to play this?"

"Nicci and I will stay with Lilith—"

"You think that's wise?" Tim interrupted.

"What do you mean?"

"You and Cohen…face-to-face? I mean, even *with* Lilith there, he might run if he sees you up close and personal."

"I'm not letting her out of my damn sight." Chance glared over at his friend.

"And I'm not saying you should. But you may want to hang back a bit…appear like less of a threat."

Chance continued to trudge up the hill in silence, considering the man's suggestion despite the looming fear it summoned.

"*If* we're gonna go through with this insane plan, it makes no sense to sabotage it from the start. That would make it all risk and no damn reward, and you know it," Tim continued.

"Fine," Chance reluctantly agreed. "Six feet."

"Fucking seriously? Six feet is still in spitting distance."

An aggravated huff rattled past Chance's lips. "Fifteen."

"Thirty," Tim countered.

Chance shot him an openly hostile glare.

"Hey, I get it, man. But if you're going along with this, you need to give it a chance to succeed. Believe me. I wish I could keep Eileen away from all this shit too."

Chance's lips slanted into a smirk. "That's what we get for falling for fierce women."

Tim chuckled. "I want so bad to protect her, but I fell for her in part because I didn't need to. Fucking sucks, ya know?"

"I do." Chance grinned. "It's like being torn between terror and pride. When Lily left to face Ashcroft in the Phipps Bend basement alone…with a damn pistol because she refused to leave anyone behind, I thought my heart was gonna explode."

Tim smiled over at him. "Lily is as loyal as they come, brother."

Although the man meant it as a compliment, Chance's smile dimmed. "I know. That's what scares me."

"How so?"

"This bond she has with Cohen…despite every reason why she should cut ties…despite everything he's confessed…everything he's done. When is she finally gonna learn?"

Tim patted his shoulder with a heavy sigh, bringing them both to a stop. "She sees the good in people, even when she shouldn't, but it's not like she's ignoring everything. She was the first to admit this is a trap. Lil might not share your loathing for Cohen, but she isn't blind, and she hasn't forgiven him."

Chance cocked an eyebrow at his friend. "And how do you know that?"

Tim flashed a wolfish smile and started walking again. "Because if she'd *truly* forgiven Cohen, she wouldn't let *you* within five miles of him."

"Fair point." Chance chuckled, feeling a fraction lighter.

They crested the hill before the comfortable silence ended.

"This will make a good spot." Tim paused near a rock formation overlooking the meeting site and fished the sniper scope out of his tac vest. The man crawled over to the edge, lying in a prone position, and peered through the scope. "I've got clear views of the whole area, including the parking lot, all the way out to the road. I'll see any cars approaching before they pull in, and the terrain should hide my position."

"All right. You'll perch here with Eileen. She can cover your back and stay out of harm's way."

"What about Keller? He's a decent shot, and we have two sniper rifles."

"We need someone to stay with the RV and guard our escape."

Tim hopped back up and dusted off his jeans. "Makes sense."

"So, we're agreed? Nicci and Lilith will go out to meet Cohen, with me following at a distance—"

"Thirty feet," Tim interjected.

"With me following at *thirty damn feet*. You'll set up here, warn us of anyone approaching, and cover our backs. Eileen will be here with you, and Keller will be on standby with the RV."

Tim nodded. "Makes the most logistical sense. Still don't fucking like it, though."

Chance peered down at the park's entrance with a growing sense of dread. "I don't either. Luminita is downright diabolical, and we have no idea what tricks she might still have up her sleeve."

"We can always say fuck it and haul ass to Knoxville," Tim offered with a faint glimmer of hope.

Chance wanted to take the out. He would have no problem turning his back on Andrew, regardless of the possible consequences. Even if Luminita released a new plague or inflamed the current pandemic, even if thousands or millions lost their lives, none of it was worth sacrificing Lilith. Luminita might not want to kill her, but Chance knew all too well there were far worse things than death.

Unfortunately, Lilith would carry the weight of every sacrifice. She still had empathy for others—far more than Chance did anyway. Lilith had never witnessed, much less experienced, the true depravity people were capable of. Surviving Boston had been her darkest brush with the underbelly of society, thank God.

The thought of Lilith living through half the shit he had endured, especially when bouncing around foster homes, one house in particular …A white house with a blue door and creaky stairs…

"Chance? You okay?"

Tim's concerned voice yanked Chance back from the precipice, from the deep pit full of memories he had desperately tried to forget. For years, they had remained safely buried, but ever since the talk with Orchid, those noisy stairs at night and what always followed had haunted his thoughts.

"Yeah. I'm good," he lied, rubbing a hand over his face.

"I seriously doubt that." Tim huffed a laugh.

Chance leveled a glare at the man. "I'm good enough."

"Hey, we still gotta sweep the area and ensure there's no one else here. We got time, if there's anything you want to get off your chest."

"Where do I fucking start?" Chance released a sarcastic laugh while they walked along the ridge.

"With the shit I don't already know," Tim suggested with a shrug.

He probably wanted to appear casual, but Chance felt the tension thrumming over his friend.

"You already know everything, Tim."

"Do I?" Tim raised one blond eyebrow and kept his unnerving stare locked on him.

"Everything important," Chance amended.

"Then where the hell did your mind go just then?"

Chance hesitated. It wasn't something he *ever* wanted to acknowledge out loud, much less discuss. "I was thinking about all the reasons why I'd let the world suffer to keep Lilith safe, but...*she* could never live with that."

It wasn't an outright lie, just some heavy mental editing to avoid certain topics.

Tim stopped Chance with a hand on his arm. "You're worrying me, brother."

Chance managed a half-smile. "I'm fine. Lilith is the reason I'm here...in more ways than one."

Tim narrowed his eyes. "Stop bullshitting me. Something's been off with you since your face-to-face with Orchid."

Chance forcibly expelled a breath and ran a hand through his hair. "Ya know, it's the weirdest thing, *mon ami*...Having a conversation with the abusive mother who I thought died twenty years ago put me off my game. Fuck. What do you expect, Bardow?"

Tim appeared unamused. "Now you're just being a dick."

Chance shook his head. How did the man *not* get it? Surviving his childhood had been hard enough, but the truth about his mother had made it all worse, like he had *pointlessly* suffered. Orchid was alive. She could have saved him, but she never even looked for him.

"Talk to me, Chance." Tim's voice was gentle this time, but it didn't help quell the rage which refused to be suppressed any longer.

"What do you want me to say? I'm spinning out? Yeah! I am! Between the situation with Cohen, the weird dreams, finding out I'm half Durand, almost fucking dying, and the shit seeing Orchid dragged up...I'm trying to keep it together. But the thought of losing Lilith—the one thing keeping me from falling apart—fucking terrifies me because without her..." Chance swallowed hard and squarely met Tim's gaze. "I'll crack under the weight of all this darkness."

Tim stepped closer and grabbed Chance's shoulder in a tight grip. "Brother, you are *not* alone. As long as I'm here, you'll *never* be alone. *We* will keep Lilith safe, but you need to start talking to me more…share that burden so it's not so damn heavy."

Chance nodded while rubbing his neck. The rage finally started to ebb somewhat. "I appreciate you, but…there's some things I never want to talk about with *anyone*. They *need* to stay buried."

Tim considered him for a moment. "Back there…did your mind go to one of these *buried* memories?"

Chance rolled his eyes with fresh aggravation. "Can you please just drop it?"

"That's a yes. Doesn't sound very *buried* to me."

"Damn it, Tim! Let it the fuck go!" Chance shoved away from him to continue along the hillside.

After a few steps, Tim grabbed his arm and spun him around. "No! You know why?"

When Chance merely stood there with a hostile glare, Tim continued.

"Because Lilith isn't the only one in danger here, asshole! You, me, Eileen, Nicci, Keller, Gibson…We are *all* at risk, and I need your head in the fucking game!"

"I have it under control, Tim."

"Do you? Because I'm pretty sure you just told me the fucking opposite. You're one step away from cracking, remember?"

"And you think airing out ancient history is gonna fix that?" Chance yelled in pure exasperation.

The entire argument was pointless. They didn't have time for this.

"Keeping secrets gives them power, remember? We *just* went through this shit with Cohen!"

"Do *not* compare me to him!" Chance growled, taking a step closer, hands curling into fists.

"Then stop *acting* like him! Right now, you're fixating on one thing to drive away your demons—the *same thing* Cohen fixated on, by the way! Your sanity is *not* Lilith's responsibility any more than Cohen's is! You need to right your own damn ship and stop adding to the shit Lilith is already fucking carrying!"

The words hit Chance more effectively than a punch to the gut, and all the rage tearing through him turned ice-cold.

Shit. Tim's right. I put everything on her…I rely solely on her…

"Chance." Tim's voice grew soft, compassionate. "I didn't want to go there with you, man, but…you wouldn't listen."

Chance nodded absently. The words barely registered past the roaring in his head. He had been so busy blaming everything on Cohen that he had never realized the stress *he* brought into Lilith's life. She had been holding him together since his first encounter with Orchid at the cabin, before he had even known who the woman was.

"Look, you don't have to tell me everything. God knows, we don't have time for that. Just tell me what's fucking you up right now."

Chance swallowed hard and tried to focus past the overwhelming guilt crushing his chest. His thoughts kept churning into an indecipherable mess.

"Breathe, brother." Tim patted his back.

After forcing a few deep inhalations into his constricted lungs, Chance just spoke, uncertain what exactly would come out. "I am so desperate to keep Lilith from the dark things. She's gone through so much this year. Hell, even before that, with Boston. But she still hasn't seen how far the depraved rabbit hole goes, and I never want her to."

"Not like you have…" Tim's concerned expression deepened. "You don't think she's seen some shit in her line of work?"

"Seeing it and experiencing it are two very different things."

A dawning expression of understanding lit Tim's face. "Shit. You aren't just talking about being locked in closets, bruises, and broken bones, are you?"

All Chance could do was shake his head. The fear and panic those particular memories summoned strangled any words he tried to get out.

"Jesus, Chance." Tim rubbed a hand over his face and took a step back. "The fucking foster home? The one you never talk about?"

Shameful tears burned Chance's eyes. He still couldn't say it. "She never even looked for me, Tim. She believed Luminita, moved on, started a new family, a new life…all while I…suffered."

"There's no way she could have known what was happening to you…" Tim held no confidence in those words, and it showed.

"She saw pictures. *Pictures*, Tim. Luminita showed her pictures of me, dead, and that's all it fucking took. If something happened to Lilith, I wouldn't believe it until I held her dead body in my arms. And *even then*, I'd fight the truth. My mind would run through the worst-case scenarios…like what if this isn't real and she's alive? What if someone's hurting her? What if she needs me to save her? They *never changed my name*, Tim. One search would have been all it took."

"But that's you. You were raised in worst-case scenarios. You were trained to see the worst in people. It's what makes you damn good at your job, but not everyone sees the world that way. What I don't get, though, is why all this is coming up now. What does this have to do with Lilith?"

Chance straightened and faced the horrific realization he had come to—the one he had been trying desperately to purge from his mind.

"Luminita doesn't want to kill her, Tim. She wants Lily alive…to cage her…use her blood, and if it works…" He met Tim's stare with steely determination. "Do you think her experiments will stop there? Lilith is the *last of Gregor's line*…unless…"

Chance left the rest unspoken, mostly because he couldn't make himself say the words.

Tim paled when the meaning sunk in. "Fuck. Well, that's a whole new nightmare I hadn't considered."

"Yeah. That's the current worst-case scenario I can't get out of my mind, and Cohen…kissing her…has *not* fucking helped." Chance released a slow exhale, and the tightness in his chest lessened. Somehow, just getting all that out there, acknowledging the fear head-on, actually helped.

"All right. Well, our mission is pretty damn clear—keep Lilith away from Luminita. Anything else we need to tackle?"

"Can we just finish the sweep and get back?"

Tim eyed him carefully. "We good?"

Chance nodded. "You were right, Tim. I needed that. I'm sorry for being a dick."

The man shrugged. "I'm used to it by now."

Chapter 61

Lilith inhaled through her nose and slowly exhaled through her mouth while Chance double-checked every strap on her Kevlar vest.

Cohen is the key to finding out what Luminita is up to. This will work. It has to work.

"I had Tim replace the damaged plate in the back with one of mine," he stated, running his fingers over the front straps one last time.

It took a second for the words to register past the chaos in her head. "What? No, Chance. That puts you in danger."

He shook his head but didn't meet her eyes. "Luminita doesn't want me dead. It's better it comes from mine than someone else's."

"She wants me alive too," Lilith reminded him.

"And Aaron hates you more than me. If he's really working with Luminita, we need to be cautious." Chance stepped behind her, readjusting the back for what felt like the tenth time.

"Chance?"

"Yes, *cherie?*" The fear in his voice was becoming far too familiar.

Lilith turned around to face him, but his gaze seemed fixed on the NPYD letters on the front of her vest, as if he couldn't bear to look at her.

"Hey." Lilith reached out and slid her palm over his stubbled cheek.

Chance closed his eyes and leaned into her touch, placing his hand over hers to keep it there.

"Chance, look at me."

His throat bobbed, and when his hazel eyes finally met hers, they were brimming with tears. The pained expression on his handsome face tore at her heart.

"I'm sorry," she whispered.

Confusion drew his brows together. "What could you possibly have to be sorry about?"

"Seriously?" Lilith blinked in surprise. "We are standing here, facing a crazy plan of mine for the third time…and the other two failed pretty spectacularly. Maybe you should just slap duct tape over my mouth and lock me in the bedroom."

That, at least, earned her an amused grin.

"I won't lie. The thought *has* crossed my mind more than once."

Lilith eyed him suspiciously, but it was all for show. They both needed a brief reprieve from the pressure suffocating them.

"Because of my idiotic plans or"—she pulled on a flirtatious smile despite the nervous panic still rippling through her body—"other reasons?"

Chance brushed his lips over her cheek until they reached her ear. "Well, *cherie*," he whispered. His gravelly voice was full of dark promises. "We are sharing an RV with five other people, and you…tend to get quite…vocal."

The most delicious shiver raced through her body to clench her thighs. The man's voice alone was magical. Chance could recite the phone book in that tone, and it would be erotic as hell.

"That's entirely your fault," Lilith teased, unable to fight her grin.

Chance pulled back enough to consume her field of vision. Although his eyes were banked with heat, sadness lingered there too. His thumb skimmed over her jaw and across her bottom lip.

"I will happily accept the blame for that the rest of my life, *mon fiancé.*"

Lilith fought off the sudden tightness in her throat and blinked back the tears threatening to spill. With a new sense of determination, Lilith cradled his face in her palms and searched his eyes while she spoke.

"Chance, the paper is only a formality. I've already made my vows to you. I am yours, and you are mine, *mon mari.*"

The shock was unmistakable, and a few tears escaped, trailing down his cheek.

"And yes…I looked it up. Did I say it right? My husband?" Lilith asked in a burst of nervousness.

Chance nodded but had to clear his throat several times before he could talk. "Say it again." His voice still cracked, but the smile stretching his lips nearly stole the breath from her lungs.

"*Mon mari.*"

Wormwood

As soon as the last syllable passed her lips, Chance drew her against him and claimed her mouth. Every kiss was fantastic with Chance, but this one…It burned through her until her knees buckled. Lilith slid one hand into his hair while the other gripped his shoulder to keep herself upright.

Chance snaked his hand up her back to hold her nape, keeping her close. The world just fell away. In that moment, no one else existed, just Lilith and Chance.

If only it could stay that way.

All too soon, Chance broke the devastating kiss, panting heavily. "I love you, *ma femme*." He whispered the words like a fervent prayer against her lips.

My wife. She had looked that one up too.

"And I love you, always." Lilith pressed her forehead to his, tears burning her eyes, and just breathed him in. She wanted to absorb every single detail of this moment, right down to the smell of leather and sunshine on his skin.

"Ahem." The sudden intrusion broke the blissful bubble. "You guys done sucking face? I swear, between you two and Tim and Eileen, it's like chaperoning horny teenagers."

Nicci grumbled, but Lilith could hear the smile in her voice. It made her wonder just how much Nicci had overheard.

Lilith peered around Chance's shoulder, her flushed cheeks burning. "Sorry, partner."

Nicci chuckled and winked. "No, you're not. I get it, but we need to go."

"We'll be right there, Nic," Chance called over his shoulder without taking his eyes off Lilith. Apparently, there was something else he wanted to say—without an audience.

"All right. You got thirty seconds." Nicci jogged down the stairs to wait outside.

"Okay, Lily. Tim and Eileen are already in position. Remember, we're keeping the walkies on channel seventeen because Cohen knows the other channels we used. Do you remember where I showed you Tim would be set up?"

Lilith nodded.

"Good. Stay out of his sight line. Don't put yourself between him and *any* hostiles. That *includes* Cohen, okay?"

"I know." The thought made her uneasy, but they had gone over this several times already.

"We'll try to take Cohen for information, but if anything starts going wrong, I won't hesitate to take him out."

Once again, Lilith nodded, although it was her least favorite part of the plan.

"Don't take unnecessary risks. You are bait to draw Cohen out, nothing more. Once he's away from the car, I want you out of there. Haul ass back here."

Okay, now this *is my least favorite part of the plan.*

"Chance. I can't just—"

"Yes, you can, *cherie*, because I *need* you to, please."

"Time's up!" Nicci hollered from outside. "Let's move our asses, people!"

Chance pressed the mic button. "Nic, we have radios for a reason. Over."

"Yelling is more fun! Let's go!"

"I'm serious, Lily. Once you draw out Cohen, run. I'm begging you."

She couldn't promise him that. What if something happened? What if he was in danger? Lilith couldn't just run off and leave everyone else to clean up her mess.

"Lily."

"I'll consider it. Come on." Lilith pushed Chance toward the exit, which he *allowed* her to do, of course.

They only had enough full mags for two assault rifles. Keller carried one to guard the RV, and Eileen had taken the other to protect Tim. Of course, they both had sidearms as well.

Nicci had her service weapon, and Lilith had her Beretta. Tim was manning the sniper rifle but also carried his SIG P226. Chance preferred his SIG-Sauer, a standard issue pistol for the Secret Service, which made sense. He had been the vampire equivalent most of his adult life.

Chance approached Keller once they stepped out of the RV. "As soon as you hear the signal, drive straight for our location."

"Yes, sir." Keller nodded at Chance. "On your command—Sunset."

Chance pressed the mic button again. "Bardow. We're heading into position. Let me know when you have us in your scope. Over."

"Copy. Over." Tim's voice crackled through Lilith's earpiece when she popped it in.

After about a five-minute walk, they entered the clearing, and Tim's voice came through the walkies again.

"In my sights. Over."

Chance held his arm up with the okay sign for Tim before pressing the mic button. "Keller. RV still secure? Over."

"All clear. Over."

"Hersch, coms check. Over."

She checked in loud and clear.

Everyone was in position and as ready as they could be.

Here's hoping this plan actually works.

Chance stopped about thirty feet from the low split-rail fence separating the parking lot from the nature preserve. Lilith immediately turned around.

"What's wrong?"

"Nothing, *cherie*." Chance sucked in a breath, as if speaking was a challenge. "I don't want to spook Cohen, and you want him alive, so…I need to keep my distance."

Alarms began blaring in her head. This *wasn't* the plan. She didn't like this at all, not one damn bit.

"Heads-up. A car is coming down the road…slowing down. Over," Tim reported.

"Chance, this isn't the plan. You are supposed to stay with me." Lilith eyed him and took a step closer.

"A necessary change, *ma femme*." Calling her his wife in this moment felt like emotional bribery.

"Car is entering the lot. Over." Tim's voice held more of an edge now, but Lilith continued to stare at Chance.

"Nicci will be right with you, *cherie*. Go on. I've got you covered."

After narrowing her eyes at Chance, Lilith finally tore her attention away from him and faced the lot. A dark blue sedan was rolling to a stop near the entrance.

"Come on, partner," Nicci urged.

Lilith glanced back at Chance one last time. Leaving his side just felt wrong, but they had come this far. It was too late to turn back now, and Chance obviously wasn't budging on this.

She jogged over to her partner, and they quickly covered the distance to the fence.

The sedan came to a stop a few feet away, and Lilith's heart hammered against her ribs. The tint on the back windows made it impossible to tell for certain, but it seemed like Cohen was alone.

Perhaps she was wrong. Maybe it wasn't a trap and Cohen truly had just wanted to see her.

The driver's side door opened, and Cohen's blond head appeared. In an instant, his haunted eyes snapped to Lilith's with a physical weight. Her heart leapt right into her throat in sheer panic.

This is a bad idea. The thought was pure instinct.

"Bardow. Do you have him in your sights? Over." Chance's voice rumbled through the line, snapping Lilith out of her trance.

"Affirmative. Over."

Cohen walked around the car, dressed in a crisp grey suit, like the ones he preferred, but something was different. His gait held less confidence. His eyes remained fixed on her, as if she was the only thing that mattered.

He didn't take in his surroundings or look for the threats he had to know were out there. But what truly caught her attention were the flickers of guilt in his expression. He was doing a good job of suppressing them. If she hadn't been looking for them, she might not have noticed.

Lilith swallowed her rising apprehension. She'd known this was a trap going into it. None of this should have been a surprise, but somehow, it still felt like it was. Maybe it was that one moment of doubt when she had thought maybe, just maybe, Cohen hadn't been lying.

None of it matters. It doesn't change the mission here.

Lilith resolutely put one foot in front of the other, walking out to meet Cohen while popping the snap on her holster. Nicci stayed a few feet behind, giving her a little space.

When Lilith drew close, Andrew lowered his gaze to the concrete. It made things easier. The weight of his stare had summoned memories of Duncan's basement, his confession, the kiss, his sacrifice. A free-for-all of indecipherable emotions gripped her chest, and suddenly, she was grateful Chance wasn't next to her.

Maybe that was the real reason he had hung back. Perhaps Chance didn't want to know what she would feel in this moment.

Hell, what am *I feeling?* Everything seemed like a convoluted mess.

Cohen came to a stop in front of her, close enough to touch, and slid his hands into his pockets. "Thank you," he said in a raspy voice. "For meeting me."

Reluctantly, Lilith took in his dress shirt, then his unblemished face, and finally, the swirling amber of his eyes, which were already glassy. After everything, she still wanted to see Cohen for who he was, and that knowledge both relieved and terrified her.

"Tell me what's going on, Andrew." Her words came out shakier than she had expected.

The man's throat bobbed several times. "It's so good to see you." A faint smile tugged at the corner of his mouth.

"I'm glad to see you too." It was the truth. As fucked up as the entire situation was, she *had* missed him. "I thought Ashcroft—"

"Nearly," he said in a quiet voice. "Luminita…she helped me."

Lilith took a step closer and searched his eyes. "Andrew, what happened? What did she do?"

Cohen pinched his brows together. He swallowed hard again with tears in his eyes. "It's *my* fault."

The pain emanating from him nearly overwhelmed her, and Lilith gripped his arm to steady herself. Of course, that only made things worse. Heart-wrenching sadness flooded her system. It felt like he had dragged her into arctic waters, drowning her in the icy depths.

"We have a second vehicle inbound. Over."

Lilith let go of Cohen's arm and took a step back. Her hand gravitated toward her gun. "What is happening, Andrew? You need to tell me."

"Entering the parking lot. Over." Tim's anxious voice was barely audible over the alarms screaming in her head.

"Lily." Cohen stepped forward, grabbing her right arm, the one poised over her gun. "Don't. You *need* to stay with me. Please." Sheer desperation infused every word.

"Bardow. Do you have a shot on Cohen? Over." Chance's voice growled through the earpiece.

"Negative. Lilith, you need to move aside. Now! Over." Tim barked the order, but she was frozen in place by the panic in Cohen's golden eyes.

This was all wrong.

"I'm sorry," he whispered the words, hovering far too close, crowding her vision.

"Cherie! Move!" Chance yelled from behind her.

It wasn't supposed to happen this way. She had to get through to Andrew, get him on their side.

"Cohen, you don't have to do this. We can help each other," she pleaded with open desperation. "Please. Just come with us."

The man's face crumpled with fresh tears. "I *am* helping you."

"Lilith!" Nicci slammed into her partner, knocking her to the side.

Lilith stumbled to the ground.

A thunderous shot cracked through the air, and Lilith's heart stopped for an instant. Panic rang through every nerve as she slowly turned to look back, terrified of what she would see.

Cohen stood there, just as mystified as she was. There was no blood. But Tim was an excellent shot. He wouldn't miss.

Everything happened impossibly fast.

Nicci scrambled to her feet, but Cohen kicked her square in the chest, knocking her backward. The second car came to a screeching halt. Shots were fired—probably Chance—and Andrew grabbed Lilith, hauling her against his chest.

"Back up, Deveraux. I don't want anyone to get hurt!" Andrew hollered over her shoulder.

"Bardow! Do you have a fucking shot? Over!" Chance screamed into the walkie, but there was no response. "Bardow?!"

Nothing.

"Hersch?"

The line buzzed with silence. Dread blossomed in Lilith's chest, turning into sheer horror.

"DeLuca! I need you to check on them!" Chance ordered.

"I can't leave her," Nicci yelled back.

"He won't hurt her, Nicci, but Tim and Eileen—"

"Nicci! Go!" Lilith peered over her shoulder.

Chance had his gun trained on them. Nicci reluctantly lowered her weapon and took off like a shot, sprinting for the hill.

"Sunset, Keller. Fucking Sunset!" Chance screamed into the walkie as he raced toward Lilith.

There was no answer.

"I'm so sorry, Lilith. This is the only way."

Andrew's words drew her attention. Lilith turned back to stare up at him.

"What did you do?"

She had known this was a trap, knew the odds weren't in their favor, but she hadn't expected Andrew to be so…complicit.

His fingers drifted over her cheek. The agony in his expression cracked her heart. "I had to…for you. There was no choice. Neither of us have a choice."

"For me?" Those words summoned her anger until it burned in her gut like lava. She shoved at his chest, but his hold on her only tightened until she was flattened against him. "Let me fucking go!"

The car door opened, and the familiar sound of heels clicking on pavement echoed in Lilith's ears.

"I can't." Tears fell from Cohen's golden eyes, and he leaned his forehead against hers. His trembling breaths washed over her skin, betraying the agonized guilt tearing him apart. "I am so sorry...for everything. I never wanted to hurt you. Never you."

Lilith lost the fight against her tears, and they streamed down her face. There was no getting through to Andrew. He was set on a course, bound and determined to see it through, no matter what she said or did.

I was wrong, so fucking wrong, and it might cost everything.

"Mr. Deveraux. If you value the lives of your compatriots, I suggest you stop and lower your weapon."

Luminita's voice soured Lilith's stomach.

"Let her go!" Chance bellowed in a war cry.

Lilith tried to pull away, but Cohen's arms were like iron bars around her. She couldn't move, could barely breathe. Everything was falling to shit.

A shot split the air a second before Chance yelled a warning. "Luminita! Order him to let her go, or I swear...my next shot goes in your fucking forehead."

"I would not advise that course of action," Luminita stated calmly. "I'm the only thing keeping Aaron from slaughtering your friends. And believe me...if you harm me, his wrath will extend much farther than *your* death."

Her heels clicked closer, and each step felt like razors embedding into Lilith's skin.

This is all my fault. Lilith had thought Cohen would try to help them, but she had once again put her faith in the wrong person. *I should have listened to Chance.*

"And why should I believe you?" Chance yelled, closer this time. He was still moving toward them, maybe ten feet away now.

"Andrew," Lilith whispered, her voice shaking. "You need to let me go, please. We can still stop this."

"I can't..." Andrew's tear-stained voice broke, and his heart thudded violently against his ribs. "It's *my* fault."

Jenny Allen

"You don't have to take my word for it," Luminita said. "See for yourself."

Chapter 62

Luminita's ominous words rattled in Lilith's skull, summoning a host of terrifying scenarios.

Tim wouldn't miss…Something happened to him…to Eileen…to Keller…maybe Nicci.

Lilith's body burned with a desperate need to turn around, to see what was happening, but the effort was futile. Cohen banded his arms around her, pinning her firmly to his chest with more strength than he'd had in Duncan's basement.

Suddenly, she was in the earthen tunnel of her nightmares, the walls crushing in on her, suffocating her.

Breathe…Just breathe.

Lilith hesitantly looked into Andrew's face, which hovered far too close. She kept hoping she would see hazel or grey or anything else, but when she stared into his molten gold eyes, it felt like a personal betrayal. Despite *everything*, she *still* wanted to see *him*, have faith in *him*, and he knew it.

Tears freely fell while Cohen stared back at her with a convoluted mess of emotions. His gaze fell to her lips, only for an instant, before he cleared his throat and averted his eyes.

"I would listen to her, Deveraux." Aaron's condescending voice brought reality crashing back in.

Lilith turned her head to the left, peering over her shoulder as best she could. A mixture of relief and dread washed over her. Tim and Nicci stood a few feet away, with their hands behind their heads. At least they were alive—for now.

Aaron lurked nearby, next to a dark-haired stranger. Luminita stood between them and Cohen.

Motion caught Lilith's attention. Two figures moved into view, their rifles aimed at Nicci and Tim. That's when the world ceased to make sense.

Special Agent Eileen Hersch and former Green Beret Brian Keller came to a stiff halt. *No way* were they working for Luminita. Neither of them would *ever* double-cross the group. It was *not* possible.

Lilith snapped her attention back to Nicci and Tim. They both showed every marker for fear, sadness, defeat, and guilt, but *not* betrayal.

What the hell is happening?

"You're fighting a losing battle, Chance." Aaron strolled forward with his hands in his pockets—the very picture of calm indifference.

Chance. She couldn't see him.

Lilith whipped her head to the other side and finally caught sight of him. His gun was trained in Aaron's direction.

"I have very little interest in seeing *any* of you survive," Aaron continued.

Something in his voice drew Lilith's focus. Her gaze collided with Aaron's malicious stare, and fear exploded in her chest, like an atom bomb.

Lilith had always known her uncle disliked her, perhaps even despised her. He had never kept his contempt secret, but until now, she'd had *no idea* how deep his loathing ran. The unrestrained hatred contorting his features was on open display, for all to see, and it chilled her to the marrow.

"I won't let him hurt you," Cohen whispered against her ear. His heated breath warmed her clammy skin but sent chills skittering down her spine.

The promise left her conflicted, like everything about Cohen did. Lilith had wanted so badly to believe that, once they got here, Cohen would be on *her* side, that he would help them. She *wanted* to trust him.

Hell, if she was still seeing his true eye color, part of her *obviously* still did. Yet, here he was, holding her prisoner for Luminita and Aaron, refusing to let her go.

The sound of an approaching vehicle drowned out everything else. Lilith peeked over Cohen's shoulder toward the road. A panel van was pulling into the lot.

"Killian. As we discussed." Aaron's strange words were barely audible over the roaring in Lilith's head.

Cohen took a step backward with her, toward the parking lot, toward the van, away from Chance.

"Brian Keller." The strong Irish accent confused Lilith at first—it had to belong to the tall stranger with Aaron. "Drop your rifle."

The gun thudded to the ground, and Cohen took another step back.

Lilith frantically looked for Chance again. This time, his tear-filled eyes were already on her. Lilith's throat tightened at the sight.

Chance shifted, heartache and frustration clearly etched on his face. His hand flexed around the pistol grip, and it drifted between targets.

This is his nightmare, and I made it all happen.

"Let her go!" Chance ordered, but his voice held more desperation than authority. "Please! Cohen!"

Andrew's backward steps didn't falter.

"Draw your pistol." The Irishman's command drew Chance's focus away from Lilith. "Place the muzzle to your right temple."

"Wait! No!" Tim hollered.

"Stop!" Chance tossed his gun to the ground and held up his arms. "There! I'm unarmed!"

Dread twisted around Lilith's lungs. Silent seconds ticked by, but the sensation didn't just belong to her. It infused the very air until each breath felt poisonous.

Cohen tightened his arms around her.

"I'm sorry." The apology was so quiet, Lilith wasn't sure she had actually heard it.

"Squeeze the trigger."

As soon as the order left Killian's mouth, a shot echoed with a chilling finality, followed by a heavy thud. Lilith flinched in horror, grateful she hadn't been watching.

"Andrew," she whispered between shaky sobs. "*Please.*"

Lilith met his golden eyes in desperation. She couldn't let anyone else die.

"Stop this. There's still time. Help us. *Help me.*" She sent a silent prayer to whatever deity would listen that she could still reach him.

Like most of her prayers, they were useless.

Andrew's face crumpled while he studied her eyes. Lilith knew his answer before he hovered closer.

"Please…*trust me.* I *am* helping you." He closed his eyes, sending tears streaking down his cheeks. Cohen gently pressed his forehead to hers.

He expelled a heavy breath against her lips, and the rush of misery and longing left Lilith breathless. *"Everything* I've done has been for you."

Despair twisted her stomach, drowning out the chaotic shouts and screams behind her. Lilith fought to drag in any air past the sudden boulder lodged in her throat.

Andrew thought he was doing the right thing—for whatever reason. He wouldn't change his mind, she couldn't reason with him, and he wouldn't stop all this from happening. Keller was dead. The others might join him, and Luminita would hold Lilith prisoner, slowly draining her of blood.

The finality of that, the complete ruin of everything she had worked for, the life she wanted slipping away…It all burned in her aching lungs like napalm.

"You broke our deal, Mr. Deveraux, and turned my best agent against me. Did you think there would not be consequences?" Luminita's question cut through Lilith's panic while the van came to a stop a few feet away.

"Eileen Hersch."

A fresh stab of terror tightened Lilith's chest when the Irishman spoke the agent's name.

"No! Please! I'm begging you!" Tim's heart-wrenching scream brought fresh tears to Lilith's eyes.

"Luminita!" Chance yelled. "Is the offer still on the table? My life for Lilith's!"

The words hit Lilith like a physical blow. Luminita just wanted her blood. Chance would face much worse in her vicious clutches.

"Drop your rifle," Killian commanded.

The weapon hit the grass, and Lilith's heart plummeted.

"Stay where you are, Bardow!" Aaron's stern voice boomed.

Shouts were exchanged, but Lilith focused on the sharp clicks of Luminita's retreating heels.

"My life for Tim and Eileen's!" Chance shouted in pure panic.

The clicking heels stopped.

Another tense silence blanketed the space.

Lilith stared over Cohen's shoulder at the stiff lines of Luminita's back. Slowly, the petite woman turned around to face Chance.

"I don't *need* your deal. I possess the one thing you want more than anything." When Luminita gestured toward her, shame burned Lilith's cheeks. "You'll come to me, willingly, at a time of my choosing."

Lilith peered back at Chance and wanted so badly to take this whole idiotic plan back. He paced, raking his hands through his hair, desperately trying to breathe. Chance was powerless. He couldn't stop this, any of this, and it was eating him alive.

"Draw your pistol," Killian commanded.

"We aren't armed! We surrender! Please!" Tim pleaded until his agonized voice broke.

Luminita's heels clicked farther away until a car door opened and closed. Lilith buried her face in Cohen's shoulder while her sobs consumed her.

This is all my fault.

An engine roared to life. Andrew continued to move Lilith toward the van.

Commotion erupted behind her—shouts, a deafening shot, racing footsteps, grunts, pounding blows. Lilith couldn't bring herself to look. She couldn't fight off Cohen, and she couldn't help. Lilith was nothing but a liability, the angel of death, and everyone she loved would suffer for it.

"Enough!" Aaron's booming voice echoed across the vast space, and Cohen's steps halted.

Terror vibrated under his skin, and for the first time, his hold on Lilith loosened. It wasn't enough for her to escape, but it did enable her to take in the scene.

Lilith found Eileen first. She was sprawled out on the ground, not moving, but there didn't seem to be much blood. Killian hadn't given the order to pull the trigger.

Chance and Tim hovered close by, with their hands in the air. The wide-eyed stares of horror on their faces made Lilith follow their line of sight, to the car idling near the van.

All the air seized in Lilith's chest.

Aaron stood with one hand twisted around Nicci's ponytail, the other holding a knife to her throat.

"We already have the target, Aaron. It's enough." Cohen's voice trembled slightly. "You've proven your point. This isn't necessary."

Aaron slowly turned his head toward Cohen, a grin creeping over his mouth. However, the man's vicious stare wasn't for him. It landed solely on Lilith.

Haunted memories of the Phipps Bend basement flooded her mind. Ashcroft had already stolen one partner from her this way. She *couldn't* lose another.

"Aaron," Lilith called. "Stop! I'll give you what you want, willingly. I won't fight you. *Please!* Just let her go!"

Nicci's glassy eyes met Lilith's with a thousand apologies. It tore Lilith's heart wide open. They both knew her word meant nothing to Aaron.

Her uncle kept his cold glare on Lilith. "Killian, get in the car. Cohen, do your fucking job."

Lilith finally drew in a deep breath while Aaron doled out orders and dragged Nicci to her feet. Perhaps her word *did* mean something, after all.

Cohen continued guiding Lilith toward the van, and she let him. She kept her eyes locked on Nicci while Aaron backed up to the car. Once he reached it and his grip on Nicci's hair began to slacken, Lilith finally looked back at Chance.

He shifted his gaze between Lilith and Nicci in abject failure. Not a single thing had gone right, and he would only blame himself.

"Chance." Lilith's voice broke, and she swallowed hard. The flood of tears made her vision waver. "I'm so sorry."

His chest heaved with each labored breath, hands clenching at his sides. "I'll find you, *ma femme.*"

A pang of sadness infused Cohen's suffocating embrace, but Lilith kept her gaze fixed on Chance. This was really it. There was no escaping, no last-minute rescue. She belonged to Luminita and whatever hell she had planned.

"Niece!"

The derisive tone tore Lilith's attention from Chance, but the satisfied grin on Aaron's face made the blood freeze in her veins. His brows were drawn down and together, upper eyelids lifted, tightness below his eyes. All the microexpressions of premeditated violence appeared so fast, Lilith barely had time to scream before the blade ripped across Nicci's throat.

Shouts and movement filled Lilith's ears, but her world narrowed to the crimson pouring down Nicci's chest. "No!" She shrieked the word over and over, thrashing against Cohen's chest, but Aaron wasn't done.

A malicious sneer curled his lip while he raised the knife. In a split-second, Lilith realized Nicci's vest was lying on the ground. Her mind descended into endless screams.

Aaron brought the knife down with brutal strength, driving it right into Nicci's chest. Shock rattled every piece of Lilith while she watched Aaron toss her partner to the ground.

Aaron disappeared into the car, and they peeled out before Tim reached Nicci's still form.

"Fuck." Cohen moved faster while Lilith just stared at the blood soaking the grass.

Tim crashed to his knees. He clamped his hands over Nicci's neck in a desperate attempt to stop the bleeding.

Then Lilith flew sideways into the van.

"Cohen!"

Chance's snarling scream brought Lilith back to the present. She scrambled to her knees, but Cohen climbed in, blocking the exit. Chance was only a few feet away.

"Drive!" Cohen hollered while grabbing the door.

"Stop! Or you're fucking dead!" Chance scooped up a discarded gun off the ground and kept running.

"I'm sorry, Deveraux. It's the only way to save her." Cohen slammed the door closed, tires screeched, and then the van lurched into motion.

Shots thudded against the metal, and the vehicle swerved, sending Lilith sideways until she slammed into the van's side.

Blood. There was so much blood. Lilith could barely breathe. Each inhale tightened her lungs in growing panic. *This can't be happening.*

"Lilith." Cohen's despondent voice slowly drew her attention.

When her gaze finally landed on his warm brown eyes—Nicci's eyes—anger boiled over into hatred.

"What the fuck have you done?" Lilith forced the words past gritted teeth. Tears stung her eyes.

Cohen hung his head and smoothed his sandy blond hair against his scalp. "This wasn't supposed to happen. Fuck!"

"Keller and…" Lilith had to clear her throat before she could say it. "…Nicci is dead because of you!"

Cohen closed his eyes, and his shoulders slumped forward. His guilt became thick enough to choke on. "I had no choice."

The words were barely audible.

"Why?" Lilith shrieked. She lunged at him, but strong hands gripped her from behind. Lilith had been so focused on Cohen, she hadn't realized they weren't alone.

Something sharp jabbed her thigh while she continued to struggle. An odd warmth seeped from the injection spot, and the vise around her lungs loosened.

Fuck. They drugged me.

Lilith stopped fighting the men behind her. It would only make the drugs work faster, and they were already hitting hard.

"Lilith…I'm so sorry. Aaron wasn't supposed to—"

The warmth spread, and Lilith's ragged breaths slowed. Her eyelids felt so heavy.

"Fuck you, Cohen." Tears flooded her vision again while arms lowered her to the van's floor. "I trusted you."

Lilith's eyes fluttered, and tears fell in a steady stream. Cohen's face hovered into view, and his fingertips glided softly over her cheek. But Lilith couldn't move. She was so tired.

"You can still trust me, Lilith. I had to do this…to save you."

The words didn't make sense. *To save me? Save me from what?*

Lilith opened her mouth to respond, but a wave of drowsiness pulled her under, and the world went dark.

Chapter 63

Chance emptied his entire clip into the van while he chased it to the road. Not that it did any good. He could only watch in horror as it disappeared around the bend.

She's gone. Lilith is gone. The thought repeated in a terrifying loop until he couldn't breathe.

"Fuck!" Chance screamed and flung the useless gun across the road. The growing pain in his chest doubled him over. He barely managed to drag oxygen into his lungs while his fists tightened in his hair.

She's gone. Lilith is gone.

"Chance!" Tim's ragged scream interrupted the loop. "Chance! I need you! Now!"

After one last look down the road where the van had disappeared, Chance tore his attention away from it and tried to swallow the rising despair threatening to consume him.

"Right fucking now!" Tim yelled with growing anger.

Chance hurried back to the park, forcing himself to move against every instinct, away from Lilith, away from where she had gone.

Tim's tac vest lay discarded on the ground, and he had his balled-up shirt pressed solidly against Nicci's small chest. Blood covered his arms and hands.

Tim's red-rimmed eyes snapped up to Chance. "Fucking help her."

Chance jogged closer, shifting his gaze from Tim to Nicci's slack face. She was already so pale.

The memory of Gregor in Farren's courtroom flashed through his mind, along with what Cohen had told Lilith in that moment.

You can't bring him back. He's already dead.

"Does she have a pulse?" Chance asked, kneeling across from his friend. He already knew the answer.

"No." Tim sobbed between heaving breaths. "Please. Use your fucking demon blood and help her!"

Chance expelled a pained sigh, tears burning his eyes. He put a hand on Tim's shaking shoulder. "Tim—"

"No! Don't you fucking say it!" The man shook Chance's hand off and cried angrily. "Help her, Deveraux. Please!"

Chance swallowed hard. Nicci's lifeless face was splattered with blood. "It won't help. Her heart's not beating. It won't circulate—"

"Do it!" Tim demanded. "I'll do CPR. It will work! It has—"

His voice broke with heaving gasps.

Chance lifted his tear-filled eyes to Tim's desperate face. He couldn't refuse his friend. Chance grabbed the knife Aaron had dropped—the one already covered in Nicci's blood—and sliced the underside of his wrist. Blood welled along the cut, and he held it over Nicci's mouth.

Tim drew in a trembling breath and knelt over her, locking his hands together on the center of her chest. While he pumped with furious tears, the blood spurted from the deep incision across Nicci's throat.

"Put pressure on her neck," Tim barked.

Chance complied, his heart sinking further with every compression. Even her lips felt cool against his wrist.

"Tim—"

"Shut up! It will work." He pumped harder.

The blood seeping around Chance's fingers slowed.

"Tim, she's gone," Chance said gently.

"Don't you dare give up!" Tim snapped.

"Tim!" Chance grabbed his arms, stopping him. "She's gone. She's not even bleeding anymore. There's nothing we can do."

Tim drew in heaving breaths while tears splashed against his bloody hands. "We *never* gave up on you!"

The pain in Chance's chest flared, stealing his breath again. He had been so certain he was dying that night, that he wouldn't make it, and Lilith...

She's gone. Lilith is gone.

Chance cleared his throat. "Tim." His voice broke on that one word, and he released a slow breath. "I know. I'm sorry, but...Nicci is already gone."

Wormwood

Chance dropped his gaze to her face, already devoid of color, devoid of her jubilant personality, lifeless.

Fuck. Everything went wrong. So fucking wrong.

Slowly, Tim sat back on his heels, his wide shoulders shaking. "I was supposed to keep her safe…keep all of you safe. Keller…and Nicci—" The man collapsed, weeping from his very soul, and rubbed his face. The blood on his hands mingled with his tears.

"Is Eileen…" Chance started but couldn't bring himself to finish that sentence.

"I got the gun away from her in time," Tim replied with a heart-breaking sigh. "I had to knock her out."

Tim's grief-stricken eyes met Chance's again.

"I had to punch my domestic-abuse-survivor girlfriend unconscious to keep her from shooting herself." His face crumpled, revealing all the agony contained in that admission.

For Tim, crossing that line, regardless of the reasons, hurt as much as losing one of his best friends—the woman he considered his little sister.

Tim fell quiet while he stared down at Nicci despondently.

"What the fuck happened?" Chance asked, with as much sympathy as he could.

Fresh tears filled the man's eyes. "Killian, the man with Aaron…he's like the siren, but it only seems to work on humans. Whatever he told Keller and Eileen to do, they did."

Chance nodded at the confirmation, but it didn't make the concept any less frightening.

"They knew…" Tim said in a haunted tone. "Keller and Eileen. They knew what was happening. I could see it in their eyes." Another sob broke free, and he dragged in quick, shallow breaths. "They were aware of what was happening, but they couldn't stop it, any more than I could stop this…"

Tim brushed aside a few strands of hair from Nicci's face and wept.

"Keller…he looked right at me…begging for my help before he pulled that trigger." Tim ran his hands through his blond curls and clenched his jaw.

"This isn't your fault, Tim. You hated the fucking plan. *I* should have said no…I should have made Lilith see reason."

And now she's gone. Lilith is gone. Keller and Nicci are dead, and Lilith is gone. Chance buried his face in his hands, still unable to force a full breath into his lungs.

"It's not your fault, brother," he admitted on a sigh. "It's not Lilith's either. We couldn't have known about the Irish fucker."

No, but someone did. Cold certainty began to settle in Chance's gut. *Tim is right. It's not my fault or Lilith's or anyone else's. There is only one person to blame.*

"Tim?"

The soft voice barely registered over the blood thundering in Chance's ears like a war drum.

Chance looked to Eileen while she sat up, rubbing her head. Tim was on his feet in an instant, hurrying over to her.

She's okay. She's alive. She's here…unlike Lilith.

The image of Lilith wrapped in Cohen's arms, with his forehead pressed to hers, burnt in Chance's chest like a raging forest fire.

This is all on Cohen. Every drop of blood, every second apart from Lilith, everything that would happen to her…This was *all* Cohen's fault.

The rage spread through his chest, invading every single cell until there was nothing but static surrounding him. Chance slowly rose to his feet.

Tim called out to him, but he ignored it. Crimson colored his vision, tainting the world while he stalked toward the car Cohen had arrived in.

It was unlocked. Chance popped the trunk and ripped out the carpeted liner, tossing it to the pavement. Voices behind him joined the chaotic noise in his head, but they didn't register. Chance grabbed the tire iron and slammed the trunk closed.

Someone moved in his periphery, but he didn't care.

The world was nothing but an ocean of red after that. He tightened his hand around the metal until his knuckles ached. Chance slammed the tire iron down on the car over and over. Glass shattered, the side mirror went flying, dents gave way to the metal frame below. Each time it struck, the vibration burned through Chance's arms, but he held on.

When he finally stopped, it was only because the metal slipped from his hands. His chest heaved, and sweat covered his body, but the rage still burned brighter than ever inside.

It isn't enough. It will never be enough.

Chance drew back his fist, but someone grabbed his arm.

"Chance! Stop!" Tim's voice cut through the frenzied delirium. "Hurting yourself won't get her back. *Lilith* needs you. Come on."

Sorrow began to eat away at the anger.

She's gone. Lilith is gone.

Wormwood

The tightness in his chest returned, along with the tears. Every muscle hurt now that the adrenaline had worn off, and Chance sank to his knees on the pavement.

"She's gone. Lilith is gone," he sobbed.

Tim rested his hand on Chance's shoulder, and there were tears in his voice when he spoke.

"*Lilith* is still alive. We'll find her."

Chapter 64

Andrew sank to the floor and leaned his head back against the cool cinderblock outside of Lilith's cell. Tears burned his eyes.

Could this have gone any worse? Fuck.

Nicci had never liked him, and the detective had a strong tendency to ensure Cohen knew it, but he had respected the woman's tenacity and loyalty.

The memory flashed through his mind for the hundredth time: Aaron's fast blade slashing across her neck, blood gushing from the wound, cutting off her Kevlar vest, plunging the blade deep into her chest. Andrew wiped his eyes, which were already impossibly raw.

All Nicci DeLuca had been guilty of was protecting her people. When Tim tackled Eileen to keep her from following Killian's commands, Nicci had bolted straight for the Irishman, intent on eliminating the threat.

She had almost succeeded.

The fierce woman had managed to knock him down and break his nose before Killian even reacted. Nicci had been seconds away from slicing his throat when Aaron snatched her.

Fucking Aaron. I should have tried harder…made Luminita see he's a damn liability. The man hadn't killed Nicci because she was a threat. The woman hadn't deserved to die. Aaron murdered her solely to spite Lilith, to cause *her* pain.

Lilith. His very soul crumpled at the memory of her snarling at him in hatred. *I trusted you.* She had hurled those words like the weapons they were. They had cut him far deeper than he would ever admit.

It was all for her, to save her. If he had let her go, Keller and Nicci's deaths would have been for nothing. The virus would take hold, destroying Lilith from the inside, and she would have died painfully. He *refused* to let that happen, no matter the cost.

Cohen closed his eyes and concentrated. Lilith was still asleep. It wasn't peaceful—her sleep rarely was—but she was still unconscious.

Lilith's tear-streaked face appeared in his mind again. She had stared into his eyes—his *true* eyes—and begged him to help her, just like she had in that dream, the one which still haunted him, the one where he had kissed her.

Holding her tight against him and *not* kissing her had been as difficult as denying her sobbing pleas. He could still feel her warmth, still smell her lavender shampoo, still feel her breath on his skin, but what hurt most…She had been happy to see him when he had first arrived.

Lilith had said as much, but the things she felt had told him far more than she had voiced.

And now…they've all burned to ash, like I knew they would. No matter what happened, he would never have that back. Lilith would never look at him that way again, and *that loss* was devastating.

A spike of confusion and fear reached him from inside the cell.

Lilith's awake.

Cohen turned his head toward the door and swallowed hard. He had to talk to her, warn her about Aaron, make her understand the real danger, but he feared what he would find in that cell.

Lilith no longer considered him a friend. He was the enemy, the last person she would ever trust again, and his soul was so tired.

Can I really handle this? Can I stand there in front of the woman I love and allow her to hate me for it?

Andrew smoothed his hair against his scalp before wiping his red-rimmed eyes. Lilith's confusion transitioned to fear, sorrow, guilt, and finally, to soul-crushing grief.

After drawing in a deep breath, Andrew got to his feet. His feelings had no place here. Lilith deserved the truth. She needed him, even if she hated him. His hands trembled while he smoothed his dress shirt, but the action helped calm his rattled nerves.

"Okay." Andrew shifted his attention to the guard. "Let me in."

The man nodded, twisted the lock, and opened the heavy door. Andrew inhaled deeply and exhaled slowly before he stepped into the room.

Lilith sat on the cot with her back to him, facing the small window. She was hugging her midsection, shoulders shaking with silent tears.

More than anything, Andrew wanted to hold her in his arms again, but she would find no comfort in that now.

"Lilith." The name escaped his lips like the gentle prayer it was. A useless one, perhaps, but he couldn't help hoping for a reprieve.

Her back stiffened, and anger rose to the surface. His hope withered away in that instant.

"I need to talk to you," Andrew said softly.

"Get out."

He had anticipated the clipped words, but they still hurt.

"I know I'm the last person you want to—"

Lilith whirled around with a glare that made the words instantly die in his throat. "The last person I want to see?" The question dripped with venom, and she rose from the cot to face him. "Chance *warned me*…He *fucking warned me* not to trust you…that you're dangerous."

Every word hurt like a fresh cut to his already battered heart, and he hung his head. Cohen couldn't bear to see the hatred in her eyes while she stalked closer.

"I knew this was a fucking trap when you called, Cohen."

That caught his attention.

Despite every instinct of self-preservation, he met her livid stare. "Then why did you come?"

Lilith furrowed her brow, and for a moment, guilt outweighed her fury. "For you. I thought you were in danger…that you were trying to help us…to give us information."

The instinct to touch her, hold her, was almost overwhelming. *I thought you were in danger.* The very idea of Lilith risking not only herself, but her friends, for *him*.

God, no wonder she hates me.

"I trusted you."

Cohen refocused on the floor while her rage built.

"I had *faith* in you!" Lilith stepped closer. "I risked our fucking lives when *everyone* thought I was insane for creating this plan. Hell, even Tim wrote you off."

Andrew slumped his shoulders, but he peeked up at her from beneath his heavy brow. The sunset streaming in through the window gave her blond hair a reddish glow, making her righteous anger downright ethereal.

He deserved her wrath, every drop of it.

"And now…" Panic and grief billowed to the surface. Lilith shoved Cohen's chest, making him stumble backward. "Keller is dead!" She shoved him hard again. "Nicci is…" Her voice broke under the strain. She steadied herself for a moment. "Nicci is…"

Tears flooded her eyes, and she trembled.

"I'm so—"

Lilith's face hardened, and she slapped his cheek with brutal force. "Don't tell me you're sorry! Nicci is dead! She's fucking dead because of you!"

Lilith lashed out with hard strikes to his chest, but as the grief overcame her anger, the fight lessened with each hit. Still, Cohen took every one of them.

"She's dead…You could have stopped it." Lilith sobbed between labored breaths. She stopped hitting him and covered her face, coming completely undone.

Without any conscious thought, Andrew wrapped his arms around her shaking shoulders and drew her against his chest. To his amazement, Lilith collapsed against him, weeping. Her whole body shook.

It was far more than he deserved, but Andrew closed his eyes and cherished the moment. He would hold her for as long as she would allow.

When she didn't move away, Andrew slid down the wall, taking her with him, and pulled her into his lap. Lilith continued to cry, her tears soaking his shirt. He didn't dare speak a single word. It would only shatter the fragile moment. Andrew just held her and softly stroked her hair.

Minutes ticked by, stretching into an hour or more, before Lilith finally spoke again. "Why?"

Her raw voice held no malice. He had no clue what to say.

When she softly pushed away from his chest, he let her, despite the heart-rending loss the action caused.

"Why did you do it?"

Lilith's red eyes finally met his, and when they did, it struck him to the core.

She saw him—*truly saw him*—still, after everything. The realization stole every response he had prepared.

"I know you *think* you're doing the right thing…Why?" she pleaded.

Fuck the plan. I won't lie to her, not anymore.

"You're infected."

A deep frown wrinkled Lilith's brow, and she scooted back a bit. He felt every inch, like a physical loss.

"What?"

"The Wormwood virus the cult created, Lilith. You're infected, and…Luminita has the only cure."

Lilith shook her head. "That's *not* possible, Andrew."

Cohen released a heavy sigh and lowered his gaze to the floor again. "It is…It's *my* fault."

"What do you mean?" Lilith asked, with more disbelief than apprehension.

Andrew closed his eyes. This was the true moment when she would realize the cost of his selfishness. After this, Lilith would hate him.

"I infected you…when I kissed you."

Silence filled the room until his ears rang.

"I swear, I didn't know, Lilith. That's why I was hearing voices…It was all because of the virus."

"Luminita told you that?"

Something about her tone surprised him. He looked up at her.

Lilith sat there with the most unexpected expression of sympathetic misery.

"Yes…"

Lilith's shoulders fell, and fresh tears glistened along her lashes. "Why didn't you say something on the phone?"

"Lilith, you constantly try to sacrifice yourself for others. I didn't think you'd listen. I didn't think you'd take the risk to save yourself. I can't let you suffer and die because of me."

"I'm not." Lilith sighed and rubbed her face.

"Not what?"

"I'm *not* infected. I can't be."

Cohen frowned while Lilith got to her knees.

"Andrew, I'm a pureblood, a strong one. I know how this virus works. It would take hundreds of exposures to infect me, if it's even possible."

The knot in Cohen's chest tightened with every word until he could barely breathe.

"Andrew, Luminita lied to you."

"No," he whispered, despondently staring at the concrete floor. He couldn't believe that. If it were true, then everything that happened, everything he had done—Alexis, Noah, Keller, Nicci—it was all meaningless. "I was infected…I kissed you."

"Andrew, look at me." Lilith waited until he met her eyes. "Even if you were—which I strongly doubt—you couldn't infect me with one kiss or a hundred, for that matter."

Lilith slumped back against the wall with a defeated sigh and ran her hands through her hair.

While Andrew's mind spiraled into soul-shattering chaos, the heavy door swung open. Luminita's heels echoed off the walls.

"That *would* be true *if* Andrew was infected with the same Wormwood strain used to infect Goditha's blood supply. Unfortunately, that was not the case."

Hatred radiated off Lilith in nearly suffocating waves, and Andrew glanced up.

Aaron hovered over Luminita's shoulder.

Andrew surged to his feet. "Get him the fuck out of here!"

Aaron cocked an eyebrow, and a deviant smile stretched his lips.

"Andrew, it's a bit late for theatrics." Luminita sighed. "You knew sacrifices would be made."

White-hot rage scorched every vein and clenched his hands into fists. "I *begged* you to keep things civil…to let the others go unharmed."

Luminita appeared unmoved by his accusation. "Which I considered, but…examples had to be made."

"Are you not familiar with bargaining from a position of strength?" Aaron's voice held far too much amusement while his appraising glare raked over Cohen. "Hmm. I suppose that shouldn't surprise me. You and *my niece* have that in common—weakness."

Lilith's rage turned feral. Cohen spun just in time to catch her around the waist when she lunged for Aaron.

"Fuck you! Monster!" Lilith screamed, trying to fight her way out of Cohen's grip. "I'll fucking kill you!"

Aaron smirked. "I seriously doubt that."

Lilith's shrieked response was more of a war cry than actual words.

"That's quite enough." Luminita turned back to Aaron. "Why don't you wait outside?"

The humor drained from Aaron's face, and Lilith finally started to calm down.

"Sălbatic." Luminita reached up to stroke the madman's cheek. "I need to speak with Lilith, and you are a…distraction."

Aaron shifted his vicious glare from Lilith to Cohen, but when he looked at Luminita, his expression softened into something deeply intimate.

"Right outside the door," Aaron reluctantly agreed.

After one last malicious scowl at Lilith and Cohen, Aaron strolled into the hall.

"I have nothing to say to you!" Lilith snapped at Luminita before pushing away from Andrew.

Once again, he acutely felt the loss of her warmth.

"Then listen," Luminita said in a calm voice. "Dr. Scott is working for me...here. I believe you know him?"

Lilith shot her a piercing glare. "I'm sure you *know* I do."

"I do. He uncovered a specialized strain of the virus when he examined Andrew's blood. The cult most likely infected him when they abducted him. It is *not* the same one spreading across the South. It's far more contagious and transmittable to vampires, even purebloods."

"Bullshit." Lilith didn't even hesitate.

Andrew's gaze swung between them in confusion. Luminita had never mentioned a different strain.

"Dr. Scott can provide you proof of both the virus and its cure."

Lilith folded her arms over her chest and shook her head. "I don't believe you."

A soft chuckle passed Luminita's lips. "*Crin*, you are a woman of science. I do not expect you to believe me without proof, which I have."

"I'm a pureblood." Lilith's tone sounded less certain this time.

"So is Aaron. He's far older than you and has a stronger heritage. He isn't even affected by the sun, like your father and uncle were, and *he* was infected by the virus."

The blood drained from Lilith's face, and she sat on the edge of the cot.

"Andrew."

Reluctantly, he pulled his gaze away from Lilith.

"We should allow her time to rest. It's been an exhausting day." Luminita gestured toward the door, but Andrew looked back at Lilith, conflicted.

He didn't want to leave her.

Lilith stared despondently at the floor, seemingly oblivious to his inner conflict.

"Come on, Andrew," Luminita urged.

"Go on," Lilith said softly, not bothering to look at him. "I'm tired."

Without another word, she curled up on the mattress, keeping her back to the room.

Andrew watched her shoulders shake for a moment, felt her slipping into despair and grief. He couldn't help her this time. She wanted to be alone, and after everything, he didn't blame her.

With his head bowed, Andrew paced past Luminita and Aaron, heading for his own private cell of self-loathing.

Chapter 65

"I need to pull the RV around." Tim's voice sounded hollow, even to him.

"Tim." Eileen grabbed his arm when he started to walk away.

He didn't look at her, *couldn't* look at her. The black eye was already forming, along with light bruises that would soon darken.

"Just stay with Chance and…" His throat constricted, and he blinked back the fresh tears threatening to spill. "…the bodies."

Saying it soured his stomach.

"Tim." Eileen tried to turn him around, but he slid away from her hold.

"Please." He didn't care if she heard the shattered vulnerability in his voice. Anything else would have been a lie. "I'll be right back."

She didn't reach for him again, and he was both grateful and saddened by that.

The trek back to the RV felt eternal. Horrific images of Nicci's lifeless body, his fist connecting with Eileen's face, and Keller's brains misting the air tormented him endlessly. It was a nightmare he could never wake up from.

Tim trudged up the RV stairs and abruptly stopped. Keller's duffle sat on the couch, and Nicci's laptops were still on the table next to her mug. Hours ago, they had all been gathered right here.

He moved over to the table and traced his fingertips along the rim of Nicci's NYPD mug—the one she had brought back with her from New York because it was her good luck charm. It was still half-filled with the pitch-black coffee the pipsqueak had loved so much.

It was cold now.

Tim's vision blurred into a watery mess, and he turned away. He didn't have time to break down any more than he already had. Tim couldn't leave Chance unsupervised for too long. The way he'd utterly destroyed that car had been unnerving, but when he had reared back, intent on bare-knuckle fighting the thing, that was terrifying.

Tim sank into the driver's seat and twisted the cables together, sparking the ignition. The engine roared to life, but he felt the ghosts at his back. The RV should have been full of voices, people, life…

And now it wasn't.

After adjusting the visor to cut the sunset's glare, Tim drove the short distance to where Chance and Eileen waited. He parked, leaving the engine running, before walking back to the bunks.

Tim had found extra bedding in the drawer beneath the bottom bunk during their first stop. He grabbed a pair of sheets, along with two medium-weight comforters, and made his way outside.

"Chance, can you wrap up Keller?" Tim held out some linens, and Chance took them without complaint.

On some level, relegating his war-brother to someone else's care hurt, but Tim had to be the one to take care of Nicci. In a few short months, the woman had weaseled her way into his life, become his sister, a friend—hell, his best friend, if he was being honest.

Tim loved Chance like a brother, but that shit with Boston, lying to him, using him…It had cut deep. They hadn't been the same since. There were things Tim just couldn't talk to the man about anymore.

Gut-twisting grief wracked his body all over again when he knelt beside Nicci's pale form. He had never met someone so fierce in such a tiny package, except perhaps Eileen.

"Can I help?"

Eileen's voice was so gentle and timid it made his heart ache.

Tim nodded, unable to speak. He still couldn't bring himself to look at her and the damage he had inflicted.

Tim didn't know specifics about Eileen's ex, but he understood enough. There was no way she could look at him the same after this, and Tim refused to allow her to excuse his actions, like she had done for the asshole she'd married.

It wasn't okay. None of this was okay.

They carefully wrapped Nicci's body in silence. It didn't take long for red to seep through the fabric. There was so much blood. He had seen too much in the past few weeks—a goddamned ocean of it.

Tim slid his arms beneath Nicci's petite form and cradled her against his chest when he stood. He couldn't fight back the tears after that. Eileen rested her hand on his back, a little sliver of comfort, while he carried Nicci into the RV.

Chance lifted Keller's bundled body and slid him onto the top bunk. "I figured I'd leave the bottom one open…in case you need to rest, Eileen."

Rest…after I beat her unconscious. Bile rose in Tim's throat.

Tim drew in a steadying breath and carefully lowered Nicci to the couch before he sank to his knees. He couldn't believe she was gone. Tim kept expecting her to bound up the steps, her long ponytail swinging like a pendulum. He knew what she would say right now.

Suck it up, big fella.

Eileen caressed his shoulders, but Tim felt impossibly unworthy of that touch.

"I'm so sorry." Her tearful apology only sharpened the pain.

"Don't apologize." Tim slowly stood. He avoided her gaze while he stiffly moved to the driver's seat. "This isn't your fault."

After clearing his raw throat, Tim did his best to sound normal.

"We need to get out of here. I'll drive us into town, and then we can figure out our next move. I think it was about fifteen miles."

"Okay," was all Chance said before the bedroom door shut.

Tim threw the RV in gear and pulled through the parking lot. When he turned onto the main road, the sounds of splintering wood and breaking glass emanated from the bedroom.

Better that than a fucking car.

Eileen remained silent the entire drive back to town, not that Tim blamed her. What could she really say? Aaron and Killian had destroyed everything. They had killed more than Keller and Nicci today.

Tim was just thankful Eileen hadn't said the words out loud yet. It was one more loss he simply couldn't take, not right now.

Tim parked in a gas station lot and collapsed against the seat. The weight of the world rested on his shoulders. Losing Xander had been hard, but Keller, Nicci, Lilith…Eileen…It was too much.

"Tim." Eileen's quiet voice beside him sent a jolt of absolute dread through his weary body.

"I know," he said on a defeated sigh. "But can we not do this now?"

"Do what?" The confusion sounded genuine.

Tim rubbed his face roughly and tried to breathe. She was going to make him say it.

"I know…what I did." His throat became impossibly tight. "You don't have to say it. I understand."

"Understand what?" She hovered closer, and Tim lowered his tear-filled gaze to his raw knuckles.

"Tim. Please. Look at me." Her voice trembled.

"I can't." The words emerged as more of a pained sob than actual speech.

Suddenly, Eileen was straddling his lap, and his heart leapt into his throat. The dark purple smudges around her vivid blue eye immediately made him look away.

"Look at me," she demanded, gripping his chin and pulling him back.

His eyes instantly gravitated to the bruises, the dark puffy skin, the tiny cut above her eyebrow. Tim's stomach pitched, twisting into painful knots.

"You…saved my life," Eileen said softly. Tears spilled from her eyes.

Tim's face crumpled, and he shook his head. "I hurt you." He was unable to hold eye contact. "You could **never** look at me the same way. You shouldn't. I could have pinned you to the ground, but…I was so scared that if you got away…"

"Stop. Please." Eileen cradled his face in her palms and moved closer, crowding his vision. "Look at me…right now…and tell me I see you any differently."

The words sounded nice, and he wanted so badly to believe them, but he couldn't do it. Seeing that instinctual fear in her bright blue eyes would simply gut what remained of him.

"Tim. I love you. I know you would never hurt me." She moved, trying to force him to look at her.

He closed his eyes, sending tears streaking down his cheeks. "I *did* hurt you."

"To save me. To save my life," she insisted.

"It doesn't make a difference. Not to me. And it shouldn't to you."

"*You are not Karl.* You could *never* be like him." The conviction in her voice made him finally open his eyes.

Eileen stared at him with such excruciating tenderness, Tim felt his heart might explode.

How? How can she look at me like that?

Wormwood

She brushed her thumbs over his scruff. "You did what it took to save me, without any regard to what you thought it might cost you. You think you hurt me, but you put my life first. You are *not* a monster, Tim. You're the farthest thing from one. I love you, and I'm asking you—begging you—to love me back."

Those words shattered every remaining piece of his heart, and Tim pressed his forehead to hers. "I do love you. I could never stop."

Eileen closed the short distance, capturing his lips in a fervent kiss. It stole the breath from his lungs, said everything, promised everything, and it shocked Tim to his core.

She broke the kiss to collapse against him, nuzzling his neck with panting breaths. Tim wrapped his arms around her, holding her tight, terrified of letting her go.

They stayed that way for a while, clinging to each other.

A loud crack followed by the sound of more splintering wood intruded on the moment.

"Is he going to be okay?" she whispered against his neck.

"No."

"What do we do?" Eileen slowly sat back, and he reluctantly let her.

Tim tried to rein in his chaotic emotions and think. "I should call Antonio and tell him what happened. We need help."

The bedroom door creaked when it opened, and they both turned.

Chance lumbered out of the wrecked room with heavy breaths. Blood dripped from the knuckles of both hands. "We need to find Luminita's compound."

"Agreed, but the three of us can't do it alone. Orchid said the place is a damn fortress."

"I know," Chance agreed in a sullen tone.

"I can call Antonio—"

"We aren't calling him," Chance interrupted sharply.

"Chance—"

"We're driving to his fucking doorstep. The Elders will give us what we need. We aren't leaving until they do."

When Tim stared at him in disbelief, Chance shot him a glare that left no room for argument.

"Call Gibson. Tell him we won't be meeting him in Knoxville. We're heading to Ocate, New Mexico…to Cattaneo Ranch."

To be concluded in book 6, Hellebore.

Acknowledgements

<u>Test Bunnies (Alpha Readers)</u>
Jennifer Saviano
Kayla Bowers
Danny Nagel
Marissa Atchison

<u>Beta Readers</u>
Chandra Marie

<u>ARC Readers</u>
Jenny Fraser
Holly Kuhns
Brooke Rogers
Mandy
Sammi Dyer
Angel Webster
Tiffany Ewald
Miracle Whitley
Kristy Hurst
Catalina Ashley
Stephanie Vincente
Christi Nunn
JoAnn Boothby
Stephanie Silvestri
Isolette Chaves

About the Author

Jenny Allen (Deardorff), the author of The Lilith Adams Series, also published poems and short stories in university journals while spending time as a reporter and photographer for the Chattanooga State College newspaper. Allen studied forensic science, compiled extensive research in world myths, and applied them into a thrilling supernatural series. Her background as a published photographer and award-winning artist helps her visualize scenes when writing, contributing to her unique style of vivid imagery.

Born on a Royal Airbase in Lakenheath, England, she left the U.K. at age nine to travel the United States and Germany. In her sophomore year, she began writing poetry after the suicide of a close friend. She later graduated to short stories and narratives until, in 2002, she wrote her first novel, *Lilith in London*, which was never published but still exists as 432 handwritten pages. Over twelve years, it underwent a metamorphosis, eventually becoming her first published novel, *Blood Lily*.

Currently, Mrs. Allen (Deardorff) lives in York, Pennsylvania, with her husband, Eric Deardorff, and their two sons, Kaidan and River. When not working as a full-time RN, she is writing and researching other books in the Lilith Adams Universe. She plans to continue her book series while pursuing her medical career.

"Writing has been a tremendous benefit to my mental health. It's provided me a way to trap certain issues in the paper and allowed me to work through them in a safe space. My characters have grown exponentially since the first book, and I'm excited for the continuing journey!"

Suggested Reading

These are not paid advertisements or endorsements. These are simply books and authors that I personally enjoy!

Jennifer Saviano
Saviors MC Series
An intense slow-burn MC Romance/Thriller series with all the emotional depth and trauma response. Clever, bold, and endearing!

Avanne Michaels
The Beta Series and much more!
A gifted author in the Omegaverse realm who deals plenty of emotional trauma. Why choose at its best!

Desie Marie
Whiskey & Weights
A delightful Polyamory novella debut with female empowerment and positive plus-sized representation.

Trisha Wolfe
The Hollows Row
Trilogy & More!

Extremely smart and twisted dark romances that are absolutely addictive! The obvious research and exceptional writing bring the characters to life in every book.

Samantha Moran
Dealings in the Dark,
Bound & Betrayed

Supernatural, demonic possession horror at its finest! The intricate mental health questions woven into these books, especially the second one, are brilliantly handled.

Kelsey Humphries
Heartlanders Series

These audiobooks are a must-have for rom-com lovers. Voiced by Paige Reisenfeld & Ryan Lee Dunlap, these quirky books make us anxious introverts/extroverts feel seen & deliver heart-touching stories.